I0760324

THE ILLUSTRATED MARSHALL DRUMMOND CASE FILES

STUART JAFFE

ILLUSTRATED BY TED WOODS

Copyright Information

THE MARSHALL DRUMMOND CASE FILES: CABINET 4

Cover Art by Mari Morgan
Illustrations by Ted Woods

ISBN: 978-1-963517-22-4

First Hardcover Edition: December, 2025

This compilation includes the following stories:

THE BUTCHER'S WITCH

This story first Appeared in the anthology *We Are Not This* (Falstaff Books, 2016)

THE AMNESIA DEALER

WITCH'S BREW

THE FATE OF LAURA MCCULLEN

APARTMENT 2A

THE ESSENCE OF THE PROBLEM

BONES IN THE WOODS

For all you wonderful fans of Marshall Drummond

He's blown away by your love and support

ALSO BY STUART JAFFE

Max Porter Paranormal Mysteries

Southern Bound
Southern Charm
Southern Belle
Southern Gothic
Southern Haunts
Southern Curses
Southern Rites
Southern Craft
Southern Spirit
Southern Flames
Southern Fury
Southern Souls
Southern Blood
Southern Graves
Southern Dead
Southern Hexes
Southern Hart
Southern Kin
Southern Lies

Nathan K Thrillers

Immortal Killers
Killing Machine
The Cardinal
Yukon Massacre
The First Battle
Immortal Darkness
A Spy for Eternity
Prisoner
Desert Takedown
Lone Star Standoff
The Puppeteer
Blowback
Prime

The Pathway Ring

Pioneers of the Pathway
Lions of the Pathway

The Ridnight Mysteries

The Water Blade
The Waters of Taladoro
Waterfire

The Parallel Society

The Infinity Caverns
Book on the Isle
Rift Angel
Lost Time
Pages of Glass
The Bold Warrior
City of Infinity

The Malja Chronicles

The Way of the Black Beast
The Way of the Sword and Gun
The Way of the Brother Gods
The Way of the Blade
The Way of the Power
The Way of the Soul

Gillian Boone novels

A Glimpse of Her Soul
Pathway to Spirit

Stand Alone Novels

After The Crash
Real Magic
Founders

Short Story Collection

10 Bits of My Brain
10 More Bits of My Brain
The Bluesman
The Marshall Drummond Case Files: Cabinet 1
The Marshall Drummond Case Files: Cabinet 2
The Marshall Drummond Case Files: Cabinet 3
The Marshall Drummond Case Files: Cabinet 4

Non-Fiction

How to Write Magical Words: A Writer's Companion

For more information, please visit ***www.stuartjaffe.com***

THE ILLUSTRATED MARSHALL DRUMMOND CASE FILES

Contents

CASE 01

THE BUTCHER'S WITCH

MARSHALL DRUMMOND KNOCKED on the chipped wooden door to room 2F. It had been a chilly morning in Winston-Salem, North Carolina, and Marshall had opted for his favorite trench coat and Fedora. He knew his attire made him look like a classic G-man, but his days working in the public sector had ended a few years back when he left the police department after a rather unsettling experience. One that opened his eyes to the world beneath the surface.

As a private investigator, most of his cases tended to involve that other world — the one with ghosts and spells, the one with witches and curses, the one most people never saw nor wanted to see. When his old patrol buddy, Cooper, asked him to handle the current matter in private, he welcomed the idea of a case that did not involve the need for trips to the cemetery or discoveries about how deep the underworld went. He should have known better.

Drummond raised his fist to knock on the door again when a charming gal opened it up. She was small, though most people were small compared to Drummond, and she wore her hair much like Vivian Leigh whose popularity continued to rise since starring in *Gone with the Wind*. In fact, if not for the tear stains on her cheeks, the woman holding the door open had the looks to grab a man's heart and walk away with it in her purse.

"Ms. Parker? I'm Marshall Drummond. Our mutual friend, Detective Cooper, sent me. Said you needed some assistance."

The worry on her face told Drummond everything — this would be a more complicated case than Cooper had let on. Of course, Cooper always had been light on details when it came to work, so Drummond should not have been surprised.

"Please, call me Anne," she said, stepping back to let Drummond into the apartment.

Like most of the apartments Drummond had seen, the Depression had taken its toll on this one as well. Even ten years since the Crash, people still suffered. Sparse furnishings and a threadbare tablecloth bore witness to Anne Parker's losses. He saw no signs of silver picture frames and Anne wore no jewelry of any kind — all pawned off, no doubt.

Though the single window in the room had been shut, Drummond could feel the cold seeping through. To try to stay warm, Anne wore a brown-and-white knit cap and a wool scarf with brown fringe. One door, leading to the toilet and single bedroom, had been shut to warm up the room.

The air smelled damp and stale. Anne's rose petal perfume did little to cover it up. In the summer, the window would have been open, but the odor of cars clogging the street would have been little improvement.

"Would you like some coffee?" Anne asked.

Drummond glanced at the open kitchen area which was separated from the rest of the single room by a white counter. He saw nothing on the counter to indicated that she had much in the way of food let alone coffee.

"No, thank you. I think it best if I just get to work."

Fidgeting with the frayed ends of her coat, she sat on a wood chair by a small round table next to the window. "I didn't realize the detective had sent anybody."

"Well, you know Cooper. Just give him a sweet and simple matter to sweep under the rug, and he's going to make sure even the filthiest of us is as clean as possible."

"Yes, I suppose so."

"Now, as I understand it, your ... friend is missing?"

Anne forced a sad chuckle. "Is that what we're going to call it?"

"We can call it whatever you want."

"She's ... my wife, I guess. Not according to the law, of course, but we loved each other. Does that shock you?"

Now it was Drummond's turn to chuckle. "Doll, if you saw half of things I've seen in my life, a couple of queer ladies ain't going to be the beginning of shock. Now your wife — please tell me her name, when she went missing, and exactly how you found out about it."

"Her name is Xia, but I don't know much more than that. She just didn't come home. A couple days ago. I do hope she's okay."

Drummond pursed his lips and tapped his chin. His gaze shifted from the nervous, young woman to the closed, bedroom door. He clapped his hands together once, strong and loud. The girl jumped in her seat.

"A picture," he said. "I don't see a picture in this room of Xia. Do you have something? Perhaps in your bedroom."

As Drummond stepped towards the door, Anne bolted from her chair.

"Please, don't go in there. My unmentionables are out. I'll get you a picture."

"Thank you. I sure appreciate that."

Opening the door the minimum necessary, Anne slipped through and shut the door behind her.

Not suspicious at all, Drummond thought, as he ambled into the kitchen area. He poked through the cabinets and drawers — mostly empty. Squatting, he pulled back the curtain under the sink. What he saw gave him pause — three candles, black, red, and green; a jar of salt; a jar of a gray powder. Not enough to definitively say that one of these two women was a witch, but given the paraphernalia's hidden nature, Drummond's internal warnings sounded.

A few moments later, Anne returned empty-handed. "I'm so sorry. We don't have any."

"None? Not a single photograph?"

Anne gestured to the empty room. "Times have been hard."

Drummond had no idea why financial hardships meant she could not hold onto their photographs but decided to let the matter go. He would not get the answers he wanted here.

As politely as possible, Drummond said good-bye and promised to return once he had some news. He had no trouble spotting the relief on Anne's face. He didn't like it.

In the hall, Drummond pressed his ear against 2F's closed door. He waited but heard nothing to indicate panic nor did he hear any other voices. He walked down two doors and knocked. No answer. Another door down and knocked. No answer.

However, the door across the hall opened, and an old lady no more than five-feet tall poked her head out. "You a cop?"

Drummond took off his Fedora and smiled. "No, ma'am. Private investigator. Do you know anything about the two women in apartment 2F?"

"I know they're funny. And I don't mean with jokes."

"Besides that."

The little lady crossed her arms, pushing her ample bosom near her chin. "You calling on here because of the trouble they had?"

"Exactly. Tell me about the trouble."

"Don't know much. Just that Mr. Rankin came hollering at them. Don't know what about though."

"Mr. Rankin? Who's that?"

The old woman pointed down the hall. "He's the butcher. Got a shop on the corner a block up."

"And you heard this Mr. Rankin arguing with the ladies?"

"I told you that already. You need to listen. He yelled on and on about his kids and how she promised to deliver right away. That's all, but I don't know anything."

Putting his hat back on and giving the brim a polite flick, he said, "Thank you, ma'am, for your time. You've been immensely helpful."

"Times is hard. We gotta help each other out. Right? Like how I'm sure the police got a reward for this information."

"They very well might. I'm not with them, remember? I'm a private investigator."

The woman's face tightened. She huffed and stormed back into her apartment, slamming the door behind her.

As Drummond took the stairs to the street, he weighed the likelihood that Anne Parker had murdered her lover. Perhaps Xia and Mr. Rankin had started up together. Parker catches them and loses her restraint. Next thing she knows, she's killed them. Possible — except Anne Parker's behavior did not seem like that of a woman who had killed her lover. Still, she was hiding something.

He turned left and headed up Patterson Avenue toward the corner. Well before he reached Rankin's Butcher Shoppe (with a silhouette of a pig's head on the sign), he knew things had turned bad. Two police cars had been parked across the street and a crowd had formed outside the store forming a sea of hats. As he approached, he spotted Detective Cooper standing on the sidewalk.

With his head down and his hat low, Cooper smoked a cigarette while the RJ Reynolds smokestacks puffed away in the skyline. He offered a slim nod to Drummond.

Drummond struck a match on the side of the building to light his own cigarette. "This can't be a good coincidence — you having a case just a block away from this matter you wanted me to look into."

"I was thinking the same thing." Cooper extended a pudgy hand, and as the two men shook, he exhaled a smoky sigh. "In fact, I think when you take a look in there, you're going to say there's no doubt these cases are related."

"Maybe I shouldn't go in there, if this is going to become an entirely police matter."

"Don't start that with me. When you see it, you'll know that coppers ain't going to be able to figure this one out. We need somebody like you."

Drummond couldn't miss the two beat-cops keeping the crowds at bay. They peeked over their shoulders at him as if to say *You're not one of us. You don't belong here.*

Patting Cooper on the shoulder, Drummond said, "You got any good news for me?"

"A few months back Hitler took over Poland."

"That's good news?"

"I never liked the Polish much."

Drummond frowned. "I'm a quarter Polish on my mother's side."

"That's why I don't like a quarter of you."

Cooper led the way into the butcher's shop, and Drummond understood the trouble right away. Rankin lay face up on the floor. His eyes wide open. His throat slit. Dried blood left a trail over his cracked lips and down his work apron. His legs and arms had been spread wide as if preparing for a Medieval torture. A large, incomplete pentagram had been painted black atop him and the floor. And if that weren't enough, the man's tool of trade — a butcher's knife — had been lodged into his sternum.

Drummond clicked his tongue. "Somebody was more than a little angry at this fellow."

Cooper flicked cigarette ash onto the floor. "You can see here why I know this is related. And if all that witchy stuff on the floor ain't enough, I also found this." On the counter, he placed an empty, glass vial. It reminded Drummond of a woman's perfume bottle.

Drummond said, "You think he had another woman? What's that got to do with witchcraft?"

A young police officer entered the shop and Cooper pointed at him. "You! Get out! Don't let anybody in here." The young officer bolted away as if he had been fired. Cooper gestured to the vial. "I know that has to do with witchcraft because I have one exactly like it at home."

Drummond stepped closer to the counter, keeping his eyes on the vial, not wanting to see Cooper's face. "Oh."

"Look this ain't anything I'm proud of. Heck, I didn't even believe any of this until I met you. But I was having some problems and nothing seemed to help. So I went to Madame Xia. She gave me a bottle just like that one."

"What kind of problems?"

Cooper tapped the tip of his shoe against the counter. "I'd rather not say."

Drummond leveled his dark eyes on Cooper. "I'd rather not ask. But you've put me in a position where I need to know."

"Well ... let's say it had to do with potency ... in the bedroom."

"Oh."

Drummond picked up the bottle and sniffed at its open mouth — fragrant like Spring morning flowers. He crouched next to Rankin's body — no scratch marks on the arms, no torn clothing, no sign of a struggle.

"Strange. Such a clean kill, you'd think it was a professional job. Slit neck from behind, unsuspecting victim. But this butcher's knife in the chest — that's violent, angry. That's personal."

"Well, that potency spell — I was only supposed to take two tablespoons. He emptied this thing. So, either he was dead inside beforehand —"

"Or he was trying to please a lot of women."

"Maybe one of them found out about the others and didn't take to it too kindly."

"Yeah. Which doesn't bode well for your missing Madame Xia."

"You think whoever did this killed her too?"

"Probably. Or maybe she's lucky and the killer is going to try to force her to perform a spell."

Drummond checked Rankin's left hand — wedding ring. "Where's Mrs. Rankin?"

"Not home, yet. Neighbors said she does a lot of shopping. Butcher's wife does pretty well. She can afford a lot. We expect her back soon, though. It's been several hours, after all."

"They live here?"

"Upstairs."

"Mind if I take a look?"

"Not at all. Let's go."

They stepped around the counter and through a swinging door. The back area consisted of thick wooden tables stained with animal blood and large slabs of pork, beef, and poultry hanging from hooks. Large blocks of ice formed a pyramid in one corner and chilled the room. Next to a closet, a narrow staircase circled up to the second floor.

Cooper opened the door onto a well-furnished apartment with a ceiling fan for the summers and a wood-stove for the winters. Oriental carpets lined the floor. Two bottles of whiskey stood on the kitchen counter, blue bows tied around their necks. The room smelled of cigars and money. A card had been attached to one bottle. It read: *It's time for a change.*

"If you want the hooch," Cooper said, "I can look in the bedroom for a moment. Won't even remember those bottles were here."

Drummond licked his lips but shook his head. "I shouldn't tamper with anything that might be evidence."

"You kidding? I say live it up a little while you can."

"Then you take it. I've got plenty of my own stash."

"I bet you do," Cooper chuckled.

Drummond glossed over several framed photos on the walls, but noted that he saw no children. In fact, none of the furniture bore signs of a child — no damage, no stains, nothing. And no toys anywhere, either.

"Hey, look at this." He turned around a chair that had been facing the window. Black lace underwear had been draped over a cushion like an invitation. "Maybe the missus found this and knew it was for another woman?"

"Why would Rankin lay that out on a chair in his own home, if he didn't want her to see it?"

"Maybe he did want her to see it? Maybe it was a sick way of saying *you're done*. Like the card on the bottle. Maybe that was the change he was talking about."

"Maybe ... but then why isn't there any sign of a fight in here? Or anger? If she found that and thought it meant another woman, and she had the rage to go stomp downstairs and kill him, then why isn't there anything in here to suggest that level of violent emotion? Not a chair turned over or a glass shattered or something burned. Neither of those bottles was tossed across the room. Nothing."

From a side table, Drummond snatched a photograph of Rankin and his wife huddled against a snowfall — bright smiles as she snuggled against his chest. "Look here. Do these two actually look like a miserable couple?"

"Well, no, but that could've been years ago."

Drummond didn't hear Cooper. The world dropped away as he stared at the photograph. He didn't see the snow or Rankin's goofy grin. He didn't register the satisfaction or the loving way Rankin had his arm around his wife. Drummond only focused on Mrs. Rankin's familiar face and the brown-and-white knit cap and wool scarf she wore.

Racing out downstairs, he yelled back at Cooper, "Send men to Madame Xia's apartment. The killer is there!"

He leaped over Rankin's body and bolted out of the butcher shop. Shoving bystanders out of his way, Drummond rammed his way back to the apartment building. How long had he been gone? Would anybody still be alive? Or even there?

If Mrs. Rankin was just a killer, Drummond knew she would have been long gone. But from what he could tell, this was about rage and love and magic. That last one was the most important because magic takes time.

He turned the corner and sprinted for the building. The whole case spread out before him as the pieces found their place. Rankin loved his wife. He had bought her everything he could, financed her shopping sprees, and took her on winter trips. But they had no children. Not a single photograph of a child in that apartment. Rankin had the same problem as Cooper — potency.

Whatever methods Rankin tried in the past, they had failed. He must have been desperate — that was the usual way a man like him discovered a witch like Madame Xia. He wanted the potion from her and planned for a special evening with his wife. But Xia was late delivering or perhaps he wanted more of a guarantee. Whatever the issue, he argued with Xia at her apartment. It must have worked because he got his potion in time for a night to conceive a child.

But while Rankin cut apart pigs and cows downstairs, Mrs. Rankin returned early from her shopping and discovered the booze and the card, the lacy underwear, and the potion. She knew he had seen a witch — they would have talked about it — and she knew that their dream of a child might finally come true. But she misunderstood the use of the magic. She drank the entire potion.

Drummond burst through the front door and into the lobby. He soared up the stairwell to the second floor. The old woman peeked from the corner of her door as Drummond zipped down the hall. When he reached 2F, he leaned back and thrust his foot to the side of the knob. The door smashed open.

The woman who had called herself Anne Parker spun around. She stood in the middle of the sparse room with a book in one hand and a lit, red candle in the other. The book bore a pale cover, and Drummond cringed inwardly. He had seen covers like that before on occult books — made of human skin. On the floor, she had drawn a circle in chalk and lined the edges with strange symbols.

"Mrs. Rankin."

An embarrassed grin trembled on her lips. "That's me."

"And the real Anne Parker?"

"Tied up in the other room."

Drummond glanced at the closed door leading to the bedroom. "And Madame Xia?"

Mrs. Rankin's face chilled. "Dead. Just like my loving husband."

No mistake — Drummond heard her say the word *loving* with

sincerity. These murders were not done by a woman in a jealous rage. *Got to keep her talking.* "Why kill the man you love?"

"I didn't. She did."

"She?" Maybe he was wrong. "Did your husband cheat on you?"

"Never," she said, insulted by the mere suggestion of infidelity.

"Then I am right. Listen to me. I know you drank that potion. The bottle smells of your rose petal perfume. But that potion was not meant for you."

"I know that now!" She shrieked as if the words escaping her lips caused pain in her chest.

Drummond had no doubt that the potion had warped her mind beyond reason. "Please," he said, "you're not a witch."

"I have this book. And if this one doesn't work, there are half-a-dozen more in the bedroom."

"You can't bring him back. Even if it's in that book, you'd have to study for years and —"

Mrs. Rankin's eyes blazed as she pulled her head back. "I wouldn't dare disturb my husband. And that witch can rot forever as far as I'm concerned."

"Then what are you doing here?"

She looked back at her book. "Making things right for the living."

"And a spell will do that?"

She pointed to the closed door. "That poor girl in there — the real Anne Parker. The witch twisted her little mind so that she thought she was in love. A woman in love with another woman? That poor thing was under a witch's spell, helped that witch because of magic, so she might as well help me, too."

"Help you?" But before he could ask *How?* the answer came to him. "You drank the potion because you assumed it was for you because Rankin isn't the one having trouble making a baby. It's you."

Mrs. Rankin shivered. "And all this time, that young thing in there is given the ability to have children and she throws that away to lie with another woman. Well, I'll take care of her. I'll get this spell to work and she'll fall in love with me and do anything I say — even have my child."

Drummond held back his tongue. There was no sense reasoning with her. Her mind had been poisoned by magic and upbringing. Nothing he said would stop her.

He considered rushing forward and tackling her, but what if she pulled off her spell? He knew a lot about magic, but not enough — what would happen if the spell went off but got disrupted? What if the spell on the floor did more than try to force love? Many spells could achieve polar opposite results depending on slight variations in the casting.

The knob on the closed door leading to the bedroom turned. Both Drummond and Mrs. Rankin froze at the sound as the wooden door squeaked open. Anne Parker entered the room.

She reminded Drummond of Alice from the children's books, except this Alice had a dark look in her eyes and a strength in her tight jaw. She dropped the rope that had bound her. Singed pieces drifted smoke into the air. She wore a simple brown frock but this struck Drummond as more menacing than any of the elaborate clothing he had seen witches wear.

"You're a witch too?" Mrs. Rankin said.

"No," Parker said, her voice windy and sweet. "But I know a thing or two of magic."

Mrs. Rankin jutted her head toward Drummond. "You see? You don't have to be a witch to pull off a spell."

Parker crossed her arms. "You can't make me fall in love with you."

"Why not? Xia did it to you."

"No. Not like that. I fell in love with Madame Xia because she was beautiful and kind and dangerous. She cared about me, and she welcomed me without question. The only magic she used was stealing my heart with her smile."

Mrs. Rankin snarled. "Then you're a disgusting monster."

"I'm not the one trying to use magic to force a lesbian love affair."

"What? No. I'm not going to love you back. You're going to be my slave."

Parker slapped the kitchen counter. "You arrogant twit. You think it's so easy to pull off a spell like that?"

Drummond often found women baffling, but he could see these two storm fronts colliding into a hurricane, if he didn't stop things from escalating. To Mrs. Rankin, he said, "Don't do this. You're not thinking clearly. You ingested a witch's potion and it has addled your brain. You killed your husband who you love very much. You're not in control of your actions."

"She most certainly is."

Mrs. Rankin's face fell. "W-What?"

With the predatory grin of a trophy hunter, Parker said, "Drinking all of that potion caused your momentary insanity. So, yes, killing your husband was beyond your conscious control. But after that, you were entirely in command. Coming here, murdering Madame Xia, tying me up, pretending to be me for Mr. Drummond, and attempting to cast this spell — which will fail — all of it could have been stopped at any moment by you."

Drummond pictured the crime scene. All the signs of the occult had to have been done *after* the murder. The bloodstains showed blood dribbling downward from the mouth and neck over his shirt, but the body had been found lying flat. The arms and legs had been spread apart and the incomplete pentagram had been painted over the body. None of those things followed any witchcraft Drummond had seen before. Clearly, these had been the desperate acts of Mrs. Rankin as she hoped to cover up her behavior, trying to pin it on Madame Xia, but not knowing the proper way witches did things.

"But you tried to set up Madame Xia for your husband's murder. Why come here?" Drummond asked.

"Exactly," Mrs. Rankin said. "If I had set her up, why did I come here to murder her? It doesn't make sense. And that's proof that I didn't know what I was doing."

"You didn't finish, though," Drummond said.

"What are you talking about?"

"The pentagram. You didn't finish it."

"So?"

"It suggests that at some point, you changed your mind. I think you started framing Madame Xia as part of this spell-intoxication you were under. But then, your mind cleared. You saw what you had done, and you knew who you blamed. So, you stopped trying to frame her and stormed over here to murder her. You're guilty Mrs. Rankin, and no amount of acting, false spells, or other nonsense you want to play out will change the fact that you know exactly what you are doing."

Mrs. Rankin's dark eyes darted from Parker to Drummond to the spell book in her hand. Her chin quivered as tears slipped down the side of her nose. She slumped her shoulders. "I am the monster," she whispered.

She started a slow, steady moan — quiet at first, but growing in volume and intensity with each passing second.

Drummond's gut lurched. "Mrs. Rankin?"

Her head snapped up, her face a twisted gargoyle of shame and rage. She raised the candle in the air like a carving knife. "I am the monster!"

Three holes appeared in her chest before Drummond registered the loud bangs from behind. He whirled around to find Cooper standing with legs apart and a service revolver gripped between both hands for a steady shot. He did not look at Drummond but kept his focus on the falling body of Mrs. Rankin.

"Cooper, she wasn't any harm. That was a candle, not a weapon."

Cooper slouched. "I've seen enough magic for a lifetime. No way would I let her use that spell — whatever it was. Besides, she already killed two people."

Drummond turned to Parker. "You okay?"

"No," she said, and dropped to the floor, finally weeping for her loss.

After a few minutes, Drummond quietly left. The police didn't need him mucking around, and Cooper would find it easier to put together a more plausible story that the department could accept.

He turned away from the direction of his office and walked east. He needed to clear his head and rid himself of the shakiness that magic always left in the air. On the corner, he flicked a nickel to the paperboy for a copy of the Salem Journal's afternoon edition. Skipping the front page news about Germany's push through Europe, he read over the local society pages — an old habit.

Looking at photographs from the latest gala thrown by the Reynolds tobacco family — one attended by prominent members of the Hanes and Hull families — Drummond focused on the smiling party faces. He wondered how many of them harbored dark hearts like Mrs. Rankin. After all, magic in a bottle couldn't change the soul of person. Like alcohol, magic could only accentuate what already festered there.

On the next page, he gazed upon photos of nuptial engagements. How many of them had the open love that would leave them on the floor weeping?

It's too easy to blame the witches, he thought. He folded the newspaper and tucked it under his arm as he walked deeper into the city he loved.

CASE 02

THE AMNESIA DEALER

MARSHALL DRUMMOND TIPPED BACK HIS FEDORA with a pencil and tried to contain his exasperation. "Look, pal, the harder you make this on me, the harder it's gonna fall on you."

The man in the interrogation room looked like a classic ghost — pale white and wearing nothing but a sheet. He gripped his bald head with both hands as if trying to hold his skull together. "I swear, I don't know."

"All I'm asking for is your name."

The man wasn't even looking at Drummond. Instead, he stared at the wood table.

"How about where you're from? You know that?"

The man shook his head. "Nothing. I don't know where I am — heck, I don't even know what day it is, what month, or what year."

Drummond scratched his chin. "You're telling me you don't know that it's 1937."

"Is it?" The man's shoulders shuddered and tears dribbled down his face.

"Aw, come on. Don't start crying." But Drummond knew that once a suspect started with the tears, it would be a long night of wailing before anything useful could be gained. Then again, he wasn't even sure if this guy should be called a suspect.

Only an hour earlier, the evening had looked like it would be a short one — a quiet, Winston-Salem night. Thanksgiving had ended a day ago and winter had yet to kick in. The private investigator business had been quiet lately, though usually Christmas brought along a few cases. Drummond planned to close up early, knock back a few drinks at Tommy's Bar, and maybe strike up a chat with the new waitress, Penny.

But then Detective Cooper called. Baldy had walked into the police station wearing a toga and a dazed look in his eyes, and he claimed that somebody had stolen his mind. Normally, Cooper would have called in the wacky wagon and had this guy sent away to the local asylum. But he knew Drummond handled the stranger cases, and it was a slow night. Besides, they had been partners back when Drummond walked the streets as a beat cop, and he figured it'd be good to see his old pal. At least, that was what he had said.

Drummond didn't buy all that his old pal was selling, but he also knew what a horrible place the asylum would be. He figured ol' Cooper had been spooked by something he didn't want even the asylum to know about. Besides, it wouldn't hurt to give this bald man a few minutes before condemning the guy to such conditions. Except after spending five of those minutes, he had yet to get as much as the man's name.

"Heckuva racket we're in." Cooper said as he walked in with a mug of coffee. "Peter Lorre here say anything?"

The bald man perked up. "Is that my name? Am I Peter Lorre?"

"No," Drummond said. "Tell you what. Let's skip over who you are for right now, and why don't you tell me what happened. How come you were found walking around like, well, like this?"

Stroking the sheet that clothed him, the bald man looked even more lost. "I swear, I don't know anything. I woke up in a room, the door was open, and I couldn't remember anything, so I ran."

"Okay, that's a start. Where was this room?"

"A big house, but I ran and I don't know where I was. I just kept running until I saw the police lamp outside. That's it. That's all I know."

Drummond leaned in closer and in a low voice, he said, "You've got to tell me something. If you don't, Cooper's going to throw you in an asylum. Trust me, pal, you do not want to go there."

From across the room, Cooper said, "Hey, did you tell him about the glowing man?"

Drummond bore his eyes onto the bald man. "What's he talking about? Tell me about the glowing man."

"I-I can't. If I tell you, you'll definitely lock me up. You'll think I'm crazy."

"Oh, don't worry about that. I've seen more crazy things in my life than you can even dream up. Now, tell me."

The bald man appeared to weigh his options and quickly realized he had none. "Okay," he said. "First, it wasn't a man. It was a woman. After running around for a while and before I found the police station, I ended up in the park. And there she was. This woman stood near a tree. She was glowing like a greenish kind of color. I thought I was dreaming. She said she'd been looking for me and it was time to go back. I didn't know what the heck was going on, but I knew I didn't want to go anywhere with her. So, I ran again. Then I ended up here."

"That's it?"

"Isn't that enough? She was glowing green, for Pete's sake."

Drummond tapped his lips with his pencil. "What was she wearing?"

"Huh?"

"Her clothes. What did they look like?"

"I don't know. Like a long robe-type thing."

"Anything else?"

The bald man's face brightened. "Yeah. She was drawing in the air."

"Drawing?"

He swooped his hands around in the air. "Like this. Over and over."

Drummond nodded and stepped out of the room. Cooper followed.

"What do ya think?" Cooper leaned against the wall. "He's nuts right. I shouldn't have bothered you."

"He's not nuts. At least, not because of this."

"Wait. There really is a glowing green woman?"

Drummond shrugged. "Maybe. Do you really want to know?"

"Not on your life. I hate this stuff. I'm happy to hand it all over to you."

"Gee, thanks."

"Heckuva racket." Cooper chuckled, then sipped his coffee. "So, what now?"

"Put him in the drunk tank for the night. I'll go look into this."

From behind the door, they heard a muffled cry. "Detectives!"

Drummond threw open the door to find the bald man cowering in the back corner. Cooper came in with a baton at the ready. The bald man's eyes widened and he covered his head with his hands. The sheet he had been holding up dropped and Drummond saw an arcane symbol carved in the man's stomach.

The man blubbered tears. "Don't hurt me."

"Nobody's going to hurt you," Drummond said, but the man continued to panic.

With a sharp cry, the bald man spread his arms wide against the wall. Sweat covered his body. Blood dribble from the strange symbol.

"What the hell is this?" Cooper said.

Drummond kept his eyes on the bald man. "Stuff you don't want to see."

As if in answer, the bald man let loose one final cry. Then the skin around the symbol imploded as if a cannonball had struck him in the belly. A big hole broke through. Blood splashed out his back and the bald man collapsed in a heap.

"W-What the h-hell?" Cooper stumbled out into the hall.

A voice from further down called back, "Hey, Cooper. I got another one of those bald togas roaming the streets for you."

"Crap," Drummond said. This was going to be a long night. He stepped out of the room and as he walked by Cooper, he said, "Get that mess cleaned up before anybody sees it. I'll take of this."

It all sounded good, but he had no clue how he would take of anything. He snatched the latest case sheet from the front desk. The officer on duty protested but by then Cooper had recovered enough to yell down the hall that Drummond had his permission.

The sheet detailed a disturbing the peace complaint. Apparently, this bald man in a bedsheet had been stumbling around the southern districts just outside the city. Nice area of town but more than Drummond could afford.

He drove out to Queen Street — a peaceful tree-lined neighborhood with tiny houses and plenty of kids. The address on the sheet turned out to be an empty house with a *For Sale* sign stuck out front. Since no other sightings had been reported before Drummond left the police station, he decided to check out the empty house. There was a chance Baldy had slipped inside.

Footprints on the dusty porch confirmed Drummond's suspicion. The front door stood ajar, so Drummond entered. From the right pocket of his trench coat, he pulled out a .38, and from his left pocket, he brought out his ward. A witch who owed him one had made the ward from a smoky-white crystal. It supposedly protected against minor magic, but when she delivered it, she gave him a curious wink. *Damn thing will probably never work*. He had yet to see it in action and hoped this wouldn't be the time to discover he had been hoodwinked. Yet he still did as she had instructed — kissed the front of it to enact its magic — and after returning it to his pocket, he had to admit, he found comfort in feeling its weight bounce against his side.

The house was a typical affair — staircase right from the entrance leading to a second floor, living room off to the side, long hall leading back to a kitchen and bathroom, brown walls and hardwood floors. All quite compact and functional. On the walls, a few rectangles of darker brown showed where the previous occupants had hung pictures of one kind or another.

Drummond followed the footprints back into the kitchen. The bald man cowered on the floor in the opening where an icebox would be placed. Heavier than the first man, this one also had a thick, dark brow. His bottom lip protruded giving him a persistently angry expression. The sheet he wore covered his waist and below, but he made no effort to hide the symbol on his stomach.

He gazed up at Drummond. "What's going on? Who are you?"

Lowering his weapon yet keeping it at the ready, Drummond said, "I'm Marshall Drummond. I'm a private investigator, and I'm trying to figure out what happened to you. Do you remember anything?"

The man scrunched up his features as he thought. "I don't know. I can't even ... what's my name? Why can't I think of my name?"

"Do you know how you got here?"

"I woke up in a room and I saw a guy running out the door. I tried to follow him, got out of this big house, but then I couldn't recall anything and everything looked unfamiliar and I got confused."

"Don't start crying." Drummond searched over the dust on the floor. He saw only his shoe prints and the footprints of the bald man. "You been in here alone? Have you seen a woman wearing a cloak? Kind of glowing green?"

"Glowing green?" Tremors rolled across the bald man's skin. "What is happening to me?"

"Stay calm."

"How can I stay calm? Look at me!"

There were only two ways into the kitchen — from the hall and from a door that led out to the backyard. Drummond's focus shifted from one entrance to the other. "I know you're scared. I know this is all very strange. But if you haven't seen the green, glowing lady yet, then this ain't over."

"So let's find the green, glowing lady and get this over."

Drummond leveled a cold stare at the bald man. "You don't want that."

Somebody opened the front door of the house and stepped in. Drummond put out his hand and the bald man snapped his mouth shut. Drummond inched towards the hall and lifted his weapon. With a brisk motion, he snatched a peek around the corner and down the hall.

"Well?" the bald man said, bringing his knees up to his chest. "Is it her?"

Drummond nodded. He had not seen the cloaked woman, but he did catch the glowing green — there was no mistaking the unearthly light created by magic. To alleviate any doubt, a creaking voice with a thick North Carolina accent came from down the hall.

"Now, now, you've been naughty. Running away from our kind benefactor — why, you and your little friends have caused me a lot of trouble tonight. But like I told you so many times before, once you've got my mark on you, there's no escaping your fate."

Drummond looked back at the bald man. "You remember meeting

her?"

The bald man shrugged. Whatever curse this witch had put on him, it had wiped away his memory more thoroughly than anything Drummond had seen before.

Two light footsteps and the heavy thunk of a cane. Two more steps and another heavy thunk. The witch closed in.

Drummond considered grabbing the man and dashing out the back, but he had had enough experiences with witches to know better. She would not be giving up. At least by confronting her, she would be stuck in the confines of the hallway. With one hand out, he gestured for the man to stay put. Then Drummond stepped into the hall.

The woman hunched over her cane, wearing a long cloak. She had scraggly black hair with wisps of gray stripped throughout. She was not old but rather weathered as if years of using magic had robbed her of her youth. A greenish hue pulsed off her body, reflecting on the narrow walls of the hallway.

As she lifted her head, a hole marred where one of her eyes had been. "Be a smart lad — turn around and leave. That man in there, he belongs to me."

Trying to act casual, Drummond leaned a shoulder against the wall. "Well, now, that's going to be a problem. I don't like leaving anyone in the hands of a witch."

Her mouth opened wide. "Oh, so you know the truth about the world."

"Some. But who can ever know the full truth?"

"A philosopher, now. Mr. Court would have fun talking with you."

Drummond cocked his head. "Mr. Court? Is that your boss?"

"Nobody is my boss." The witch hissed the words and her glow brightened. After a breath, her body relaxed and the glow dimmed. "But I do assist Mr. Court from time to time. Right now, I'm trying to clean up the mess he made when he left a door open."

Drummond glanced over his shoulder. "How many more of these baldies did you make?"

The witch lifted a gnarled hand. "You best leave now, or I'll have to make another."

Pushing off the wall, Drummond said, "Okay, okay. I can tell when I'm outmatched. He's all yours." As he turned back down the hall, he whirled around, taking quick aim with his .38 and fired off two rounds. The first shot went wide and buried into the wall. But the second shot caught her in the arm. Unfortunately for Drummond, the witch had expected his move — her green light burned with fury as she cast her spell.

WHEN DRUMMOND AWOKE, he sat in a beautiful reading chair in an even more beautiful study. The walls had built-in bookshelves of deep, rich wood. Volumes upon volumes of books old and new were stacked from the hardwood floor to the high, vaulted-ceiling above. A mural had been painted on the ceiling depicting the constellations and the images their connections created.

To his left, Drummond saw a small table with a gold lamp. Another reading chair had been positioned on the other side of the table. In front of him, on the floor, a bear skin rug stared at him. Beyond that, an enormous fireplace with a small fire flickered amber light across the floor and walls. On the far wall, he spotted a short radiator under a narrow, barred window. Everything about the study had been designed to both comfort and intimidate.

Drummond stood, noting that he had not been bound to the chair, and checked under his hat — still had hair. He felt his stomach, too — no carved symbols. At least, she hadn't cursed him. He had no intention of waiting around for her to change her mind.

He headed straight for the cherry wood door. Unsurprisingly, he found it locked. While he had not been made immobile, he was certainly a prisoner. He glanced out the barred window — the dark, moonless night blacked out any landscape Drummond could use to figure out his location.

From the other side of the door, he heard an echoing voice. "Ah, he's awake. Good."

Drummond moved back five feet from the door and reached into his pocket — no weapon there, of course. He had probably dropped it in the hall when the witch attacked him. The door unlocked and for an instant, Drummond considered rushing forward and fighting his way free. But the nature of the study and the fact that they had not trussed him up suggested a less violent approach might be favorable.

A man entered, and Drummond fell back a few more steps. The man was uncommonly short. No taller than four feet. He had a thick, white beard matched by long, white hair that formed a horseshoe around his bald head. A fine tweed suit with a checkered bow tie, a thin, crimson scarf, and thick, black glasses that enlarged his eyes gave him the appearance of a marionette.

After closing the door, he looked back and offered a warm, sincere smile. "It's a pleasure to meet you, Mr. Drummond."

"You know my name?"

"Why should you be the only one knowing names around here?"

"Then I take it you're Mr. Court."

The man gave a slight bow before walking toward the reading chairs. "Please, join me."

Drummond did not move. "Forgive me, but I'm not in a sociable mood."

"You may want to change your attitude. Chances are, you're going to be here quite a long time."

"Where exactly is *here?*"

Mr. Court smirked and walked to a small, wet bar in the back corner. "Care for a drink?"

Drummond wanted to down a shot or two of whiskey but thought it unwise for the moment. "No, thank you. I'd rather just have answers."

Setting down his glass with a perturbed thud, Mr. Court said, "You are being rude. Now, take off your coat, relax, have a seat, and let's talk."

Drummond crossed his arms and remained standing. "I don't think I'm going to be doing any of that. Not until I know why you're cursing these men, wiping away their minds."

"Well, then, I suppose I have to tell you. I can't abide your rudeness for much longer. But remember, we could have done this a far easier way." Mr. Court sighed and sipped three times before placing his glass back on the bar. When he turned around, his affable expression had vanished. With a calculating sternness, he said, "Have you ever heard of the Hull family?"

"Who hasn't? Reynolds, Hanes, and Hull — the big three families in this town."

"Correct. But what most people don't know is that whereas Reynolds makes their money off tobacco and Hanes off textiles, the Hull family uses magic. All the magic in North Carolina is permitted only through their rule. They are, if you will, the local government of magic. And they collect taxes for that, too."

"I always thought your kind were anarchists."

"Oh, I didn't say the witches want it to be this way, only that the Hulls had that power. And, please, don't lump me together with them. I'm no practitioner of magic."

Drummond lowered his arms, relaxing into the conversation. "Fine. You're not a witch, and the Hull family controls all the magic usage around here. What exactly is going on with these men?"

"I am a sort of sub-contractor. The Hulls hire me to handle certain people and situations that they need handled discreetly."

Dropping his head, Drummond said, "I thought we were going to be direct, honest, about all this. Can we not play the game of ambiguous statements?"

Mr. Court tapped the side of his nose. "I like you. I didn't think so at first, but I definitely do like you. Okay, Mr. Drummond — in the world of magic, there are many dangers. If you are a family like the Hulls, if you want to control the magic usage, then you have to also dole out punishment. That punishment can take many forms. The Hulls preferred method is to curse people. However, sometimes leaving a cursed person alive with the information concerning the Hulls still in their heads is too dangerous. That is when they hire me."

"These men I found. They were all victims of you and the Hulls?"

"Not victims. Criminals. Ones who have now been punished with a curse of amnesia. I get paid a large sum to insure that these people have all memory erased."

Drummond strolled toward the reading chairs and sat. With a satisfied grin, Mr. Court took the other chair.

"Why do the Hulls bother with you? Can't they hire a witch directly?"

"There are always layers in an organization. It helps insulate those at the top from connections to those at the bottom."

"So, you're a middle man."

"We all have our place. Frankly, I'm sure the Hulls could cast the spell themselves. I probably could learn to do it, too. It's rather simple, I'm told. But we prefer to keep our hands clean of such things. And there are plenty of witches more than willing to help out if it gains them favor with the Hulls. I can see on your face that you don't quite understand. Allow me — the Hulls have a problem with someone, they decide they want him cleaned, they send him to me, I have my witches wipe their memories. Simple. I also have a curse placed on their bodies so that should they escape, or if the spell fails to clean fully and they start to remember, they are ... put down, as veterinarians often say."

Drummond's eyes narrowed. "That's what happened to the man at the police station. You executed him through a spell."

"He should have stayed here."

Drummond looked around the study, the size and scope of it, the wealth behind its design. "How many of your victims are living here? How big is this place?"

"It is quite an operation, but we treat them well — they're really nothing more than giant babies once they've been cursed. I see to it that they have a calm, peaceful life until they die of natural causes."

"This is like some kind of hospital for people cursed by you?"

"Cursed by order of the Hulls, but yes, I suppose, for lack of a better description."

Drummond remained quiet, letting it all sink in. But then a thought hit him that burned like a hot ember in his gut. "Why would you tell me all of this unless you're not going to let me leave? You're going to curse me as well."

"Don't be foolish. I won't curse you. I only follow the orders of the Hulls, and they've never even heard of you. But you did insist on learning all of this information, and I promised it would not be the easiest route. I will have to notify the Hulls of our conversation, and chances are that they will be unhappy with you knowing all of this. But enough for now. We can talk more at dinner. Please, make yourself comfortable. You can toss your coat anywhere. We won't hold it against you."

Drummond glared.

Mr. Court backed up to the door. "I see. You need more time to acclimate. That's fine. Quite understandable. Relax. Help yourself to a drink. I shall return later and we can finish our talk." With that, he made a hasty exit.

Once alone, Drummond took a quick tour of the study, checking for any possible way out he had missed. He found nothing. On the bar, he saw the two glasses Mr. Court had poured.

At least if things turned out the worst, he could smash them and cut his own throat. No way would he let a witch steal all of his memories.

"But it won't come to that," he muttered as he jiggled the locked door once more.

A few minutes later, the radiator pinged followed by the soft hiss of steam. Heat warmed the room. The fire still burned. What was Court trying to do — sweat out Drummond's compliance?

Drummond removed his hat and set it on the chair. With his sleeve, he blotted his brow as he tried to put the pieces of this strange day into place. Clearly he had stumbled upon something he had not been meant to see. Now, those involved were playing clean up. But why had they not destroyed him? Why not wipe his mind and leave him a bald, blubbering mess before finally killing him? Even now, Court left him in the study, a prisoner but still capable of thinking. It didn't add up.

Sweat trickled down his side, and Drummond started to shimmy his coat off. That's when he heard the door unlock. And he understood.

When Court stepped in, he glanced at Drummond, and his face dropped. Drummond snickered. "Little too eager there, aren't you?"

"My parents always said it was my worst trait."

With a sharp motion, he brought his coat back up and pulled it tight. "This is about the ward."

Court sauntered over to the chairs and sat. "I don't know where you acquired such a powerful ward, but it protected you from having your brain scrambled. When my witch attempted to remove your coat, it burned her hand clean off."

"Really?" Drummond said, snatching his hat and setting it back on his head. "I had no idea it was so strong. Heck, I could've used it a long time ago. Can't say I'm sorry about your witch, though."

"I wouldn't expect you to be."

Drummond sat, crossed his legs, and tapped his fingers on the arm of the chair. "So, now what? You can't harm me with magic, and I don't care how hot you make this room, I ain't taking this coat off."

"We do seem to be at a stalemate but for one crucial difference. You are my prisoner."

"For now. But people will miss me. Detective Cooper is the one who sent me on all of this. He'll want a report tomorrow to find out what happened, and when I don't show up, he'll start to get concerned."

"That's only a problem if he can find you, and if I were in your situation, I would not be expecting that level of success from Detective Cooper." Court patted his knees and stood. He brushed off his suit and slid one finger along the top of his scarf. "I'm afraid you are stuck here. I suppose I'll have to starve you out, unless you want to be a helpful sort and take of the coat."

"Not a chance."

"Then we shall see what happens. But I prefer my odds. We'll chat later. I still have one more escapee to recover."

OVER THE NEXT SEVERAL HOURS, Drummond sat in the chair, moving as little as possible. He couldn't be sure he was alone. He figured chances were good that Court or one of his employees spied from some unseen corner of the room. Besides, there was no place to go.

Instead, he sat and thought. Because something itched at the back of his head. Some small thing he had missed. He started at the beginning with Detective Cooper calling him into the station and followed events one by one in his head. He recalled the bald men, the fear shaking in their eyes. He recalled the abandoned house and meeting the witch. He recalled every aspect of being in this study. The numerous times Court tried to get him to remove his coat and the regular offer of drinks.

Drummond looked at the bar — probably spiked with either poison or a spell that would neutralize his ward.

Then it hit him — *why hadn't Court simply removed the coat?*

The witch had magical energy which the ward fought against. It burned her. But it wouldn't have had any effect on Court. Unless ...

He had found it. The missing piece. The only question now — how to use it.

Gazing at the stacks and stacks of books, he considered digging deep into whatever arcane knowledge he could find. But he knew better. Even if he happened upon the key information, he probably would not recognize it. Knowing of magic and knowing magic were two vastly different things. Besides, if he had wanted to have his nose stuck in books all day, he would have become a librarian. Taking action suited him better — another reason he preferred being a PI over a police detective.

Instead of research, Drummond paced the room and thought. Twenty minutes later, he still had no plan, but that did not worry him. Most plans fizzled away the moment the action began. He would simply have to wait for Court to return and improvise with what he knew.

This time, when Court arrived, he brought the hunched witch along with him. She scowled as she entered the study. With more gray in her hair and a heavier thud from her cane, Drummond swore she had aged years since they had last met. The hole where her eye had been now matched the empty space where her hand had been. Perhaps the loss had caused the change in her. Or perhaps she had spent too much time playing with spells she couldn't control. He had seen that before.

Magic required more than simply knowing the words and drawing the symbols. A true witch had to study, build up strength, and learn how to control these powerful forces. Otherwise, the forces controlled the witch.

Court and his witch spread out, one to either side, and he checked over Drummond. Seeing Drummond's stubborn refusal to give in, Court wrinkled his nose, adjusted his thick glasses, and clasped his hands behind his back.

"I thought you were more pragmatic than this, Mr. Drummond. I expected your coat to be folded over the chair and your acceptance more apparent. You know you cannot escape, that your fate has been set, yet you persist nonetheless."

"Looks like you're not willing to give up, either. Unless she's here for decoration."

"Well, one must be cautious."

"Very true," Drummond said. Though he kept his eyes on Court, he heard the witch's cane continue to thump as she positioned herself on the opposite wall, directly behind him. "This could go on a long time. So, I'll tell you what — we both know your witch can't move on me. Not as long as I have this coat on. But that's not true of you. If you can take my coat off, then I'll let you do whatever you want to me."

Court raised an eyebrow with a practiced expression. "Hardly a generous offer when we both know that you are more capable at fisticuffs than I. The chances that I would be able to successfully remove your coat are slim."

Drummond put his hands out. "Fair enough. How about this? I won't stand in your way at all. You only have to walk over here and slip my coat off."

Court did not move. "I'm sure there's a trick in here somewhere."

"No trick. I promise on all that is holy in the world — all you have to do is take my coat."

Court still did not move. He chuckled. "So, you know."

"That you use magic, too? Yeah, I figured that one out." He turned his head to the side. "How about you, witch? Did you know your boss here can cast a spell or two?"

The witch snarled. "Don't talk to me if you want to keep your skin on your body."

To Court, Drummond said, "I guess she didn't know. Unless she saw you burn off a finger or two."

"Not after I saw what happened to her," Court said. "I wouldn't dare touch your coat."

"This brings us to a tough spot. What to do? You two don't seem to want to let me leave, yet you can't lay a hand on me."

Court's head lowered. His eyes darkened. "I wouldn't say that."

Crap. Drummond whirled around to find the witch on her knees. Her eye had rolled upward, showing only the white, as she mumbled ancient words. She swayed in a circular motion and her one hand traced shapes in the air. Drummond had never seen a spell cast this way before, and he certainly didn't want to witness the results.

He checked his pocket for the comfort of the ward when he heard Court mumbling words, too. He spun back. The short man mimicked the witch's swaying motion and a diabolic grin stretched out on his face. With both hands, he made gestures in the air similar to those of the witch.

Drummond stepped toward the door. Green flames erupted from the floor, blocking his exit. He turned back and another wall of green flames formed, reaching to the ceiling, obstructing his way, keeping him stuck between the witch and the madman.

The heat intensified behind him, forcing him forward and closer toward the green flames in front. Court laughed. "Careful, Mr. Drummond."

While Drummond knew the ward protected him from magic, feeling the heat from this ghostly fire did not fill him with confidence. Perhaps the ward had weakened or perhaps the witch had discovered a loophole — magic seemed to be filled with those.

The fire grew hotter, yet it did not consume any of the wood or the books or even the bear-skin rug. Then it moved. The wall of green in front crept towards him. He could feel the flames reaching closer from the fire behind, too.

This is not good.

The witch raised her arms toward the ceiling, arched her head back, and let loose a high-pitched ululation. Her crazed cries visibly rolled up her throat. The horrendous sound chilled Drummond's skin as did the sight of her charred stump.

Whatever else this spell could do, that sound announced that the worst was coming. Unless Drummond did something fast.

With a yell of his own, he launched towards the witch. Two feet away from her, green flames shot up from the floorboards — directly under Drummond's feet. His primal war cry turned into a garbled scream of pain. He flailed backwards. His heel caught on the floor, but as he went down, his momentum sent him reeling into Mr. Court. On instinct, Court put out his hands to brace against the impact. The sound of sizzling skin and the smell of burnt flesh filled the air along with the man's dire shrieks.

Though smaller than Drummond and positioned at a poor angle, pain and adrenaline must have given Court a sudden burst of strength. The man found the power to shove Drummond forward. Once back on his feet, Drummond took the initiative. He barreled across the room, dove into the air, through the flames, and tried to flip his body over at the last moment so that his coat-clad back slammed into the witch.

The two tumbled up against the side of the fireplace. With her head next to his ear, her anguished screams vibrated down his spine. He tried to stand, but the green flames he had soared through now barred his way.

"I'm sorry," he said — and he meant it. He could not stop the pain she endured. While his hope had been to disable her from hurting him, he never intended to cause her demise. Not like this. He heard her body dissolving beneath him. The screams, the sizzling, the sounds that he would never stop hearing in his nightmares went on. Only when he felt her mass disappear beneath him, only when he saw the green flames dissipate into the air, only then could he stand.

When he clambered to his feet, he discovered Mr. Court on the floor. The man wept as he stared at the tortured stumps that had once been his hands. Drummond heard something crack and felt a bump in his pocket. Reaching in, he found the dusty remains of the ward — all five cracked pieces.

Drummond stomped over to Court. With a sharp motion, he grabbed the man's scarf and whisked it off. Stepping behind Court, he used the scarf to gag the man — just in case Court knew spells that could be cast without hands.

THE NEXT FEW HOURS reminded Drummond one of many reasons why he had left the police force. After calling Detective Cooper, he had to wait around for the police to arrive. Then he had to help fabricate a reasonable explanation for the unexplainable events of the evening. Cooper knew enough not to ask too many questions.

They found several more victims of Court's "cleaning" process locked away in the house. Each one was rushed to the hospital, but Drummond didn't hold out hope that they would have their memories restored. Fixing magic with medicine rarely worked. At least no other would fall prey to Court's sadistic methods. Unless the Hull family found a new Mr. Court to continue the practice. For now, however, the case was closed.

By the time Drummond returned to his office, he wanted to sleep but knew such a luxury would be far from easy to achieve. He slumped behind his desk with an open bottle of whiskey and a full glass. The sun peeked over the horizon for a new day.

"Helluva racket I'm in." He raised his glass and thought of Cooper.

He tipped back the glass until it emptied and poured another. "Helluva racket."

CASE 03

WITCH'S BREW

FOR THE THIRD TIME, Marshall Drummond turned his head and tried to relax his body as a fist plowed into his cheek. Slick with blood, his face swelled while his captors pulled back for another strike. This was going to be a long day.

Only an hour before, Drummond had been sitting in Vera's Diner, enjoying his morning coffee. Looking over the front page of the Winston-Salem Journal, he read the latest about mass unemployment, soup lines, and the dwindling sense that anything would dig the country out of its economic despair. FDR certainly had nothing new to offer. Things ahead looked bleak.

Clicking a nickel on the table, Drummond stood, set his Fedora on his head, put on his long coat, and planned to head into his office to start another day as a private investigator. That was when the two thugs walked right up to him. They were big, square-jawed men wearing cheap suits and expensive handguns — a combination that suggested organized crime.

Strange. While being a private investigator meant coming into contact with criminal types, Drummond specialized in cases of the supernatural variety. He never had any cases involving mobsters. For that matter, Winston-Salem never reached the size to attract mobster business attentions — at least, none that Drummond knew of.

Drummond tipped his hat. "Morning, fellas. What's this all about?"

One of the thugs grabbed Drummond's arm. "I guess you want to take me for a drive." The other thug grunted as they escorted him outside.

That was it. They stuck him in the backseat of a 1928 Cadillac Town Sedan — a few years old but still in good condition — took his .38, checked his legs for an ankle holster — he didn't have one — and drove to a warehouse on Northwest Blvd. They dragged him into a large open building and brought him behind a low wall of crates. From there it took only a few minutes to tie him onto a wood chair and unleash a flurry of punches.

They never asked questions. They never made threatening remarks. Just punch after punch after punch. By the fourth strike to his head, Drummond thought learning a few witch curses might be a good idea in the future.

The assault continued until they heard a door in the back open and the steady clicks of expensive shoes on the warehouse floor. Both men stepped back and stood at attention — clearly former Army.

"Okay, boys," a voice said, filled with enough gravel to pave roads all the way to New York City. "Go on out and wait by the car. I'm gonna talk with Mr. Drummond alone."

The two thugs gave a short nod and simultaneously said, "Yes, Mr. Popper." They walked out attempting to hide their hurried steps.

Drummond didn't know whether to be pleased that the beating portion of his abduction had concluded or fearful of what Mr. Popper had planned next.

Mr. Popper walked into Drummond's view wearing a dark blue suit and a gray Bowler. He had the bulk of a man who once had an impressive physique but had let it atrophy into flab — still strong but not like before. Thick lips and a broad face made his grin potentially charming but, without doubt, threatening.

He dragged a chair over and sat before Drummond. "My name is Wex Popper. Pleasure to meet you." Gesturing to Drummond's face, he added, "Sorry about the rough-up. Under the circumstances, I had to make my men believe you deserved it."

Drummond ran his tongue over his split lip. "You telling me you had me beat up for show?"

"Afraid so, pal. See, I'm planning on hiring you, but if word gets out what this is all about, I'm finished. So, I put up this little charade here. Make it look like there's a different reason we're talking."

If this was a *little charade*, Drummond hated to think about what a real beating would look like from Popper. "If all that's true, then how about untying me?"

Popper grinned, sending a chill over Drummond's skin. "First, I want to make sure you're not going jump and try to choke me to death or sucker punch me."

Drummond had to admit he had been thinking just that, but assaulting a mobster did not seem like a healthy way to cap off his morning. With a sigh, he said, "I won't attack you."

Popper nodded. Displaying a surprisingly dainty touch, he undid the ropes that kept Drummond in the chair. When he finished, both men sat back. Popper reached into his coat and produced a pack of Camels. He offered one to Drummond.

"Don't mind if I do." Drummond put the cigarette in his mouth and leaned forward to accept a light. He inhaled a long, slow drag before saying, "Okay, Mr. Popper, time to talk. What the heck is this all about?"

Popper smoked his cigarette. He stayed quiet, observing Drummond like a scientist watching an animal for aberrant behavior. Drummond did not want anything to do with this, but he figured that giving Popper a moment to think would feel a lot better than giving Popper a reason to start punching.

At length, Popper said, "This is difficult for me. It's hard to believe. Hell, I keep going back and forth between believing it and thinking I've gone crazy. I don't even know where to start with you."

"You went through an awful lot to quietly get me here, beat me up for no reason other than appearances — that would suggest to me that you know exactly what you want to say. Stop being a chump and say it."

Anger flared in Popper's eyes, but he cooled it back fast. "You're right. Why have you here if not to tell you this? Okay, Mr. Drummond, here it goes. I'm being haunted by the ghost of a girl."

"Yeah, I figured it was something like that."

Popper's shoulders dropped. "Oh, thank goodness. I thought for sure I'd gone crazy."

"I don't know about that, but seeing a ghost doesn't make you crazy. Ghosts are real."

Tapping out another cigarette and lighting up, Popper said, "Okay. What do I have to do? How do I get rid of her?"

"That depends. Let's start with where you're from."

"What does that have to do with anything?"

"You're not from around here. I know most of the criminals working this town, and you're not one. So, if I'm going to help you, I need to know where this ghost has been haunting you."

"I may not be local, but the ghost is. I come down here for vacation, y'know. Get away from the stress of my life. Okay? Been coming down here for years. Got a little place near Salem Lake. But last week, she started showing up. First, I thought it was just a bunch of vivid dreams. But then I started seeing her when I knew I was awake. She won't leave me alone."

"Fair enough. Tell me this — do you know her?"

Thrusting his arms out, Popper said, "What do you mean by that? What's that suppose to be all about?"

"The question is quite simple. Do you know this girl that's haunting you?"

Popper hesitated. "No."

"Too bad. Usually, something like this is caused by a relationship, left over business, that kind of thing. If you know who the ghost is and what the problem is, then you can talk to the ghost and often get them to move on without any trouble. But if she's targeting you at random, she might be a full-on poltergeist or close to it. Either way, you ought to get a priest to come in here and perform an official exorcism. You mobsters are mostly Catholic, right?"

"I ain't calling in no priest. I told you — this has got to be kept quiet. So, how do we do it without a priest?"

"You say the girl was local. Do you know where she's buried?"

Popper nodded.

"In that case, you go dig up her body, salt it, and burn it. Pretty standard stuff."

"And that'll take care of it? She'll be gone and stop bothering me?"

"That'll take care of it."

Popper jumped to his feet. "Sounds good. Let's get to it."

Drummond froze. "Me? Go get one of your goons to dig up a grave. You don't need me to throw salt on bones and burn them."

Despite his bulk, Popper's arm moved in a flash, grabbing Drummond by the front of the shirt and wrenching him forward. "You're going to do this because I'm telling you to do it. And I don't want to ever have to explain it again that nobody is to ever know about this. You understand?"

"Sure, pal, whatever you say." Drummond lifted the side of his mouth into a half-grin.

As they walked outside, Popper pointed to the Cadillac. "You're driving." He then pointed to his men. "Stay here."

Drummond got behind the wheel and with Popper in the passenger seat, he drove off down Northwest Blvd. Other than giving directions, Popper said nothing. Drummond didn't ask for more. He figured the less he knew, the better. But that didn't stop his mind from wondering.

In particular, he wondered if he should go along with any of this. He didn't mind getting rid of a ghost — even for a mobster — but something stunk bad. Popper's evasiveness did nothing to help ease Drummond's suspicions. And as Popper's directions lead them out of the city, Drummond worried that perhaps this whole excursion was a ruse.

Had he crossed the wrong people at some point? Possible. He certainly had crossed many bad people. But mobsters? He could not recall anything he did that involved mobsters.

Drummond shook off his thoughts. All he had to do was take care of the bones, and that should fix the matter. Then he could return to his quiet life of fighting the witches and ghosts of Winston-Salem. He could forget all about the underworld of organized crime. One underworld was enough.

After driving through acres upon acres of tobacco farms, they entered the shadowed roads of a forest. The air cooled. The afternoon sun fought to even dapple the ground with light. Popper indicated a dirt sideroad, and five minutes later, he told Drummond to stop the car. From the trunk, Popper grabbed a can of gasoline and handed a shovel to Drummond.

Raising his eyebrows, Drummond said, "Just one shovel?"

"I don't dig." Popper reached in and picked up a small box of salt. "Follow me."

Trudging through the woods, Drummond's internal alarm sounded off — constant and loud. It bothered him that they were alone. It bothered him that Popper kept the important details a secret. Most of all, it bothered him that Popper had a shovel, gasoline, and salt at the ready.

"Here," Popper said, pointing at a patch of dirt near a pitch pine tree. "Get digging."

With no better options, Drummond thrust the end of the shovel into the dirt. He cringed at the resistance of the Carolina red clay. It wasn't the first hole he had ever dug and it wouldn't be the last — it never got easier.

Five minutes in and he could feel the sweat trickling down the back of his neck. With each shovelful of clay, he glared at Popper. The large man leaned against a white ash tree and smoked a cigarette as he watched Drummond work.

Drummond continued digging, but he made his shovelfuls as light as possible. The longer this took, the better. He had no illusion about the situation. He was digging up a body in the middle of the woods for a mobster — they don't like for people to know where the bodies are buried.

"Y'know," Popper said, blowing smoke rings, "I never really believed in ghosts and all that spooky stuff until this happened."

Interesting. Then there really was a ghost. "Tell me something — are we cleaning up your mess or is this somebody else's?"

Popper's thoughtful expression darkened. "Don't you worry anything about me or my men. You just dig."

"Not that simple. You want those ghosts to stop haunting you, then you're going to have to tell me a little about what's going on."

"I thought you said all we had to do was burn and salt the bones."

"You obviously expected that it's not that simple. You already had the salt here — you must've talked to somebody or read it somewhere. So, why bother coming to me? Unless you need an expert, and I'm telling you as an expert that I need to know some details."

The dilemma played out on Popper's face. At length, he kicked a stone off to the side. "Okay. Ask a question, and maybe I'll answer it."

Drummond kept his head down and shoveled more dirt. He had not expected Popper to be so accommodating. After a moment's thought, he said, "This girl — how old is she?"

Popper chuckled. "All you people. Everybody judging. What does it matter how old the girl was?"

"Matters a lot. The younger a person is, the more innocent they are. The more innocent they are, the harder it is for them to haunt you. So, if she's been haunting you and if she's very young, it'll be more difficult to stop her." None of that was true, but Drummond figured he might get an answer with a careful lie.

"I don't know. At least fifteen. Maybe seventeen."

"And did she deserve this? To die? Or did she just see something she shouldn't have?"

"Everybody dies. Some just get on with it sooner than others. That's all there is to it."

As Drummond wracked his brain for a good way to ask another question, he shoveled loose more dirt. He noticed the dark skin of a hand poking up from the ground. Dragging his foot, he quickly covered it back up.

Popper stepped forward. "What's wrong?"

Drummond looked up. "Nothing. Why?"

"You got pale. You look scared."

Think. Quickly. Think. "I am scared. I'm starting to realize I won't be leaving these woods, will I?" Popper shrugged. Drummond went on, "So, come on and tell me. What did you do to her? Why is it that you buried a black girl out here in the woods?"

All the casual calm drained from Popper's eyes. His bulk transformed into muscle as his face took on a dark scowl. Popper whipped out his Colt 1908, a small but powerful semi-automatic, and pointed it at Drummond. "You finish digging and you salt and burn that corpse, or you will definitely not make it out of these woods alive."

"You don't know what you're dealing with here. Salt and burn these bones all you want. She's not going to go to rest."

"You're lying."

"I don't think so."

"I don't care what you think. I'm going to ..."

Popper looked beyond Drummond and his eyes widened. All his bluster faded. His chin quivered and he staggered back. "Quick. Take care of the bones. Now! She's right here."

Drummond looked behind him and saw nobody. "Where is she? Tell me. I'm not tuned into her. I can't see her."

Shaking his finger, Popper said, "She's right there. Standing right next to you. Do something!"

Drummond opened his mouth to speak when he noticed the wet stain running down Popper's pant leg. In the next instant, Popper whirled around and sprinted off.

Drummond watched as Popper receded into the woods. "Well, I'll have to thank that ghost for saving my life." He climbed out of the shallow grave he had dug and walked away. That's when he felt a cold spot in his path. "Oh, crap."

Only a fool would stick around, and Drummond's mother had taught him never to be a fool. He was, however, too slow.

A shard of ice shot through the back of his skull causing a freezing headache to wrap around his brain. The pain burst straight through into his eyeballs and rattled his teeth. He dropped to his knees as the source of the icy shocks worked its way around his skull. And he finally saw the cause.

A pale spirit floated before him — a young, black girl, no more than fourteen years old. Her arm stretched out with her hand embedded in his head. He had read about this — a ghost could connect a living person with the ghost realm. The book mentioned there might be pain.

Might!

The excruciating bolts of iced lightning blasting through his skull and into the marrow of his bones made it difficult to concentrate. Tears trailed down his cheeks as he tried to focus on the ghost, tried to understand what she wanted him to see — all this pain had to be worth something. From the look on her face, the experience did not feel any better for her.

Maintaining her connection to Drummond, she moved to the side and pointed further ahead. A short distance away, Drummond saw another pale figure. A black boy, this time. He stood next to a clump of gray stones with his hands in his pockets and his head hung low.

The ghost girl thrust her face in Drummond's view. With great strain, she shrieked a harsh, mournful cry like a tortured animal, and one word cut through to the center of Drummond's pain-riddled brain — *brother!*

Pulling her arm free, the ghost girl vanished. Drummond collapsed forward, his head pressing into the earth. For five minutes, he remained motionless. Sweat drenched his body, and breathing proved to be the only thing he had enough strength to do. When he finally lifted his head, he stared at the unmarked grave of the young boy.

Snatching the shovel, he attacked the firm ground with renewed vigor. Each shovelful brought him closer to what he feared would be the truth. When he finally found the boy's leg and dug further up to reveal the torso, Drummond stopped. He had seen enough.

Glancing back at the girl's shallow grave, he understood more and more the ugly truth. Popper had attempted to destroy these bodies with salt and fire, but he botched the job. He used the salt to ring the bodies and burn them inside the salt circle. It probably seemed like a magical way to do things, but it had the opposite result. A circle of salt protects and contains. Popper had managed to create a poor man's incinerator — great for burning bones, terrible for ending ghosts.

From the looks of it, he realized it wasn't working and doused the flames. But the damage had been done. The bones were burned without the salt on them. Drummond could not free the souls — at least, not the traditional way.

"I never meant for the girl to die." Popper stood at the girl's grave.

Drummond stepped back and looked over his shoulder. "You going to tell me what happened?"

"Doesn't matter."

"Of course it does."

Popper lifted his eyes onto Drummond, cold and lifeless. "The boy there is her brother. Last year, I came here on vacation. Me and the boys tied on a few too many. We were driving along the backroads and saw this colored boy and his sister walking along the side of the road. I don't remember who said to do it, but we thought it'd be fun to scare them. So I turned the wheel and sped up the car — aiming right near them. But then I changed my mind. I ran him down."

"Why?"

"Same reason I had my boys beat you up. I've got power and strength in my position, but that's based on fear, and that fear is an image. I've got to maintain that image or lose everything."

Drummond could not hide the disgust on his face. "And the girl?"

"After killing one, I wasn't going to leave a witness. I backed up with the pedal hitting the floor and ran her down, too. We took the bodies out here into the woods. We were drunk. We were —"

"It doesn't matter. You killed a fourteen year old girl and sixteen year old boy on a whim. What kind of monster are you?"

Without any remorse, and with all of his threat, Popper said, "A real one." He kicked at the grave. "If you want to live through this, you're going to finish what we came here to do."

Drummond shook his head. "It can't be done here. You screwed it all up. We need to go a different route."

"Don't be lying to me. You see what I did to a couple kids who meant nothing to me. You don't want to see what I'll do to somebody who has let me down and lied to me."

Drummond set his hat on the back of his head and wiped his sweaty brow. "I want to see these kids move on and no longer be trapped here, haunting the earth — probably more than you do. But I'm telling you, it can't be done here."

"Then what do we do?"

Drummond had been wondering the same thing. He had two questions in his mind. The first was answered easily — he knew exactly how to get these ghosts to move on. The second question was more problematic — what to do about Popper.

Drummond's head snapped up and he held back a sly grin. "We're going to go see a witch."

Popper stood still, absorbing Drummond's words. Like a child throwing a tantrum, he stomped on the ground, kicked the stones, picked up a couple sticks and hurled them into the woods, before storming down the path towards the car. Drummond picked up the shovel and followed.

During the drive back, Popper tried to ask three times before finally managing to simply say, "A witch?"

Drummond nodded. "You know ghosts are real. Witches, too. Shouldn't be that much of a leap for you."

"But aren't they evil?"

"Yeah. But I know one that's a friend. She'll help me."

"I don't know about this. Bad enough I got to be haunted by ghosts, but dealing with witches — seems like I'm getting further away from being done with this stuff."

Drummond wanted to slam on the brakes to make his point but figured that would only anger Popper more. "It's my life on the line here. You've made that clear. So, you're going to have to trust that I want to solve this problem the best way possible."

Popper grumbled, leaned his head against the window, and watched the trees roll by. As evening approached, they parked outside a small house with a smaller yard.

Heading up to the porch, Drummond said, "This woman's old. She goes by the name of Madame Zabrinski. If you're smart, you'll keep your mouth shut."

"Don't be a wise guy."

"I'm not joking around. All this mobster attitude you've got — it's going to hurt you in there."

"I ain't afraid of an old lady."

As Drummond knocked on the door, he frowned. How much of an idiot could one man be? But a quick glance over told him that Popper's words were spoken mostly out of fear.

When the door opened, Madame Zabrinski stepped forward. She was short, five foot even, and looked to be in her nineties. Pudgy and wrinkled, she reminded Drummond of a fairy tale godmother. For the most part, she treated him the same — with kindness and concern. But he knew better than to be lulled into that persona. Madame Zabrinski was a witch. The babushka covering her head and the warm cookie smell coming from the kitchen could not hide the fact that when she wanted to, she could curse a person with such imaginative evil that suicide would seem a better option than suffering another day under her thumb.

Madame Zabrinski gazed upward and her face opened into a bright smile. "Marshall Drummond! It is wonderful to see you again."

Kissing the top of her hand, Drummond said, "It's wonderful to see you, too. This is an associate — Mr. Popper. I hoped you might be able to help him out."

"Anything for you. Come, come."

She led the way into her living room — a sparse square with only one table and four chairs. Candlewax pasted the middle of the table. A tabby slept in one corner. Otherwise, she had emptied the room of all furniture and decoration.

Everyone took a seat. Madame Zabrinski chose a chair at the front specially designed to give her an equal height with her guests. "Mr. Popper, what is it that brings you here?"

Popper leaned his elbows on the table and pushed his bulk forward. "Drummond here tells me that you can get rid of the ghosts haunting me."

Madame Zabrinski glanced at Drummond. He didn't need magic to read her mind — she wondered why he couldn't handle this himself. But a witch would never make it far in life if she couldn't read people and situations, and Madame Zabrinski had lived a long life.

With what Drummond hoped was a nod of understanding, she turned her attention back to Popper. "Of course I can help you. I would be happy to do so."

Popper raised his eyebrows. "Great. I thought it'd be tougher with you kind of witchfolk."

"Oh, I never said it would be easy."

With his brow dropping low, Popper said, "Yeah, it never can be. What is it that we have to do?"

"Not *we,* but *you.* I don't do anything for free."

Popper laughed. "Money? Is that all? How much you want for this?"

Madame Zabrinski tsked. "Witches don't need money. We require a different form of payment."

Putting his wallet away, Popper said, "What does that mean?"

"In this case, it means I require one of your fingers."

Popper looked from Madame Zabrinski to Drummond. "My what?"

Madame Zabrinski spread her hands on the table. "I require a finger. Your little finger will do, but I will need it in order to banish this ghost from haunting you."

With an uncomfortable chuckle, Popper leaned back in his chair and crossed his arms. "That's crazy. Drummond didn't require anything like that. He said that we only had to salt and burn the bones."

"And if that had worked, you would not be here with me. Obviously, what you're dealing with requires something stronger. In order to cast the kind of a spell to defeat such magic, I need a finger from the victim being haunted — that would be you."

"Lady, you belong in the looney bin. I'm not giving you crap."

Madame Zabrinski turned to Drummond. "Why are you wasting my time?"

Drummond put on a bashful shrug. "I thought he wanted this thing taken care of. I'm sorry." He shifted to face Popper. "Are you sure you won't give her your finger? Because that's it. I've got no other options to help you out, and I say that knowing full-well what that means."

Madame Zabrinski put her hand on Drummond's wrist. "Is he going to kill you for this?"

"I believe so. But what else can I do?"

"Unfortunately, that is it. Without a finger, there's nothing you can do."

Popper smacked his hand on the table. "I don't believe any of this. I'll go find another witch. Somebody'll help me. And Drummond, you're coming with me."

Madame Zabrinski made a show of rolling her eyes. "You will not find another witch willing to do this magic for just one finger. I am a friend of Drummond's, and I was giving you the job for free."

"For free? You wanted my finger."

"Any witch willing to cast this spell will require you finger — for the spell. But they'll also require payment, and I don't mean money. You'll have to make a deal with them, and trust me, you do not want to make a deal with a witch."

"The hell with you both. I'll just leave this state and never come back. I can take my vacations in Virginia."

"No, Mr. Popper. Now that the ghost has found you, she will not let you go. Wherever you live, she will appear. She is not bound by the tragedy of one location. She is bound by her hatred towards you, and that will allow her to follow you, no matter how much pain it causes her. In fact, the further you go, the more pain it will cause her and the more she will hate you, causing your haunting to get worse and worse. Maybe she'll go after your own family."

With a crack in his voice, Popper said, "Then what am I supposed to do?"

Madame Zabrinski reached into her pocket and produced a small knife wrapped in a handkerchief. She pushed them across the table. Popper stared at the knife. He looked at his fingers. For an instant, Drummond thought the mobster might shed a tear.

Instead, the man swiped the knife. "Can I have some privacy?"

Madame Zabrinski pointed to the hallway. "Door on the left is the bathroom. Please don't make too much of a mess." Once he left the room, she scooted off her chair. "Come on. To the kitchen. Let's get things ready."

Following her, Drummond said, "Wait, there really is a spell that needs his finger?"

"Of course."

Entering the kitchen, she grabbed a pot, filled it with water, and stuck it on the stove. As she gathered various roots and herbs, cut them up and dumped them into the pot like a chef preparing a gourmet soup, she also asked Drummond for the details. He laid it all out for her — starting with his breakfast that morning, being beaten and threatened, and ending with all he learned from digging up the graves and encountering the bodies.

When he finished, she chuckled. "Huh. I'm not one to get premonitions, so when I woke this morning and had the sudden urge to prepare to release two ghosts, I listened." She walked to her kitchen table and pulled back the tablecloth. On the table she had drawn a circle with numerous symbols all around it.

"What's this?" he asked.

She dug around her pocket until she found a small piece of paper. Handing it to Drummond, she said, "When you get his finger, put it in the center here and recite these words."

"And the stuff you got boiling on the stove?"

"That was the other part of my premonition. You'll know what to do when the time comes. And, if I'm wrong — premonitions can be tricky — well, then it's a good eating. Enjoy it."

"What about you? What are you going to do?"

Madame Zabrinski offered a kind smile and patted Drummond's hand. "When you get as old as I have and never once had a premonition, and then suddenly, you have two — well, you wake up knowing exactly what that means."

"I don't know what that means."

"You'll see in a moment."

"I don't understand."

"You will."

"But what about —"

"All I have to say is the magic words. And they are 'Yes, Marshall, we are going to betray Popper and then kill him.'"

The kitchen door banged open. Popper stepped forward brandishing his pistol. "I knew it. You think I'm so dumb that I'd go cut off my own finger? You think I'd trust a witch?"

Madame Zabrinski made a claw and pointed it at Popper. "I will curse you for all eternity." She spat in his direction.

Drummond could not understand what she was doing — curses didn't work that way.

"Nobody's cursing me," Popper said, and shot Madame Zabrinski twice in the chest. He then walked straight up to her and shot her once in the head.

The gunshots tremored through Drummond's body as if he had taken the bullets. Even in his shock, he heard rumbling behind him. As Popper swung his arm across to take aim, Drummond finally caught on. Without looking, he reached behind, grabbed the pot handle, and threw the boiling mixture at Popper.

The mobster screeched and flailed backwards. His pistol dropped to the floor and he followed, banging his head on the hard wood. Smoke drifted up from all parts of his body, and for a moment, Drummond thought perhaps the brew had been some type of acid. But then Popper's skin bulged and twisted into knots. He screamed until the skin on his throat followed the same pattern. In ten seconds, he was dead.

Drummond stared at the corpse. The smoke continued to rise as the skin turned black. Bits of it flaked off like ash off charred wood.

Moving fast, Drummond yanked out kitchen drawers until he found a sharp knife. Grabbing Popper's hand, he cut off the man's little finger. The bone gave way with ease, and Drummond hurried over to the kitchen table and set the finger in the center of the circle. From his pocket, he fished out Madame Zabrinski's paper and read the incantation which she had been kind enough to write out phonetically.

When he finished, nothing happened.

He thought about re-reading the incantation — perhaps he had messed it up somewhere — but then saw he had only been impatient. The finger lifted into the air. It hovered for a few seconds and with a pop, disappeared.

A cold spot passed through him, but it did not cause pain. Deep in his chest, he developed a strong sensation of satisfaction. The ghosts had just said *Thank you.*

Drummond leaned against the kitchen counter and let out a long breath. He hated to leave Madame Zabrinski lying dead on the floor, but he hated going to jail even more. Placing his hat on his head, he winked at the witch.

"You were one of the good ones."

He went to his office that night, pulled out his copy of *Tom Sawyer*, opened it, and then pulled out the flask of whiskey sitting in the carved out book. He raised the flask into the air. "To you, Madame Zabrinski. Some days are far too strange. I'm glad you were there to help me through this one."

In the morning, he would start a search for the parents of the murdered children. It wouldn't be easy — he never got the children's names. He would get a lot of pushback from law enforcement, too. None of them would want somebody poking around, digging up old cases about murdered black kids, not in the South. But while the ghosts had been taken care of, those parents were living each day haunted. They deserved some peace, too.

Tipping back the whiskey, letting it warm his belly, he wondered how long it would take him to sleep that night — if he would sleep at all. But at least those two children would sleep. And Madame Zabrinski — she deserved to sleep well, too.

CASE 04

THE FATE OF LAURA MCCULLEN

MARSHALL DRUMMOND COULD PUSH THE MODEL A only so fast before he risked the old Ford burning up on him. Driving from Winston-Salem to Greensboro always required a solid two hours, but this time, the minutes seemed to drag and taunt him simultaneously. With the sun setting and the headlights barely good enough to meet the road, he worried he might be forced to slow down even more.

Lighting a cigarette, he readjusted on the seat. "Go over it again," he said to the woman sitting next to him. "We won't reach your farm for a bit, and the more I know what to expect, the better."

He meant what he said; however, he withheld the fact that the more times a story was told, the more details he could glean from it. Plus, having a person retell their story made it easier to spot lies — a trick Drummond had picked up back in his days on the police force, back before he had ever seen a ghost, back when the idea of being a private eye for the weird and unexplained never even crossed his mind. He didn't doubt Amanda McCullen's tale, but he had the gut feeling that she withheld a few key items.

"Give me that," she said, swiping the cigarette from his mouth. She took a long drag while staring out the window, wincing as if the act caused her pain. Her eyes sunk deep into her troubled brow as her cracked lips found the cigarette once again. She handed it back to Drummond and rubbed her temples. The bracelet around her bony wrist jangled as it slid toward her elbow. Most of her bones pressed against her skin. The economic depression had lasted for so many years now that many people had wasted away to almost nothing.

But that wasn't the reason for her malnourished look, and he knew it. After all, the McCullen tobacco farm had done well enough for several years — especially with the rising war in Europe. People were nervous enough and if Hitler followed through on his threats, there would be lots of panicking people who needed something to smoke. For Amanda, though, the loss of weight, the lack of eating, came from a different fear, one that could destroy any adult no matter how strong — she feared for the life of her daughter.

"Can you drive any faster?" she said.

"Won't do your Laura any good if we die on the way there. Tell me the story again. Put in all the details you can remember. Especially about that book." He stabbed a finger down at the large book sitting between them.

She shifted her body, making an obvious effort to look out the passenger side window. "Where should I start?"

"The beginning, of course. Just like you told me before."

"Well, okay. There's my husband, Roy. He's a religious man. Church every Sunday. Prayers before every meal. Reads the Good Book every night before he goes to bed. When I got pregnant with Laura, he was the happiest I'd ever seen him. Even more than on our wedding day. He thought the Lord had blessed him with the greatest of gifts."

As the lights of downtown Greensboro appeared on the horizon, Drummond settled back and nodded. This was good. The details Amanda chose to reveal signaled that she spoke the truth. If she had been lying, everything would have matched up nearly perfect — the mark of a well-rehearsed bit. But this time, when she described Roy's conviction to his church, she did so through all of his praying. Earlier that day, she had focused on his devotion to hard work and charity.

"Those nine months," she went on, "were some of the happiest we ever lived. All the anticipation, all the preparation. I know a lot of families wouldn't welcome another mouth to feed, and for many, having another baby is just another baby, but this was our only one. This was something we wanted for a long time and couldn't have. She's more important to us than just being our daughter. She's our miracle."

More details she had not expressed before. Until now, Drummond knew only that their daughter suffered from a botched spell. This new information meant the McCullens would be more desperate than he had originally thought — and he knew they were desperate from the start.

Amanda grew silent, the thickening smoke in the car hiding some of her expression. Drummond cracked a window to air things out and prodded her along. "You told me that your husband couldn't accept Laura after she was born."

With a mournful shake of her head, she said, "Laura didn't form right. Especially her brain. She's slow and she's missing three fingers. Her eyes give it away the most, though. After she was born, Roy was convinced we were being punished for some sin we had committed. It didn't matter what the doctors said, he wouldn't listen. That was hard on her. And me. But Roy spends most of his life out in the fields, so the majority of the time it was just me and Laura. That's when this all really started." Careful not to touch the book on the seat, she turned to face Drummond. "Please, understand that I love my husband and my baby girl, and I only wanted to do something to help them both."

"Of course. What mother wouldn't? You wanted the two most important people in your life to love each other like they should."

"Exactly. That's all I wanted. I saw the brilliant, charming, sweet little girl in Laura every single day. But Roy worked hard, and when he came in, he was exhausted. He had no patience for Laura's outbursts, and she often was cranky after a long day with me. He kept getting the worst of her."

"Is that when you decided to turn to magic?"

"No. I told you that already. At first, I followed Roy's ways. I prayed." The answer satisfied yet another test by Drummond. He was convinced more than ever that she told him the truth. That suggested that his original suspicion might be false — that she was a witch trying to fool him. She continued, "For months, I prayed, but nothing happened. Laura didn't get better, and Roy grew more distant. One afternoon, I was in town and my friend suggested I see a fortune teller. I think she meant it is a distraction, but the idea intrigued me. I'm pretty sure the whole thing was a trick, but afterwards, while my friend freshened up, the fortune teller came to me and said I should visit a woman by the name of Rachel Higgins. She also went by the name Madame R. The fortune teller said that Madame R knew real magic that might help."

Amanda broke from her tale to point out the turn off the main road. The old car bounced hard as they drove across a long dirt drive. Fields surrounded them. Though the moon offered limited light, it was enough to see the overgrown acres on the left. Those on the right grew tobacco, but the plants looked small and many had not bloomed at all.

"It took me another three months before I could pull together enough money and a good excuse to visit Madame R. She listened to my problems, took a look at Laura, and she pulled out that book. After reading it for a bit, she closed it, set it on her table, and shook her head. She refused to help me. Said that Laura was perfectly fine and didn't need magic messing with her head. I begged her — I mean, I really got on my knees and begged — but Madame R said she couldn't help. Too dangerous, too expensive — she threw out any excuse to turn me away. Then she started coughing and rushed for her washroom." She rested her head back, closed her eyes, and crossed her arms. "I'm not proud of myself, but you know exactly what I did. I couldn't accept that there was an answer in that book and this woman refused to help. So, I swiped the book and high-tailed it out of there."

This part of the tale bothered Drummond. The few experiences he had with witches suggested Amanda had been set up. For whatever reason, Madame R purposely left that book in a position to be stolen. She made an excuse to leave Amanda alone and waited for the book to disappear. Drummond had been searching for an answer from the beginning — why would a witch that just met Amanda want to put her in this position? What did the witch gain?

"You've not been contacted at all by Madame R since you left with the book? You're sure?"

"That woman scared me. I mean I was hopeful she would help — heck, I'd take help from Al Capone, if he offered — but that doesn't mean I felt comfortable about her."

"You didn't answer the question. Did she contact you since —"

"No."

Drummond tapped his chin. Maybe he read too much into it. Maybe Madame R really had a cough and truly was absentminded enough to leave a dangerous spellbook on her table.

Up ahead, the dirt road opened into a dirt area. Off to the right, a large barn loomed like a blank wall in the growing darkness. To the left, the farmhouse — two stories, square, large, but old. White paint had peeled to the wood while the porch bowed inward from neglect.

Drummond cut the engine. "Finish before we go in."

"But Laura —"

"I can't help her until I know what I need to know."

"But I've told you before —"

"You came to me for help. This is what I need in order to help you. If we go in there now, I'm going in blind — mostly. Trust me. If you can't, let me know now because this'll go down very different."

Though her eyes stared intently at the second story windows, she nodded. "I hid the book in the basement, so Roy wouldn't find out. If he saw that thing, he'd have thought the Devil had taken me over and ... well, I don't want to think about what he would have done. For about a week, while he was out in the fields, I studied those pages, tried my best to make sense of them, tried to figure out some way to help my daughter."

"You told me the book was blank."

"It was. All except for five pages. The book wanted me to see those pages only. At least, that's what it felt like. And when I thought I understood as much as I could, I went upstairs to Laura's room, waited until midnight, and cast the spell." With a shaking hand, she covered her mouth. "That's when everything went to Hell."

"Can you describe the spell? Did you use any colored candles? Perhaps you —"

"Stop it! No more!" Tears streamed from her eyes. "My baby is right in there. Go and help her. That's why you're here. Go do whatever you have to do, and save her."

Drummond paused. Back at his office in Winston-Salem, Amanda had told him that Roy had gone berserk when he found out what she had done. He had pulled a rifle on her and ordered her out. Now, sitting in front of the farmhouse, Drummond wondered if the man might be lining up a shot from one of the darkened windows.

"Please," Amanda said, putting her cold hands near Drummond's arm but refusing to touch him. "Go help my baby. Roy's dangerous. This spell is dangerous. My Laura is in trouble. Please."

He couldn't think of a way to approach her that would calm her down and get specifics about the spell. She had yet to give him a clear indication of what the spell had been. She balked at letting him touch the book, but at his office, she did leaf through it in front of him. When he had looked over her shoulder, all the pages had become blank.

He grabbed his Fedora. The inner-lining had begun to fray and he rubbed the loose threads with his thumb. He hated to admit it, but he had agreed to this job solely for the money. With every passing minute, he regretted that decision more. But what could he do? The economy had hurt him as much as the next guy.

He stepped outside. Gazing up at the second floor, he spotted Laura's bedroom — unmistakable considering the green and gold light flickering against the dark.

His feet crunched the pebbles in the dirt as he walked toward the porch. Halfway there, he heard Amanda's tentative steps. She sniffled and exhaled a shaking breath. Each step he took closer to the house, he expected to hear the report of a rifle or the heavy thud of a shotgun. He considered bolting for the front door, but what would be the point? Either he would be shot now or he wouldn't. If he ran, and if Roy actually had a gun trained on him, chances were the bullet would find him.

A few steps more — they seemed as if they took an hour — and Drummond reached the porch. He let out a long sigh as sweat dappled his cheeks. Amanda stopped only a few feet away from the car. Drummond understood — she wanted to be brave, she had been, but her mind had a healthy dose of fear. Either that or she wanted to see if Roy shot the first person through the door.

"Roy?" Drummond called as he banged the knocker.

From behind, Amanda whispered, "It should be unlocked."

Drummond turned the knob. The door opened with ease. "Roy? My name's Marshall Drummond. I'm a private investigator. Your wife hired me to help with Laura. I'm coming in the house. If you're planning on shooting me, you might want to hear me out first. I really can help."

Amanda yipped — a cry of pain mixed with the fear of being heard. Drummond glanced back. She had run off somewhere. He moved towards the car — perhaps she hid behind it — when a thick voice called from the kitchen. "Back here."

Clutching his .38, Drummond entered the house. As he walked down a short hall, he noted the lack of furniture. Marks on the walls denoted where portraits had been hung — only two left. Candles melting into the old sconces provided the only light.

In the kitchen, behind a square table that would've been at home aboard a navy vessel, a burly man sat on one of only two wooden chairs. On the far corner of the table, Drummond noted an open bible, and beyond it, leaning against a corner of the room, he spotted Roy's rifle — the kind soldiers used in the Big One. The man raised his eyes at Drummond like a confused dog. "Please, help me."

"Are you Roy McCullen?"

He nodded.

"Okay, Roy, let's start with what the problem is and go from there."

Roy uttered a bitter laugh. "I don't even know how to explain that much. You'll think I've gone crazy."

"I'm the guy who doesn't think the crazy sounds too crazy. That's why Amanda hired me."

Roy's top lip trembled. "She hired you?"

"That's right. Just a few hours ago. I'm here to help you and Laura."

"My Amanda hired you? A few hours ago? How?"

Drummond paused. He had been so happy to be getting paid for anything, he never bothered to ask the obvious questions — like how she could afford him. Hell, if he wanted to be honest with himself, he didn't ask anything pertinent. One look at Roy's terrified eyes, however, and Drummond knew the answer to the current question.

"The book told her to, didn't it?"

Roy reached over to rest a hand on his bible. "That book." He spat the words out as if they were poison in his mouth.

Holstering his .38, Drummond moved closer to Roy. "Did she see my name in that book? Is that how she found me?"

In a cold, dead tone, Roy said, "Why don't you go look in the thing for yourself?" He glanced over at the washbasin.

Drummond's skin prickled as his eyes shot toward the kitchen counter. The edge of a large book poked over the washbasin rim. He glanced over his shoulder, back up the hall, as if he could see through the front door all the way to the car where he expected the book to be sitting on the front seat. With his throat constricting, he had to remind himself to breathe.

"How many books of spells did Amanda have?" he managed to ask, his voice sounding small in his ears.

Roy closed his eyes and leaned his head back as if the mere thought of his wife and those books caused him pain. "Just the one. But it was more than enough."

Wishing he could be anywhere else, doing anything else, Drummond stepped closer toward the washbasin. And he saw it. No mistaking that horrid cover. "How did you get hold of this?"

Roy uttered a sharp cry and lowered his head into his hands. "That damned book. It wouldn't leave me alone."

Drummond's stomach tightened as he moved even closer to the washbasin. Blood painted the bottom corner of the book. "Roy, what did you do?"

"In the dining room." He sniffled and shook his head.

Drummond rushed out of the kitchen, checking the doors along the hall, heart pounding straight into his head, fearing that behind every door he would discover Laura's body, wondering how he would tell Amanda — all of it blending together into a dark pit deep in his chest. He entered the dining room. Like the rest of the house, the room was empty. Except for a woman. Her bludgeoned body lay in a crumpled heap against the back wall. Face smashed in — a crimson pulp. Blood and urine pooled beneath her.

"I didn't want to do it," Roy said, standing behind Drummond.

Despite years of police and detective work, Drummond jumped. He whirled around; his hand dropped to his revolver. "Take a step back."

"I had to do it. I didn't want to, but I had to do it."

"Okay. We can talk about that. But right now, you need to go back into the kitchen. It's safer in there. Can you do that? Please?"

With his thick, bottom lip quivering, Roy shuffled his way down the hall. Drummond peeked at the corpse once more before leaving. No mistaking what he saw — every point where the book had smashed into her body, he noticed a burn mark on her skin.

Back in the kitchen, Drummond opted to remain standing in the doorway. If he needed it, he had a clear shot straight outside the front entrance to his car. For the moment, though, Roy appeared placid. Besides, money or no money, there was the daughter to think about. "Can you tell me what happened and stay calm?"

Roy pressed the heel of his palm against his eyes. "I'll try."

When he said nothing more, Drummond prompted, "Let's start simple. Who is the dead woman in your dining room?"

"My Amanda." He burst into tears again.

The world tumbled over Drummond. It gripped his chest and squeezed. Rubbing his temples to ward off the pounding, he shook his head. "That's not right." She never touched him, never let him touch the book, and the cold he felt around her. "But I met your wife. She hired me."

Through soft sobs, Roy said, "I killed my sweet wife."

Drummond stumbled down the hall like a drunken sailor. The walls kept him standing. Halfway down the hall, he saw one of the family portraits on the wall. Inspecting it closely, he crossed his fingers that the woman standing next to Roy would look nothing like the woman waiting outside. But it was her. Amanda McCullen. No mistake.

Pushing onward, fighting the sickening feeling rising up his throat, he reached the front door. He threw it open, not sure what he hoped to find. He saw nothing but an empty dirt lot and his car parked a few feet away. No sign of Amanda.

The night air braced him. He inhaled deeply and trudged toward his vehicle. Peering inside, his jaw clenched.

Nothing.

No Amanda. No book. No sign of anybody but himself.

He lit a cigarette and stared at the glowing tip — he had shared a cigarette with her. Except he recalled that she winced in pain while smoking. From what he knew, ghosts suffered physical pain when they touched the corporeal world.

He paced the length of the car. One of the great benefits of investigating the bizarre cases proved valuable at that moment — he could jump to strange conclusions and oftentimes be right. It seemed clear to him that the Amanda who drove out to Greensboro with him was a ghost. He had never seen such a lifelike ghost before, but the evidence in the house could not be denied. While Amanda told her story in the car, the real Amanda had been bludgeoned to death with the book.

He glanced back at the house. The flickering light from Laura's window taunted him. "I know, I know," he said. The idea of checking out that room twisted his stomach, but the idea of leaving her to the mercy of whatever spell Amanda had unleashed hurt worse. Should he check on Roy again? The man had a rifle with him. Yeah. Roy shouldn't be left alone.

Drummond tossed his cigarette aside and hurried back to the house. He closed the front door and froze. Part of him refused to go any further down the hall. Roy's crying echoed back. But it was more than that. Drummond's conscience broke through — he had to go upstairs. Roy could wait. The man had hours of tears left in him and had he wanted to hide his murder, he would have attacked already. But the girl ...

Each step upward caused a loud creak in the wood, and Drummond couldn't help but think about the picture he had seen earlier that week — *Horse Feathers*. The antics of the Marx Brothers seemed ages ago and miles away. If the house had some furniture still in it, the sounds wouldn't echo so terribly, but the economy hit everybody hard in one way or another.

At the top of the stairs, he saw a short hall. To his left and right were bedroom doors. The door on the right stood ajar. Peeking in, he spotted a bed in the otherwise dark room. No daughter. Nothing but a mostly empty room.

Turning back to the the other bedroom door, he narrowed his eyes and approached. The doorknob felt icy cold. He pushed open the door and his heart dropped.

Laura McCullen hung in the air — her head askew, her eyes blacked out, her skin rotting. But there was no rope. She wore a nightgown, fouled in front and back, and her body floated in a tight circle. She made a gurgling sound. The smell of feces permeated the air.

Fighting back the gorge in his throat, Drummond stepped closer. On the floor, green-gold light flickered up through a hole in the wood. A casting circle made of salt surrounded the hole. Whatever Laura's mother had attempted to do, it locked the girl in this state and imprisoned her body in the circle.

Though her eyes followed his movements, she never attempted to speak to him. For that, Drummond felt deep gratitude. He did not want to learn what horrid sounds might come out of that thing. No. Not a thing — a girl. He would have to be careful not to lose sight of that. Beneath this spell or curse or whatever it was — Laura McCullen was still a little girl.

Next to the bed, he found the container of salt. He used what remained to draw a line of salt across the two windows. As he backed out of the room, he formed another line of salt across the doorway. Then he closed the door.

"She came out wrong," Roy said from the top of the stairs.

Drummond whirled around, dropping the salt and grabbing for his pistol. How did that huge man keep sneaking around so silently?

"All kinds of problems," Roy went on. His bottom lip drooped and his head hung low. "Her feet weren't formed right. Her lungs worked twice as hard to breathe. And she couldn't speak — or wouldn't. Stuff like that. We prayed hard. Every night. We prayed for her to be made whole. Amanda did all she could to help Laura. While I was out plowing fields, she spent every waking hour trying to teach that baby to make do with what she had. After two years, we couldn't deny anymore what we both knew to be true — Laura's problems went far beyond the physical. Amanda — she couldn't accept it. She spent a good month or two crying for an hour and sitting motionless for another hour and only taking care of Laura when absolutely necessary. I told her, my wife, I told her that she shouldn't give up. Keep praying. But she had lost her faith. Said it didn't do her any good. Said she'd find a better way. I could tell by the tone in her voice that she meant something bad. I just never imagined it would be this."

Drummond noticed that Roy held his bible against his stomach. He had his rifle with him, too. He used it like a cane, but a practiced hand could have the weapon up and ready in a flash.

"She went to see this strange woman," Roy continued. "Madame Zarn. What kind of name is that? Zarn? Don't know how Amanda found this woman, but she said the lady was a nutjob. Don't know what was said there or what happened or anything, but Amanda looked so upset, I thought surely this would end it. She even came to church next Sunday." He gazed up at Drummond, tears rolling down unrestrained. "She came to church with me. I really thought things were going to be okay, then. I thought she had accepted the gifts the Lord had blessed us with and that we would do our best with Laura just as He wanted us to do. But on the next damn day, she started driving all over the state, going from one bookstore to another, real out of the way kinds of places, until she found that cursed thing."

Drummond tried not to look at the rifle. "You know where she got that book?"

"Could have been a dozen places. I was so angry with her — hell, I didn't bother asking something that."

"I take it she thought she could perform the spells on her own."

Roy slammed the bible against the banister. "I don't know what the hell she was thinking. I took one look in that book and I could feel the evil inside it. I forbid her to try anything with our Laura. Told her she had to take the book back wherever it came from. Get rid of it. But when I went out to work in the fields, she disobeyed me. I knew it the moment she started. Dark clouds rolled in over the sun. They came on so fast, I stopped to stare at the sky. When I looked down, my crops were dead. That's when I understood. I ran to the house — damn near had a heart attack I ran so fast — and when I came in, she was sitting on the floor chanting. I came up here, saw what had happened to Laura, and I came right back down. I yelled at Amanda, but she couldn't hear me or anything. She was in some kind of trance. So, I hit her. Slapped her in the face. Hard. That didn't stop her. She had that book sitting in front of her. I picked it up and she went crazy. Jumped on my back, screaming and hitting, and hell, she even tried to bite me. That's when I lost my temper. The next thing I know, I'm sitting on the floor, holding the book, and she's like you saw her."

"But you're calm now."

Roy shrugged. "I'm numb." He looked at Laura's closed door, put out his hand, but snatched it back. "You can save her, can't you?"

Not waiting for an answer, Roy turned around and thudded downstairs. Drummond rushed to the banister to watch where the burly man went. No need, though. Roy shambled through the hall until he returned to the kitchen.

Not the kitchen, Drummond thought. *The book*. Roy wanted to be near the book.

A shiver worked its way up Drummond's legs. His knees buckled and he dropped to the ground. Fearing his reaction might be the work of witchcraft, he clasped his revolver, aimed at Laura's door, and waited.

The end of his .38 shook. He stared at it as if it belonged to somebody else. At length, he inhaled sharply and holstered the weapon once more.

"Think," he whispered.

From the conflicting stories, he knew this much to be true — Amanda and Roy McCullen had a daughter, Laura, who had been born with physical defects and possibly mental ones as well. Despite Roy's objections on religious grounds, Amanda sought out witchcraft as an answer. Whatever spell she had cast went horribly wrong.

This much he suspected to be true — when things went awry, Amanda formed a salt circle to lock Laura in her bedroom. She then hoped to find some way to save her daughter. Perhaps she wanted to call Madame Zarn or Madame R or whatever name she went by, but Roy, distraught by this betrayal, lost his senses and murdered his wife with the book that had caused all this trouble in the first place. That act and the decaying of his daughter left him in his current stupor — a state of mind that could easily be pushed into madness. Amanda's will to save her daughter, a powerful force indeed, cast her ghost into Drummond's life.

But what did she expect him to do when he didn't even know what spell she had cast? Perhaps he could seek out Madame Zarn, but any witch willing to send a novice into the depths of a book like the one in the washbasin — well, that witch had no interest in helping save anybody. She thrived on the discord.

It all came back to that book.

Drummond perked up at the thought. Wiping his sleeve across his brow, he used the banister to hoist back to his feet. In his time with Amanda, he had been unable to see anything on the pages of that book — but that had been an apparition. The real book might bring a different result. If he could use the book to find out what spell Amanda had cast, then he had a chance of learning how to stop whatever she had started. He could still save Laura.

He hastened his way down the stairs, through the hall, and to the kitchen. He came to an abrupt stop in the doorway. Roy stood in the middle of the room. With his bible open on the table, he rocked back and forth and mumbled words. Both hands clutched his service rifle close to his chest.

Drummond resisted the urge to grab his own weapon. That would only intensify the situation. "Roy? I have an idea how we can help you and your daughter."

"Go away."

"I can't. Not with Laura upstairs. Not with you needing my help."

Continuing to rock on his heels, Roy lifted his head enough to see Drummond. "I'm beyond help."

"Everybody can be helped. Have a little faith." Keeping to the walls and counters, Drummond edged his way nearer the washbasin. He worked behind Roy until he could see the top of the book resting on the back rim. Though he told himself it had to be a trick of the light, he swore he saw a face on the cover. It beckoned him to come closer.

"You're wrong," Roy said, clutching his weapon tighter. "Everybody gets a choice, but those of us who fail the choice do not deserve help."

"But you haven't failed."

"My wife is dead by my hand."

"In defense of your daughter. You wanted to stop Amanda from using a witch's spell upon Laura. Surely the duties of a father outweigh those of a husband." Drummond inched closer. A little more and he would have the book. "And you're still doing a good job as a father. You've let me come to help fix this. All I need is some information."

Roy halted his rocking. Drummond froze. In a deeper voice, one calmer and frighteningly in control, Roy said, "Go ahead. Take the book."

Drummond frowned. He had expected Roy to stop anybody from delving into that book ever again. He figured once the man had regained his composure, perhaps in the morning or in a few days, he would turn his attention toward attacking that thing. He would use his bible and his muscle to rid the world of the book — probably by digging a deep grave and burying it with the Holy Word.

"Go on," Roy said. "I'm sure the answer is in there. It has to be. Right?"

Taking two wider steps, Drummond reached the washbasin. He gazed at the book — no face on the front. And no blood. The corner of the book where Roy had bludgeoned his wife to death had no blood on it. Drummond searched over the counter and saw no sign of a rag. The cover had no streaks either. No sign of being cleaned other than the missing bloodstains.

Like a two hundred fifty pound wall, Roy slammed into Drummond, pressing him against the edge of the washbasin. In a guttural growl, Roy said, "The book demands more."

Drummond's hands gripped the edge of the counter, his arms straining to keep from being shoved headfirst into the washbasin, his legs spread wide for balance. Despite the meaty hand on the back of his head, he managed to turn enough to see Roy. The man's eyes flickered green and gold while his face flushed a fiery red.

Roy said, "It wants you." His right hand flashed by and Drummond felt a sharp sting on his forearm. Glancing down, he saw that Roy had cut him with a steak knife.

The book in the washbasin opened on its own. Its blank pages flipped through as if an invisible hand searched for the right spot. When it stopped, Drummond watched drops of his blood hit the empty page. The book absorbed the blood like a thirsty farmer on a scalding day. An image formed on the page — his own face staring back at him — not a mirror image but rather an illustration in blood depicting his anguished expression.

His arms shook from the pressure. He couldn't hold out, and even if he could, staying by this evil book did him no good. Doing nothing but holding his ground would not work. So, he waited for the moment that Roy would shift back in order to attack again. When that happened, Drummond let go. His arms, his legs, every muscle relaxed.

He dropped straight down to the floor. Roy stumbled over him, his hand slamming the backboard. He yelled both in surprise and pain.

Drummond didn't wait. As he shot back to his feet, he barreled his shoulder into Roy's gut. The large man toppled backward and smacked his head against the floor. Drummond hurtled over the man and bolted up the hall.

Yanking the front door open, he sprinted outside. Across the dirt lot, he dashed by his car and continued into the dark fields. He would have kept running but his foot stubbed a rock and he collapsed to the ground.

Sweat dampened his forehead as he flipped onto his back. Propped up on his elbows, he stared at the house. Roy McCullen stood in the doorway, peering into the dark while on the floor above, his daughter's room flashed green and gold. Snorting like a bull, Roy paced the porch for a full minute. Drummond held still. He tried to slow his breathing, keep the noise quiet, avoid moving a muscle. A soft breeze rustled through the dead fields, stirring up the rich smell of manure. Sweat salted Drummond's mouth.

When Roy finally returned inside and closed the front door, Drummond dropped onto his back and exhaled a long breath. "What the hell was that?" he whispered to the night sky.

Roy teetered on the edge of insanity — that had been clear from the start. He had dipped his head over the side, murdered his wife, and pulled back onto the edge. If Laura had not been in the equation, Drummond would have called the police and had Roy arrested for murder — case closed. But if he brought the police in, they would see Laura floating, rotting, yet still alive.

Some would come up with excuses to dismiss what they saw, but enough would believe. Eventually, the truth would come out and a new era of witch hunts would begin. Drummond didn't care for witches, but he didn't think they should be hunted down and tortured. Plus, the number of false accusations and innocent deaths would be too high. No. Police were not an option. He had to handle this himself.

Which brought Drummond back to the same problem. He sat up and gazed at the house. How could he break the spell on Laura when he didn't know what the spell was?

Start with what you do know.

He paused as his thoughts whirred over each other to the music of cicadas. His mouth dropped open — he didn't know anything for sure. He had been told one story by Amanda's ghost and a second story by Roy. Neither struck Drummond as a reliable source. Amanda had died a violent death which made her ghost's intentions suspect. And Roy — everything about him was suspect.

As if he could hear Drummond's thoughts, Roy stepped out onto the porch carrying his service rifle. With the butt planted firmly in his shoulder, he raised the weapon and aimed into the dark. He moved in a half-circle — searching, searching. Lowering the rifle, he marched off the porch. The only luck Drummond had all night came at that moment — Roy opted to head off to his right while Drummond crouched in the fields to the left.

Drummond held still and counted to twenty. He had no real plan other than to take advantage of the fact that Roy had left the house. He couldn't rely on much that he had learned from either parent, so he would have to save Laura by improvising. And the first thing that came to his mind centered around the book. That was a constant in the entire evening and an obvious source of trouble.

Fine, then. I'll destroy the book.

Popping to his feet, he dashed across the ground, up the porch steps, and into the house. He headed down the hall toward the kitchen. As he came closer, the air thickened around him. Breathing became tighter and his movements required more effort.

"Don't fight me," he said, not knowing if cursed books could hear.

Regardless of the magic involved, the book could not hold back the man. Drummond had real muscle, not just mystic power, and he forced his way into the kitchen. Once he stepped over the threshold, the strain released. He moved and breathed with ease.

At the washbasin, he glared at the book, wondering how to destroy the thing. Fire felt like the logical choice. He dug out a pack of matches, struck one on the counter, and tossed it on the book. It stuck to the cover, but the flame did not spread. He struck another match and threw it in. Again, it made contact but did not burn. Seconds later, both flames snuffed out with a trickling trail of smoke.

"Couldn't just be easy."

The front door banged open. Huffing like an angry beast, Roy stood in the doorway with his head down and his glazed eyes zeroing on

Drummond. He dragged the rifle behind him, the muzzle caked with dirt, as if he had no use for the weapon.

"Crap," Drummond said.

Roy clumped down the hall, picking up speed as he went. No time to weigh options. Drummond winced as he reached out and picked up the book.

The next few seconds crawled by as Drummond lived in two moments simultaneously. In one, he watched Roy's barbaric approach — the man tore down the hall like a ravenous beast. He knocked over the family portrait, dropped the rifle onto the floor, slammed against the doorjamb, and burst into the kitchen. An anguished roar built from deep in his gut and spewed out his open throat.

In the other moment, Drummond saw that twisted face from the book's cover. It snaked out of the book and turned back to watch him with gold-green eyes.

"Save me," a voice cried out.

Laura?

Roy's thick fingers curled together to form a fist the size of a sledgehammer head. He pulled back his arm.

The face floating before Drummond changed its shape until it looked like a healthy version of the girl upstairs. "It's going to get me. Please, help."

Life returned to its normal speed as Roy's fist bashed the side of Drummond's head. Spots formed in the air as the floor smacked the other side of his head. The book flew out of his hands. It spread open inches from Roy's feet.

Roy pulled back his fist for another attack when the voice from the book cried out, "Papa! Stop!"

He hesitated. The feral look in his eyes disappeared. Turning his head slowly, he took in the room, the open book, and Drummond on the floor. Rubbing his sore knuckles, his bottom lip trembled as he put together what had happened.

"It's not your fault," Drummond said. "You weren't yourself."

But Roy dropped to his knees, clasped his hands, and prayed. Drummond sat up. His head throbbed and blood clotted one nostril closed. He waved a hand in front of Roy, but the man went on praying.

"Roy," he said, snapping his fingers. No answer. Grunting as he clambered to his feet, Drummond went on, "It's okay. I'm starting to understand what's going on here. Like I said — this ain't your fault. You're up against something much stronger than you. Don't worry, though. I think I can handle it."

In the hallway, Drummond spotted the service rifle. Ignoring the pain sparking along his side, he shuffled to the weapon and checked it over. All appeared fine. After wiping the dirt from the barrel, he brought it back into the kitchen.

"That book is like a living thing." He raised the rifle. "Only one sure way to end this that I can see." He aimed the rifle at the book.

But Roy's thick hand wrenched the barrel downward. The beast had returned to the man's eyes. He growled as he rose to his feet. With a hard motion, he yanked the rifle free from Drummond's hands and tossed it aside. Drummond raised his fists while stepping into a boxer's stance. He did not want to fight this man — no, not a man, a beast at the moment — but he had to get to that book. As long as that thing continued to exist, this would not end.

Roy, enraged with a mind possessed, rushed forward, took a punch on the chin, and tackled Drummond to the floor. Gasping for air, Drummond had no hope of getting his arms free from under Roy's immense weight. In a swift motion, the large man reached over, grabbed the book, and held it overhead, ready to strike.

"Papa! No!" Laura's voice screeched from the pages.

Roy's face twisted in horror. He threw the book into the corner and rolled across the floor.

Not wanting to see Roy turn back into a monster, Drummond crawled to the doorway, got to his feet, and stumbled down the hall. He hated leaving the book behind, but any attempt to retrieve it would only bring the monster back. Besides, the final pieces had fallen into place.

He chastised his short-sightedness. He kept focusing on the book and Roy and even Amanda, when he should have been paying attention to the daughter. It was all about Laura.

As Drummond reached the staircase, he felt sharp pains with every deep breath. Trying not to think about the possibilities of his body quitting on him, he forced his legs to start climbing to the second floor. To Laura.

He saw it now — Amanda and Roy had lied about Laura. She never suffered birth deformities or mental retardation or any other defect. Her only problem, as far as Drummond could tell, left her unable or unwilling to communicate. That's why Amanda sought the book — it wasn't a spell book. It was a conduit — meant to link Laura with its pages so that they could give her a voice. But magic provided by witches always comes with a steep price. It craved more than a simple link — it wanted all of

Laura.

Halfway up the stairs, Drummond heard the clatter of Roy getting to his feet, snorting like an animal, knocking things aside. Drummond wished he had the salt with him. That was the key — the salt circle around Laura had not been drawn in an effort to trap her but rather to protect her. Amanda must have seen the way the book had taken possession of her husband, or perhaps it had gone after her first — either way, in a moment of maternal clarity, she found a spell to protect her daughter and attempted to cast it. It only half-worked.

From that moment on, the book fought for control. It forced Roy to murder his wife. Her ghost had managed to escape the book's grasp, find Drummond, and hire him, but once back at the house, she lost to it again. The book dispatched her, leaving her terrified yip echoing in the night. Then it attempted to pull Drummond under its influence. The only thing that could break through the books lure was the voice it had been meant to give — Laura.

An idea sparked in Drummond's head as he reached the top of the stairs. He glanced back to see how much time he had before Roy showed up. But Roy stood at the bottom of the staircase, rifle in hand.

"Changed your mind about that, huh?" he said, wondering if the book controlling Roy could understand him.

With the surety of a well-practiced maneuver, Roy lifted his weapon and shot. The bullet pierced Drummond's thigh, knocking him to the floor. His shoulder dragged down Laura's bedroom door.

"Great," Drummond said through clenched teeth. "Now he decides to start shooting."

Roy came up two stairs, his weapon still aimed. Drummond fumbled for his revolver as pain seared up his leg.

"Roy? You in there anymore? Come on out. Stop this thing from using you like this." Roy reached the halfway point but he hadn't fired again — the real Roy must have been fighting back. "That's good. Hold that thing down in you. Laura's counting on you. I can save her for you, but you've got to do your part." As he spoke, Drummond reached up for the doorknob. "Don't shoot me, Roy. Fight for Laura."

The strain within the large man played out on his brow. The constant shifting of wrinkles showed concern followed by hatred followed by shock, and in between, emotions that ran the gamut from sorrow to struggle. He arched back and bellowed an indecipherable word.

Drummond turned the doorknob but the angle made it difficult to open.

Roy gazed at the weapon in his hands. He threw it aside as if it were a snake ready to strike. The sudden motion — or perhaps the fight within him — caused him to lose his footing. He tumbled down the stairs.

Not willing to miss his opportunity, Drummond pulled hard on the doorknob and pressed his back into the wood. The door flung open and he flopped backward into the room. He tried to scoot his body over the salt line crossing the doorway, but with his injured leg, the effort failed. The salt container was too far away to bother with. By the time he dragged himself to collect the container, Roy would be in the room — no telling which version of Roy, though. Besides, a salt line would only continue the problem. Laura didn't need such protection anymore. She needed to be set free.

Crawling on his elbows like an infantryman training under barbed wire, Drummond worked his way toward the girl. Each breath echoed in his head as he moved closer. The green-gold light flashed from beneath Laura. She floated above, every bit the horrible sight she had been when he first saw her. Only now, Drummond knew better. She was no monster. The decayed skin, the fouled clothing — all of it was a result of the initial attack upon her before Amanda had managed to form the salt circle.

As he inched closer, he pictured the way the book had betrayed Amanda's intentions. The way it used her to get near Laura, the way it formed a hole in the floor — a hole that led nowhere but created a green-gold light, energy that would drain Laura's soul away.

Thump. Thump. Roy climbed the stairs.

Drummond crawled faster as the thumps grew louder. He saw how Amanda must have fought for control of the book upon her mind, drawing that salt circle with the last of her sanity, knowing that it would prevent her from being near her daughter — especially the version of her under the spell of the book. Then the book shifted to Roy. But Roy's religious beliefs were too strong. And like his wife, Roy loved Laura more than anything.

Thump. Thump.

But he also blamed Amanda for the troubles they endured. That blame, that anger — the book used that against the family. Through that anger, it hoped to force Amanda to open the circle and give up Laura. She refused, of course, and for that, the book had Roy murder his wife.

Drummond checked behind him. A trail of blood from his leg led out into the hall, but no sight of Roy. Just the sound of his steps. Not many left. He rolled back to his stomach and crawled onward. A few more feet and he'd be able to reach the circle.

If Amanda's ghost watched on, he hoped she would see what her salt circle had done. Far more than merely protect her daughter, the circle gave Laura time to figure out how to fight back. That's why she was able to call her father briefly to his senses. And that's why she would be able to save them now.

All Drummond had to do was reach over and break the circle. But as he stretched outward, Roy appeared. He stomped over and slammed the corner of the book into the back of Drummond's hand.

Drummond screamed. Cradling his hand, he had no time to think. Roy swung the book like a golfer and smashed Drummond in the forehead.

The world tilted around him. Red pain became the prominent sensation. Drummond tried to get to Laura again, but something pinned him to the ground — Roy's knee bearing down on Drummond's chest.

As his vision returned, Drummond watched Roy open the book with the care and reverence he used for his bible. A soft chant began. At first, Drummond thought other people had somehow entered the house, but when the ringing in his ears subsided, it became clear the only voice chanting archaic words belonged to Roy.

As the chanting continued, Roy's eyes rolled back. Drummond waited for the man to gaze at the book or at Laura, but only the whites of his eyes remained. Drummond tried to arch back, but between his broken hand and the bullet in his leg, he couldn't budge. That left one choice.

Using his good hand, Drummond reached for his revolver. He pressed the short barrel against Roy's thigh. As he squeezed the trigger, Roy's eyes opened wide in shock.

The weapon blared. Roy leaped back out of instinct only to discover that his move exasperated his pain. While he clutched his leg and rocked on the floor, Drummond moved. He flipped onto his stomach, crawled closer to the circle, and swiped his hand across the salt spraying it over the floor in a wide arc.

Laura darted through the air. Her rotting skin shed into dust as she settled above Roy. Her arms went wide and she inhaled deeply. For a moment, it appeared as if she were going to sing — a big opening note expected from an opera. But instead of beautiful music, a horrid shriek belched forth.

The green-gold light vomited out of her and into the open pages of the book Roy held. His body jittered like a prisoner executed in the electric chair but he made no sounds of pain. When it ended, Laura lowered to the floor. An audible rush of air whisked through the room until the book closed.

Only Laura's muted cries remained.

USING A CANE, Drummond hobbled up the path leading to the Friends School for the Deaf. Laura held his hand as if it were a life ring thrown from a sinking ship. Though she could hear fine, she needed to learn sign language in order to communicate. She had a pad and pencil to write her thoughts as well, but after a short talk, she agreed this would be a good place for her. After all, she couldn't stay at the farm, and though she had enjoyed living at Drummond's office, she understood that he would not be taking on the responsibility of raising her. Which left foster homes or an orphanage. Neither appealed to her, and Drummond thought he was in for a bad choice. But his old pal, Detective Cooper, came up with the suggestion of the Friends School for the Deaf — a place that would also board her throughout the year — and it clicked for everybody. At the school's entrance, Laura stopped.

"It's going to be fine," Drummond said, hoping that his words were true. "If you have any problems, you know how to get hold of me."

She gazed up at him with a hollow look — she understood. Though he would not be upset if she came to him because of trouble at school, the problems he referred to were of a supernatural inclination. Because when the two of them found the strength to leave the McCullen house the night they rescued each other, they could not find the book. They searched the bedroom, the stairs, the kitchen.

Despite the horrible scenes of blood, destruction, and death, Laura did not give up until she had exhausted all possible locations in the house. It scared Drummond. She combed over her mother's body as if it held no more importance than a chair.

Even all these weeks later, she still had not reacted as he would expect of a child after losing both parents. Perhaps she was tougher than most. Or perhaps the spell cast upon her had left her different than most. He could only hope that she would do fine, that she would never need to call on him, and that neither of them ever saw that book again.

Burying her face in his belly, she gave him a strong hug. When the headmaster arrived, Laura broke away and took the man's hand. He ushered her into the building and to a promising future.

That was it. No wailing. No screams. No reaching back for him as they tore her away. She simply accepted her new fate and walked in to face it.

Drummond turned away and hobbled toward a fate of his own.

CASE 05 - APARTMENT 2A

SOME DAYS, MARSHALL DRUMMOND WANTED nothing more than to say *No* to a new case. But as the only private investigator willing to look into the weird, other-worldly problems of Winston-Salem, those tended to be the kinds of cases that came his way. And though the analysts promised that 1934 would show serious improvement to the economy, Drummond's empty wallet did not agree. That was how Marshall Drummond found himself standing in the entrance way of a three-story walk-up on West 7th Street.

"If you ask me, this whole thing is hogwash." The landlord, Mr. Cornstall, barely came up to Drummond's chest. He had a squat body and more hair poking out of his shirt collar than on the top of his head. He smelled of cigars and the lunch that stained the belly of his shirt — strong onions and garlic. "I don't believe a word of it. But everybody in this building won't shut up about it. They're saying I got to get a priest, I got a get a rabbi, somebody — Ms. Olson in 1B even made me call a psychic. What's a fortune teller gonna do?"

"So you called me," Drummond said, tipping his Fedora back.

"You're the cheapest. And since this is all really a big song and dance to get my tenants off my ass, I figured you're worth it."

"Thanks for the confidence booster."

"Look, fella. The only reason I'm doing any of this is because these people still pay their rent. You know how rare that is these days? I can't afford to let any of them leave because they're scared of some kind of noises in the walls. So you go in there, you look around, make a couple hand motions or whatever it is you gotta do, and you tell them everything's okay. Hell, you do a good enough job that they shut up, and I'll pay you ten percent extra."

From the outside, the place resembled any other building on this row of dilapidated apartments. "Did you gather everybody together?"

"Yeah. They're all in Sullivan's apartment — second floor, 2B." With a sneer, Mr. Cornstall added, "Any other requests?"

"That's it." As Drummond moved toward the stairs, he noticed Mr. Cornstall staying at the front door. "You're not coming?"

Thrusting his hands in his pockets, the landlord gazed up at the ceiling as if he expected ghosts to come flying out — though he probably imagined them to be of the two holes in a sheet variety.

"Tell you what," Drummond said. "I'll do my work, and I'll stop by your office later when I'm done. You can pay me then."

"Sounds good to me. I got to check on some of my other buildings." Without another word, Mr. Cornstall scurried off.

Until that moment, Drummond had been of the same mind. He thought he was being paid to come in and put on a little show. He had not been given many details — only that the tenants complained of strange noises. Nobody would go on record beyond that. In his experience, real hauntings, real problems with magic, resulted in such fear that the victims willingly blabbed far more than they should.

Perhaps the landlord simply took cowardice to a new level — running away based on nothing but a few words. However, the back of Drummond's hands tingled, and he got the distinct impression this day would not be going his way.

He climbed up the wooden stairs to the second floor, walked down the short hall, and knocked on the door marked 2B.

A long-faced man opened the door — thin, bald, wireframe glasses, wearing a white shirt, black suspenders, and tan pants. "Are you the private investigator?"

"That's right. You Mr. Sullivan?"

"I am. Please, come on in."

Sullivan led Drummond into a quaint one-bedroom apartment — nothing more than a living room, kitchenette, and a bedroom. The bathroom was shared on the floor with the apartment across the hall.

In the living room, a middle-aged woman in a brown housecoat sat on one end of a threadbare couch. A young couple wearing patched clothing sat on the other end.

Drummond noticed the lack of furnishings. Not unusual, though. In these hard times, a lot of people had to sell off whatever they could to survive.

After closing the door, Sullivan gestured to the people sitting on the couch. "This is Ms. Olson, and those two are the Lukowskis."

"Pleased to meet you all," Drummond said. To the Lukowskis, he added, "The two of you live across the hall?"

"No," Mr. Lukowski said with a heavy accent. "We are on the third floor."

"Who lives across the hall?"

Everybody exchanged an unsettled look. Sullivan cleared his throat. "That would be Ms. Turner and her daughter, Milly. But they haven't been around in a while."

"Skipped out?"

Ms. Olson perked up. "Oh no. Not them. They love it here. And we'd sure hate to see them leave. I think Ms. Turner mentioned some work in the fields."

"That's right," Sullivan said. "R.J. Reynolds tobacco has been hiring day laborers and such. I think she has a sister who lives in the countryside and thought she could get some work. I guess she did because we haven't seen her in at least a week or so."

Drummond didn't believe much of what he had heard, but he decided to let it be for now. "Anybody else live in this building that's not here?"

"No. There's two apartments on each floor and the one on the third floor and the one of the first are empty. Have been ever since I moved in."

"Okay then. Since the four of you are the only regular residents, why don't you tell me what's going on here so I can figure out how I can help."

Ms. Olson clutched her coat tight around her. "I guess it all started about a month ago. Ain't that right?"

Drummond frowned. "A month? And you said the gal across the hall, she and her daughter left a week or so ago?"

"I suppose. Unless, whatever's causing the trouble in this house got them."

Drawing on her cigarette, Mrs. Lukowski rolled her eyes. "She is too superstitious to even say. She's thinking that we're haunted."

"Please," Sullivan said. "Let's not start bickering again. Just because you don't believe in such things —"

"And you'll believe anything, if it makes you a buck."

Turning back to Ms. Olson, Drummond said, "Tell me about how it all started." He figured the woman who believed in ghosts would be the most talkative.

"Well, I don't know about the others, but for me, it began with banging in the walls." She waved her hand to stop anybody from speaking. "Don't go telling me that it's the pipes knocking about. I know what it sounds like when I turn on my radiator. I know pipes. This ain't that. This is more like cracks of thunder in the wall. I swear the whole apartment shakes."

Stroking his chin, Drummond said, "How often does this thunder in your walls happen?"

"Well, like I said the first was about a month ago. Happened around midnight. Scared me so bad I fell right out of bed. Don't think it's happened during the day, but usually at least two or three times a week the noise comes."

Drummond looked at the others. "Is it the same for the rest of you?"

Sullivan shrugged, and the married couple shook their heads. Drummond waited for them to elaborate, and the pressure of all eyes on them finally got Mrs. Lukowski talking. "What do you want me to say? I haven't heard this mysterious banging. We haven't experienced any of these things. The only reason we agreed to come to this meeting is because we don't want to lose our apartment. The landlord says to come to the meeting, we come to the meeting."

"You said the word *things,*" Drummond said. "What else has been happening besides loud banging?"

"Nothing as far as I'm concerned."

Sullivan's face flushed red. "You are such a liar. You want to sit here and pretend you're better than the rest of us, that were just a bunch of superstitious folk from some backwoods country, but you're no different than any of us. Your husband isn't sitting there shaking because of nothing happening in this apartment building."

"Mr. Sullivan, you need to shut up, or you will regret —"

Ms. Olson said, "You people can't do anything right. We have a private investigator here and he needs answers, yet the two of you want to pick at each other like you're having a lovers' spat."

Mr. Lukowski's head perked up, but his wife put her arm around his shoulder and patted the side of his face. To Sullivan, she added, "You are a viper. No, you're worse than that. You're a buzzard chewing on flesh before it even dies."

"All of you," Drummond said, "be quiet." In the shocked silence that followed, he walked across the room at a slow pace, letting his footfalls click loudly against the wooden floor.

What had he gotten into? The next time somebody came to him with a job that sounded like easy money, he would have to remind himself that no such thing existed. Especially in his line of work. "I'm going to make this clear. You are each to go back to your apartments. Stay there until I have interviewed all of you. Is that understood?" He paused a moment, and when nobody objected, he added, "Then get moving."

The two women stared at each other, seeing who would flinch first. When it became clear that neither would move, Drummond cleared his throat. That was enough to get them responding. Everybody cleared out of the apartment, and Drummond hoped they would follow his instructions. He remained behind.

To Sullivan, he said, "I'm already here, so we might as well start with you."

"Me? I got nothing to say. You want to know who you should be talking to, it's Ms. Olson. She's the one behind you even being here. She's the one that's causing all the ruckus, calls the landlord, makes all the trouble. The rest of us are fine. If she would just keep her mouth shut, we'd all have a more peaceful life around here."

Drummond liked this guy — not the man's personality, but rather interviewing him. A guy like Sullivan thinks he's smart and is willing to yap away because he's always convinced he's one step ahead of the cops — or in Drummond's case, the private investigator. Of course, guys like Sullivan are almost always wrong.

Holding his hat in hand and tilting his head slightly downward so that he looked a bit on the dumb side, Drummond said, "So, you're telling me you've never experienced any of these banging sounds? Never had any problems like the ones I'm hearing about?"

"Well, I may have heard a banging noise or two. But come on. It's the pipes or rats or who knows what's in those walls."

"Nothing else? Never seen anything strange?"

Sullivan's eyes darted to the front door before he could shake his head with a bashful look. "I wish I could help you, but frankly, the only reason we're doing any of this is to humor her. We want her to be happy so that she's not ticking off Mr. Cornstall. In case you didn't realize it, times are a bit tough around here. I can barely afford this place."

Setting his hat back on, Drummond said, "Tough all over." He headed toward the door.

"That's it?" Too much hope trembled in Sullivan's voice.

Drummond paused before slowly turning back. "I have one more question. Those neighbors across the hall, the woman and her daughter, what can you tell me about them?"

"Nothing." Sullivan shrugged. "I mean I'd see them in the hall now and then. On the way to the bathroom and such. But they were quiet, kept to themselves."

"And these disturbances that you know nothing about, they started around a month ago?"

"If you believe Ms. Olson."

"Your neighbors — they left a few weeks ago?"

"I suppose. I don't really pay attention to the comings and goings of people around here."

"No husband? No man in the picture?"

"Like I said, I don't really pay attention. Though, now that you mention it, I don't recall ever seeing a man come around. I think she mentioned some guy once. Lost during the war. But if that was her husband, then her daughter's way too young."

"Oh?"

"Yeah, the daughter couldn't have been more than fifteen. I guess that works, age wise and all, but it sure seems fishy to me. I think Ms. Olson once mentioned something about a guy. You should ask her. I'm sure she'll be happy to tell you her entire life story." Sullivan wiped his hands on his pants. "Thanks for asking me all the questions first. I got places to go, so I didn't really want to have to hang around here much longer."

Drummond winked. "Pal, you and me both."

He was out in the hall and closing the door before Sullivan could force a fake–friendly laugh. The door across the hall looked like any other. Drummond placed his hand on the wood — didn't feel any different. Nothing special. The obvious thing — obvious for Drummond — flashed through his mind. A witch. He suspected that if he entered the apartment, he would find a casting circle painted on the floor filled with archaic symbols, primed to cause the mischief in this building. But if that were the case, then the witch would have cursed the building with purpose. Though anything was possible, Drummond had yet to come across a witch who cast malicious spells for no reason at all.

And from his short conversation with Sullivan, one thing was clear — Ms. Olson had a word or two about the missing neighbors. Which meant that before he could leave, Drummond would definitely have to speak with her. If all went well, he could interview her and be done. A quick report back to Mr. Cornstall, get paid, and go home. Maybe stop at a bar for a few drinks. Maybe chat up a new waitress.

Yeah. The more he pondered this case, the more it seemed like a lark — one tenant's fears or imagination causing trouble for the rest. He tapped out a cigarette, put it in his mouth, and lit it up. Waving the match out, he headed down the hall.

As he went downstairs, he noticed the front door wide open. The late day sun warmed the air, and the fresh fragrance made him want to be done with these interviews.

He could walk out. He had dealt with enough nutty people in his line that he became quite good at spotting them. Everything about this case suggested it was all in Ms. Olson's head. Well, most everything.

Less than five steps before he could leave, the front door slammed closed. Drummond stood still and watched the door. The light breeze had been blowing inward, and he couldn't feel an air current that would cause the door to close on its own.

"Damn." Not so nutty, now.

Though he knew the outcome, he still walked up and tried the knob. The door would not open. Of course not. That would have made his life simple. On the other hand, at least he now had proof that something supernatural was happening.

He turned around and gazed down the hall at apartment 1A — Ms. Olson's place. The hall was dark and dirty. He could barely make out the edges of a metal door knocker.

With a steady pace, he approached the door. Turned out the knocker took the shape of a gargoyle. He checked the floor. No signs of protective magic — no salt, no symbols, no charms. Lifting the ring threaded through the gargoyle's mouth, he knocked twice.

Ms. Olson opened the door as if she had been waiting for him since leaving Sullivan's apartment. Stepping back, she motioned for him to enter.

"I'm so glad you're here," she said, fidgeting with her coat pockets. "It's about time Mr. Cornstall did something to help us. I'll be honest, I don't think I could sleep another night knowing that I have to go through all that banging noise again. It's dreadful."

Drummond tried to keep his face noncommittal. He didn't want her clamming up because he reacted strongly to the condition of her apartment. But it was appalling.

Cluttered with endless stacks of junk. Whereas most people who had fallen on hard times sold off their furniture, their possessions, anything to keep going, he had heard about the other types, too — the collectors. These people walked the streets picking up anything that they convinced themselves had value. Of course, little of it did, and their homes became rummage sales with no customers.

But knowing it and seeing it were two different things. Nobody mentioned the smell. Stale and acrid — reminded Drummond of the way his mother smelled right before she had to be committed. West Carolina Insane Asylum wasn't the worst place for her, but the memory still turned his stomach.

"Would you like some tea?"

Removing his hat but tightening his coat, he shook his head. "Thank you, but I'm not here for a social visit."

"Of course not. Why don't you sit and I'll answer any questions you have."

He glanced around the room for a chair. With a self–deprecating chuckle, Ms. Olson wobbled into the room and moved aside stacks of old newspapers. Gesturing to the wooden chair she had revealed, her lips formed an awkward grin.

Drummond took his time sitting down. His eyes swept the floor looking for signs of a casting circle. He checked as many book titles as he could catch hoping to spot any of the classic witchcraft tomes.

But he found nothing.

Clearing his throat, he decided to take one more stab at the possibility that Ms. Olson was a witch. "Tell me, what exactly do you think is going on around here?"

"Isn't that why you're here? To tell us."

"You've been the one living through this. I'd really like to know your take on it all."

Ms. Olson exhaled, her cheeks blowing out as she gave the idea thought. It struck Drummond that perhaps nobody had ever asked for her opinion about anything before.

"I guess the first thing I'd want you to know is that I'm not a kook. I don't go around claiming ghosts and spirits and all of that are after me lightly."

"You think this is about you, specifically? That you are a target?"

"Indeed I do. I've lived in this building for many years. Longer than anybody else who's here now. I also have more things than most. You saw Mr. Sullivan's apartment. Bare to the bone. The Lukowskis aren't doing much better. So, I understand why there's jealousy. I'm not saying I condone what they're trying to do — of course not — but they have my sympathies."

"You believe Sullivan and the Lukowskis are doing this to you out of jealousy for your good fortune?" Drummond tried not to roll his eyes. "Yet even knowing this, you forgive them?"

"I don't know how they're making the noises, and I don't know how they made me see that thing or even set off that vision, but they are aiming to run me out of here."

Trying hard to keep stoic, Drummond said, "You saw something? You had visions? You didn't mention those before."

Ms. Olson scowled toward the ceiling. "I didn't want to give them the satisfaction." She narrowed her eyes on Drummond. "But I'll tell you everything now."

He winked and smiled at the woman. And though, at the moment, he wanted nothing more than to step out of this foul-smelling apartment, he settled back in his chair and said, "I'm all ears."

"Well, I don't even know where to begin. If you ask me, I suppose the real problem is the Lukowskis. Mr. Sullivan is nice enough, though he never stood up for me. He's a bit wishy–washy. The Lukowskis on the other hand — well, let me tell you, they brought nothing but trouble from the day they moved in."

"What kind of trouble?"

"All kinds. The two of them fight constantly. This one's mad about being on the third floor. That one's mad that they can't be in a better neighborhood. Nothing wrong with this neighborhood. Lots of fine people around here. Oh, and they hate how poor we all are. That's why she's so jealous of me. I'm not saying I'm rich or anything, but look around here. I've got more than most. Another thing — Mrs. Lukowski always cooks the most horrible smelling food."

Drummond could not imagine how Ms. Olson could smell anything beyond her grimy walls. "Did they ever cause you problems? I mean directly."

"Not directly. But then, it's rare that anybody in the building would come down and talk with me. They can't stand seeing my full apartment."

"How about Mr. Sullivan? Do they cause him problems?"

"Some. The real trouble was between them and Ms. Turner."

Drummond reached into his coat and pulled out a small pencil. Fishing out a notepad next, he flipped through to a clean page. He knew his little bit of theatrics had made the difference. Ms. Olson wanted to feel important, and this small act signaled that her words mattered. Not that he expected any difficulty getting her to talk, but by filling her with a sense of value, he hoped that either her words would be more truthful or her details more revealing.

Tapping the pencil against the notepad, he said, "About how long ago did problems arise between the Lukowskis and Ms. Turner?"

"Almost immediately. The Lukowski's apartment is directly above the Turner's. Ms. Turner — she's a lovely lady, makes me little rolls and always checks in to say *hi* — well, she used to tell me that the Lukowskis would dance and bang their feet around and make all kinds of noise. Remember, Ms. Turner has a sweet little daughter. That girl needed to get a good night's sleep for school and, besides that, who wants to live with all that noise? I've only had to put up with this weird banging a few weeks and it's driving me crazy. I can't imagine how awful it must be for her."

"Did anything else happen? Did Ms. Turner ever confront the Lukowskis?"

"Oh my, yes, plenty of times. It got so bad the two of them could barely walk by each other in the hallway." Ms. Olson stepped a little closer, and Drummond noticed her right eye did not move in conjunction with her left. He didn't want to stare, but he suspected she had a glass eye. With a conspiratorial whisper, she said, "I didn't want to say anything when we were all together upstairs, but if you ask me, I don't think Ms. Turner and her daughter left to go work on any farm or visit any family. I think they're trying to find a different place to live, so they don't have to deal with the Lukowskis."

"I think I get the picture. You've done a great job of painting a clear image."

Ms. Olson blushed — a rather unpleasant sight on her scrunched face. "I do try to be thorough."

"Then let's get to the heart of things and be thorough. Tell me about these other instances of strange things happening — the visions? Sightings? Whatever has happened in addition to the banging noise."

Ms. Olson glanced at the door while her fingers danced at her side. She walked off a moment and returned with a small stool that she set close enough where her knees bumped his. "One night, after the banging woke me up, I went out into the hallway."

"Is that something you did often? When you couldn't sleep or when these noises woke you up?"

"No." She reddened.

"It's okay. I'm not judging you."

"Oh, no. Nothing bad. I just — I had to use the commode. Anyway, I was in the hall and that's when I saw it."

"And what was it?"

"Hard to explain. It was bluish, and it floated over in the hallway between me and the bathroom. It had a little bit of shape to it, but I wouldn't say it was a person. More like a child's drawing of a person. However, that was just the shape. There were no details — no face or limbs or anything at all. Just a blue light that made me think of the drawing. I know how that must sound."

"That's hardly the strangest thing I've ever heard."

"I wish Mr. Sullivan had been as understanding. I mentioned it to him the next day, and all he could do was list the reasons I was mistaken. Just a car driving by with the headlights streaming across the walls — that was his favorite explanation. Twice after seeing this thing, Mr. Sullivan suggested — and not too subtly, I might add — that I'd been drinking. Well I'll have you know, I haven't drunk a drop since Prohibition began."

"How many times have you seen this light?"

"It started shortly after the noises began. Maybe once a week. I didn't mind after the first time. That first time scared me, but then nothing much happened. At first, I thought it was more jealousy — trying to push me out. But even after I got used to the light, it kept coming back."

Drummond studied Ms. Olson's face. He thought she had lied, but he couldn't be sure about what. Perhaps the apparition scared her more than she wanted to admit. Perhaps the apparition never happened at all. However, the locked front gave him direct evidence that something was going on here, so why not a ghost floating around the bathroom?

"I thank you for giving me so much of your time."

"Not at all," she said, a slight shake adding to voice. "I hope you don't have to leave yet. There's more to tell."

"I do need to interview the Lukowskis, but before I do that, I have one more question. You mentioned visions, as well. Can you tell me about them?"

Unable to hide her relief, she said, "I'd be delighted to tell you everything."

Drummond wriggled in his chair, trying to find some way to be comfortable.

"You should know that what I'm about to say is something I've kept a secret. If those people above me knew, why their jealousy would be tenfold. I wouldn't be surprised if they tried to run me out this very night." Ms. Olson adjusted her coat as if it were a princess ball gown. "I have what Grannie used to call a gift. I've heard people call it a *sensitivity*, too. It means that I can see all the subtle differences in the air. Not this air that you're breathing but the other plane of air. You understand me?"

"Yes, Ms. Olson. In my line of work I've met people with gifts before."

Her enthusiastic grin faltered. Only for a second. She regained her composure, and continued, "Of course. How silly of me. Well, anyhow, my gift is that I can talk with the dead."

"Really? Perhaps you can make this lot easier on us. Let's talk with whatever entity has been causing you problems, making all this noise, appearing to you, and figure out what it wants." He only half–believed what he said. On the off-chance she really could speak with the dead, he didn't want to pass up that kind of opportunity.

But as he had suspected, she balked. "It doesn't quite work that way. You see, I can speak to them, but they are very picky when it comes to responding. They don't simply talk to me as if over the telephone. Instead, I see things. In my dreams. Images. What I like to call visions."

"And have you had any visions about your current situation?"

"I have," Ms. Olson said, raising her eyebrows. "You *are* good at this."

Unable to tell if the woman had attempted to flirt with him, and unwilling to find out the answer, Drummond said, "Thank you. Please, tell me about your vision."

Leaning forward with her fingers plucking at her coat, she said, "I saw gold."

"Gold?"

She nodded. "In my vision, I walked into this large room. It was all dark. And when I flicked on the lights, I was in a huge warehouse filled with gold. Like Fort Knox. That's when I knew this was a vision and not a dream."

"Because it looked like Fort Knox?"

"I've never been there. How would I know what it looks like? Plus, at night before I went to sleep, I spoke to the ghost. I said to it that I was listening and if it sent me a vision, I would pay attention. What you think of that?"

Drummond thought he had enough. Standing, he pocketed his notepad and pencil. "You've given me far more than I could ever ask for. You've been a tremendous help."

Ms. Olson jumped to her feet. "Oh, please, you don't need to go now. I have plenty more I want to share with you."

"Don't worry. I'm not leaving this building. But I do need to interview the Lukowskis. If I have further questions, and I just might, I hope I'll find you here in your apartment."

"Then I'll be here. Waiting." Her eyelids fluttered, and once more, Drummond wondered if she actually had flirted with him. It took him another two minutes to extricate from the apartment, but then he climbed his way to the second floor. He walked down to room 2A, and as before, he placed his hand on the door. He stood there, waiting for banging or noise, but nothing happened. It bothered him now — not the silence, but the missing women. Ms. Turner and Milly had left only a few weeks after the noises began. His suspicion that a witch might be involved increased with every moment.

Ms. Olson clearly could not be the culprit. But, if she was to be believed, Ms. Turner and the Lukowskis had some terrible arguments.

Perhaps Ms. Turner had cursed the building before leaving with her daughter. Drummond lifted his head to look up at the ceiling. Perhaps Mrs. Lukowski was the witch and it was her spell that got rid of Ms. Turner. Either way, he swallowed down the knot in his chest as he approached the staircase and climbed to the third floor. He walked down the hall and knocked on apartment 3A.

Mrs. Lukowski opened the door, barely glanced at him, and walked back with a cigarette burning at the end of a long holder. "Would you like a drink? Only the best — made in some back alley, no doubt."

"Selling alcohol is still illegal in this country."

"So is a lot of things I like to do." Glancing over her shoulder, she added, "Don't tell me you never had a drink."

This woman's flirting was worse than Ms. Olson's — especially because Drummond knew Mr. Lukowski had to be around somewhere. Nobody was getting out of this building.

Off to the left, Drummond spied a door that would most likely lead to a bedroom. He didn't bother trying the knob — he expected Mr. Lukowski had locked himself in there.

Puffing on her cigarette stem, Mrs. Lukowski said, "I imagine you've spoken to the rest. If you have any sense, you found Mr. Sullivan to be a bore and Ms. Olson to be a fool."

"And how am I going to find you?"

"Unhelpful, I'm afraid. I told you — I don't believe in any of this supernatural nonsense, and I don't know anybody well enough to offer you assistance in figuring out who is behind this."

"Maybe you can help out with one thing."

"Oh? I'd love to hear it."

"I have a few questions about your relationship with Ms. Turner."

The eager amusement drained away. "Don't really have much to say about her. She and her brat were not very welcoming when we moved here. I can't say I'm sad that she's gone."

"I thought she was off making money doing some fieldwork. Expected back anytime. You're saying she's moved out?"

"She's not here now, so she's gone. Frankly, anytime with her out of the building is a reprieve to me. Who knows? Maybe I'll be lucky and she'll never come back."

The door leading to the bedroom thumped twice. Drummond looked to Mrs. Lukowski, but she showed no evidence of noticing the noise. "Is your husband okay?"

"Of course. Why do you ask?"

"It sounds like he's not feeling well."

Mrs. Lukowski waved at the door as if dispersing a foul odor. "Don't worry about him. He gets moody."

Drummond held in check the urge to kick that door open. If he had to bet money on it, he would guess that Mr. Lukowski was having a very bad experience with a ghost. Thumping doors aside, nothing pointed to Mrs. Lukowski being a witch. Other than Ms. Turner and Milly missing. But he saw no books, no candles, nothing in her apartment or demeanor to indicate that she had control of the situation like a witch.

The witches he knew reveled in their power. With their trap sprung, with nobody able to leave, they would have revealed themselves by now. Certainly, no true witch would bother denying the supernatural. Not even to be coy.

Damn. Drummond had hoped either Ms. Olson or Mrs. Lukowski would prove to be the cause of the disturbances.

"Mr. Drummond, I can't spend the entire day cooped up in my apartment. If you've got nothing else to ask me, then please, go. Do whatever investigative work you need to do to stop this hassle."

Drummond did not like this. He especially did not like the people in this building. He most especially did not like the strange thumping coming from the bedroom. He decided that would be the best route to go. Breakdown that door if he had to, but he needed to find out what Mr. Lukowski had going on in there.

When Drummond stood to make good on his thoughts, a tormented scream erupted from one floor down. A quick look at Mrs. Lukowski proved to Drummond that she had not been expecting the outburst.

He rushed through the hall, down the stairs, and up the second floor hall, until he reached the open door of Mr. Sullivan's apartment. When he entered, he found Sullivan sprawled on his back with blood pouring out of a gash in his forehead. Off to his left, Drummond spotted a towel folded on the kitchen counter. He tossed it over to Sullivan who quickly applied it to his wound.

"You okay?"

"Do I look okay?" But Sullivan waved Drummond back from approaching. "I'll be fine. Strangest thing happened, though. I got fed up waiting for you to finish this nonsense, and I said to myself *That's it. I'm leaving.* When all of sudden, I got the worst chill. Freezing cold. I don't mean the kind of cold where you need a sweater or even the kind of cold that you get when Mr. Cornstall lets the heat go off in the middle of winter. It was as if somebody threw ice down into my bones yet even deeper than that. Scared the hell out of me. I jolted forward, slipped, and banged my head on the counter."

Drummond glanced at the counter again. Sure enough, blood splatter showed where Sullivan had hit. From down the hall came the unmistakable voice of Ms. Olson. "Did you see it? Did you see it?" She rushed in, flushed with excitement, and upon viewing Sullivan, her mouth formed a big O. "You poor man. Look at you." She rushed to his side and took control of the towel pressed against his forehead. "I knew it would happen eventually. The ghost attacked you."

Trying to push her off, Sullivan said, "There was no ghost. Nothing like that."

"I heard you scream, and I came upstairs as fast as I could. In the stairwell, I saw it. That same blue light." She snapped her eyes to Drummond. "Are you going to tell me that wasn't a ghost?"

Drummond lit a cigarette. "No, ma'am. I won't deny what you saw. There's something wrong in this building, and now, it looks like it got a little bit of Mr. Sullivan here."

Sullivan grabbed the towel and pushed Ms. Olson aside. "This is ridiculous. I got scared, I'll admit that. Then I slipped and fell. I hit my head on the counter. That's all that happened."

"Cold spots like you felt can be signs of the supernatural."

"But I didn't see any blue light. I didn't see anything ghostly. For that matter, it's still dusk. Don't ghosts come out late at night?"

Drummond dragged on his cigarette, letting Sullivan stew for a moment. "Ghosts come out whenever they want. Most people don't see them ever. You have to be attuned to them, and it's the rare person that can do that."

Ms. Olson crossed her arms as if feeling a new chill. "And I do."

"I think you have some of it. Not a lot. If you truly had a gift, you'd be able to see a full ghost, not just a bluish color. But you do have some sensitivity, there's no denying that."

Her chill appeared to wash away with triumphant warmth. She lifted her chin at Mr. Sullivan. "And you thought I was crazy."

Sullivan sneered. "Oh, you're nuts alright. Collecting all that trash. I swear some mornings I can smell your apartment all the way up here."

"That's a horrible thing to say. You know what your problem is ..."

As the two tenants argued, Drummond turned his attention to the apartment door across the hall. If Ms. Olson was to be believed — if she truly saw a blue light and was not simply being opportunistic — then perhaps her dream of gold actually connected with the situation. The sounds, the vision, the ghost — perhaps it all added up to something more substantial. And since Ms. Olson was not the witch and Mrs. Lukowski was not the witch and Sullivan did not appear to have any abilities, including balance, that left two possibilities. Either Ms. Turner was the witch or Mr. Lukowski had been dabbling in magic. Either way, the time had come to take a look inside apartment 2A.

"The two of you stay here," Drummond said, but the level of bickering had reached a fiery stage — the two of them did not even notice him leaving the room and closing the door behind.

He considered picking the lock, but before he could get to work, a brighter idea struck. He tried the doorknob. The room was unlocked. Inside, he found both the familiar and the unexpected.

The familiar — the apartment layout mirrored Sullivan's place. The same small room, the same small kitchenette, the same small second room off to the side.

The unexpected — the floor was missing.

Every floorboard had been yanked free and tossed aside. The plaster on the walls had been cut down, and several holes in the ceiling suggested that the job had not been finished yet.

At least now I know why Ms. Olson heard all that banging.

Stepping from one beam to the next, Drummond made his way into the center of the room. From this position he could see that several of the cabinet doors had been removed and even the radiator had been pulled off — the exposed pipes sealed shut.

Not only did he have a ghost, an image of gold, and loud banging, now the criminal had to understand the basics of a radiator.

With the question of the banging answered, Drummond thought about the vision. He did not think Ms. Olson's dream should be taken literally, but clearly something of value had been hidden in this apartment. Or, at least Ms. Turner seemed to think so. She and her daughter had ripped the place apart. Then again, what were the chances those two women knew how to dismantle a radiator. Perhaps somebody else helped them.

Only problem with that idea — Ms. Turner and Milly left a week or so ago, and according to Ms. Olson, the banging had continued.

Surveying the damage, Drummond said, "Doesn't look good for Turner and daughter."

A murder would explain the ghost and other supernatural behaviors in this building. The continued banging suggested that whatever treasure the criminal sought, he had yet to find it. The ghost had assaulted

Sullivan — a pretty strong argument against him. But Lukowski's odd behavior and hiding in his bedroom did not scream of innocence either. And if Mr. Lukowski was guilty, that also suggested Mrs. Lukowski was in on it with him. Or she was willing to help him cover it up.

Looks like the only one I can trust is Ms. Olson.

Drummond also allowed for the possibility that he was completely wrong. Everybody in the building could be innocent, and they were all simply victims of a crazed ghost.

"My, what happened in here?" Ms. Olson said, standing in the open doorway.

Behind her, Sullivan peeked inside. "I don't think the Turners will be coming back anytime soon."

Drummond locked eyes with Sullivan and paused. Ms. Olson looked genuinely surprised. But Sullivan?

Drummond said, "The two of you, please return to your apartments. I think I'm almost done here."

"I don't know," Ms. Olson said, fingers twisting the fringe of her coat. "I don't feel quite safe downstairs all alone. Not after seeing this room."

"Trust me on this one. You won't want to stick around here. Not when I'm about to do what I'm about to do."

Sullivan frowned. "And what exactly is that?"

"You got a ghost problem. I'm going to talk to the ghost."

Ms. Olson found the inner–strength to hustle downstairs and slam her apartment door. Sullivan, on the other hand, shook his head and meandered back to his own apartment.

Drummond grabbed one of the cabinet doors off the floor and brought it to the center of the room. He rested it across two beams and squatted close to it. From his coat pocket, he produced a small metal flask. In the old days when he wore a uniform and walked a beat, he kept it filled with cheap whiskey. Since taking on the world of ghosts and curses, he kept it filled with witch's water.

Drummond thought of it as unholy water. Created by witches, the cursed water could be used to form a specific casting circle — one that would allow a person to speak directly with an otherworldly entity. It worked faster than a normal summoning circle and did not require arcane knowledge. Any fool could use it. But witch's water had two major drawbacks. One, the connection would be strained at best. And two, the stuff was unstable.

Drummond didn't like the idea of blowing up. But he needed to talk to that ghost.

As he dribbled the water on the back of the cupboard door, he wondered what the witches would say if they could see this. Because of its volatile nature, witches rarely agreed to create the water. The small amount he owned had been a gift from Madame Turosk for disposing of a nasty poltergeist. If she knew that he had put it into his whiskey flask, she might've cursed him instead.

After completing the circle, he pocketed the flask and stepped back. Nothing happened. He tried to remember if Madame Turosk had instructed him to use a phrase or another symbol or even some other ingredients to enact the spell. But he recalled the directions clearly because there were so few. Witch's water would do all the work once it had been put in a circle.

"Hello? I'm trying to talk with the ghost in this building. Anybody there?"

Maybe he hadn't completed the circle. Easy enough to miss a spot pouring from a flask. Not a lot of precision control.

Moving closer on the beam, he inspected his work. Though the wood on the cabinet door had soaked up a lot of the water, the wet marks were clear enough to see. A solid, full circle.

Crap. He really thought this would work.

Standing straighter, he arched his back and stretched out his arms. That was when the spell kicked in. Flames followed the line of water to make a perfect circle. They shot up four feet high, sending Drummond stumbling backwards.

He tripped. Hard wood slammed into his back and shoulder, but he managed to keep his head up — avoided cracking his neck. "Okay, okay. I got it. You're here."

The fire lowered until it formed smoldering coals around the circle.

Getting back on his feet, trying not to moan, he said, "My name's Drummond. I'm here to help. But I need you to tell me why you're so angry."

A young girl spoke as if talking through a long, metal tube. *"They did this. He does this. Still. Oh mama! Oh mama!"*

"Why don't you be a little more helpful and give me a name?"

"Don't know names. Did I ever? Mama won't let me. Is she in charge? Am I?"

"You know where they live, right? How about that? The person who hurt you, does he live upstairs?"

"I warle gcol frustraaaa"

"I don't understand."

"Not again, Mama! Listen to the doctor. Take your pills."

The smoldering coals reignited into flames. The flames grew high. Forced to step back from the heat, Drummond said, "Please."

A moment before everything went bad, Drummond had a simple thought — a circle made with witch's water was not a secure summoning circle. In the case of a summoning circle, the caster could contain the spirit or creature. But this — this was just a phone line opened straight to the ghost.

The upside down cabinet door began to spin. With flames reaching three feet high, the fires swirled around each other like mating snakes. The few kitchen drawers opened and closed as did the cabinet doors still intact. The one bare bulb in the center of the room flickered on and off.

"Calm down. I can help you. We can make this work."

In answer, the flaming door spun off, flipping through the air until it smashed into the exposed wall studs. Drummond whipped off his coat and used it to pat out the flames. If the whole building went up, they'd all die. Unless the ghost would be willing to let them free, and he doubted that.

Though the circle of witch's water had been demolished, the ghost's voice still found a way through. *"Not our fault. Never was what they wanted."*

"I believe you," Drummond said. "I want to help you rest."

The door to the apartment slammed open. A rush of wind from behind pushed Drummond toward the hallway.

"Okay. I got it." When he stepped into the hall, the strong rush of wind pushed him towards the staircase. "You want me to go upstairs? Talk to the Lukowskis again?" A garbled shriek rang in his ears. "I'll take that as a *yes*."

Before Drummond could step down the hall, Mr. Sullivan opened his door. The thin man no longer looked so frail. In fact, he came off rather threatening. And Drummond was a man who knew how to read a threat.

"Stay in your apartment," Drummond said.

"I heard a noise. Everything okay in there?"

Drummond glanced back at the Turner's apartment. Black smoke rolled over the lip into the hall. "Looks fine to me."

Sullivan raised an eyebrow. "Come on in here. I've got something to share with you."

Drummond did not move. "I've got another interview to conduct upstairs. I'll come back later and chat with you."

"Not a good idea. Those Lukowskis are strange people. They've caused most of this mess."

That caught Drummond's attention. Stepping into Sullivan's

apartment, keeping both hands loose and ready to fight, he said, "What exactly do you know?"

Incredulous, Sullivan gestured back out to the hall. "All of it. You think I like being stuck in this building?"

"That is something, isn't it?" Drummond strolled around the main part of the apartment, his eyes roved over every space, every piece of paper or dirt, anything he could see that might clue him into Sullivan's role.

"Look, I'll make it simple. The Lukowskis are responsible. For everything."

"But you and the Lukowskis insisted that this is all in Ms. Olson's head."

"Are you thick? That was all talk."

As Drummond came around toward the kitchen, his eyes fell upon the sink basin. A checkered curtain hung off the rim to hide the plumbing underneath. Squatting, Drummond pulled back the curtain. He found an open toolbox. All the usual were there — hammers, screwdrivers, levels, as well has a few particular items. Backflow stopper, pipe wrench, steam gauge — the tools of a plumber. The kind of man that would know how to cap off an exposed radiator pipe.

"Oh crap."

He tried to whirl around, but it was too late. Sullivan slammed the side of Drummond's head with something large and metallic. Drummond's brain never had time to figure it out. All went dark.

WHEN HE AWOKE, he was not surprised to feel the bump on his head. The surprise came from the fact that he was not bound. He fully expected to wake up sitting in a chair with his hands tied behind his back and possibly his legs tied as well. Instead, Sullivan had dragged him across the room and plunked him down on the couch.

Night had arrived. Rubbing his head with one hand, he checked his watch on the other. Only out a few hours.

As his attention finally took focus on the apartment, Drummond discovered why Sullivan had not bothered tying him up. The man had taken Drummond's gun. He sat in a chair on the opposite side of the room brandishing the weapon and making it clear that he aimed directly at Drummond.

"He's awake," Sullivan said.

From across the hall, footsteps. Mr. and Mrs. Lukowski entered the apartment.

Drummond eased back on the couch. Sudden movements rang in his head like a hangover. "All three of you?"

Sullivan scowled. "All three of us nothing. Whatever went on between the Lukowskis and the Turners had nothing to do with me. They were fighting forever. From the moment they met each other." Sullivan shot a fierce glare at Mrs. Lukowski. "I don't really care what your fight was about. I don't want to know."

"I see," Drummond said. "You came into this about a week ago."

"That's right. All that banging and noise coming from across the hall annoyed me. It went on and on, and I'm sure that's half the reason these two were constantly arguing with them. But then Turner and her daughter left. At first, I bought into the story that they were trying to get work. But they never came back. And that banging didn't stop."

"So one night you went in there to see what was going on."

"I was trying to help. I figured they had done something stupid and caused a problem with the pipes. Before it got any worse, I wanted to go fix it."

"And if you succeeded, you'd send a nice bill to Mr. Cornstall."

"Hey, I don't work nothing for free."

"That's when you found the two of them. The Lukowskis. I'm guessing they were pulling down the walls by that point."

Sullivan's body slouched. "I just wanted to stop that noise."

"Sure. I understand. You just wanted to help. That is, until you heard about the treasure."

The Lukowskis exchanged a quick look. Mrs. Lukowski stepped forward. "What do you know about it?"

"I think I know more than you do. After all, I actually spoke with the girl."

Mrs. Lukowski smirked. "Oh really? I sincerely doubt that."

As the pieces fell into place for Drummond, he struggled to find an escape from his current situation. But as long as they were talking, nobody was getting shot. "I understand. After all, you got Ms. Olson to buy into the ghost story. It's a clever enough ploy when you consider Ms. Olson's personal beliefs. Only problem for you is that it's real. There is a ghost."

Mrs. Lukowski chuckled, but her husband did not share her amusement. "Mr. Drummond, I've seen desperate men grasp at all kinds of things to keep themselves safe. But a ghost?"

"That was the reason I was hired. Do you really think Mr. Cornstall would pay any money to me if he didn't think there might be a chance something was wrong in here?"

"Mr. Cornstall would pay anything to make sure his four remaining tenants stayed."

"Fair enough. Perhaps you should ask your third partner here. I believe Mr. Sullivan had an encounter with the ghost as well."

Sullivan waved the gun at Drummond. "Leave me out of this."

"Afraid you're stuck in it. All of you are. You may not want to believe it, but that doesn't really matter. That ghost is in this building, and in trying to communicate with it, I was forced to use witch's water."

Mrs. Lukowski forced out a laugh. "Witch's water? That's even more absurd than the idea of the ghost."

"You see, I can use this water, witch's water, to communicate with a ghost. Not very effectively, and it has the nasty problem of bringing the ghost closer to our plane of reality. What all that means is that she's in the building and a little more capable of touching us." Drummond narrowed his eyes on Sullivan. "You know what a cold touch she has."

Sullivan involuntarily shivered. That small reaction gave Drummond a glimmer of hope. An idea for a way out. But before he could push Sullivan into the actions he wanted, he would have to sow greater distrust between these two groups. His gut told him that the truth would suffice.

Shaking his head, Drummond looked at the Lukowskis. "I feel sorry for you two. You've gone through a whole lot of effort for nothing."

"Shut up."

"Sure. Not a problem. At least, not for me. Both of you, on the other hand, you've got plenty of problems."

Mr. Lukowski took one strong step forward. But when he spoke, his voice sounded timid and thin. "Only problem we have is you."

"No, I'm not the main problem. I imagine your wife would have no trouble seeing me dead. Although Mr. Sullivan may not feel the same."

"There won't be any killing," Sullivan said.

"Not by you. But when they realize there is no treasure in that apartment, I think they might get a little mad. They may not be thinking straight after that."

Mr. Lukowski shot forward and grabbed Drummond's coat lapels. "Stop saying there's no treasure!"

"Leave him alone," his wife said. "He's just screwing your head up. We know there's treasure."

Drummond smoothed out his coat as Mr. Lukowski stepped back. "That's not what the ghost said."

"That's enough from you about ghosts." Mrs. Lukowski put her arm around her husband and guided him closer to the hallway. Talking to him as much as she was talking to Drummond, she said, "I was standing right there in the hall when I first realized what the Turners were up to. We had just moved in, and Ms. Turner gave me the evil eye as I walked from door to door introducing myself. She wanted nothing to do with me. But Milly, that girl, she came rushing up and yanked her mother back inside. And she smiled at me and shook my hand and welcomed me to the building. And do you know what happened?"

Her husband nodded. "I remember."

"I saw it. They had pried up two of the floorboards." Stepping closer to Drummond, she continued, "There's only one reason a mother and daughter have for doing that."

"You thought they were hiding something in there," Drummond said.

"I did. But I was a little wrong. I realized that once all the banging continued. They were ripping up *all* the floorboards. That meant they were searching for the treasure, not hiding it. So I did a little private investigation work of my own. Talked to Cornstall and he admitted that when they came to the building they specifically asked for that apartment. He even admitted that Ms. Turner said her late husband had left something for her there."

"And you thought it was money."

"Oh, it is. Or jewelry. Something valuable. According to Cornstall, Mr. Turner came out several months earlier. But something happened to him. Cornstall doesn't know what — the fellow just stopped showing up with rent. Disappeared. A few months later, in walks wife and daughter."

Drummond snickered. "Sorry, but you're wrong. About pretty much all of it."

Mrs. Lukowski walked up and slapped Drummond across the face. "Shut up."

Drummond looked to Sullivan. "Is that what you want? Want me to shut up?"

Sullivan's gaze passed from Mrs. Lukowski to Mr. Lukowski, then back to Drummond. "I'd like to hear the rest of what you have to say."

Drummond made sure to keep his face relaxed. "For a start, let's dispense with the lies. Mrs. Lukowski never spoke to Cornstall or if she did, he certainly never told her some tale about Mr. Turner. When I was hired to do this job, Cornstall made it clear that the tenants in this building had been the only ones for a very long time. That's why he's worried — doesn't want to lose his last paying tenants. But that's okay. I know why you lied." Drummond winked at Mrs. Lukowski. She crossed her arms. "A little lie like that makes the truth easier to swallow down, doesn't it? Now, I believe you that you went to say hello to your new neighbors and that they were rather rude to you. I also believe that you saw the torn up floorboards, and from that point on, you decided there had to be something worthwhile in there. Especially when you continued to hear banging night after night. But here is where you went wrong. There is no treasure. There never was. No Mr. Turner, no secret goals, nothing of value in those floors."

Mr. Lukowski slammed his fist against the front door. "We know that. We pulled up all the floorboards. And cut down the walls, too."

"And now you're working on the ceiling. You won't find anything in there, either."

"I've had enough," Mrs. Lukowski said. "I suppose you're going to tell us that your ghost friend explained this all to you."

"As matter of fact, that's absolutely right. She did. She tried to. See, Ms. Turner was a sick woman. Mentally ill. Her actions — ripping up the floorboards — that was not a woman searching for treasure. That was a woman searching for something that never existed. Something in her mind. Milly struggled to keep her safe. But then you came along. Isn't that right, Mr. Lukowski? All of this was your wife's doing."

"Don't say a word, dear. This man is trying to turn you against me."

Drummond put up his hands. "I wouldn't dream of it. Mainly because I know I can't succeed. Your husband must love you very much. He's taking you at your word that there is a golden treasure. He's broken into this apartment and pried up the floors and walls and now the ceiling — all for you. And worst of all, he killed a little girl for you."

Sullivan snapped to attention. "Is that true?"

Here we go, Drummond thought. "Of course, it's true. You really think that the Turners just walked away? I mean, after all, if you believe what Mrs. Lukowski said, then you believe that the Turners were destroying their own apartment looking for treasure. Why would they simply walk away?"

Sullivan stood, the gun in his hand trembling. "What did you do?"

Mrs. Lukowski's face scrunched together. "Don't be a child. We had a problem, and we took care of it."

Mr. Lukowski cleared his throat. "I took care of it," he said with more than a hint of disgust.

Interesting. Drummond had thought there was more of a united front with the married couple. Perhaps Mr. Lukowski's gaunt appearance came more from guilt than anything else. "Is that right? You killed that little girl? She couldn't have been more than sixteen years old. And you murdered her."

"It was an accident. I went for the mother. Tried to get her to confess where the gold was. But she just babbled nonsense, and the daughter started hitting me in the back with a bat."

"Be quiet, dear." Mrs. Lukowski's stern eyes bore down on her husband.

"Sullivan deserves to know the truth, and this cheap detective might as well know why he's in the fix he's in."

With his voice cracking, Sullivan said, "You killed that sweet girl? You killed her. And there wasn't even a treasure."

Drummond wanted to get off the couch, but he suspected any movements on his part would result with a bullet in the leg. If not worse. "It was an accident. Right? Come on, Mr. Lukowski. Tell us how it was an accident. You tried to get them to fess up, and Milly Turner started hitting you with a bat."

"She kept at me until I finally spun around and grabbed that bat out of her hand. I didn't mean to kill her. Just wanted her to know what it felt like." His bottom lip quivered.

"So you swung it at her?"

He nodded. "I don't know how it happened, but I cracked her in the head. Just once. But that was it."

Mrs. Lukowski rubbed her husband's arm. "Yes, yes. But we've taking care of it. It's like it never happened. It was unfortunate, but once we get our treasure, it'll have been worth it."

Sullivan took aim on the married couple. "I did not agree to any of that."

With a roll of her eyes, Mrs. Lukowski said, "Put that away. It's an empty threat. If you're mad at us for killing somebody, it makes no sense for you to kill somebody."

The way the barrel unsteadily wavered, Drummond didn't think anybody was in serious danger of a fatal shot. In fact, if Sullivan fired, the recoil alone would probably send him spinning to the floor. Drummond could leap onto him and disarm him with ease.

But as the standoff continued, something bothered him. Something was missing. Before he had a chance to put his intuition into words, Mrs. Lukowski answered it.

She stepped closer to Sullivan. "I understand. You're angry. You feel we lied to you or that we betrayed you. But we were protecting you. We didn't want you to have to deal with the burdens that we have to deal with. Oh, I can see it in your eyes — you believed his nonsense about ghosts. That's not a burden we have to worry about. After all, if any of what this charlatan said was true, then why hasn't the ghost come in here and hurt us all? I mean, if you believe everything he said, my husband and I are guilty of murdering that girl."

Drummond snapped his fingers and stood. Pleased that Sullivan did not shift the aim of his gun, Drummond said, "I'd like to thank you, Mrs. Lukowski. You've made me understand the situation a little clearer." To Sullivan, he added, "You can put down the gun. In fact, I'd like to have it back. We won't be needing it anymore."

Sullivan peered at Drummond with a side-eyed glance. "If I put down my gun, they're going to run."

"They won't get far because you and I both know that there really is a ghost. And as Mrs. Lukowski has pointed out, that ghost has not attacked. I know why. Because throughout their whole story, they've never once mentioned the death of Ms. Turner."

Sullivan cocked his head towards Drummond. "The mother? She's still alive?"

"That's why Milly hasn't attacked. She led me out into the hall and wanted me to go upstairs. But then you clocked me in the head, and I've been stuck in this room with you clowns. The way I see it, Milly's waiting for me to help her mother." In a louder voice, he went on, "And I will. You hear me, Milly? I'll protect her."

Mrs. Lukowski scoffed. "You should join the theater."

Still focused on Sullivan, Drummond said, "Now that Milly knows I'll save her mother, the second either of them steps out to that hall, they'll be ripped to pieces. So, how about handing me my gun back?"

With tentative motions, Sullivan lowered the weapon. Nobody moved. He reached over and placed the gun in Drummond's hand.

"Thank you," Drummond said as he holstered the weapon. To the Lukowskis, he added, "What's the matter? You don't believe anything I said. Go on out. We won't stop you. You can even go back to excavating that apartment. Go find your treasure."

The fire in Mrs. Lukowski's eyes blazed at Sullivan. "You're a moron. We could've had everything. Instead, you give him your gun."

Sullivan shrugged. "It was his gun to begin with."

"I'm surrounded by worthless crap for brains. What do you think he's going to do the minute we turn our backs? Either he'll shoot us or arrest us."

Drummond lifted his hat from the couch and placed it on his head. "No, ma'am. I already explained this to you. I won't have to do anything. Milly Turner will take care of it."

"Oh, that's right. The ghost." She cocked her head toward her husband. "Do us all a favor and step out into the hallway to prove to Mr. Sullivan that he's an idiot."

Mr. Lukowski hesitated. He licked his lips and inched closer towards Drummond. Mrs. Lukowski reached over and slapped her husband upside the head.

"I can't believe this. You would rather have me risk my life? Your own wife. Where's the chivalry in this world?"

With a little more strength to his voice, Mr. Lukowski said, "No need for chivalry when you say there is no such thing as this ghost."

"Fine. I'll do everything myself." With a huff, she stepped out into the hall, made a pirouette, and faced the men. "You see? Nothing is going to happen to me. I'm absolutely—"

A scream as forceful and high-pitched as a locomotive whistle rippled down the hallway. The walls shook. Mrs. Lukowski had only enough time to reach toward her husband. A blue mist slammed across the hall taking the top half of her with it.

Drummond had seen many horrible things in his time, but watching those legs crumple to the floor as they spewed out blood turned his stomach. The other men in the room fared far worse.

Sullivan stumbled back a few steps before dropping to the floor in tears. He gestured toward the hallway, tried to make words, but only a wheezing whine uttered out of his throat.

Mr. Lukowski whirled back on Drummond. "How?"

Drummond's hand slipped down to his holster. "I warned her."

Mr. Lukowski rushed over to the kitchen basin and threw up. When he no longer had substance in his stomach to heave, he coughed, grabbed a towel, and wiped his lips. Leaning back against the counter, he had the shake of a shell-shocked veteran. "That bitch took my wife."

"She's going to take you down, too, unless you give up."

"You think that turning myself in is going to appease that thing? It just ripped my wife in half."

"Listen to me. You're in shock. It's understandable. But here's what you need to know — it's obvious to me that Ms. Turner is still alive. You didn't kill her which means you either sent her off somewhere or you're hiding her around here. Either way, if you want to get out of this building alive, then you need to tell me where I can find her."

Mr. Lukowski shook his head and mumbled to himself. He wagged a finger at Drummond. "You can't fool me. If I tell you that, I'll never get out of here alive. That was my wife." He stepped toward the hallway. "You hear that? You hear me ghost? If you want your mother to live, then you better not lay a hand on me."

"That won't work," Drummond said — though, he wasn't so sure.

"Of course it will. At least, it'll work long enough."

"Long enough for what?"

Mr. Lukowski paused in the doorway. He winked at Drummond — a dark, malicious wink. "Revenge."

With that, Mr. Lukowski ran into the hallway.

Drummond darted after him, leaping over the remains of Mrs. Lukowski. It would've been convenient if the ghost had taken care of Mr. Lukowski as well, but the witches Drummond knew told him long ago that touching the corporeal world caused pain to a ghost. Ripping a person in half must have delivered quite a punch to Milly. She would be out of sorts for a while. Which meant the rest was on Drummond's shoulders. And if he didn't stop Mr. Lukowski, then that ghost might blame him for the death of her mother.

Sprinting down the hall, he glimpsed Mr. Lukowski stomping up the stairs. In the seconds it took Drummond to catch up, he considered drawing his weapon and taking a shot. But hitting a moving target while also running and navigating a hallway and stairwell — that bullet didn't have a chance of finding its target.

By the time he hit the first step, Mr. Lukowski neared the top. "Stop," Drummond said. "Killing that old lady won't save you from the ghost."

Mr. Lukowski continued climbing and yelled back, "I'm not trying to save myself."

Drummond feared as much. A man with nothing to lose on a suicide mission — not a good combination. Skipping steps, Drummond gained a little ground.

Mr. Lukowski reached the top. Gasping for air, he said, "You'd be better off trying to get out of this building. Nothing's going to stop me." He dashed off.

Drummond hit the third floor landing and raced down the hall. Mr. Lukowski had stopped at his door and fumbled with the keys. Drummond did not slow down.

He slammed into Mr. Lukowski, tackling him to the ground. Though Drummond's head still ached, his adrenaline kept his strength up. Two jabs into the chin and Mr. Lukowski eyes rolled.

Though Mr. Lukowski remained conscious, he rocked from side to side, dazed and without control. Drummond snatched the keys from the man's hand and unlocked the apartment door.

Like an angry bear, he stormed across the room and kicked open the bedroom door. Ms. Turner sat in the back corner, bound and gagged. The bed had been set on end against the wall leaving the majority of the floor space open. And yes sir, it was open — half the floorboards had been torn up. All the thumping Drummond had heard — some of it may have been Ms. Turner, but the rest was Mr. Lukowski prying up floorboards, trying to get to the treasure from above.

Seeing Drummond enter, Ms. Turner did not struggle or scream or strain against her bindings. She had been tucked away in this room for weeks. Any fight she had left, she would not waste.

Drummond crossed over to her, pulled down her gag, and got to work on the ropes. She smelled awful — apparently, the Lukowskis had never bothered to bathe her.

"You're safe now," he said. "I'm going to get you out."

Ms. Turner leaned her head back as if enjoying the summer sun upon her face. "What a sweet gentleman you are."

"I don't know about that, but the people who kidnapped you are not getting away. One of them is already dead, and I have friends in the police force — they'll take care of the others."

"How lovely. You're a fine looking fellow, too. You know, I have a daughter. She is a tad young for you now, but if you're willing to wait, she'll be quite a catch in a few years."

Drummond paused before returning to the rope knots. "Ms. Turner, do you know where you are? Do you understand what's happened?"

"Do you know that when I was young, I had four different gentlemen trying to win my hand. Isn't that something? Four gentlemen."

Drummond's heart sank. "I'm sure you were quite fetching in your time. Frankly, you've still got the good looks."

Ms. Turner giggled. "Oh, you are a charmer."

The last knot refused to loosen. Drummond stood. "I'll be right back. I promise. I'm just going into the kitchen to get a knife so I can cut these ropes."

"Would you like me to sing you a song? Those gentlemen I knew always said that I had a lovely singing voice. I'm not trying to brag mind you, but I often feel better when there's music in the air."

"If it makes you feel better, sing away."

Ms. Turner rocked her head back and forth in time with the melody she sang. She had a surprisingly strong voice as the old 1911 tune *Some of these Days* floated from her lungs. The corner of Drummond's mouth raised. The lady was right. Life did feel a little better with music. All that potential joy vanished as he stepped into the main part of the apartment. Mr. Lukowski stood in the kitchen.

"Looking for this?" Brandishing a knife, he lunged at Drummond.

It happened too fast. Before Drummond could process what he had seen, Mr. Lukowski's fist found Drummond's stomach and the knife had dug into his arm. The two men wrestled to the floor. As they rolled toward the center of the room, Drummond spotted the knife only a few feet away. He did not recall it falling to the ground. Never heard the clatter. But there it was.

As Ms. Turner's melodic voice carried above them, Drummond and Mr. Lukowski continued to struggle. Drummond brought his knee up and gouged it straight into Lukowski's side. Lukowski responded with an elbow to the ribs. Each time one of them reached for the knife, the other took advantage of the opening with punches and kicks.

The third time Lukowski went for the knife, Drummond had had enough. He dug his knuckles into the side of Lukowski's neck. Lukowski groaned and rolled over in a strange effort to get away. Rather than reach for the knife himself, Drummond kicked it, knocking it all the way towards the wall.

With a small amount of distance between them, both men got to their feet. Neither rose quickly, and they eyed each other warily, ready for the next assault.

Drummond took a wide stance to ensure that he did not fall. "It's all over now."

"It won't be over until she's dead."

"That won't happen. Listen. Do you hear her singing? You better believe that Milly hears her singing, too."

"Don't care. My wife is gone. I don't really care to live at all."

Drummond leaned back against the wall. "Okay. But I'm warning you, that ghost is still vicious. She won't make your death pleasant."

Lukowski glowered. His hands twitched at his sides like a gunslinger staring down the sheriff. For a second, Drummond had to hand it to the man — he almost convinced Drummond that he meant every word he said. Probably believed it himself — a little. Then his eyes betrayed him. Keeping still, he gazed around the room — clearly, looking for signs of the ghost.

Drummond understood. He had come close to death enough to know the difference between bravado and truly having lost the will to live. Lukowski had a broken heart. That and a guilty conscience. He had done horrible things, and he knew that the time to pay approached. Drummond had one question still. Which was more important — revenge or survival?

Turned out to be revenge.

Lukowski bolted for the bedroom door. He managed to get one foot across the threshold. But then it was over.

The ghost grabbed him from behind, yanked him back into the apartment's main room, and tossed him against the kitchen wall. His body flopped to the ground only to be thrown to the ceiling. The ghost took a tour of the walls and doors in the apartment concluding by smashing Lukowski's head against the glass window. A long crack spidered out from the point of impact on both the glass and his forehead.

Lukowski whimpered. Crawling on his knees, he gazed up at Drummond. His face streamed blood, and he reached out as if begging for help.

Drummond tapped out a cigarette and lit up. He took a long, slow inhale. He watched as the ghost dragged Lukowski out of the room and into the hall. He heard Lukowski screaming but only for a few seconds. A loud crack of bone was followed by silence.

The silence lasted only two seconds. Then the charming voice of Ms. Turner returned to finish her song. Drummond walked over to where the knife had come to rest against the wall. He picked it up and entered the bedroom. Ms. Turner sat straight up with her head bobbing from one side to the other as she sang.

When she concluded, she said, "I have a wonderful daughter. She always takes good care of me."

"That she does." Drummond knelt behind the chair and sawed through the last rope knot. "In fact, it's because of her that I came here."

"She sent you to help me?"

"I believe so."

Ms. Turner touched his wounded arm. "Looks like you've been cut."

"I'll be all right. Why don't we help each other get out of here?"

"That would be wonderful."

Drummond eased Ms. Turner to her feet. She moved slowly, her knees giving out after a few steps. But he held her up. They leaned on each other as they headed toward the door.

"Wait," she said. "We can't leave without Milly."

"She's with us in our hearts now." It sounded corny in his head, but he didn't know much about consoling a mother half out of her mind. It would have to do.

Ms. Turner pulled away from Drummond's light grip. She swayed as she approached a closet door. The accordion fold on the door poked outward as she slid it aside. On the floor was a large duffel bag with a dark stain at the bottom. She looked back at Drummond, tears dribbling down her face.

"Is that her?" he asked.

She nodded.

"Then I give you my word, after I get you settled in, I will return here, and I'll take care of that."

"I can't leave her here."

"You won't have to worry. Milly will watch over this room just fine while I'm gone. And when I get back, I'll see that she is laid to rest properly. That's really what you want, isn't it?"

She nodded and took his arm. They walked down the hall to the stairs. Drummond saw no sign of Mr. Lukowski's final moments. No blood, no corpse, not even scratches on the walls.

As they carefully went down step-by-step, Ms. Turner patted Drummond's hand. "Where am I to go now?"

He knew the answer. He knew it the moment he saw her. She would need professional help — the West Carolina Insane Asylum. "I know a place. Good people there. And I even have a friend for you."

"You do?"

"My mother lives there. She'll be very happy to meet you."

"If it's good enough for your mother, then I'm sure all of it will be fine. Because any woman good enough to raise a man like you has to be a decent person."

Drummond chuckled. "I never said I was an angel."

"Neither did I," she said with a wink. "Besides, I already have an angel looking over me."

"That you do."

At the bottom of the stairs, Drummond reached out for the front doorknob. It turned easily, and the door opened without any problem. Before they could leave, however, Ms. Olson came rushing down the hallway.

"Mr. Drummond, Mr. Drummond, is everything okay? Is it over?"

Holding the front door open, he said, "It's all going to be fine. The Lukowskis are gone, and the Turners won't be here anymore, either. Mr.

Sullivan is in his apartment. Probably still crying. You may want to go give him some comfort. But I wouldn't be too long about it. He's going to be getting a visit from the police later tonight."

As he turned away, he heard Ms. Olson rushing up the stairs. Once he got Ms. Turner settled in at the hospital, he would call his old pal, Detective Cooper, and explain about Sullivan. If Cooper wanted to arrest the man, he could. Drummond didn't worry about Sullivan running. The man could try, but Drummond doubted he would. Plus, if he did, he wouldn't get far — Sullivan didn't have the brains or willpower for an effective escape.

Ms. Turner inhaled the night air with deep satisfaction. "You know, people don't realize how the simple pleasures are the real wonders of the world. And the world around us is filled with so many great wonders. I always tried to make sure my Milly understood. That's why I know I'm going to like meeting your mother. Meeting new people can be a joyful experience. It is one of the many great treasures of the world. You mark my words — everywhere you look there are treasures to be found."

As they strolled along the sidewalk, Drummond tipped back his hat. "You keep talking like that, you'll have people seeing treasure everywhere."

CASE 06

THE ESSENCE OF THE PROBLEM

IT WASN'T THE FIRST TIME THAT MARSHALL DRUMMOND had a midnight meeting in the Winston-Salem railyard nor the first time the meeting would be with the cops. He understood, though. Back when he was a beat cop, before the crash of '29, he would never have dared talk in public to a PI who specialized in ghosts, witches, and other unworldly creatures. He would have been laughed out of a job.

So, when his old friend, Detective Cooper, set up this meeting, Drummond knew there had to be a serious problem. Worse than that, really. After all, Cooper had contacted Drummond several times over the years whenever his cases became unusual. Cooper had even visited Drummond's office on occasion. A clandestine meeting like this promised trouble of a greater magnitude.

With a long drag on a cigarette, he tipped back his hat and let the cool night breeze tickle his skin. Summer neared its end but not before striking out with a final sweltering week. A rainstorm earlier that day did little to help, and the humid air wafting off the giant steam locomotives only made things worse.

Two figures approached. The dim yard lighting made them little more than shadows. Still, Drummond recognized them right away — the sturdy frame of Detective Cooper and the rounder shape of Chief Carter.

The Chief of Police, huh? Things had definitely gotten worse.

"Thanks for coming out here," Cooper said as he shook Drummond's hand. The Chief kept his hands at his sides as he continually scanned the area.

Readjusting his hat, bringing the brim lower, Drummond said, "What exactly can I do for you?"

Before Cooper could respond, the Chief snorted and spit off to the side. "I'm going to be straight with you. I don't believe in any of this crap. Never have. Never will. But Pearl and I are at our wits end. We don't know what to do and Cooper thinks you can help."

From the derisive way Chief Carter spoke Cooper's name and from the uncomfortable look on Cooper's face, Drummond guessed that his friend's job rode on the success of the night.

"Well, you've established how much you don't want me to help you," Drummond said. "Tell me how I can help you."

The Chief scowled. "Now I remember why I was happy to see you leave the Department. Damn smart mouth of yours."

Cooper put a hand on each man's shoulder. "Come on gentlemen, let's not forget why we're here."

Poking his cigarette in the Chief's direction, Drummond said, "I don't know why I'm here. You can cut the games; I don't work for you anymore. You want my help? Get on with it."

For a second, Drummond thought he had ticked the Chief off enough to cause Cooper trouble, but then Chief Carter snorted and spit again. "You listen to me — I don't buy any of this dog-and-pony show of yours. You understand? Only reason I'm here is 'cause I got no other choice. And my Pearl deserves every chance, so here it is — somebody broke into our house and terrorized our maid."

"Your maid?" Drummond received a nod from Cooper confirming the claim. Then he frowned. "A break-in and an assault? This is all your domain. You got the whole Department at your disposal, and I'm sure they'd turn every stone for you. Why are you bringing this to me?"

"Use the police? Gee, that's brilliant. Why didn't I think of that? Oh, wait — maybe, any moron with half-a-brain would realize that I'm meeting them out here at midnight because I want this kept quiet. Your genius pal here suggested you could help and that better be the case — especially considering the odd nature of this."

"Odd?"

Now it was the Chief's turn to receive a nod from Cooper. Stepping closer to Drummond, the Chief's mouth twisted in disgust. Out of his coat pocket, he produced a light-blue cloth no bigger than a napkin. "Mrs. Carter and I went out last night, went to a show at the Colonial, and when we got back, Ms. Daggett was standing in the corner of our living room shaking and talking gibberish. Shock, of course."

Drummond wanted to hurry the Chief along. He didn't need to hear the normal details. In the last twenty-four hours of a normal case, the Department would have brought every suspect in and questioned them. All the leads would have been followed up on. Standing in the railyard on a humid midnight and hearing the word *odd* meant something unnatural. The normal way of doing things would not help — not necessarily. It depended on the nature of the *odd* part of all this.

But if Drummond pressed too hard, the Chief would remember he didn't believe in magic. This was 1932, and he was a modern, civilized man. Ghosts were for superstitious chumps. He would curse out Cooper and storm off determined to use his own men. And whatever had frightened Ms. Daggett would continue to haunt the Carter's house —

because if the Chief used the word *odd* and Cooper thought this meeting worthwhile, Drummond had no doubt the regular police would be way out of their depth.

Chief Carter stared down at the light-blue cloth, his thumb rubbing it, and he shuddered. "This was clutched in her hand." His voice choked as he thrust the cloth over.

Drummond opened it, pretending to ignore the Chief's stifled blubbering. His heart fell as he saw the symbol drawn on the cloth — a swirling line wrapped around a downward pointing arrow. The drawing had been made with a crimson substance that all three men recognized — blood.

Cooper gestured to the symbol. "There's more."

"I figured," Drummond said. "Nothing so far is worth getting this upset over."

"The Chief isn't telling you where Ms. Daggett found that cloth." Cooper peeked over at Chief Carter. When he got no response, he took it as permission to continue. "It was sitting atop a — well, um, a sort of altar, I guess. This horrible thing in her room made of the furniture and a disemboweled animal — a calf, maybe a wolf. I don't know. Blood everywhere. Between that and the strange symbol — well, I thought of you."

"Gee, thanks." Rifling through the various occult symbols Drummond knew, he could not place this one at all — of course, he only had limited experience with occult symbols. "I'll need to check out the crime scene. You said she found this cloth in her room?"

Chief Carter stabbed a finger in Drummond's direction. "I'm not having you and your voodoo nonsense stepping foot in my house. All you'll do is upset Pearl and my maid. It'd be pointless anyway. I already had the rooms looked over."

"I thought nobody from the Department knew about this."

"Something bad happens and you think I'd call for you first? Sheesh, you must be more deluded than I thought." Speaking slow as if giving directions to a bratty child, Carter said, "I had an old friend — retired — come over. He checked out the house, and he talked with Ms. Daggett. Tried to, anyway. She wouldn't say anything. But he found the cloth in her hand. When I saw that symbol, when I saw what it was drawn with, that's when I remembered that Detective Cooper had stayed in contact with you. That's the only reason I had this meeting set up. But there's nothing else to be found in the house, and I'm not putting my loved ones through any more of that."

Clearly trying to salvage the situation, Cooper said, "That symbol looks like the stuff I've seen in your office. Am I right?"

Drummond shrugged. "It's not a spell, if that's what you mean."

"A spell," Chief Carter sneered. "This is the kind of crap I wanted to avoid."

Pocketing the cloth, Drummond said, "You don't have to believe it, but you better accept that others believe it. Not only that, but they guide their lives by it. So, instead of acting like an ass every time we mention spells and such, you might want to remember that we're all sweating and tired tonight because we want to help you." Before the Chief could rebut, Drummond turned away. Passing Cooper, he said, "I'll look into this."

Back in his car, Drummond checked his watch — 12:24am. The Chief should have come to him sooner. Either the perps were idiots with the bad luck to pick the house or they had targeted the Chief. Unless, of course, the attack had been meant to intimidate the maid, and the fact that she worked for Chief Carter had been an unfortunate coincidence. But Drummond thought that would be an amazing bit of bad luck. No. This all felt very specific and not at all the work of amateurs.

Driving along East 11th Street, Drummond considered requesting an interview with Chief Carter. But given that the Chief only agreed to meet in a railyard at midnight and that he had a near-conniption at the idea of Drummond checking out the crime scene, he did not like his chances of getting any requests approved.

He pulled up to Raymond's Diner — one of the only all-nighters in the city. It had been fashioned out of an old railcar and had plenty of charm despite being narrow and cramped. The place was good for late-night thinking. It always smelled great and had only a few people hanging out on the long counter — mostly truckers grabbing a meal before hitting the road.

As Drummond settled into a booth near the back, Catalina walked up to him, set a mug on the table, and filled it with hot coffee. She had a weathered beauty that always left him wondering how she had ended up at such a dead end. Though he knew Hollywood could be quite prejudice against brown-skinned women, he would have paid money to watch her dance alongside Fred Astaire or fight the bad guys with Gary Cooper.

"The usual?" she asked, only a slight hint of a Mexican accent.

"Just the coffee for now, doll."

"Suit yourself. But Marcus is on the grill tonight."

Drummond raised an eyebrow — Marcus made a mean omelet that never failed to satisfy no matter how late at night. "Okay, then. The works."

"Hushpuppies on the side?"

"What kind of man would I be, if I didn't eat hushpuppies?" As she turned to go, Drummond added, "Hey, Cat, let me ask you something."

"Sure, but I like my full name."

"Catalina it is, then." His hand reached into his pocket and gripped the cloth. "Were you a good kid?"

She shrugged. "I did my share of things, but I was no troublemaker."

"You knew any kids that got in trouble a lot?"

"No more than the next kid. What's this about? You got a new case?"

Catalina knew Drummond was a private investigator, but she had no idea of the kinds of cases he undertook. Pinching the clothing between thumb and forefinger, he said, "I'm working on something a bit odd, and I'm trying to make sure it really happened." She raised an eyebrow. Grinning, he said, "I mean that sometimes kids will pull all sorts of tricks to get Mommy and Daddy's attention."

"How old is the girl?"

Drummond had to laugh. He had not mentioned anything specific, yet Catalina had picked up on the image in his mind. "I don't even know if there is a kid. Just trying to think all the angles."

"Shouldn't you already know something like if there's a kid or not?"

"Of course. I don't know why I even thought that way. I must be more tired than I realized." He swigged back some of the coffee.

"Most kids are good, though. Even the bad ones are usually not trying to cause any real harm. They just want to be seen."

"I guess that means you've got a kid."

"Two. Both boys."

A heavy-set fellow with a heavier beard waved his hand from the far end of the counter. Catalina headed off to take care of her other customers, and Drummond watched her every move.

It wasn't an infatuation. Drummond simply appreciated a fine woman when he saw one. Especially when what made her so fine came from inside. Catalina was bright and caring. The fact that he found her beautiful only widened the smile on his face.

"What's got you so happy?" she asked when she returned to his booth.

"You came back."

"I'm your waitress."

"But my food isn't ready yet."

She flashed her smile and glanced back at the two men finishing their meals. One threw some cash on the counter, knocked his knuckles a few times atop the cash, and walked out. The other joined his friend a moment later.

"See that?" she said as she slid into the booth bench opposite Drummond. "You're the only customer I got left."

"Lucky me." He tried to sound casual, but for some reason, his heart raced in his chest.

Before his blood rushed to his head, Catalina reached over and snatched the light-blue cloth out of his hand. "Is this part of your case?"

Drummond frowned. He did not recall taking the cloth from his pocket. "It was left behind — presumably, a message."

When she opened the cloth, Drummond saw the change come over her face. He wanted to jump across the table and ask her what she knew, but that approach would have failed. Part of being a good detective was reading people. A woman like Catalina would not respond well to an aggressive tactic.

Instead, he sat back and sighed. "I've seen plenty of weird, little groups in my time — cults and covens and such — but I don't know that logo at all."

"Covens."

Not a question. Not a surprised look, either.

"There are groups that call themselves covens. Consider themselves witches. You know anything about that?"

Catalina raised her eyebrows. "*Las brujas?* Witches? Where I come from, they're either respected or feared. Either they're good or they're horrible monsters."

"Is that what the symbol is? Some kind of Mexican witch?"

All the charm in Catalina's face drained away. She handed the cloth back with a cold, disappointed gaze. "I don't know that symbol. Doesn't look like a witch-thing, though. Those are usually more geometric. You know? Pentagrams and circles with other basic shapes inside. That kind of thing."

"Then what spooked you? I saw your reaction. Come on, doll. Tell me the truth."

Marcus dinged the order bell. With a relieved roll of her eyes, Catalina swooshed out of the booth and grabbed Drummond's omelet. She returned and set his plate down hard enough to slosh the omelet across to the edge.

"Look," she said, jutting her hip out to the side, "I don't actually believe in witches or anything like that. My *abuela* — my grandmother

— she is the superstitious one in the family. That's how I know anything about any of it. And I'll admit that there's plenty of strange things in the world, plenty of things we don't understand, but witches flying around on broomsticks? No. That's just old superstitions."

Drummond unfolded his napkin and placed it across his right leg. "I had to say this earlier tonight, and it still holds — doesn't matter if witches are real or not. There are those who believe. That's what matters."

"*Verdad*. In that case, I'd say that I haven't ever seen that symbol before, but my grandmother does have several books in the apartment. Quite a few of them have all sorts of symbols similar to that one. If you want me to, I could take a look for you." This last sentence came out halting and unsteady.

Setting his fork down before he had his first bite, Drummond gazed up at her. "I would greatly appreciate that. When do you get off work? There are lives at stake here." Not entirely true, but he never minded stretching the truth a little bit.

With a dismissive gesture, she said, "Phil and Douglas were the last two regulars of the night. A few might trickle in, but it's Wednesday. Very slow. Marcus can handle it for a bit without me."

"Shall I join you?" The words sounded suave in his head, but Drummond inwardly cringed as he heard them leave his mouth.

"You need to go to where that cloth came from. If this is the work of a witch, then you need to find her. Best way to stop magic is at the source. My *abuela* always said that if you kill a witch, you undo all her magic."

"I wish that were true — the undoing, not the killing — but it's not been my experience."

"That's what she told me. But it's all in their heads anyway. It's not like you cast real magic spells. It's just ritual. Like any religion."

Drummond snickered as he slid from the booth. "I think the Vatican might not like you equating their priests with witches and witchcraft."

She gestured to the omelet. "You're gonna leave that?"

"Unless you can guarantee that the guy threatening everyone will take a break while I do, then food'll have to wait. Please, go find your grandma's books." From his coat pocket he pulled out a business card. "That's my office address. If you don't mind, please meet me there tomorrow morning. About nine?"

"There's a number here. Can't I call you?"

"I'll be out all night. Just in case *abuela* comes up empty, I've got my own sources to call on."

Catalina ran her eyes up and down. "*Abuela,* huh?"

"Did I say it wrong?"

"Not one bit." With a high school grin, she walked into the kitchen. Drummond detected a little extra sway in her hips.

DRIVING OUT OF THE CITY, Drummond made his way southwest towards Mocksville. His Model A made good time despite the backfires and puttering engine. He worried the old automobile might not last much longer, and he could not afford a new one. But getting shot at and racing away from angry ghosts had taken its toll.

He would rather have been on his way to Chief Carter's house, though Carter had made it clear he was not welcome. Eventually, he would have to visit the crime scene. Besides, Carter most likely went home to be with his wife for the night.

As the city shrank in his rearview mirror, the Carolina forest took over — thickening trees that darkened the roadway like an unending tunnel made by Nature. It would take over an hour to reach Leroy Parker's house — plenty of time to think.

Most of that time should have been spent mulling over the case. Drummond's mind, however, drifted repeatedly to thoughts of Catalina. Her electrifying smile, the rhythms of her speech, and her openness all reached deep into his chest. But her casual willingness to accept those things that would have sent most people screaming into the night weakened his knees.

Careful, Drummond warned himself. Getting smitten on a case is a good way to end up dead.

Closing in on three in the morning, Drummond pulled off the main road onto an unmarked gravel drive — one lane, dark, leading deep into the forest. After three minutes of winding turns and uneven terrain, Drummond finally stopped before Leroy Parker's home — a dilapidated shack which may never have seen better days. Oil lanterns hung from strategic points along the front porch and more were visible inside the house.

Drummond had expected Leroy to be awake. As far as he knew, the man never slept.

"Who the hell are you?" a thickly accented voice called. The front door cracked open. "I got a shotgun and ain't afraid to use it."

Leroy was also a bit blind and a bit more paranoid.

"It's Marshall Drummond. So put down your shotgun and crack open a whiskey."

The front door flung open and Leroy's hefty figure stood in silhouette. He was a tall, black man, full of charm and a belly laugh that could be contagious. He was also among the smartest people Drummond had ever met.

Leroy loved knowledge. He spent all of his time reading books on any subject that grabbed his interest. Those interests were wide — everything from agriculture to economics, from machinery to meditation, and of course, the unnatural worlds.

Several years back, Drummond helped Leroy out of a jam with a witch, and that birthed a strong friendship which had lasted ever since. It also led to Leroy's obsessive investigation of all things in the unseen world. Any books he could get his hands on, he read. He knew the full history of witchcraft around the world, he knew their scarce folklore and myths, and Drummond hoped that he knew their obscure symbols, too.

"You about near got your head shot off," Leroy said, beckoning for Drummond to sit on a wooden bench near the warm fireplace. "What kind of fool thing you doing comin' around here near the witching hour?"

Drummond snickered. "It's been hours since midnight."

Though he shook his head, Leroy opened the drawer from a small wooden desk. He pulled out a pair of thick glasses. Even wearing them, he still squinted. "There's more than one witching hour, my friend. You got your midnight, you got your three in the morning, you even got a four. All depends on where your witch came from."

The inside of Leroy's house looked more rundown than the outside. Bare-bones, too. Hard wooden furniture and dusty shelves had been pressed against the walls. An old army cot had been placed next to a small desk. The only form of decoration — not really a decoration at all — tons of books. Between the dust, the wood furniture, and the endless books, Drummond marveled that Leroy had not died by an accidental fire from his oil lanterns.

"Now, whiskey." Leroy set out two shot glasses, somewhat dirty, and produced an unopened bottle of whiskey. After he poured the drinks, he said, "Okay, we have our drink. Tell me what's brought you out here."

"I'm working on a new case. Don't know much about it yet, but I got this." Drummond placed the marked cloth on the desk next to the whiskey.

Keeping his head back and squinting downward, Leroy picked up the cloth. Squinting harder, he brought the cloth closer to his face. His breath and his mouth dropped. He thrust the cloth under the table and backed away, pressing against the wall.

"Have you plumb lost your damn mind? You bring that into my house during the witching hour? You want to get us killed?"

With frantic momentum, Leroy doused every lantern in the house. He stumbled out onto the porch and shut off those lanterns as well. When he returned, he started about lowering the flames in the fireplace.

Drummond said, "This was given to me at midnight, and nothing happened. You can relax."

"All the more reason to worry. Obviously, if it ain't got you during the first hour, then it's more likely get you going into the next."

"At least, tell me what it is."

Leroy checked that his shotgun was loaded and handed it over to Drummond. He then pulled out an old service revolver from under his pillow and checked it over.

Drummond tried to remain calm, but the shotgun in his hand ignited his nerves. Despite his paranoia, Leroy did not panic easily.

Snapping his fingers, Leroy pointed at a large bag of salt sitting in the corner. "Stop staring at me like a frightened girl seein' her first willy and get to work."

Drummond went over to the bag, grabbed a metal scoop, and lined the doors and windows with the salt. When he finished, Leroy indicated the hearth, too. Drummond got another scoop and made a small arc in front of the fireplace.

"So this is some kind of ghost?" Drummond asked.

"Salt works on more than just ghosts."

"Any chance you're going to fill me in?"

With a lick of his lips, Leroy hurried behind Drummond — inspecting the salt lines and shuttering the windows as he went. "That there cloth — it's a calling card and a threat. It's also part of a spell."

"Summoning? I thought that's all done with circles and some special writing and candles and such."

"Usually, but there are other spells. Darker spells. Far more dangerous. Kind of magic used to summon in a circle or even more dangerous, a triangle, well that's used to bring up your regular ghost. Want to call up old grandpappy — a witch uses a summoning. But this — this ain't about raising no ghost."

Icy fingers crawled up Drummond's spine. "What then?"

"It's used for making objects — things that use essence for a wish."

"Wishes, huh? You serious?"

Waving his gun in the direction of the salted windows, Leroy said, "Doesn't look like a joke, does it?"

"Sorry. I just never heard of this kind of thing. Is it like Aladdin's lamp? A genie or something?"

"More like a philosopher's stone. The fact is, somebody's trying to call upon something serious, you understand? Somebody who knows a lot about what they doin'."

Drummond let this settle in his brain. "The symbol on the cloth — is that whatever essence is being raised? Is that like its name or something?"

"Kind of. It's kind of like Mojo — it's a word that encompasses a lot of undefined magic, things that we know exist, but we don't know enough about them to give them a proper name."

Drummond surveyed the room — the closed windows, the salt lines, the pressure of dark. "You think this essence is coming here."

Leroy shrugged, but it turned into a shudder. "I can't say I right know what that thing is going to do. But I know you brought its calling card in here." Leroy whirled toward the shelves. "I might have something."

From across the room, Drummond asked, "What can I help you find?"

Snapping his face right up, Leroy said, "Start by using your brain. Lotta good it'll do havin' you looking for books when you should be guarding all the entrances."

Before Drummond could respond, a loud thud hit the front door. Like a small explosion, it struck the door again, sending a plume of dust and dirt toward the center of the room. The door held. The salt had not been disturbed.

The men shared a look — eyes wide, faces chilled. Without a word, they broke from each other. Leroy returned to the bookshelves, and Drummond aimed the shotgun at the door.

A horrible sound erupted. Like an enormous and powerful claw dragging through the wood, the sound ripped across the wall, from the doorway toward the first window. Tracking the sound's movements with his shotgun, Drummond eased his finger onto the trigger.

He expected another thud at the window. Perhaps a hit strong enough to shatter the glass. Instead, he heard the claw sound turn into the ear-shattering screech of nails digging into glass. When it passed over to the wall again, heading toward the next window, Drummond snatched a glance at Leroy.

Leroy sat on the floor, hunched over a large text, his finger tracing the words as he read.

The screeching of glass ignited the air once more. Drummond aimed at the second window. He fought against a natural urge to squeeze the trigger and blast away whatever lurked outside. But he was no novice when it came to dealing with such things. Ghosts often tried to trick people into breaking their own salt lines. A shotgun blast would definitely disturb the purity of the salt protection. Drummond had the shotgun for one reason only — to destroy anything that reached through the walls of the house.

"I got it! I got it!"

"Great. What's the symbol mean?"

"Not that. That's not a symbol I recognize, and I probably don't have the appropriate book because if I did, then I would recognize it. There's a few books I can think of which might hold the answer, but —"

"Leroy! What is it you've got?"

"Right, right. Says here that if you want to summon an Essence, you have to fashion summoning bait — that'd be the calling card. Once you done that, the Essence will come to wherever the calling card is."

As the deep scratching continued against the walls, the creature outside pounded hard, sending dirt falling from the poorly constructed ceiling.

"I think we know that part already," Drummond said.

Leroy read faster. "This is saying that you gotta make an offering. You've got to build an altar and offer up something of value to the Essence. If it likes what you offered, then it will leave some of itself in the object you want to imbue with it."

"In case you missed it, we don't have an altar. What happens if it doesn't like the situation?"

"It leaves. Then it comes back the next night during the witching hour. It'll come back three times."

"This all went down last night. So this Essence didn't like what was offered the first time and now it's here for another. That about it?"

"Yeah, and it'll come back tomorrow night looking, too."

The window next to the chimney shattered. The wooden shutters protected Leroy and Drummond from sustaining any injuries, but they heard the tinkle of glass against the wood like sinister windchimes. "I don't have time for twenty questions. What are you telling me?"

"If the third time comes and still this here Essence is not satisfied, then all that summoned it perish."

"Perish? Can't say I like that word."

"That's what it says here."

"Hold on, there — we didn't summon it. I swear I did not say any summoning spell."

"I don't think that matters to it. Anybody that's touched the calling card is considered guilty. Think of it as guilt by association."

Drummond eyed all the salt lines. "What if it can't get in? If it can't see the offering, then it can't reject it."

Leroy frowned. "Maybe. We don't have an offer for it anyway."

"It doesn't know that."

An unearthly gust of wind howled down the chimney. It smashed into the ground, spewing ash and sparks into the air. As it pressed outward, it scattered the salt on the floor. A red tinged object flew into the room. It moved too fast for Drummond to get a solid look, but the semi-transparent creature flowed like a shredded blanket in a strong wind.

It bowled over Leroy and battered Drummond back into the wall. He tried to get a shot off but the thing moved too quickly. Before he comprehended what had happened, the shotgun lay in two pieces on the floor. A rapid series of strikes rippled up Drummond's abdomen. As he tumbled to the ground, he saw Leroy's head jack to the side.

The creature tossed books from the shelves and overturned the furniture before soaring back up the chimney.

Groaning as he held his side, Drummond said, "Guess it didn't like our lack of an offering."

Leroy spit blood onto the floor. "We better figure out fast with it does like or we're not going to be around here in twenty-four hours."

DRUMMOND DROVE BACK to Winston-Salem with Leroy in the passenger seat. Before they had left, Leroy dug out an old miner's headlamp which he used to read and reread passages from his books as they traveled. Fine by Drummond. He did not want to have a conversation anyway. The entire drive back, his mind swirled around thoughts of Catalina.

She had touched the cloth back at the diner. Detective Cooper had touched it as well. And, of course, Chief Carter, his wife, and their maid, Ms. Daggett. If Leroy was right, then all of them would be destroyed by this Essence should it not be satisfied with tomorrow night's offering.

Catalina hurt the most. Drummond cared about Cooper and Leroy, and though he did not like Carter and he did not know Carter's wife or maid, he still did not want to see them die. But Catalina — Drummond's spot for her had grown from a small part of his heart to a hole large enough to cover his entire chest. And he swore it was still growing.

It felt strange. He had not fallen hard for a woman in years. Not since Patricia Welling. That had ended horribly — considering she was a witch. But there was no denying it. Catalina caused his pulse to quicken and his breath to catch.

Of course, if anything did happen between them, they would have to be secretive about it. Nobody would look too kindly on a Mexican and a white man dating. If it got out, her life would be in serious jeopardy.

In fact, she had more to fear from that situation than anything involving the Essence. After all, in a little less than twenty-four hours, they would either please the Essence or they would fail and all of them would be dead. But if she were to fall for Drummond as much as he had fallen for her, if they decided to embark upon a relationship, the threat to her would never end.

By the time they reached his Fourth Street office, Drummond had only one thing left on his mind — sleep. Sure impending death hung over his head, but that problem had another twenty-one hours to wait. He would be no good for anybody with his head fuzzy and his reflexes slow. Leroy, on the other hand, appeared to have hit his stride and asked Drummond if he might use the office desk to continue his research.

"Be my guest," Drummond said as he crawled onto his old, lumpy couch — the lumps molded to his exact needs. "I've got good witchcraft references on that bookshelf. Help yourself. It's not going to be anything like you have back at your place, but it should cover all the basics."

"Thank you. Now get some rest. You are going to need all you got."

"If you want some more whiskey, just open Moby Dick."

Drummond lowered his Fedora over his eyes, and in seconds, he snored. His dreams were uncommonly vivid and tactile. And always the Essence made itself known. He would be enjoying ice cream with Catalina on a beautiful summer afternoon when suddenly the sky would darken and that amorphous Essence would arrive. In another, he walked to the park, holding hands with Catalina, admiring the way people did not sneer or ridicule them, when without warning, the Essence arrived. Its shredded blanket form hovered in front of him, just out of reach. Its features blurry and unreadable. In a third dream, he visited his mother at the asylum. She was small and frail, and it brought her great pleasure to hear that he had fallen in love. Until her face crystallized and then blew away like salt in a strong wind. A loud thud followed the arrival of the

Essence. It closed in on him and as he endured a rapid-fire attack to his body, he jolted awake.

Seeing Catalina sitting in a nearby chair, her lovely gaze upon him, left Drummond wondering whether he had woken at all or if he remained in a dream. Leroy sat at the desk with Drummond's copy of Moby Dick open flat. The flask of whiskey kept hidden in the hollowed book stood next to an empty but used glass. Leroy had his face pressed close to the pages of a large volume and appeared to notice little of his surroundings.

"Good morning," Catalina said.

"Morning," Drummond glanced at the clock on the wall — 9:15 am. He plucked his hat off the floor and sat up on the couch.

"Coffee?" Catalina asked.

"Absolutely."

Scratching the stubble on his chin, Drummond watched Catalina's graceful movement as she poured coffee from a metal thermos into a mug she had swiped from the diner. She sat next to him and handed it over. With a grateful gulp that burned his tongue, he allowed himself a few extra seconds to awaken.

Releasing a satisfied sigh, he looked over at the beautiful woman to his side. Her brown skin formed the perfect backdrop to allow her eyes to sparkle. Like an unexpected wind gust, Drummond had the harsh sensation that Catalina would melt away before his eyes and the Essence would reappear. He stared at her, counting in his head, waiting for this dream to fall apart.

She placed a hand on his shoulder. "It's okay. Your friend Leroy explained to me what happened. I want to help."

With those words, reality solidified. Drummond gulped more of his coffee, stood, and let its caffeinated warmth flow through his veins.

Nodding his appreciation, he set his coffee mug on his desk. "Okay. What have y'all learned?"

Catalina glanced at Leroy, but when the man did not lift his head from his book, she sat straighter and gazed up at Drummond. She crossed her legs, revealing her knees, and the world threatened to disappear around him. A devil whispered in his ear that they would never stop the Essence — so why not simply sweep this beautiful woman off her feet and enjoy each other until the end? Thankfully, Catalina spoke, snapping him away from his infatuation.

"I talked with my *abuela* and showed her the symbol. She had a lot to say. First, the symbol was crudely drawn which suggests an amateur.

Possibly the first time this person has ever attempted using dark forces. But this kind of magic is not something a novice would stumble upon."

That perked Drummond's attention more. "Set up?"

"Anytime you deal with a witch, you're asking for a set up."

"So, your grandmother thinks a witch is behind this?"

"Not exactly. A witch certainly provided the information on how to do the magic — that is clear — but beyond that, it does not appear that a witch is involved."

"Because the symbol is not drawn well."

"Also because of how you described the maid. She has seen something horrible. Been petrified by it. If a witch had performed the summoning, she would have made sure to get the offering right on the first try."

Drummond tapped his chin as he paced the office. "If the maid had a problem with either Mrs. Carter or the Chief and she resorted to this kind of solution, it would have to be a big problem. Which makes me think it has more to do with the Chief of Police than the running of the house. Maybe somebody she cares about has been arrested. Or maybe she's fearful of somebody and wants police protection. I could see her go to the Chief, figuring that she might have a little pull, being their trusted maid."

"It can't have gone well, since she sought out a witch."

"Carter's a bit of a bastard. Pardon my language. She might be their maid, a close member of their lives, but she's still a colored girl as far as the Chief's concerned. I'm guessing he made that distinction quite clear to her."

Casting a grim look downward, Catalina said, "Everybody has a point where they take no more. She was not asking for a simple favor or help. She had to be desperate. No matter how much she thought that the Chief would consider her more than the maid, she's no fool. Nobody who could end up being a maid in that household is an idiot."

"Meaning what?"

Catalina stepped in front of Drummond. Only when she had his full attention did she speak. "You do not go see a witch casually. Especially for something this big. This maid is desperate. She had to have exhausted all other options. The last effort, she risks losing her job to ask her boss and the Chief of Police for a favor. A black girl asking a white man."

"A huge favor. One that he denies."

"This must have pushed her beyond being reasonable. She sought out a witch, and the witch took advantage of the situation. It's what they do."

"Not all of them are bad," Drummond said and turned to Leroy so that Catalina could not catch the expression on his face. "We've got a working idea of what might be behind all this. No proof, but an idea. You got anything?"

Without looking up, Leroy said, "You think I found something and I'm holding out on you? I'll tell you when I figure something out to tell you. You know what would help, though? Some damn quiet."

"Always full of charm." Setting his hat on his head, Drummond opened the office door and gestured for Catalina to join him outside. As they stepped onto the sidewalk, he offered his arm both from polite habit as well as a desire to feel Catalina closer. She blushed but kept her arm at her side. Her eyes darted from one passerby to another. Drummond headed along, trying not to scowl.

"Sorry about that," he said.

"It's okay." Though he could not be certain, he swore she walked in a manner that continuously brushed her arm against his.

As they continued northward, he watched the faces of those trudging to work. He paid attention to their eyes — did they look at Catalina? What expression did they wear? Did he put her in any danger by being so close to her? He stopped.

"What's wrong?" she asked.

"You may not want to come with me for this next part."

"Because of that?" She tossed her head in the direction they had come. So, he had read the situation right. Perhaps he had read everything else between them right as well.

"I don't want to cause you any trouble."

Catalina laughed. "You brought a witch symbol into my life that might cause my death. I don't think you can cause me any more trouble."

He chuckled. "I only meant —"

"I know. And I appreciate the concern. Just don't ever do it again."

As they walked on, Drummond thought he understood what she meant but decided he would need more time to think about it later. If they survived. "You know where I'm going?"

"It would make sense that we're headed toward the police station. I'm guessing you want to talk to the Chief."

Smart and beautiful. He wanted to hug her, but he kept his hands in his coat pockets and his head tilted down.

In less than fifteen minutes, they passed under the stone archway of the Winston-Salem Police Department. It had been a long time since Drummond had stepped foot in this building, yet the sounds and distinct aromas had not changed. Footsteps echoed on the tiled floor while voices bounced around the cavernous lobby. The strong stench of burnt coffee floated through the air, and Drummond offered a little thanks for having Catalina in his life to prepare a far more palatable morning wake up.

He did not recognize the desk sergeant — must have been a new man — but the desk sergeant certainly recognize him. Stabbing his pudgy finger in Drummond's direction, the man said, "What are you doing here?"

"I need to see Chief Carter."

"He said you'd try. I didn't think you'd be stupid enough. I'll be nice, though. I'll give you ten seconds to turn right around and get the hell out of my station. And take that brat with you."

Drummond kept his face cold. He knew that if *brat* was the best the desk sergeant dared to throw as an insult, then Drummond could ignore most of the man's bluster.

Catalina stood her ground. Never once flinched. Drummond could not hold back the crack of a smile.

From off to the right, a man coughed and spluttered his morning coffee. Drummond looked over to find Chief Carter holding his coffee out in one hand and a file folder in the other while he glanced down at his suit. His head snapped up to focus his fiery squint at Drummond. "What the hell are you doing here?"

"Got a couple questions about a matter that you —"

Attempting to hide the worry on his face, Carter thrust his hand in the direction of his office door, sloshing coffee onto the floor. "Get in there. Not another word." As Drummond and Catalina stepped toward the office door, Carter said, "She's with you? Tell her to wait in the lobby."

"I need her to —"

"Keep arguing with me and she'll have a worse time than sitting in a cushionless chair."

He stormed into his office and all eyes turned quietly on Drummond. What had promised to be a dull morning for the police had now become a story for the officers to tell their wives later that night. Drummond could feel their anticipation, their hope, that he might push Chief Carter into even more hysterics.

Instead, Drummond felt Catalina pat him on the arm as she walked back to the lobby. He held his anger in check and entered Carter's office.

The front wall consisted of dark-stained wood and numerous glass panels so that the Chief could watch over those beneath him. As Drummond closed the door, Carter stomped along the wood wall, pulling dark shades down over each glass pane. When he finished, he continued stomping across the room, set his coffee on his desk with a chilling thud that shook the photograph of Chief and Mrs. Carter dressed up at a dance. "I know you're an idiot, but you're not suicidal. You should have enough brains not to come in here."

Drummond slowly walked along the perimeter of the room. "The case took an unexpected and rather urgent turn." He had never been in this office and marveled at how precise everything had been placed. The paintings of deer and duck had all been hung at the exact same height, perfectly level. Next to the door, an umbrella stand contained a single umbrella which did not appear to have been tossed in but rather carefully placed so that the curved handle could be easily grasped as one walked out. Even the large key rack — with labels for car, home, cell one, cell two, cell three, office, and more — had been situated with such care that Drummond knew Carter's anger was pure. No acting needed. The idea that a PI would enter his little kingdom and disrupt his planned day infuriated the Chief far greater than having been forced into a position of hiring Drummond in the first place.

Chief Carter stood behind his desk with his fists pressing into the top. "You tread real light in this office. Say what you've got to say and get out. That is if you don't piss me off and I throw you in a cell."

"My team and I are starting to get a clear picture of what's going on."

"Is that who the dark floozy out there is? Your team?"

Drummond stopped to level his own cold glare at the Chief. "I'm not the only one who should tread lightly in this office."

Both men held a silent standoff until Drummond remembered the stakes were far greater than his scoring points against the Chief. Looking away, and trying not to feel the burn of Carter's gloating eyes, Drummond said, "Your maid, Ms. Daggett, did she recently ask you for a favor?"

"What kind of favor?"

"Something big — perhaps help with a jailed love one or maybe she's found something personal in your house or—"

"Whoever's causing trouble in my house, it's not my maid. Geez, is that the best you can do? Somebody broke in and made that horrible thing."

"If I got to see this horrible thing —"

"I told you that you are not stepping foot in my house. Your presence would be bad enough upsetting my wife, but now you want to go after my maid. I've got no more time for your crap. You have something else besides moronic accusations?"

"Whatever you're hiding, it will come out. You've got years of police work behind you to know that's how this will play."

"And you don't. You never made it beyond a beat cop. Couldn't hack it. Oh, you couldn't even quit with any dignity. Had to start talking about ghosts. You sounded crazy just like your mother."

Drummond clenched his fists. He saw the Chief spot the action and both sized the other up like boxers in the ring. "Just because you hate me, doesn't mean I won't be right."

"About what? You haven't said anything worthwhile."

"You hear me this time — I promise you that by tomorrow morning this will all be over."

Drummond whirled around and made his own show of stomping out of the office. As he approached the lobby, Catalina took one look at his stern face and walked alongside without a word. They left the police department and continued on for another block before Drummond allowed his face to open into a smile.

"What's going on?" she asked.

Drummond opened his clenched fist and revealed the keys to Chief Carter's house. "I think it's about time we find out everything we need to know."

THE CHIEF LIVED on the northwest side of town in a section of homes that wished to be as wealthy as the R. J. Reynolds' estate but could not actually afford it. Politicians, successful small business owners, and police chiefs all found a comfortable upper-middle class life — practically unheard of in these horrible economic times. The well-paved roads and tree-lined drives suggested wealth while a few overgrown yards and one abandoned home suggested reality.

Drummond parked across the street from the Carter home and cut the engine. He watched the house in silence for a full three minutes.

"What are we waiting for?" Catalina asked, trying hard to sound more curious than impatient.

"Any sign of what we might be walking into."

"I haven't seen anything. Did I miss something?"

"I haven't seen anything, either. Perhaps nobody's home. Normally the maid would be cleaning the house, but after what happened, she may not be willing to step foot in the place. And who knows what kind of schedule Mrs. Carter has? Perhaps she spends all day playing bridge with her friends at the club, trying to impress the truly rich people."

"Then we go inside?"

"Give it a few more minutes."

Drummond waited another fifteen. When he failed to spot any sign of activity, he figured the house must be empty. Exiting the car, he made a line straight for the front door, moving swift and confident as if he had every right to be there. Catalina's heels clicked behind him as she hustled to catch up. The key worked without trouble, and in seconds, they were standing in the entranceway of the Chief of Police's home.

Like the neighborhood, the house attempted to appear more prosperous than reality. Above them hung a chandelier — but it was small and the ceiling lacked the height to show it off. The floors were polished hardwood, but the rooms were too small to take advantage of their shine. And while the furniture had certainly cost plenty, it was well used — small stains and worn sections betrayed them.

A stale odor permeated the air but it did not come from the kitchen. Drummond moved quietly down a hall, passing the Chief's study, a family room, and a dining room — all well-appointed and as precise as his office. Catalina stayed close by, and Drummond tried not to be distracted by her nearness.

At the end of the hall, he saw a door that stood a bit open. The floor had kitchen tiles — so, presumably, the kitchen. But the stench — like spoiled meat that sat out in the heat too long — had grown stronger and it came from the closed door on the right.

Covering her nose and mouth, Catalina said, "You sure you want to open that?"

"Don't have much of a choice." Drummond reached for the door and pushed it open.

The maid's room — not much larger than a walk-in closet, enough to hold a twin bed, a small dresser, and a rack for hanging her uniform. On the dresser, she had a picture of herself with an older gentleman. They shared the same bright eyes, same shade of dark skin, and the same jawline. Drummond guessed the man was her father.

If he could have stopped his observations there, if he could have ignored the massive structure taking up the center of the room, he would have gladly done so. But even without the horrendous odor that threatened to knock him down, he could not avoid the terrible sight before him. His stomach threatened to revolt, but Catalina gasped and turned her face into his chest. He had to keep together.

Taking up most of the available space in the room, Drummond saw a monument of horror. Several chairs had been stacked to form the skeletal structure of the offering — a T-shaped object with the arm formed from two long pieces of wood. Two animal skins hung from the arms of the T — wolves, probably, and freshly stripped. Blood congealed on the floor from where it had dripped off the meaty flesh the night before. Muscle still clung to the skins in odd-shaped chunks.

That would have been bad enough, certainly enough to traumatize the maid and frighten the Chief, but it went further. Resting in a basinet that had been situated near the top, the small bones of an infant poked out. The perpetrator had robbed an infant's grave, and dirt splotched the white bones.

As the shock wore away, Drummond noticed the lack of flies. The stench smelled fresh with Death, yet no flies, no maggots, nothing. Covering his mouth, he stepped closer to the monstrous structure to get a glimpse in the basinet.

The infant's skull had a large hole in the side and many of its other bones were missing. A mound of dirt filled the bottom half. He could not see how the thing managed to stay balanced atop the chairs.

"Come," Catalina said, backing into the hallway. "This is the offering rejected by the Essence. There's nothing here to help us."

Drummond did not feel so confident, but he relished any excuse to step away from the horrible sight. He closed the door behind him and headed toward the front door. The fresher air made breathing easier. As he reached for the door, he heard a disturbance from upstairs.

He froze. He listened.

When the sound came again — a distinct clump of something heavy against the floor — Drummond turned toward the staircase. Catalina put out her hand. "Perhaps we should leave."

"We're here to find out all we can, and that means *all*. There won't be a second chance. Once Chief Carter realizes I nicked his house keys, this all ends for us."

Her gaze drifted upward. "But there are things not meant to be disturbed. Perhaps —"

"Too late for that kind of caution. People have already broken the rules, tried to mess with magic they don't understand. That thing back there — what kind of twisted mind thinks that's what this Essence wants?"

"But —"

"I'm going up there. I want you to go back to the car, start the engine, and be ready to rip out of here if I come running. Okay?"

"I'm not leaving you alone in here."

Drummond forced a playful wink. "I've been dealing with this kind of thing for years. Don't worry. But still, make sure the car is ready."

As he started up the stairs, Catalina followed him. Stopping, he turned back but she did not budge. When he tried to nudge her toward the door, she grasped his shoulders and pulled in, her eyes much larger so close up.

"Listen to me," she said. "I'll go back to the car like you say, but you've got to make me a promise. You promise me that you won't do anything stupid. You go up there only to see what's making that noise. You don't do anything else. Just observe and get out of there."

"Doll, it'll be fine."

"Promise me."

He wanted to lean over and kiss her. He wanted to assure her everything would be okay. But that wasn't reality and they both knew it. Instead, he brushed her cheek with the back of his hand.

"I'm just going to check things out up there. That's it. But I want you in the car, ready to go, because sometimes these things turn bad. I hope not, but it's the nature of my job, and that means that you always need to be prepared for any outcome. So, I'll do my best not to tick off anything up there and you do your best to help me get the heck out of here should anything go bad. Deal?"

She nodded, and he swore he could see her mouth part open as if inviting that same kiss he had imagined delivering. Moments later, she was out the door, and he had turned to face the climb to the second floor.

It wasn't the first time Drummond had climbed a staircase expecting some kind of unnatural horror awaiting him at the top, and he had come prepared. He pulled out his .38 and checked that it was loaded and ready. He knew the answer — yes, of course — but checked anyway.

The creaking of each step tightened his muscles as it prickled his skin. It happened nearly every time. Something about that sound unnerved him. More than the horrid whine formed by spirits lost between life and death, more than the pained gurgles of a man dying from a gunshot, more than the deadly shrieks of a witch consumed by her own magic, the simple sound of a creaking stair filled Drummond with dread.

At the top, he saw a hallway running straight back to the end of the house — two doors on either side and a bathroom at the far end. The faux-wealth of the downstairs extended up here as well. Three portraits in expensive frames hung on the walls. A small table sat against the wall about mid-way in the hall. Flowers sat in a gold-trimmed vase.

The heavy clump came from the door on the left at the end. Always at the end. Never the door he could reach without taking more than a step or two. Of course not. That would have been a simple matter.

Grumbling as he walked along the hall, he listened to each footfall, felt each heartbeat, smelled every bit of the horror below seeping into the sticky air above. When he reached the far end, he pushed the bathroom door fully open. The small toilet and chipped sink lacked the comfort of the truly wealthy. He had been in enough rich homes to know — those with money liked their bathrooms spacious and comfortable. In fact, a rich man's bathroom often was the most comfortable room in the house.

Turning to the door on the left, the one where the latest *clump* emanated from, Drummond wondered if the Essence had decided to make its third call a little early. With his handgun pointed chest-high at the door, he reached forward and turned the knob with his free hand. As the lock released, he pushed the door open, stepped back, and used both hands to control his weapon.

Gazing into the room, he thought he might prefer the maid's room over this — a large, empty room, bright white, with padding on the walls, no furniture save a wheelchair, and Mrs. Carter. She sat in the chair and stared out one of the three windows flooding the room with sunlight. Her smart dress spoke to her wealth — an illusion promoted by the stylish hat she wore — but the stark reality surrounding her betrayed the false image.

Just observe and get out. Catalina had wanted him to promise that much, and though he had refrained from saying the words, he wondered if she had the right idea.

He inched forward, his fingers flexing against the grip of his weapon. "Mrs. Carter? You okay?"

She had one leg stretched up, resting on the ledge of the windowsill. The foot slipped and smacked against the floor — *thud.* Without moving any other part of her body, she lifted her leg and reset it upon the windowsill.

"Mrs. Carter, my name is Marshall Drummond. Your husband hired me to investigate the problem you and your maid encountered the other night. Would you be okay with talking to me?"

He could not be sure, but he thought her shoulders tensed. Moving further into the room, he saw the side of her face — lean, sharp-boned, stern.

"Mrs. Carter, I think I might be able to help you out. I understand that your maid has been dabbling with forces she doesn't understand. It seems to me that you may have witnessed some of that dabbling. I know how that can be. Quite disturbing. If you want —"

Like a thoroughbred charging out of the gates, Mrs. Carter bolted from her chair, her hat flipping to the floor. She lunged at Drummond, caught him by the lapels and shoved him back against the wall with the strength of a wrestler. Despite her withering arms, she kept him pinned. Milky white clouds covered her eyes yet she acted as if she saw clearly. Snarling with her top lip, she closed her hand around Drummond's throat.

"The souls are mine. Their hearts are mine. I will have the truth. I will have justice."

She tossed Drummond to the floor, before stumbling back as if inebriated. Her hand grasped her chest. Moving like an elderly woman, she flailed about searching for the wheelchair. When she found it, she settled in, breathing heavy and shivering.

Drummond holstered his weapon as he scrambled to his feet. He suspected that whatever had taken over was now gone, but he had no plans to wait around for a return visit. He hurried out of the room, rushed down the hall, and took the stairs two at a time. Out the front door, he raced for the car, idling at the ready. When he dropped into the passenger seat, he said, "Drive."

Catalina did not ask any questions. She sped off and headed across the city.

They ended up at a little dive on the eastern edge of town. Built out of a converted townhouse, the establishment boasted half a dozen tables with a fairly serviceable kitchen in the back. No sign outside, and only people south of the border inside.

Catalina rattled off something to the man in the back who returned with an equally rapid-fire response. The only words Drummond caught were *Si, si.*

"Have a seat," Catalina said indicating a table fit for only two chairs by the window. "I ordered a couple grilled cheese sandwiches and coffee. That okay?"

Drummond nodded. He didn't feel much like talking but knew he would have to anyway — if only to be polite. But the coffee warmed his body and provided a jolt of energy that sparked his thoughts. So far,

Catalina had accepted everything with ease. Perhaps as a result of her grandmother's influence. He hoped she could handle the rest.

"Okay," he said, his mouth suddenly dry despite the coffee. "You sure you want to hear this?"

She tossed a look that felt like his father smacking him upside the head when he was little and behaving stupid. Suppressing a grin, he explained all of what had happened upstairs in the Carter house. When he finished, he gave a small shrug. "I know you don't believe anything your grandmother says, but in my experience, there's more truth to it than we like to admit."

The food came, and Drummond discovered that not all grilled cheese sandwiches were the same. This one had a spicy tomato, cilantro, peppery spread on it — Catalina called it *salsa.* Quite good. "I think I like Mexican food."

She chuckled. "Grilled cheese and salsa is far from Mexican. Stick around me though, and I'll have your taste buds singing."

Drummond wanted to smile. He wanted to reach over and hold her hand. He wanted to tell her that he would stick around and he would learn to love her food.

But even if they weren't facing an evil Essence that would kill them before the next dawn, he knew there were too many people who would act as horribly as the Essence if given the chance. Even in this makeshift diner, surrounded by Catalina's people, he did not dare show too great an affection for her.

People liked to segregate themselves. They felt safety by creating arbitrary walls. He had seen it between the whites and the Mexicans and the blacks and all the other groups. He'd seen it between the witches and the civilians. Heck, even behind the walls, people wanted to segregate. Get a bunch of white people together, and they soon found more reasons to wall off from each other — rich versus poor, tall versus short, it didn't matter.

Underscoring his point, the diner door jingled a bell as it opened and in walked a black woman wearing a maid's uniform. All the patrons stopped their meals to stare at her. All the eyes that had been trained on Drummond's back lifted to fall upon this newcomer.

"A white man and a black woman in one day," Drummond said. "These people will be talking about this night for years to come."

Catalina winked. "You don't know the half of it."

Drummond reached over and grabbed the chair from a neighboring table. As he set it down, Catalina glanced questioningly.

"Even if she wasn't wearing a maid's uniform," he said, "there's no way that woman is not Ms. Daggett."

He gestured to the chair, and the woman walked over and sat. She placed her purse in her lap and folded her hands atop. She sat ramrod straight with her head held up, though the corner of her mouth betrayed a slight tremble.

"You're Mr. Drummond?"

"I am. And you work for the Carters."

She nodded. "I apologize for barging in on you, but from everything I understand, you're my best chance for surviving the night."

Every warning inside Drummond's head blared as a hundred questions crammed through him. The fact that Ms. Daggett had sought him out had to be a good sign. He didn't think she was a witch, so he hoped she wanted to be as helpful as she appeared.

Drummond sipped his coffee and observed Ms. Daggett's face. She waited patiently, though she wore a pleading gleam in her eyes that volleyed between Drummond and Catalina. At length, he said, "Normally, we would talk around the subject until I had a good idea of what you knew."

"But there's no time for that," Ms. Daggett said.

"That's right. It's a good thing, your coming here. Shows me that you're not a monster. So, why don't we begin with something simple? You tell us why you're trying to hurt the Carters after they've been so good to you?"

He caught a flash of shock before her face clamped down into an emotionless blanket. Keeping her eyes forward, no longer making contact with anybody at the table, Ms. Daggett said, "I understand. I'm just the colored maid and that horrible thing was in my room. I know you saw it. I watched you come running out of the house." Cautiously, she turned her face to look directly at Drummond. "But I swear — I swear on everything holy in my life — I had nothing to do with that."

"Are you telling me that Mrs. Carter has always been in the condition I saw her?"

Ms. Daggett shook her head. "That started after. Before all of this, she ran the place tight. Very strict woman. Everything had to be perfect for her. A lot like Ron, er, Mr. Carter. But if he found something wrong, he fixed it himself and told me how he wanted it in the future. Mrs. Carter, however, she could be vicious. Sharp-tongued and not afraid to use a slap in the face."

"You want me to believe you had nothing to do with that display in your room?"

"It's the truth."

"And you just happen to be outside the house when I came running out? So you decided on a whim to follow us?"

"Not at all. I was there looking for you."

Drummond glanced at Catalina. He expected to share a mocking look but he only saw her concentration on Ms. Daggett. She was falling for this woman's line, and what little he knew of Catalina suggested she didn't fall for lines easily. After all, she even doubted her own grandmother — wasn't her fault that the grandmother spoke the truth.

Ms. Daggett dug around in her purse. "This is coming out all wrong. I'm trying to help you — I mean, get some help — I mean, I don't know what I need. This is all rather new to me." From her bag, Ms. Daggett pulled out a light blue cloth. Before she placed it on the table, Drummond knew what he would find — another summoning symbol. Turned out this one resembled the letter K with half-moons hanging from its arm.

"I'm still listening," he said, his voice lowering, nearing a threatening tone. "I'm not liking what I'm seeing, though."

"I don't imagine you do. If you know what that thing is, then you know what I'm facing." She turned to Catalina. "Please, ma'am, you've got to believe me."

Catalina reached out and placed her hand atop Ms. Daggett's. "You need to tell us everything. Start with that. Then we'll see what we can do."

Drummond folded his arms, then covered his mouth with one hand as if in deep thought. He did not want Catalina to spot the warm smile on his face.

Dashing the tears from her eyes, Ms. Daggett nodded. She sat back in her chair, still managing to look rather straight and poised. "Mrs. Carter hates me. From the first day I got hired, she wanted me out of the house. I do good work and I don't talk back, but she was determined to make my life miserable. Especially after she failed to fire me. Mr. Carter wouldn't have it. He said that good help was difficult to find, especially in these hard times — everybody says they can do the job just so they can get a job, but it's harder than it looks. Especially for demanding bosses like the Carters. So, you can't just grab any old fool off the streets and expect the job done right.

"She accepted her husband's word on the matter, but she never stopped hating me. Doesn't surprise me that she gone found a witch. I know what you thinkin' — Ms. Daggett has gone a little loopy. But I assure you, my head is screwed on tight. I didn't believe any of it myself. Never was much for superstition. But after I saw that ... thing ... in my room, well, I knew somebody had it out for me."

Drummond said, "You think that's Mrs. Carter?"

"Can you imagine anybody else wants to kill me? And I wouldn't believe the magic, if I hadn't seen it firsthand. That thing came into my room while I was standing there — still in shock from finding those skinned offerings. And then, this ghost — I don't know what else to call it — it comes floating in. I thought for sure it was going to kill me. Instead it passed right up through the ceiling. I heard Mrs. Carter scream, and when I got up to her room — well, you saw her.

"Later that day, Mr. Carter padded the upper room and locked her away there. He told me not to worry, that he was going to contact an ex-cop he knew who could handle the situation. That night, he went off to meet with you — I'm assuming it was you he was talking about — and I rushed back home to meet with Mrs. Jackson."

"And she is?"

"Just an old lady who lives the floor below me. But she knows all about this kind of stuff. She told me about the summoning spell, told me that our lives are in danger, and that sent me looking for you. Turns out you're not too hard to find."

The corner of Drummond's mouth lifted. "If you're looking for a detective willing to take on the weird cases, there ain't another in the city."

"Certainly seems that way."

Leaning forward, he snatched up the cloth — having already touched one, he figured it hardly mattered if he cursed himself a second time. The Essence could only kill him once. He flipped it over to see the symbol had been burned around the edges.

Answering his frown, Ms. Daggett said, "I don't know. Mrs. Jackson wouldn't touch it, wouldn't even come close enough to look."

Rolling the cloth between his fingers, Drummond tried to place all the pieces together. He thought he had a reasonable picture of events, but nothing that presented a solution. And no solid proof as to who caused this whole mess. But, unless he was mistaken, there were only three people who could've set this summoning in motion.

He shifted to face Catalina. "I need another favor from you."

"Careful or I'll have to start charging you." Despite her playful tone, he could see the nerves hiding beneath — she had no idea if he could save their lives or not. Well, neither did he, but he knew one thing for certain — he would give everything he had to beat this.

"I need you to stick with Ms. Daggett. Make sure the two of you show up at the Carter house tonight. You've got to be there before midnight — the first witching hour."

"I promise I'll have her there on time."

"Maybe you can take her to your grandma, and maybe while you're there, you could grab something for me — a necklace or a ring or any kind of jewelry that has a stone or two in it. Nothing fancy or expensive. Just something she won't miss."

"Sure. With the economy so strong, people love to throw away jewelry. I see people on soup lines just tossing away —"

"Can you do it or not?"

"It's that important?"

"I wouldn't ask otherwise."

"Okay. I'll do it."

He tossed a few dollars on the table to cover the meal and then handed Catalina a few more. "Call a cab. Be careful." He swore her hand lingered in his. Breaking away, he turned to Ms. Daggett. "I appreciate you tracking me down and telling me what you did. I've got to meet with some people to figure this all out. I'll do what a can to help us all." He pocketed the cloth without asking if he could keep it and walked out of the diner.

ENTERING HIS OFFICE, he found Leroy Parker asleep on the couch, a tattered book covering his face. The old man started at the sound of the door closing.

"So, you do sleep," Drummond said as he placed his hat and coat on the stand.

Rubbing his eyes, Leroy sat up. "I got bored waiting for you to return and I finished your whiskey." Stifling a belch, he added, "Sorry about that."

"After all I've put you through, you've earned an indulgence or two."

"That's a fact."

Drummond pulled out the second cloth and handed it over. While Leroy inspected it with his mouth agape and his eyes narrow, Drummond brought his friend up to speed. When he finished, he walked over to the tall windows and gazed out at Winston-Salem. "I sure hope you found something useful. If we all die tonight, there won't be anybody to stop the witches from taking over."

"Hell, you think you're the only fool stupid enough to fight the unnatural forces? If we die tonight, nobody'll notice. Least of all, them witches. They been hiding from guys like you for longer than before you been waddling around in a diaper. They'll be doing it long after. Ain't no witch that wants to get burned at the stake, so they've learned to keep scarce. And trust me on this one, they ain't about to get all high and mighty just 'cause you ain't around anymore."

Drummond bit back his laughter. "Suppose I deserved that."

"Aw, don't get all down on it. None of us is important to the big picture. But we are important to lots of little pictures around. That's why we fight."

"You mean I shouldn't worry about the city — just focus on helping the Carters for tonight."

"I mean leave the big picture to the Almighty." Leroy stood and put the cloth on Drummond's desk. "Now, what you brought here is an interesting wrinkle."

Clapping his hands together in one sharp motion, Drummond spun to face Leroy. "I knew you'd figure out what the symbols mean."

"No, no. I ain't got that. Told you I probably wouldn't and I meant it. But if you'll stop letting your brain travel you all over the map and take a look at this thing, you'll see what I'm trying to show you."

Drummond crossed his arms as he leaned closer. "I'm listening."

"See how this second symbol is all burnt up? That's important. Tells me that this ain't the second but the first symbol. Tells me we're dealing with two summonings."

"We've got two Essences to deal with now?"

Leroy tapped the cloth with a boney finger. "Just the one. See, this first one worked. That's why the symbol is burnt up. It's been used. Somebody already succeeded in dealing with a summoned Essence. What's odd right here is that this person did a good job the first time around and botched the second."

Drummond crouched over his desk and scrutinized both cloths. "The burnt symbol has stronger lines. A surer hand. Something happened between the casting of the two spells. Something injured the person so they couldn't do as good a job drawing the symbols."

"I'd guess it was the offering. Whatever the caster used to appease the Essence must've been something brutal."

"Could it be part of a person? Like could you offer up blindness, maybe a bad leg, maybe a bit of insanity?"

"That's some specific supposing you're doing."

"Would that work though?"

"How should I know? I ain't ever summoned an Essence before."

"But —"

"Yeah, yeah, it probably would work. Depends on the kind of Essence you're calling out. That's probably what went wrong here. The first time worked, and if like you say, they offered their eyes and legs and such, well, that don't leave you much to offer next time around. Whatever offering was made for this other Essence didn't go so well. See what I'm saying?"

"Then that's the one that came after us last night."

"I suspect so."

"Why would she want to do it again?"

Leroy rubbed the back of his neck. "I don't understand why anybody would do it in the first place. But if you're of the mind to go down that dark road, then I guess you got mighty strong feelings about something or someone. And this business with an Essence, well, it's like making a deal with a witch."

Drummond grabbed the cloths, stuffed them in his pockets, and crossed to the coatrack.

"Where you going?" Leroy asked.

"If this is all like dealing with a witch, then it has all the trappings, too. I think I know who did this, and I've got a inkling why. But I know for sure that whoever did it, asked for something which didn't happen. They screwed up the wording and got a literal interpretation. You follow?"

"Like if you ask a witch to see that your spouse kicks the bucket and the witch casts a spell making your loved one walk around kicking buckets all day."

"Exactly. So, this person doesn't get the results —"

"And they go back to the well and try to call up another Essence."

Drummond donned his hat. "Am I right?"

"Probably."

"Then I'm off to figure out the final part of this thing. You meet us tonight at the Carter house. Address is next to the phone. Be there before the first witching hour."

Leroy perked up. "You know how to stop this?"

Pausing halfway through putting on his coat, he cocked his head toward his friend. "That was your job. What have you been researching all day?"

"What do you want from me? All my good books are back home."

Shrugging his arm through his coat sleeve, Drummond said, "You got a few more hours left. Do your best and find us a solution. I might be able to figure out the who and the why of all this, but that won't stop this Essence from shredding us up."

"If that's the case, then forget your end of it and help me here."

"Not that simple. Besides, if you fail, we'll need to find another way out of this. The answer to that will come from knowing the truth of what happened to get us all here. Understand?"

Leroy slid behind the desk and picked up a book. "You've got my best."

"I knew I could count on you."

"Just one thing."

"Name it."

"You got more whiskey?"

MARSHALL DRUMMOND HAD ENDURED many uncomfortable conversations in his life. It went with the territory of being a private detective. People hired detectives to take care of uncomfortable things, and usually, those people withheld crucial information to spare themselves extra uncomfortable questions. But Detective Cooper was not a client to Drummond. He was a loyal friend, and that made the upcoming conversation weigh hard on the shoulders.

Drummond called Cooper from a payphone several blocks away and let his friend pick the meeting location. Cooper opted for the public library. When they settled in a back corner on the main floor, Drummond set his hat on the table and glanced around to make sure they did not have any eaves-droppers.

"Of all the places to meet, you picked a library. Too much hidden in these books. Ever since I started this line of work, it seems I never get any happy news here. I can't stand libraries."

Cooper smirked. "I know."

"Oh, so this is a joke. You like making me squirm."

"I'd like you to stop complaining and tell me what the heck you found out."

From all he knew of Cooper, he decided the quick strike would be better than a slow build up. Drummond said, "You should be prepared to lose your job."

"That bad?"

"It ain't good. Chief Carter's wife has gotten herself in a real mess, and I think the Chief is a whole lot to blame for it, too."

"I don't know. The Chief is a daily pain in my ass but he's not the kind to get caught up in anything like this — like your kinds of cases."

"I'm not saying he did it. I'm saying I think he's the cause. Part of it, at least."

"And I'm telling you that you're wrong." Cooper raised his voice enough to garner a sharp look from the librarian at the desk in the middle of the room. In an over-compensating hush, he went on, "I put myself out there for you. The Chief could have taken his problem anywhere, but I'm the one who told him you were worth it."

"Don't pretend this was all for me. You did this to advance your career, and now that it's looking bleak, you want to throw the blame elsewhere."

"Hey, pal, I like you a lot. You've been a good friend, but I'm not losing my job over you."

"Doesn't matter what you want. This case is going down this particular road. You can't change it."

"Except nobody believes this stuff but you. If you start spouting off that the Chief's wife is practicing witchcraft, where do you think it'll get you?"

Trying not to yell, Drummond said, "You're the one who brought me this damn case. It's not my fault your boss is married to a —"

"Stop it," Cooper said, his face reddening as the cords on his neck popped. "I'm trying real hard to make you see that this is not the path we want to take. Do you understand what I'm saying? Taking on the Chief, in any manner, is not just a surefire way to get me thrown on my ass, but it'll end your detective agency, too. No more cases coming your way from me or any other cop. Heck, the Chief will probably revoke your license."

Drummond rested his elbows on the table and rubbed his eyes. "Look, I was on the job, too. Not as long as you, but I know how it is. Y'all want to protect each other, and you seriously want to protect the Chief." Drummond paused as a memory clicked in his head. "It's like the way the Chief would show up to all the police functions alone. Always claiming one reason or another for his wife's absence, but did you ever believe that? Of course, not. He was protecting his reputation for some reason. Maybe she had an illness or maybe she was touched in the head. Same thing here. You want to protect him, but I'm telling you — after tonight, things won't be the same. For any of us. Admit it or not, fight it or not, doesn't matter. The truth comes out tonight. You should be prepared."

The conversation continued for another fifteen minutes, but it only circled its way back again. Though Drummond could not get Cooper to cross the blue line, he did get his old friend to agree to come by the Carter home later that night — before midnight. "And come with an open mind. You may not like everything you'll hear, but I trust that you'll listen."

With that Drummond left the library. He still had the early evening before his life might be cut short, but he could not think of a thing to do. In the end, he opted to spend more money than he should and had dinner at Joey's — steak, potatoes, green beans, a little wine, quiet atmosphere. Charming place, but dining alone soured the meal a little. If this was to be his last, he wished he could have Catalina sitting opposite him, her bright smile lighting the table, her melodic voice overcoming the murmur of patrons.

Instead, he had to dine in silence. At least, that gave him time to mull over the case yet again. And usually, time spent thinking about a case's details revealed solutions he had missed earlier.

When the meal ended, however, Drummond felt no surer of his ideas than when he had started. Which left one thing to do — visit the Carter house and find out the truth. Even if it was the last truth any of them would hear.

WHEN HE TURNED DOWN CARTER'S STREET, he found two cars parked along the curb in front of the house. Good. People had already arrived.

As he strolled along the walkway, Cooper parked behind his car and hurried to catch up. They exchanged a nod but stayed silent. Ms. Daggett greeted them at the door while Catalina sat on the living room couch with her knee bouncing a strong rhythm. Leroy had also made his way there — standing by a brick fireplace and holding a glass of brandy.

Chief Carter hunched in a large reading chair, the lines of his scowl deepening as he glowered at the growing number of people invading his home. When he saw Drummond, his top lip lifted in a sneer. "I knew asking you to look into this was a mistake. Knew it from the get-go. Only reason I went along with it was for my dear Pearl."

"Now, now, Chief. Let's not start with lies." Drummond stood in the archway and waited until he had everybody's attention. It did not take long. "Tonight is about honesty. Tonight, whether you believe or not, a dangerous reality is barreling our way. If we lie to each other, if we pretend this isn't happening or that it couldn't be happening or any such nonsense, the result will not change — we all will die. And that includes Pearl Carter." Pointing to Cooper, he added, "Will you please escort her down here? She needs to be part of this."

"Hold on there," the Chief said. "You are not about to disrupt my wife's rest —"

"She'll be dead in the morning, if she doesn't come down here. And frankly, she's a major cause of all our problems, so I don't care what you want."

The Chief bit in his lip before whirling at Leroy. "And what's this colored boy doing drinking my good brandy?"

Drummond took one strong step into the room and glared at Carter. "Everybody in this room is a friend of mine. Everybody but you. If we live through tonight, you'll owe Leroy your life. I think a sip of brandy is the least you could offer. And you can cut out the racist talk. I know it's an act for you."

"You come in here and start insulting me? You're the one putting on an act. We both know you're full of beeswax. What the hell do you really want anyway?" Despite his bluster, Chief Carter sat back in his chair and pulled his arms in as if fighting off a chill.

"Just the truth. Armed with that, I think we'll find our way out of this hole."

The slow clumping of Cooper and Mrs. Carter descending the old stairs quieted the room. All eyes turned toward the entranceway. Drummond stepped aside to allow them easy access to the only empty chair — one that Chief Carter insisted nobody sit in but her. Apparently, they had assigned seats in this house.

Mrs. Carter moved with her hands held out front and her ears guiding her way. Gone was the violent creature that had attacked Drummond. He saw only a woman stricken and sad.

"I hear a lot of people," she said as Cooper helped her to the seat. "Are we having a party?"

"Be quiet, Pearl," the Chief said. "This ain't no party. If anything, it's going to be a kangaroo court."

Drummond checked his watch — 11:42 pm. Cutting it close, if the Essence decided to be punctual. Once again, all the attention focused on Drummond, and he tried not to show his discomfort. Laying out a case in front of one or two people never bothered him. But an entire roomful — might as well stand before a pack of hyenas while wearing a suit made of raw meat.

Catalina pushed off the couch and approached him. "Come on, now. These people won't stay calm all night long."

Her words did not matter as much as her presence. She eased to his side. Tipping back his hat, he took one last survey of the room, particularly focusing on Ms. Daggett.

She had sat on the opposite end of the couch from Catalina and had not moved much since Drummond's arrival. He watched her narrowing eyes and her tightly held mouth.

Drummond cleared his throat. The time had come to set it all straight. "To avoid all the denials and protests, allow me a few minutes to explain how we all ended up here. The first thing you all must understand is that Chief Carter loves his wife."

"Of course, I do. What kind of idiot way to start this is that?" the Chief said but remained in his chair.

"Not all marriages have love. I want to assure everyone that yours does."

"If you're going to spend this whole night assuring everyone here of the obvious —"

Mrs. Carter sat erect. "Please, Ronald, hasn't this whole thing gone far enough? Just sit and be quiet. If he can help us, then we should listen."

"Thank you," Drummond said. "And I'm sorry to have to say this part, but while Chief Carter loves his wife, he is no longer *in love* with her. He is a loyal man — keeps Pearl's photo on his desk, makes sure to be home at a respectable hour every night, and never behaves in a manner that would cast shadows on their name. But the two rarely did anything together. Detective Cooper reminded me that the Chief went to all the police functions alone, always finding excuses for the absence of his wife."

Standing behind the couch, Cooper shifted from one leg to the other. "I never said anything about that. You blurted it out, that's all."

"True, but our conversation helped me to remember it. And that doesn't change the fact that until the other day, Pearl Carter was in excellent health. It was only after this business with the Essence that she was blinded and taken ill. Only then did the Chief pad her room and lock her away. So, before that, they had simply grown apart. He cares greatly for Pearl — they've lived an entire life together — but she no longer holds his heart. That honor belongs to another woman, and that fact is the root of all our troubles."

Drummond turned toward Ms. Daggett. "He fell in love with you." Before the gasp in the room could expand into a commotion, he raised his voice, "What's more, you fell in love with him. Now, in any other case, a man falling in love with his maid would be scandalous but otherwise, not particularly interesting beyond a few days gossip. But in this situation, we're dealing with the Chief of the Winston-Salem Police Department and a black woman."

Chief Carter wriggled to a new position in his chair. Whether from his experience as a detective or his stubborn refusal to yield an inch, he stayed quiet. He would let Drummond speak, and then Drummond expected a long-winded rebuttal. But if he did his job right, Drummond thought there would be nothing left for the Chief to say.

"When Mrs. Carter learned of the affair," Drummond said, "it hurt her far more than she realized. Because here's the part that the Chief did not understand — not at first. Pearl loves him. She never stopped. She woke every day in hopes that she could lure him back. The fact that he no longer felt the same passions for her did not dissuade her. She would take whatever scraps she could get.

"But then Ms. Daggett stole his heart. Forgive me here, Mrs. Carter, but I can't say with certainty if you hated Ms. Daggett because she was nothing more than a maid or because she was black, but you did hate her."

Mrs. Carter lifted her chin. "I still do. As for the reasons — I only need the one. She took Ronald away from me."

"I understand that, but the kind of hatred you have goes deeper. This is hatred that led to not only vengeance but to you playing with dangerous magic. I suppose it doesn't matter. Either you're a snob, a racist, or the most jealous woman I've ever come across. Perhaps you're all three."

Ms. Daggett's concerned brow wrinkled her entire face. "She's the one who cast the spell? Who put that grisly thing in my room?"

"Yes and no. There have been two spells cast, but she only did the first one." Drummond placed the burnt cloth on the coffee table. "This one here. And it worked. She called an Essence to this home, and in exchange for its help, she sacrificed her eyesight and her leg. But it didn't go as she planned. You wanted Ms. Daggett dead. What did you say that backfired on you?"

With a hawkish chuckle, Mrs. Carter said, "You don't have it quite right. I only sacrificed my leg to the Essence. Then I told it that I didn't want to ever see Ms. Daggett again." Her chuckle grew into a sickening laugh. "That's why I'm blind. That's why I didn't do another spell. Even if I were stupid enough to attempt it, I can't see anymore."

Drummond took a moment to explain the idea of the Essence so that they all had the same understanding. Then he placed the second cloth on the table. "This is the spell we're still dealing with now. I believe Mrs. Carter when she says she would not cast the spell again. In fact, it's quite clear that's true — a brief look at the two symbols shows a distinctly different hand involved. Both are careful and precise, but Mrs. Carter's has the strong lines of a determined, angry disposition. The second symbol is less sure of itself, less able to believe what he knows is happening, less able to accept that magic is real."

With his face buried against his fist, the Chief said, "More ridiculousness. It's obvious you think I'm behind this, but I wasn't —"

"Yes, I know. You have an alibi. You were at the Colonial watching a movie. But you told me that you were there with Pearl. Of course, that's not true. Why would you take a blind woman to a movie? Also, the Colonial is known for showing lesser-quality films. Not the kind of thing you'd want your wife to go see, if she could. But you were definitely there. The Chief of Police knows how to establish an alibi."

"This is hogwash. Why would I ever bother hiring you, if I'm behind this?"

"Because of what happened next. You cast the spell, but you didn't expect any of it to be real. You still don't believe in any of this. So, when you came home and found Ms. Daggett petrified by the discovery of that bizarre horror in her room, you became frightened. You figured somebody was trying to scare the Chief of Police, and you brought me in on it to kill two birds with one stone. You hoped I'd discreetly take care of the matter for you, but if I failed, you'd be able to hang me out, ruin my career, and never have to deal with me again."

The Chief lifted his cheek from resting on his fist. "All I've done was prove that magic is a load of bunk. Pearl did not go blind from magic. She had a stroke. I did that second spell to show her that it's all in her head. I found the instructions she had gotten hold of — and Pearl, dear, I don't ever want to know how you found that — and I followed what it said. Even left five dollars next to the blue cloth. I figured that was more than enough to satisfy an imaginary spirit."

"You did what?" Ms. Daggett said, her hand flattening on her chest.

"I'm sorry, my sweet angel. I didn't want to scare you so bad, but I had to prove that I was right. And see, no magical being visited me at all. Never even got to make some kind of wish."

Before Ms. Daggett could say more, Drummond pushed on. "The problem is that the Essence did come that night. It rejected your offering and left that monstrosity as a sign of its displeasure. Of course, Ms. Daggett also covered for you. She lied about the timeline but it was too late. I already knew she loved you. She called you Ron."

To the Chief, she said, "I'm sorry."

"It's not your fault," the Chief said.

Before he could blubber on, Drummond interrupted, "The next night, I had the cloth, the calling card, and so, the Essence came after me when I was at Leroy's home. We didn't have an offering because we didn't know what was going on. According to Leroy, it'll come one more time — tonight. If we don't satisfy the creature, then it'll kill us all. But while I spent my time figuring out that you all were caught up together in this business, Leroy and Catalina have been researching how to stop it. Leroy, the floor is yours."

The poor man nearly spilled his drink. "Er, well, I'm not much a speaker. And, well, to be honest here, I ain't got anything to say."

Chief Carter jutted his chin at Leroy. "You mean to tell me that you've been standing there, drinking my brandy, and all this time you ain't got an answer for us?"

"Oh, I got an answer, but y'all ain't gonna like it." Leroy set his glass on the fireplace mantel. "Fact is, there's only one way this ends without us dying, and that's to give the Essence an offering it likes."

"You're kidding me. All this talk and in the end, nobody has an answer but give the criminals what they want."

"What criminals?" Catalina said. "You? Your wife? You two are the only ones who misused magic. The rest of us are innocent victims in all of this."

Smacking his fist on the arm of his chair, the Chief's face reddened. "There is no such thing as magic! But somebody is trying to shake us down and that's who we should be going after."

Drummond pursed his lips. "Sorry to say it, Chief, but I thought this might be the way things would work out. See, Leroy is among the best when it comes to understanding the world of the unnatural. The longer he took to find out information on this spell, the worse I felt were your chances."

"*My* chances?" the Chief said. "I thought we were all in this, all our lives on the line. See that? The closer we get to the final hit in all of this, the more his story of magic Essences falls apart."

Mrs. Carter clicked her tongue three times as she shook her head.

"You'll have to forgive my Ronald. He can be thick sometimes. He's a brilliant cop, but not so smart when it comes to love."

Ms. Daggett suppressed a chuckle. "I can certainly agree with that."

Unsure of which woman to reach for, the Chief locked his hands under his legs. Staring at the space between the women, he said, "What is it I'm being thick about?"

With the patience of a schoolteacher, Mrs. Carter said, "When you call upon an Essence, you have to make the offering worthy of what you intend to ask the Essence to do. You want it to help in a minor matter, then you don't have to offer much up."

"That's where you screwed up," Ms. Daggett said. "You offered five dollars, but it wasn't enough."

The Chief said, "How much money does —"

"It doesn't want money." Mrs. Carter spat out the words. "When I wanted to be rid of your mistress, I sacrificed my legs. I offered my ability to walk so that she might walk out of my life."

Drummond said, "It hasn't let you go, either. When I saw you, it attacked me through you."

The Chief barked, "I told you to stay away from —"

Pushing to the edge of the couch, Ms. Daggett twisted her gloves. "Ron? What did you ask the Essence for?"

"Huh?" Sweat beaded along the Chief's forehead. In a quieter voice, he said, "This … this isn't real. It's all nonsense."

A loud click preceded the lights going out. Drummond checked his watch — midnight. Detective Cooper's hand dropped to his service revolver while Leroy's attention darted to the windowsills. Ms. Daggett's focus remained on Chief Carter while Catalina nudged closer to Drummond.

A large bang reverberated through the house as if a boulder had crashed upon it. The walls shivered and the wood creaked.

Leroy snapped his fingers at the Chief. "Hey, Mr. Chief of Police, pay attention. We need to salt the windows. You got any?"

"Salt? What good —"

Cooper whipped around the couch. "I know where it is. I spent two winters shoveling the driveway. There's salt by the side door. Come on."

Drummond locked his focus on the Chief. "The Essence is coming. You can argue all you want, but it is a force of Nature. And like all natural forces, pretending they don't exist won't help you. Go ahead and deny gravity all you want. You're still going to plummet to your death if you walk out of a five-story window."

"This doesn't make sense," the Chief said, clutching his head between his hands.

"Sure, it does. And I'd wager you understood it completely all along. The problem you have is that you're not willing to admit what you want the Essence for. Yet another reason you hired me — so you could tell your wife and your girlfriend that you had tried everything. But you've been hoping all along that either I would get myself in such big trouble that you could dismiss me as a crackpot loon or that I would defeat whatever evil I found. Either way, it would all end up well for you."

Cooper and Leroy returned with two large bags of salt. They got to work on the windows and doors while the Chief's astonishment kept him from talking more. Ms. Daggett gathered a handful of candles from the drawer of a side table and distributed them around the room. The flickering flames provided light but created eerie shadows that Drummond could have done without. Taking advantage of the momentary respite, he turned to Catalina.

"Did you bring the jewelry?"

"Of course," she said, pulling out a necklace with a half-moon plate of silver and two small emeralds. "Is this good?"

"Perfect." He handed the necklace to Ms. Daggett. "Please, take this to your room and set it on that rejection from the Essence."

Her eyes rested on the necklace, then lifted to meet Drummond — her fear taking control of her cheeks and brow. "You want me to look at that horrid thing again?"

"That depends — do you feel like living through the next hour?"

As Ms. Daggett rushed down the hall, Chief Carter found his voice again. "That's enough. You've gotten everybody here spooked and you're making no sense at all."

Mrs. Carter slapped her hand at him but missed. "Honestly, Ronald, you are being more pig-headed than usual. The truth has been spoken. We all heard it. No amount of denial is going to free you from that."

Before he could respond, a loud thud cracked around the house. Catalina stepped closer to Drummond, her hand clenching his arm. The Chief yipped while the others let out grunts of surprise.

"We don't have long." Drummond strode across the room until he towered over the Chief. "This is your doing, and much as I hate the fact, it also means whether we live or die is up to you. There's no stopping what you started. Understand?"

With panic seeping through his throat, the Chief said, "I don't understand any of this."

His wife reached farther and made contact with his side. Pinching him sharply, she said, "He means that because you cast the spell, you are the one who has to make the offering. You've failed twice. Don't screw this up."

Ms. Daggett returned in time to catch these final words. She pointed to the window and screamed. "Something's out there."

Drummond said, "Make it good, Chief. Otherwise, we all die. Including the one you love."

"The one I love?"

Grabbing the Chief by the shirt, Drummond lifted him to his feet. "You thought you could cast a spell and wish away one of these women, didn't you? Your wife gets it. And so does your mistress."

Another thud — this time the front door rattled but held.

Mrs. Carter leaned forward, her milky eyes sparkling in the candlelight. "There are only three of us in this, Ronald — you, me, and your lady. You saw what I had to give up. And if you do nothing, she'll die right in front of you. So, it's your turn. But if you summoned the Essence the way I think you did, with what I think was on your mind, then you're asking a lot from it."

Drummond nodded. "That's why it turned down your offering. You've got to make it bigger — more meaningful."

"But what?" the Chief said, the desperation in his voice oozing like an open wound. "Does an Essence want my job? That's the biggest thing I've got."

"You've got me," Mrs. Carter said, her head drooping.

Ms. Daggett stepped forward, her lip quivering. "And me."

The Chief stared at both women before pulling free of Drummond's grip. He straightened his tie and fixed his shirt.

Mrs. Carter slapped her knee. "I knew it. I can hear your stubborn breathing. You thought you could have us both, didn't you? That's what you're askin' for, isn't it?"

"Pearl, I love you. I truly do. But you're not a warm woman anymore. And I'm a man with a pulse, with needs."

"Your needs are going to kill us all."

"That's not what I wanted and you know it. I just thought —"

"You just thought that frail, little Pearl screwed up the spell but you're smarter. You're a big man. You'll do a better job at it."

The Chief's mournful face turned toward Ms. Daggett. "She's wrong. If I have to choose between the two of you, then I choose you. I don't care about the consequences. We'll leave the South. We'll find a town that accepts a mixed couple."

Leroy paused his covering the front door ledge with salt. "Good luck with that. The Northern states hate black folk all the same. They just hide it better."

The Chief took Ms. Daggett's hands. "Please. I love you, Bernice. I've loved you since the moment you walked into this house. I choose you."

She pulled her hands back. "You understand what you're saying? Not about us, but what choosing me means."

Drummond said, "She's trying to tell you that choosing either woman means the other becomes the offering. At least, that's what we all think the Essence is going to want."

Leroy said, "No doubts on this side of the farm. If you ask me —"

The front door blew off its hinges and clobbered Leroy to the floor. A gust of wind followed. Drummond rushed to his friend's side. As he cleared wooden shards off, Leroy's alcohol-soaked breath greeted him. "What in blazes? How'd I end up on the ground?"

"You're okay. But the Essence is here."

"I wouldn't say any of us is okay, then."

With Drummond's aid, Leroy managed back to his feet. Once he appeared stable enough to stand on his own, Drummond stepped towards the living room. He never got further. An unseen hand dug under his ribs and hoisted him into the ceiling — hard enough to crack the plaster. As his groan widened into a full-throated yell, the hand let him drop to the floor. Then it was Leroy's turn to aid Drummond back to his feet.

Doubled over and catching his wind, Drummond expected terrified screams and wailing cries of pain. Instead, he heard nothing but frightened held breaths. Lifting his head, he gazed into the living room. To his surprise, Catalina had brought everyone together near Mrs. Carter's chair. Following her stern finger, Cooper had formed a rough circle of salt around them all.

All except Chief Carter. He stood in the middle of the living room. Floating before him with its shredded gown and out-of-focus face, the Essence waited.

That didn't seem fair to Drummond. When this thing came into Leroy's shack in the woods, it attacked them with vicious abandon. When it entered this house, it did the same. Why should the Chief get off so easy?

But it wasn't easy. Drummond had known this outcome to be the most likely, and that was not an easy outcome at all. The Chief glanced over at the salt circle. Ms. Daggett stood at Mrs. Carter's side. They held hands as they stared at the Essence. Drummond had a strong feeling that Mrs. Carter's blindness had been granted a temporary suspension — at least, enough that she could see the Essence.

Leroy spread salt in a circle around him and Drummond. That didn't matter, though. Drummond figured either the Chief made his offer or no amount of salt would save any of them. The Essence would stick around until they starved to death or left the circle in a fit of madness. No — it all rested on the Chief.

Drummond saw the answer in the Chief's final grim grin. He wanted to feel relief, but a swift jolt of cold horror flooded his system. This would not be pleasant to watch. This would haunt them all for years to come.

When the Chief's gaze returned to the Essence, his grin dropped. Tears dribbled down his cheeks. Whispering, he said, "I-I'm so sorry, my loves. I hope someday you'll understand."

He nodded to the Essence, and it placed a ghostly strip of its flesh around his throat.

"No!" Ms. Daggett said. She tried to bolt free but Cooper held her back. She cried out, reaching her heart forward but unable to break loose.

"You can't break the circle or we all die," Cooper said.

The Essence raised the Chief into the air. His legs kicked out as his hands involuntarily reached up in a useless attempt to find air.

Mrs. Carter stood. "Ronald, don't do this. We'll find another way."

Catalina took charge of keeping Mrs. Carter in her seat. "It's too late. There is no other way."

As the Essence continued to choke the Chief, Drummond watched with a heavy heart. He had hoped there would have been a better solution. He had hoped Leroy would have found an answer, or Catalina's grandmother would have offered up a little-known counter-spell, or even the Chief might have admitted the truth right away and got everybody working the problem.

But as the Chief's body went limp, Drummond saw how there had never been another way. The Chief could never admit he had cheated on his wife — a betrayal of her trust. And he could never admit that he would not leave his wife for Ms. Daggett — a betrayal of his word to her.

There was no other option. The Chief had only one thing to offer the Essence — himself. His last act of loyalty to the women he loved. An act that he refused to betray.

* * * *

Two days later, Drummond met Catalina as her shift at Raymond's Diner ended. Following her directions, he drove them to the Mexican side of town on the eastern edge of the city. Neither one said much on the drive — he still felt raw from recent events and imagined she did, too. With any luck, they would be able to fix that shortly.

"Over there," she said, pointing to a wide swath of cleared land where starter homes were going up.

He parked the car. From his pocket, he pulled out an envelope, and from the envelope, he pulled out the necklace Catalina had provided at the Carter house. "You sure about this? The man died for this. That's a big price to pay. I imagine anything you wish for would be granted."

She refused to look at the necklace. "It's not mine to wish on. Mrs. Carter or Ms. Daggett have a real claim to using that thing, but neither of them wanted it. Why should I?"

"I don't know. I hate to see it wasted."

Catalina placed her coat down, covering the necklace, and leaned closer to Drummond. "Those two women only have each other now. When we left that night, I heard Ms. Daggett promising Mrs. Carter that she'd stick around and take care of her. Your detective friend, Cooper, will get to keep his job, right? Without Chief Carter, there's nobody to fire him. Leroy's back in his home, probably drinking and reading to his heart's content. See? Everybody ended up in a good place."

"Except the Chief."

"I'm not so sure. I think he was in a lot of pain over the trouble he caused. I'm not saying he wanted to die, but I get the sense that he did not mind dying for the sake of a glorious gesture to his beloveds."

Drummond glanced out at the construction site. "Doll, that's why you should use this necklace. You didn't get anything out of a night that could have killed you and probably shaved a few years off a good life."

"Stop it," she said with a grin. "I don't want it, and I won't wish upon it for the same reason you won't either."

"Oh? What's that?"

"We both know too well that messing with magic is always a bad idea."

He put the necklace back in his pocket. Smart gal. "You really think it's best out there?"

"My friend, Fernando, works that site. He said their pouring concrete on the back four houses today. You slip that necklace into the concrete, and nobody will ever have to worry about it again."

Drummond exited the car. As he walked around the side, he admitted she was right. Neither of them would dare play games with the power of that necklace, and they couldn't let anybody else use it, either. He had considered having Leroy research a method of destroying the thing, but that would take too long, offer too much temptation. Best to be rid of it right away.

As he crossed the street, Catalina rolled down her window. "One more thing."

He trudged back and leaned over the door. "What is it?"

"You're a fool if you think I didn't get something out of this already."

Drummond tried to keep his chest from puffing up. "Oh? What might that be?"

She glanced up and down the street before pulling his head in. She kissed him. For a long time.

CASE 07

BONES IN THE WOODS

OVER THE HANDFUL OF YEARS that Marshall Drummond had been a private investigator of the strange and unusual, he had come to one solid conclusion — it always traced back to a witch. No matter what the *it* referred to, if the case involved the supernatural or the paranormal, it always traced back to a witch. It simply had to. Because for the most part, witches played the role of the conduit between every day human beings and the other worlds out there. So when Leroy Parker called saying that he had found a body with strange and unusual properties, Drummond suspected he would end up dealing with a witch.

He was wrong.

Rain had fallen for the last seven days and North Carolina had become one enormous mud pit. Drummond worried his old Model A might not be up to the challenge, but Leroy would never have called unless the problem required Drummond's unique skills. By the time he had traveled out of Winston-Salem and into the Mocksville area, by the time the trees had grown thick and the winds had picked up, Drummond considered going back to his downtown office, calling Leroy, and telling his friend to wait until tomorrow. But he did not stop driving. He did not turn around. How could he? When dealing with witchcraft, he had learned not to second-guess his instincts. Besides, if he waited until tomorrow and Leroy ended up dead, Drummond would blame himself for the remainder of his life.

He came to a stop alongside the road. His car coughed and wheezed as he idled. Normally, he would take the dirt path that wound through the woods all the way back to Leroy's remote shack, but wagon wheels would have had an easier time dealing with the mud than the Model A.

No way around it — the car had to stay. After shutting off the engine, Drummond reached into his coat pocket and pulled out a flask of whiskey. If not for the heavy rain and thick clouds, a full moon would have shown that night. Stepping out of the car, Drummond scrunched his head down as he put up the lapels of his long coat. He nudged his Fedora tighter on his head and trekked into the woods.

The cold rain pelted his face, and the whiskey did not warm his belly up enough. As he trudged through the mud path, he wondered why he continued to put up with this. Back when he was a beat cop, he had the police force on his side. A thankful citizen or acknowledgement from

Chief Carter could make his day. Even had his picture in the Winston-Salem Journal once — standing between his fellow cops as they arrested a thief who had been troubling the same several downtown blocks.

But after seeing a ghost, after learning that magic was real, Drummond could not turn back to that life. He resigned from the force, hung out a shingle, and got to work protecting North Carolina from witches and ghosts.

The only problems — getting paid and getting recognition.

He did not need to make a lot of money nor did he need constant pats on the back. But more often than not he wondered why he put up with it all. Especially when he found himself trudging through the cold rain to risk his life when he would rather be back at his office in the arms of Catalina.

They had been seeing each other for only a few months, and getting time together had proven difficult. She had two young sons and an *abuela* that would never look approvingly on her dating a *gringo*. On his side, he had all of North Carolina society saying it was wrong to have relations between races.

But to Marshall Drummond, the whole thing was a crock. He had fallen for this beautiful, Mexican woman and saw no reason to deny himself his emotions. The fact that she reciprocated brightened every moment. Still, they understood the world they lived in. The 1930s continued to bring marvel upon marvel of technological changes, but many people's minds had remained in the past.

They knew not to hold hands in public. They knew not to go to her family's apartment. They knew to keep their growing connection a secret. In fact, they pretty much stole their time together by finding moments of pleasure in the one safe place they had — Drummond's office.

But all of Drummond's fretting disappeared as he came upon Leroy's home. The small, dilapidated shack contained one room that met all of the grouchy man's needs. A wide awning stretched out, and oil lamps hung on the inside corners. Leroy stood in the doorway waiting.

Drummond waved as he stepped under the awning. It felt good not to be spit in the face by the constant drenching of the clouds.

"Thanks for coming," Leroy said.

Leroy Parker — an old black man, a cranky sort, and one of the smartest men Drummond had ever met. The man devoured knowledge as if it alone could sustain his life. After a short run-in with a witch several years back, he became enamored with witchcraft, witch lore, and everything else in the paranormal world.

Shaking off his hat, Drummond said, "I didn't think I'd be seeing you for a long time. It's only been a few months since my last case. I figured that experience would've been enough to keep your head stuck in books for a few years."

"I ain't happy about it, neither. You'll understand when you see what I got inside. Come on."

Drummond entered the home to find it had not changed at all since his last visit. The same narrow bookshelves, the same stone fireplace, the same hazardous oil lamps, the same plain worktable. The only difference — the table had been moved to the center of the room, and upon it, Leroy had laid out the bones of a human being. They were bleach-white without a single bit of grit, gristle, or even skin attached. They looked more like the kind of bones used in a medical school for instruction than a body Leroy had turned up in the woods.

Drummond jutted his chin toward the table. "Is this what's so odd? A bunch of very clean bones?"

"Do I look like a dang fool? You really think I'd haul your sorry rear all the way out here just for that?" Leroy wiped the rain drops off his thick glasses before setting them back on his nose. "Normally, I take a walk every day. But with this rain for the last week, I've barely gotten out of the house. So this morning, I decided I'm going on a walk no matter how wet I get. I was out probably about an hour when I saw one of the ribs on the sorry fella poking out of the ground. Looked like he was given a shallow grave, and all the rain turned our wonderful Carolina clay into soup — made it easy to spot the bones."

"And you dug this guy out and hauled him all the way here?"

"Well, I wasn't going to leave him there. A dead body would either attract scavengers or somebody else was going to find it and the next thing I know I got the police knockin' on my door. I don't live all the way out here in the woods because I like having visitors, you know."

"I only meant that you aren't a young man anymore."

"I'm strong enough and don't you forget it. Also, I hiked all the way back to my house, got the wheelbarrow, came all the way back out to the body, and dug it up and hauled it that way. I ain't an idiot."

Stepping closer, Drummond looked over the bones. "I certainly see one odd thing — the skeleton's practically complete."

Leaning in from the other side of the table, Leroy said, "Fact is, the rest of the bones are probably out there and I missed them in all that mud."

Drummond did not know a lot about interpreting a victim's appearance just from the bones, but he had seen enough to know these bones belonged either to a man or a very large woman. The rib cage was spread wide which led him to think that perhaps this man had quite a few pounds on him. He wasn't sure if bones actually worked that way, but that's how he pictured it. Looking at the ribs, Drummond spotted another oddity.

"This mark on the sternum — is that why you called me?"

Leroy inched away from the table, his chin quivering. "That be it, right there."

For such a small mark, it had an impressive amount of detail. At first glance, Drummond saw a simple triangle. But the closer he put his face toward the bone, the more unraveled before him — thorny vines snaked around the edges of the triangle, a circle within the shape, and inside the circle, a carefully carved number three.

"What's the number mean?" Drummond asked.

"I was kind of hoping you'd tell me."

Gesturing to all the books on the shelves, Drummond said, "You're the one who does all the research. How should I know?"

"I done some looking and ain't found nothing. But I haven't had time to dig into the really deep stuff."

"Then why'd you call me out here in the rain? You need somebody to hold your hand because you're scared of a skeleton?"

Leroy puffed his chest. "I ain't scared. And I didn't call you out here to hold my hand, neither. I wanted you to see this so you knew what we're dealing with before I show you the last thing."

"There's more?"

Leroy paused before going to a bag in the corner. "There's always more."

Drummond turned back to the skeleton. He noticed a smell like the embers of a campfire. Reaching over, he rested his index finger on the sternum just above the carved symbol. Warmth. He could feel slight heat radiating off the bones. Perhaps Leroy had the right idea — Drummond stepped back from the table.

"The bones," Leroy said as he walked over to Drummond. "When I came across them, they wasn't just loose in the open. What I mean is they were clothed. The pants and shirt was torn up and covered in mud, but I did find a wallet."

Leroy tossed over a brown billfold. Catching it with one hand, Drummond flipped it open. A couple dollars in cash, a small photo of a young woman, and a detective's badge. Drummond dug deeper into the wallet and found an ID card — Derek Richmond.

"According to this, Derek was born sixty-seven years ago. That means his badge is retired." Drummond closed the wallet and tapped it against his chin. "Detective Derek Richmond — doesn't sound familiar, but when I was on the force I didn't hang around with the detectives much. Not at all, really."

"It's a place to start, though. Right?"

Drummond nodded. "You keep searching in these books and find out what you can about that symbol. I'll go find out who Derek was and why he's buried out here in such an unusual way." Drummond turned to the door, hesitated, and looked back. "You might want to cover those bones with a tarp or something. I don't like the way they felt."

"Me, neither."

BY THE TIME DRUMMOND trudged through the rain and mud back to his car, got the old Ford rumbling down the road, and saw Winston-Salem in the distance, midnight had come and gone. He would have to wait until morning to pursue his investigation on Derek Richmond. But he still had one investigative option available, and since it also involved a beautiful woman in his life, he had no qualms about staying up a few hours later.

Catalina often worked the graveyard shift at Raymond's Diner. It afforded her the luxury of seeing her children in the morning before they went off to school and spending time with them in the evening before they went to bed. Normally, she slept in the afternoons, but since hooking up with Drummond, much of that time got filled, too. He had no idea when she actually slept.

When he entered the diner, he could feel his world brighten. She walked over to his table with a secret smile on her lips and poured a cup of coffee. He wanted to reach over for her hand. He wanted to stand and slip his arms around her waist. He wanted to kiss her. Instead, he merely thanked her for the coffee.

"You got good timing," she said. "We just finished a midnight rush."

Drummond gazed over the diner. Three people remained at three different tables. Several spots on the counter still had dirty plates.

"If it's a bad time, I can go."

"Don't you dare. Seeing you is the best part of the night."

He grinned as he smoothed back his wet hair. Part of him pushed the idea that he should sit back, enjoy his coffee, and bask in this woman's presence. But the rest of him knew it could not be that easy.

"Leroy brought a new case."

With a quick check that her customers did not need her, Catalina settled in the chair opposite him. "Is this going to be like the last one?"

Good question. The last time — the only time Catalina had experienced one of Drummond's cases — they all came close to dying. "I hope not. I'm not sure how this is going to turn out. It might be something minor — an old cop messing with magic he didn't understand. But there's this symbol."

Catalina's eyebrows lifted. "Oh, a symbol. That's how the last one started."

Sipping his coffee, Drummond tried not to show his thoughts — because she was right. A symbol had started the last case, and that bothered him. He had come to the diner with the intention of asking Catalina to take the symbol to her *abuela.* The old woman believed in a lot of superstitions, but she also had a good grasp on the real magic in the world. She might know something about the symbol and the number three.

But he did not want to use Catalina or her *abuela* that way. Not only because doing so threatened to bring the dangers of the paranormal world into their lives — more than already had happened — but also because he did not want this to become a habit. Catalina had enough problems on her plate. No reason to make her life more complicated by adding witch symbols to the mix. Heck, his romantic involvement was complication enough.

Setting his coffee down, he waved off the case like an annoying fly. "It won't be like last time. Just another case, that's all."

Catalina sighed, making a hissing sound through her teeth. "Don't start lying. I can always tell. And there is no *just another case, that's all* with you. Never will be. Not with your kinds of cases."

"Well, that's certainly true." Hoping to catch her with a charming grin, he said, "Are you coming by later?"

"I've seen you every afternoon this week. I need to be at home, too."

Despite her serious tone, her lustful gaze spoke otherwise. One of the men in the back rose from his chair and approached the cash register. With a playful pout, she got up and headed back to work. Before she left, she managed to pat Drummond on the shoulder. Just a quick tap but enough to send his heart racing.

Probably a good thing that she get some rest and give him a little space for a day. He had a case to follow, and he did not want her anywhere near the witches and other horrors that he faced. He did not doubt her ability to handle it — simply, he wanted to preserve a little bubble of happiness, untouched by the real world. For as long as possible.

DRUMMOND WAITED UNTIL NINE in the morning to start making calls. Partly, he wanted to be respectful of anybody he might disturb. Partly, he needed to sleep in before facing this case.

The phone directory listed four Derek Richmonds or D Richmond. Drummond hit bingo on number two — Detective Derek Richmond's wife answered the phone. He asked if it would be okay to visit and inquire about a matter concerning her husband. Mrs. Richmond acted hesitant, even suspicious, but she did agree. That told Drummond a lot. Whether her cautious approach came out of fear that he was a kidnapper calling with a ransom demand or that she had done away with her husband and worried Drummond might be on to her — that remained to be seen.

Before heading out, he pulled down his copy of *Moby Dick* and opened the false book. From the cut out pages, he took his whiskey flask. He poured a finger into a shot glass, sat behind his desk, and kicked his feet up. As the alcohol slid down his throat to warm his belly, he wondered if he had a way out of this case. After all, he wasn't being paid. But no. Those thoughts were lack of sleep talking — plus a little bit of magic fatigue. Just once it'd be nice to have a simple case. A straight-forward theft. Heck, even a complicated murder would be nice.

Donning his Fedora and coat, Drummond made his way down the wood stairs to the first floor. Stepping out onto the street, he took a moment to appreciate the lack of rain. Still overcast, but no rain. At least, not yet. The sidewalks, the cars, the pavement, the YMCA on the opposite side — all of it had begun to dry out. It gave the world a sense of rebirth. Enough that Drummond chanced a smile.

But then he heard his name called. He turned around and saw Detective Cooper approaching. They had been beat cops together and Cooper continued to use Drummond's services whenever he came across *the oddity* cases.

"I got too much to do already," Drummond said. "Can't take on another case."

Cooper pointed down the street at Drummond's Model A. He walked right by Drummond and headed for the car. Drummond had seen plenty of odd behavior from Cooper over the years, but he never saw the man's face as pale with concern as he did at that moment.

When he got into the car, he turned to Cooper. "Should I drive us somewhere?"

"We can talk right here." Cooper glanced out every window before continuing. "The second this case started I knew your name would be coming up."

"What did I do now?"

"I got a call from Cindy Richmond."

"That can't be good."

"Do you have any clue what's been going on since Chief Carter's death?"

A few months ago, Chief Carter enlisted Drummond's help in a brutal case that ended up taking the man's life. Drummond looked closer at Cooper and he understood. "New chief not to your liking?"

"Chief Murdoch has been playing the bad cop role since he got to the desk."

"That's why we're talking in my car. You don't want to be seen with me."

"Can you blame me? You think I'll still have a job if it gets out that I'm involved with the kinds of cases you make a living off of? It's bad enough you're in my file as my former partner."

"Gee, I'll be sure to shed a tear. You want to tell me why the police are concerned that I'm trying to talk to Mrs. Richmond?"

Cooper scowled. "You know exactly why. Derek Richmond's been missing for a few days now. His wife is all worried. I've been assigned the case, and I told her to contact me if anybody called asking about him. When she told me that you called, I knew we were sunk." He shifted in an attempt to appear less threatened, but Drummond knew the man too well. "The fact that you're poking around tells me things are going to take an ugly turn. So, help yourself out and tell me what went on."

"I'm not sure yet. Honest. But I can say this much — the chances are real slim that Derek Richmond is alive."

"You have a body?"

"Just bones. And if they are actually Derek Richmond, then he was messing around with bad magic."

"Is there such a thing as good magic?" Cooper picked at his fingernails as he thought.

Drummond understood the dilemma — this new chief, Chief

Murdoch, would want the discovery of remains to be reported, but if Cooper did that, he would also have to report the stranger aspects of the case. After all that had happened with Chief Carter, Cooper's career teetered on the edge of collapse. Getting involved in a Drummond case would toss him over the edge.

"As far as I'm concerned," Drummond said, "we never had this conversation. I never saw you. Never told you about any bones, never heard about any case."

"I appreciate the gesture, but I can't forget we had this talk. However, I'm willing to buy you time. If you want to meet with Richmond's wife, don't do it at her house. Don't do it over the phone. Nowhere that I'm going to see it, hear it, or know it, because then I'll have to report it. If you can keep things quiet, then I'll delay as long as I can. But eventually, I'll have to know about those bones."

"I'll keep everything quiet, and I'll bring the bones straight to you the moment I can guarantee the case belongs to you and not me. If it's my case, I'll either bring those bones to you or make sure nobody ever finds them. Deal?"

Cooper swallowed hard before lighting up a cigarette. With his head surrounded by nicotine clouds, he nodded. "One more thing — and this is probably important. Your last case we worked on together, the one that killed Chief Carter, remember how it started?"

"You recommended me to Carter because of the problems with his wife."

"Before that. Before Chief ever came to me, he had one of his retired buddies look into the case. He was trying to keep everything quiet and away from police eyes."

Drummond leaned his head back. "I take it that retired cop was none other than Detective Richmond."

"None other. That man helped Chief Carter and ended up dead, involved in something that's one of your cases. This whole thing is pile of —"

"Don't worry. I'll handle this."

After Cooper left, Drummond sat in the car for several minutes without moving. Even if he could manage to get Detective Cooper to call Mrs. Richmond and vouch for him, he doubted the woman would provide anything useful. She had as much to lose, if not more, as Detective Cooper. If Drummond sullied her husband's name, if the police got a black eye over a case like this, all the support Mrs. Richmond received from the department would evaporate. Some of that came in the form of friends. Some of that came in the form of a pension. And if Richmond's death was not equated to such an unsavory situation, she had the support of death benefits coming her way, too.

Nobody deserved to lose everything because of a spouse's mistake. Which meant he had to find another way to investigate Derek Richmond without involving the wife. Unfortunately, the solution that Drummond could see involved another spouse who would not want to speak with him.

"Guess it's going to be one of those days," he muttered as he started up the car and headed off toward the ritzy side of town.

WALKING UP TO THE FRONT DOOR of the late-Chief Carter's house left Drummond's heart sinking in his chest. The last time he had been here, the chief ended up dead, his wife came close to losing her mind, and their maid — also the Chief's mistress — had seen her livelihood fall to the floor along with the man she loved. The idea that they might be happy to see Drummond, let alone might provide him with information, sounded more ludicrous with every step he took.

When the front door opened, Drummond discovered that Ms. Daggett, the comely black maid he had expected to see, had been replaced with a stout German woman. "I've been warned about you," she said in a terse greeting. "You are not welcome here."

"I only need thirty seconds of Mrs. Carter's time. I just want to ask her one question."

"Leave now or I will call the authorities."

She tried to close the door, but Drummond stuck his foot in the way. No point in arguing this further. If she called the police, Detective Cooper would be sunk. "I'll go. I promise. Just tell me one thing — where can I find the previous maid, Ms. Daggett?"

He could see it on her face — she knew. She looked around as if some unseen hero might swoop in and save her. When no such rescue came, she looked back at Drummond.

"I do not want to lose this job. You go now."

"All I need is an address. Mrs. Carter had to have sent final payment somewhere. Please, this is important."

Perhaps the new maid felt some sympathy for Drummond, but he suspected more than anything, she simply wanted him gone. She stepped away for a moment and returned with a scrap of paper and a hastily written address. "Now go."

She pulled the door open for some momentum, and she slammed it shut. Drummond got his foot out with no room to spare.

MS. DAGGETT LIVED IN A POOR SECTION of Winston-Salem. Rows of townhouses backed up against railroad tracks and abandoned lots. Raccoons and stray dogs fought for scraps found in the trash.

Walking toward the place, Drummond wondered how much of the current day's poverty could be accurately predicted by the surrounding area. Before the Crash, one look around and he would easily call this the poor area. But he had seen enough homes that looked well-off from the outside yet had been gutted to the pawn shops on the inside. At least this place was honest about its standing.

Halfway up the short walk, Ms. Daggett stepped out onto her porch. She carried a Browning Auto-5 hunting rifle at her side. "You can turn right around and go home, Mr. Drummond."

"I'm not here to cause you any trouble."

"Last time we met, the man I loved ended up dead. I got nothing to do with you, so your being here means trouble."

"I just need a little information. A name."

"What you need is to get off my property." She lifted the long-barreled rifle.

"Put that away, please. We both know you won't try to shoot me."

"Why? Because I'm black? You took away the man I love and I got no job no more. Seems to me, I don't have much left to lose."

Drummond noticed several folks watching from their porches and windows. Quite a show for an afternoon.

"Okay, okay, you win," Drummond said turning away. "I just figured you didn't want to end up like the Chief's pal, Derek Richmond."

Before he took two more steps, she said, "What happened to Detective Richmond?"

Drummond hid his grin. With Ms. Daggett and the Chief being lovers, he figured the Chief might have mentioned his close friend — and Richmond had to be a close friend, otherwise, Carter would never have entrusted the man with his paranormal troubles.

Drummond turned back with serious concern on his face. "The way I read it, Mrs. Carter didn't just learn all that magic from a book. Somebody had to show her what to do. I think Detective Richmond figured that out, too. Only he found her."

"Her?"

"The witch."

Now it was Ms. Daggett's turn to notice her neighbors watching. Talk of witches would not go down well. Lowering her rifle, she approached Drummond. "What do you know about witches?"

"Not enough. But that witch killed Richmond, and if I'm right, she's trying to clean up the whole mess that you all created when you started playing around with magic you didn't understand." He had no idea if the two cases were actually related, but he figured Ms. Daggett would believe him. One glance at her widening eyes confirmed this belief.

"I didn't mess with any of it. Mr. and Mrs. Carter — they're the ones that cast spells."

"I know that, but I'm not certain the witch does. Or cares. If you want to protect yourself, then tell me the witch's name."

Again, she checked to see the interest level of her neighbors. Leaning close and speaking softer, she said, "What makes you think I know any witches?"

"Because we're still having this conversation. Now, I've got to go find this woman, and if you're not going to help out, it'll take a lot longer. Might even take too long. But I can't just stand here admiring the lovely surroundings."

Her muscles tightened. "No reason you need to be rude. This is my home."

"You're right. I apologize. I'm a little testy under the circumstances."

"I give you that name, you promise to leave me alone? After you leave, I don't ever want to see your face again."

"You have my word."

Ms. Daggett sighed. "Murphy. Sylvia Murphy." Drummond nodded his appreciation and turned away. Speaking louder, she said, "How will I know if you succeed?"

Without looking back, he said, "You'll wake up in the morning."

BY THE TIME DRUMMOND drove all the way out to Mocksville to check on Leroy's progress, night had fallen. He had hoped to visit Raymond's Diner for a cup of coffee and a chance to see Catalina, but he lacked the opportunity. Mostly because part of him wondered if his bluff might be true — that the witch Sylvia Murphy might be targeting those involved with Chief Carter's last case. Considering that among those making the list were Leroy, himself, and Catalina, he thought it of paramount importance to make progress.

The path to Leroy's shack was still too muddy for the car. Drummond plowed halfway through the woods, his shoes sloshing deeper into the mud with every step, when Leroy caught up with him.

"I would've thought you'd given up your hikes," Drummond said. "The last one didn't go so well."

"Clears the mind." Leroy pointed back the way Drummond had hiked. "We've got to get to the city. Got plenty to tell you."

Drummond didn't like the urgent tone, but he turned around and started for the car. "Got a few things to share myself. Should I be worried about Catalina?" He kept thinking about that bluff — that the witch was getting rid of anybody involved with Chief Carter's death.

"No, nothing like that. Unless ... that is ... yes, she might be in trouble. We all might. But no, not really."

"I'm going to slap you silly if you don't give me a straight answer."

"Now, now, ain't no reason to get like that. This is complicated. Let me try to explain."

"That's kind of what I'm trying to get out of you."

"Well, if you'd shut up a minute, let me speak, maybe you'll learn something." They reached the car, and as Leroy clambered in, he asked, "You bring your whiskey flask?"

"Sorry, it's back in *Moby Dick*."

With a disappointed huff, Leroy waited until Drummond got the car moving. "It's like this — that symbol carved in the detective's chest is a very odd usage of a very odd spell. Now, most spells are cast within a casting circle. That's the most common. You can also cast within triangles and there are other ways too, but that gets more complicated. In all those normal cases, the person inside the casting circle is a witch. Now a witch has an aura of magical energy around her."

"An aura?"

"It's the best way I can describe it. Just know that she's got like a gas tank for the magic in her, and she uses the circle and the symbols to focus that magic into creating a spell. Make sense?"

"I learned long ago that none of this makes sense. I just do my best not to get bucked off the horse."

"Fair enough. Try it this way — the circle helps a witch cast a spell, but other people — non-witches — can do magic too. Chief Carter's wife and the Chief both tried it. Of course, the results can be bad for amateurs."

"Nothing you're saying is making me feel any better about Catalina. Or you and I, for that matter. Is this witch coming after us or not?"

Tapping the window with his knuckle, Leroy said, "That's the thing — I'm not convinced we're dealing with a witch."

"We are. Her name's Sylvia Murphy. I was told she was a witch."

"You may have been misinformed. See, every time somebody casts a spell there's a release of energy. Like with a gunshot. When you shoot, there's a release of energy and some of the leftover energy is in the air. You can smell it, right?"

"Gunpowder? Yeah, you can smell that."

"You can't smell magic, but like gunpowder in the air, it can get on you. According to two of the rarest texts I have, some spells can utilize that residue. No matter who it's on."

"You think Sylvia Murphy is using that spell?"

"I do. It works by drawing a triangle within a circle and then placing a person with this residue on each point of the triangle."

Drummond recalled the number three as part of the carving in Detective Richmond's chest. "She numbered them?"

"Afraid so."

"Does this mean we're headed to a graveyard? You want to go dig up the other two bodies?"

Leroy shook his head. "I think those two are still alive. Whatever spell Sylvia Murphy attempted to cast using the magic on these people — well, you saw what it did to Richmond. If the same thing had happened to numbers one and two, they would've all been dumped together. Possibly, they would've been buried spread out nearby, but I checked that area again while you were out. Nothing there."

"She could have buried the bodies anywhere. Put one in the woods, one in the city dump, one on the other side of town."

"That's probably too much work. This woman is casting a spell using magic off of other people because she doesn't have it herself. Doesn't strike me as somebody who is willing to take the patience route."

Drummond felt a chill across the skin. "If what you're saying is right, then she needs a new number three. And all of us that were at Chief Carter's the night he died, we all have that magic residue on us. Right? You, me, Catalina, all of us — we're all viable targets for the spell."

"Exactly."

Drummond pressed down on the accelerator. "Let's just hope there aren't too many Sylvia Murphy's living in Winston-Salem."

* * * *

TURNED OUT THERE WERE TEN. After the first half-dozen, Drummond and Leroy had established a routine. Drummond would approach the front door, introduce himself as a detective, use Detective Richmond's badge to bluff his way into the house, and sit down with Sylvia Murphy to ask questions.

As he interrogated the subject, Leroy snuck around the back of the house. If there was a basement door, he would take it. If not, he found some way into the house — a kitchen door or a backyard entrance — and searched for signs of either witchcraft or the witch's victims. When Leroy found the house to be clear, he signaled Drummond and left the way he came in. Drummond would find an excuse to leave, and they were on their way to the next Sylvia Murphy.

By the time they reached Sylvia Murphy Number Seven, the evening had turned into night, making their outing far more dangerous. There had been several obvious risks to their actions — among them, the fact that Leroy might get seen by a "helpful" neighbor. Catching a black man snooping around the backs of houses would not end well for him. They had been lucky so far.

"When this is done, I'm going to get ahold of an entire bottle of whiskey and it's yours," Drummond said.

Leroy chuckled. "That's liable to get me in more trouble than if I get caught breakin' into houses."

"But it will be a lot more fun."

This particular Sylvia Murphy lived in a neighborhood as poor as that of Ms. Daggett, but these people pretended that they had more in their pockets than they did. The outsides of the homes had many of the trimmings seen on wealthier houses, yet they were off. The gold-plated doorknobs turned out to be flaking paint on wood. The charming picket fences were peeling and missing several slats. And though the yards looked full and well-kept from a distance, up close they were patches of weeds and clover.

Right away, Drummond's inner-warnings went off. Years of being a detective of the strange informed him that this place did not feel normal. The house sat back from the other homes on the street as if it strained for a little extra privacy. The walkway leading toward the front door used six shrubs and dark shades to create an unwelcoming atmosphere. The place only lacked a guard dog to make it clear that the owners did not want anyone's attention.

From the time Drummond knocked on the door to the time it opened, he had the opportunity to peek in the window and look over the porch. Heavy curtains blocked his view, and the porch had been kept clean and boring. When the front door finally opened, complete with a soft whine, Drummond had a moment of doubt — Sylvia Murphy did not act like anything evil.

Drummond found it hard to believe this five foot tall, old woman had hurt anybody. She looked like a storybook grandma, not the evil witch in the woods. Her brittle gray hair could have been a wig, and her large round glasses could have been unnecessary. The warm smile on her cracked lips, however, beheld an authenticity that Drummond could not deny.

"Sylvia Murphy?"

"Yes?"

"I'm Detective Marshall Drummond." He flashed Richmond's badge. "Sorry to trouble you, ma'am, but your name came up in an investigation, and I'm required to follow up. If I could just have a few moments of your time, ask a few questions, I'm sure I can leave you to the rest of your day."

"Why, I cannot imagine why you would want to talk with me. I'm an old lady who doesn't venture out of the house. Nothing I can really help you with. But please, please, come on in. I was affixing to have some sweet tea. You're welcome to join."

Drummond's warning systems reignited. Honest people tended to answer questions quickly and with the truth. Babbling on and on with denials mixed in amongst rambling suggested trouble. Of course, Sylvia Murphy might simply be a babbler. But if other warnings popped up, Drummond would have confirmed this was the right Sylvia Murphy.

She led him through a dark living room with a black cat curled in a reading chair. They entered the kitchen, and he sat at a chipped, wooden table. A glass pitcher filled with tea sat on the counter next to a tin of sugar. Sylvia scooped sugar two more times, stirred the pitcher with a large ladle, and poured two glasses. She handed one to Drummond as she sat at the corner of the table.

"I don't get many visitors," she said, letting her feet dangle off the edge of the chair. "So, tell me about your investigation. Was anybody hurt?"

Drummond left the glass of sweet tea untouched. "Why do you ask?"

"I see all kinds of terrible things happening out my window. The world is changing around us, and I can't say it's for the better. Having a big police detective in my house — well, you aren't here because you think I went and stole something. Best I can guess, you think I saw something out my window."

"As it is, I'm afraid somebody was hurt."

"I knew it." She added a little glee to her voice, playing up the part of the lonely old lady looking for any excitement in her life. "Tell me about it. What can I do to help?"

Drummond caught a shadow pass across the window — Leroy. Leaning onto his elbows, Drummond pulled in Sylvia's attention to keep it off of anywhere Leroy might go. "I'm afraid one of our own, a fellow detective, got hurt." He watched her face closely for any twitch or grimace — any reaction at all.

"That is serious," she said, holding a cryptic smile.

"When it's this serious, you can be guaranteed we're going to find out who did it." Again, no clear reaction.

"I don't recall seeing a police detective getting hurt out my window. Don't know what else I can do for you."

"There is something. You see, the nature of this particular case is a little odd."

"Odd?"

There it was. She said the word with a hint of recognition as if she had the thought — *now we're getting to the meat of things.*

Drummond snatched glances at the shelves and countertop, looking for any object that might confirm the use of witchcraft. Nothing jumped out as strange for an old woman's kitchen. In fact, everything he saw pointed to the possibility that Sylvia Murphy was in fact just an old woman. Maybe he had made a mistake. His gut screamed at him that this woman was the one, and much of her behavior supported that conclusion. But it was all circumstantial. No hard evidence pointed toward her guilt.

He peeked at the back door. No Leroy yet. Perhaps his partner had found a basement entrance.

Tipping his head back, Drummond crossed his arms and frowned. "You never saw anything, did you?"

"I suppose not. It certainly is nice having a visit, though." She nudged his glass of sweet tea closer. "At least finish your drink with me."

With a nod, Drummond lifted the glass to his lips. He tried not to wince as the over-sugared tea ran across his tongue. Then he saw two things that froze his body.

First, another shadow passed the kitchen window — a brutish-sized man with curly hair. Second, he noticed Sylvia's wrist. When she pushed the glass towards him, her wrist poked out of her sleeve, and on it, he saw black wax.

Placing the glass down, he looked all around the room. No candles. He did not notice any candles coming through the house, either. Even if he had, black candles were not a common color — unless you were casting spells.

Drummond spit hard and wiped his lips against his sleeve.

Sylvia Murphy chuckled — a soft, unkind sound like the creaking of floorboards. "Don't worry. It's not poison. You're no good to me dead. But, before you lose consciousness, tell me one thing — how did you find out about Detective Richmond?"

Drummond's head felt thick as if his skull had grown more bone. At the back door, he spied Leroy waving urgently. With a bang, the door burst open and Leroy entered with his arm wrenched behind him. The brute with the curly hair did the wrenching.

"Look what I found, Granny."

Sylvia glanced behind her. "Well, it looks like the detective brought a friend. Good work, Junior."

"Should I get rid of him?"

"Haven't we learned anything from losing our last number three?"

Like a schoolboy reciting his lessons, Junior said, "We always need to have a backup."

"That's right. Mr. Drummond here is going to fill in just fine. If we make a mistake and can no longer use him, this colored fellow will do the trick. Be a good boy and take him downstairs. I'm not finished with this detective right yet."

Drummond heard all the words and understood them, too. But his body did not want to react. He tried to move his arms, tried to make eye contact with Leroy, tried to make a plan — but his thoughts muddled together into a thick sludge.

Sylvia hopped off her chair and dumped the sweet tea into the sink. Adjusting her big glasses, she turned back and folded her hands gently in front of her. "I need to know how you found what was left of Detective Richmond. Can't have any more of our mistakes popping up for the police to catch. Now tell me."

Drummond wanted to keep his mouth clamped tight, but something in her tone compelled him to speak. No, not her tone — her spell. Whatever mickey she slipped into his drink, she had control over him now. At least, to some degree.

Fighting it nonetheless, he still said, "Mud ... shallow grave."

"There, there. That wasn't so hard. I think I understand now, so you can rest. You'll need your strength for later."

When Drummond managed to crawl from the murky depths of his unconsciousness, he found himself tied to a metal rod stuck into the concrete cellar floor. They had positioned him on his knees, and he could tell by the lack of feeling in his legs that he had been there for quite some time.

The cellar had a low ceiling and two bare bulbs casting shadows in all directions. Most of the area had been cleared for the large casting circle that dominated the floor. Heavy, black lines had been painted on the concrete. Drummond had been placed at one point of the triangle within the circle. The other two points were empty for the moment, and neither had a post with which to tie somebody.

To his right, near the staircase going up to the kitchen, a fancy chair had been placed on top of two wooden crates. Sylvia Murphy's makeshift throne.

Leroy had been tied and gagged at the foot of the throne. Junior, the curly-haired brute, stood at the opposite side of the cellar like a courtroom guard ready to put an end to any disruptions of their ceremony.

Flexing his fingers, Drummond tried to pull free from his ropes. No give. Not even a slight shift. The knots were tight and would take a long time to saw through if he had anything sharp at hand. Even if he did, he wasn't sure he could get a good angle to cut with.

"Finally," Sylvia said. "I was about to ask Junior to break out the smelling salts." Tilting her head toward the ceiling, she yelled, "Millie! Janice! Get on down here."

Loud thumping and louder giggling followed the call. In seconds, two women trundled down the stairs. They looked to be in their early-thirties yet they dressed as if they were teenagers with bows in their hair and frilly laces around the edges of the dresses they wore. With a quick curtsy toward Sylvia, each girl sat cross-legged at the other points of the triangle.

Sylvia beamed as she said, "Mr. Drummond, I'd like you to meet my grandchildren. To your left is Janice and to your right is Millie. Both wonderful women. And, of course, you already met Junior."

With a giddy bounce as she spoke, Millie said, "Granny, are we going to do a new spell today? Can we? Can we?"

"I think that's an excellent idea." From the side of her throne, Sylvia lifted a large book with a strange, leathery cover. Drummond had already encountered human skin covers before but the sight still bothered his stomach.

Janice said, "Is it time to try the big one again? Can we do that today?"

Sylvia made a show of thinking it over. Like a circus ringleader teasing the audience for one more death-defying trick, she said, "You know, with the energy I feel coming off this man, I think it just might be time. It might indeed."

The girls rocked back and forth with wide eyes and wider grins. Janice licked her teeth while Millie seemed to conjure up a daydream of what the future held.

"Which one of us is it going to be?" Janice asked.

As she flipped through the pages of the book, Sylvia said, "Now, now. You know Millie is the oldest, so she gets to go first."

Millie reached over and flicked Janice on the shoulder. "That's right. You'll get your chance soon enough. I've had to wait a couple years more than you for this."

Drummond wanted nothing more than for those two girls to shut up. Every word they uttered spun circles of dread around him. Though he had no idea what twisted spell they could be so excited about, he didn't want to know. He looked to Leroy, but his friend could barely lift his head. Either they had beaten him terribly or they had given him a dose of sweet tea to cloud his thoughts.

Once more, Drummond shifted his weight and attempted to get his hands in a good position to work the knots. Once more, he failed. No matter how he arched his shoulders or turned his wrists, he could not get started on those ropes.

"Here we are." Sylvia set the book flat on her lap and ran a finger under the sentences as she read. "Yes, yes. I think we're ready to finally do this."

"Does that mean we're going to be real life witches?" Janice asked.

"What kind of question is that? Witches? Those are evil things. You say your prayers at night, don't you?"

"Yes, ma'am," Janice said.

"Every Sunday you go to church, don't you?"

"Yes, ma'am."

"Well then, tell me how is it that a good churchgoing girl like you could be a witch? You don't really want to be a witch, do you?"

Though Sylvia's question had been said with a gentle tone, Janice looked as if she had been slapped across the face. "No, ma'am. Never. I was just worried that might happen to us. Just wanted to make sure we were going to be okay."

"Well, that's good thinking. We have to be careful when using these spells. We can't just go throwing them around. We do them wrong and bad things happen."

Millie said, "Like what happened to the Detective Richmond?"

With a solemn nod, Sylvia said, "Exactly like that."

Drummond scanned the room for anything that might help, but empty was empty and it wouldn't get filled anytime soon. Only out of frustration, out of the desire to make sure his mouth still work, he said, "Doesn't matter whether you're a witch or not. Casting spells is going to take you down an evil road."

Everyone stared at him, and briefly he thought Junior would come over with a punch or two. But Sylvia let loose her nasty chuckle. "We're casting spells of love. There ain't no evil love."

Drummond's gaze fell upon Leroy. A spark lifted in his chest. Though difficult to see, he noticed Leroy's shoulders and arms making slight motions — he had been working to loosen the ropes binding his hands. Where all eyes had been focused on Drummond, none paid attention to Leroy.

Drummond averted his eyes so as not to draw any attention that way. He did not have a lot of options open, but there was one thing he could certainly do. He could buy Leroy time.

"Let me get this straight," he said with a sarcastic wink. "You think that if you cast spells with love in your heart, somehow that will protect you from the evils of witchcraft. Is that right?"

Millie snickered. "You got it all wrong. We're not casting with love in our hearts. We're casting to bring love to our hearts."

Drummond raised an eye over at Sylvia. The old woman shrugged. "What can I say? A grandma will do anything for the love of her grandchildren. Millie and Janice are good girls, and they deserve good men in their lives. I've taught them manners and virtue, and I've cast a spell or two to make sure that they follow those guidelines. Sadly, most men in the world lack the qualities necessary to make a good husband."

Drummond could not hide his scoff. "So you've been playing with magic to create a love spell? You want to put that on me?"

"Don't be a fool. I said *a good husband*. Besides, love spells don't really work."

Millie tapped her chest with her thumb. "Granny's going to get me a husband."

"Your Granny is completely right about me. I am not husband material."

With her hands laid open on the spell book, Sylvia inhaled the air as if taking in the spell itself. "This book has shown me so much. We've worked hard on spell after spell, learning the basics, until we were ready to try this difficult bit of magic. But magic it is. Wonderful magic. We are going to use the magic surrounding you and the life inside of you to give us the essence of a man my Millie deserves. From that, we will begin to grow her husband."

Drummond had no idea if such a thing could be done, but he knew for certain that these women could not do it. The bones of Detective Richmond proved that. Drummond pitched a glance at Leroy but couldn't tell how far the man had come.

"Okay, girls," Sylvia said with a clap of her hands. "I'd say it's time."

Millie and Janice rocked on their knees with big grins.

"Wait a minute," Drummond said. "If all of this is about getting husbands for your granddaughters, why did you tell Mrs. Carter about a spell that murdered her husband?"

"She was a dear friend of mine. She came to me because she was convinced Chief Carter was having an affair. And like so many men, he was. The fact that he had fallen for a colored woman only made matters worse. So, I let her into my confidence. She had been a good friend for a long time and deserved better than she was getting from that man. I showed her my book, and I showed her what she needed to do in order to fix her marriage." For the first time, Drummond saw the darkness rooting across Sylvia's face. With a shiver, she threw it off and returned to a gentle smile. "You see? I approached my friend's problem with love. My love to her through friendship, and her love for her husband through marriage. It was in that light that I encouraged her to use the spell."

"Well it killed her husband and destroyed her mind. You really want to risk that with your granddaughters?"

"Her failure came as a results of her lack of faith. My convictions are stronger, and I have no doubt that my granddaughters have greater faith, too."

"Most definitely," Janice said, her eager eyes begging for approval.

Drummond said, "But what about —"

"Enough," Sylvia said, slapping her hand on the book. "It is time. Girls, do just as we have been practicing all along."

Even with those big glasses, Sylvia had to hold the spell book close to her face to read it. She mumbled through a chant, over and over like a Buddhist monk reciting a mantra. The girls laced their fingers together in their laps, closed their eyes, and made a bowing motion — back and forth to the rhythm of Sylvia's voice.

Leroy had opened his eyes as he struggled to free himself. Sweat beaded on his brow. Drummond could see it in the man's face — he knew time was running out.

Drummond took a chance and looked at Junior. The large man chewed on a fingernail as he played with the crumbling bricks in the wall. Since Drummond had not tried to escape, Junior had no opportunity to do anything. He was bored. Of course, he was — he would not get a turn for a wife for many years. Both his older sisters got to go first.

Drummond's chest spasmed as a gentle tingle covered his skin. Millie and Janice felt it, too — they moaned and arched back, thrusting their chests in his direction.

He wanted to say something, but before he could speak, a pale light formed between the two girls. It reached out from their chests like a snake made of smoke. What it lacked in color, it made up for in brightness. Blindingly so.

Janice's body jerked, and a second line of smoke snaked out of her chest — this time headed for Drummond.

Its languid approach allowed him one last look at Leroy. From what he could see, Leroy would break free but never in time. Drummond struggled against his bindings once more, and as with each time before, he failed.

The smoke hovered in front of his chest as if the snake readied to strike. When it snapped into him, he felt a sharp blade pierce his skin. Janice cried out in perverse pleasure.

Millie's body followed the same patterns as her sister. And like Janice, a pale smoke came out of her, snaked its way toward Drummond, and snapped into him.

Drummond thrust his chest out. Each breath sunk the knives deeper. His eyes locked open. And with his peripheral vision, the most frightening sight yet — Junior grinning.

"Ready Granny?" Junior asked.

Without breaking her chant, Sylvia gestured toward her grandson. The man strode out of Drummond's view, but when he returned, he held a long branding iron, glowing white hot.

Drummond had no doubts now where Detective Richmond got the mark on his sternum. Junior stepped into the circle, stepped over the smoky beams connecting Drummond to the two women, and settled in the middle of it all. He raised the branding iron and let its glow shine in his twisted grin.

Drummond struggled and bellowed but could not break free. The smell of burning metal intensified as Junior stepped closer. The girls writhed and moaned in time to Sylvia's steady chanting.

Ever since leaving the police force and taking on the bizarre cases that came his way, Drummond always thought he would die at the hands of a witch. It never occurred to him that he would die because a wannabe-witch did not know how to cast a spell properly. Death by incompetence — not as noble as he had hoped.

A vicious yell roared to life from Drummond's right. Leroy! The man jumped to his feet and knocked over Sylvia's throne. As Sylvia cried out, the startled look on Junior's face made Drummond's chest burst with joy instead of pain.

Continuing his battle cry, Leroy rushed across the cellar and tackled Junior. Their bodies crossed through the smoky light, severing the connection in the triangle. Millie and Janice were thrown backward. Bright sunlight erupted from the center of the circle along with an explosive blast. Drummond's ears popped. He could see nothing, hear nothing.

Time shifted. He thought that perhaps he had been knocked out. When his eyes watered open, he found Leroy sitting in front of him. Nobody else.

"They're gone." Leroy looked at his empty hands. "They got away."

ONCE FREED, Drummond helped Leroy check through the house. The Murphy's had fled. From the looks of it, they had no intention of returning. Rooms had been hastily packed, several books had been taken, and much of the house had been rifled through.

Drummond checked his watch. Between searching through the house and having been unconscious, they had lost an hour. The way his head felt, he figured he'd been out far longer.

He stood in the center of the living room, surrounded by wooden furniture and a crocheted blanket. The black cat had either gone with the family or curled up in some dark corner. He tried to focus on what to do next, but his head still fought to regain a sense of normality.

Leroy, however, had his wits completely about him. And his anger. He kicked a nearby chair, splitting the leg. "All the stupidity. What is the matter with folks these days? Why would they want to go given up everything they believe in just to get their daughters married? Makes no sense."

"People have a way of mucking up their thoughts in order to get the results they want."

"There is no way they can truly believe that the Bible tells them this is okay. Any of this."

"Come on, now. You know that can be made to say just about anything."

Wagging his finger, Leroy said, "Don't you start on that. There's plenty good enough in that book."

"Maybe so, but the Murphy's seemed to have missed those parts."

Leroy stomped on the broken chair again, splintering parts of the back. "I'm sick of this. I just want to be home with my books and a bottle of whiskey. Is that so much to ask?"

"Then go back. We lost one. It happens."

"What you say? You really think this is over?"

"For now." Drummond gestured to the empty room. "They're gone. I'm sure they'll surface someday, and when that happens, we can act. We'll remember who they are. Certainly won't forget this. We'll get our payback."

"I think you got your brain all churned up. This ain't over. That fool woman that thinks herself a witch, she ain't going to stop. This whole thing was to get her granddaughter's men. Right? From the looks of those girls, they don't have that many breeding years left — and you better believe that's the old woman's goal. She wants herself some great-grandbabies."

Leroy was right. And that meant Drummond could not go back home to lay down his aching head and get some rest. "Okay. You win. Let's figure out what their next move is."

Leroy slumped on the couch arm as he focused on thinking through the problem. Good. Drummond needed Leroy sharp as ever — especially when his own mind was not up to par.

"Well," Leroy said, "those girls were damn scared of their grandma, but they also struck me as quite spoiled. They going to be whining and complaining that they didn't get their man tonight."

"And the old woman knows we're not going to give up. Ever. She knows of the results that happened to the Carters, too."

"That's right. So she's feeling pressure from her grandkids and from us. You ask me, I think she's going to try it again tonight. If at all possible, she'll try to get herself another number three and attempt to pull off the spell before we can catch her."

Drummond agreed. "She doesn't want to hear her grandkids screaming about how she failed them. So, what does she do? Maybe she has Junior go grab the nearest guy, haul off somewhere, and get moving on this."

"If she's panicking, then maybe. But she didn't strike me as the panicking kind. Everything she did was calculated — even the way she looks and acts is meant to disarm people into thinking she's a sweet old lady. Doesn't seem like she's going to let her setback stop nothing."

"She needs one of us — the guy with magic still attached."

Leroy's head jerked towards Drummond. "She doesn't need a guy. She just needs the energy of a life. Anybody who has magic on him will do."

Drummond's world slipped as his stomach sank. "Including Catalina."

In seconds, the two men sprinted out of the house and jumped into Drummond's car. Speeding through the streets, Drummond raced away like a gust of wind. Leroy had the sense not to say anything encouraging on the drive. Drummond needed to boil — which did not take long.

When they arrived at Raymond's Diner, Drummond shut the car off and hopped out before it had completely stopped. He hurried toward the restaurant with Leroy at his side. Only one thing mattered — Catalina.

Bursting into the diner, he garnered some startled looks from patrons. He scanned every waitress in the establishment. She wasn't there. He stormed over to the manager.

"Where's Catalina? She should be on her shift."

The manager, a portly bald fellow, scowled. "Yeah, she should. She asked to take a break, and I felt generous towards her. She's always been a good worker. So I said sure, take ten minutes. You know what she did? She up and left. Never came back. Left me hanging with the tables that I have to take care of myself now." As the manager moaned on about how unfair life had treated him and how betrayed he felt by Catalina's disappearance, Drummond's world lost all bearing. He stumbled back and would probably have fallen if not for Leroy being there to catch him.

"Take a breath," Leroy said. "But just one. Get your head back, and we can start thinking again. The girl's only got us now."

Leroy escorted Drummond back to the car garnering a few more subtle looks of disdain from the patrons. Drummond held the steering wheel and stared ahead at the diner. He wanted to drive but had no idea where to go.

"She wouldn't do that. She wouldn't leave this job. She's got two boys and her *abuela*. They rely on her. She wouldn't just go."

Patting his shoulder, Leroy said, "I know. I'm sure you're right."

"You know, she and I, well, I don't know how you feel about that kind of thing, but we've been seeing each other."

"I know. I'm happy." Leroy gave Drummond a final pat on the shoulder. "You've had your one breath now. Time to get to work. We know what the spell is all about, and we know that they took Catalina in order to finish the spell. So the only question that's important that I can see is where do they go to get this thing done?"

Drummond licked his lips and tapped his chin. Work the case. Forget about the risks. Focus. "They would need someplace quiet. Private. And dark. That spell created a lot of light and they wouldn't want somebody to see it coming through a window or stumbling upon them in the woods."

"The woods. They must've done something in the woods, at least when they were first learning, because they buried those bones out near my place."

"They were dumping evidence. They could have put it anywhere."

"If they were just getting rid of those bones, they had no reason to come out that far. There are miles of woods between Winston-Salem and my place. Any one of those would've been good for burying the bones."

Drummond perked up. "You think they have a second-place?" He thought about the Murphy's home. "They managed to recover from the explosion, gather everything they needed, and kidnap Catalina in a very short time. That suggests to me that they were prepared."

"You think they knew we were coming?"

"Well, we had been searching Sylvia Murphys all day. It's not that hard to imagine they got wind of it. But that's not what I mean. I'm talking about contingency plans. The grandchildren did not waste time packing what they didn't need. They rifled through their house for very specific items — plenty of useful stuff had been tossed aside. They knew what they were doing."

"Which means they knew where they were going, too."

"Exactly. I think you're right about those bones. It's our best chance, anyway."

He started the car, pulled away from the diner, and headed back towards Mocksville.

* * * *

DRUMMOND AVOIDED TWO ACCIDENTS on his way out of the city, and he could feel Leroy's rising tension. He thought about assuring Leroy that he could handle the car even at high speeds, but he did not want to spare the energy. He focused on the road, the car, and most of all, Catalina.

Memories of her threatened to push all else away. He pictured the way she smiled at him at the diner. He remembered the way she felt hugging him after the trauma of the Chief Carter case. He recalled being in bed with her in all its glorious variations.

When they reached the turn off for Leroy's place, Drummond did not stop. He let the car fishtail in the mud and managed to force the vehicle almost halfway before it finally bogged down. Without pause, both men jumped out and continued on. They only stopped at Leroy's home for a few moments — long enough to grab Leroy's shotgun and some extra ammunition.

With Drummond's flashlight revealing the path forward, they hustled through the woods. Leroy pointed the changes in the trail as they came upon the first house. Empty.

"Probably somebody's hunting lodge," Leroy said.

Though the rain had finally stopped, clouds kept the moonlight from helping them. Drummond's eyes locked on wherever the flashlight went. The dark woods would have to remain dark. Leroy gestured to where he had discovered the bones. Drummond acknowledged this with only a quick, single nod.

They came across two more homes. The first was empty like the previous one. The second had a young couple honeymooning in their parents' forest getaway.

"How many more places are out here?" Drummond asked as they hurried along.

"Don't know for sure. But I don't expect its many more. Maybe three? Four?"

They only had to go to one more house. Drummond knew it was the right place as they approach from the side. Wards had been tied around several trees making a circle surrounding the house. Drummond pulled out his handgun and motioned for Leroy to go around to the left. Drummond took the right.

An oil lamp flickered in a second story window. No light could be seen from below — Drummond could not tell if there were window slits in the basement at all. Probably not. But there was a cellar door.

He tried lifting the heavy door. Only an inch up, he heard the rusty squeal and stopped. Gently, he returned the door to its resting position. Even through that small crack, no light came up his way. Either they had not cast the spell yet or Drummond was too late.

He scurried along the side of the house until he reached the porch. Placing each footstep with care to avoid any telltale sounds, he gradually made his way toward the front door. Each second of wasted time felt like an eternity of loss. He wanted to rush in there, grab Catalina, and race off.

With only a few steps left till he could attempt a quiet entrance, he heard Sylvia Murphy's voice. "Junior, the girls are both ready. How much longer?"

Junior's beefy voice replied, "I got the casting room all cleaned up. Looks even better than the one back home." Sounded to Drummond like Junior was yelling toward the upstairs. "Granny? You want I should take the waitress downstairs?"

"Well, of course. We can't do the spell without her."

Peeking through the front door window, Drummond saw Junior across a bare wood floor. Like many cabins built for a weekend away from the city, this one consisted of a large bottom floor — a big room that could be used for just about anything and a small kitchen tucked in the back corner. Stairs led up to a second floor where Drummond guessed Sylvia helped her granddaughters clean up, calm down, and get ready to finish the spell. Bound and blindfolded, Catalina had been propped against the wall next to the fireplace. She looked unharmed but she also looked scared. Every sound caused her to flinch. Drummond could see how Junior purposefully stepped louder and made unusual sounds to mess with Catalina's fears.

He waited until Junior squatted in front of Catalina to untie her hands from the metal ring embedded in the stone. *How many people have they brought here?* Drummond wondered.

Catalina kicked out. Junior tried to hold her legs, so she clunked her head forward, slamming into his shoulder. He backhanded her which freed up her legs, and she started kicking again.

With Junior's back toward the front door and his attention focused on wrangling Catalina, Drummond figured he would never get a better opportunity. He reached for the front door. Locked. He expected that. Sort of hoped for it, too.

Making no attempt to hide noise, he stepped back from the door, raised his foot, and thrust forward. The lock splintered the jamb and as the door flew open, Drummond thundered into the house.

Junior whirled around too fast and flopped onto his rear. Drummond blitzed across the room. He slammed his foot down on Junior's chest.

"Catalina, I'm here," he said, his voice resonating deep in his chest.

Her shoulders dropped with relief even as her ears stretched toward his voice. "Drummond?"

"You expecting somebody else?"

As her sudden smile washed over him with warmth, Junior grabbed his foot and twisted hard.

Pain sprang up Drummond's leg. As he tumbled to the floor, he pointed his weapon at Junior and pulled the trigger. The shot burst a hole in the floor as his arm smacked into the hard wood.

"Granny, we got trouble!"

As Junior rolled onto all fours and slowly pushed his bulk to a standing position, Drummond looked for his gun. He did not recall dropping it, but it certainly wasn't in his hand.

The next few seconds happened so fast that it would be weeks before Drummond put it all together. In the span of a couple breaths, Drummond spotted his handgun next to Catalina's hip. As he tried to roll onto his good knee, Junior stepped up behind him. The man's thick arms locked Drummond's head and cut off his air. Catalina's struggles managed to pull loose one hand from her ropes. She pushed up her blindfold and saw Drummond's predicament. Spots formed in front of his eyes. He saw her focus drift to her left. Unable to turn his head, he had no idea what shocked her, but he heard the steady steps of somebody coming down the stairs.

In the next breath, Leroy's shotgun erupted. The blast reverberated in the floor. A chunk out of Junior's head pinwheeled into the wall, and as Junior fell over, the big man's body spun Drummond off balance.

A scream erupted from the staircase — deep, guttural, old with disbelief. Sylvia Murphy stood on the bottom step. Her sweet, grandma countenance evaporated into a tight, red-filled rage. With a gasping breath, she said, "You think this will stop me? You think there isn't anything I wouldn't do for my granddaughters? I may not be a witch, but I am every bit as dangerous."

A hole appeared in her head — small and crimson. Blood oozed down the front of her face, filling in her cracked and wrinkled skin. Her legs gave out and her body folded to the floor. Drummond looked over at Catalina to make sure she was not hurt. She held his handgun. He never heard the shot.

Hobbling over to her, he took the gun away and finished untying her from the wall.

Answering the unasked question, she said, "The woman wasn't wrong. She was never going to give up. We couldn't spend the rest of our lives worrying about her."

Drummond held her tight. In her ear, he said, "It's okay. You did the right thing."

She pushed back. "I did what was necessary. But it wasn't right."

From behind, Leroy said, "Are you all okay?"

Drummond and Catalina helped each other onto their feet. Drummond said, "As good as can be expected. Thanks for keeping me alive."

"Anytime." Leroy winked.

"I'm not looking forward to hiking all the way back on this foot, but it's better than being dead."

Leroy cracked open his shotgun to reload its two chambers. Once he had the weapon ready to go, he stepped out front, his eyes roving for any possible threat. Helping Drummond limp toward the front door, Catalina said, "You know, there are better ways to impress me."

Drummond chuckled. "I'll try to remember that in the future." He laughed harder. "Cooper's going to blow a gasket when he finds out he'll have to hide this mess."

Millie's high-pitched screech broke through the air. She flew down the stairs and across the room. Wielding a knife high above her head, she lunged toward Catalina. Though her words garbled together with her screams, Drummond thought she said, "If I can't have someone special, neither can you."

Perhaps Catalina's words echoed in his head. Perhaps he merely wanted to protect her. Perhaps he let anger get the better of him. More likely, a blend of all three put him into action.

In one swift motion, he pulled out his handgun and shot Millie in the heart. No hesitation. No second chances.

She stumbled forward a few extra steps but her momentum stalled. The knife nosedived from her hand and stuck into the wood floor. She stared at Drummond, confusion wriggling across her face. Gently, she touched the bleeding wound and lifted her hand to look at her fingers. "I just wanted a husband."

She fell over and moved no more.

With tentative steps, Janice descended the stairs. She had her hands raised high and tears cutting rivers down her cheeks. She looked from one corpse to the next. Each caused her to gasp and sniffle, shudder and cry.

Leroy returned with his shotgun up and ready. Drummond put his hand on the barrel and pushed down.

"That's not necessary." He looked to Catalina. "That's not right."

Leroy said, "You let her live, she's going to want vengeance."

Janice settled on the bottom stair and cradled her dead grandmother. Over her cries, Drummond said, "Maybe so. Maybe not. That's her choice. Coming after us because of the consequences of her family's actions is also not necessary or right. But she has to make that choice herself."

They turned away and walked outside. Drummond added, "Either way, we'll be ready."

CASE 08

THE HAUNTING

MARSHALL DRUMMOND WATCHED A SPIDER CRAWL across the uneven ceiling in his office, and for a few seconds, he considered that the spider had it made. No knowledge of the stranger world surrounding it, the creature simply went about its day looking for food, a good place to rest, and a good mate. Drummond worked on getting those things, too, but he could not ignore the stranger world around him — not for long, anyway.

Catalina, the woman in his life, rested her head on his bare chest. The two pillows and the rough blanket did little to cushion the hardwood floor, but neither minded. Both breathed soft and strong after an enthusiastic afternoon. He knew she listened to his heartbeat — she had once commented on how peaceful it made her feel to hear his calm pulse after such vigorous pleasures — and that gave him a sense of peace, too. After all they had been through in the last handful of months, he welcomed any peace he could snatch.

Dealing with the economic depression after the Crash of '29 caused enough stress in the lives of everyone, but Drummond had the added benefit of being the sole investigator of the bizarre for Winston-Salem. Possibly for all of North Carolina. He had seen so many terrifying things, had escaped the clutches of Death so many times, that he wondered how much longer he might last. All the more reason to focus on the pleasures life had to offer.

He kissed the top of Catalina's head as the sounds of the city rumbled below.

"I wish I didn't have to go to work," she said, playing her fingers across his chest.

"I don't think I've got energy for another round. Not yet, anyway."

Her naked body pressed warm against his side. "I'd be happy to just lay here."

"Me, too."

"I don't want to go outside and see the world." She raised up to look him in the eye. "How much longer do you think we can keep this up?"

He knew exactly what she referred to, but he didn't want to think about it. Just another source of tension in his world. Unfortunately, he knew her well enough now — if she wanted to discuss a topic, there would be no evading it. Sitting up, he rested his back against his beaten, office couch.

"Nobody's bothered us yet," he said.

"Nobody's bothered you. That's because you're the white man in this relationship. But a brown woman like me — I notice the way people look when you visit the diner during my shift. Mrs. Carlisle and Mr. Cook, in particular — they don't approve. Heck, the entire country doesn't approve."

"I don't recall asking anybody for permission."

She smacked his chest. "This is serious. At some point, people will decide that what we have is more than a friendship. They suspect now, but they either can't tell for sure or are content lying to themselves. But I know how this story goes. Somewhere along the line, one of us will smile a little too much at the other or we'll brush by the other a little too closely — whatever it is, something will set off those who bother watching. And when that happens, my life is in danger. And so are the lives of my boys and *mi abuela*."

"Are you saying you want to stop seeing me?"

"Don't be an idiot. I don't want that at all, but I can't live in constant fear, either."

Drummond chuckled.

"This isn't funny," she said, hitting him harder on the chest.

"No, it's not. I was just thinking about the kinds of cases I deal with. A bit of constant fear is a daily occurrence for me, too. Just not over the same things."

A loud banging rattled the office door. Drummond jolted at the sudden disruption, and Catalina hurried to dress. Pulling on his pants and donning a shirt, Drummond eased across the room. He glanced at his .38 tucked in its holster, sitting on his desk. The pounding on his door had an angry feel to it. Perhaps one of his neighbors didn't like listening to his carnal activities. Perhaps Catalina's prognostication regarding the more hateful nature of people had come true early.

"Okay, okay," he said over the constant thumping. "Hold your horses." He grabbed his handgun before approaching the door.

With a quick look back, he checked on Catalina. She nodded and did a good job of muting her shiver. Flicking a match against the door jamb, Drummond lit a cigarette. As he opened the door, he raised his weapon and let it lead.

The banging ceased.

Nobody stood there.

Drummond peered out the door, up and down the hall — empty.

Turning around, he heard Catalina gasp. She stared at a spot on the wall above the couch. A dark stain had formed — deep crimson like dried blood — and the longer he looked at it, the more convinced he became that the mark had taken on the appearance of a face. An anguished face. A round-faced man glaring outward while locked in endless pain.

Catalina dropped to her knees, crossed herself, and muttered a quick prayer. As Drummond closed the office door, he watched the stain, half-expecting for it to move, perhaps start talking — nothing would have surprised him.

"Well, crap," he said. "Looks like I'm being haunted."

Though he could feel Catalina's shocked eyes fall upon him, he kept his focus on the wall. When nothing about the horrid image changed after a few minutes, Drummond sat behind his desk, finished his cigarette, and leaned back in his chair. He always thought this day would come. Considering his line of work, it surprised him that a haunting had not occurred sooner. Now that the moment had arrived, his mind blanked as to the best course of action.

Catalina, however, stepped to his side, her eyes never wavering from the evil portrait. "Do you know who it is?"

"The ghost haunting me? I haven't a clue. That wall painting doesn't ring any bells, and frankly, the list of possibilities is longer than the number of citations I gave out back in my beat cop days — and we handed those out every single day."

"Then you better start with finding out what ghost you've pissed off."

"You're right." Drummond straightened. This simple, clear suggestion kicked his brain into action again. "I've got a few witches who owe me. They'll be able to figure this out."

"Are you *loco?* Why would you want to deal with a witch? Even if they owe you, they'll find some way to twist the whole thing around so you end up owing them. Never owe a witch."

"Better than being haunted. Banging doors and blood on the walls is the minor stuff. I've seen what happens to people. It's annoying, startling things like this at first, but it can quickly escalate. Dangerously so. I don't want you to walk in here one day to find my head twisted backwards, a hole in my chest, and my heart on the other side of the room."

Checking her watch, she said, "I've got to leave or I'll be late. You listen to me. Forget all this witch nonsense. You call *mi abuela.* She'll be able to find out who is pestering you, and you won't have to sell your soul in the process."

"Your Granny is not going to see me. I'm the white man sleeping with her granddaughter. Heck, you won't even let me visit your house because of her and your boys. I mean, does she even know who I am?"

Leaning over, Catalina kissed him. "Promise me that you won't go see a witch. I'll talk with *mi abuela* and arrange for you to meet. Okay? But no witches. Promise me."

"Fine, fine. I promise."

She kissed him again and left for work. He remained at his desk, staring at the face on the wall as if it might poke through the wood at any moment. Though he had put on his bravest face for Catalina, he had to admit that the incident troubled him. Not because of scary noises or unnatural happenings — he had long grown comfortable around such things. Rather, he knew that no matter what Catalina's old granny had to say, things would get worse. Not once in his career had he seen a haunting nipped in the bud where the victim only suffered some banging doors or bloodstained walls. Not once. Things always got worse.

DRUMMOND DID NOT LIKE WAITING. He understood, of course, that Catalina had to show up for her job. With so many people out of work, pawning off everything they owned and starving on the soup lines, having any kind of employment meant the world. She had a family to provide for, too. But that did not make the waiting any easier.

Drummond liked to deal with a problem, not sit around wondering when somebody else would come along and fix it for him. His entire business had been built around the idea of arriving at a person's home to be the fixer, not the other way around. But he also knew that Catalina was right.

No good would ever come from dealing with witches. If there was a way around that, he would be a fool not to take it.

So, he waited.

Eventually, she would get off work, go home, kiss her boys *Good Morning,* and after seeing them off to school, she would tell *abuela* all about the haunting. The old woman would probably refuse at first, dig in like a soldier unwilling to risk stepping over a line, but her granddaughter could be very persuasive. Plus, she had eyes that mesmerized with their beauty and depth. It would take a bit of effort, but at length, her *abuela* would agree. She'd set some terms, if only to feel in control, but she would agree. Once that played out, Drummond would get his chance to find out who haunted him. In the meantime, he had to live with being stuck in his office, caged up with no action to take — at least, no sensible action.

He reached for his copy of *Moby Dick*. Not to read. The book had been hollowed out long ago. Inside, he kept his trusty flask of whiskey.

Except he pulled back from the bookshelf. Getting drunk would not be a good idea that night. Not when a ghost — or something — wanted to hurt him.

Sitting at his desk once again, he pulled out a piece of paper and a pencil. At the top, he wrote: *People (living or dead) who want to kill me.* Going through his cases, he listed all the names of the witches and ghosts he had come into contact with. He even tossed in the names of a few gangsters.

After two minutes, he stopped. Far too depressing to look at the full page. Especially when he knew he could fill another with ease.

Rubbing his face, he stood and donned his Fedora and coat. Just because he had to wait did not mean he had to wait in the office. A short walk might clear his mind, help him focus, or at least, get him moving — even if it was only around the block.

The last edition of the day's *Winston-Salem Journal* had hit the streets, and Drummond spared two cents for the paper. As he strolled along the sidewalk, absorbed in the latest news from around the world — things still looked unsettled in Europe — he let the cool air cleanse his spirits. This town had been good to him, and he often felt a kinship towards it, as if it had a vested interest in his well-being. Winston-Salem understood that he protected her from the witches and ghosts, and in return, he did not end up homeless.

Shaking his head, he smirked. He had seen an endless stream of folks bargain in their minds to justify all manner of supernatural deals. It appeared he was just as susceptible. Although, he would argue, there existed a massive gulf between a light-hearted belief that he had a deal with the city itself and bargaining with witches.

As he walked along, someone gripped him by the shoulder and yanked him into a dank, narrow alley. A gut punch doubled him over, and as he strained to inhale, a hefty blow to the back of his head sent him face first into the ground. But in that half-second of falling, he knew that no human had assaulted him. When he lifted his head and saw the empty alley, it only confirmed his thoughts. He never saw an assailant, never heard the scuffle of shoes during the assault, never glimpsed the attacker rushing away. But more than all of that, a cold chill had accompanied each blow to his body like a winter breeze growing colder off the snowy ground.

Drummond sat up and rested his back against the brick wall. On the plus side, he knew for certain now that the ghost haunted him directly, personally — instead of haunting his office. On the minus side, that meant Catalina would be in danger by simply spending time near him. Of course, he could hear her reply — *I'm always in danger being near you.* And they both knew she did not refer to the supernatural.

When he stood, Drummond paused, bracing himself for another attack. He gazed up the dark alley, wondering if the ghost floated nearby, ready to chill his skin as it struck at him hard. No attack came. At length, he stepped out onto the sidewalk and made his way back to the office.

Once inside, he pulled a hammer from one drawer of his desk and clawed back three slats in the floor. Reaching in, he found the two ghost wards that a witch had prepared for him during one of his many cases. After chastising himself for not thinking of these sooner, he threaded a coarse rope through one and created a necklace with a ghost ward pendant. Made of polished quartz mixed with Carolina red clay, the witch had carved it into the shape of an ouroboros. Its deep coloring matched the blood image still staining his wall. He placed it over his head before making a second necklace out of the pendant shaped like a lion's face.

With the ward safely around his neck, Drummond decided to partake in a little *Moby Dick* after all. Two swigs. That's all he allowed himself. But the sharp warmth eased the edge off and helped him focus better than his walk had done.

When his office door slammed open, he jolted in his chair and, thankfully, managed to keep the startled shriek frozen in his throat. Catalina stepped inside. Her grim pallor and the fact that she still had several hours left on her shift told Drummond everything.

"This thing isn't just haunting me, is it?" he said.

She shook her head. "The diner got slow, so I went in the back for a cigarette. This invisible thing shoved me against the wall, I could feel icy fingers around my throat, and then when the new cook, Joey, walked in, the ghost released me. Just gone." She swiped his whiskey flask and took a long pull. "My heart is still racing. I called Cynthia to come in early and cover me. Told her I wasn't feeling well. The second she showed up, I came straight here."

Drummond hugged her, kissed her softly, and then tied the lion-faced ghost ward around her neck. "This'll help. I don't know how strong a ward it is, but the witch that made it had a lot of power."

"Had?"

"Long story. Point is, it'll help for the short term."

She patted the stone against her chest. "We have to go to my apartment right away."

"Won't that tick off your *abuela?* She's not going to like seeing me."

"She'll get over it. Especially when she sees that her own granddaughter is being haunted, too."

"Your boys?"

"This late at night? They better be asleep or they'll be sorry."

Drummond set his hat on. "Lead the way."

FOR DECADES, immigrants from Mexico and further south congregated in the southeastern section of Winston-Salem. Many of the signs and stores catered to Spanish speakers, and the sounds of Mariachi bands played alongside bilingual blends wherever one listened. Even so late at night, Drummond could hear the distinct tones of this transitioning culture surround him.

Catalina's apartment shared this mixture of cultures. The overall layout of the place felt distinctly American — she had enough room for her family, barely — while hints of her Mexican roots popped up in the colorful blankets on the practical couch or the spicy aroma in the cigarette-stained air. Seeing the thin blanket used in place of a bedroom door, Drummond could not imagine how her boys would sleep through his visit. Especially when Catalina and her grandmother spit out their rapid-fire argument.

At length, Catalina walked over to the kitchen area — a corner of the main room that had a sink, an icebox, and a few cupboards. *Abuela* stood in the room glaring at Drummond. She bent over an old walking stick and wore all black — mourning for her husband who had died twenty years ago. A black knit shawl covered her shoulders and her dark brown skin seemed to bleed right into her clothing. Only her stark gray hair altered the color pattern.

With a trepidatious smile and a slight wave of the hand, Drummond knew he would never be able to win over this woman. It did not help that, in many ways, she reminded him of the witches he fought against on a daily basis.

Catalina returned with a glass of water. As she handed it to the old woman, she gestured to the couch along the back wall. "Please, have a seat."

Drummond removed his hat as he settled on one end. Catalina sat close — but not too close.

"This is my *abuela*," she said. "You can call her Mrs. Medina."

Mrs. Medina huffed. "He doesn't even know our language."

"Now, *Abuela*, you promised to be nice."

Though he knew it would piss off Mrs. Medina, perhaps *because* he knew it would piss her off, he placed his hand on Catalina's knee. "It's okay," he said. "Your granny and I don't need to become good friends. All I need from her is a little help identifying this ghost. That is, if she's capable of doing anything."

Fire burned behind the old woman's eyes. "I've known the dead far longer than you've been alive. Show some respect."

"So, you're a witch?"

She looked to Catalina. "What kind of man is this? *Estupido.*"

Slipping out from under his hand, Catalina said to Drummond, "She's a medium. She's had the gift since she was fourteen. And unlike a witch, she doesn't require any kind of devil's bargain to help us out. She has spent her life identifying ghosts, talking with them, and helping them move on." Shooting a bladed glare between Drummond and her grandmother, she added, "There is serious trouble going on here, so the two of you need to stop this right now."

Mrs. Medina gripped her walking stick tighter. "I don't want to see you hurt."

"Then help me."

"I meant your heart."

"My heart will be just fine. Besides, that won't matter if I have a ghost haunting me all the time."

"Of course, dear. *Lo siento,*" Mrs. Medina said, but she didn't look too sorry to Drummond.

Spreading the shawl over her head, the old woman approached the couch. She clasped Catalina's hand and with some hesitation, reached out for Drummond. He placed his hand on top, her leathery skin cold to the touch, and he tried to focus on the ghost issues rather than the relationship issues. She rolled her neck, closed her eyes, and slowed her breathing.

While Drummond's cases had brought him into contact with many sorts of strange creatures and stranger people, he had yet to spend any serious time with a real medium. Unlike a witch, the medium did not require geometric shapes drawn on the ground, arcane symbols painted with undesirable substances, or any of the other paraphernalia witches utilized in casting spells. He guessed a medium did not need those things because she cast no spells. Her gift allowed her to see what others could not. In some cases, she could communicate with these unseen forces. But that was the limit.

Mrs. Medina's hands clutched tight around Drummond and Catalina's wrists. With her head back and her eyes rolling upward, she moaned. A long, creaking tone that vibrated the floorboards.

Drummond glanced at the bedroom. Not even a curious peek from behind the bedsheet. *How could those boys sleep through this?*

As abruptly as it began, so it ended. Mrs. Medina released them and stepped back. She fumbled for her walking stick, and Catalina rushed over to help.

"That it?" Drummond asked, inspecting his hand. "Do you know what's happening to us?"

"Sí." The old woman set her shawl back around her shoulders. "The ghost is a man. Once a very powerful man. His name is Carter."

"Chief Carter? Damn."

Mrs. Medina flinched at the swear but said nothing. Drummond ignored her as he swallowed down the idea that the former Chief of Police had come back from the grave.

A short while ago, Chief Carter had hired Drummond to investigate an odd occurrence at his house. Turned out the Chief had been cheating on his wife with the maid, and Mrs. Carter attempted magic in revenge. It did not go so well. But the Chief loved both wife and maid, and in the end, he sacrificed his life to protect the two women from the unnatural horrors that had been unleashed.

Drummond swore under his breath. "I should've known."

Shaking her head, Catalina said, "You couldn't have possibly —"

"That case is the only one you've worked closely with me on. The moment I learned that you were being haunted, too, I should've known."

"What does it matter? You know now."

"At the least, I would've saved your granny from straining herself."

Mrs. Medina snapped a sharp glare at Drummond. "I'll have you know that I'm strong enough to handle anything the world of the dead has to offer. And before you go on with your mouth, you should listen better. You'd have realized that I wasn't done talking."

"Oh? Did the Chief say something to you?"

"Keep talking and I'll never get to tell you. I'll probably die before you shut up long enough."

Drummond opened his mouth to throw a sarcastic comment but

stopped. Sparring with Mrs. Medina would not accomplish anything, and it might piss off Catalina. Best to stay quiet and let the old woman have her say. Besides, the whole point being here was to listen to what she had learned. Might as well be smart and let her talk. Gesturing toward her, Drummond nodded.

Mrs. Medina raised an eyebrow. "Didn't think you could catch on so fast. Good for you. Now, both of you listen close because this is an angry ghost."

"They always are," Drummond muttered.

"This ghost has come back from the Other for you."

"The Other?" Catalina said.

"When a person dies, their spirit usually moves on to what is after — Heaven, Hell, whatever. But some spirits remain stuck here as a ghost. These ghosts can take many forms depending on what keeps them from moving on. Many are cursed to roam the lands where they died, but some do have one refuge from the mortal world — the Other. Not being dead, I don't know what it is exactly like, but it seems to be another plane where only the ghosts can go. A limbo for them while they wait to move on."

"The Chief left that to haunt us? Why?"

Grinning with pride, Mrs. Medina said, "Good question. Sometimes, a ghost gets angry and wants to torment those he holds responsible for his death. Sometimes, a ghost gets confused."

Drummond looked up at the ceiling. "C'mon, Carter. We did the best for you that we could. And you hired me, not Catalina. If you're mad, be mad at me. Just focus it all my way."

A thin boy with hair shooting out in different directions stepped from behind the bedsheet. Rubbing his eyes, he frowned. "Mama? What's going on?"

"Pablo, back to bed," Catalina snapped.

"Who's that man?" Pablo asked.

Catalina never responded. She never had the chance. Both Pablo and Mrs. Medina lifted into the air. As the boy's eyes flew open, wide awake, Catalina shrieked.

Drummond tried to rush for the boy, but his legs would not move. Not from fear. Rather an unseen force froze him to the floor. One glance at Catalina told him that she suffered the same affliction. She reached toward her son, but her legs would not move. He looked from one terrified face to the next but could offer no help.

Pablo's mouth opened to scream but no sound came out beyond a tight gurgle. The ghost choked him, and his mother and grandmother would be forced to watch.

"Abuela," Drummond called out. "Try to connect with this ghost again. Try to call it off."

He did not have much hope for that to work, but doing nothing would not save them. For her part, Mrs. Medina closed her eyes and concentrated hard.

Nothing.

Pablo's brother — apparently the heaviest sleeper in all of Winston-Salem — finally wandered in. He gazed around the room and clearly wondered if he might still be dreaming. Until the ghost grabbed him by the chest and hoisted him to the ceiling. He screamed.

But Drummond noticed a thawing in the legs. Holding five people at once seemed to strain the ghost. He thumped one foot forward, the effort forcing a harsh breath out of his lungs. Catalina thrust her arms toward her two flailing sons even as her eyes darted toward her *abuela.* The tears streaming down her face matched those of her sons as they stretched towards her embrace. Drummond thumped another step forward.

"Try to walk," he said to Catalina. "This thing can't control all of us."

Indeed, the more Drummond stepped towards the group, the easier his movements became. It appeared that the ghost no longer choked Pablo, too.

Groaning as her face tightened, Catalina forced her left leg forward. She exhaled with the same force Drummond had done only moments before, and the anger in her eyes flared. "You let my boys go. You hear me, Carter? Let them go now." She forced her right leg forward. Thump. "You think you're tough? You have no idea how I'll torture you, if you hurt my boys."

"That's it. Keep going." Instead of feeling like he moved through a thick bog, Drummond's legs now felt as if he waded calf deep in snow.

The boys lowered — still hovering above the ground, but only by inches. As Drummond and Catalina moved closer towards them, Drummond felt his body straining less. He saw the smile trembling on the corners of Catalina's mouth. If they could just reach the boys.

Mrs. Medina's eyes snapped open — milky white and filled with shock. A wave of energy blasted from her in all directions. Drummond fell to the floor. The boys were thrown against the wall before crumpling down. Catalina stumbled backward against the kitchen counter.

With her arms held wide and her entire body slowly turning in the air,

Mrs. Medina began to speak. The voice did not belong to her. Drummond heard Chief Carter — a Chief Carter locked in painful struggle. "Please — help. Please — find a way. Please — I need —"

Mrs. Medina's eyes closed and her body dropped hard on the floor. Catalina rushed to her side, beckoning her children towards her, and they hugged — clinging together with desperate energy as if holding onto life preservers on a sinking ship. As she fawned over her boys and cared for her ailing granny, Drummond got to his feet and dusted off his hat.

"You take care of your family," he said. "If you need a doctor for your *abuela*, go ahead and call one. I'll cover the cost."

"What if he comes back?" she asked. "These ghost wards did nothing."

"Yeah, I'll be having a chat with the witch that made them. But not now. You care for your family, and I'll go take care of that ghost." He could see the debate within her — the need to be there for her boys and her granny versus the need to be by Drummond's side, to fight the ghost with him, to protect her family through action. "Don't worry. I've done enough of these things to know that I'll be needing your help eventually. But not yet."

He did not give her an opportunity for further protest. Setting his hat low, he left the apartment.

ARMED WITH THE KNOWLEDGE of the ghost's identity, Drummond headed straight for the Salem Cemetery. In the world of magic and ghosts, there were many different types of hauntings. Drummond felt certain this was the simplest. This was about Chief Carter's anger and revenge. Thankfully, a simple haunting had a simple solution. Drummond merely had to dig up Chief Carter's grave and purify the man's corpse. Purification could be attained by numerous methods — salt, fire, and holy water among the most common. As he pulled his car up to the cemetery gates, he could not repress a slight grin. He was on firm ground now — in his element.

Once he stopped this haunting, he intended to return to Catalina's apartment. There would be a long, uncomfortable conversation with her family explaining how he knew Catalina and how serious he felt towards her. They may not be happy about it; however, he would be returning the hero. He would be responsible for having saved them from a malicious ghost, and that had to count for something. With any luck, he would be more than a few steps closer to gaining Mrs. Medina's trust and the boys' acceptance.

Drummond's growing confidence disappeared like a scream on the wind. Even before he identified the gravestone, he knew which grave would belong to Chief Carter. It had to be the one with a pile of disturbed earth, two lanterns, and the caretaker standing over it. Swallowing back the dread rising in his throat, Drummond gave the caretaker a nod and looked at the deep hole in the ground.

Flicking his tongue, the caretaker said, "As long as I do this job, I will never understand this. Who in their right mind would want to go digging up dead people?"

Drummond peered down the hole. Chief Carter's coffin could be seen despite the dark of night and the dirt covering the top end. Somebody had taken a hatchet to the bottom section.

Frowning, Drummond said, "Don't grave robbers usually pull up the whole thing?"

"That's the normal way of it. They pull them up, open them up, take all the jewelry and valuables they can find. They'll even pry out a gold tooth. Then they just leave the caskets in the open. Sometimes the body is pulled out and face down in the grass."

"You ever seen this before? Somebody put back the casket and cover half of it with dirt?"

"Can't say as I have."

Drummond gestured to the hole. "Mind if I poke around down there for a moment? Don't worry, I'm not some lunatic. Just a private investigator."

"You looking into this grave robber?"

"Sorry, no. But I think whoever did this might be connected to a case I'm working on. I'd like to get an idea of what they might have taken. If that's okay."

The caretaker tossed a shovel toward Drummond. "Long as you finish the job for me, you can do what you want."

Drummond did not know whether to be pleased or disturbed by how easily the caretaker gave up the grave. But as the man walked back toward his workshed mumbling about dealing with weirdoes so late at night, Drummond decided he didn't care. He needed to take a look in that grave. Simple as that.

THE DIGGING WENT SLOW. Drummond wanted to simply crack open the rest of the casket with the blade of his shovel, but he saw no good reason to provoke the ghost further. Besides, a dark feeling manifested in his gut. The disturbed grave meant that this was no simple haunting. Somebody had messed with Carter on purpose.

After a time, when he had finally excavated enough of the casket to pull it open, Drummond found what he feared. The left femur had been pulled through the open section of the casket — torn skin and clothing had snagged on the sharp edges. The rest of the corpse remained intact — gently rotting away but intact.

"What does that all mean?" the caretaker said from the top edge of the grave. "I ain't ever seen a grave robber interested in body parts. It's like that Frankenstein, ain't it?" The caretaker snorted a laugh. "Is that what this is? You chasin' some mad scientist tryin' to bring life back from the dead? I swear, you night folk are the craziest sons-a-guns I ever dealt with." Shaking his head, the caretaker walked away again.

Drummond closed the casket, climbed out of the grave, and started shoveling dirt back in. With each shovelful, he thought about the caretaker's question. Not a mad scientist, of course — but perhaps a witch. There was no shortage of enemies wanting to hurt Drummond, and any witch paying attention to his career would know about the Chief Carter case.

Running down that list in his mind, thinking through one witch after another, Drummond tried to figure out if any of them would risk coming at him this way. Not that disposing of the city's only magic-fighting investigator would be such a bad thing for them — might even bring a witch some fame — but it might also expose their presence to the city. And though Drummond had yet to figure out the hierarchy within the witch community, it had become clear to him over the last two years that somebody stood at the top. That person or group controlled all the witches in the state. A big move such as coming after Drummond might require approval of those higher-ups.

In fact, the more he thought about it, the less likely it seemed a witch would be doing this of her own volition. Shoveling more dirt, the answer hit him like a dark howl on a full moon night. Janice Murphy — not a witch at all.

The last case he had worked on involved a twisted family that dabbled in magic without any proper training. These non-witches had provided Mrs. Carter with the magic spell that destroyed her and her husband. Not only did Drummond's investigation lead to the destruction of the Murphy family, but they also attempted to take Catalina's life. And while the grandmother, the brother, and the sister all perished, Janice had survived. She made it clear that vengeance now stoked her heart. Since the cases connected to Drummond and Catalina, it made sick sense that she would target them both.

With a sharp thrust, he stuck the shovel into the dirt and stormed back to his car. If Janice was the culprit behind this, then he and Catalina had a lot to fear. Janice had no real experience controlling magic. If she played with these kinds of spells, she might as well be putting a gun to her head and those around her. She would have no control.

Drummond sat in his car and drummed the wheel with his fingers. Janice's family had a home in the city and another out in the woods of Mocksville. He did not think she would go to the second home — her family had been slaughtered there. Too many bad memories. She was such a child in her head that Drummond expected she would want to return to her real home. It was also a closer drive which made that the sensible location to check out first.

DRUMMOND CALLED UPON a frightening level of self-control when he parked his car across the street from the Murphy residence and stayed sitting. The rage within urged him to rush across the yard, up the long path toward the house set back from the street, and bang on the door. Kick it in if necessary. Find Janice Murphy. His imagination grew cloudy from there, but he figured by the end, she would be more than happy to end whatever spell she had cast upon Chief Carter's bones.

Instead, Drummond settled back in his seat and watched the house. He had dealt with the Murphys before. He knew that his fantasy assault would not result in a satisfying solution. After all, he had seen the look in Janice Murphy's eyes.

The night he walked out of her family's cabin in the woods, the night she sat on the floor cradling her dead grandmother, he witnessed her pained glare. If he roared into her house now and attempted to force her cooperation, she would merely dig in her heels and refuse. He could pull a gun on her and threaten to put a bullet through her skull, but she would only laugh. Her eyes had promised — Janice Murphy would gladly die if it meant tormenting Drummond and Catalina. Anything for her vengeance.

So, Drummond sat in his car and waited. And watched. Part of him wanted to drive off at high speed to his good friend, Leroy Parker. Leroy knew the arcane books of witchcraft better than anybody Drummond had ever met. That man would solve this in an instant. But Drummond did not want to take his eyes off the house. If Janice got away, he feared that he might never be able to stop this, never be able to protect Catalina.

Besides, Leroy deserved a break. It wasn't right for Drummond's dangerous lifestyle to impede upon his friends. He felt bad enough the way it had turned against Catalina. He had no intention of going any further.

With these thoughts swirling through his head, Drummond's eyes closed. He could not remember when he had last slept — possibly over twenty-four hours ago. Within seconds, he snored deep and steady.

The honk of a car woke him. The morning sun shone bright on the street. Drummond tipped his hat back and through puffy eyes, he looked at the Murphy residence.

"Crap." He had been out for several hours. If Janice had any inkling that he watched her, she could have slipped out easily. He might have blown his best chance.

Ignoring the stiffness in his neck, back, and legs, he left his car. A dozen people strolled the sidewalks — some heading to work, a few pushing baby carriages, a few headed to the market. A normal day for normal people. None of them had a clue that ghosts floated through the world like the dead leaves in Autumn.

Halfway up the walk toward the Murphys' front door, Drummond felt the temperature drop. Something popped on his chest. He glanced down. His ghost ward had snapped in two.

Drummond halted.

The ward had not done its job protecting him earlier, but clearly it now reacted to this house. Gazing up at the darkened windows, the dead bushes, and the unwelcome gloom hanging over the home, Drummond discovered a trickle of hope. Janice had been here. And he would bet a lot that she had cast her spell from this house. The energy that he felt and the reaction of his ghost ward proved it. With any luck, she remained in the house.

Ignoring the plummeting temperature, he tightened his coat and pushed onward. He banged on the door and waited. Twice more, but nobody came.

If she had wanted to watch him suffer, she would have answered the door. She would have laughed in his face. But perhaps she hid from him, fearing he might stop her spell.

He walked around to the back of the house. A car shed stood several feet away adjacent to the back alley road. Peeking through the windows, he saw that the family car was gone. He had no idea if Janice could drive but he figured that if not, she could certainly find somebody willing to drive for her.

He hurried back to his own car. Whether or not she had been in the house that night, he did not know with certainty. But he felt certain she was gone now. She had set the spell and left.

Once again, he called upon his willpower to stay in the car. It would be simple to blunder into that house in a foolish attempt to break the spell. But he knew the depths of Janice Murphy's desire for vengeance. He would never forget those eyes. And that cautioned him. If she left the house open and her spell accessible, then she wanted him to rush in blindly. She must have other surprises waiting for him. Which meant he had to be smart about this.

Time to get Catalina. He drove off.

WHEN DRUMMOND ARRIVED at Catalina's apartment, he found the boys had gone off to school, the grandmother rested in the back bedroom, and Catalina waited with open arms. Like an angel's light breaking through hellish clouds, her smile and embrace crushed the mounting gloom within him. For a time. No amount of warmth could change the fact that they still had to deal with the ghost of Chief Carter.

After explaining what he had seen and experienced at the Murphy house, Drummond settled on the couch and rubbed the back of his neck. "I didn't want to burden Leroy with this. And quite frankly, I don't feel like driving all the way out to his shack. Not when Chief Carter's ghost is so active right now. And especially not after I felt that terrible ghost chill surrounding that house. Going out after Leroy would take too long. Too many opportunities to be attacked. Too much time wasted for answers I can hopefully get elsewhere. Even coming here, I'm worried that when I get back, the spell will have dissipated."

"You don't have to convince me," Catalina said, leaning her head on his shoulder. "I know you're here to ask for my help, and you know I'm going to give it to you. No questions asked. No problems."

Drummond had an idea of what to do. Part of it was based on his experience as a private investigator of the bizarre. Part of it was guesswork based on what he thought he would find inside the house. But he wanted to run it by Mrs. Medina. Unfortunately, the attack on the old woman had been harsh enough that she needed rest for the remainder of the day.

The more he thought about it, the more he decided letting her in on his plan would be a bad idea. Even if she agreed with him, she would say everything she could to dissuade them. Because any attempt to end this haunting required risk to Catalina. No way would Mrs. Medina allow that.

As if she could sense the psychic energy in the room, Mrs. Medina entered with soft shuffling steps like a ghost slipping out from the bedroom. Catalina popped to her feet and rushed over, but before she could utter a word, her grandmother waved her off. The old woman stood firm in the center like a graveyard statue watching over the dead.

She glowered at Drummond, but when she spoke, she directed her words toward Catalina. "Take this paper." A small yellowed paper shook in her hand. "You go down to Mr. Drummond's car. You read that paper. It'll tell you how to stop this ghost."

Catalina took the paper but did not leave. "You need to get back to bed. You need rest."

"Go now." Her stern voice forced Catalina back a few steps.

"You've suffered a —"

"I told you to go down to that car."

Catalina's chin quivered, and Drummond thought she might shed a tear or two. But she had better control than that. She stiffened her back and left without another word.

"You've really pissed her off," Drummond said. "But I imagine she'd be even more pissed off if she heard what you planned to say to me."

The old woman wriggled her lips — perhaps fighting the urge to grin. "You keep surprising me. You're not half that idiot I thought you were."

"Look, I know you're not crazy about me seeing your granddaughter. And I'm sure you're worried about how all of this might affect you and the boys, too. I don't know what I can tell you other than we're both adults, we both understand the dangers of what we're doing, and if there were any other way, I would take it. I don't want to see Catalina or any of you hurt by this. By anything."

Mrs. Medina remained standing in the center of the room. "Having a relationship with Catalina is selfish. But if that were it, if that were all I had to worry about, then so be it. Nobody with brown skin lives a life without feeling the sting of the bigot. But this other world you've brought her into — that terrifies me. If the Klan comes to our door, maybe they'll run us out of town. They'll scare us and threaten us, but as long as we leave, then that'd be the end. That's usually the worst of it. Only the truly terrible events, those where people stand up against the bigots, only those times do we end up with one of us dead. But you —

your line of work — people connected to people like you die all the time."

Drummond sat forward. "I've tried my best to keep her out of it. And once we clear this ghost so that it's not haunting her, I'll do all I can to keep her away again."

"No, you won't."

"You think I'm lying?"

"I think you're unwilling to do what is necessary. You want to protect her from this world that you're involved in? There's only one way. Break her heart now. Leave her. Let her hate you, if necessary. No good is ever going to come from your relationship. And more likely than not, she's going to end up dead. Don't do that to me. Don't do it to her boys."

"It's not that simple," Drummond said, but Mrs. Medina had turned away. She shuffled back into the bedroom, leaving him on the couch alone. He knew he would be thinking about this moment for many hours to come. But at the moment, Catalina waited for him down in the car. They had a ghost to fight.

Leaving the apartment, Drummond thought, *I just have to make sure Catalina lives through this.*

ONE OF THE FIRST LESSONS Marshall Drummond ever learned as a beat cop was the importance of focus. Most criminals failed because they lacked focus. They were so intent on whatever greed or depravity brought them to the point of committing their crimes that they neglected to focus on how to get away with it. Of course, some of them were simply stupid.

Drummond did not want to be stupid. And he did not want to lose focus on what mattered at the moment. So, despite part of his brain's desire to recount every word and gesture Mrs. Medina had made, he forced his mind to focus on getting rid of Chief Carter's ghost. Fail at that, and nothing else mattered.

Although Mrs. Medina's yellowed paper provided little more than Drummond had already planned to do, she did offer one tidbit that had never occurred to him — surround the entire house in a salt circle. Circles were usually used for casting spells. Witches used them all the time. Being an element of purity, salt was usually used to block ghosts — salting the entrances to a home such as the doors and windows. Drummond had even seen salt circles used to protect small groups of people. But an entire house?

After stopping at the hardware store and picking up several large bags of salt — the owner assumed Drummond had a desire to prepare for a harsh winter — they headed for the Murphy house. All throughout the trip, Drummond could feel Catalina's unasked questions weighing on him. She wanted to know what her *abuela* had said to him. She wanted to know how dangerous the road ahead would be. She wanted to know if what they had between them would be enough to survive all the challenges the coming years might hold.

He kept his focus on driving.

When he finally parked near the house, they both paused to stare at the building. It seemed to stare back. Though the late-afternoon sun kept the area filled with light, a grim darkness hung over the house. Drummond could not be sure, but he suspected that even the pedestrians avoided the area — going out of their way to cross the street rather than spend too long passing the front of that impersonal, gray dwelling.

"You don't have to do this," Drummond said. "There's always another way."

"Was she really that blunt with you?" Catalina stared at her grandmother's shaky handwriting on the paper. "She's usually subtle. Or at least, her version of subtle. She must really be shaken up to go right at you with some version of keep my granddaughter out of this mess."

"She's just trying to protect her family." Drummond said nothing more for a moment. He thought about her grandmother's words. At length, he said, "Then let's get this over with."

Together, they hauled the heavy bags of salt into the front yard. A few passersby glanced in their direction, but nobody dared step onto the Murphy property to inquire further. If two strangers wanted to throw salt around that horrible house, so be it.

They each took one bag and began outlining the circle in opposite directions. A narrow gap had been left open near the front. The salt line had to be thick and wide. For a few moments, Drummond worried they did not bring enough. Having to drive all the way back to the hardware store, collect more salt, and come back did not factor into his plan — namely, get all of this done before the daylight died. But by the time he reached the back corner of the house, he knew they would be okay.

At least, as far as the salt went.

Breaking into his third bag, Drummond arched his back and wiped the sweat from his brow. Physical labor had never bothered him, but as he got older, his body disliked the acts more and more. No, he had to be honest — he was out of shape, he drank too much, and he suspected repeated exposure to magic probably affected his health as well. He couldn't prove any of that — except the lack of exercise — but he had his suspicions.

Lighting up a cigarette before shouldering another bag of salt, Drummond glanced at the house. The windows were empty, but his skin crawled nonetheless. Even in the daylight, those windows followed him like the eyes of a painting. The house watched. And in the darkness of the windowpanes, he sensed anticipation. Something inside waited.

No — not something. Chief Carter. Drummond did not know how much longer the ghost would wait. He could not be sure how much control Janice had over Carter. But he knew for certain that one or both of them would not wait forever. Opening the salt bag, he got back to work. They had to finish this fast.

Once they completed the circle, Drummond and Catalina met up at the gap facing the front door. He pulled her in close and gave her a long kiss. Pulling back, he gazed at the house, his skin prickling as much from the ghostly energy as from his thoughts of what lay ahead.

"You make sure you have that salt ready," he said. "If all goes well, I'll walk out of there with no problems, but things rarely go well."

"Let me come in with you."

"We have a plan, and we should stick to it." He continued to stare at the house and in a dark tone, he added, "If for any reason I don't come out of that house, you do not come in after me. You need to go straight to your granny. Tell her what happened."

"Don't talk like that."

"And Leroy. You go see him, too. He'll know people who can shut this place down fast. Witches. People we don't want to have to deal with unless there's no other choice."

Though he could feel her fears hovering upon his shoulders like another ghost, he lowered his hat and headed in. His footsteps on the wood porch sounded dead and hollow. The doorknob felt cold. The entire place had become a giant tomb.

If the front door had been locked since the family's death, Janice clearly wanted him in there now. The door opened with ease. As if expecting a shot to ring out, he paused. When nothing happened, he stepped inside.

What he saw did not resemble the house in which he had once interviewed Janice's grandmother. It had never been a charming place, but it had originally felt lived in. Now, the rooms had been gutted. The dark shadows of the house looked like the remnants of a fire. It only lacked the charred odor.

He recalled the kitchen had been set off to the right and the living room to the left. But he doubted Janice would make things so easy. The basement had the conjuring room — a horrible place where the Murphy family had attempted to cast their spell upon Drummond. But he did not think Janice liked the basement all that much. That had been her grandmother's domain.

Drummond gazed up the dark staircase. Janice's room — upstairs, one of the doors would lead to Janice's room. That would be where she felt most comfortable. That would be where she had cast her spell.

Climbing the stairs, Drummond reached for his handgun. He stopped, clicked his tongue, and brought his hand down. A .38 wouldn't do any good against a ghost.

The second floor of the house consisted of a narrow wooden hall with four closed doors. A window at the end brought in a little sunlight, but nothing could alter the gloom surrounding this house. Death and anger permeated the wood.

Drummond tried the first door. The room — empty. Scuff marks, dust-riddled sections, and old blemishes sketched where furniture had once been. The second door. Also empty. Moving further down the hall he noticed where pictures had once hung on the walls — the outlines like ghosts themselves.

The third door turned out to be Janice's bedroom. Like the other rooms, the furniture had been removed, but here a large casting circle had been painted to cover the bare wood floor. Symbols of witchcraft surrounded the edge of the circle. Sitting in the middle — Chief Carter's femur.

Drummond stood in the doorway, his eyes scanning the room over and over. It couldn't be this simple. He glanced back the way he had come, half-expecting to see Janice leading a gang of thugs with baseball bats and a crowbar. Part of him hoped for it. At least, then, Janice would not have cast any spells. She merely would have wanted him beaten up.

But nobody threatened him from the hall. He looked back at the casting circle. He'd seen enough of these to recognize an amateurish job. No doubt in his mind — Janice had done this.

Even the bone had been handled with a lack of professionalism. A real witch would have cleaned the bone. Bits of dirt and chunks of flesh still clung to this one.

Carefully easing his foot into the room, Drummond stayed alert —

his eyes roved across every shadow, his ears perked up at every sound, he even sniffed the air for subtle changes. But nothing happened.

It didn't make sense. Why had the haunting stopped? Chief Carter had attacked them several times, but as soon as Drummond zeroed in on the Murphy house, the attacks stopped. Janice wanted him here, that much was clear, yet nothing more had happened. The constant cold in the air spoke of ghosts, yet none had manifested.

"Chief Carter?"

No answer.

Drummond stepped fully into the room. When nothing attacked him and he could sense no change in the air, he walked along the edges. Careful not to touch the circle, he checked the closets and windows.

But he knew he was stalling. The longer he went unmolested, the more his fingers tapped along his side, the more he held his breath, the more he perspired. Only one answer came to mind, and he did not like it. The spell — the trap — waited for him to take that bone. Until then, all would remain safe, calm, and quiet. But if he simply walked away, left the house and resumed his life, Janice would unleash Chief Carter once again.

"Okay, you win. Let's see what you've got." Drummond stepped over to the circle, crouched down, and picked up the bone.

A shard of ice cut through his brain. He arched back, his mouth locked open in agony. The frozen blade pushed deep into his head creating a blinding migraine that brought him to his knees. Gasping, he cradled the bone close to his chest.

Moments later, the pain disappeared. The icy attack had been removed. But Drummond knew not to get hopeful. As if in response to that thought, an invisible force slammed into his face, rocking him onto his back. Blood gushed from his nose, and he struggled to get to his feet.

Bluish flames sparked to life on the walls and crawled across the ceiling like undulating tentacles of fire. They created no heat but gave off a horrendous stench. Drummond did not want to find out what would happen if he came into direct contact with them.

Before the flames could reach the doorway, he sprinted for the hall. When he stepped into the corridor, Janice's bedroom door slammed behind him. He tried to move forward. Something grabbed hold of him and pulled him against the back wall. Down the hallway, out of the dark, emerged a spectral head — stretched from floor to ceiling. A pale, ghostly light emanated from the head as its skin shredded away from the mouth. Jagged teeth remained in their constant skeletal grin.

A revolting moan coursed through the walls. It made Drummond think of a man with his tongue cut out. It made him think of the wet, hard sound of maggots crawling over each other. It made him think of retching. The sound wormed its way into his brain, causing pain equal to the icy blade he had suffered only moments before.

As his stomach twisted, his grip weakened. Chief Carter's femur dropped to the floor. The head disappeared. The force holding Drummond against the wall released. He fell to his knees, and the terrible sound stopped.

"Marshall?" a voice sang out. "Marshall, where are you?"

Drummond knew the voice. Knew it wasn't real. Knew he had to ignore it.

"Marshall?"

"You're not here, Mother. I know you're alive." He tried to stand but his legs would not offer support. He feared if he picked up the bone, then the full force of evil in the house would come upon him once more. So, he crawled. Nudging the bone in front of him, he crawled down the hallway. And all the time, the voice of his mother called out to him, prodding him, begging for his attention.

Never. Acknowledging a specter like that would give it power. Drummond pushed aside all thoughts of his mother, of Chief Carter, of the house, of the cold, of the evil surrounding his every movement. He merely brought his knee forward and pushed his body a few feet down the hall. With his knuckles, he shoved the bone further on. Drag his body, push the bone. Drag, push. Drag, push. Drag ...

With one final push, he sent the bone careening down the stairs like a drunk. His mother's voice shrieked. Back on his feet, Drummond followed the bone toward the bottom.

As the high-pitched wail settled down, it distorted into a voice part-human, part-beast. "You think that is going to save you? You think you're ever getting out of here?"

The stairs wobbled under his feet. Or perhaps his legs did the wobbling. Pressure built around Drummond's head. He bumped to the side, the handrail digging into his ribs. Each step closer to the first floor thickened the strange sensations. Wooziness weaved through his thoughts. He tried to draw a breath but nothing entered his lungs. His eyes rolled up and his body dropped.

The world muted around him. When he next opened his eyes, his cheek pressed into the floor. His legs stretched straight against the stairs while the rest of him had reached the bottom. The angry bruises on his chin, shoulders, chest, and spine answered any question he had towards what had happened. He fell. Hard.

With gentle care he got his legs under and managed to stand once again. Nothing broken. Not dead, either. Both good signs. At least, he hoped they were good signs. Either he had been lucky in his fall or the things that Janice brought into this house to torment him had no intention of letting him escape through death.

The front door stood only ten feet away, and the bone had stopped halfway along the floor. Drummond consider making a run for it, but the burning in his right leg muscles suggested more damage had been done then he had first thought. Though running appeared to be out of the question, he could not remain standing there.

"Aw, the hell with it," he said and started moving.

His first steps sent jolts from his feet right up his spine. Limping helped a little. If he was willing to ruin his leg further, he thought he might be able to run for a short distance. And to reach the front door, he only needed a short distance.

As he neared the bone, blurry shapes fluttered off to the sides. Turning his head in that direction, he found nothing. But the second he refocused on the bone, the shapes reappeared. They were real. They were there. He had no doubt.

Another step closer.

He heard a car drive by and the gleeful shouts of children running along the sidewalk, oblivious to the terrible things happening so near.

Five feet — maybe six. He simply had to pick up the bone and run.

He could feel the ghosts surrounding him. The other things, too — the nameless spirits, half-ghosts, and other forms of dead that he had not encountered yet to know what to call them. Janice had summoned everything she could, stashed it all in this house, and waited for Drummond to foolishly enter.

She must really hate me.

He crouched in front of the bone, and he could hear the house inhale. It was a runner setting into the blocks, anxious to hear that starter pistol. He glanced ahead at the five feet he would have to race to reach the front door finish line. The temperature of the house dropped a few degrees. He licked his lips, rolled his shoulders, and reached for the bone.

Launching into as much of a sprint as his body would allow, Drummond bolted for the front door. But the world twisted around him. Like running through a kaleidoscopic hallucination, a funhouse hall of mirrors, and a horrific nightmare of a psychotic mind all rolled together, the walls bled and the ceiling mutated into an angry, snake-filled mouth. Ice cold hands grabbed at his feet while tentacles smelling of sulfur slithered across his shoulders. Screams howled like coyotes crying in the night.

Drummond focused on the small cracks of sunlight cutting through the edges of the front door. That became his world. Five feet, he reminded himself. Five feet towards that little glimpse of light.

"You've left me to waste away in a nuthouse," his mother's voice cried out.

"You killed us," a guttural growl announced. "It's because of you we're here."

Drummond could not identify the voice nor did he want to. The spirits wanted him to look away, wanted him to step toward them. Just one step. Anything off the path to the front door and he might be lost forever.

He could not feel his heart beating. He could not recall the last breath he took. He only knew the cold on his skin and that sliver of light before his eyes. While it seemed to last hours, the part of his brain clinging to reason and rationality knew he had crossed those five feet in mere steps. Faster than the otherworldly creatures could grab hold of his body. Faster than the hallucinations ripped from his dark thoughts could seize his mind. He opened the front door and sunlight burst through. Even brighter — he saw Catalina's smile.

His joy lasted only a brief second. He stumbled forth onto the lawn, the chill sliding along his back. Catalina's smile faltered, and Drummond wondered exactly how bad he looked. No time for such thoughts, though. The ghosts had caught up to him.

Their cold touched his skin and reached deep into the bone. His teeth chattered. The pathways in his brain felt as if they had shrunk. He fell to his knees.

He could see Catalina reaching towards him, yelling at him. But the words came out garbled to his ears.

Through thick and muddy thoughts, he managed to recall that he held the bone. That all of this had been about the bone. That he was supposed to do something with it — if only the cold would leave his brain. That sharp, painful cold.

He doubled over, wanting to throw up, and the thought of the hot liquid racing up his throat, how warm that would make his body feel, cleared his mind for a few seconds. Enough time to recognize his situation. Without pause, he swung his arm back and hurled the bone high into the air.

It landed several feet beyond Catalina. He smiled at her. The instant the bone left his hand, the shivering touches of the ghosts withdrew. But he had no illusions that they would let him go.

"Close the circle," he said.

Waving urgently, Catalina said, "Get over here. We'll close it together."

But Drummond did not move. His heart cut under his chest and tears wet his eyes. "The only reason they haven't tried to get away is because I am right here. All of this has been set up by Janice Murphy against me. If I cross the circle, they'll come with me. Do what you came here to do. Get the salt and close the circle."

"No," Catalina whispered, her head shaking as much as her voice.

"Do it. Close the circle. Take the bone, go to your *abuela*. She has to finish this."

She smashed her palm at the tears on her cheeks. "Just walk over here. It's only a few more feet."

Drummond stood straight and firm. He didn't know how much longer the spirits surrounding him would stay interested. Soon they would realize the way out stood open. They could leave, and they would. Catalina stared back at him, and he saw the answer in her eyes — she would do what he asked. She understood.

"I love you," he said.

He turned away and limped back toward the house. He could hear her crying, hear her frustrated scream, but he closed his eyes in thanks — he did not hear her follow him. As he climbed onto the front porch, he knew she finished the salt circle. She would pick up the bone. She would head home to her granny. That old woman would know how to neutralize the spell upon Chief Carter, but that would not end the haunting Janice had placed upon Drummond.

That was the other reason he had turned back. Because though he did not touch the bone anymore, he could still feel the presence of evil. What he knew of witchcraft suggested that when Mrs. Medina dispelled the bone, he would need to be ready with a final strike against the remaining spirits. They were connected to that bone through Janice's poor magic. They could be destroyed through the same.

In other circumstances, he would have set dynamite on a long fuse. Time it right and the house would go up, purifying the spirits in fire. But that would not work since he was locked in the house, too. Well, it would work, but he still hoped to live through the experience. Plus, he didn't have any dynamite on him.

Salt and holy water would also cleanse spirts, but again he lacked the materials — the former sat in a circle outside, the latter he neglected to bring. In fact, he could only think of one thing he had available to purify with — his blood.

Stepping into the house, his eyes roving along the walls and ceiling, he whispered, "This won't be any fun." At least the hallucinations had left. The house looked like a house again.

He had time but not infinite. Catalina would be driving as fast as possible and though there would be traffic, she would manage to get home soon. Which meant he needed to find where Janice had hidden her totems — pieces of the spirits, like Chief Carter's femur, or specially made objects spelled to connect with the ghost world.

A frosty streak sliced across his chest. He grimaced. It hurt, but without the cursed bone in contact with him, those spirits had far less power. He did not fool himself into thinking he could not be killed, but at the least, it seemed he would not have to see their dark manifestations. He hoped his assumptions would be true.

A hard blow to his back shoved him ahead several steps. "Okay, okay. You can hurt me more than a little." He opened his mouth for a few more sarcastic comments but halted. He did not have time to play defense. He had to find those totems.

He knew they were in the house. They had to be. Otherwise, the spirits would have located somewhere else long before he and Catalina had arrived. Cursed ghosts tended to be tethered to the places they died, the spell that cursed them, or the object they were cursed upon. Two out of three of those options pointed to this house.

Another arctic punch hit him in the gut, sending a wave of cold up his throat. Coughing, he fought the pain under his ribs and took in as much air as he could manage. These ghosts were toying with him. Soon, however, their attacks would escalate. They always did.

Since most of the house had been gutted, he did not have to worry about searching the furniture. Perhaps she had hidden the items within the walls or the floorboards or even the ceiling. No. Back when they first met, Janice Murphy had been a meager, sheltered girl looking for love. She only wanted a husband. Using magic to achieve that goal was her downfall. And though her impassioned anger focused on Drummond for vengeance, he did not see her suddenly gaining the skills to rip open a wall, use a hammer and nails, have the knowledge of basic house architecture, or even the foresight to hide things in such a manner.

The next attack struck at his knees. He fell over, yelling as he grabbed hold of his bad leg. He didn't know if they could read his mind — he had no idea if such a thing was possible — but it sure appeared as if they disliked where his thoughts had led him.

And if he was on the right track, then the totems he sought would be in plain sight. Gasping as he got back to his feet, and making sure to favor his good leg, he hobbled toward the stairs.

Janice's room did not have the totems. That had been the exclusive area for Chief Carter's curse. But there were three other doors up there. All empty rooms — unless he missed something.

Gazing up the dark stairwell, Drummond paused to think. Janice had used her own room as a personal point of power in the house and it only controlled the one ghost — Chief Carter. If she could have gained dominance over more than that one from her bedroom, she would have. So, she needed a far more powerful room to take control of numerous spirits. He turned away from the stairs and headed toward the kitchen — toward the basement stairs.

Sylvia Murphy, Janice's grandmother, had performed all their serious magic down in that dank, barren basement. Janice and her sister must have spent hours of their lives down there. They would have witnessed all the unique, startling, wondrous, and horrific aspects of magic in that one room. The basement would be perfect for the kind of dangerous spell Janice wanted to perform. Good for hiding her work, too — especially from Drummond. Based on his own terrible experiences down there, she would assume he would avoid that part of the house as much as possible.

To some extent, she had been right.

As he walked through the empty kitchen, the wall-mounted cabinets rattled. As if struck by an earthquake, the entire kitchen erupted into violent shaking. The cabinet doors flung open and closed. One ripped off its hinge and spiraled toward Drummond's head. He ducked and the cabinet door cut into the wall. Chipped pieces of floor spewed outward like shrapnel. A vile odor like raw sewage sifted through the air.

Drummond tried to step toward the basement, but his bad leg did not follow. His limp caused too much pain. Glancing down, he saw a large splinter of cabinet wood sticking out of his calf. He pressed up against the wall, and rested his head, taking a moment to just breathe. Sweat soaked his collar. Then, moving as fast as his body would allow, he reached down, snatched the wood, and yanked it out. He groaned and spit on the ground.

With his leg dragging behind and his arm supporting him against the wall, he made his way to the basement door. The quaking room settled. Glancing back, he saw a thin line of blood marking his trail. Could have been worse — at least, he didn't think he'd bleed out from that.

He opened the basement door and stared at the steep staircase down. He uttered a few choice swears before finishing with a simple, "Perfect."

Closing his eyes, he pictured Catalina. Had she reached her apartment yet? Was Mrs. Medina working whatever skills she had to save him? Or perhaps the old woman decided that since he and Catalina would not break off their relationship, she would do it for them.

The stairs beckoned him like the open mouth of a shark, the uneven wooden steps like the beast's jagged teeth. Putting most of his weight on the handrail, he hopped down once, then again.

"Hey, ghosts," he said as he dropped down another step. "I know you're having fun tearing me apart." Another hop. "But just remember that if you knock me down the stairs, I'll probably be dead." Another hop. "You do that, you won't have any more fun with me. Trust me on this, it's no fun to torture a corpse."

As the basement came into view, he saw the large casting circle marked with seven black candles. They were thick enough to burn a long time — all night, probably. In front of each candle, situated within the circle, Drummond spotted the totems — cloth from a shirt, a tooth, several sticks fashioned into a doll, some hair tied in a pink bow, a pencil with teeth marks, a wood pipe, and a photograph.

"Well, well. I hate to tell you this, but I think you all are screwed."

The answer came not with a frosty punch or a simple pain-inducing strike. Rather his feet left the ground. The spirits hauled him into the air and flung him onto the floor. He tucked his head saving himself a cracked neck at the last moment. Dust sailed into the air, and Drummond uttered a harsh grunt.

He did not bother getting back on his feet — they would only knock him down again. Instead, he crawled across the floor, heading for the circle. With a nasty chuckle, he said, "Y'all better be careful. You throw me like that again, and you might accidentally blow out your own candles."

That clearly gave them pause for he managed to crawl several feet without trouble. Unfortunately, they overcame whatever fears stayed their hand, and as Drummond reached the edge of the circle, he felt bitter cold cut into his head. The pain flattened him to the floor and he tasted blood on his lips.

Steady pulsing waves of heat and cold surged through his head and threatened to knock him unconscious. Just when he thought sweet oblivion would take over, the attack halted, only to be replaced with a similar attack on his wrecked leg. As he bellowed and cried, he swore he heard laughter echoing around him.

"Catalina!" He wanted her to hurry up, wanted her *abuela* to end this torture, but could only manage to call her name again.

Sweat broke over his body, chilling his skin. The attack on his leg ended — even ghosts had to take a break. Shuddering, Drummond got up on his hands and good knee and proceeded to crawl into the circle. Once there, he collapsed to his side. Breathing heavily, nose running, sweat wetting through his shirt — he allowed himself one minute to rest.

But the floor rumbled, and Drummond braced for another quaking attack. Nothing came. He lifted his head and gazed around the dark basement. He could feel their presence — the ghosts and spirits — as they hovered at the edges of the room.

Catalina? Mrs. Medina?

Pushing aside the raw aches that filled every movement, Drummond pressed against the floor until he rose to a seated position. His bad leg stuck out at an odd angle like a ragdoll losing its stitching. A dark stain bloomed around the knee.

The house rumbled again, and he heard a strange moan from the spirits. A startled moan. A moan of fear. Definitely Catalina, then. She must have reached her granny and they had begun the process. He did not have much time left to do his part.

Digging around his coat pocket, he produced a small knife. As he cut into his pant leg, he sensed the agitation of the ghosts growing. Like him, they recognized the shift in the air. They knew something had happened in the house around them, but they didn't know what. Drummond had no intention of telling them that Chief Carter's curse unraveled upstairs in Janice's room. Revealing that truth just to gloat was the mark of a fool or an amateur. Instead, he focused on the task at hand.

With a good length sliced into his pant leg, Drummond grabbed the two ends and ripped the fabric all the way to the ankle. He tried not to look at the mangled, deformed object that had been his leg. For the moment, he did not care about it — only what it could do for him.

He reached over and dipped his fingers in the dark liquid pooling near his knee. Sufficiently soaked, he stretched toward the cloth totem and painted across it with his finger.

He did not know what words to say, but everything Leroy Parker had taught him suggested that the words themselves did not matter. Circles, symbols, and words existed to help focus the intention of a spell. He needed no help this time — his intention pulsed out of every pore in his body. He picked up the bloody cloth and held it over its candle, his focus fully on destroying the vile thing.

As the flames consumed it, he heard a soft pop. The thought struck him — *Was that it?* — when a horrid whine rippled through the room. The walls rumbled again, and this time the remaining spirits took up their cries like a lamenting Greek chorus.

Drummond ignored the sounds, focusing on each step of his task — reach over to his knee, coat his fingers with his blood, reach over to the next totem, douse the totem with the blood, burn it with its own candle's flame.

The temperature plummeted as the ghosts worked together to stop him. They could not touch him within the circle, and even if they could, they would not dare risk disrupting the spell that let them live, but if they could freeze the room, slow him down, break him, then perhaps they might survive a little longer. At least, that was Drummond's supposition of what went on in a ghost's mind. Another dip of blood, another burning totem, another pop and cry.

Drummond could see his breath puffing in white mist. Frost formed along the moisture of the walls. He shivered, and his fingers shook as he dipped for more blood. If it got cold enough, perhaps he would have trouble getting the blood to flow. If that didn't stop him, the incessant howling would drive him crazy and do the trick. Like a disorganized song, the remaining spirits bayed and bawled, filling the air with their erratic sorrow.

"I'm trying to help you," Drummond said as he took the old photograph soaked with his blood over the flame. "I want to free you from being cursed. Show some gratitude."

As the temperature continued to dwindle downward, Drummond's thoughts slowed. His movements, too. His eyelids grew heavy and he hugged his arms close against the cold.

Two more. He had two more of something to do, but his mind had trouble focusing on the process or the purpose. The world had frozen around him. The only good side: the extreme cold had numbed his leg.

A little rest. Yes. He needed to rest for a bit, and then he would finish whatever he meant to be doing.

With a loud crack like thunder hitting directly overhead, the entire house shifted. Drummond startled awake, his heart pounding against his ribs. "Focus," he commanded and emptied all his energy into finishing those last two totems. At least, then, there would be quiet.

DRUMMOND OPENED HIS EYES to a white room with bright sunlight and murmured voices. Despite his foray into the paranormal, he had no clear idea what the afterlife might be like. One sharp sniff, however, told him exactly where he had ended up — a hospital.

"He's awake," Catalina's sweet voice said.

And there she was. Standing over him, smiling down, caressing his cheek with her hand. Lifting his head, he saw Mrs. Medina sitting in a chair next to the hospital room window, her arms folded, her scowl severe.

"How long?"

"Just a day. The doctors gave you some pretty strong stuff to keep you asleep while they worked."

He glanced down — a large cast covered his right leg. "I guess that's a good sign."

"You'll walk again. But on crutches for a while."

"And Carter?"

Catalina gestured toward her *abuela.* "All taken care of."

"Then that only leaves Janice. Right? I did take care of all the totems?"

"You did. But don't worry about Janice or any of it right now. Just focus on getting better."

Drummond squinted. "Why are you being so nice to me? I expected you to be angry."

"Oh, don't worry, I'm furious with you. When I got down to that basement and found you lying in a pool of blood, your leg bent all crazy, I was so mad I nearly broke the other one." She leaned close. "But love makes you do crazy things."

A nurse walked in, and Catalina immediately pushed back to stand by her grandmother. Mrs. Medina glanced at Drummond with a raised eyebrow. Catalina understood how the world would see their relationship. If he loved her, shouldn't he want to protect her from the judgment of the nurses, the diner customers, the housewives? From everybody who thought they shouldn't be together because of differing backgrounds? Whatever Mrs. Medina saw on his face as a response, she did not approve. With a dismissive sniffle, she looked away.

But Drummond had been haunted by enough for the last few days. He leaned his head back, let the nurse do her work, closed his eyes, and decided to take Catalina's advice. For now, he would rest and get healthy. The rest of his problems would have to wait.

CASE 09

THE BLOOD WITCH

OF THE MANY THINGS MARSHALL DRUMMOND HAD LEARNED since becoming the private detective of the bizarre for Winston-Salem, one stood out to be as important as the golden rule — never trust a witch. When negotiating, when partnering, and especially when fighting, a witch only ever held one allegiance — herself. So, when Drummond entered his office one autumn afternoon and found a young, beautiful witch patiently waiting for his arrival, warnings flashed throughout his brain.

"It's one-thirty," she said with a thick Carolina accent. "You always take such a leisurely lunch?"

Removing his Fedora and long coat, Drummond said, "I've only been back on my feet a couple weeks. Just trying to appreciate walking again."

His previous case had mangled his right leg and stuck him on crutches for two months. Catalina, his beautiful gal, played nurse for about a week, but she had to get back to working at Raymond's Diner. Her two boys and her *abuela* relied on her to earn income. Plus, she tried to be careful about her relationship with Drummond becoming too obvious — the sensibilities of modern man had come a long way, but too many people would frown upon a white man and a Mexican woman together. Even in 1932.

"Tell me, what could I possibly do for a witch?" Drummond eased behind his old desk. Casually, he slipped his hand underneath to rest upon the grip of his .38 sitting in the gun tray and aimed directly at his guest.

She raised an amused eyebrow. "My, my. What gives me away?"

The small earring studs that, when looked at closely, resembled pentagrams. The large handbag overflowing with horded clutter. The black nails and the smell of burnt leaves. Most of all, Drummond had come to know the unique look in a witch's eye — as if the world had told her a secret she could barely contain blabbing to everybody she met.

"Nothing really," he said. "Just a good guess, I suppose. Question still stands — what is it that brings you to my door?"

"I should think that's obvious."

"Sorry. I don't work for witches."

"That's because you are a smart lad. Handsome, too." As she spoke, she rummaged through her large bag. A moment later, she plunked a heavy book onto the desk. "You'll need that book."

Keeping his eyes on the witch, he said, "And why is that?"

"Well, do you believe in prognostication?"

"Ever since I started dealing with witches and ghosts, I've learned not to discount anything too fast. I take it, then, that you can see the future."

She shook her head with a deep smile. "But I've tried. People tend to think it's an easy thing to do. Beginner magic. But that's far from the truth. The universe does not like to give up her secrets. And even if you succeed at peeking into tomorrow, there are so many variables that can change the outcome. All you ever truly glimpse is one possible future."

"And you saw something involving me? Something that required you to bring me this book?"

Gathering her things together, the witch stood. "I know you'll not believe a word I say, but the truth is the truth. Not all witches are bent on causing harm. Some of us just want to be left alone to study our spells and live our lives. Now, far be it from me to meddle in the affairs of others, but I find myself in a predicament which I hope this book will help prevent. You see, while practicing my prognostication, I saw a horrible time ahead. It was a fleeting glimpse — no more — but it was enough to frighten me. It was enough to make me take the trip all the way here and give you that book. I can't tell you how any of it will work out, but I promise you this — later today, you will be starting a new case, and it will bring you up against a horrible and powerful adversary. It is my hope that my little gift to you will tip the scales."

Still keeping his eyes on her, he drummed his fingers on the desk. "That book is going to help me live through a tough fight?"

"Oh, I don't make such claims. I don't even care if you live or die. I only know that if I don't interfere, the outcome will be far worse for all of us. For me, in particular. This person you are up against is not entirely sane, and the result of allowing such a person to continue their madness — well, in this case, it may cause certain troubles for the witch community." She shouldered her bag and headed toward the door.

"Hold on. I don't even have your name."

She paused in the doorway. "Now why would I ever give you that kind of power over me?"

"What if I need to speak with you? I've got to have something to call you. Unless you want me yelling *Hey witch* all around town."

"I don't hope to ever see you again." She chuckled. "Then again, our paths may cross more than I'd like. Shoot, I guess you need some kind of name. You can call me Miss Fox."

"Ah, going for the pretentious alias."

"Pretentious yet still dangerous. Watch what you say." She clicked her nails against the doorframe as she left the office.

Drummond finally looked down at the book. Wrongness pulsed out of it. The cover had a flaking texture — cowhide that had seen too much sun — and tiny beads of various colors lined the edges like encrusted jewels. The title had been written in a fanciful hand, but Drummond could not read the language — a hint of Korean or possibly Japanese, but there were too many sudden swirls in the script to be either. Probably some language long forgotten by all but the witches.

He walked over to his bookshelf and pulled out *Moby Dick*. Inside, he kept a flask of whiskey at the ready. After taking a swig, he returned the flask and the book before sitting at his desk again. And perhaps it would have ended there. Perhaps the warnings from Miss Fox would have proven false, and Drummond could have moved on with his life. But the first of two terrible things happened — his phone rang.

Before Drummond could offer any form of greeting, Leroy Parker's static-filled voice said, "We got a problem."

Leroy had helped Drummond on a few cases. The old black man spent most of his time reading up on anything to do with the supernatural. He was the closest thing Drummond had to an official expert, and considering Leroy's high intelligence, he was all Drummond had ever needed.

The worry in the man's voice prickled Drummond's skin. Coupled with the fact that Leroy did not have a phone in his house, that he lived far from any convenience, that he had to have gone out of his way to make this call, turned the whiskey in Drummond's stomach into a whiskey sour. "What's happened?"

"I got jumped last night. In my own damn home."

"You okay?"

"What kind of stupid question is that? 'Course I'm not okay. You think I'd want to leave my house and drive all the way to the store so I could make a call to talk to you if everything was okay?"

Even though Drummond knew Leroy could not see him, he fought back the grin rising on his lips — cantankerous as ever. "Sorry. You need anything from me?"

"You think I'm calling you just to let you know that something happened to me? Dang fool. What's the matter with you? I'm the one that got popped on the head. Why are you acting like an idiot?"

Drummond sat straighter in his chair as the situation started to click into place. Leroy lived in the woods far off near Mocksville. Nobody would just happen upon his place and decide to rob the old man. Whoever did this had targeted Leroy, and Leroy only had one thing of value — his library of witchcraft.

"What did they take?" Drummond asked.

That direct question calmed Leroy. He always appreciated honest and logical thinking. "A book. Only one. But it's a bad one."

Drummond's eyes shifted to the book on his desk. "It wouldn't happen to be covered in rotting leather and have cheap, fake gems around it."

"How did you know that?"

"You better get over to my office."

AN HOUR LATER, Leroy sat next to Drummond and stared at the book. For several minutes, neither man said a word. After several minutes more, Drummond guessed Leroy might take a while, so he poured them both a glass of whiskey and leaned back in his chair.

Without taking his eyes off the book, Leroy reached over and picked up his glass. He sipped the whiskey, set the glass back, and leaned closer to inspect the spine of the book. "She just came in here and dropped this off?"

"Told me she could see the future. I was wondering if this book is meant to help me or hurt me."

For the first time since arriving in the office, Leroy looked up from the book. "She's a witch. You really have to wonder?"

"It's your book. You tell me? What's it for?"

Leroy sipped more of his whiskey before finally easing back in the chair. "This book was a grimoire belonging to a witch coven. They're no longer around — a few members died and the rest dispersed to join other covens."

"A grimoire? That's like their spell book, right?"

"Spell book, rulebook, everything book — all that's important to keeping a coven running."

Drummond pursed his lips. "How come you have it?"

"There was a bookshop on East 10th Street about five years ago. Phil, the owner, he had just gotten into the stock market around '28. Crash destroyed him. Took the store out, too. But back before all that, I'd frequent the place. They often had very rare and unique texts."

"And this bookshop, operating in the open in downtown Winston-Salem, just happens to be selling grimoires?"

"Phil had no idea what he was selling. More than the Crash, his incompetence is probably why the bookstore is no more. So, yeah, that's where I got this book. And here's the kicker — I can see that there are a couple pages missing."

Drummond froze as Leroy's words sunk in. "You sure?"

"This book belongs to me. What do you think? I looked through it many times. Based on how wide the spine is, there should be two maybe three more pages in the middle. For cryin' out loud, you can practically stick your finger through the gap."

Ignoring the hyperbole, Drummond sat forward and peered at the book, trying to discern the same clues Leroy had picked up on to prove there were missing pages. "How long are you going to make me sit here and wait for you to open this thing?"

With a scoffing chuckle, Leroy said, "Either this witch or somebody working for her came to my place, conked me on the head, and stole this book. Then she brings it to you and drops it off. And in between those two moments, this witch or somebody working for her has removed a handful of pages. And you want me to simply open the book? Are you out of your damn mind?"

"I can't just leave it here on my desk."

Leroy stayed quiet for a moment as he thought. At length, he said, "You have any salt?"

"No."

"Are you kidding me? You deal with ghosts and magic all the time and you don't have salt on hand? It's amazing you're still alive."

"I've got a little holy water from an older case. You want that?"

"We need salt. And a pure white candle. Get me those things and we'll cast us a little spell to make sure this book is okay."

As Leroy muttered at Drummond's incompetence, Drummond donned his hat and coat and headed out of the building. He strolled up to the corner store on 5th Street. The bustle of the city swarmed around him with men smoking pipes and cigarettes as they stomped up or down the street. Women walked together gabbing while others pushed carriages with their babies for an early autumn stroll. Cars weaved around on the road honking at each other like geese while two boys played tag around the adults.

It all looked so normal.

Yet just a few buildings behind Drummond, a witch's book sat on his desk. Just a few buildings behind him, a man waited for the tools necessary to cast a bit of magic. There had always been more than one world and few ever saw beneath the surface layer. Drummond often wondered if he would prefer to go back to being one of these people trudging through their days, worrying about food and money and love, but never having to fear the unseen, the unknown, the hints of power beyond anything a human being could or should tap into.

After he purchased the salt and candle, he tried to clear his head on the walk back. The weight of the salt refused to let his mind wander. It kept him thinking about the strange world he lived in. The dark and nasty people who populated it. The way it drowned those around him with the same horrors he faced regularly. People like Leroy. Or Catalina.

When he entered the office, Leroy grabbed the shopping bag and quickly drew a salt circle around the book. He then quartered the circle with salt lines right across the top of the book. After lighting the candle, he dripped wax at the crossroads on the center of the book and stuck the candle secure in the wax.

This was the reason — more than any other — that Leroy lived hidden in the woods. He knew witchcraft. He knew their techniques, their secrets, their spells. If not for his morality keeping him in check, Drummond suspected the old man could out-witch even the strongest of witches.

Leroy put his hands above the flame, closed his eyes, and mouthed words that Drummond could not hear. It lasted only a handful of seconds. The flame flashed red before blowing out. As gray wisps of smoke trailed upward, Leroy lowered his arms and relaxed his shoulders.

"It's safe now," he said.

Drummond stepped further in and realized he still wore his coat and hat. Taking them off, he said, "So there was some kind of spell on that book after all. That witch brought it here as a trap."

"Maybe. It's also possible that she needed to cast a spell on the book in order to remove the pages, and I simply removed the residual of that spell. No way to know for sure except to ask her."

"With any luck, that won't happen." Drummond walked over to his desk. "Should we open the book? See what pages are missing?"

Leroy removed the candle and brushed the salt aside. Drummond had never been too fastidious about his office, but he cringed nonetheless as salt sprayed across his floor. No time to complain, though. Leroy opened the book.

Drummond leapt back like a housewife terrified by a mouse. "You could warn a guy before you open the book that might kill us all."

"Quit your whining and have a little faith in me. I wouldn't have touched it if it was that dangerous."

Finding his heartbeat again, Drummond approached the desk. "Well?"

Leroy had the book opened flat. Three ragged edges poked out from the spine where the three pages had been torn. Leroy stuck his nose close into the spine has he inspected the book.

"I remember this now." He sat back and finished his glass of whiskey.

"And? What did the witch take out of the book?"

"No idea."

"But you just said —"

"I remember this book because it was a big pain trying to translate. Witches use a lot of old and long-forgotten languages, but some of these covens — especially when writing in their grimoires — mix-and-match their languages. Heck, some of them make up their own. And if they're really paranoid about protecting their coven secrets, they'll use a mixture of languages and then put it all in code. I worked on this book for a couple months several years back."

"I take it you didn't succeed."

"Go sit on a wasp's nest — I'm no quitter. I certainly did succeed. But, it was rather time-consuming and I had other things to do. And frankly, the opening pages were rather boring."

Running his finger over the remnants of the torn pages, Drummond said, "Clearly, this part wasn't."

"If we're lucky, the page we have before the torn section and the page after might clue us in as to what was taken."

"You still remember the code?"

"Do I still remember the code?" He thrust his empty glass at Drummond. "Make yourself useful." Grumbling to himself, Leroy grabbed a pencil out of Drummond's desk and a piece of paper. "Don't you dare hover over me while I'm working on this. It's going to take a while."

After filling up Leroy's glass, Drummond set it on the desk and donned his hat and coat. As he climbed downstairs, his intoxicatingly lovely girlfriend walked up.

"Catalina? I was just on my way over to the diner to see you."

She still wore her waitressing outfit and smelled of cigarettes and sandwiches. Drummond put his hand on her waist and tilted his head for a kiss. But her brown skin had paled and her eyes glistened with tears.

"What's the matter?" he asked.

And that began the second terrible thing to happen that day.

* * * *

THERE WERE PLENTY OF THINGS about North Carolina weather to despise, but autumn was never among them. If not for the urgency in Catalina's voice and the concerned frown on her face, Drummond would have been content to drive in silence and enjoy the cool air swirling around the car. But 1932 did not appear to be the year of contentment for Drummond.

"I'm sorry to be bringing this to you," she said. "Especially because I doubt anybody can pay you. But if you don't take a look into this, nobody will."

He reached over and put his hand on her arm. "It's me. If you can't bring me a case, then what am I good for?"

"Don't start acting noble just yet. I can bring you a lot of trouble."

With bright warmth in his voice, he said, "We've been through enough already. You should know I'm always here for you."

"Good — because this is bad." She took a deep breath and as she spoke, her fingers rolled and unrolled the edge of her waitress apron. "There's a group of Mexican laborers working out in some fields near Greensboro. One of those workers is a friend of *mi abuela*."

Drummond snickered. "A friend?"

"Not like that."

Of course, Drummond knew that Catalina's grandmother would never take a lover. Not even a casual boyfriend to walk in a park with. Though her husband had passed away many years ago, she still mourned his death and wore all black all the time. Drummond had merely been trying to lighten the mood, but the stern tightness on Catalina's brow told him the time had come to be quiet and listen.

"His name is Roberto." She arched back her shoulders and focused on the road ahead. "The field hands don't make a lot of money, so when he called, you know it had to be important. They have to pay for their calls.

"He's worked this farm on and off for many years. Last week, a younger man named Matteo disappeared. This is not so strange — plenty of times workers leave without notice. Sometimes they find better jobs. Sometimes they have family problems. And of course, sometimes they are on the run from the law. But Roberto said that this was not true of Matteo. He was a good kid and seemed to be very excited about the money he could earn working that field for the next month."

Drummond rolled his window down further and lit a cigarette. "You think this boy's been kidnapped?"

She lowered her head and swallowed a short whimper. With a sharp sniffle, she said, "Yesterday, in the fields, the workers found the boy's arm. No other limbs. Just his arm. And, well, in his hand, they found his heart."

Catalina covered her face and sobbed. Drummond smoked his cigarette. She needed to get this out and he needed to think. It was a strange way to murder somebody — clearly leaving a message behind. He did not know of any witch rituals that involved this type of behavior, but Leroy would be a better resource for that answer.

And, of course, there was the matter of the book. The witch's arrival, the missing pages, and now this murdered boy — even the most green detective would guess that these things were connected. "This boy's arm and heart were found yesterday?"

"Yes. Roberto called *mi abuela* late last night and she spent most of today deliberating what to do about it. She called me right before my shift ended, and that's when I came to you."

"Do we know how far the police of gone in their investigation? Do we know who the detective is on the case?"

She gazed over at him with unveiled disgust. "Don't you understand? Don't you see why I'm asking you to look into this?"

"Because this is a strange murder that clearly has some kind of witch connection."

"I don't know about that. Maybe it does, maybe not. But do you really think the police are going to care at all about the murder of a Mexican field hand? Haven't you spent enough time with me to know a little about the world I live in?"

"Of course. I'm sorry. I didn't mean it like that."

"But you did. You just didn't realize it."

Drummond knew he had stepped in something foul and accidentally spread it all around him, but his screw-up did not change the current problem. "Okay, the police won't look into this. That's why you need me. Were the police even notified?"

"I doubt it. If they notify the police, all work would be stopped, and these people cannot afford to miss a day's pay. They'll be waiting for us after the sun goes down. The farmer has a few crappy little shacks he lets them live in while they work his land. We'll meet them there. Unless you'd rather ignore them like the rest of the world."

Drummond did not take the bait. Instead, he threw the last of his cigarette out the window, exhaled a cloud of smoke, and finished the drive to Greensboro in silence.

THEY HAD TO WAIT over an hour before the workers came in from the fields. Drummond tried to engage conversation with Catalina but either she had not forgiven him for his insensitive comment or she worried too much about the murder. Probably both.

As the field hands cleaned up and tried to unwind, a few of the wives brought out food they had been preparing. A large circle formed as all the workers ate in a group.

Drummond suspected that on a normal night, there would be plenty of conversation, laughter, possibly even music. But not this night. As he and Catalina walked up to the circle, the folks ate with a solemn attitude. A few murmured words of Spanish drifted between them while plenty of suspicious eyes watched Drummond's arrival.

Though Drummond's Spanish had improved being around Catalina, he did not want to insult them by attempting to communicate in their own tongue. He knew enough to understand that Catalina had introduced them, and he caught her mentioning her grandmother. When the circle opened up enough to form a couple new spots, Drummond and Catalina sat. They were offered plates of rice and beans which they graciously accepted, and as Drummond ate, Catalina repeated the story of Matteo as told to her by Roberto.

Throughout the tale, Drummond observed the numerous field hands. Most wore stoic expressions — the glazed-over look of men who had put in hours of hard labor. The desire to simply eat and go to sleep before enduring another backbreaking day read evident in their eyes, their lowered shoulders, even their simple slouch. Their bodies were exhausted. And now they had to deal with a crazy person killing and cutting up one of their own.

Roberto clearly had the group's respect. Partly because of his age — he looked to be in his mid-30s which made him one of the elders of the group — but he also spoke in a way that reminded Drummond of Leroy on a good day. There was a commanding intelligence behind the man's tone. A confidence that suggested a good education, one that was wasted cutting cabbages at the end of the growing season.

When Catalina finished the last of Roberto's words, Drummond let the air grow still. He wiped his mouth and handed the plate to one of the ladies, making sure to nod and say *gracias*. He did not need to look at the group to know all eyes were on him. He could feel it.

"What did you do with the arm and heart?" he asked.

Catalina listened to Roberto's answer and translated. "They burned it. They were worried it might be cursed, and even if it wasn't, it was certainly bad luck."

"Probably a good idea. Though I wish I could've inspected it. Did Matteo have any enemies?"

"No. They say everybody liked him. He was a hard-working kid and good-looking. Very charismatic."

"How about new people in his life? Did he make any new friends recently?"

Catalina relayed the question and Roberto shrugged. He looked at the group for an answer. After a moment, he pointed to one young man. They exchanged a few words and the young man stood. With his head bowed and a straw hat held between his two shaky hands, he said in stilted English, "Matteo had girlfriend." The young man checked with Roberto, received a nod, and as if saying the words caused physical pain, he said, "White girl."

Miss Fox had been young but no way would she have been described as a girl. This was somebody else. "Did any of you see this girl?"

All the heads shook *no*. Roberto spoke and Catalina said, "Apparently, Matteo bragged about the girl a bit."

"How long ago was this?"

"A few days before he disappeared."

"What about a white woman? Maybe the girl's mother or older sister? A young woman. *Muy bonita*."

A heavyset man with a thick black mustache nodded. "*Si, si*." Beyond that, Drummond caught only a few words.

Catalina said, "A white woman — very pretty like you said — stood at the edge of the field watching them work around that same time. This is José, and he said he caught her eye at one point. Says her stare caused his bones to freeze. She had the eyes of a witch."

Drummond nodded. "I'll bet she did."

The expectant looks pressed against him. He knew they wanted an instant solution and that it would not be coming. "Can somebody show me where this woman stood?"

Roberto and José rose causing the entire group to stand. The two men escorted Drummond and Catalina back toward the fields. The rest of the group followed, but they stopped at the edge of their little half-circle of shacks. None dared go further.

With the sun down, the air cooled fast. José led them along the edges of the fields in the dark, the large acreage like a canvas of black. Only the group's weak flashlights provided a view of the ground.

Twice, José stopped and spread his light on the tree's forming the edge of the property. He stepped one way, then another, peering at the trees as if trying to pick out an old friend. But then he shook his head and walked further up. As they moved on, Drummond wondered if the man remembered the spot at all. Roberto asked them to be patient — José would never forget the strange woman staring at him all day long. It was simply a matter of finding it again in the dark.

The third time they stopped, José's flashlight lingered on a dead tree with a large broken branch. He turned to the group. "Here."

Drummond stepped forward and the others backed up to allow him space to work. Through Catalina, he asked everybody to shine their flashlights on the ground. It did not take long to find where the witch had stood. Clearly, she wanted to be seen.

A small circle had been burnt in the grass. She had waited in the spot long enough that her footprints marred the center of the circle. No symbols, though. So, she had not cast a spell. Yet, she obviously wanted somebody to know that she had been in this specific location.

Drummond waved Roberto over. "The boy, Matteo — is this where you found his arm?"

Roberto nodded.

"She wanted you to find the arm." This witch had to have known Mexican laborers would avoid the police, preferring to deal with it themselves. Since she also knew the connection of Leroy to Drummond, enough so that she brought the book to the office, he could assume she probably knew the connection of Catalina as well. Not that much work for anybody to tie Catalina's grandmother to Roberto. This witch understood all the roads that eventually led to Drummond. The big question looming in his mind — why?

The young man who spoke of Matteo's girlfriend came racing up. With an abrupt halt, his eyes fixed on the burnt circle. Sweat dripped off his nose and Drummond half-expected the boy to run away screaming in terror. Indeed, the boy took a couple steps back before finding his courage. He cupped his hands around Roberto's ear and whispered. When he finished, Roberto gazed off into the dark before he spoke.

Translating, Catalina said, "This isn't the first time this has happened."

Despite his detective instincts jolting into high gear, Drummond kept his tone calm and respectful. "Just how many more times has it happened here?"

"Not here. Two other times at other farms. All within the last bunch of weeks. This boy heard about one of them while working at a different farm. And it happened again to an older gentleman at the last farm the boy worked. And now it's happened here."

"Why didn't he tell us before?"

Not even bothering to translate the question, Catalina said, "You really think he's simply going to trust you because you showed up with me? When terrible things happen to these people, they don't look outside for help. They learned the hard way that sharing their problems with outsiders only causes more trouble for them and their families. In fact, there are only a few reasons they're willing to talk with us at all — I'm one of them, but more importantly, they're scared out of their minds. They don't know how to handle it within their own community. That's why they reached out to *mi abuela,* and that's why she reached out to me. Understand?"

With a sheepish nod, Drummond turned his focus back to the immediate problem. "These other murders — did this witch show up like she did here?"

Catalina asked the question. "Yes. He says she showed up every time. And there was always the same burnt circle where the victim's arm and heart were found."

"And which farms did this happen at?"

Through the translations, the boy gave enough information that Catalina could write down the farm names and a rough idea of where they were located. Drummond promised he would do his best to take care of the situation, and Catalina promised that he was a man of his word. With that, they walked back to the car and drove off to Winston-Salem.

By the time he reached the office, Drummond had mulled over the few facts of the case he had at hand. He did not expect to glean much more in his considerations, and in fact, nothing new came to light. He simply did not know enough yet. But the habit of going through a case over and over gave him comfort. When he walked through the door, the look on Leroy's face gave him even more comfort — even a glimmer of hope.

"Well, I got the good and the bad," Leroy said. When he saw Catalina enter behind Drummond, he popped to his feet and offered a slight bow. "Ms. Catalina, it's always a pleasure to see you."

Drummond chuckled. "Quit it with the smooth talk. She's tired. Probably wants to go home and put on some clean clothes. I'm tired and definitely want to go to sleep. What did you find out?"

Despite the ominous nature of what he said, Leroy spoke with enthusiasm and a joy of learning something new. "I translated the first page before and the first page after the removed section. It took a while. Thankfully, this wasn't in any sort of code. It is, however, a mixture of various languages, so an exact translation is next to impossible. At least, for me at this stage in my life. Maybe some big brained professor could do it, but not me. I'll keep working on it, though, and eventually this kind of thing should be easy. Well, easier."

"Yes, yes, we all know how smart you are. Get on with it."

Leroy threw a sarcastic wink at Drummond. "You better watch it — you're starting to sound a lot like me."

"You don't have to worry about me until I start wanting to research through the books like you do."

"Lucky for you, I do like this work. What I found here is that this page before the removed part is the end of a section on basic spells the coven expected its members to know." Leroy moved his hand over to the page after the ripped out section. "Over here is where things get a little different. See the symbols?"

Drummond looked closer and saw two triangles with markings on the various sides. "I take it those aren't words."

"Correct. These are diagrams of what to draw for these particular spells. You're familiar with triangles used in magic, right?"

"The witches use that shape instead of a casting circle for their darker and more dangerous spells."

"You actually listen to me now and then. Good to know. Yes, you're correct. And this page is the end of a very dark spell. Could be anything, but two triangles is big trouble."

"Why should this bother you? The witch doesn't have this part of the spell. It's right in front of us."

Holding Drummond's whiskey flask, Catalina sat behind the desk. After taking a swig, she said, "Leroy is trying to tell you that since the first page he translated was the end of the basic spells and since this is the tail end of a very dangerous spell, then the part ripped out is most likely also a dangerous spell. But a complete one."

"Listen to her," Leroy said. "She keeps proving to be smarter than you."

Drummond scratched his chin. "Any idea what this complete dangerous spell that the witch stole from this book is?"

"Actually, yes." Leroy flipped to the back of the book, his triumph evident in every motion of his fingers. "Here. This particular coven thankfully did something most do not — they provided an index. Based on the page numbers, and several hours of translating, I was able to figure out what was on those pages. At least, what some of the keywords they used were."

"And?"

"And that's the bad part of all this. We're dealing with blood magic."

Drummond sighed. "Not surprised."

"A lot of blood."

"Still not surprised."

"I don't have much else. I do have the name of the spell that I think the witch is using, but it doesn't match any of the other languages that were written in the grimoire. My guess is that the name is something the coven made up. But for what it's worth, the spell is called the *yag-dath*."

Drummond took a few minutes to fill in Leroy on the murdered field hands. Leroy listened closely before walking over to Catalina and clasping her hand between his. "I'm so sorry."

"I appreciate that," she said. "Hopefully we can stop this witch so that nobody else gets hurt."

"That would be nice."

"But I can tell that won't be happening tonight. I'm exhausted. I better go take care of my boys." Catalina stood and walked to the door. Drummond inched towards her for a good night kiss but instead got a simple pat on the shoulder. "I'll see you gentlemen tomorrow. Good night." She left.

Drummond stood at the closed door for a moment before turning to Leroy. "You're a colored fellow. Maybe you can explain this to me."

Leroy turned back to the book. "Anything starting with that sentence, I want no part of."

"I've obviously said something wrong, but I don't quite understand why. I mean she made it clear enough, and I understand that much now, but why is she still mad at me? All I said was that these people should've gone to the police first before bothering with us."

Falling back in his chair, Leroy laughed hard and long enough that it left him gasping for air.

* * * *

DRUMMOND AWOKE with his muscles stiff and his back aching. He had fallen asleep in his desk chair. Leroy hogged the couch, but Drummond figured the old man had worked hard enough that night and deserved the more comfortable furniture. Rubbing his eyes, Drummond checked his watch — 7:32 AM.

He shook Leroy awake, and the two men caught breakfast a couple blocks up the street. With coffee flooding their systems and eggs curbing their hunger, Leroy suggested they get back to the office to translate more of the text. Drummond agreed that Leroy should do that, but he had a different avenue he wanted to pursue.

"I'll be back in a couple hours at the most."

Leroy shook Drummond's hand. "You be careful with whatever you're planning. Oh, also, it sure would help my concentration if I had a couple cigarettes."

Drummond smirked and handed over the last of his open pack. He waited until Leroy turned the corner. Then, he set off for the police station.

He walked straight up to the front desk but didn't recognize the young officer who greeted him. In fact, so many years had gone by since Drummond was a beat cop that he recognized fewer and fewer faces every time he entered the building.

"Can I help you?" the young officer asked.

"I'd like to see Detective Cooper."

As the message of Drummond's arrival made its way back to his old partner, Drummond sat on a stiff, wooden bench in the waiting area. From there, he could see the Chief's office. Though the blinds were closed, he had been in there enough times to know it well. Although, it had to have been redecorated. After Chief Carter died, the new chief took over and that always made things change fast. Unfortunately, this time around, those changes were for the worse. Cooper had expressed enough dissatisfaction that Drummond kept expecting his old friend to transfer to another town just to get away from the new boss.

When Cooper arrived, Drummond saw that dissatisfaction in the man's tense body. Red-faced and tightlipped, Detective Cooper glowered at Drummond as he walked over. "What the hell are you doing here?"

Perhaps Drummond had misread where Cooper's anger was directed. "I've got a case I'm working on and need to ask you a question. Nice to see you, too."

"I can't be seen with you. Not here. Wasn't I clear enough the last time? The old days are gone."

Drummond pushed close to Cooper. "Then meet me outside somewhere. But I need to talk with you. People are dying."

Cooper glanced around to make sure nobody paid too close attention to them. "Give me ten minutes. I'll meet you out front of the library. Nobody will ever believe that you're going to a library."

Drummond left the police station and headed several blocks over to the public library. He tipped his hat to a few ladies that strolled by and he grabbed the morning edition of the *Winston-Salem Journal.* Sitting on the library steps, he read the news and waited.

If somebody took the time to watch him, they would have seen the concern on his brow as he thumbed through the paper. But it wasn't the articles about the struggling economy or the violence in Europe that troubled him. And it wasn't even the mistreatment by an old friend.

It was Cooper's casual acceptance at Drummond suggesting that people were dying. His old partner did not question things any further. Some would take that as an ultimate sign of trust. But Drummond knew better. In fact, by the time Cooper arrived at the library steps, Drummond wasted no time jumping right in. "You already know, don't you?"

Cooper flashed a salesman smile before reading Drummond's face. Then he turned serious. "It's no secret that you've been shacking up with your own little bit a dark meat."

"Watch it."

"Hey, I don't judge. You do what you want to do. All I meant is that I know you got this Mexican girlfriend, so it's no surprise to me that you're looking into these murders of Mexicans."

"Does that mean you're looking into it, too?"

"It's not our jurisdiction. It's all on Greensboro."

Drummond folded the newspaper and stuck it under his arm. "If this is Greensboro's problem, how come you even know about it?"

"I don't. Not really." As a young couple headed toward the library entrance, Cooper gestured for Drummond to join him in a walk. "It's like this — Chief Murdoch brought me and the other detectives in and told us we might end up hearing about this case. But that it's not a case. Nobody's officially reporting it, and nobody's being assigned to look into it."

"Why is he telling you at all then?"

"That's what I was wondering, but the case is over in Greensboro so it won't be coming here. I don't know why he was making a big deal of mentioning it and I didn't care. Didn't give it another thought. Until you show up asking about it. Look, I gotta keep my nose clean right now. No department in the entire state will touch me if I get involved in screwing over the Chief. So whatever you got going on, do your ol' pal a favor and leave me out of it."

Cooper did not wait for Drummond to respond. Adjusting his hat, he rapidly walked away.

AS DRUMMOND STEPPED INTO HIS OFFICE, Leroy leapt across the room. "Come here, come here. You've got to see this."

Rarely did Drummond ever get to see Leroy with such wondrous excitement on his face. The old man pulled Drummond toward the desk like a child tugging a parent by the sleeve to show off a picture he had drawn. While Drummond had been out having a surreptitious and unpleasant conversation with Detective Cooper, Leroy had been investigating the locations of the murders.

"Once I finished the translations, I found out that you had actually been close to the truth. See here?" Leroy pointed to the page after the ripped out text. "You had wondered if this might be connected to the actual spell, that it was the end of the spell, and we dismissed it because why would the witch leave behind part of the spell — but that's exactly what she did."

Drummond looked closer. "Those diagrams of triangles are part of the spell she killed those field hands for?"

"That's right. It's only this little part in the first column that's about her spell. The rest is not important for us. Now, the reason she didn't take this page is that it only explains where the bodies needed to be placed. And, assuming this witch has even a modicum of intelligence, she could remember that much."

"Shouldn't she be able to remember it all? I mean, it's her grimoire." Drummond paused. "Isn't it?"

"I don't think so. I suspect she tore these pages out because she needed them. Whatever spell this is all for, she heard about it through witch gossip and decided to try and take it for herself. There are many grimoires out there that have legendary status from the covens that had once existed. Plenty of witches would love to get their hands on them. If this particular witch heard that I had it, it's no surprise she came after me."

"But then why bother sending the book to me? Why not just keep the book?"

Leroy shook his head. "No idea. But I know where we can find out some answers." With an even bigger grin, Leroy pulled out a map of North Carolina. On it, he had drawn three circles. "These are the three farms where the field hands were taken and their arms and hearts returned. Notice anything?"

Drummond saw it right away. Anybody dealing with the things he dealt with would have seen it. "Connect the three points and you got yourself a triangle. From the looks of it, pretty close to an equilateral triangle."

Leroy used a ruler to draw the triangle. "You are absolutely correct. From the page I translated and from this map, I can say with fair certainty that the point in the middle of that triangle is where we're going to find our witch. And, hopefully, some answers."

Drummond eased back as of putting distance between him and a hungry, vicious animal. "Let's put aside the fact that none of this is adding up very well. I'll ask you something — doesn't it all seem rather easy?"

"You know how many hours I spent sweating over that translation? Nothing easy about it."

"Granted we've all put in a bit of effort, but the solution wasn't that difficult to find. The witch who stole your book and ripped out the pages gives it to me, your regular colleague. She could have sent the book to a bookstore or some other private investigator. But she gives it to me. This same witch could have ripped out all the pages of the spell, but she leaves behind one page that has the very information we need to put a lot of these pieces together. For that matter, she blatantly murders these field hands, including one working on a farm with a man who would no doubt call Catalina's grandmother. Heck, she stands in the field long enough to be seen."

"I think you're the one that's stretching. That's a lot of machinations to do what I think you're implying."

"Which is what?"

"You think this is all a trap. You think this witch is purposely pointing where she's going to be so that you and I will go out there and be her victim. Right?"

"When you say it aloud it sounds absurd, but yeah, that's exactly what I'm thinking."

Leroy clicked his tongue. "Good. I was beginning to think I was the only one who thought it sounded as absurd in my own head. Worse — I agree with you. I think this is a convoluted way to force us out there."

From the doorway, Catalina said, "But why would this witch want all three of us?"

Drummond jumped to his feet. "Hold on. There's no need for you to go out there, too."

"There's every need. It wasn't your grandmother that asked for this help. And without me you couldn't even talk to the field hands. You need me out there. And if all of this adds up the way you two are suggesting, then the witch expects me to be along as well."

Drummond's mouth formed a hard line but he did not say anything.

Leroy stepped back and gestured toward the map for Catalina to see. "If we go out there now, it'll be broad daylight. Not even close to any of the witching hours. It would be the safest and smartest time to go."

"I agree," Catalina said as she glanced at the map. "Besides, this whole conundrum you're worried about isn't that hard to understand. She wants us out there as part of a larger plan. This spell is part of that plan, too. Clearly from what Leroy has figured out, the spell requires a lot of blood — three bodies worth — and that they form a triangle over a large area. Nothing too crazy about it — she's killing two birds with one stone."

"Terrible choice of words," Drummond said. "But you might be right. And the only reason she visited me and gave me the book was to ensure that we would come."

Leroy nodded. "She couldn't just tell us to come because why would we listen to a witch? This way, she's forced us to look into it, and really, we have no choice now. Not unless we're going to ignore the three dead people."

Drummond opened up his desk drawer and pulled out a box of ammunition. He checked that his .38 was loaded and put a few more rounds in his coat pocket. Pointing at the map, he said, "Bring that with us. And maybe the book, too. Take anything else you think we'll need or can use. We probably won't be able to come back until we finish dealing with this witch."

Leroy gathered the map and book. "I'll cross my fingers that I'm completely wrong about all this."

A few minutes later, they left for Drummond's car.

* * * *

HEADING OUT OF THE CITY with the sun stretching towards late-afternoon, Drummond's nerves rattled on edge. Bad enough that he knew a trap awaited him, but bringing along Catalina and Leroy twisted his guts into braided pigtails. If this had been a normal case, the kind of case Detective Cooper could handle, then Drummond would never have dreamed of driving out there. But with a witch involved, with magic involved, often the best solution proved to be among the most dangerous.

Or perhaps that was merely what he told himself to justify his actions.

Because part of him — the part that loved to uncover answers — that part of him simply wanted to find out. That part of him had no interest in waiting. No interest in being safe or cautious. That part of him would not be satisfied until he knew why this witch had gone to all this crazy trouble.

It was the same part that forced him out of the police department and into being a private investigator of the bizarre. He knew it brought peril into his life. He recognized that it might be the most destructive force within him. But, usually, the only life at risk was his own.

I can't start lying to myself. The truth — plenty of times he put other people's lives at risk, too. He took no pleasure in it, but he recognized that sometimes it became necessary. The only real difference this time was that he cared a lot for Leroy, and, if he dared to admit it, he loved Catalina.

Rustling the map as he refolded it to a new section, Leroy said, "There should be a turnoff coming up soon."

Drummond followed Leroy's directions and soon they cruised through endless fields. Beef cows grazed in a massive pasture to the left while on the right Drummond spotted several horses in the distance.

"You sure you've got the right farm? I thought you said this place grew tobacco."

"I said that it was around a tobacco farm. It's not like we had exact coordinates. Just drive down to the end of the road — about another mile or two — and if we don't see what we're looking for, will keep rolling around the farms in this area. It's going to be here somewhere."

"And what is it exactly that we're looking for?"

"Abandoned barn, old drying house, maybe a dilapidated outbuilding of some kind. How should I know?"

"You're the one that translated the damn pages."

Catalina turned in the passenger seat and put a hand on both men's shoulders. "Enough. We will drive around the farms and we will keep our eyes open. Considering how obvious this witch has been up to this point, I don't think she's going to make it too hard for us to figure out."

Turned out, Catalina called it. After two more turns and about four miles, Leroy indicated a field on the right. An old tobacco drying house stood a short distance away from a crumbling barn. Both the barn and the drying house had been painted red originally, but over the years, sun and whether had done their damage. What paint remained looked more brown than red.

Except for the symbols.

Freshly painted in white, two large symbols on each side of the drying house stood out like a blazing lighthouse beacon. Of course, any such symbols would have drawn attention, but these came directly from Leroy's translated pages.

Drummond parked on the side of the road. Weeds covered most of the land, and it made walking toward the drying house difficult. The uniform rows that once thrived with tobacco plants now bred thorny vines, wild bushes, and knee-high grasses in haphazard paths. It looked like another victim of the Crash. Whoever owned the property now — probably the banks — had yet to unload it.

"Watch where you walk," Leroy said. "This is fertile ground for copperheads."

Drummond paused mid-step. Leroy was right. Copperheads tended to mind themselves, only striking out when disturbed. But they blended in well with fields growing wild, and it would be easy enough to accidentally step on one.

Catalina said, "Should we check out the barn, too?"

"No need," Drummond said. "This is only going to happen in the drying house."

"How do you know?"

"Look at the place."

Tobacco drying houses came in many shapes and sizes. Some were actual barns converted to the purpose of hanging the big tobacco leaves to dry out. Others looked like square sheds with a wide awning all the way around and a tower in the middle. But this one had been built with two steep sides coming out straight from the ground at an angle to meet in a point at the top — like a giant triangle.

As they reached the drying house, the weeds and grasses receded, leaving nothing but arid land surrounding the building. Drummond put out his arm to hold his friends at the edge of the grasses. He slipped his hand into his coat pocket and gripped his handgun.

Leroy said, "There's definitely another entrance in the back — probably big barn doors to haul all the leaves. Sometimes these places have one on the side, too — poking out or cut in like a little hallway."

"You go around and check it out from the back. Catalina, see if there's a side entrance and take that. I'll be the one to go through the front door."

Catalina narrowed her eyes on him. "You don't have to be a hero. Miss Fox will be expecting you through the front door. Any trap she has would be based on that, right? Why don't you come with us around the place?"

"Because if it is a trap, then no entrance will be safe. I'm the one with the most experience here, so I'll go in the front. And believe me, I'm not trying to be a hero. I intend for all of us to leave this place alive and well."

Leroy walked off, giving the building a wide berth, staying in the overgrown patches as much as possible. Catalina followed. As they left, Drummond steeled himself for whatever might be waiting behind the front door. Once he saw Catalina stop at the side and Leroy break away toward the back, he knew the time had come.

The dead ground crunched beneath his feet as he marched up to the drying house. It felt strange at every step — the crust of the ground brittle and crumbling while beneath was packed clay as hard as a city street. Despite the building being in disuse for so long, Drummond swore he could still smell the tobacco in the air.

With his .38 at the ready, he threw open the front door. The place was empty. The back sliding door lay open and Leroy stood there with his eyes darting around. Catalina walked in from the side entrance, standing just inside the shadows.

The long wooden framework running on both sides of the building were designed to hang the heavy tobacco leaves for drying. But in this empty, forgotten place, they looked like scaffolding meant to hold up a malformed creature. Old crates and boxes filled up much of the area's sides — apparently, the last owner used the drying house for storage in the final years.

Beyond the painted symbols on the outside, the only indication they had come to the right place rested in the center. An old metal washtub sat in the middle with a casting circle dug into the ground around it. At the head of the tub, a clean drinking glass sat empty. A triangle had been formed encompassing the circle, and each point of the triangle held a single black candle — unlit.

As he carefully approached the washtub, Drummond scanned the boxes on the sides searching for any hint of an ambush. Just dust and decay.

Leroy stepped in from the other side. "Looks like all her prep work is done. Maybe she's just waiting for us."

"Or the witching hour."

"I don't think so. It wasn't entirely clear from the fragment on that page, but I got the sense that this spell can be done at any time. Still, better we're here in the daylight."

Drummond walked further in and noticed the wet patches in the dirt around the washtub. Footprints. He put out his hand. "Nobody else move." Once he saw that Leroy and Catalina had stopped approaching, he walked further forward until he could see into the tub.

Dark, thick, black blood filled half of the tub. On the sides, a handprint displayed where somebody clasped the rim. Drummond's first thought — Miss Fox had filled the tub with the field hands' blood and then bathed in it. But the handprint was too small, the footprints too narrow.

He turned his head toward Catalina. "Is it possible that Roberto didn't tell us everything?"

She pulled back, her face going cold. "Like what?"

"Maybe there was a fourth person abducted. Maybe another young man — a small teen or maybe even a child. One that they have yet to get the arm and heart from."

"They didn't say anything about any of that. And I didn't hear anything that would make me think they hid something that big. Why? What are you seeing in there? Is it — is there a child in that tub?"

"No. It's filled with blood. But I think there was a young person in there. I think maybe Miss Fox bathed someone in there."

Catalina covered her mouth and turned away. Leroy stepped over and glanced into the tub. "Yep. That looks about right. But you can tell she didn't force some kid into that blood. Look around — no scuff marks on the ground. Nothing to indicate struggle of any kind. Besides, with most of these blood spells — except for the acquisition of blood part — you usually have to be a willing participant."

Drummond stumbled back. "Hold on. Are you telling me that somebody willfully got into this tub? Is that right?"

"Looks to be the case."

Drummond did not want to believe it, but he had to agree with Leroy's assessment. The ground was smooth, and if there had been a struggle, blood would've splashed everywhere. Drummond squatted down and looked at the candles. They had been lit before. Recently. The wax was still soft.

"Whatever happened here, whatever the spell was, it's already been cast."

Keeping her back to the tub, Catalina said, "Isn't that a good thing? I mean, the spell wasn't a trap for us."

"But then what is the trap?" Drummond pursed his lips and tapped his chin. "You two should take the car and go back to the office. See if you can figure out anything else from that book."

"What about you?" Catalina asked.

"I'm going to hunker down behind some of these crates and stakeout this tub. There is no doubt we were meant to come here, and it wasn't just to see the leftovers of a spell. Miss Fox will be coming back. I intend to be here when she does."

Before Catalina could turn around, Leroy said, "We can't just leave you here. That's crazy."

Drummond shook his head. "If all three of us are waiting here, she'll see us. She'll hear us or somehow know what we're doing."

"Nonsense. You hide right on that side behind the crates, and I'll hide in the alcove that leads to the side door."

Catalina said, "And what about me?"

Leroy looked to Drummond for help. Drummond clamped his mouth tight to avoid swearing. At length, he said, "If we're going to do it this way, I'm not even going to pretend that I could get you to leave."

"Good."

"But I do want you at a safe distance. And I don't want to hear arguments. We have our car parked right on the road in front of this building. So, you go back to the car and move it down the road. Far enough away that Miss Fox won't be able to see you but close enough that you can see the top part of the drying house. I have a feeling that if anything happens, it won't be subtle. Look around us. None of this is subtle. You'll know when we need help."

Catalina wanted to argue. Drummond expected it, but he also saw her recognize the full situation. She nodded and left for the car.

Waiting. Again.

Situated behind a tall crate with enough gaps that he could see the tub, Drummond tried to find a comfortable way to sit. But the drying house had not been designed for comfort — especially the angled sides which were only intended to hang tobacco leaves. Besides, Drummond knew his discomfort came less from his cramped conditions and more from the ache in his heart.

As the hours went by, he focused almost entirely on Catalina. He saw in the way she had held her body, in the way she had looked at him, that things were changing. She seemed to be pin-wheeling away, and due to their strange situation, he had no opportunity to catch her.

A few times, he tried to clear his head, but that only left him with a washtub of blood to think about. From his vantage point, the handprint stood clear against the metal tub. The longer they waited, the dryer the blood became, the darker that handprint.

Not wanting to become nauseous, Drummond forced himself to start thinking about Catalina again. Every minute longer he sat there, his mind played games — trying to convince him that Miss Fox would never come back, that this whole thing was a waste, that he should leave now and run to the car — to Catalina. Surely if they simply had time to sit and talk, they could work out however deep her concerns went. Surely all he had to do was bare the truth of his soul. Let her know, without doubt, that he —

The front door opened and in walked Miss Fox. At her side stood a young woman coated in dried blood. Still, despite every inch of her skin painted in cracking crimson, despite her lost expression that drifted away from reality, despite the drool stringing off her lips, Drummond knew exactly who she was — Janice Murphy.

All the questions that had plagued him crystallized into a solid clear answer. Why had any of this happened? Janice Murphy.

This young woman had been behind all of the horrible events Drummond had suffered in the past year or so. Her grandmother had contributed to the spell that killed Chief Carter and Drummond had been involved in destroying the magic that eventually led to Sylvia Murphy's death as well as that of Janice's sister. The loss drove young Janice mad with an unquenchable thirst for vengeance. From the psychotic determination in her eyes, Drummond saw that she had only grown worse since their last encounter.

Even without the caked blood, she would have borne the look of a corrupted mind. While most of her insanity traced to the loss of her family, Drummond suspected some of it to be caused by her use of magic.

The Murphy family was not made of witches. They were novices that played at being witches. But when dealing with dark, oftentimes evil, magic like blood magic, nobody should be playing at all.

"One last bath," Miss Fox said. "You're almost there. Soak in that tub and all you asked of me will be true. One last bath and there will be nothing that Marshall Drummond could do to stop you. Your grandmother and your sister will look down upon you and smile knowing that you have honored them through such great sacrifices. You should be proud."

Janice faltered forward a few steps. Her body shivered as if she had emerged from a cold shower and the night air chilled her. She wore a blood-drenched shift that flapped against her body like peeled skin. With her head down at a slight angle and her hair wet and dangling, she gave Drummond the sense that she had burst from the belly of a large animal.

If she had been anybody else, Drummond might have felt sorry for her. He might have stepped out from behind the crates and attempted to bring her back to sanity. He might even have expressed a warning that no good would come from dealing with this witch.

But this was Janice Murphy.

When Drummond stepped out from behind the crates, he aimed his .38 at her forehead. "Sorry to disappoint you ladies, but there is no way I'm going to let you finish this spell."

As Leroy stepped out of the alcove, Miss Fox brought her hands together in a quiet little clap. "You both came. I'm delighted. What about the Mexican woman? Did you bring her, too? No, no. Don't tell me. Let it be a surprise."

"You can play the fool all you want, but it won't change things."

"Oh, bless your heart, you are charming. You actually think that the spell has not already been completed. Janice, honey, why don't you show Mr. Drummond exactly what you can do."

Janice lifted her head and licked her lips. A strand of gore speared out of her shoulder. It stretched across the drying house and latched onto Drummond's handgun. Before he had time to comprehend what had occurred, the taut strand — like a tendon dripping with blood — yanked the weapon from Drummond's hand and tossed it into the shadows. The tendon loosened and snapped back into Janice's body.

Stepping further into the room, Leroy watched Janice as if trying to comprehend the arrival of a unicorn or gargoyle. "What on Earth —"

Two new tendons shot out of Janice's sternum. One slammed into Leroy's chest, lifting him up and thrusting him against the drying racks. The other caught Drummond in the gut.

He had been punched by many tough customers, but even the biggest bruiser never hurt him like this. He crumpled to the ground, unable to inhale without pain, his eyes watering, and even his ears ringing. With a hand gripping the nearest crate to keep from falling over, Drummond watched as the bloodied tendons snapped back into Janice's body. Gazing across the room, he saw that Leroy sat on his knees and focused on trying to breathe.

"Don't fret now," Miss Fox told Janice. "I know you can't control your new body so well just yet, but it will be yours in time. Finish your last bath and you will marvel at the horrors you will create."

Janice scrunched her face up questioningly.

Miss Fox lifted an eyebrow. "Do they look like they can cause you trouble? And I have yet to do my part with them. So stop dawdling and get yourself in that bath. You wait too long, and nothing will work the way we have it planned."

Rubbing his stomach with one hand, Drummond glared at Janice and Miss Fox as the two women ambled toward the washtub. Janice continued moving straight into the tub — lowering down as if indulging in the soothing pleasure of a hot bath. At the same time, Miss Fox lit the three candles on the triangle points.

When she struck a match for the candle nearest Drummond, she offered a sympathetic shrug. "If it were up to me, y'all would be dead right now. But she wants you to suffer something awful. I can't imagine what you did to enrage such a sweet child."

Groaning as he spoke, Drummond said, "She ain't sweet. You look at what she's willing to do, she ain't sane, either."

"I agree with you there. She is most definitely not right in the head. But then, how could she be? What kind of sane young woman tracks down a witch like me? Not only did she find me and tell me what she had in mind for you, but she did not even put up a fuss when negotiating the deal. With a witch. Can you imagine?"

"And what do you get out of it?"

"Me? A little insurance. The ruling family of magic in North Carolina is quite strong. Nobody would dare mess with them. But we witches can live a long time, and that means we need to be ready. Nothing lasts forever. Those who are strong today will be weak tomorrow. A witch like me — I need all the advantages I can get. Little Miss Bloodbath here is going to leave me with quite a bit of power."

Drummond tried to stand but ended up on his backside. "That's it? Seems like an awful lot of trouble for a little bit of extra power."

Miss Fox chuckled. "If it had been my choice, I would never have gone through such a circuitous route to get to you. But this is how she wanted it. And, admittedly, this spell is old enough and complex enough that it sort of called for such games. It won't hurt, and it will only help enhance my reputation. Not many witches could pull off this spell."

Brushing off her legs, she stood and plucked a hair off Drummond's head. She sprinkled the hair over the candle and it sizzled away. She then crossed to Leroy, plucked his hair, and burned it under the candle near him. Finally, she returned to Drummond and said, "My reputation will also improve as the witch that killed you. Granted, you're not that big of a name, but any witch who takes out our enemies is notable."

From his shoulder, she pulled a long, feminine hair. This she lingered over the third candle's flame. It ate Catalina's hair with vigor, and the instant the flame finished, all three candles snuffed out.

Miss Fox turned back to the washtub. She bowed her head, mumbled a few words, and placed her hand atop Janice. With slight pressure, she guided Janice under the surface of blood. A moment later, Janice came up, spluttering a deep breath, as blood washed over her skin.

Miss Fox crouched by the side of the tub and put her hand out. Janice clasped it and took a long inhalation before dipping back under.

While this revolting ritual played out, Drummond tried to summon the strength to stand. He felt sure he had broken a rib, but he still should have been able to get up. Yet even breathing seemed a struggle. He felt as if a giant stone sat on him.

Leroy had one hand clutched against his chest and appeared to have the same struggles. "What is this evil?"

The witch smirked. "Well, I'm fairly certain that Janice intends to torture you all, but I didn't like the idea of you spoiling our play. Don't worry. My little spell won't do you any harm. It'll just keep you in place, that's all."

Drummond spied movement near the open barn door. He glanced over, but he already knew what he would see — Catalina. He should have assumed that she would ignore his orders to stay in the car. At least her timing was good.

She spent a short moment watching the witch and Janice. A range of emotions battled across her face starting with confusion, passing through disgust, and settling into bold determination. When she finally locked eyes with Drummond, he did not see the sweet woman he had come to know, the woman who loved and cared for her two boys, who cherished her *abuela,* who warmed his life and helped him ignore the brutal world around them. She had pushed all of that aside. Her eyes told him everything — she embraced the brutal world so that she could be brave enough to enter that building.

It would not help, though. Watching Catalina plan her approach was like watching a squirrel sniffing around an old box trap. Drummond wanted to warn her off, but his mouth would not work. Another wonderful aspect of Miss Fox's spell.

Catalina decided against crossing the open barn doors to get onto Drummond's side of the building. She clearly hoped to slink along Leroy's side and disrupt the spell when she got closer. But the moment her foot crossed the threshold, her black candle ignited.

With a shark grin, Miss Fox gazed at the candle. "Finally, the Mexican girl has joined us."

A lesser woman might have frozen in a poor attempt at hiding by not moving. Not Catalina. Recognizing she had been found out, she launched forward, rushing toward the candles. Drummond could not have been more proud.

"Stop," Miss Fox said, her voice filling up the entire drying house. She whipped around and put out her hand like a police officer.

But Catalina had dealt with witches before. She would not be so easily intimidated. In one graceful motion, she crouched down, grabbed a rock from the dirt, and flicked it like a professional baseball pitcher.

It sailed across the air with impressive speed. Miss Fox flinched, and that instinctive motion saved her face. Her arms took the brunt of abuse from the rock as she yelped.

Catalina never stopped moving. She followed the rock straight through and checked Miss Fox with her shoulder. The witch flailed toward the washtub, and for a few precious seconds, she focused on not tumbling into the blood.

With her attention divided, Drummond could feel the power of her spell weakening on him. Catalina swept her foot across the ground, destroying the lines of the casting circle and triangle. She then knocked over all three candles.

Though his ribs still ached, the invisible force that pressed Drummond into the ground lifted. As he stumbled to his feet, he noticed Leroy also rising.

Breathing hard, Catalina said, "Bet you boys could use a little help."

Drummond stepped forward, and it appeared as if Catalina might be opening her arms for a hug — but he had no time for that. "Down," he said.

Her eyes widened as she dropped to the ground. Drummond swung hard and knocked Miss Fox in the jaw. The witch fell over, rolling against the side of the tub, and hit the dirt hard. She moaned as she tried to get to her knees.

Drummond actually thought they had won. But that moaning of the witch mutated into a dark chuckle. And as Janice Murphy rose from the tub full of blood, Miss Fox's dark chuckle turned into a macabre laugh.

From the other side, Leroy said, "Drummond, are you all —"

Janice's blood-slick tendons daggered out in numerous angles. One flew from her back at Leroy while two shot forward toward Drummond and Catalina. Two more burst from her legs and ripped open the metal siding of the tub.

Catalina tried to dodge the attack but still took an impact on her left arm. Leroy and Drummond had experienced it before. They managed to avoid the vicious blows.

The open tub, however, flooded crimson across the ground turning it into thick mud. Doused, Miss Fox did not move. She remained on all fours, cackling like a hyena.

Janice's tendons retracted with a vile slurp. Leroy tried to take advantage. With a deep growl, he jumped Janice from behind, wrapping his arms around her in a tight bear hug.

Drummond knew this would end badly, but he could not let Leroy face it alone. He raised a fist, hoping he might clock Janice dizzy enough that Leroy could get free.

He never got close.

Before he could take a second step forward, Janice lifted her eyes to stare right at him. Baring her teeth, she made a slight motion with her shoulder and thrust one of her deadly tendon attacks out her back.

The shocked look on Leroy's face reverberated through the air. He was a smart man, but the world of books and knowledge played out far different in the world of action.

Still trying to punch Janice, Drummond made the mistake of forgetting about Miss Fox. The witch threw herself forward, clobbering Drummond in the shins. He went down, splashing in the blood-soaked mud.

Tangled in the witch's limbs, Drummond struggled to get back to his feet. He heard the slurping noise and a painful groan from Leroy. Pushing Miss Fox over with one arm while propping up on the other, he tried to see the extent of damage Leroy had suffered. That's when Janice attacked him.

With two tendons, she pierced under both clavicles. Drummond could feel the assaulting parts of her grip his bones and lift him up. He screamed at the unforgiving pain.

In a voice more monstrous than human, Janice said, "All you have taken from me, I will take from you."

He wanted to say something to undercut her pleasure, but he did not trust his voice to remain steady. To the right, he saw Leroy — on his back, holding his side as blood seeped between his fingers. To the left, Miss Fox lay on her back, laughing as she wriggled in the blood and mud. And Catalina — where was Catalina?

The loud reports of Drummond's handgun filled the air. Janice's shoulder flung back. She cried out and instantly retracted her tendons. Drummond flopped into the mud.

With both hands clenching the .38 tight, Catalina stepped from behind the crates. She kept her aim on Janice as she walked forward. When she stopped at Drummond's side, she lowered one hand to help him stand.

Miss Fox's laughter ceased. She huffed as she got to her feet, crossed her arms, and forced a casual attitude. "If you have to kill her, I quite understand. Though, I would greatly appreciate it if you would reconsider."

Drummond could not stand completely straight, but at least he had found his voice. "We're not waiting around. My friend is going to die if he doesn't get to a hospital."

"If you don't mind me saying, you are not faring much better. You ought to be focusing on your own condition. In fact, the three of you should just leave. I can handle Janice."

"Forgive me if I don't think it's a good idea to trust you."

Miss Fox put her arm around Janice. "Of course, dear. That would be foolish of you. Unless we had a deal. Because a witch always keeps her word."

Janice gazed up with hope in her eyes.

Catalina glanced over at Drummond, but he shook his head. "Don't take that gun off her."

To Janice, Miss Fox said, "Oh, I see. You really thought that I was going to let them leave. Well, I wasn't. I've not made a deal with them. But don't worry, I made you a promise, and I have kept my end of that bargain. Have a not?"

Janice pushed away. The scowl on her face betrayed both her anger and wariness.

"Now, now. There's no need for that. You asked for this vicious strength, and I have provided. You asked for this convoluted trap to bring your three enemies here in one place. I have provided that, too. I even cast a spell to prevent them from bothering you on your last bathing. All of which I gave you free in exchange for your power when you were done."

"Not done," Janice said with a gravelly growl.

Miss Fox pointed back at Drummond. "Do you mean because he's still alive? Well, I'm afraid that is your concern. Our deal was for when this spell was done. I made no such promises regarding these three. You had ample opportunity to kill them, but like a dog that toys with her food only to have it snatched away by a hungrier dog, you've wasted your chance."

Janice's face, already covered in crimson, flushed an angry red. She arched her back and thrust out her stomach — but nothing happened. She whipped her arms around as if pitching the tendons from her body — but nothing emerged.

Her shoulders drooped and the horrible monster disappeared from her face. Drummond saw only the young woman who had been raised to believe so many fairytales, to follow such destructive faith, that her end seemed inevitable. Tears drew through the dried blood on her cheeks.

Miss Fox took Janice's arm and placed it over the empty glass on the little table. With a quick motion, she produced a blade from her mud-caked pocket. A simple slash of the wrist, and Janice's blood poured out.

When the glass filled to the top, Miss Fox set it aside. She mouthed several words and tapped Janice on the forehead. The young woman collapsed, banging her head on the sharp edge of the torn washtub.

"Oh dear," Miss Fox said, taking a step back from Janice's lifeless body. "I guess she didn't get quite what she wanted out of our deal. But then, you already know to never make a deal with a witch." She turned her attention toward the mess of her clothes. "It does appear that I need a change of outfits. And since all of this business is concluded, and your weapon will keep me from killing you, I don't see any reason for us to continue to pester each other. Good day."

"Don't you dare move." Catalina tightened her grip on the .38. Drummond moved in toward her, putting his hand out for the weapon. She brushed him away, her narrow focus never leaving Miss Fox.

The witch cocked her head to the side. "Well, well. Shoot a confused girl in the arm and suddenly you think you're ready to kill a person."

Drummond peeked at Leroy — if this became a drawn out affair, the old man would not make it. "Now look — nobody is talking about killing anybody."

"I am," Catalina said. "Do you really think a witch like this went through all the trouble of manipulating Janice Murphy just for a glass of blood? This spell was one of the most complicated I've ever heard of — killing three people and separating body parts all over the state to form a triangle. And that was just the first step. Do you really think she's done with us?"

Miss Fox said, "I am for now. Regardless of my motives, your boyfriend's line of work near guarantees that our paths will cross again. So I would be lying if I said I never had plans. I always have plans for the likes of him. But not today."

"You hear that? She even admits it. The only way we can stop her is to put a bullet through her skull."

Drummond inched closer to Catalina's side. He made no further motions to take the gun. Instead, he lowered his voice so that only she would hear him. "Don't do this. Everything you said is probably right, but don't do this. If you squeeze that trigger, it'll change you. Trust me — you won't like what you become. You'll spend every morning looking in the mirror and despising who you see. Think of your boys. They'll see the change. They won't understand it, but they'll see it."

Out the side of her mouth, she said, "I can't just let this witch go. I'll be living in fear for the rest of my life."

Leroy coughed hard, and a small amount of blood beaded on his lips. The old man gazed over at them, but Drummond could not tell if Leroy saw anything. The sense of death drifted off the old man.

Hold on. Drummond watched Catalina's face closely. Unwavering.

"Damn," he said. Removing his hat, and holding it against his chest with one hand, he stepped toward Miss Fox — careful not to block Catalina's line of sight. "Seems to me there is only one solution. You and I are going to have to make a deal."

"You can't," Catalina said.

"Oh, please do." Miss Fox ran her tongue across the top of her lip. "Tell me what is it you want."

Drummond set his hat back on and turned so that he did not have to see Catalina out of the corner of his eye. "The first thing you're going to do is heal Leroy right away."

"I'm afraid I can't do that. But I can stabilize him enough that you should be able to drive him to a hospital."

"Fine. You do that. Second thing — you leave Catalina and her family alone. You don't talk to her, you don't visit her, you don't watch her or observe her, you have nothing to do with her. I don't even want you to speak her name. That goes for her kids and her grandmother and any other family that might be connected to her now or forever. As far as you're concerned Catalina and her bloodline no longer exist."

From behind, he heard Catalina say, "Stop it. Don't do this for me."

Drummond glanced back. When he caught the tears in her eyes, he looked away. "It's the only good choice I have. And I'm not saying it's good, but it'll have to do."

Miss Fox said, "Anything else? Or do you two need to discuss it further?"

"That's it," Drummond said.

"I should think so. That is quite a tall order already. The big question, of course, is what do I get, if I do all this for you?" She overacted her thought process, pantomiming the weighing of two ideas and mimicking Drummond's pursed lips. She paused to throw a wink at him.

"She's stalling," Catalina said. "The longer she waits, the sicker Leroy becomes."

Drummond said, "And the more desperate she thinks my negotiating position will become."

Miss Fox snickered. "Aren't the two of you the bright ones? Very well. I'll make it simple. All I require is a few drops of your blood. Three should suffice."

Drummond kept his face unmoved, but inside, his brain screamed at him for even considering such a bargain. Except he refused to let Leroy die. He refused to allow this witch to plague Catalina and her family for years to come. If he tried to negotiate further, he might be able to talk her into something less dangerous, but the risk to Leroy would only get worse.

Catalina must have gone through the same calculations. However, she arrived at a slightly different result. "You can't have any of his blood. Leroy would rather die."

"Be quiet, child," Miss Fox said. "I doubt Leroy agrees with your value of his life. And your opinion does not matter. This is not your blood to negotiate with."

"But I'm holding the gun. Look in my eyes. The deal is this — not one drop. Any more and I'll blow your damn head off."

Miss Fox hesitated as she stared directly at Catalina. Whatever she saw in those eyes brought a change about her that Drummond could not miss. A slight bit of respect. A lot of concern. Between Catalina's threats and Drummond's demands, Miss Fox would soon be searching for ways to destroy them both.

"One drop," Drummond said before he realized he had opened his mouth. "You can have one drop and that's it."

Without taking her eyes off Catalina, Miss Fox said, "Very well. One drop."

RAYMOND'S DINER. Drummond waited until the dinner rush had finished before taking his usual booth. Catalina saw him, and he saw the dread come over her. It killed the last thread of hope he held for them.

She walked over — a brisk, businesslike gait. Far different from the way she once sauntered toward him, the way she moved to make sure his eyes lingered on her hips. When she reached the booth, she lifted her order pad. He said nothing, and when she finally allowed her eyes to meet his, she put the pad away.

"I'm going on break," she yelled over her shoulder. She slid in across from him. "How's Leroy?"

Tapping his fingers against a water glass, he said, "That old man is an annoying brat to those sweet nurses, but he's recovering well. Two weeks down, probably only one more to go. How about you?"

With a guilty drop of her eyes, she said, "I'm sorry I haven't called you back. I'm sorry I haven't come by your office."

"It's okay. I understand." He dropped his hands into his lap and sat back. "Actually, I don't understand. You've been through tight spots with me before."

"That's exactly why. At first, it was exciting. Fun, a little reckless, and you are so confident. It's very attractive. But with each of your cases that I got involved, the danger kept getting worse. I have my boys to think about, *mi abuela*, the future."

"And I'm too big of a risk."

She aimed for a lighter tone. "We had a nice little bubble world for a time. But that's all it was. Look around us. We were never going to work out."

"I don't care what the world says about that. I never have."

"But I do. I have to. I care about it for my boys. Their lives are hard enough. And you — you may not care, but you have the ability to not care. The world will not punish you for not caring. I don't have that same luxury."

Drummond said nothing for a moment as he locked down emotions threatening to overflow. "This is goodbye?"

Her face dimmed. "I'm afraid so. I've already given my notice. My boys, *mi abuela*, and I are leaving."

"For where?"

"I'm not going to tell you. Not when a witch has control of your blood."

Straightening, Drummond said, "Hold on. You're leaving Winston-Salem because of that deal I made?"

"We're leaving the entire state. After everything I've seen with you, I will never trust a witch. I think you are crazy for doing what you did. Leroy will never know how much he owes you, but I appreciate it. I still think sometimes, maybe, in some way, you should have let me shoot her."

"I'll never regret that decision. It would've destroyed you, and that would've destroyed your family, too. If losing this love we had built is the ultimate price I have to pay to protect you from the horror of killing someone, then I'll happily pay." Leaning awkwardly across the table, he kissed her. "Go have a good life, Catalina. A long and good life."

She picked up the napkin from the place setting and wiped her eyes. She forced out a smile. "Go. Before I really start crying."

Drummond watched her long enough to commit this final image to memory. Then he set his hat on and strolled out of the diner. He meandered down the blocks of Winston-Salem. The autumn leaves floated through the air, dry and brittle and full of glorious color.

They had shared a good thing, but Catalina was right to leave. Especially because in a few weeks, when Leroy felt ready, Drummond intended to learn all he could about blood magic. There had to be a way to counter whatever she could do with his one drop of blood.

And if that failed, he would put a bullet in her brain.

CASE 10

THE CONNECTED ONES

MEZMO
the MAGICAL
and the
AMAZING
LIONMAN!

GRABBING BREAKFAST should have been east for Marshall Drummond, but then few things were ever easy for Winston-Salem's only detective of the unique and bizarre. As he walked along the street, he considered the corner diner. Unfortunately, right after resigning from the police and hanging out his private detective shingle, he had enjoyed two brief but vigorous relationships with the waitresses — neither of which would want to see his mug again.

He thought about the Blue Ribbon Diner three-and-a-half blocks over. He had helped the owner, Buzz, when the guy courted serious trouble for selling hooch out the back. Prohibition had ended years ago, but the bootleggers and the protection rackets continued to operate. Just because booze was legal didn't mean all those who made money off it went away. But Drummond convinced the gang that wanted to destroy Buzz to back off (possibly with the help of a witch), and Buzz was eternally grateful.

So was Charlene. His waitress.

Of course, the best scrambled eggs and coffee could be found at Raymond's Diner, but it hurt too much to enter the place where Catalina had worked. She had been the real thing. She understood the world he lived in, knew about ghosts and witches and magic, and accepted it all. He had envisioned days ahead spent in her arms, being a father figure to her two boys, becoming something more than another guy in a long coat and Fedora. Unfortunately, after a series of cases that eventually threatened her family, they had to part ways. Whoever said that it was better to have loved and lost deserved a gut punch.

His best option looked to be buying a newspaper and making a cup of coffee on the hot plate in his office. Well, maybe not the best, but certainly the safest. A bleating car horn erased all chances of that.

Drummond's attention snapped to the sudden break in the morning routine. The other pedestrians moved like a herd. The shift of hats in the same direction looked like a choreographed number from the latest Broadway hit. Instead of music kicking in, however, gasps and screams followed.

Two blocks up, a brown 1938 Ford Standard Coupe barreled down Fourth Street without regard to anybody on or off the road. Other cars swerved away while people dove to the sides. More horns yelled their anger, and screams ignited the air with panic.

"What's she doing?" a paperboy said.

Drummond came close to asking how the boy knew the driver was a woman, but the boy had not been looking at the car. At the far end of the block, a middle-aged woman pushed a baby carriage across the street. She cooed and grinned and pointed at the little bundle in the carriage, oblivious to the boulder of metal rushing toward them.

People pressed in to gawk with horrible expectation. The growing throng prevented Drummond from backing up to run down the sidewalk. Though a few in the crowd yelled at the woman, their voices drowned in the overall commotion.

One quick peek up the street — that car already neared the top of the block. Damn. Drummond had not planned on racing against an automobile this early in the morning.

He darted onto the pavement. The voices around him erupted — Get back on the sidewalk! What the blazes are you doin'? — but Drummond pushed harder, his hat flipping into the air behind him. He wanted to wave his hands and scream to get the woman's attention, but the motions would throw him off balance and she clearly paid no mind to the shouting around her.

Somebody tried to yank Drummond off the road. The woman with the baby carriage was halfway across. Drummond shoved away the hands grabbing for him and swerved into the center of the road. Nobody could stop him there. Except for the car.

The roaring engine grew louder. Drummond didn't dare glance over his shoulder. His brain conjured enough terror without seeing the hungry bumper nipping at his heels.

Before he had time to think further, he scooped the woman onto his shoulder with one arm and shoved the carriage off to the left with the other. The baby shrieked as loud as the woman. Drummond dashed to the sidewalk on the right as the car blasted through the intersection.

The car turned sharp, tipped for a second, then shot straight at the corner. As Drummond set the woman down, he saw the car swerve oddly before ramming into a man with a gray coat and hat. The man flew back against the brick wall of a building and blood splashed upward from his head.

A chorus of shocked gasps rippled through the crowd. Drummond glanced down at the woman. "You okay?"

"The baby!" the woman said, and the odd sound of her words explained everything. She was deaf.

Keeping a protective arm around her shoulder, Drummond guided her across the street. Traffic had stopped, though, as people hurried to witness the bloody scene. Thankfully, one young woman had taken control of the carriage and returned it with the baby safe and snug. The deaf woman bawled as the young woman patted her back.

Convinced the two ladies had the matter well in hand, Drummond looked back up the street for his hat. Long gone. Damn. He liked that hat. Though he probably needed a new one anyway.

Several women screamed anew. The ghoulish onlookers surrounding the street corner all took a large step back. Drummond pushed forward. This group did not appear too concerned with helping others, and if the injured man had survived, he would require first aid fast.

But the man stood straight, his stark white hair standing out amongst the crowd of black and brown hats, and he offered an uncomfortable grin. "I'm fine. I promise," he said, as he picked up his gray hat and headed across the street. "I'm sure it looked awful, but he only grazed me."

Nobody dared stand in his way. They parted for him with miraculous speed, and when the distinct cry of sirens announced the arrival of law enforcement, the crowd dispersed as if nothing had happened. In seconds, the majority had returned to their morning hikes toward work. Drummond, however, hurried down the street and followed this strange man.

Even if the man spoke the truth, even if he had only been grazed, he should never have been able to walk away so easily. And Drummond had seen the hit. Not a graze at all. That man should have been heading for the morgue.

"Hey, Mister," the paperboy called.

Drummond glanced over to see the boy jogging toward him carrying his Fedora. "Thanks, kid."

The boy hesitated long enough for Drummond to get the message. He dug into his coat and pulled out a nickel. With a flick of his thumb, the coin flipped through the air. The paperboy caught it, smiled, and scurried off.

Setting the hat at a slight angle, Drummond felt more like his job title — the city's only detective of the bizarre — and Gray Hat who should have died certainly fit the description. Drummond headed after the man. Better that than spending another twenty minutes debating where to eat breakfast.

* * * *

FOLLOWING THE MAN proved simple. His gray hat and tall figure were easy to spot in the busy morning. Only a few blocks north and the hubbub of the car accident had drifted away like a leaf flowing down a stream behind them. Nobody on these streets had any clue that something terrible had occurred nearby. But that's the way of all cities. Heck, Drummond had interviewed people who failed to hear a murder on the other side of an apartment wall.

Gray Hat cut down an alley before joining another stream of people moving crosstown. Drummond did his best to keep up without being seen. From what he could tell, Gray Hat never once threw a suspicious eye in any direction. He strolled ahead without any concern that somebody from the car accident might be tailing him.

Four more blocks and he turned into a narrow alley. Drummond waited on the street to make sure he could follow without getting caught. However, Gray Hat did not continue through to the next street. Instead, he entered a door on his left.

Skipping the alley, Drummond walked further along to find that the building belonged to the Afternoon Playhouse. While motion pictures continued to compete with theatres for spaces, Drummond guessed there would always be a hankering for live entertainment. Especially the kind Gray Hat provided — a poster of the man under the name Mezmo the Magical hung outside the theatre doors. Mystic smoke swirled off his fingers and in the background stood a large creature — half-man, half-lion — with the imaginative title Lionman printed beneath.

This early in the morning, the ticket booth was closed, but the performance schedule had been posted on a typed paper. Mezmo's first show was at one o'clock. That gave Drummond quite a few hours to kill.

Further up the street, he spotted a corner diner he had never been to before. "Looks like breakfast, after all."

AFTER A DECENT FARE of eggs and coffee — nothing special in taste and the waitress was sixty-something going on ninety — Drummond thought about paying a visit to the police department. Not too far to walk, he could be there in no time, and his old pal, Detective Cooper, would be arriving soon to start the day.

But whatever information Cooper could acquire regarding the car accident would not be helpful. Mezmo had left the scene before the police arrived. People might report what they had seen, but no copper would take it seriously. Not if he wanted a healthy career in the department.

Talk of ghosts, witches, and magic — not to mention a man smashed against a brick wall who simply up and walked away — well, those in charge did not like such tales. The first time Drummond saw a ghost, he knew he would have to resign from the police force. He couldn't deny what he saw. Fighting against these unnatural occurrences — that was how he chose to handle it all.

Detective Cooper, on the other hand, dismissed the oddities he had witnessed. He tried to straddle a narrow line, tried to hold onto his job while making sure these things were dealt with. Drummond did not think his old partner could manage it much longer.

With a click of the tongue, he decided to leave Cooper out of this one. Instead, rather than waste the morning, Drummond thought he should check out the area. Most people worked, ate, and lived within a few blocks of home, and Mezmo had walked to work. Seemed like a good place to start.

Unfortunately, the city surrounding the Afternoon Playhouse offered nothing beyond the ordinary. Not that Drummond expected a sign pointing and flashing the words WITCHES HERE in bright lights, but anything out of place would have been appreciated. Instead, he found brick apartment buildings, a few corner shops, and the strong tobacco aroma that permeated all the sections of the city situated close to the R.J. Reynolds factories. At length, after plenty of walking and taking the time to read the full newspaper, Drummond made his way back to the theatre, bought a ticket, and settled in for the show.

The building bore the standard traits of any theatre — large proscenium, heavy stage curtain with advertisements, balcony and box seating above, architecture from three decades gone. Sitting in the lumpy chair, Drummond wondered if the owners ever thought to update anything. He noticed that the curtain ads had been carefully placed to cover holes in the old fabric. With only a handful of people catching the early performance, the owners would be lucky to have enough money to keep the lights on, let alone repair or update the place.

An old woman emerged from a side door and sat at an upright piano perched near the stage. She adjusted her ancient glasses, arranged some sheet music, and jumped right into playing a piece that felt more at home in a silent film. Drummond half-expected the stage lights to be operated by candle.

The curtain rose and Mezmo walked out to center stage. Gone were the gray hat and suit. He now wore a black tuxedo, a shimmering cape, and a flashy turban bearing a single peacock feather. Without speaking, and always in time with the music, he meandered through a series of standard magic tricks — all well-performed as far as Drummond could tell, but nothing particularly unique or special. Until Mezmo pulled out a large piece of chalk and drew something on the stage floor.

Drummond's stomach tightened. He wriggled in his seat. Part of him wanted to stop the show before anything bad happened. Another part of him wanted to see what Gray Hat had planned. Drummond figured nobody would cast a dangerous or harmful spell during a show like this — not unless this was to be Mezmo's final performance.

He double-checked the program — Mezmo would be engaged at the theatre for two more weeks.

After lighting a green candle, the magician concentrated. For the first time since the whole show began, Drummond could see that the man actually put some effort into things. Of course, he did. This wasn't an illusion. Casting magic — the real thing — required effort far beyond skillful sleight-of-hand.

Sadly, as Mezmo levitated two feet above the stage, his audience had become bored. A smattering of applause fluttered through the theatre, but nobody understood that they witnessed a man actually floating in the air.

After the curtain dropped, Drummond remained seated, waiting for the few audience members to leave. None of them paid him any mind with the exception of an overweight drunk who weaved along the straight aisle, caught Drummond's eye, and waved with a half-hearted smile. Once alone, Drummond strolled to the front, climbed up onstage, slipped behind the thick and musty curtain, and checked the floorboards. His jaw clenched — casting circle.

He worked through the labyrinth backstage until he found an exit leading toward the dressing rooms. The name Mezmo had been typed on a piece of paper and pinned underneath a chipped and fading star painted on one door. Drummond knocked.

"Enter," a stern voice said.

Drummond opened the door to find a lean, vibrant gray-haired man sitting on a wooden chair with his legs crossed and sipping hot tea. Other than a makeup table with a large mirror and a small rug with concentric circles of color like an archery target, the dressing room matched the man — sparse and practical — leaving Drummond full of questions.

Setting his cup of tea upon the table next to a box filled with makeup tins, Mezmo said, "You are a surprise. I don't often get gentlemen asking for an autograph. Mostly youngsters and the occasional lonely woman with a pretty smile." Before Drummond could respond, the man cocked his head to the side. "Oh, I see. You're not here for an autograph."

"Afraid not. But I did catch your show. It was quite something."

"Not my best work. However, this is not the best theatre, either. Still, in these hard times, we all must do what we can to earn what we need." Keeping his eye on Drummond, the man managed to pick up his tea, have a sip, and return it to the saucer. "What can I do for you?"

Drummond considered stepping into the small dressing room but decided intimidation would not play well. Instead, he opted to lean against the doorframe, push back his hat in a friendly manner, and light up a cigarette. He offered one to Mezmo, but the man declined. "I saw you earlier today, too. This morning. Car screaming down the street, out of control, slammed right off the road. Looked like it hit you hard. Just wanted to make sure you were okay."

"How thoughtful. As you can no doubt see, I'm fine. Enough to perform a show even."

"Yeah, that part really amazed me. Might've been the best trick of all. There you were with your head bashed against a solid brick wall, your blood sprayed it a whole new color, and then a couple hours later, your prancing about onstage like nothing happened."

Though he acted calm, Mezmo's eyes narrowed, and Drummond caught a twitch in the corner of the left. "Obviously, you were mistaken in what you saw. It must've been somebody else who was hit by the car and thrown into this wall. Because no man could survive that, and clearly I'm quite unharmed."

"It's just that I tend to be an observant fellow, and I am positive the one I saw having his head cracked open was you."

Mezmo glanced at his watch. "And yet, you waited close to four hours to check up on me. Even then, you took another hour to enjoy my show. I don't think you're being entirely honest with me. Are you with the police? Have I committed a crime?"

"I'm a private investigator. Name's Marshall Drummond."

A miraculous change overcame the man. He sat straighter, inching forward to the edge of his seat, and shook Drummond's hand with all the enthusiasm of meeting Humphrey Bogart. "My apologies. I was not trying to be rude, but you'd be surprised as to the strange types that I have to deal with."

Extracting his hand free, Drummond said, "I think you got me confused with somebody else."

"I doubt it. North Carolina is not exactly brimming with men like you, men who investigate ghosts and magic."

It was Drummond's turn to keep a calm face while his insides roiled. "Can't say I'm usually noticed for the work I do."

"That's because you don't travel the circles that I do."

"The Amazing Randall? The Death-Defying Swami? Mezmo?"

The man laughed. "No, not stage circles. And please dispense with Mezmo. You can call me Mr. Howe."

"Well then, now that we know who we really are, perhaps we can try this conversation again."

All of Mr. Howe's boyish exuberance drifted away. "I'm afraid that my answers are not going to change. Not significantly."

"You're still going to pretend you didn't use magic to survive that accident?"

"Oh, I did not survive. But I did use magic to return."

"Return? You saying you're some kind of ghost?"

Mr. Howe chuckled with a patronizing tone that grated Drummond's ears. "I am no ghost nor walking corpse nor any other form of undead or apparition. I am every bit a living man as you are."

"Then you've got a lot to explain."

"I think not. I'm hardly answerable to you. Although, I am curious who hired you to investigate me."

Drummond hesitated. "Well —"

Mr. Howe crossed his legs and resumed sipping his tea. "Oh, I see. Nobody hired you. This was to satisfy your own curiosity."

"Look, pal, I don't know your story, and I'm pretty sure I don't care, but you're playing with a stick of dynamite. Witchcraft — by definition, that's the role of witches and their covens. They do not take kindly to people stealing their secrets. Especially men. My advice to you — stick to card tricks and illusions. The real stuff is only going to get you killed."

Mr. Howe sipped more tea and smirked. Turning away, Drummond flicked the brim of his hat. The corridor ended in a metal door which led out to the alleyway. As he headed up toward the street, he muttered, "Serves me right."

After all, what had he expected? It wasn't Drummond's job to save this guy from himself. Nobody watching a show would suspect that any of the magic was authentic. In fact, even the danger that somebody might try to mimic Mr. Howe's act was muted by the fact that all the real elements — the casting circle, the candle, the arcane symbols — would all be seen as merely props to help create a spooky and mesmerizing atmosphere. As long as Mr. Howe did not take it further, did not try to control or harm others, then Drummond couldn't see what else he should do.

Owning a gun did not make a man a criminal. Shooting a person with a gun did. Having an interest in witchcraft should not make Mr. Howe a bad guy. Casting spells on himself was dangerous but only to himself. As long as he didn't turn it on others.

"Mr. Drummond! Mr. Drummond, please, wait!" Mr. Howe waved from the open door.

Drummond planted his feet firm. "Yeah?"

With a furtive glance up and down the alley, Mr. Howe said, "I've decided that I'd like to hire you."

"I don't think that's a good idea."

"I'll pay you double your normal rate."

"Guess there's no harm in hearing you out." Drummond tightened his coat as if buttressing against a hard, cold wind and walked back.

"Not here." Mr. Howe came down the alley, swirling his coat around his shoulders and donning his gray hat. "Is your office far?"

"Far enough that you'll have told me everything by the time we get there."

"Then let's walk around the block a few times. I have another performance in a couple of hours and I can't afford to miss that one."

Thrusting his hands in his pockets, Drummond said, "A walk around the block it is. What's your story?"

Oftentimes, Drummond found it necessary to pull information out of a client through a mixture of friendly commonsense statements and a little tough-guy bullying. Not surprising — most clients did not want to admit that their problem might be paranormal in nature. But Mr. Howe jumped right in. "Have you ever heard of the Fraternity of the Elder Bones?"

"That's a new one to me," Drummond said. "But the list of secret fraternities and brotherhoods is long. Add in all the witch covens, and nobody could remember them all."

A passing woman wearing a hat with a shoulder-wide brim raised an eyebrow when she heard the words witch covens but clearly dismissed the idea as she walked on. Most people kept to themselves, buried in their concerns about work or home or the myriad aspects of daily living.

The few walking behind Drummond and Mr. Howe either didn't eavesdrop or found ways to not believe the things they heard.

Mr. Howe went on, "The Fraternity of the Elder Bones started a long time ago. Long before North Carolina joined the United States. Long before the British even bothered with the States. From what I've been able to ascertain, the Elder Bones reaches back to a small village in France, or possibly, Switzerland."

"Not to be rude, but do I really need the history lesson?"

"Only to understand that these people have had centuries to perfect what they do."

"Based on this morning, I'm guessing they dabble in longevity."

"In a sense. The group took such a focus — longevity, immortality, anything resembling the chance to continue their lives. They have spent ridiculous amounts of money and time attempting to perfect this single spell."

They turned the corner and headed uphill. "Why not cut a deal with a witch? Some of them know how to extend life for hundreds of years."

Mr. Howe chuckled. "If you could even find a witch willing to part with such a precious secret, can you imagine the horrible price they would exact?"

"Very true. So, I take it that you're a part of this Fraternity?"

"Lord help me, never. Bunch of insane hooligans. I mean, of course, they aren't crazy about the spell they've worked on, but beyond that, they are out of their minds. I'd rather be a part of some ancient cult sacrificing virgins into a volcano. At least that had some twisted logic to it."

Drummond tried to keep his voice neutral but suspected his growing disdain for Mr. Howe crept in. "Would you please get to the point? I'd rather not spend all afternoon walking in circles."

With a haughty lifting of his chin, Mr. Howe said, "I believe I'm the one overpaying for your services. If I want to give you the full details, that's what I will do."

"You haven't paid me a dime, yet."

"Shall I finish my story or not?"

"Allow me to speed it up. If you weren't part of this Elder Bones nonsense, then you either bought or stole their spell. Right?"

Mr. Howe paused. "Well, yes, I suppose. That is, well, you're confusing things. Just listen. There was a group of us — myself, Henry, Eustace, and Sarah. Henry is a stage magician like myself and Eustace is his assistant. Sarah is Eustace's friend. For us, it all began back when Henry was in a used bookshop."

"Do I really need to hear this part?"

"Er, perhaps not. Well, I'll be quick. Henry stumbled upon a spellbook and on a lark he tried one of the spells out. Of course, it worked. Not exactly, but enough that he showed us that witchcraft was real. We formed our little group to study it. Through those years we became better at the basics, though none of us was very good, but while we were mediocre practitioners, we were excellent theorists."

Drummond nodded. "You're not alone. A lot of people who learn the truth about the world can't learn to make use of it. So, they study the history, they collect the books, they become experts in lore, all to satisfy that itch."

"Then I suppose that is what we did. However, a few months after I learned of the Fraternity of the Elder Bones, the group had broken apart. Sarah's husband didn't like her spending so much time away from home. Henry and Eustace couldn't find a steady gig and decided to try a traveling tour. I remained here."

"I still haven't heard how any of this adds up to you hiring me."

Mr. Howe stopped walking and glanced around the street. "Because yesterday, Sarah's husband, a brutish man named McAllister, he threatened me. He said Sarah's gone missing and he blames me."

"She didn't quit playing with witchcraft, did she?"

"None of us did. You see, we took a page from the Elder Bones way of doing things. We each had some aspect of witchcraft that fascinated us the most and decided to devote our studies to that one aspect."

"I take it you like the whole immortality idea."

"Not exactly. I don't wish to live forever. I simply desire to live a full life. Not have it cut short by foolishness or accident."

"And the others?"

Mr. Howe resumed walking. "We never shared that with each other. On purpose. Understand that over the years, we came into contact with a few witches. They were not pleasant visits. Mostly, they were warnings. On one occasion, a witch sent Henry to the hospital. When the group split up, we agreed to stay quiet about our pursuits as a measure of safety — in case a witch decided to come after us."

"You think that's what happened to Sarah? A witch did something to her and now her husband can't find her?" Drummond watched Mr. Howe's face. "No, it's more than that. You're worried about yourself. You think Sarah might betray you somehow."

Bristling, Mr. Howe said, "The poor woman is in trouble, and I highly doubt the police will be equipped to handle the situation. But this is your specialty. And there we are. See that? We've only walked the block twice. Not too bad. So, will you take my case?"

They stood outside the front of the theatre. From about halfway through Mr. Howe's story, Drummond knew he would take the case. Heck, he had started investigating the moment he saw the car accident. At least this way he'd get paid.

DRUMMOND HAD THREE NAMES — Henry Peyton, Eustace Harding, and Sarah McAllister. He also knew that McAllister had a husband. That was more than he often started with.

First thing he wanted to do was interview the husband, but Mr. Howe said he didn't know where the McAllisters lived. "Again, for security against the witches, our group tried to keep out of each other's personal life," he had said. "I don't know where any of them live. I don't have numbers to call. Nothing like that. If they wanted to meet beyond our appointed times, they could always find me here after a performance."

Drummond knew the man lied — after all, two of the group had a very personal relationship — but he figured calling Mr. Howe dishonest would not set things off on the right footing. So, Drummond headed back to his office to check the phonebook and start making some calls.

But as he walked toward the building's entrance, Detective Cooper stepped out of his car. Criminals often develop an eye for a cop, and watching the way Cooper strode toward him, Drummond saw it, too. The stooped shoulders, the G-man outfit, the tie askew, and one hand kept close to the holstered weapon — all of it screamed police.

Drummond tapped two cigarettes from a pack. "How long you been sitting in that car waiting for me to show up?"

"Too damn long. Where you been?" Cooper accepted the cigarette and a light.

"Just started a new case. I'm guessing you're up against something bad or you wouldn't be here."

"Yeah. Can we talk upstairs?"

Drummond tried not to be offended at how Cooper glanced around. Back when he was a cop, Drummond would never have wanted his peers to see him talking with a guy that investigates ghosts, either. Only thing that could kill a career faster would be to bring in a psychic.

They climbed the stairs to the third-floor landing. He jingled out his keys to open the door with a frosted-glass window and the number 319 painted fresh.

Cooper slumped onto the old couch against the wall opposite the three large windows. The gray day did little to brighten the office. Drummond walked over to one of two built-in bookcases and pulled a copy of Moby Dick. He had recently refreshed the whiskey flask hidden inside and didn't mind sharing with his old patrol partner.

"Thanks," Cooper said, taking a swig.

Sitting behind his desk, Drummond kicked up his feet. His muscles sighed — he'd walked too many blocks today. "You wouldn't be here, and you certainly wouldn't have sat in your car for an hour or two, unless you had no choice. What kind of mess are you trying to solve without your bosses knowing?"

"In the past, I've brought you things that are supposedly witches and ghosts and such, but whenever you've solved those cases, if it ended in something I couldn't put in a report, then I managed to change the wording so nobody would question the matter."

"Or you."

"But this, well, this is something you can't call a different name. Problem is, I don't even know what to call it in the first place."

"Take another drink and tell me what happened."

Cooper tipped back the flask and winced. "It started this morning. I was called to the scene of a car accident."

Drummond's stomach dropped. "Let me guess. Car went out of control and slammed into a guy. But you didn't find a body."

"How did you — no, you're kidding me. This is your case already?"

"Afraid so. I don't think it's going to be one you can report on, either."

"Not much of a choice about that. Lots of witnesses. Oh, I just realized — you're the Good Samaritan who saved the woman with the baby but didn't stick around to make a statement."

"You should probably keep that out of your report, too. Chief Murdoch is not a fan of mine."

Cooper snickered. "I think the Chief would rather admit that witchcraft exists than give you credit for anything."

Sitting forward, Drummond tapped his finger on the desk. "You said that your case went beyond the usual witches and ghosts. All I know is that a guy walked away from what should have killed him. That's a spell. Heck of a powerful one, that's for sure, but still just a spell. Not enough for you to risk coming to see me. Did something happen after I left?"

"You didn't check out the car, did you?"

"I followed the dead man."

Cooper paused, letting those words sink in. "When I got there, patrol officers had pushed the gawkers back as well as the press — well, Joey Shultz from the Journal. Thank goodness there wasn't more to deal with. I took one look inside that car and I knew I'd be sitting here. See, the driver — this woman — she didn't look right."

"Yeah? She have an extra head or something?"

"Might as well have been."

Not the answer Drummond had expected. He figured there would have been a strange symbol painted on her forehead or, if this turned into a truly dark case, a strange symbol carved into her chest. Before his thoughts could leap ahead of the facts, Drummond grabbed his notebook and pencil. "How about you tell me everything you came here to tell me?"

Cooper set the whiskey flask on the floor, not too far away, and stretched out on the couch. "I've seen a few unfortunate souls in my time — some birth deformities, a guy burnt up in an apartment fire, and one that got mangled in a factory accident. I ain't ever seen anything like this. Half of her face — it just wasn't human."

"What was it then?"

"How should I know? I'm just a cop."

"Fair enough. Describe her for me."

"Right." A sheen of perspiration beaded on Cooper's forehead as he stared at the ceiling. "First off, the entire right side looked like a pile of rocks. All lumpy and misshapen. On the left side, she had light-brown hair, smooth and long. Probably looked really good on its own. But on the right side, her hair was nothing but a few twigs poking out. Real twigs — pieces of wood. From what I could see of her neck and arms and part of her side showed through a tear in her blouse, well, it didn't get much better for her. Her neck had a rough look to it like sandpaper, like really heavy sandpaper, and her arms had a greenish tinge. Soft, green and furry."

"Like moss?"

Cooper sprang up. "It was like she had become part-tree. Is that possible? Sheesh, listen to me. That's how screwed up this world has gotten. I'm seriously asking you if a woman could become part-tree."

"I've never heard of it, but that doesn't mean it can't be. Heck, you saw it with your own eyes. Anything else?"

He shook his head. "The rest of her was covered in blood."

"She at the morgue?"

"Yeah. But nobody is going to want to make an official report about her. They'll simply say that she lost control of the car and died on impact. The rest they'll ignore. Write up that the body was too damaged for further conclusions."

"That covers the weird. What about the normal basics? What's her name? Where does she live?"

"Nothing yet. Lady didn't have anything on her — not even a purse. No plates on the car. Nobody showing up to claim her."

Drummond tapped his chin with the pencil. "Any chance you can get me to that body? If we wait too long, they'll cremate her to make sure nobody sees a thing."

"I'm thinking the same. But I can't get you in until after hours. If I'm seen with you in an official capacity —"

"Yeah, I figured. Tonight then. Besides, I've got another lead to follow up."

All of Cooper's worry and fear vanished as the detective side of his brain kicked in. "That's right — the walking dead man."

With an awkward chuckle, Drummond said, "That's not my lead. In fact, the dead man is my client. His name's Mr. Howe."

Cooper picked up the whiskey flask. "You have the most bizarre life I've ever seen."

"Don't I know it."

Drummond pocketed his notebook. He let Cooper take a final swig before returning the flask to Moby Dick. Though he wanted to see the tree-woman's body, he already had that piece in place. Examining her only served to confirm his suspicions.

As if reading Drummond's mind, Cooper said, "This wasn't a car accident, was it?"

"I doubt it. That woman tried hard to kill Mr. Howe. And I'm searching for a missing woman."

"Same woman?"

"Maybe. Care to wager on the odds?"

"Not on your life." Cooper grinned as he donned hat and coat. "So, where are we headed?"

"We?"

He opened the office door. "I don't like it, either, but this is an official investigation. Body in the morgue and plenty of witnesses to the accident."

Drummond paused. He spotted the look in Cooper's eyes. He had witnessed it in a mirror the night after he saw his first ghost.

Had it been only the woman, Cooper could have swallowed the lie that she suffered from some rare fungal disease. Had it been only the dead man walking away, he could have accepted any number of explanations — the simplest being that the man only got grazed by the car. But with both happening, with Drummond involved, and with a possibly-missing woman apparently wrapped into the case, Cooper had to learn more.

Drummond couldn't tell which way Cooper would fall when the case finished up. Perhaps he would find some nugget to latch onto that let him toss away all this strangeness at the earliest convenience. Perhaps he would finally accept that Drummond's world was not just superstition and delusion.

Either way, Drummond recognized that Cooper wouldn't be able to pass this case off. The man needed to tag along, to see how it all played out, to know what awaited at the end of the road. "Might be nice to have my old partner by my side again."

Cooper offered a grim nod. "Thank you."

HAVING COOPER ALONG proved useful right away. Instead of spending the rest of the day dealing with phone call after phone call trying to track down the correct Peyton, Harding, and McAllister, Cooper put one of his new recruits on the task. As long as Drummond's name remained out of the picture, police department resources would be available.

"It could take a while," Cooper warned. "Recruits are eager to please, but grunt work is grunt work no matter how you cut it."

Drummond said, "We can't go to the morgue until tonight. How about the car? You guys still take them to the dump?"

"Not at first. Chief Murdoch has a deal with Doc's Auto Shop. Doc gets to take out anything worth taking out before it goes to pasture."

"And the Department gets a little something out of the deal."

Cooper tensed. "Better that than the Chief skimming it for himself. In case you forgot, the police don't get a lot of money to take care of the whole city."

"Whoa, cowboy. I just want to take a look at the car. I don't care about the arrangements."

They drove off in Cooper's Ford Model 18 — a new car specifically bundled with all the options cops wanted. Drummond had the courtesy to lower his brim in case anybody recognized him in the passenger seat. Of course, Cooper would not get in trouble for merely chatting with Drummond or driving the man someplace, but Drummond figured the less pressure on his friend, the better. If he was right, Cooper had set himself on the road toward the worst day of his life. Might as well not ruin it further.

By the time they arrived at the auto shop, Cooper had eased back a bit. He still had a constant frown on his brow and his grip on the steering wheel had not lessened, but Drummond noticed that the man no longer hunched forward, ready to bolt at every turn. Progress.

As they stepped out of the car, Drummond said, “Flash your badge and get us to the wreck. I’ll keep quiet. But once we’re there, you stay back.”

“I know how to inspect a car.”

“This is my case now, and you don’t know what you’re looking for.”

The original Doc of Doc’s Auto Shop had passed away more than a decade ago, but people still remembered the man fondly. His sons continued the business, and through a mixture of loving memory and savvy marketing they kept the name. Cooper had no trouble getting the boys to give access to the car. They didn’t even bother walking the detectives over.

Probably don’t want to know what we’re up to, Drummond thought.

“Over there,” Cooper said, pointing to the Standard Coupe with its front end smashed into a hunk of jagged metal.

Drummond began with a simple examination of the exterior. He walked a complete circle, noticing nothing beyond the damage from the accident. Except the damage itself seemed odd.

“See that?” Drummond pointed to the front of the car.

“I see a wreck. What about it? The car slammed straight into a brick wall.”

“Jumped the curb, hit the man, and kept going right into the wall. Shouldn’t this be flat?” He ran a finger along the slight concave curve of the radiator. “A man couldn’t make this dent. It looks like the car bumped a metal pole. But this would be where the car hit Mr. Howe. Right?”

Cooper crossed his arms and glanced back at the auto shop’s front office. “Hurry up.”

Drummond wrinkled his brow as he walked over to the driver’s door. It had been removed. Probably at the scene in order to get the body out. The seat, the steering wheel, the foot pedals — all of it had dark splotches of dried blood. The gear shift had been painted in gore. Probably punctured the driver’s stomach on impact. Splinters of wood stuck out of the right side of the seat, and leaves sprinkled about as if somebody had pulled a tree out of the car with too much force.

"Got a flashlight?"

Cooper pulled out a square light that fit in the palm of the hand. Drummond flicked it on and bent down near the pedals. He played the light over every part of the floor. Nothing. Before he backed out of the car, a thought struck him and he glanced up under the dashboard.

"There you are," he said.

"Got something?" Cooper made a show of leaning in but managed to avoid getting too close to the blood.

Drummond reached up with two fingers and pinched around a piece of cloth that had no business being there. With gentle care, he slid the cloth free. Turned out it was a tan ribbon tied around a knot of blond hair and a twig.

Inching back as if the package might snap out like an angry snake, Cooper said, "What is that? Why was it in there?"

"Good questions. A lot of this stuff is still new to me. I've only ever seen what the locals do for witchcraft. It's an old, old practice with depths far beyond a lifetime of study. You said that woman had become part tree —"

"Only that she looked that way."

"— and we know she targeted Mr. Howe."

"We don't really know that for sure."

"True, but I suspect when you identify the woman, you're going to find that she is either Sarah McAllister or Eustace Harding. Once we know that for certain, then we know Mr. Howe was the target for certain."

Cooper licked his lips as Drummond's words sank in. "I'm going to headquarters. I can see if they have an identity yet, and I can check on the recruits about those addresses."

It was a small thing, but seeing the man start thinking like a detective gave Drummond hope. "Drop me back at my office. I can look into this thing we found, see what kind of spellcasting it is. That should help us figure out what's going on. I'll meet you tonight at the morgue."

"Sure." Cooper clicked his tongue as he headed back. "I can't believe I'm having these conversations. It was one thing to go into your office and drop a case that gave my fellow officers the heebie jeebies. Once I left, it was out of my hands. Done and gone. But this — this is nuts."

"You get used to it."

* * * *

DRUMMOND FELT A TWINGE OF GUILT for shading the truth from Cooper. When he said that he wanted to look further into this tied up hair and twig, that much was honest. He let Cooper assume the rest. The part he left out — he would not be spending hours hitting the books to find his answer. No. Not when he could ask for the answers directly.

Once Cooper's Model 18 turned the corner, Drummond crossed the street and headed back toward the car accident. He had about two hours until he had to be at the morgue. Three blocks to get to the scene, several more to reach the theatre, a chat with Mr. Howe, then back all those blocks and up to the morgue — depending on how long the talk with Mr. Howe went, it might be tight. He picked up his pace.

When he reached the theatre, the front was dark. Without pause, he hustled down the alley and knocked on the side door. That failed, so he pounded on it.

An old man wearing an old suit answered. He had on more make-up than a Victorian strumpet. "We're just getting ready. The theatre doesn't open for another hour. You can buy tickets out front."

"Already saw the show."

The man's face brightened. "Come for an autograph?"

"I'm working for Mr. Howe."

The man's face darkened. "Oh. The magician. He's in his dressing room."

Drummond knew where to go. Though he did knock on the door with the painted star, he did not wait for an answer. Pushing the door open, he stepped in, crowding the tiny room and looming over Mr. Howe.

"How dare —" Mr. Howe gazed upward from the mirror. "Oh, sorry. I thought you were the stage manager. Solved the case already?"

"Getting closer. But it doesn't help when my client holds back on the truth."

"Excuse me?"

Drummond shifted enough to close the door, then leaned back against it with his arms crossed. "You acted like this morning was a random accident. But the woman driving that car targeted you, tried to kill you specifically, and I think you knew that. You also told me Sarah McAllister went missing, that you didn't know where she lived, but that's not true, either. And before you get all uppity and start denying everything, you should know I found this."

He tossed the ribbon-tied hair and twig onto the make-up table. Drummond found it amusing that he put on this performance in a theatre. Hopefully, Mr. Howe would not see through it all.

Drummond had no proof of anything, yet. He simply wanted a reaction.

Mr. Howe stared at the small bundle like a chess master plotting how to destroy his opponent in the next five moves. Drummond observed every motion, every facial tic, every breath. Mr. Howe stayed calm — no surprise at the accusations, no shock at the hair and twig, nothing at all. He sat and thought.

From the hall, a voice called out, "House opens in an hour."

Several other voices called back, "Thank you."

Then a knock at the door. "House opens in an hour, sir."

"Thank you," Mr. Howe said before standing. His eyes narrowed, and the thin, cold line of his lips made him more threatening than any scowl could manage. With a jerk forward, he pressed Drummond against the door, bringing his face in close enough that Drummond could smell the coffee and cigarettes perfuming the man.

Perhaps it was only the dramatics of the stage life, but Mr. Howe's large reaction surprised Drummond. Under other circumstances, Drummond would have belted the man back, but he had come to the theatre and provoked Mr. Howe to glean whatever information he could get. In fact, he would have to admit that his plan had exceeded expectations.

"You are quite rude," Mr. Howe said. "To come here with direct and veiled accusations right before I have to go on stage is disrespectful, to say the least. What's worse is that you don't even know what you're talking about."

"Are you denying what I've said?"

"The only thing you've said that displays any competent detective skills is that the driver did, indeed, target me. I agree with that. There's a plausible argument that the woman is Sarah McAllister, but she could just as easily be Eustace Harding. Neither woman cared for me much. But the idea that I know the whereabouts of Sarah is not only absurd, but frankly, suggests you lack the intelligence for your job."

"Now who's being rude."

Pressing his finger to the side of his head, Mr. Howe said, "Think for just a minute. I know it's difficult. Why would I have chased you down an alley to hire you for this case if I already knew where to find Sarah? If I was up to some nefarious plot like you suggest, why would I involve you at all? You saw the accident, came to my dressing room, and you were leaving. I would be the stupidest criminal in the world if I then asked you to investigate my crimes. And pay you double your rate, no less."

"You haven't paid me anything yet."

"You haven't done anything worth being paid."

Drummond swiped the hair and twig bundle and left the theatre. He shook off the embarrassment of his one obvious mistake and focused on the riches provided by Mr. Howe. The man's outburst suggested several important things. He confirmed this wasn't an accident. He confirmed that the driver was either Sarah McAllister or Eustace Harding. And he confirmed that the tied hair and twig held some kind of power. Anger came from fear. Nobody reacted with that much anger over nothing.

After grabbing an apple from the corner stand, Drummond made his way to the morgue. The walk took up much of the leftover time and gave him a chance to eat as well as think. Unfortunately, there wasn't a lot to think about yet.

He knew the routine when he arrived. With his hands in his pockets and his head angled down, Drummond meandered around to the back where Cooper waited in the well of a sunken door. The sky had darkened but nobody bothered to turn on the lamp hanging over the doorway. Dusk clung enough for Drummond to see his old pal, but the man's cigarette glow gave him away more than anything else.

Without a word, Cooper led the way through the basement maze toward the morgue. He used his flashlight to find the correct door for the exam room, leaned in, and popped the lights on before entering. In the dark, Drummond had not seen Cooper's distress, but now he could read the man's unease plainly.

"I didn't know the dead made you uncomfortable," Drummond said.

"Not usually. But this one's different. And frankly, with you along, I'm wondering if I should worry about the dead popping up back to life."

The body had been placed on a table in the back and covered with a dirty, white sheet. "Has anybody examined the body yet?" Drummond asked as he approached.

"Nobody wants to even look at the thing. Chances are in the morning they'll lift the sheet, say to themselves, 'That lady's dead,' and that'll be the end of it. I doubt anybody in the department will argue the matter. The sooner that thing is gone from everybody's life, the better they'll all feel."

Drummond pulled back the sheet. It was far worse than Cooper had let on. Half of the woman's face no longer existed. However, instead of the mangled, bloodied mess of an accident victim, her skin had become the rough, fertile ground of a tree — rocks and dirt, perfect for moss and fungus. Sprigs of yellow hair poked out of her earthy scalp like new plants reaching for the sun. Her eye had been covered over, half her nose flattened, and even the line from her jaw to her neck had become a solid piece of bark.

Swallowing his nerves, Cooper appeared on the opposite side of the table. "It hasn't stopped."

"Oh? She wasn't like this when you found her?"

"No, this is — I could see her face before. And there was a gash on her forehead from where she banged into the steering wheel."

Drummond noted a slight indent where the gash may have been, but since then, the rough textures of Mother Nature had covered it over. He pulled the sheet down to the woman's shoulders. The tree bark continued along the same lines. With a quick motion, he snapped the sheet up and peeked at the rest of her corpse. Tree bark, stone, and moss all the way to the thigh.

"What happened to her clothes?" he asked.

"Already burned. There was a concern this might be some kind of disease."

"But they just leave the body out?"

Cooper reddened. "With this thing, people aren't thinking straight."

"That's for certain." Drummond looked over the woman's feet. Nothing odd there. Next, he checked her hands. "Look at that."

Cooper inched in as Drummond pointed to the woman's right hand. A circle had been carved into her palm, and in the circle, a simple but identifiable image of a tree.

"What's it mean?" Cooper asked.

After returning the sheet to its proper place, Drummond stepped back and pursed his lips. "More magic cast in ways I've never seen before. Any luck figuring out who this lady is? Or did your boys track down those addresses?"

Cooper's mouth tightened as he shook his head.

"Your boys didn't check for Sarah McAllister, did they?"

"Didn't even try. I think the Chief stopped them, but I doubt they put up much of a fight."

"Then you're on your own."

"Well, I've still got you."

"Gee, do you have any good news for me?"

With a shiver, Cooper said, "Are you done here? The sooner we get out, the better. I don't want to lose my job because we're caught lollygagging."

They stayed quiet until they were out of the morgue and standing by Cooper's car. Drummond mulled over next steps. He needed to learn about this magic, but he didn't like his options.

The few witches he would trust to give him a real answer were still witches. They would exact a hefty price for the information — one that did not involve money. Going to a witch for answers had to be a last ditch, desperate move, and this case did not add up to that.

Leroy Parker would probably know the answer, too. But that man lived alone in the woods for a reason. He wanted nothing more than to sit with his books and learn all about witchcraft from the safety of anonymity. If Drummond went running to the hermit whenever there was a conundrum, Leroy would eventually stop answering the door. Or worse, he'd bring out a shotgun.

Which left Drummond with the worst option. He'd have to hit the books and research it himself.

WITH A POT OF COFFEE and a pack of cigarettes, Drummond sat at his office desk and got to work. Cooper said he had other, normal cases that needed his attention but that he would join up in the morning. Drummond assumed the idea of searching through actual witch books left a bad taste in Cooper's mouth. So, he searched alone through one tome after another. His personal library on the subject of witchcraft was scant compared to most others who studied such things, but it sufficed. Usually.

Forty minutes later, he sat back and rubbed his eyes. The thought of spending the entire night combing through these books threatened to rush the coffee in his stomach right up his throat. He really needed to hire an assistant to do all of the bookwork. Somebody who thought staring at old texts written in blood epitomized fun.

He swiveled to gaze out at the city, though the YMCA blocked most of his view. That was exactly how this case felt. He saw bits and pieces, but the full view seemed blocked at every turn. Things that should have been simple had stymied him. So much so that he had resorted to becoming like Leroy — holed up, alone, reading tomes of witchcraft.

He hated to admit it, but the roadblocks occurred right alongside the arrival of Detective Cooper. Before that, he didn't know as much, but he had a clear line toward his answers. Since Cooper's involvement began, Drummond had been ambling about, seeing fractions of what had happened, and not getting anywhere.

Pacing his office, he thought about Cooper and the man's delicate position with the police.

Cooper was a sturdy, dependable detective on the force. He had a strong record, too. In fact, the only big strike against him was his relationship with Drummond. But that could be discounted because the two men had been partners when they were beat cops, and all cops hold both a deep appreciation and a soft spot for the idea of a partner.

But then this case came along. Nobody wanted to touch it. Basic steps of an investigation had been ignored — identifying the body, performing the autopsy, interviewing the victim. Without a doubt, those higher up the ladder sought to bury the entire incident. Last thing any Chief of Police wanted to admit was that there might be magic involved and that those on the police force accepted magic as real. In the end, Cooper had no choice but to play both sides of the field.

"Which means I'm on my own."

Like a dog let off its chain, Drummond lunged across the office, swiped up the phone book, and got to doing what he knew best — legwork. Turned out there were only a dozen McAllisters listed. Number five hit — Shawn McAllister, husband of Sarah, worried out of his mind for his missing wife. So worried, in fact, that he agreed to meet with Drummond at nine o'clock that night.

Drummond could feel the excitement racing his heart faster, and he tried to curb it. McAllister was desperate. He would have agreed to meet with a duck, if the duck quacked a promise to help.

Grabbing his coat and hat, Drummond crossed the office and opened the door. Cooper had a fist up, ready to knock.

"I'm never going to sleep tonight. Can't get this crap out of my head. So, tell me what we need to do."

Drummond grinned. "Get your car."

THIRTY MINUTES LATER, they parked across the street in a pleasant neighborhood a few blocks off of the eastern section of the city. The narrow houses lining the streets looked like uniformed soldiers standing at attention. What they lacked in individuality, however, they made up for in life. The laughter, the arguments, the gleeful screeches of surprised children, the hacking cries of a baby — from all sides, the sounds of families bled into each other like an abstract choir.

Drummond and Cooper walked up to number 31. Shawn McAllister answered before the second knock had finished. He was a young man, mid-twenties, strong, square-jawed, shaved hair. Held himself with military form. But his eyes betrayed the hours of worry that had been eating away at him.

"You Drummond?" he said with a voice that should have been powerful and commanding, but fell weak and wobbling.

"I am. This is my partner, Cooper. Before you let us in, I want to make sure you understand that I'm not with the police. And I'm not your usual private investigator."

"You said all that on the phone."

"You've had a half-hour to let it sink in. Still want to talk with me?"

Stepping back to open the door wider, McAllister said, "If you can help me find my wife, I don't care who you are."

The house looked rather typical for a city home — long and narrow, staircase practically at the foot of the front door, living room barely enough for a couch and a chair, a meager bar shoved in the corner, basic kitchen in the back. A lamp next to the couch provided dim lighting. Still, Drummond could see well enough to notice that the furnishings had been set with precision. The couch, the chair, the end table — all had been placed perfectly centered against the wall. A blanket had been folded into a sharp rectangle and set exactly centered on the back of the couch. Even the three framed photographs of family members had been hung on the wall with perfection.

McAllister gestured toward the chair. "You want a drink?"

"I better not while I'm working."

"Right." He sat on the couch — in the middle, on the edge. "Tell me what you need? How do we find Sarah?"

While Cooper leaned on the stair railing, Drummond settled in the chair, crossed his legs, placed his hat on his knee, and pulled out a notebook. "Let's start at the beginning. When did you know she was missing? What have you done about it? Tell me everything that led up to me sitting here asking you these questions."

"Yessir. I can do that."

Two days ago, McAllister came home after work (he was a plumber) expecting dinner and his wife but found neither. Not even a note. He thought that maybe she had been gabbing with one of her friends and lost track of time. It happened on occasion. But hour after hour went by and still no Sarah. He called around to their family, making sure to ask about Sarah without indicating what he feared, but she had not visited any of them recently. He did the same with their friends. He even drove around the neighborhood as if he had lost a pet.

"Please, you gotta help me. I can't live without that woman."

Drummond put on a show of closing the notebook and storing it in his pocket, all the while letting out a series of disappointed sighs. "Look, Mr. McAllister, we really would like to help you out, but I can't do any good at finding your wife, if you're not going to be honest with me."

"You think I'm lying? I just told you —"

"I believe everything you've said. But you've willfully left out some important details. Namely, why don't you go to the police? I'm guessing it has something to do with your wife's connection to a man named Mr. Howe."

Even as McAllister's voice turned dark, the rest of him shivered. "How do you know about him?"

"I'm good at my job. So, you tell me your story again, but this time let's hear the full truth."

Dazed as if he had taken a right cross from a prize fighter, McAllister shook his head and cleared his throat. Drummond let the man stall for a short time, but eventually he had to clear his own throat in response. McAllister reddened but looked no closer to speaking.

"What's holding you back? Is it the fact that your wife had some kind of relationship with Mr. Howe or is it that she was involved in witchcraft?"

McAllister's chin quivered. "You know everything, don't you?"

"Not enough or I'd have found your wife already. So, quit dancing around things and tell me everything."

He rubbed his palms against his eyes. "Okay. Here it is. Sarah has always had an interest in that witchy spell stuff. Long before I ever met her."

"You were okay with that?"

"I saw it as a dark streak, that's all. She likes horror movies and Edgar Allan Poe and anything like that. Loves Halloween. It's not like I believe in any of it, and I certainly didn't think it was more than entertainment for her. You know? Just a thing she liked to think about."

"But that changed."

"It's my own damn fault. I saw an ad in the paper for Mezmo and thought it'd be a fun thing for Sarah. Right up her alley. I bought tickets, and we went to the show. But near the end, she practically burst out of her seat. On the way home, she said that Mezmo had performed magic. I laughed — I actually laughed about it back then. But, I mean, the man was billed as a magician. Of course, he did magic. Guess the joke was on me. Once we go to the house, she dove into her books. I fell asleep, and she woke me up at close to three in the morning. She had found the spell he had used. You sure you don't want a drink? You might need it."

"I'll be fine. I've heard a lot stranger than this before." Including Mr. Howe's version which did not match this one.

McAllister headed to the small bar in the corner and fixed himself a gin and tonic. He knocked it back and set about making another. "I still didn't understand the seriousness of what was going on. I had to go to work. I had to make sure we could pay the bills. Sarah, well, she went to Mezmo's show the next day, and afterward, she approached him backstage. That set everything in motion. Within a month, they had befriended Eustace and her husband, and the four started their little club."

"Club?"

"The Magicians of the South. As far as I could tell, it was like any kind of club. They'd get together and talk about witches, magic books, and spells, and all of that nonsense. Well, it seemed like nonsense at the time, but now she's missing."

"Why do you think her absence is connected to this club?"

"Because we had a fight right before she left. I told her I couldn't take what she was doing anymore, that I needed her to stop, I needed her to forget it all and remember us. You know what she said? She told me she was doing all of it for us. She slammed the door and promised when she came back, everything would be perfect. But she hasn't come back."

"You have any idea what she meant? What kind of spells she was working on?"

With an odd reticence in his voice, McAllister bowed his head over his drink. "I guess I should show you her room. Otherwise, you'll just keep asking questions and wasting time."

Drummond gave the man a moment of quiet to summon the courage he clearly needed. Thankfully, Cooper maintained his quiet observation. Drummond appreciated this as a sign of respect. Cooper knew he was out of his depth and didn't balk at playing second chair. Less than a minute went by before McAllister set his empty glass down and shuffled toward the stairs. Drummond and Cooper followed.

The second floor consisted of a narrow hall with a bedroom on the left side and a smaller room and bathroom on the right. A tiny window at the end overlooked their tiny yard. A few pictures hung on the walls — notably, a photograph of Sarah in her wedding gown.

She had a healthy, plump look to her. Though she didn't smile — most people held a serious, stern look in photographs — she sparkled with joy in her soft eyes. She exuded a sense of confident strength mixed with subservience that must have appealed to the military side of Shawn.

Most importantly, she had strands of dark hair visible beneath her headpiece. The half-tree woman had blond hair. Looked like Eustace Harding drove that car into Mr. Howe.

"Here," McAllister said, opening the door to the smaller room. "Light is to the left. I don't go in there."

Indeed, he stepped back as if the door led to a blazing furnace. Drummond entered the room, saw the lamp on a small table, and turned on the light. For someone with no real knowledge of the spectral and magical, poor McAllister must have thought his wife had gone insane. Cooper's soft gasp said the same thing.

The entire room had been painted black. Heavy curtains blocked the windows. The bed and dresser had been removed. Only a handful of bookcases and the small table with the lamp remained. A large casting circle had been painted on the floor, and rows of half-melted candles lined one wall for easy access. And the books — each one a volume on spellcraft or witch lore.

Leroy would love to nick a few of these.

Though the circle itself had been painted in thick, yellow lines, the symbols had been made with chalk. Easy enough to erase and change for other spells. Drummond noticed that the current markings — even the simple, straight lines — had a shake to them. An unsure hand.

One book sat on the floor, opened to a specific diagram, and the same symbols had been diligently copied onto the circle. He cocked his head to read the page — For the Conjunction of Multiple Minds. With his foot, he nudged the cover closed and checked out the volume's title — Witchcraft for Influencing Others.

He glanced over the bookshelves. All of the books had been professionally published, and none looked older than a decade. Many of the cover designs mimicked the true witch tome look, but they were only facsimiles.

A real witch library had many books that were one-of-a-kind, handmade, and given from one generation to the next. Plus, authentic books tended to be covered in skin — animal or human. Even the books that were published commercially (with paper covers) had runs of less than a hundred. Some has few as thirteen — one for each member of a coven. Sarah McAllister's library belonged to a novice. A dabbler.

Sorry, Leroy. You wouldn't have liked this, after all.

That thought stopped Drummond. If this room had belonged to Leroy, it would have looked much different. The bookshelves would have better books, of course, but the rest of the place would not have been so blatant, so witchy. In fact, Leroy's home looked like any cabin in the woods. Only when one observed closely did the truth reveal itself.

That held true for all the witches Drummond had ever encountered. Despite depictions in motion pictures and in fiction, witches had learned to hide their presence quite well.

Years of being burned at the stake will do that to a group.

Yet here Sarah McAllister had converted a bedroom into an overt room of witchcraft. To Drummond, that spoke of something more than simply being a novice. It was like a show. Perhaps she thought this display would impress those in her club — in particular, Mr. Howe. After all, he appeared to be the only one amongst them that had any real power.

Based on this room, Sarah would never accomplish much more than a few parlor tricks. Eustace had attempted something far more difficult and failed horribly. Whatever spells Henry had played with, Drummond figured the man had not fared any better or he would have been able to help Eustace. Only Mr. Howe had displayed the real deal — and a big spell at that. Coming back from that attempted murder via automobile showed a man quite capable with complicated spells.

They returned to the living room downstairs. Finishing yet another drink, McAllister looked over with glazed eyes. "I swear I didn't know things had gone so far. That room was her private place. I didn't go in there."

"What about the Club? Did you call any of them?"

"I went through Sarah's little book and found Henry's number, but nobody answered. I didn't find an entry for Eustace. But I knew where to find Mr. Howe." McAllister's head lolled with his slurring speech. "Went right to that theatre and yelled at him, tried to get him to tell me where Sarah went off to, but he acted dumb."

"You don't believe him?"

"He was the center of the Club. He called the meetings, he decided what they would talk about, he controlled everything. How could he not know? But I ain't got proof, and if I go to the police, they'll find out about that room and they won't believe anything from that point on.

They'll think my Sarah was up to no good and they won't try too hard to save her. Or they might think all that crap is mine and think I killed her or something."

Drummond figured he only had time for a few more questions before McAllister passed out. Direct had to be the way. "Do you think Sarah might be having an affair with Mr. Howe?"

Bracing for anger or possibly violence, Drummond instead received a short sob. McAllister wiped his nose against his sleeve. "I've been thinking it a lot these last hours. Maybe she was slipping away from me for all these months since she got into that witchy stuff. Maybe I missed the signs. But I do love her. I want her back." With a furious stab of his finger, he went on, "And you explain this to me — if she was planning the whole time to run off with that bastard magician, then why would she be so nice to me last night? We were together, you know what I mean, and afterwards, I held her in our bed and she was telling me about her plans for our future."

"Dreams of kids and a larger house?"

"Not like that. I know we don't look well off, but it's worse than that. We're going to lose this place in a few months and have nothing. But she said that soon all of our money troubles would be gone. She had a way to make us rich. I thought it was a little pillow talk. Some wishful thinking. Maybe it was, but tell me — why would she be intimate with me, why should she say all those things, if she was planning on leaving me? Maybe she was unhappy, but she's not a cruel woman. That ain't like her."

He stumbled to his feet and swayed over to make another drink. Drummond guessed the man would be unconscious before he could down half of it. Turning to go, Drummond caught a look from Cooper — his pal had something.

Cooper stepped closer to the couch. "Mr. McAllister? You mentioned calling around while looking for your wife. You said you called Henry Peyton. May we see the address book she kept all those phone numbers in?"

3:23AM. 273 LINCOLN AVENUE. Drummond and Cooper sat in the car watching Henry Peyton's apartment building. The phone number had led to this address and pinned Henry to apartment 4D. Light still shined through 4D's window. Drummond tapped Duke Ellington on his knee as he stared at that light. But Cooper suggested they wait a few minutes to better get a feel for the place. Maybe this was the official way to do things, but Drummond had left that world a long time ago. "Enough waiting," he said as he left the car.

Getting into the apartment building could have been trouble but not during such a late hour. As Cooper caught up with him, Drummond merely ran his finger down the call buttons, pressing one and waiting a few moments before moving on to the next. Nobody liked waking to a doorbell in the middle of the night, especially by a drunk who can't find his own keys.

On the fourth ring, a voice said, "Huh? Who is it?"

Drummond mumbled and slurred until the voice tossed out a few expletives and buzzed him in. Simple as that. Cooper stayed silent, and Drummond wondered if he disapproved or was taking mental notes.

No elevator. They took the stairs to the fourth floor. Faded green wallpaper lined the hall and the brown paint on the doors looked several years worn. Cooper knocked on 4D.

A muted voice muttered, a door closed inside, and then a bone-thin man opened up — just a crack, just enough for Drummond to see a gaunt face, salt-and-pepper scruff, and sallow eyes that had not enjoyed a descent night's sleep in over a week. Those eyes gave Drummond and Cooper a once over.

"What do you want?" the man asked, his cigarette-soaked voice grating hard.

Donning his most authoritative tone, Cooper said, "You Henry Peyton?"

"Yeah?"

Cooper shoved the door hard, knocking Henry back as he and Drummond entered. "A lot of people are looking for you."

"Hey, what's the big idea? You can't barge in here. I'll call the police."

"Go ahead. Call 'em."

Drummond had to admit it — he never liked Cooper more than at that moment. Before the situation turned ugly, though, Drummond stepped forward. "I'm Marshall Drummond. I'm a private investigator. This is Cooper. I've been hired to find Sarah McAllister. We thought you were missing, too. But clearly you're not."

A quick scan of the apartment presented an orderly, well-maintained place. Not particularly well off but not struggling to make ends meet, either. Nice touches like area rugs and floral curtains suggested Eustace Harding's hand.

Cooper thrust Henry against a wall. "Look, pal, if you know where

Sarah McAllister is, you better start talking. I've seen too many horrible things since I woke up, and I don't plan to see anymore."

Through a trembling jaw, Henry said, "She doesn't want to be seen. Not like this."

"What does that mean?" Slamming Henry to the wall again, he went on, "What did you do to her? You turn her into a half-tree like your girlfriend?"

"I didn't do that to Eustace. I didn't do anything to anybody. It was an accident. We're all working together and things just went wrong. That's all. Horribly wrong."

Drummond tilted back his hat and lit a cigarette. "Let him go." He waited for Cooper to comply. "Mr. Peyton, I'm sure you can see that my friend here is upset. We both are. He's shaken by what your little group has done — accident or not. Me — I'm angry that you attempted to do any of it in the first place. You've been trying to catch the Devil's tail and that's a stupid thing to do. So, unless you want Cooper to beat you senseless and then have to deal with me — and I haven't even shown you how angry I am — well, the best thing you can do is take us to Sarah McAllister. Now."

Henry nodded hard enough to pull a muscle in his neck. He winced but stifled a groan. His eyes darted to a closed door on the opposite wall.

"Sarah McAllister?" Drummond called out as he crossed the room. "Are you okay in there?"

Cooper pulled his .38, and though he had yet to point it in any particular direction, Henry's hands shot straight into the air.

Drummond knocked. "Mrs. McAllister?"

Now Cooper raised his weapon toward Henry. "Why isn't she answering? What did you do to her?"

But Henry's eyes had locked on the door. He shook his head as tears dribbled down his cheeks. "Don't go in there."

Swallowing down the rise in his throat, Drummond thought Cooper might have the right idea. Pulling out his own .38, he turned the doorknob.

Like the room in Sarah's house, this one had been devoted to witchcraft by non-witches — black walls with white symbols painted in vertical stripes, yellow casting circle on the floor, candles and books, plus heavy curtains to keep out the light. Only one big difference — Sarah McAllister.

She hung on one wall like a human tapestry. With her arms and legs spread as if caught in the middle of a jumping jack, she looked frozen in place. Her dark hair hung limp and sweat-soaked, and her head lolled forward. Her bones pressed against her skin. But the worst part of it, the part that made Cooper whisper a few curse words from the other room — bloody, pulsing ribbons of flesh covered all but her head, plastering her against the wall like a mummy from a twisted mind's nightmare.

Drummond felt his body break into a sweat. He wished he could blame that on the room — it must have been ten degrees hotter than the rest of the apartment — but the shiver prickling his neck suggested otherwise. He wrinkled his nose at the stench — death and … chlorine? Yeah, a strong chlorine odor permeated the air — not from cleaning, though. The smell emanated from the things stuck to Sarah. Covering his mouth, Drummond saw a book on the floor opened to a page dotted with blood. He swiped it up and backed out of the room.

As Drummond closed the door, Henry crumpled to the floor. He buried his head in his arms and convulsed through several deep sobs. Cooper holstered his weapon as he stepped back toward the window.

Drummond crouched near Henry. Holstering his weapon, too — didn't want to upset Henry even more — Drummond said in a gentle tone, "Tell me."

Henry shuddered. "We just wanted to know what Mr. Howe knew — we wanted to learn to cast spells, make our lives better, that sort of thing."

"The Magicians of the South."

"No, the Magicians of the South is nothing. We fed that story to Sarah's husband and anybody else who might've gotten nosey." Tears flooded down Henry's face. He tried to talk more but ended up in a coughing fit.

Drummond patted the man on the back. "I think I've got a good idea what happened. I'm guessing that the three of you thought you were smart, trying to cheat your way to riches, and you made a deal with Mr. Howe. He gave you the spell to perform, right?"

Nodding, Henry took a deep breath, coughed twice more, and then appeared to pull himself together. "He brought us those books and explained how to draw the symbols and what words to say and how to make the offerings."

"What did you give him in return?"

"Money. Not even that much. Said he didn't want to cause us problems with family or anything."

From the window, Cooper said, "Wanted to keep you quiet. You spend too much and suddenly Sarah's husband is asking questions, causing problems."

Henry sniffled. "But that spell wasn't worth any of it. We did it exactly how he said and it didn't work. It went all wrong. I know you're thinking we screwed it up somehow, that we're novices and that we don't know anything at all, but that's not true."

"Looks pretty accurate to me."

"No. I mean, yes, we're novices, but we knew that going in. We spent weeks going over every bit of it. We understood that it could be dangerous, so we made sure to get it right. I'm telling you, we did not mess it up."

Drummond thought about Eustace. "Your gal, she wanted to be thinner. Stick thin. Instead, the spell turned her into a tree. And Sarah, what did she want?"

"Money. Not to be filthy rich or anything. Just enough to live comfortably. Sarah's like that. Never been greedy. If she had gotten her chance, she would've wanted something simple. Just a good life for her and her husband."

"What do you mean if she had gotten her chance?"

Henry looked up at both detectives. "You think we'd keep going after Eustace? We're not insane."

Cooper spun back. "Shawn McAllister said his wife's been missing for two days. You're telling me she's been like that for two days?"

"Almost. We met here two days ago. It took most of the first day for Eustace's spell. When we finally got the thing to kick off, there was a flash of light that knocked me on the floor. Took a bit before I could see. And when I did, Eustace was already starting to change, and Sarah was like ... I tried to get her down, but — you didn't touch her, did you?"

Drummond placed a placating hand on Henry's shoulder. "I've learned not to touch something like that until I know what I'm dealing with."

"Good. It hurts like hell. Makes your heart start pounding like a heart attack is coming. You know? And then it releases this horrible smell."

Drummond nodded. "You tried to get her down, found you couldn't, so what then?"

"After everything, well, I've just been trying to turn it all back. I figure if a spell got them like this, then another spell should reverse it all. Nothing works. I've barely slept. But I must've dozed off a little bit yesterday morning, and that's when Eustace left. I don't know where she is, and I can't go looking for her because I have to stay with Sarah."

"She's dead," Cooper said. Not the way Drummond wanted to break the news.

Henry did not seem surprised. "Killed herself, didn't she?"

"She tried to kill Mr. Howe with a car. Smashed him into a wall. She died on impact, but he didn't get a scratch."

Drummond frowned. The stories about this group were all different enough to be a problem. None of it tied together like he wanted. Unless—

He leafed through the book from the casting room until he found the spell. Having been in the witchcraft world for several years now, Drummond picked up a little knowledge regarding the symbols and casting practices. He would never be crazy enough to attempt any of it, but reading over the spellbook, he could piece together how it worked — mostly. One of the key symbols he noticed — three circles in a row with a horizontal line cutting across them all.

He tapped his chin. Gazing down at Henry, he said, "You and Eustace are shacked up here together, right?"

Henry's face dropped in shock.

"I don't care about that. The point is you share this place which means you share the casting room, too. At the McAllister's, Sarah had a casting room. In fact, she had drawn the same group of symbols from the spell. Just like in your room."

"That's how the spell works. We had to have separate circles that connected their power. At least, that's how we understood it."

Cooper said, "But Sarah fought with her husband. She came over here. You said all three of you cast a spell from here." He glanced up at Drummond. "They had to be at both circles, right?"

"It's worse than that," Drummond said. He walked over to a small table and set the book down.

Cooper squinted at the book. "Am I supposed to understand any of that?"

"Not at all. These are usually written in about three different languages, one of which has probably been dead for centuries. Might even be in code. But if you know witch symbols, you don't need to read the instructions. The symbols explain most everything and they don't change no matter the language of the text."

"I take it you know the symbols?"

"Only a few. That squiggly line that turns straight and then shoots off in different directions — that means transformation."

Unable to hide his enthusiasm, even at this grotesque moment in his life, Henry said, "Exactly. And this symbol here, the rounded W on top of a cross, that means offering."

Drummond shook his head. "You idiots didn't even translate this correctly. That is not the symbol for offering. It's the symbol for sacrifice. Your spell was never going to work. Your offering was rejected. That's why Eustace was deformed." He glanced at the door to the casting room. "And Sarah — oh, I see. The hair and the stick were smashed together through Eustace's body. She became part-stick part-woman — human and tree. But the offering which should have been a sacrifice had been presented bound in a tan ribbon — almost flesh-colored. That's why those strands of flesh have wrapped Sarah to that wall. It's part of the same rejection."

Henry said, "If that's true, then why didn't it do anything to me?"

"Good question. But before we deal with that, we need to stop what's happening to Sarah."

Cooper said, "You know how?"

"I've broken a few curses in my time. Stay in here and keep guard on Henry. I'll take care of this."

Drummond saw the mixed emotions cross Cooper's face. The man did not like the idea of being relegated to guard duty, and he hated the idea of letting his temporary partner face dangers alone; however, he sighed relief that he could avoid stepping into that room. After all, Cooper had seen Sarah's casting room and that caused him enough strife.

With a strong stride, Drummond moved to the kitchenette and rifled through the cabinets, trying all the doors and drawers. Once he found a box of salt, he turned to Henry. "You got a hammer? Anything I can pry up wood with?"

"In my car. Got a tire iron."

"That'll do. Cooper, take him with you and get it."

"What are you going to do?" Cooper asked.

Drummond stepped toward the closed door to the casting room and Sarah. Nobody said a word.

ONCE HE HEARD THE MEN leave the apartment, Drummond's body drooped. He had seen a lot of weird things but this vied for the top of the list. With a shudder, he reached for the doorknob. No sense in waiting for the tire iron — if he waited, he might lose the will to push onward. He opened the door.

The putrid odor slammed in his face, and bile rushed up his throat. Words like Stop! Run! Don't be an idiot! screamed in his head. At least some part of him still had the sense to be afraid.

"We're going to get you out of this," he said.

He didn't exactly believe his words, though he hoped they were true. She didn't seem to believe him, either. But there was a glimmer of emotion in her eyes, not truly hopeful — perhaps a hint of faith.

"Here you go," Henry said from the doorway.

Drummond grabbed the tire iron. "Thanks," he muttered as he shut the door.

Approaching the casting circle with caution, he kept his focus on Sarah. More importantly, he paid attention to the horrid strips binding her to the wall. If anything would try to stop him, it would be those abominations.

Just focus on the task — each piece, step by step.

At the edge of the circle, he snatched a glance at the uneven floorboards. One stood out — not only did it cross the main lines of the circle, but it poked up enough to make his work easier. Stepping around the circle, he stopped at the chosen floorboard and used the tire iron to pry it up.

Drummond kept expecting some reaction as he yanked the wood free and broke the circle. He thought the strips might make some noise or lash out at him. He hoped breaking the circle would break the curse and release Sarah — Curse Breaking 101. But no such luck.

"Why should it be easy?" he said, tossing the floorboard aside.

He pursed his lips as he stared at the room, the strips, and Sarah. He still had the box of salt. Then again, breaking the circle had failed to produce the slightest reaction. Salt was an even more basic approach — Remedial Curse Breaking. Not really curse breaking, anyway. More like defensive measures.

But nothing else came to mind, so Drummond started by laying down a line of salt across the doorway. That would stop a lot of otherworldly things from getting out of the room — at least, through the door. Next, he put a handful of salt in his coat pocket for quick access should it become necessary. Finally, he stood before Sarah, grabbed another handful of salt, and tossed it onto the strips that bound her.

A sharp hissing erupted like a nest of snakes angered by an intruder. Sarah's head snapped upward, her eyes blazing bright, and she shrieked. The noise raging from her shook the walls and set Drummond's pulse racing. It sounded like two voices — Sarah's and a deeper, more masculine cry.

Possession? Drummond had dealt with the phenomenon only twice and both times scared him to the bone. But when Sarah's mouth shut and her head drooped forward, the male voice continued — from the other side of the door.

Drummond stormed into the living room to find Henry on his knees, clutching his stomach, and crying in pain. Cooper stood over the man, bewildered by the sudden shift in behavior and lost as to what he should do. "He just started screaming."

Drummond grabbed Henry's arms. "Lift your shirt."

"Huh?" Tears soaked Henry's cheeks, but the odd demand appeared to bring him back to the moment — and to the fact that the pain had ceased. With a wary motion, he lifted his shirt. Red welts marked his torso at the same points that the strips covered Sarah.

Drummond stepped back. "Now we know that you didn't walk away from this unscathed."

Jumping to his feet, Henry cried out, "What did you do?"

The harsh look from Drummond withered the man back. Henry turned to Cooper but didn't dare say a word. The only other direction he could move was toward the casting room, and he could hardly look in that direction. He dropped back to his knees. "What's happening to me?"

Drummond had been thinking the same question, but he had an idea about the answer. "Looks like I've got a good news/bad news situation for you. On the good side — Sarah is not cursed. At least, not in the normal way."

"There's a normal way?" Cooper said.

"Yeah, but this is different. Especially because of this one symbol in the spell. Circles with a line through them. I think it's the reason Henry felt what happened to Sarah or why Sarah felt what happened to those things on her."

With a shiver in his voice, Henry said, "Are you saying we're all joined together?"

"Sure seems that way." Drummond's face tightened. "Now, the bad news — when you're dealing with something that needs a sacrifice and is tormenting you, it usually means that you've still got to make the sacrifice. Otherwise, this thing won't stop."

"A sacrifice? I can't kill anybody."

"Not that big of a sacrifice. But it has to be personal. That's what a real sacrifice is."

Henry's face screwed up as he thought. "I don't have anything to give up. I mean I've got some cash. I could burn that. Or my bed. I don't know. This apartment?"

"Material things won't work. Those kinds of sacrifices are sometimes good, but since this thing already rejected you once, you've got to make it count big. There won't be a third chance."

"Then what? What should I do?"

"If I were you, I'd cut off a finger."

Cooper and Henry stared at Drummond as if he had stripped naked and started dancing.

With a shrug, Drummond said, "Go stand in front of Sarah and that thing, announce that you're making a true sacrifice, and cut off one finger. If it doesn't let her go, cut off another. I wouldn't bother with a third. If after two, it still isn't working, then we'll have to think of something else."

A new stream of tears covered Henry's face. "I can't do that."

"Then you and Sarah will suffer until you die."

"But … does it have to be a finger?"

"Not at all. Some of your toes, an ear — heck, you can castrate yourself, if you want. I just assumed a finger was the sensible way to go."

Henry peeked at the door to Sarah and firmed up his body. "None of this is her fault. She was the one who acted cautious. Eustace and I — we pushed things too fast."

Bobbing his head toward the kitchenette, Drummond sent Cooper without a word. Cooper searched a few drawers and found a carving knife. He walked it over to Henry.

"You need help?" Cooper asked.

Though every part of Henry's face suggested he needed a good sedative, a shot of bourbon, and somebody else to do the cutting, he shook his head. "It's got to be me."

Henry took the knife, walked back to the kitchenette, grabbed a hand towel, and then entered the casting room. When he closed the door, Cooper let out an exasperated huff and turned toward Drummond. "Is this the kind of thing you do when I send you a case? Make a guy cut his own fingers off?"

Exhausted anger flared in Drummond, but he tamped it down. The corner of his mouth lifted. "I do whatever's necessary to save people."

"That what we're doing? We're saving them?"

Drummond considered staying quiet, but then Cooper would fixate on the sounds that would soon emanate from the casting room — sounds of Henry screaming and crying as he mutilated his own flesh. "When you have a case, somebody's broken an actual law. A legal one.

There's procedures and rules that you can follow to catch the guy, lock him up, and if you do your job right, get him in a court to be sentenced for a long time. It isn't easy, but you can do it, and at the end of the day, you can rest knowing you helped the victim get some bit of justice. But with my cases — all of that goes out the window."

Using a handkerchief to pat the sweat on his brow, Cooper said, "Then what's the end for you? How does this stuff work out?"

"Even without official procedures, there are rules. Not that I know them all. Of course, there aren't any arrests, no jail time, nothing like that. But you do get a chance to bring peace to people. To put things right."

Henry stifled a sharp screech, but Sarah bellowed for a time. The sound weaved around them, leaving Cooper green and clearly ready to vomit.

Drummond said, "These people played with witchcraft like it was a lark for an evening. It's a shame, but there's no way that they get to walk away from this clean. Now, if I do my job right, they'll still have plenty of time to get their heads screwed on tight and make sure they never do something this stupid again."

The door opened. Henry walked out with the bloody towel wrapped around his hand. He glared at Drummond. "Nothing. She's still stuck on the wall."

"Damn."

Cooper frowned. "What does that mean? The sacrifice wasn't good enough?"

Walking toward the room, Drummond said, "It means that we still don't know what we're dealing with. It's not a curse. It's not an Essence. It's not something that wants a sacrifice. I keep thinking about that connection symbol. It's the only solid bit of the spell that I understand. We've all seen it in action."

"Right. That part of the spell connects Sarah, Henry, and Eustace."

"Maybe the problem is Eustace." Spinning toward Henry, Drummond said, "Think now — yesterday morning, did you and Sarah suffer an attack of pain at any point?"

Henry answered immediately. "Yes. I was trying to get her to drink some water, and we both screamed. I felt like somebody had punched me in the chest. It only lasted a moment."

Cooper said, "You didn't think that worth mentioning?"

"I, well, everything's so confusing, so frightening. And I was busy chopping off a finger."

Drummond put out his hand to silence the two men. "What if we have this backwards? I said it wasn't a curse or an Essence-related thing or even a spectral thing, but what if it's actually all of them?"

"Instead of Sarah, Henry, and Eustace being connected?"

"It's the spell-side of things that's connected together. Because they all failed to make the proper sacrifice, they were cursed by each of the connected pieces. It's the curse that ties these three together. Eustace died in the process — well, she killed herself, but the point is she's gone — and through it all, Henry and Sarah have been feeling each other's suffering."

"Okay," Cooper said. "If that's correct, what then?"

"Maybe we treat this like a haunting. Salt hurt the thing which lends the idea some credence. Normally, we'd have to go find the body of the ghost to salt and burn the remains."

"You want to go back to the morgue?"

"I don't think that'll help. This isn't a normal situation. Two of the three culprits are still alive."

Henry whispered, "And we're all connected."

"I think this connection you all share is being created by having casting circles bound with the same spell. Sarah has an identical one in her house, so perhaps we can treat the circles like extensions of the people. Perhaps these circles can be a substitute for the bones — at least, to the extent that the spell is concerned."

"What does that mean for us?"

Drummond picked up the box of salt and headed back into the casting room. "You both stay back." Neither Cooper or Henry had tried to move.

Not giving Sarah even a glance, Drummond set about lining the casting circle with salt. He added small salt piles on each of the symbols around the edge. In the center of the circle, he spotted the dead worm of Harvey's finger. He threw a hefty amount of salt to cover it.

Once he finished, he pulled out a pack of matches, struck one alive, and tossed it into the circle. Despite having no fuel but the wood itself, the fire spread as if burning gasoline. The flames flared knee-high in a dazzling deep green.

Sarah lifted her head but had no other reaction.

Damn, Drummond thought. He started to turn away, to head back into the living room with the hope of regrouping and coming up with yet another solution, when the flames shot toward the center of the circle. With the sound of sucking air, the fire engulfed Henry's finger. A deep red pillar rose straight from the middle like a burning geyser. The strips holding Sarah secure burst into green flames. They hissed and whined like young pine in a campfire.

Drummond leaped across the room to catch Sarah as she fell off the wall. Not wanting to give the spell a chance to change its mind, he hustled out and stretched her on the couch. Cooper and Henry crowded behind him.

"Is she okay?" Henry asked. "How did you do that? Are we free from this curse?"

In answer, Sarah's muscles convulsed as her eyes rolled up to whites. A pop from the other room announced the end of the fire. It disappeared leaving a gray smoky residue in the air. As Drummond tried to hold Sarah still, Henry flailed back before collapsing onto the floor and entering seizures of his own.

Drummond rolled Sarah onto her side. "Help out Henry," he said, and Cooper sped over to the man on the floor.

As fast as it began, the seizures ceased. In the unsettled quiet, Cooper looked straight at Drummond. "Is it over?"

"Almost," Drummond said as he covered Sarah with a blanket from the end of the couch. "There's another circle in Sarah's house. Based on all we've seen, I don't think it'll be done until I go over there and do everything the same as I did to this one." His gaze settled on Henry. "Everything."

Cooper's face paled. "What? More fingers?"

"Unless he wants to come up with something else."

They waited fifteen minutes until Henry had recuperated enough to sit up and think clearly. Drummond did not hold back. He explained the situation with cold, blunt words.

"Toes," Henry said, at length. "Can I give up a couple toes?"

Drummond nodded. "Give me three, just in case."

BY THE TIME Drummond arrived at the McAllister home armed with a box of salt, a tire iron, and three toes wrapped in a handkerchief, the dawn lightened the sky. Drummond had not slept in over a day, and the road blurred. But seeing the joy on Shawn McAllister's face when informed that his wife had survived helped wake his senses.

"There's still something I've got to do, though," Drummond said.

"Anything. You found my Sarah. I'll give you anything you want."

"I've got to destroy that room upstairs."

McAllister's mouth twisted with a mixture of a sneer and a smile. "Let me help."

"Better not. Some of these things feed off of strong emotions — at least, the energy associated with strong emotions. Either way, I don't think you should be in there."

Not bothering to explain further, Drummond trudged upstairs. Before starting, he took a moment to inspect the circle once more. He wanted to make sure nothing had changed — either through magic or a dishonest hand. Thankfully, all remained the same.

With the tire iron, he pried out one floorboard, breaking the circle. Then he took the two smallest toes and placed them in the center of the circle like a kid getting ready for a grotesque game of marbles. He thought about announcing his intention to offer a sacrifice but figured it wasn't necessary — the spell's connection meant that the sacrifice had already been heard earlier. Last, he salted the circle and the toes, and lit the whole thing on fire.

Drummond heard the whoosh and stared at the green flames licking the air. The heat warmed his skin, but he couldn't detect any scent — good or bad. He felt off. Admittedly, for a detective of the strange, this case had been more off than usual. No witches but a witch curse. No ghosts but a ghost burning. The whole endeavor had left him unsettled.

He thumped down the stairs to find McAllister boozing up again. "The sun's barely up."

"I'm celebrating. It's all done now, right? My life can go back to normal?"

"Sure. Whatever that is. Where's your phone?"

Knocking back his drink, McAllister said, "Kitchen."

Leaving the man to his numbing pursuits, Drummond called Henry Peyton's apartment. Cooper answered.

"It's me. I'm finished here. How are they doing?"

Cooper said, "Can't you hear?"

Drummond had thought the high-pitched noises came from a bad connection, but the moment Cooper uttered his question, Drummond's heart sank. Henry and Sarah both cried out in torment.

Cooper said, "They've been rolling around on the ground and screaming like they're on fire and trying to put it out. It's backed off a bit, so I'm guessing they'll calm down soon. I hope."

"Calm down and be okay, or calm down and be like they were before I left?"

"Sorry, but I don't think they're any better off than before."

This case kept sucker punching Drummond, and he had tired of it. He went back to McAllister, told the man to drink up, and left. He stormed over to his car, yanked open the door, took his seat, and waited. The muted sounds of a city still asleep weighed against him as his eyes felt heavy and his body weak. He had no idea where to go. Rubbing the stubble on his jaw, he played over the case in his head.

Three people bound over an interest in witchcraft. They find a source, Mr. Howe, who knows enough about it all to be a danger to everybody he talks with. Lacking any other contacts in the witchcraft world, they put their faith in Mr. Howe. He provides a spell that will link the three together and, they hope, will strengthen the power of the spell. They're not wrong on that aspect. Drummond had come across linked spellcasting before.

Each of the three wants to use the spell to gain some sort of personal benefit — beauty, security, wealth. But they screw up — mistranslate sacrifice for offering — and cause themselves to be hit three times. Once, with a curse. Twice, with the rage of a rejected sacrifice. Three times, with Eustace's death and the creation of a haunting.

All those threes, all linked together. That symbol of three circles connected had taken on more than just —

Drummond's skin prickled as he stared at the steering wheel. Circles. The only thing in this case that didn't come in threes. Sarah had a circle and so did Henry. But no third.

Starting the car, Drummond's stomach growled — part hunger, part anger. There was still one more circle that needed to be destroyed. And Drummond knew exactly where to find it.

6:29 AM. AFTERNOON PLAYHOUSE. Drummond hustled down the alley to the side entrance. He didn't bother knocking. Nobody would be at the theatre this early in the morning. Other than matinee performances, stage entertainment was a nighttime gig, and despite its name, the Afternoon Playhouse only had matinees twice a week. Nothing going on the stage until the night.

Picking locks had never been Drummond's forte, but give him enough time and he could manage. Though he did have the privacy of a deserted alley, the time of day suggested that he might get seen by people walking to work, if he dawdled. Pulling out his kit of small tools, he got started. Thankfully, the theatre had not invested in heavy security. Drummond had the door opened in three minutes twenty seconds. Not bad for him.

Storming down the hallway, he clenched his fists and gritted his teeth. When he reached Mr. Howe's dressing room, he found it locked. But it was a flimsy door and nobody was around to watch. No need for lockpicks. One strong kick smashed it open.

With one hand, Drummond flicked the lights on. With the other, he grabbed the makeup chair and tossed it aside. Mr. Howe had not decorated the room save for one small touch — the colorful little rug of concentric circles. Like a target.

He whipped the rug against the wall to reveal a casting circle painted on the floor. Bad enough this two-bit charlatan thought he could pull one over on some naïve and desperate individuals. But that he thought he could pull one over on Drummond, that made the detective's blood burn.

"Not this time, pal," Drummond said as he jammed the tire iron into the wood to pry open the casting circle. Two strong motions and a few whining, rusty nails later and a wood plank popped out. Drummond let the wood and the tire iron clatter to the floor. He dug out the box of salt and generously applied it to the casting circle. Placing Henry's third toe in the center of the circle, Drummond then formed a pile of salt over it.

Breathing heavily and sweating even more, he stepped back to inspect his work — making sure he covered all the necessary points. Satisfied, he opened his matches and struck one on the side of the box. But before he could toss the burning stick onto the casting circle, a rough-skinned hand grabbed him by the back of his collar and threw him into the hallway.

Drummond rolled against the wall, trying to put some distance between him and his attacker. With two hops back, gaining several more feet in distance, he raised his fists and finally got a look at the situation. Kind of wished he hadn't.

The mountain before him stood at least six feet tall and must have weighed over two hundred fifty pounds — most of it muscle. That alone would have had Drummond feeling the bruises before they had even been inflicted. But in Drummond's world, it was the rare case in which he only had to deal with an overly-muscular thug — this world held magic.

The beast had sharp incisors, lengthened to the point of fangs, and the bone structure of his face resembled more of a lion than a man. While his skin, eyes, and general facial features remained human, the abundance of hair and the muscles upon muscles all suggested a large feline. Even the way he moved — the casual power of a born predator — held the threat of a hunting cat.

Drummond peeked at the dressing room door. If he could rush in there, strike a match to the circle, and run off, there would be no need to deal with Lionman. But he couldn't reach it without being in striking distance of the brute.

Lionman moved closer, blocking the dressing room door entirely. So much for even dim possibilities. Drummond rolled his shoulders and readjusted his arms, taking on a boxer's stance.

In an asymmetrical fight, there were a few avenues toward success, but Drummond could only recall one. Usually, big guys like Lionman were slower and less fit. A smaller man could move faster, dodge and weave, try to tucker out the lug until it became easy to either land a hard blow or escape. But Drummond had no room to maneuver in the hallway.

"I've clearly upset you. Is this your place? You take care of the theatre when the curtain's down? Maybe you live here all the time. I don't care." Drummond continued babbling whatever came to mind. It wasn't a song to soothe the creature, but he hoped a stream of words might help to distract Lionman long enough to catch him off guard and hit a vital point — probably the crotch.

However, the words did little to cast a spell around the brute. Drummond inched back further. He could whirl around and make a run for it. He would have to negotiate the dark stage, though. If he succeeded in reaching the edge without falling into the orchestra pit and dying, he would still have to make it through the empty house to the lobby and out the building — all before Lionman grabbed hold and broke every bone in his body. Drummond didn't like the odds.

Apparently, Lionman didn't want to give Drummond a chance to gamble. The beast shook off whatever buzzed in his head and stomped forward. With a guttural noise that could have been the beginnings of a quaking roar, he thrust out an arm to take hold of his target.

Drummond blocked with one hand and used the only option he could think of — he spun toward the danger. With a simple step, he closed the distance and punched. If he landed that groin shot, Lionman would fall to the knees, and Drummond would follow up with a strong cross to the head.

But the brute shifted his hips. Instead of landing a solid hit between the legs, Drummond slammed his fist into Lionman's pelvic bone. Probably didn't even register in Lionman's thick head. But Drummond's fingers sure noticed. He felt a pop in his ring finger. Snapped in two or dislocated — either way, the hand would not be easy to use.

Lionman glanced down, confused by Drummond's audacious move, but not too confused to act. He lifted Drummond with ease and smashed the detective into the ceiling. Then he dropped Drummond onto the floor. As the ground knocked the world into spinning circles, Lionman kicked hard into the ribs. Another pop.

"That will do," a voice said.

The beating stopped. Drummond tried to lift his head, to see through his blurring eyes who commanded this beast, but he knew the answer already. There was only one person it could be — Mr. Howe.

THE WORLD WOULD NOT STOP CAREENING. Drummond's muscles felt like overstretched rubber bands. When Lionman took hold of Drummond's ankle, the detective could not even muster the tension in his calves or thighs to put up resistance. Lionman dragged Drummond along the hall floor like a giant lumbering through the forest, hauling its evening meal.

They came out onto the stage. A bare bulb atop a black-painted stand held its bright vigil in the center. As Lionman thrust Drummond onto a chair and tied his arms around the back, the detective looked out at the empty seats of the audience.

Guess I could've run this way, after all.

Mr. Howe strolled across the stage, his shoes clicking on the hardwood, his stern face holding all the controlled mystery he wore when performing as Mezmo. Gesturing to the light, he said, "You know what this is?"

Sitting upright in the chair had settled Drummond's head a bit. Not being thrown from ceiling to floor had something to do with it, too. "I believe it's called a lamp. Though usually they have shades around the top."

"It's called a ghost lamp, and its main purpose is to provide light in this auditorium when no one is here. Without any windows, a theatre is so dark you cannot see anything in front of your face — not even your own hand. Pitch black. Now, it got the name ghost lamp because some people believed the light also kept spirits from haunting the stage."

"I'm guessing you're going to tell me that it's not a superstition and that the light actually does keep away theatre ghosts."

"Oh, no, it's pure superstition. However, you and I both know ghosts are real. We know that there are many more real things in this world than most people believe. That is precisely my point. Just because something has a name does not mean it is what we believe it to be."

Drummond wondered how hard Lionman had hit him because he thought he understood Mr. Howe's point. "You're talking about witchcraft."

"Precisely." Mr. Howe brought his hands together as if in prayer. "Just because it is called witchcraft does not require a witch to be involved. I believe I have proven that with a few of the displays during my shows."

Keeping one eye on Lionman at all times, Drummond said, "You're more right than you know."

"Oh?"

"It's true that you don't have to be a witch to harness these powers. But it's also true that the word witch itself is a misused term. Most people hear witch and they think of a craggy, old lady stirring a pot of boiling eyes of newt and talons of eagle, trying to create some spell that will manipulate the world or, at least, those around her. But really, at its most basic form, the term means nothing more than a woman who studies witchcraft. Somebody who has devoted her life to better understanding the forces of Nature around us."

"You really do understand."

"The only problem is that whether you're a witch that has studied and practiced for decades or a stage magician who barely understands the forces he's playing with, the end result seems to be the same — people toying with great power and becoming corrupted in the process."

Mr. Howe straightened his tie before holding his hands firmly at his sides. "I assure you that I am far from a corrupted individual."

"Lionman over there suggests you've been messing around in very corrupt ways. Not to mention the Magicians of the South."

"His name is Jasper, and I did not create him. I met him several years ago when he was performing in a circus freak show. Most of his facial anomalies are simply defects of birth. The rest is stage makeup. As for the Magicians of the South — they corrupted themselves. Nobody forced them to reach out to me. They came to my show, learned what I could do, and pestered me until I would share my secrets."

"Nice speech, but I'm not buying what you're selling. You gave these three novices a very complicated spell. For what? They said you wanted money, and while I'm sure you took anything they offered, I find it hard to believe that was your motivation. Especially considering the risk you take if any real witches happen to notice what's going on."

Mr. Howe seemed to weigh Drummond's words carefully. He walked over to Jasper and whispered in Lionman's ear. Drummond tried to show no emotions. He had hoped to keep Mr. Howe talking, to play on the man's hubris, and have him reveal whatever nonsense all this added up to. But Drummond could not ignore the fact that he had been tied up and that a large, dangerous brute wanted to pulverize what remained of the detective's head.

With a surreptitious glance at Drummond, Mr. Howe whispered a few more words and patted Lionman on the back. The huge lug walked off the stage, up the aisle dividing the audience, and left for the lobby. Mr. Howe picked up a stool and gently set it in front of Drummond. He sat.

Drummond could not help himself — his relief came out in an audible sigh.

"I don't want to hurt you," Mr. Howe said. "I find it frustrating that you cannot understand what I want to accomplish, yet I must admit I'm also delighted to meet you. It's rather lonely being one of the few non-witch practitioners. As you can imagine, covens don't want to talk with me, witches don't want to talk with me, anybody involved with that world generally doesn't want to share their secrets with the likes of me."

"You think I'm going to spill what I know to you?"

Mr. Howe chuckled. "It would be nice, but no, I don't have any illusions as to that. But with you here, I have the opportunity to speak about the things I know without having to mask it in stage dressing or fancy riddles. I won't have to pretend that I'm only talking in a fictional sense."

"Is that what this is all about? Are you trying to recruit these young, foolish people into becoming your followers? People who want nothing more than to listen to you?" Before Mr. Howe could reply, Drummond's mind jumped ahead. "No, it had nothing to do with that. You gave them the spell, but you did not require contact with them afterwards. In fact, you don't even know where they live. You hired me to find them. The spell had to do with connecting things together. Three things, specifically. All in threes. Brings to mind something that's been bothering me from the start — there's four of you. Three casting circles, one of which is right here with you, yet there are four individuals involved."

Mr. Howe smirked. "It is a conundrum."

"Unless somehow Henry and Eustace were counted as one person.

Perhaps Henry never really meant to cast the spell for his own benefit. That's it, isn't it? The three were you, Sarah, and Eustace. Interesting — the spell didn't backfire for you."

"I am a much more accomplished spellcaster."

"This required all three to work together." Drummond leaned forward as much as his bindings allowed and his eyes widening. "Unless it never did. Unless the two of them did exactly what you wanted. You set them up, waited for them to create these connections, watched them closely — all so you could siphon something off of them."

Clapping his hands, Mr. Howe said, "This is delightful — seeing your mind spin circles around itself, when the answer has been sitting in front of you from the moment we first met."

Drummond frowned. "We met when I saw you die."

"Yet here I am."

Drummond leaned back to put some distance between him and Mr. Howe. Because he saw it all now and his stomach soured at the thought. Mr. Howe had never intended to help these young people. He used them.

He wanted to perform a powerful spell, one that could keep a man alive after being slammed into a brick wall by a car. That kind of spell required a witch with great skills — or the great sacrifice of a bunch of novices. Drummond's jaw tightened as he stared into the empty theatre.

Mr. Howe knew they would fail, and that was what he wanted. Only through their failure could he succeed with his spell, the real spell, the one this was all about.

"You told me the first time we met," Drummond said. "You're not looking for immortality."

"That's right. I don't want infinite time. Just a little more than I've been given."

"By linking their circles to yours, all of the energy they put into their spell would flow through to you," Drummond said. "When they failed and enacted a complexity of curses and worse, they would die and you would grab hold of their — what? souls? — which then became your Death shield. Is that right?"

"It's right enough."

"But it didn't go that way. While Eustace and Sarah suffered, Henry tried to heal them. He would never be able to do anything significant, but he did delay their deaths. Enough that you were starting to worry. And you weren't the only one. Shawn McAllister paid you a visit. That told you he was searching for her, and if he found her before she died, all of your plans went away. Still, you held out hope that by the end of the day, they would be dead and you would be shielded."

Drummond pictured Eustace in that car, the pain of each physical movement blending with the mental anguish she suffered over what had become of her.

"Except things fell apart," he continued. "You didn't hear from McAllister or the police, so you were thinking all was well. Until Eustace searched the blocks around the theatre, found you, and ran you down. The impact killed her instantly. You, however, lingered long enough for your spell to kick in. Had you died first, none of this would be happening. Instead, she helped you confirm that the spell was working."

Mr. Howe grinned. "I knew you were smart enough, but allow me to finish your thoughts because I really must go."

A cold lump formed in Drummond's chest.

"You see, there is a part you missed." Mr. Howe poked Drummond's knee. "I had to make sure this would all happen without pointing a finger at me. After all, gaining a protection against dying is useless if I were to be jailed for murder."

"That's why you don't know where they are. You fed them lies upon lies to keep your distance. Only then along comes Eustace — alive and full of wrath. That's why you hired me to find Sarah. You wanted to make sure this spell ends well for you."

Spreading his arms, Mr. Howe stood. "Well, yes, that's quite obvious. But you keep missing parts of this."

"I haven't told you where she is, so you tie me up here. I guess Lionman will be coming back with a lead pipe or something to beat the address out of me."

"Why would he do that? His fists are plenty strong."

That was true. Drummond had the throbbing bruises to prove it. That cold lump spread up the back of his neck as he saw the final piece of this nasty case. "You had me followed. You know where their holed up."

"Precisely."

"Then Sarah and Henry are dead. Wait, no, that's not right. If they were dead, we wouldn't be talking. Lionman! You sent him to kill Sarah, and all this chatter — you've been stalling me."

Drummond tried to stand, but he fumbled with the chair. Except he noticed his arms had moved up slightly. Apparently, Lionman never spent time as a scout learning to tie good knots.

Taking the stairs off the stage and down into the audience, Mr. Howe said, "Before you attempt anything rash, you should understand your predicament. I have no doubt a man of your skill can find your way free of these bindings, so I want you to listen and think clearly."

Drummond thought about strangling the bastard — quite clearly. "Let me guess. Either save Sarah and Henry or stop you."

"Not at all. You can make an attempt to save their lives, but Jasper will be out at Henry's apartment shortly. He won't hesitate. And I'm not a fool. Why would you sacrifice Sarah and Henry in order to capture me when we both know the police won't see a crime — not one that I'm guilty of? Poor Jasper might end up in prison, but he would never betray me. Even if he did, what court would believe that I had those two killed as part of a magic spell?"

Relaxing his shoulders, Drummond scooted as far back against the chair as he could manage and gently pressed his legs. His arms eased up creating enough slack that he could untie the knots with some effort.

From the middle of the theatre, Mr. Howe said, "This isn't over for me. That's what I want you to understand. If you save Sarah and Henry, if you interfere any further with my spell, I will make you pay dearly for it. I will cause you such agony that you'll beg me to send you to Hell. However, let them die, let me walk away with my protection against Death, and you'll not see or hear from me ever again. That's your choice to make — it's their lives or yours."

As Mr. Howe reached the back of the theatre, he paused to turn around with a flourish. Though Drummond could not make out the man's face, he felt the malevolent grin sitting on the man's lips. Mr. Howe clapped his hands. "By the time you're free, I'll be far gone."

Drummond glared. "I'll be coming for you."

"I certainly hope so. It will make all this far more interesting. Especially when you know you can't kill me." Mr. Howe made a large, theatrical motion of checking his watch. "I suppose you might be able to stop Jasper, but he's had such a head start."

"You bastard."

"It appears your eloquence has left you and so has my interest. I win today. In a short time, I will even win over Death. Until next time, my new friend." With another theatrical touch, Mr. Howe bowed as if in a Shakespearean drama and left the building.

For a few seconds — ones that stretched out in Drummond's mind — the detective crouched on the chair, torn, locked in place, his rage urging him to rip free and chase down Mr. Howe while the rest of him advocated for helping Sarah and Henry. Mr. Howe suggested

Drummond had a choice, but that was a lie.

Working the knots took a few minutes, but he freed himself eventually. He stomped to the edge of the stage, part of him already barreling after Mr. Howe. But that would not happen. Not today. Racing across the stage and back down the hall, he stopped at Mr. Howe's dressing room.

The arrogant prick had left everything untouched. The salt lines, the pried wood plank, and Henry's sacrificed toe — none of it had been moved. It suggested that Drummond was already too late. If Lionman Jasper had already killed Sarah and Henry, then Mr. Howe had no qualms about Drummond destroying the circle. It had already served its purpose.

Then again, for all Mr. Howe's cocky attitude, he had missed the key person in all of this. He never once mentioned Detective Cooper. No matter how fast the Lionman crossed the city and reached Henry's apartment, he would not find it easy to walk in and murder anybody. Detective Cooper would put up quite a fight. Hopefully better than Drummond had done.

Digging in his pocket, Drummond pulled out the box of matches, produced one stick, and struck it on the side. With a flick of his fingers, the burning stick flitted through the air and landed on the pile of salt and toe in the center. As before, the circle whooshed into green flames.

He turned to go when a flash of pink caught his eye. Not from the fire but from the make-up table. Skirting the wall to avoid the unnatural flames, he reached the table and found a piece of stationary — pink with F.E.B. printed at the top. A series of numbers had been scrawled across the page along with a name — Crocker. Pocketing the paper, he slipped out of the room.

Drummond did not watch the flames any further. He sprinted down the hall, into the alley, and hurried toward his car. If Cooper had managed to stall Jasper long enough, there wouldn't be much left of his old pal to keep up the fight. He needed reinforcements, and Drummond would provide.

THE DRIVE TO HENRY'S APARTMENT WENT SMOOTHLY — a fact that gave Drummond hope even as it caused him concern. After all, if he had no traffic getting to the building, then neither had Lionman Jasper. Then again, Lionman most likely obeyed driving laws so as not to be delayed by the police. Drummond had no time for such concessions. He floored his old car, nearly caused two accidents, and shaved off about three minutes of driving time.

Any hope Drummond harbored evaporated as he tried to find parking. Cars lined the entire street leaving no sliver of space to slip into. The same held true one street over. As Drummond pulled around the block, his chest felt the pounding of his heart like a drumbeat urging him onward even as it reminded him of the dangers lurking ahead.

Right at the moment he considered leaving the car in the middle of the street, he spotted a place. He pulled in too fast and too sharp, banging the right front wheel on the curb. Other than a perturbed snort from a gentleman walking by, Drummond took no notice. He was already racing toward the apartment building.

Weaving through the last of the morning crowd busy on their way to work, Drummond bumped a woman aside and pushed a man out of his way. He left a wake of cranky pedestrians but barely heard their grumbles. Images of Sarah plagued him — Sarah seeing Lionman loom over her, Sarah crying for help from an unconscious Cooper at her feet, Sarah being torn apart like a mouse caught in the mouth of a feral cat.

The front door to the building stood ajar, the doorknob dented from a uniquely strong grip. Drummond shuddered. Lionman was definitely here.

Bolting up the stairs, Drummond had to fight the urge to call out for Cooper and Sarah and Henry. Last thing he needed to do was alert Lionman of his arrival. Instead, as he reached the fourth floor, he checked his .38 and held it at the ready.

When he stepped off the stairs and into the hallway, his heart sank. The door to Henry's apartment lay in two pieces on the floor. Even from a distance, Drummond could see the splintered doorjamb and the shattered glass of an object that had been thrown from inside.

"You listen to me," Cooper said, his commanding copper voice echoing through the hall. "I don't know what level of Hell you were conjured from, but I've had enough of this crap to last the rest of my life. Two lifetimes, in fact. So, unless you want a bullet in your head, you better turn around and go back to the hole you crawled out of. Because there's no way I'm letting you through that door."

As Drummond hustled down the hall, pressing against the wall as he came to the doorless entryway, his chest raised and he grinned. It sounded as if Lionman Jasper had only arrived. Perhaps he had a tougher time finding a parking space. If so, then Drummond would try not to curse traffic ever again — it might have saved Sarah's life.

With his weapon held in tight for control, Drummond swung around the doorjamb and into the apartment. Cooper stood in front of the casting room door, Lionman hulking closer with each step. Henry was sprawled on the floor, unconscious, with a raw welt rising on his jaw.

Moving in fast, Drummond said, "Put up your hands, Jasper. It's all over."

Lionman whirled around, extending his arm, and with a skilled backfist, he smacked the .38 out of Drummond's grip. The hunk of metal clattered into the kitchenette. With a scowl that turned Drummond into a gazelle frozen at the sight of a hungry predator, Lionman thumped forward.

But Cooper did not hesitate at the opportunity. The police detective sprang onto Lionman's back and wrapped his small arms around the beast's neck. Lionman roared and twirled about.

He hurdled back against the far wall, trying to dislodge Cooper with the pain of repeated slams into the hard surface. But the apartment had not been built for anything but cheap housing. On the second slam, Cooper's back left a deep imprint into the flimsy materials. If Lionman kept it up, the two of them would tumble through the wall and into the neighbor's apartment.

Drummond dove for the kitchenette. He rolled across the floor and snatched hold of his .38. Popping his head over the counter, he saw Lionman reach behind, grab Cooper by the shoulders, and flip the man forward. Cooper landed half-off the couch, bouncing hard and slapping the floor head first.

Lionman paused to make sure Cooper remained as dazed as he appeared. Then the brute stomped toward the door to the casting room. Drummond raised his weapon and stepped in front of Lionman's path. "Sorry, pal, but I can't let you go in there. Trust me, here — Mr. Howe isn't worth it."

Unfortunately, Lionman had no interest in debating the merits of his boss. He thrust his arm out faster than Drummond could think. The thick fingers took hold of Drummond's jaw and pressed him against the door. Sharp stabs slid down his bones from jaw to spine to feet. Whether Lionman intended to break down the door with Drummond as a battering ram or if he meant simply to crack Drummond's jaw bones under his fingers didn't matter — Drummond felt certain the beast would succeed at both. Probably simultaneously.

Blood throbbed in Drummond's skull even as it leaked out of the wounds on his face. The sound of his racing heart filled his ears. At least, he wouldn't have to listen to Lionman's heavy breathing, deep growls, or any other noises the creature made.

He did see a flash of light. As an afterthought, he swore he heard a soft pop. Seconds later, after Lionman's grip slackened, after his eyes snapped open wide, after he bared his teeth and the greasy odor of digested chicken wafted free, after he lost focus and dropped to his knees, after blood dribbled from the corner of his mouth, after he crumbled to the side, only then did Drummond understand — Cooper had faked being dazed. Drummond's old partner had put a bullet through Lionman's heart. Probably nicked a lung, too.

"It's okay, now," Cooper said in a strong, loud voice.

"My hearing's coming back. No need to shout," Drummond said.

"What? No, I wasn't talking to you."

The pantry door in the kitchenette opened. Henry and Sarah untangled as they stepped out of the cramped space. Drummond chuckled.

"I was defending an empty room?"

"If you want to think of it that way, be my guest. But you know there's more to it."

Sarah had the vacant eyes of a soldier who had spent too much time on the battlefield. Her gaze circled around the dead man on the floor. "Is it all over?"

Cooper shrugged and gestured to Drummond.

"For you, yeah, it's over." Drummond holstered his weapon. "All the casting circles are destroyed along with the spell that led to your curse. The two of you stay away from magic for the rest of your lives, and you won't have any trouble from that world. Start casting spells, and you may end up drawing unwanted attention — the kind that'll get you stuck on a wall again."

Both Henry and Sarah did not respond, but Drummond could tell. At least for the next few years, neither of them would dare to even open a book on the history of witchcraft, let alone an actual spellbook.

"What about the dead man?" Drummond asked Cooper.

"You take Mrs. McAllister home. I'll work this up with Henry so there won't be any questions."

"As in Sarah and I were never here?"

"That's a start. The police won't ever learn the cause, but I'll see to it that they figure out how this huge man came after Henry, broke down the door and everything. Luckily for Henry, I happened to be nearby, heard the commotion, and came to the rescue. I tried to subdue to attacker, but look at him. Much too big. Ended up having to shoot the man. Didn't expect to kill him, but it happens." Cooper's mouth twisted as he weighed out what he would say. "Yeah, that might work. Get going. I've got to call this."

Drummond helped Sarah put on a coat and ushered her toward the doorless exit. She placed a hand on the doorjamb. Taking a deep breath, she looked back into the apartment.

"I don't know what we were thinking," she said.

Henry bowed his head. "We were just trying to do better for ourselves. Get our piece of the pie."

"Maybe that was why we failed. We already have a piece. Well, we did, anyway. Now we've lost a lot more. Maybe everything."

Henry's eyes flitted around the demolished apartment and landed on the large dead man. "I don't mean to sound rude or ungrateful," he said, unable to make eye contact with either Drummond or Cooper, "but I hope to never see any of you ever again."

"You're not the first to say that after one of my cases." Drummond adjusted his hat and stepped into the hall with Sarah. To Cooper, he said, "See you around."

Cooper made a quick hand gesture that could have been acknowledgement, dismissal, or even a friendly wave good-bye. Drummond took it to mean all three. He suspected Cooper felt much like Henry, at the moment. The poor man's mind would be working late trying to rewrite events so that he could sleep at night.

No matter. Sarah and Henry were safe. If Cooper had to suffer a week of insomnia, Drummond thought it a worthy trade-off.

After dropping Sarah off at her home and enduring Shawn McAllister's half-drunken/half-elated blubbering, Drummond headed back to his office. Part of him wished he could be like Henry or Sarah or even Cooper — simply turn away from all of it, somehow pretend it didn't exist. But even if he had the mental fortitude to deny reality, that did not mean that reality would comply.

Mr. Howe was out there, roaming the streets of the city. Soon he would learn of Lionman Jasper's death. Soon he would know that his spell had failed.

He had been lenient on Drummond. He thought he had everything in place, in control, and in all truth, he was no criminal. Not in the traditional sense. Mr. Howe was no hardened thug who understood how to break the law. He had spared Drummond because he saw no value in hurting another person unless he got something out of it. But

Drummond wondered if Mr. Howe would make the same choices next time. He doubted it.

Placing the scrap of pink paper from Mr. Howe's dressing room on his desk, the one with F.E.B. printed at the top, a series of numbers, and the name Crocker, Drummond went to work.

CASE 11

IN THE BAG

MARSHALL DRUMMOND DID NOT BEGRUDGE people their exuberance as Christmas approached. Since the Crash of 1929, people had needed every chance for a moment or two of joy, and the holiday season brought weeks of anticipation, days of cheer, and a few more in the afterglow. But for him, the years had been hard. His business struggled — not a lot of people willing to spend money on a detective of the bizarre and unnatural even when times were good, but when their cupboards collected dust and they had to rely on a soup kitchen one or two days a week, the last thing people cared about was if ghosts haunted the attic. His personal life was empty — not a lot of women wanted to risk a relationship with a guy fighting witches and curses. And his future looked dangerous — ever since his encounter with Mr. Howe, a failed stage magician who decided to experiment with real spells, Drummond had this itch on the back of his neck. He kept waiting for a threat or an ambush or a straightforward attack. The longer he went with nothing happening, the worse he feared what would happen — because a guy like Howe wouldn't simply let it all go.

Drummond didn't have much to go on with Howe, though. Their only encounter had left behind three odd pieces of information — the initials F.E.B, a series of numbers, and the name Crocker. Over the last several months Drummond had tried numerous avenues to uncover any connection these things had to Howe, but he had been unsuccessful. Back in November, he gave the information to his old pal, Leroy Parker, and when that grumpy man called saying he found something, Drummond jumped at the chance to leave town for a few hours.

Leroy lived in a small shack in the middle of the woods over an hour away from Winston-Salem. He was the smartest man Drummond knew, driven to understand all he could about witches and magic, and as a black man, Leroy found life better alone in the woods than dealing with too many white people. It didn't help that Leroy was as personable as a sharp rock.

By the time Drummond arrived, dusk had come and gone. The night air grew cold and threatened snow. It was easy to get lost in the woods, but Leroy had a small campfire burning in front of his house, and Drummond knew the way fairly well.

Lowering his shotgun, Leroy said, "You keep not announcing

yourself, and one of these days I'm going to kill you by accident."

Drummond walked onto the man's wide porch. "I doubt it'll be by accident."

With a strong laugh, Leroy ushered Drummond inside. Books lined the walls and a beaten couch provided the furniture. One room off to the side gave Leroy a bedroom. Only other part was a small kitchenette and that was most of what the old man needed. He had a card table set up in the middle of the main room and several books were opened alongside his notes.

"I didn't get far with those numbers," he said, pouring two shots of bathtub hooch. "You'll need to find some more information before they start to make sense. Could be Bible verses, library notations, birthdates, all sorts of things. The name Crocker is also too ambiguous. Unless you plan to do the ol' gumshoe thing and check each one in North Carolina. I warn you, though — might take the rest of your life to get them all."

Drummond knocked back his shot and hissed. Taste was not a consideration by whoever made the stuff. "I take it then that you found something with those initials — F.E.B."

"Indeed, I have."

"And?"

"And you better have another shot." Leroy poured two more and waited until they both tossed them down. "Now, before I share this with you, I got to point out that them initials could refer to a bunch of folks, but considering the source, I figure I'm on the right track. But if I ain't, I don't want you betting the farm on what I say. Understand?"

"I doubt Mr. Howe would bother writing down the initials of somebody's Aunt Fanny. Come on, now. Out with it."

Leroy filled their glasses one last time, and Drummond obliged. Anything that bothered Leroy enough to drop three shots in such a short time probably meant Drummond was best off doing the same. Laying his dark hand upon the open book on the table, Leroy let out a long sigh.

Bobbing his head, he said, "I came up with only one solid answer, and I don't particularly like what it implies. There was a woman named Felicia Eustace Brown. She was a witch back in the 1600s. Burned at the stake. Now, we've only got the town magistrate's report to tell us anything and that's not likely to be all that accurate, but he claims that she used witchcraft to turn children into animals."

"Can that really happen?"

"Don't know. I've seen plenty of spells written in grimoires to suggest that witches have tried to make it work, but I ain't ever seen proof of it."

Drummond thought of Lionman Jasper — Mr. Howe's right-hand thug who died a while back. "Maybe I have. But what I saw wasn't a complete transformation and it wasn't a kid."

"I was afraid you might say something along those lines. See, in these spell books, there are always spells that have questionable veracity. It's one of the ways the witches can hide what their doing in plain sight. The real spells are buried around a lot of nonsense and superstition, so nobody can steal the witch's work."

"Can't say I'm surprised that Howe is looking into an old witch from the past. Especially if she was messing around with similar things as him."

"That's right. And then I found this spell."

Drummond's stomach clenched. "That can't be good."

"It ain't." Pointing to a second open book, Leroy indicated a page that had a diamond symbol with a curved line in the center. "This spell claims to accomplish what Ms. Felicia had been working on all her life."

"You're saying that spell will actually do it? Turn kids into animals?"

"I'm saying the writing here claims to work. I ain't tried it out. I wouldn't have believed it at all except for the connection between the spell and the witch and the fact that your Mr. Howe is looking into all this, too."

Drummond looked over the two books but didn't expect to glean something new. Hitting the books had never been his forte. "Thanks. I don't know what Mr. Howe wants with this, and I can't say I'm looking forward to finding out, but I appreciate your help."

"Anytime. Besides, it's Christmas. Now, the sun's going down and you won't be solving nothing tonight, so what say we go sit out by the fire and finish this bottle?"

"I'd say that's the kind of Christmas spirit I like."

"Better than a lump of coal, anyway."

"Indeed, my friend, indeed."

DRUMMOND AWOKE, and his heart raced like a kid running a stick along a picket fence. Tap tap tap tap tap tap tap. It was dark. Pushing up with his arms, he could feel the dirt and leaves beneath his hands — he was in a forest. His head throbbed and his mouth felt pasty dry.

Leroy Parker's place. That's where he was. He had driven all the way out, deep into the woods, to visit his old pal, get some information, and have a drink. Damn hooch.

With his head splitting and his breath shallow, Drummond wondered just how potent that washtub liquor had been. He hadn't felt this hungover since a New Year's party in 1927.

He rubbed his hands down his face. His skin had a strange texture. Not the usual numb sensation that came with excessive drinking. It felt as if his nose were bigger and cheeks fuller.

He froze, listening into the dark woods. Did he hear something or was it his imagination?

He remembered sitting with Leroy outside by a small fire ringed with stones. They repeatedly toasted to various pleasures of life — beautiful women, getting the bad guy, sitting with friends — and they watched sparks rise into the air. Drummond could not recall if they finished the bottle, but he suspected they had. That was the goal, after all. He must have wandered off to relieve himself in the woods and passed out. Looking from one dark section of trees to another, he wondered which way lead back to Leroy's home.

When he tried standing, all sense of balance swirled around him. He toppled forward. He tried again — spreading his arms out, but no good. He fell forward with his hands digging into the ground.

Strange — his fingers were all black as if covered in soot. As he started to bring one closer to his face, he heard the sound.

Definitely not his imagination. Something was in the woods. Something big. Something stalking.

Drummond raced off. Twice, he tried to stand up and sprint, but each time he ended up back with his hands in the dirt. Not wanting to waste time arguing with his drunken body, he scurried along the forest floor, his heart pounding ever faster.

He heard the predator coming closer. Instinct took control and launched him up a tree. Scrabbling along the bark and spiraling around to the opposite side of the predator's noise. With any luck, the hungry animal would simply pass below.

But as he waited, Drummond began to notice something off — he clung to the side of a tree with all four of his limbs. How? And why did his perspective seem so skewed? The tree looked enormous. Like standing at the base of a twenty-story skyscraper in downtown Winston-Salem.

At length, when he no longer heard the rustling of the predator, he scurried further up until he reached a long branch hanging out far to the side. As he crossed the branch, he worried his weight would snap the old wood and send him tumbling to a broken leg. But another part of his brain knew it would hold. He spotted the flickering of the campfire. Not too far off.

A crazy thought popped in his head — he could jump from this tree limb to one lower down on another tree. Get closer to the campfire without having to walk the forest floor. He knew he would make it, too. Before his brain could stop him, his body lurched forward and simply pushed off.

He fell through the air, but his nerves did not ignite. If anything, the sensation of cool night wind against his skin felt familiar and comforting. When he hit the other branch, his front fingers dug into the bark, allowing him to scratch his way to a sturdy perch. He then dashed across the limb, around the trunk, up to another branch, and over where he could see the campfire with ease. Leroy's house was a large dark shape in the background.

The truth began to sink into Drummond's mind. Not the specifics but the idea. Because sitting in two beach chairs around that campfire, he saw Leroy Parker and Marshall Drummond. Both passed out.

Staring at his own body was not the strangest part, though. Dealing with witches and witchcraft meant having an out-of-body experience or two under his belt. But his mind had put the other pieces together, and he only had to look back over his shoulder to confirm what he knew. He did not want to look.

No point putting it off, though. If he had to deal with it, better to get started now.

He snatched a glance back, and sure enough, he saw the bushy gray-brown tail of a squirrel. It gave a little shake as if to say Hello.

Before he had a chance to think beyond this obvious and ridiculous notion, his instincts — his squirrel instincts — alerted him to the return of the predator. His human thoughts kept him from bolting away. He was high in a tree — not much to fear from some ground-dwelling carnivore.

Below, he watched as a black and gray wolf sauntered toward the campfire. It had an odd pattern of white fur on its back — a diamond shape with a swirling line in the middle.

He had to think, but it was so hard with his squirrel brain running faster than his human brain. Clearly, he suffered from some kind of spell — Felicia's spell or something related. That wolf sniffing cautiously forward might get the bad idea that it should snack on Drummond's body.

No way would he accept being stuck in a squirrel for the rest of his life.

Before he could stop, he whipped around and darted toward the tree trunk. The animal instincts had more control than he liked. Heck, he didn't like any of this.

Up he went along the trunk until he came to a small hole — a hole filled with acorns and pine cones. Not wanting to think about what that meant for squirrel/human connections, he grabbed an acorn and stuck it in his cheek. Then another. And another. Rushing back to the limb hanging over the campfire, he found the wolf sniffing over his body.

He shouted a few choice words, hoping to scare the beast away, but only heard high-pitched chittering coming from his mouth. He fished out an acorn, used his back tail to prop him on his hindlegs without falling over, and he gave it his best baseball pitch.

The acorn shot down into the fire.

Okay, a little off. Popping out another acorn, he readjusted his aim and let loose again. This time he nailed the wolf in the back. The big dog jumped, spun around, and lowered, ready to pounce on anything that moved. It growled. But Drummond had already prepped the last acorn and threw it into the wolf's head.

Instead of barking, howling, or running away, the wolf straightened and cocked its head at the acorn. Then he glanced up — directly at Drummond. Moving with great care between the slumbering Drummond and Leroy, the wolf acted more like a pet than a predator. It ducked under Leroy's hand and looked back up at Drummond.

No. Not Leroy, too.

But of course, whatever spell had been cast upon Drummond would also have affected Leroy. Looked like his old pal got the better end of the deal.

With a claw, Drummond attempted to wave his hand. The wolf nodded and scratched at the ground. Good enough. Drummond scrabbled his way down the tree and approached the campfire. When the wolf made no attempt to eat him, Drummond climbed onto his human lap and stared at his old pal now in wolf form. That diamond symbol on Leroy's back — Drummond's human brain recalled seeing it in the book of witchcraft.

Leroy nuzzled the empty hooch bottle, but Drummond shook his head. Maybe they had been slipped a mickey, but that was it. What little Drummond knew of potions suggested this was far too complicated a matter. Maybe Leroy knew more on the subject, though Drummond thought the man focused mainly on spells, but even if he did, they weren't in a position to do much high-level communication.

"It's right on up ahead," a voice said from the path leading out to the main road.

Drummond and Leroy darted off in different directions. Drummond shot up the nearest tree, and Leroy — well, he didn't see where Leroy went.

A young man and a middle-aged woman approached the campfire. The man wore a flat cap and a heavy coat. Probably needed it, too, since his pants had big holes and a few patches. The woman had a black shawl covering two coats and walked bent over. They looked at the two sleeping bodies and shook their heads.

"Didn't work," the young man said.

"I told you not to trust that old fool. Anybody dealing in magic ain't to be trusted."

"Then why'd you cast that spell for him, huh?"

"You know damn well why. I don't want to hear no more about it. We did it and we're here. None of your complaining is gonna change that. And at least this way my sister gets some justice."

"Then maybe we done the spell wrong. Maybe that's all. 'Sides, he said it was for the colored man out in the woods. He didn't say nothing about no second man, no white man."

"Feedin' you lies. I suppose I'm hoping too much to think that there's gonna be any coin at all in that half-standing shack."

The young man leaned over Drummond's body and nudged his shoulder, then Leroy's. "They out colder than an icicle down the back."

"Quit yappin' and let's see what's what in there."

As the two entered Leroy's home, Drummond raced down the tree and crossed over to the porch. Even the most amateur detective could have put together these pieces. Clearly, Mr. Howe had given this young man some variation of Felicia Eustace Brown's spell and instructed him to use it on Leroy. They hadn't counted on Drummond being there. It also seemed obvious that they expected the spell to transform Leroy into an animal, not simply rip his mind out of his body and plunk it into a wolf. Or a squirrel, in Drummond's case. But why? What coin could they hope to find from a guy living alone in the woods? Dumb question — if anybody had a coin worth dabbling in magic, it was Leroy. Probably some coin that grants wishes or some such.

When Drummond reached the side of the house, he dug his claws into the wood and climbed up to the nearest window ledge. Peeking through, he watched the two intruders tossing Leroy's main room. They knocked the books over and yanked out the couch cushions. The woman stuck her head under the kitchenette sink.

Drummond tried to lift the window, but it wouldn't budge. Probably was locked. Thinking on it a little more, Drummond decided that even if it wasn't locked, his tiny squirrel arms would never be strong enough to open the window. If he wanted to get in there — and he did — then he'd have to find another way.

The front door remained ajar. Only one big problem — the man and woman would have no trouble spotting him. They might not care about a squirrel entering the home, but Drummond figured that since these two were responsible for the failed spell, they might suspect he was Leroy. From that point, any number of nasty things could happen to him. No. Not a good plan. When the woman waddled away from the kitchenette, however, Drummond got an idea.

Using his claws, he climbed up the corner of the house and onto the roof. Not a lot of good he could say about being a squirrel, but the climbing ability sure came in handy. He skittered across to the pipe vent. Peeking down, he thought as long as he could move slow enough to minimize the noise and as long as they didn't start cooking, he could ease down unnoticed.

He climbed under the cone on top and slipped over the lip.

"What's that?" The young man's voice echoed up the pipe.

"Rats? Coons? There's lots of critters in the woods that'll be scratching away under the house."

"Didn't sound like that."

"You find the coin yet? Or that book?"

"Naw, there ain't nothing here like a coin. And there's too many books."

"Then keep looking."

Drummond held still. His muscles tensed and he sensed the squirrel part of him wanting to bolt for a tree. Purposefully entering a dangerous situation — something he did often in his career — did not mix well with a little animal's instincts for self-preservation. But even jumping off the pipe might have made too much noise, so Drummond forced his body to remain quiet, unmoving.

As the thought hit him that he needed to create a distraction, a lone wolf howl cried out. It sounded close — so close that the man and the woman hurried onto the porch to see if they had trouble to deal with. Apparently, Leroy had kept an eye on Drummond.

Not wanting to waste the opportunity, Drummond dropped down

the pipe, holding his clawed hands against his furry body to avoid clanging around. Instead, he pushed his tail against the pipe walls to slow his descent. When he popped out of the pipe, he rolled into the belly of the stove. A quick jump onto the top and he nearly knocked a frying pan.

"We best hurry up." The woman opened the door as Drummond dropped to the floor. "I don't like being here any longer than I got to be here."

The two people returned to tearing up Leroy's home, and Drummond did his best to hide in the shadows near the walls. They said they were looking for a coin and a book. He had no idea about the coin, but the book should be the one with Felicia's spell in it. Except that was sitting in the open and they had ignored it. Then again, these idiots failed to pull off a spell with whatever instructions they had from Howe, so maybe they don't know what they're looking for.

Drummond paused.

His previous case with Howe involved the man using others to unwittingly cast magic for purposes beyond what they thought. No reason to suspect this was any different.

A plan formed in his head. A simple one, but with his mind sharing space alongside a squirrel, he figured the simpler, the better.

Peeking from the corner of the kitchenette, Drummond noticed that the book with Felicia's spell had been tossed to the floor. That little bit of luck filled him with a lot of hope. Or perhaps the rapid pulse of a squirrel messed with his senses.

When the woman stomped over to the young man to root through one of the bookshelves, Drummond dashed across the floor and under the card table. He could reach the corner of the book with minimal exposure. Not daring to waste a moment, he stretched one black claw out and snagged hold of the book. Then he pulled back with all his tiny muscles.

Not enough.

The book made an awful sandpaper scratch as it inched along the wood floor. Or maybe his hearing and proximity to the floor amplified the noise far beyond what human ears could detect. Drummond pulled on the book again, managing another few inches.

"Stop," the woman said, and Drummond froze.

"What now?"

Drummond watched the woman's legs take a few steps toward the card table. "We're making this a whole lot harder on ourselves. What was it he said he wanted more than anything from tonight? Hm?"

"Um, he said the mojo bag, I think."

"No. The mojo bag has the coin in it, and that's what we want, right? So why are we bothering with all these books?"

"Because he wants the book."

"Right. Don't know about you, but I don't care about making that spell any more — what was it he said?"

"Refined. He called it a more refined spell."

The woman laughed. "That man is thinking far too highly of hisself."

"You reckon we just find the bag and we're set. That's what you're saying?"

"That's what I'm saying."

"I'm good with that. I didn't want to have to go looking through all them books anyway. But the bag — I mean we started with the books because there right in the open. Where do we find the bag?"

"I already checked the stove, and he said when he snuck it here for the spell that he didn't have no time to be clever about it."

"Maybe under the table, then."

At that, Drummond's squirrel brain kicked into flight. Before he could stop himself, he darted from under the table. He spotted the woman ahead and pivoted to the nearest wall.

The woman screeched in surprise but quickly regained her composure. "Don't let it get away."

"It's just a squirrel."

"Reading a book in this place? That's got to be one of the ones we cast a spell on."

"You think?"

Drummond didn't catch the woman's angry response. She had picked up a broom, and he was too busy dodging for his life. He raced up the wall, jumped atop the card table, and bolted toward the fireplace. But the young man flipped the card table, and as Drummond slammed into the floor, the man used the table to block the chimney exit.

"Come on now, squirrel." He grinned — missing a few teeth — and crouched with one hand reaching out. "I ain't gonna hurt you."

Drummond backed up a few steps but heard the woman clump behind him. He snapped his head towards her — she stood with her legs wide apart, wielding the broom overhead like a sword.

The young man's hands clamped down on Drummond. "Got the little bugger."

Drummond struggled but couldn't move his arms from the tight grip around him. He heard the woman laughing — a malicious sound that lacked any mirth. He dared glance in her direction.

Barreling through the open front door, a wolf shot across the room and leapt upon the woman. Drummond cried out Leroy's name but only heard a strained squeal from his throat. The woman screamed and the young man held still. Drummond's squirrel side smelled the fear on the man, and Drummond's human side knew to take advantage.

He bit the man's hand.

The man dropped Drummond and let loose a torrent of curse words. Drummond scampered across the floor and up the nearest bookshelf. From the safer height, he peered down.

The wolf had done what a wolf does. Ripped open the woman's throat. Blood pooled on the floor, and the young man pressed flat against the wall. He would have to pass by Leroy in order to escape.

"Easy there, fella. I'm not the one done this to you. That was her. See, she wanted to get back at a witch that done her sister wrong, and this guy told us we needed your mojo bag. He gave us the spell to turn you into an animal so we could walk in and get what we had to get. Then he was gonna show us how to take out the witch. That's all. Nothing personal, you see?"

The wolf stood over the woman's dead body and growled.

"I know it was wrong. I'm sorry. I'm just gonna leave now. With her dead, there ain't no reason for me to be here." He edged toward the door. "You just stay right there and by morning, you'll be back to being you. I swear. It's only temporary." He peeked up the bookshelf. "You, too, Mr. Squirrel. I didn't mean no harm to you."

The wolf barked and lunged forward. The young man raced out the door. Drummond could tell that Leroy let the man go. A wolf wouldn't have missed in such close quarters and could certainly run the man down, if he had wanted.

It took Drummond several minutes to calm his squirrel side. Then he climbed down to the floor. They had a long night to wait through.

* * *

When morning came, Drummond woke sitting in the chair by the campfire. Leroy sat next to him, and from the look on his friend's face, they felt the same — horrible. Hangover didn't begin to describe the thrumming in his head or the stiff ache in every joint of his body. Despite it all, Leroy chuckled.

"If you're smiling because I was a squirrel —"

Leroy burst into laughter. "Sorry, no, but that is funny." From his pocket, he pulled out a small leather bundle tied with twine. "This is funnier."

"That the mojo bag they were looking for? You had it in your pocket the whole time?"

"Yeah. I found it in the eaves of the porch during one of my regular inspections."

"Remind me not to poke fun of your paranoia anymore. I think you saved our lives." Drummond inspected the bag of roots and dirt. "If this is what they were after, why did you think the hooch was spiked?"

"I didn't. Is that what you thought? I was trying to get you to pull the mojo bag from my pocket. The empty bottle was stuck in my hand. What kind of fool are you?"

"Forgive me if my ability to speak squirrel to wolf isn't up to your standards." Focusing on the mojo bag again, he said, "These things actually work?"

"It's black people's magic. Good for putting a spell on somebody from a distance. Sounds like your Mr. Howe, don't it?"

"He certainly doesn't like to get his hands dirty. But he's whiter than a cloud. I don't see how he got to know anybody that would make this for him. Then he'd need somebody to put it out here, too. Heck, he'd also need to figure out that we're friends."

"Not at all. He's working on something, you know that much, and if you're out there looking into old witches and old witchcraft and you're messing with mojo bags, it ain't too hard to believe somebody would've pointed him my way."

"Then why didn't he just come talk to you? He had no reason to go through this trouble."

"You serious? I got riches in all those books — if you know what to look for. Plenty of witches would love to see me harmed. Probably part of the deal he had to make in order to get what he wanted."

"The mojo bag."

"Nope." Leroy took the bag back and tossed it into the embers of the near-dead fire. He then dug around his pocket and brought out a large, gold coin. Looked like a doubloon. "This is what they were really after. It was in the mojo bag. Here's what I think happened — your new pal, Mr. Howe, is still playing with forces he don't understand. He's experimenting. Getting one of my books was nothing but a bonus. He's trying to find a path to get what he's after."

"And what's that?"

"Heck if I know. But this coin — this is like a calling card for whoever made that mojo bag." He flipped the coin over to Drummond. "You find who this belongs to and you'll get all the answer you need."

Drummond swiped his hat off the ground and set it straight on. He pocketed the coin. "I'd thank you for a good evening, but I'd be lying. This coin, however, might make up for it."

"You leaving?"

"It's going take time to figure out all this."

Leroy popped to his feet, swayed a bit from the sudden movement, yet still managed a stern scowl. "Don't you think you should help clean up the mess in my home? All those books and papers, not to mention the dead woman and all her blood."

Drummond sighed. "Yeah." As he walked toward the porch, he clapped his hands together. "Next year, don't bother inviting me over. I'd rather have had a lump of coal."

CASE 12

THE LOYALTY OF DOGS AND MEN

THOUGH MARSHALL DRUMMOND had only spent a short time as a rookie beat cop before becoming a private investigator of the bizarre, he knew no good would come from sitting in an interrogation room at Police Headquarters. Making matters worse, Detective Lou Piper plunked his massive bulk into the small chair opposite Drummond. On the chipped table between them, he slapped down a file equally thick.

"You really screwed up this time," Lou said, chomping on each word with unbridled glee.

Drummond didn't think much of this performance. Every cop and ex-cop knew the routine. Probably half the papers in that file were blank. But Drummond needed to leave, if he had any chance of stopping Mr. Howe that night. Unfortunately, Ol' Lou came from the school of making suspects sweat it out. He had no problem taking his time.

Trying to sound calm, Drummond removed his fedora and set it on the table. "You guys repaint in here? I don't remember it being this clean."

Lou delivered a menacing laugh. "Oh, you better change your tune fast. This ain't 1927 anymore. You don't have the Chief to protect you. New one hates your guts, and so do most of the men. I'm guessing Cooper's the only one on your side, and let's face it, he only puts up with you because you two were rookie partners."

"One friend is better than none. How does that go for you? All you got is your wife, and I doubt you consider her a friend."

Spitting his words, Lou said, "Think you're funny? Well, I got you standing over the victim of a homicide, and you are literally holding a smoking gun. All we have to do is dig out the slug and when it's a .38, you're sunk."

"Please, do me a favor — get to digging. I'd like to be home for dinner."

"You ain't getting away with blatant murder."

"Look, I know you don't like to have to strain yourself thinking in order to do your job, so let me save you some time. The bullet in the body came from the victim's own gun. He and I struggled with it when he tried to kill me."

"That's still your story?"

"It's the truth. If you bothered to examine him at all, you might be pushing me out the door instead of trying to lock me up."

"Right." He made a show of glancing over a report in the file. Then: "And this was the stage magician by the name of Mr. Howe?"

"No. The victim worked for Mr. Howe."

"Only problem is we talked to all the theaters in the area, and nobody is running a show with that guy. He's not a local resident, either. So, how is it he was in town committing a murder? Sorry, ordering a murder. Not like being a stage magician is a lucrative career. He can't afford to be traveling to Winston-Salem unless he's got a gig to perform, much less pay a chump to off you."

Drummond bit back a slew of insults. Through gritted teeth, he said, "He uses a stage name — Mesmo. You'll have to just call all those theaters again."

A knock at the door. Detective Cooper entered carrying a mug of coffee. He set it down in front of Drummond before stepping back.

"Well, well," Lou said, rocking his head from side-to-side as if ringing out the words. "Looks like your pal showed. Tell me, Coop, you believe any of this horse-apple story about a mysterious stage magician, Mr. Howe or Mesmo or whatever his name is?"

"Lou, despite you being a prick all the time, I kind of like you." Cooper gazed at Lou with far more derision in his eyes than admiration. "Just given you a fair warning — Chief Murdoch is not amused by what you've done."

"Call me a prick again and you'll learn how much the chief cares for his seasoned veterans. You new kids — and as far as I'm concerned, you're barely above a rookie — well, keep it up and you'll find out how much bigger a prick I actually can be."

"I don't know about that. When you start mistaking a dog for a dead person and hauling in a respected PI for nothing, the chief isn't going to look favorably on you."

"What the heck are you yabbering about?"

Raising a smirk, Cooper said, "Coroner is all ticked off because you sent him an English mastiff instead of, you know, a human body."

Ol' Lou's face turned bright red. "You tell that coroner that he's got his head on backwards. I stood over the body myself. Don't hand me crap that it's a dog."

"Big one. Two hundred pounds. But still a dog." To Drummond, Cooper said, "Chief says you're free to go. He ain't happy about it, so you might want to get out while you still got time."

Lou came close to overturing the table as he bolted to his feet.

Pointing a sausage finger at Drummond, he said, "You do not move." He shoved Cooper aside on his way to the door. Then to Cooper: "You watch him. If he ain't here when I get back, I'm holding you responsible."

He thundered out of the interrogation room. Drummond knew to stay quiet during the entire exchange, but now that he was alone with his old partner, he needed some answers. Setting his hat back on, he said, "That body really turn into a dog? Or are you just getting him out of here so I could leave?"

Cooper checked outside the door. "That body came from a case involving you — what do you think? Yours are the only cases where strange crap like this happens. The real question is — do I want to know what you're involved with or is it better that I just turn a blind eye and forget about it?"

"That depends."

"Do I even want to know what it depends on?"

"You. Do you want to make an arrest or do you want this to simply disappear? At the heart of it all is just a man. He can be arrested."

"And what does disappear mean to you?" Sometimes Cooper asked the wrong questions. He checked the hallway once more. Then in a sharp whisper, he said, "You'd really kill a man just for messing around with witchcraft?"

"Normally, no. But if the threat is big enough, I'm not afraid to do what's right."

"You're standing in a police interrogation room in front of an officer, and you're stating that you're going to murder somebody. Have you lost your damn mind?"

Drummond never liked involving Cooper in his cases. He knew how hard it was for the man to accept what he witnessed. And if this went bad, the blowback on Cooper would end the man's career. Drummond couldn't let that happen.

"I'm sorry, but the more I think on it, the more it's obvious — you need to make this arrest."

"Now hold on," Cooper said. "You know I don't mess with all of your mystical nonsense."

But Drummond could see Cooper's brain working it out. The moment he had heard Drummond was in interrogation, the moment he decided to poke fun at Ol' Lou, it was over. Cooper's face tightened. Chief Murdoch was angry and embarrassed with this botched-up victim being a dog. Since he couldn't take it out on Drummond, he would focus on Cooper. Unless Cooper came back with a successful arrest.

His mouth drew in and his fingers rolled into fists. "This is the last time. You hear me? I do this, and I don't even want to see you around here anymore."

"I kind of figured you'd say something like that. Sad to hear it, but I understand. If that's how you want it, then okay. One last case together." Drummond put out his hand and waited.

Cooper unrolled his fist and shook the hand. "Where do we begin?"

"Any chance we can see that dead dog?"

LONG AGO, Drummond had accepted that as a PI he would often find himself in uncomfortable situations. Standing in the Police Department broom closet, waiting for Cooper to give the all clear, certainly qualified as uncomfortable — even if not anywhere close to the oddest place Drummond had ever found himself. At least, the waiting gave him a little time.

The case had been moving so fast he feared he missed some obvious points. It didn't help that he really hated Mr. Howe. The man had tried to kill Drummond in a theater at one time. Then again during the Christmas holiday. And once more when he sent his dog-man to finish the job.

Drummond had simply been trying to get the morning paper when the dog-man poked a gun in his side with the charming greeting of Get moving.

At the time, Drummond did not know he was being accosted by anything but a man; however, he would learn soon enough. Even without the gun, something seemed off. The man's eyes had an emptiness that matched his demeanor. A killer's eyes. Someone who felt nothing about the violence he could commit. He simply obeyed his orders.

The man ushered Drummond into an empty store — boarded up and out of business for several years now. Another victim of the Depression. Dust danced through the morning sunlight seeping between the board cracks while Drummond raced through his most recent cases, trying to figure out who this guy worked for.

With a shrug, he thought the direct approach would be best. "All right fella, you got me. Who are you and what do you want?"

"Got to collect my reward," the man said, though he had difficulty getting the words out.

"Oh really?" Drummond sounded calm, but inside his guts roiled. A reward. Another name for a bounty. That was going to cause a lot of trouble.

"Yeah. I collect."

"Nothing I can do about that, huh? Before you kill me, though, I'm curious — how much am I worth?"

"No money." The man chuckled as he undid the buttons of his shirt. He revealed his chest — the smooth hair and mottled coloring of a large dog. "Collect finish the spell he made on us."

"Us? How many of you are there?"

"Don't know. Don't care. Long as I collect."

The dog-man turned out to be rather fastidious. He couldn't simply let his shirt stay open. With one hand he attempted to button it back up and that provided Drummond an opening. Blustering forward, Drummond tried to gain control of the gun. They grappled only a few seconds before the report echoed around them.

The dog-man fell into Drummond's arms, killed by his own bullet. As Drummond eased him down, he heard a noise from the back hall. Without thinking, he whipped out his .38 and took a shot. The bullet went into the wall near the hall entrance. The figure hastened away, but Drummond caught enough to know — Mr. Howe.

It was reckless to shoot blind. Drummond knew better. But this half-man, half-dog had shaken him. Mostly because of the implications — that there were enough to use the word us.

Of course, that was the moment the beat cop arrived. The world couldn't give Drummond a few more minutes to clear out. The cop had heard enough, saw what he assumed to be happening, drew his weapon, and made his arrest.

Detective Cooper knocked on the door. "Hurry."

Stepping from the broom closet as if an entirely natural thing to be doing, Drummond straightened his coat and scurried down the hall. In the back room, with enough dirt to make it clear how little the Chief thought of the coroner, Drummond and Cooper approached an exam table with a humongous dog laid out. The smell of chemicals mixed with bile and whatever came out of the victim's stomach contents weaved through the air. Despite spending more than enough time in a morgue, Drummond never got comfortable with that smell.

"How long before Ol' Lou starts causing you problems?" Drummond asked.

Cooper stood by the entrance to keep watch on the hall. "He's been causing me problems since the day you quit."

"I meant —"

"Depends on the mood he's in. But it would be best if you hurried up."

Drummond bent close to the dog's face. The eyes — cold, dead, controlled. He could see a glimpse of the dog-man who had accosted him. But only in those eyes. The rest of what lay on the exam table resembled the original animal. A large canine.

Taking a moment to watch Drummond at work, Cooper said, "You going to tell me what this is all about?"

"Remember that case we shared — the car accident where one of the victims got up and walked away after having his head splattered against the wall?"

"Not something you really forget."

"Yeah, well, the guy who was behind all that is trying to kill me."

"Mr. Howe, right?"

"That's the man."

"Any idea why he's trying to kill you?"

"It might have something to do with the fact that I stopped him from gaining immortality."

Cooper chuckled. Only for a moment. Then all humor drained from his face. "Can that really be done?"

"Howe certainly thought so. But if it can be done, people a hell of a lot more talented at witchcraft than him have yet to figure it out. That wasn't the only thing Howe messed with, though. Some of the magic he tried involved mixing people and animals together."

Stepping closer, Cooper gestured toward the dog on the table. "This really was a man?"

Drummond tipped his hat back. "This was never a man. Started out as a dog. Mr. Howe changed him into an abomination — part canine, part human. But it wasn't real. It lacked the autonomy of either man or animal. It was nothing more than a machine of flesh that obeyed Howe's commands. In the end, after this thing accidentally shot himself, he turned right back to what he always was. A dog."

Cooper gestured to the collar around the neck. "At least he's still got that."

"I already looked. The tag just has a number on it. No address, no name, no phone number. I don't know what it refers to. I had a hope, but it didn't pan out."

"Hope for what?"

"When I dealt with Mr. Howe previously, I found a piece of paper that had numbers on it, some letters, and a name, but the numbers don't match. Not even close."

"What was the name?"

"Crocker."

Cooper snickered. "Well, I don't know about your mysterious numbers, but I know who Crocker is."

"How? There's got to be hundreds of them in Winston-Salem."

"Because the number on that tag is given out by the city dogcatcher — Mr. Anthony Crocker."

Drummond straightened and rubbed his neck. "Guess we're going to give the dogcatcher a visit."

AFTER SLIPPING OUT THE BACK of the Police Department while Lou stomped around the front cursing Drummond's name, Cooper drove Drummond to the city pound. Not a very pleasant place — prison for animals — and the smell was less than desirable, too. A barrage of barks and yelps and hisses and howls assaulted the ears.

With the flash of a badge at the front desk, the brunette-bobbed receptionist directed Drummond and Cooper into the back. She had said Crocker was on lunch break. Drummond checked his watch — 4:24 pm. The dogcatchers didn't work a three-shift rotation, so apparently, Crocker took lunch at strange hours.

They headed down a narrow aisle with cages lining either side. The constant chatter of animals begging for attention or crying out in pain or simply wanting to be heard turned Drummond's stomach. He'd never been one for keeping pets, but that was out of practicality, not desire. He would love to have a loyal dog at his side. Unfortunately, being a detective of the bizarre would not provide an animal with a stable environment to thrive.

At the end of the aisle, they turned the corner and found a small office desk sitting in a square made of cages. At the desk, Anthony Crocker munched on a cheese sandwich. A lanky fellow, he had greasy brown hair and small circular glasses that appeared to be constantly fogged over.

Tilting his head back to see around the fog line, Crocker said, "You want something?" He sounded like a boy trying to be a man, yet the gray in his stubbled chin and the lines forming on his face suggested he neared his late-30s.

Cooper flashed his badge once more. "We want to ask you a few questions."

Setting his sandwich down with care as if it were a weapon and he did not want to startle the cops, Crocker said, "I haven't done nothing."

"No one's accusing you. We think you may have information about a dangerous man that we're looking for. We'd like your help."

"Okay." He wiped his mouth with a napkin and stood, brushing crumbs off his overalls.

Cooper looked to Drummond as if to say Your turn at bat. Drummond took a step forward, pushed back his hat, and stuffed his hands in his pockets — trying to appear in authority but less intimidating than usual.

"We're looking for a man who's been abusing animals."

"Lots of people do that. Pisses me off. I guess they feel too weak to fight other men so they pick on pets." Crocker turned to the back wall and tended to his many charges. "What kind of animals did he abuse?"

"We know of one dog for sure. But I've met this guy before, and I'm certain he's hurt other animals, too — cats, definitely. Any large animal, most certainly. Probably a horse or a cow. Maybe even a few more unusual things — like a bear or a lion. We don't know exactly, but we know he's out there. We're thinking you might know who we're talking about. You come across any odd animal abuses?"

Crocker's back stiffened before he returned to his animals. "Odd?"

"Well, these abuses would not fall under the standard categories. We're not talking about somebody who likes to kick a dog or put a cigarette out on a cat. This is somebody who likes to conduct experiments — pseudoscience crap."

"This fellow have a name?"

"He has several. Lately, he goes by Mr. Howe."

Crocker made an act of thinking — shifting his feet and uttering little sounds while repeating the name Howe. During that time, he opened one cage, reached in, and appeared to take care of a small animal. But in a flash, he spun back brandishing an old Peacemaker. Still one of the favorite revolvers for the everyday joe.

Though his pulse jumped into action, Drummond held still. With his hands in his pockets, he could not quickly reach for his pistol, so he decided to play it calm and quiet. Just because a Peacemaker was an old weapon didn't make it any less deadly. In a soft tone, he said, "Hold on there, Mr. Crocker. We're not trying to cause you any trouble."

"Looks like trouble found you." Crocker seemed pleased with his quip, but Drummond saw the nervous licking of the lips and the constant bobbing of the head as the man holding the gun tried to focus on a target. Bad eyesight was not his friend. Although, in such close quarters, Drummond worried that Crocker's poor vision might be just as unfriendly to him.

"This ain't smart," Cooper said. "You've pulled a gun on a cop. You shoot me, and you'll have the entire police force coming down on you."

Another lick of the lips and Crocker shifted the gun toward Drummond. "He ain't no cop."

"This ain't the way, kid," Drummond said. "Whatever Mr. Howe has over you, don't make it worse. You work with us and we can help you out of this mess."

Crocker laughed. "You think he threatened me? He ain't that sort. Besides, he don't have to threaten none. I want to work with him. He's a great man. And whatever you think you got, however strong you think you are, he's twice as strong and got twice as much."

Drummond clicked his tongue. "Well, since you put it that way, looks like you've got us beat. We'll have to call it a day and go home, I guess."

Whether from a nervous twitch or clear intent, Crocker shot. Two things hit Drummond right away — first, the idea that he had missed whatever sign Crocker gave that he would shoot. It did not happen often in Drummond's life, and it would haunt him more than all the witches and ghosts combined. Second thing to hit Drummond — Cooper. Whatever tell Crocker had that Drummond missed, Cooper picked up on it. Before the gunshot could be heard, he tackled Drummond, and in doing so, took the bullet.

DRUMMOND SAT ON A WOOD BACKBENCH at the county hospital. Murmured voices bounced around like echoes of lost lives. Heavy whispers and clutched gasps promised horrible days for those on the other end of whatever words transpired. Drummond really hated hospitals. Almost as much as the library. Which now that he thought about it, offered a lot of the same whispers and murmurs — only with a different purpose.

It had been two hours since their confrontation with Mr. Crocker, and if Cooper had come out of surgery, nobody bothered to inform Drummond. He'd gone to the head nurse's desk several times to inquire, but after the fourth visit, she made it clear that he was no longer welcome. She would let him know anything as soon as she had anything to share. She promised.

"So, you let the guy get away," Ol' Lou said as he plunked down on the other end of the bench.

"Really not in the mood for you."

"Now you know how I feel every time I see you."

He tapped out a cigarette and stuck it in his mouth. He offered the pack to Drummond. A small gesture, but enough to promise that they were not adversaries for the moment. A cop had been shot — a fellow officer to one and a friend to the other — the two men could bury their differences for a little while. Drummond took the cigarette.

"They catch him yet?" Drummond asked.

Lou shook his head. "Not for lack of trying. Half the cops on duty and another half off-duty are scouring the streets for that bastard. If Cooper doesn't pull through, you can bet all of us will be out there looking for this guy."

"Good luck."

"You don't think we'll get him?"

"No, probably not. Don't get me wrong — I'm not casting aspersions on the quality of the police force. It's just that Anthony Crocker has a friend with a unique reach."

"Mob? They going to hide him for the next few months? Take him out of the state or the country?"

"Not organized crime. But every bit as powerful. Maybe more."

Pointing with his cigarette, Lou said, "You see, this is why I can't stand you. Always talking cryptic around me. Say what you mean to say."

"I mean to say that the man I've been after this whole time is the same man Crocker is going to seek for help. This guy — he's the kind of man that'll make it so nobody finds Crocker until he wants to be found. Is that clear enough?"

Cigarette smoke fumed out of Lou's nostrils. "I tell you — I'm trying to nice and you just want me to punch you. I can't imagine why Cooper ever tries to help you."

"Then maybe we shouldn't talk any further. You're welcome to sit here and wait with me. I have it on good word that the head nurse will gladly tell us the moment something happens. Until then, don't ask her for a single thing. She'll rip your head right off."

Lou appeared to be debating within himself for a moment. He then turned his hefty body to face Drummond head on. "Sorry, bub, but we're not sitting around here any longer. You're coming with me."

"Really? The dead dog? You're still going to take me in for more questioning when my old partner is fighting for his life?"

"I can't charge you with anything over a dog that somehow shot itself. But I've watched you. You may not think much of me, but I know how to my job. I know how to observe people. I've watched you and Cooper together. There's something you're not telling me. But more important — I think you're absolutely right. I don't care how many men are out there on the streets, they're not going to find this Crocker fella. You know what else I think?"

"That brushing your teeth is sacrilege?"

"I think you can find Crocker. You want to find him because you want to find this other guy, too, and finding this other guy is a big thing to you. Yeah — you and I are going to go find them together. And when we do, we'll both have our man."

Drummond gazed up the long hospital hall. The head nurse's desk stood off to the side like an unwelcome harbor. He looked at the earnestness in Ol' Lou's eyes. He thought about his old partner lying open on the operating table.

"I guess even if Cooper is brought out right now, he'll still be unconscious for several hours."

Lou grinned. "Think how happy he'll be when he wakes and finds out that we've caught the guy who shot him."

"Okay. We can do this. I'm sure I'm going to regret it, but I'll let you follow me along."

"Hey, I'm the cop here. You are tagging along with me."

Drummond knew there was no point in arguing. If they found Crocker, if they found Mr. Howe, then Lou would be happy enough. And he could have Crocker. As long as the police didn't get in Drummond's way with Mr. Howe, there was no real argument to be had.

Stubbing the cigarette out in a little tray of sand next to the bench, Drummond stood. "Let's get started."

DRUMMOND SAT BEHIND CROCKER'S DESK at the city pound and tried hard not to look at the blood stain on the floorboards. Cooper's blood. It should never have happened.

Shaking away where his mind threatened to go, he rifled through the desk drawers in search of anything that would clue them where Crocker could be found — and thus, where Mr. Howe could be found, too. As he worked, he listened to Lou babytalk the puppies and kittens. In the bottom right drawer, Drummond found a bottle of whiskey and gave serious thought to downing it just so he could get through the rest of the day with Lou.

Slamming the door shut, Drummond said, "Other than being a slob, there's nothing here that says much about Crocker."

"I'm not so sure." Lou made kissing noises to a particularly furry tan kitten. "It's been my experience that a man's workspace reveals more than he ever intends."

"Is that what the cats are telling you?"

Lou turned back toward Drummond with a now-familiar perturbed glare. "It helps me think. Playing with animals, looking at the clouds, anything that breathes life and reminds me how good the world can be — that's a worthwhile thing. That drives away the darkness all cops have to deal with. Helps me stay sane in this job. If you'd stuck around long enough, I might've been able to teach you that one."

"Okay, Mr. Nature Lover, what is your great insight into Crocker?"

Lou rocked on his heels a moment, letting his belly push out towards Drummond's face. "I did notice that all the animals in here are wearing similar tags. That suggests there is a record being kept somewhere."

Drummond popped to his feet. "With everything that happened to Cooper, I forgot all about those tags. We initially came to Crocker because of a tag."

Without another word, Drummond rushed back to the front desk. He leaned over toward the receptionist. "You know why we're here?"

She was startled. Perhaps a little naïve. Certainly intimidated. "Yes, sir. Mr. Crocker did something bad. And he took a shot at you."

"That's right. You need to cooperate with the police now. You understand?"

"Of course. What can I do for you?"

"This tag — can you tell me what information you have on it?"

"Why certainly." She gestured for Drummond to back up a step. When he did, she crossed the room to a shelf filled with folders. Leafing through one, she set it on to her desk and pointed. "That tag belongs to a dog named Buttons. He was found by some trash cans on Trade Street. And he was scheduled to be sent to 14 Pilgrim Drive. That's a good thing. It means somebody wanted him. You see up there in that column where it has the Xs? That means the animal had been here for too long and it's fixin' to be disposed of. But there's no X on Buttons."

Drummond read over the entry. As Lou finally caught up, his heavy breathing a sure sign of his approach, Drummond glanced through the other listings on the page. From his coat pocket, he pulled out the pink paper with Crocker's name as well as those numbers that had been plaguing him since he first met Mr. Howe. "Can you find these tags for me, please?"

He expected her to look at the numbers and say they weren't tags. Or she would search for them and come back to say that there are no animals with those numbers. But in about five minutes, the receptionist returned with two more files. Running through these listings, she indicated where three of the numbers could be found. Two cats and another dog. All of them sent to 14 Pilgrim Drive.

"Lou, as much as I hate to say this, I think you really helped."

"Of course, I did. What did you find out?"

"I got an address."

With more speed than Drummond thought the old man capable, Lou darted toward the exit. "You're driving."

LOU INSISTED ON USING HIS CAR. Fine by Drummond — he could barely afford gas and having been shot at by Crocker once, he thought the likelihood of getting a bullet hole in the side of the car was high. Better it be Lou's car than his. As they wove through the city, Lou directed which turns to take. Clearly, the big man wanted to feel like a big man. Drummond let it go. They were closing in on Crocker which meant he closed in on Mr. Howe. If doing so allowed Ol' Lou to prance around a little, then so be it.

When they reached the edge of the city, Lou pointed to a road on the left. Pilgrim Drive. It ran fairly straight with row homes lined up like the cages at the city pound. Drummond parked across the street from number 14.

Stepping out of the car, Lou and Drummond scoped out the area. Quiet. Empty. Drummond checked his watch. "Strange for this hour."

"Strange? Everybody's inside eating dinner."

"You really think everybody on the street eats at the exact same time?"

"They do if they don't want to be late for work. Most people in this neighborhood are on third shift for Reynolds Tobacco."

"Yeah, but not all of them. Crocker, for one, is a city dogcatcher."

Lou stuffed his hands in his pockets and turned up one direction and down the other. "It is a little odd. But I'm more concerned about Crocker's door being open."

Drummond had missed it. The door to number 14 was a crack open. He pulled out his .38, and upon seeing this, Lou did the same. They crossed the street and approached the door as if the thing might explode in a fiery ball at any moment. Tamping down his nerves, Drummond climbed the three stone steps to the entrance and peeked into the house.

He saw a narrow hall with an even narrower staircase on the left. One door on the right about halfway, and at the end, the hall opened into a well-lit room — probably a kitchen. Sconces once rigged for gas now hung cold and dark. Old heat marks on the wallpaper surrounded them. An alcove had been built under the stairs, and the end of a little table poked out. A lamp provided the only light.

Drummond glanced back at Lou. "Normally I'd just go in, but seeing as you're a police officer, you want to follow police rules? We can announce that we're here or something?"

Lou frowned as if he looked at an imbecile. "You want me to announce to the guy who shot a cop that I'm a cop?"

"I meant that you call the Department on your two-way, but hey, if you want to run in there shouting your head off, go right on in."

"Look, I know you don't like me —"

"What tipped you off?"

"— and I sure as heck don't like you. But for the rest of this evening, we've got to be partners. You understand? I'm not stepping foot in that house until I know I can count on you."

"There's nothing I can say that you'll believe any more than you could say something to me. You're right. I'll admit that much. I won't lie, either. I wish I had somebody else following me in there. So, here's what I'll promise you — I want to live. I think you do, too. We can put our trust in that. No matter how much you despise me, I know you won't screw me over because you want to live through this. Same goes the other way. Good enough?"

Lou glowered. "You really like to hear yourself, don't you?"

"All I'm saying —"

"Shut up and get moving. I've got you covered."

Drummond held Lou's gaze for a moment longer. They were as close to agreement as they would ever get. He entered the building. Moving with great caution as if navigating through booby-trapped enemy territory, he eased along the hall. Each step he made with care and concern. He paused to listen.

Somebody rustled about below them. In the basement. Of course.

Picking up speed, Drummond hastened down the hall into the kitchen. Once bright yellow, the wallpaper had faded into a dirty brown. An open door led to the basement stairs. Standing at the top,

Drummond could see a dim light below and around the corner.

He wanted to suggest that Lou go first, but that large man would be as stealthy as a Mariachi band playing full blast at a mausoleum. At least the basement stairs followed the wall down. Drummond only had to be concerned with one side exposed.

He put out a foot but hesitated. "Crocker? I know you're there. I just want to come down and talk."

"Y-You come down here, and I'll shoot you dead." Crocker sounded terrified. Panicked.

Drummond looked to Lou. "He'll do it."

"What are you complaining for?" Lou said. "Everything I've heard about you says you have magical powers." Lou twinkled his fingers and snickered.

With a grin, Drummond said, "You know, you keep surprising me. Every time I think you're as dumb as you look, you prove me wrong. That's a good idea." He took a few steps down into the basement. "Crocker, I'm coming down."

"Then I'm going to shoot you." The last words caught in Crocker's throat.

"No, you're not. See, I didn't come all this way looking for you. You remember when we met at the pound? I was looking for Mr. Howe. Still am. Because I know all about Mr. Howe. I know about the things he does and the world he's tapped into. I'm talking about magic."

From behind, Lou stood in the doorway and whispered, "What you doing? I was joking. Don't go down there."

Drummond whispered back. "I'm telling him what he needs to hear. He believes in magic. So, I'll be magical."

"You're really as nuts as everyone says."

With a gentle smirk, Drummond took a few more steps. "Crocker, you need to understand something before you take aim on me."

"Yeah? What's that?" Good. Crocker's interest suggested he was looking for a way out.

"You know Mr. Howe, but how much have you've learned beyond that."

"Beyond like other spells?"

"Spells, witches, ghosts, covens — once you open those doors, there's a whole world to find out about. You know about all that?"

"Some."

"Well, I do know about it all. More than Mr. Howe. I've been dealing with it for years. So, I want to make you little promise. When I get to the bottom of the stairs, if you shoot me — even if you kill me — I'm promising you that I'm going to haunt you for the rest your life. And if it's possible, I'll haunt you after you're dead too. You understand me?"

"Yes, sir." A distinct shiver in the voice.

"You going to shoot me?"

"No, sir. But I don't want to go to jail, neither."

"Once I can talk to you face-to-face, we'll see what we can work out."

Drummond took a deep breath. Nothing more he could do. At a pace he hoped did not frighten the man but did not seem cowardly either, he descended the remaining stairs and entered the basement.

Like the rest of the home, the basement was narrow. Discarded items cluttered the limited space — boxes of clothes, stacks of old magazines, rusting cans of paint, a wooden barrel with a tool box sitting on top, a bicycle with a flat tire. Standing in the back with a half-packed suitcase, Anthony Crocker held his Peacemaker — the barrel pointed at his temple.

Drummond lowered his own weapon. "You don't want to do that."

Tears streamed down Crocker's face and a bubble of mucus popped from one nostril. "I killed a cop. They're going to kill me right back. But they'll make me suffer first. Real bad. Might as well go out on my own terms. Less painful that way."

"For one thing, Detective Cooper ain't dead. As long as he's alive, you only shot him, you didn't kill him. And we can make sure everybody knows you were trying to shoot me and that Cooper jumped in the way." Turning his head to the side, Drummond spoke louder. "Ain't that right, Lou. Come down here. Show Mr. Crocker he's got nothing to worry about."

With a loud huff, Lou descended the stairs. Each squeak of wood caused Crocker to flinch. But even with his finger on the trigger, he managed not to accidentally blow his head off.

Drummond did not have to look to know that Lou stopped at the bottom of the stairs. Inside just enough to see what was going on but not make himself a target.

"What do you say, Lou? Can you promise Mr. Crocker that the Police Department won't find him dead due to any unfortunate accidents?"

"If it means I don't have to go chasing his sorry behind all over Winston-Salem, then yeah. I'll vouch."

Drummond didn't think Lou's word meant much in this situation, but he hoped Crocker wouldn't realize that.

Licking his lips, Crocker said, "You really know all about spells and such?"

"Yeah. More than I ever wanted to."

"Then you understand why Mr. Howe's doing what he's doing. Right?"

"Sorry, kid. I don't understand why anybody would mess around with that stuff. The witches? Who could ever know why they do what they do? Seems to me like trying to alter the natural world isn't the smartest way to succeed in society. And every case I've ever worked on just proves that point more and more. Nothing good comes from magic. You know what I've found does come from it all, though? Death. Pain, loss, and death."

"You're wrong. Spells like the one he's been working on — they can change the world. Make it a better place. Stop people from hurting their pets, and stop cops from hurting people who made a little mistake."

"Lou's not going to hurt you."

"He sure don't look like he agrees with you on that point."

Drummond peeked over his shoulder. Mistake. He saw Lou's gruff face and the way his eyes narrowed. Lou wanted blood. Drummond could see it. Crocker must have seen it, too. Because in that second Drummond took his eyes away, the basement lit up with a bright flash, a loud crack broke out behind, and a body slumped to the floor.

OVER THE NEXT TWO HOURS as the investigating officers arrived, as the coroner removed Crocker's corpse, as Drummond answered question after question after question, the street became alive with cops. Far more than needed. Each one wanted a piece of Crocker — even if that only meant standing around the house where the bastard had died.

Drummond, however, wanted to leave. He felt Mr. Howe slipping away. He had been close. Instinct told him so. But with Crocker's suicide, Drummond guessed Mr. Howe would go to ground for a while. Disappear. He had no doubt that Howe would take another run at him — the man was bent on seeing Drummond to an early grave — but that would be for another time.

Lighting up a cigarette, he sat on a stoop two doors down from Crocker's home. With elbows on the knees, he took a drag and tried to let the day exhale with the smoke. At least Cooper had pulled through — the only good news Drummond had heard recently.

Rubbing his eyes, he leaned back against cold, concrete steps and looked off to the side. A little girl, maybe ten, pigtails and a pink nightgown, stared back at him. Drummond scanned the area but saw no parents. No adults other than cops and medics.

"Hey there," he said, aiming for friendly, but the long day cragged his voice. "You live around here?"

She nodded and pointed across the street.

"Shouldn't you be at home in bed?"

She shrugged. "Mama said I can stay up as late as I want long as I still do my chores in the morning." As if this thought just struck her, she added, "And no complaining."

"I see. That's a lot of responsibility."

"I can handle it."

"So, you decided to come out here and see what all the fuss was about?"

"Yep. Nothing much excitin' happens around here usually."

"I noticed that." Drummond blew a few smoke rings to draw a smile off the girl. Then: "I noticed earlier that nobody was around. You the only kid on this block?"

"No. There's lots of us. But most folks don't like the kids being out on account of the new guy. They say he's creepy."

Trying to maintain his calm, Drummond said, "New guy?"

"Friend of Mr. Crocker's. Moved in a few weeks ago, and people's pets started disappearing. Mama says nobody can prove nothing but she certain it's that new fella. Is Mr. Crocker dead?"

"Afraid so. Did you know him?"

"He'd sometimes give us penny candies. That's all. Guess I won't be getting those anymore."

"You know this fella's name? The new guy?"

"Nope. But I know where he lives. Everybody knows that. Because Mama says I'm not even to walk by the front his house. She afraid he'll snatch me like he snatched them pets. It's a real pain because it's on my side of the street and I gotta walk across the street down a few doors and then back across just to get to my own home."

"That does seem like a real pain."

"Ain't it the truth."

Looking up and down the street, Drummond said, "Which house is it, exactly?"

She pointed behind her. "One with the blue door."

Drummond flicked his cigarette away. "Where are my manners? I never even ask you your name. I'm so sorry."

"My name is Margaret Mae, but most everybody calls me Maggie.

Even Mama."

"Well, Maggie, I very much appreciate what you've told me. You may have helped out the police a lot tonight."

"I didn't think you were a cop. You don't look like one."

Tilting his head down, he winked at Maggie. "I'm a private investigator." With the tip of the hat, he added, "Name's Marshall Drummond. Pleased to meet you."

As he headed toward the blue door, he heard Maggie say, "You best be careful. He's a strange man."

"I'm sure of that."

As HE APPROACHED THE HOME with the blue door, Drummond watched the windows for any sign of activity. A dim amber light could be seen through one on the first floor, but otherwise, the place looked dead. No surprise. With the loss of the dog-man compounded by Crocker's trouble, Drummond figured Mr. Howe had high-tailed it out of Winston-Salem. Hopefully, searching this home would yield a location, or at least clue, for Drummond to check out.

At the base of the stoop, Drummond paused to look back at the cops. They worked the scene diligently. Nobody bothered to look anywhere else. Still, picking a lock while a police investigation went on across the street was risky — downright stupid — but Drummond did not want to wait until morning. Not when people wanted to kill him — or animals — or animal-people.

In case little Maggie was wrong about which house belonged to the new man, or in case Drummond was wrong about the new man's identity, he decided knocking on the door would be a better first move. If anybody but Howe answered, he could apologize, ask a few questions that would seem related to the police hubbub going on nearby, and move on. If nobody answered, then he'd pick the lock. But before he raised a fist to rap on the blue wood, the door opened.

"I had hoped not to see you so soon," Mr. Howe said, dressed in his stage magician regalia while stroking his waxed mustache. "Of course, I expected you, as well. Please, do come in."

Drummond paused. "How about I get you arrested right now and we call it a night?"

"Be my guest. However, you might find it difficult when they ask you what I should be charged with. I suppose you'll try to link me to Mr. Crocker, but in his current state, he won't be much help to you."

"Don't be so sure. I know a few witches who can make the dead talk."

Mr. Howe grinned and with a little bite to his voice, he said, "I'm sure you do. But the police won't accept the word of a witch or a dead man. Besides, all of the papers you could possibly point to lead only to Crocker's address. Nothing links to this house. Except rumors. And now that we are done posturing, please, come in and we can discuss these matters like civilized men."

Drummond entered the house — identical layout to Crocker's, and probably everybody else's on the street — and he followed Mr. Howe through the side door on the right of the narrow hall. They entered a room with two high-backed reading chairs separated by a small wood table and a lamp with a frilly shade. On the opposite wall, two bookshelves bracketed a slim, brick fireplace. An oval-shaped rug covered part of the floor and several paintings of dog's dotted the walls.

"Do sit." Mr. Howe walked out of the room for a moment. When he returned, he carried two open bottles of beer.

After taking a swig — quite good beer, actually — Drummond removed his hat and leaned forward. "We need to put an end to this."

"That much is clear and simple. All you have to do is stop trying to get in my way."

"The problem there is that you insist on ruining other people's lives. You destroyed Sarah McAllister, Henry Peyton, Eustace Harding and all their loved ones. Remember them? About a year ago, you lied and used those good folks. Got them to cast a spell in your foolish attempt to gain immortality. Poor Anthony Crocker just killed himself because of his association with you. Seems that people who know you don't have a very healthy future. There's also the small matter of you trying to get me killed. I don't like that."

Mr. Howe tipped back his beer for a moment. "You have to understand that I never wanted anybody harmed. They were the necessary, if unfortunate, results of my education in witchcraft. As for you, I think you'll see that there's no reason for further pursuit of me. I'm no longer harming other people."

"Oh? You finally realized this idea of immortality is never going to happen?"

Playing with his mustache, Mr. Howe said, "No, no. You don't understand. I took to heart our … shall we call it a disagreement? You were right. There was no reason to involve or manipulate innocent people. Not when I could create my own."

Drummond set his empty beer bottle next to the lamp. "The animals?

Is that why you've been trying to create dog-men and such?"

"The animals seem quite pleased with the ability to finally communicate. They hope that they will get some greater autonomy in their lives, and I don't have to feel guilty about the repercussions when my experiments falter."

With a shake of his head, Drummond said, "You're sick."

"Sticks and stones, Mr. Drummond. The fact is that I'm quite close to success. I've managed to change an animal into a somewhat human form and managed to have them maintain that form for several hours. Cognitive functions vary and degrade quite quickly, but I don't really need them for their brains. They only have to be able to parrot the incantations that I require."

"You're being modest. I met one of your dog-men. Wasn't much of a talker, but otherwise, he functioned quite well."

"I'm flattered. Thank you."

"He also looked dead-eyed, and I'm not so sure he really knew what he wanted. Said he needed you to finish the spell. I've been thinking about that off-and-on today. I mean, why only do half of a spell, when you could get a loyal follower just by finishing it up? But seeing Crocker's suicide made it make sense. See, I thought it was a carrot. Something to keep them loyal. After all, the last time we crossed paths, you had Lionman working for you. But he was man first, wasn't he? Now that you're avoiding the complications of dealing with humans, I saw that you had a new problem. Because they have to be willing to sacrifice themselves for you, right? And unlike Lionman, the dog-men won't do it unless there's a significant reward. So, you only get them halfway to functioning. It looks like a carrot, but it's really a stick."

"A small matter and one I'm willing to endure in order to gain a life forever."

"I can't let you do that."

"But nobody's getting hurt."

"Besides the animals. But even if you don't care about them, which you clearly don't, the type of magic you're playing with has repercussions. Ones that will reach far beyond you. There are ripple effects when you unleash bursts of energy like the ones you'll have created for your spell. Especially when your spell fails."

"It won't."

"I'm sorry — when your spell falters. Witches have been trying to do this for centuries — women who have studied and shared their knowledge and mastered incredible feats. And they've never pulled it off.

You're just a fellow with a couple old books and a limited idea of how to use them. You'd have more success trying to swim across the Atlantic."

Mr. Howe stood and straightened his jacket. "I'm sorry you feel that way. I had hoped to avoid this — thought some common sense might come your way — but it seems not to be the case. Oh well. We can't have everything. It seems I had been right all along in targeting you. And tonight, there will be one final human victim."

Drummond started to rise but Mr. Howe pushed him back into the chair. No — not pushed. Howe merely pressed two fingers against Drummond's forehead.

The room dipped for a moment, and Drummond looked at the empty beer bottle. Crap. He should've known better.

"What did you drug me with?"

"Nothing too terrible. If the gentleman who sold me the mixture is correct, it will soften your resolve and has a slight paralytic effect. Enough to keep you compliant and still while I perform the spell that you're so convinced will fail. You'll provide the human energy, and I'm afraid a little blood, so that I can succeed. Right here. Right in front of you. Right now."

Mr. Howe whistled a high-low pattern. From somewhere in the back, two men dressed in long coats entered the room. From their odd gait, Drummond pegged them as dog-men.

They had that same vacant look as the dog-man who had accosted Drummond on the street and started this whole mess. But as Drummond watched them closer — he had nothing else he could do — he spotted reticence in their movements. Howe commanded them to lift Drummond and the chair, and while they submitted to those demands, they did so with a machinelike, heartless workmanship. They obeyed because they had to. As if the spell that converted them into partial humans also had a bit of mind control added to it.

With one dog-man on either side of the chair, they lifted him up. Mr. Howe put out his hand and came short of commanding Stay. They held still.

With bravado, he whipped back the area rug to reveal a white casting circle painted on the wood floor. "In the center," he said.

The dog-men deposited Drummond on the indicated spot and stepped to the outer edge of the circle. Swirling patterns clashed with sharp lines like an intricate mosaic. A beautiful piece of art perhaps, but for Drummond, the whole thing looked too complicated, too messy to work as a spell.

Mr. Howe stepped forward with a knife and a small porcelain bowl. "I wonder how familiar you are with blood magic. In itself, it is hardly strong enough to achieve my goals. However, it is one of the strongest magics there is. And so, by using it, by combining it with the other casting tricks I've learned, I should be able to finally have success."

Drummond tried to say something, tried to warn Howe that blood magic was powerful because it was so dangerous, but his mouth would not work.

As Mr. Howe walked around the circle, checking to make sure his design satisfied him, Drummond attempted to get out of the chair. But there was no need to even tie him up. Most anything he commanded his muscles to do, they disobeyed. Except for his forearms and his fingers, he remained motionless.

"Don't worry," Mr. Howe said. He grinned as he set the bowl in Drummond's lap. "I'm not going to kill you. I don't require that much blood." He unbuttoned Drummond's shirt and spread it wide to reveal the detective's broad chest. With the knife in one hand, Mr. Howe carved a line across Drummond's skin. As blood dribbled down, he caught it in the bowl. When he had collected enough, he pulled Drummond's shirt closed and pressed against the wound. He did not hold the pressure on the wound for long as if the mere thought of doing so was all that mattered.

From inside his coat pocket, Mr. Howe produced a paintbrush. He moved with a graceful flow as if performing his stage show. He dipped the brush into the blood and painted crimson over the white lines of his casting circle.

The entire time, the two dog-men stood at attention. They watched his movements and exchanged looks with each other, but Drummond could not read whatever communication occurred — if any.

Straining to move his mouth, Drummond tried to warn Mr. Howe again. He had seen witches in covens cast highly complex spells. Even with his extensive experience in the witch world, Drummond would admit that he knew far too little. Yet he still could look at Mr. Howes's casting circle and realize it would never succeed. The kind of magic Mr. Howe attempted — the very idea of reaching immortality — would require more than one witch. Probably four at the minimum — one at each compass point. And all four would have to be experienced. Highly skilled. Mr. Howe was but one man with great enthusiasm but no more than an amateur.

Drummond tried to gain the dog-men's attention, tried to express his concerns. The dog-men never looked his way. They stared straight ahead with the empty eyes of a guard at Buckingham Palace.

If only he could move his feet. If he managed to scratch a break into one of the spell's lines — or better yet, break the circle itself — then he could guarantee the spell's failure. But he only had limited control of his forearms and fingers. Not to mention, his head felt woozy since giving up that blood.

The blood!

Concentrating on his work, Mr. Howe paid no attention to Drummond. The detective took the chance. Reaching up to his shirt, he slid it open and dug his fingers into the wound across his chest. As he coated them with his blood, he saw that the dog-men watched. But they said nothing. Either they didn't understand what he intended do or they didn't care. Or perhaps it was more than that. Drummond wondered if perhaps they understood completely and wanted him to do as he planned.

Wincing at the sharp-knifed sting along his cut skin, he lowered his arm, letting his wet fingers dangle over the armrest. And he watched. And waited. It had been an exhausting maneuver. If he failed to soak his fingers with enough blood, there would be no second chance.

But then he saw it. Pooling on the tip of his finger, forming a large drop, gaining weight, stretching, holding on by the thinnest margin, containing all of Drummond's hope in a teardrop of dark red, until finally it broke free and fell.

Mr. Howe returned to the head of the circle and did not appear to notice the small splotch marring his spell. Smaller and weaker spells can be accomplished with bits of sloppiness in the circle, but something as complex and powerful as seeking immortality required every line, every symbol, every phrase to be perfect. Especially with blood magic. Not a single drop could be in the wrong place.

As Mr. Howe knelt and began chanting, Drummond could only hope that when the spell failed — and it would fail now — that being stuck in a chair in the center of the circle would not destroy him.

He closed his eyes. For a few endless seconds, he drifted away from the world around him. There was no need to be in that awful room anymore. No need to listen to Howe and wonder if the power of the spell backfiring would incinerate everything in the room.

Instead, Drummond pictured a green hill with knee-high grass surrounded by lush woods. The big, blue North Carolina sky filled the space as the hot summer sun baked the ground. Sitting atop that hill, a lovely home with a fence and a dog — the kind of place idealized in the movies. And as he climbed that hill and reached that house, he heard laughter. Wonderful, youthful laughter. He heard Spanish. He walked to the backyard. There he saw Catalina, her abuela, and her boys.

It would've been nice.

Habit told him to brace for whatever might come. But he could not move his arms or grip with his fingers anymore. Mr. Howe's chanting grew louder and more feverishly paced, but Drummond found it easy enough to ignore. He kept his eyes closed and focused on Catalina and that magical house on the hill.

If ever there had been one woman who he regretted losing, she was the one. He tried to reach out toward her, sought protection in her smile, wanted to surround himself with the love he felt for her and her family.

And with a fleeting warmth, he was with her.

They had met somewhere other than that old diner. They had fallen in love without the shunning eyes of the people around them. They lived in that perfect house on that perfect hill and never once did Catalina or her abuela or her boys have to deal with the fallout of his life. In this moment of perfection, they knew nothing of magic or witches or curses. Only love.

A bright flash reddened his eyelids. He felt the chair lift off the ground. He flew backward as flames licked at his feet, and he ignored it all. Keeping his eyes closed, he watched Catalina reach out towards him. Watched her mouth part for a kiss.

Smashing against the wall, the chair splintering into pieces, Drummond felt his arm snap. When he hit the floor, the air rushed out of his body. His eyes snapped open as he heard the screams.

Mr. Howe slouched against the opposite wall, covered in blood, shrieking in pain, with one arm held out, gripping a dog wearing the remnants of a burnt and shredded long coat. The animal barked at him, snapping its vicious jaws just shy of his face. No longer part-man, the dog clearly expressed its displeasure with what had been done to it. Green flames died along the lines of the casting circle. And on the edge of the circle, the other dog did not move. It had been split in half.

The door to the hallway slammed open and Lou burst in. He took one look at the mess, his eyes widening for a second, and then shot the dog in the flank. It yelped and limped off to the corner.

Sidestepping closer to Drummond, Lou said, "You okay?" When Drummond did not respond, Lou turned his head toward the door and used all the force of his large lungs to yell. "I need an officer. I need a medic."

Keeping his .38 trained on Mr. Howe, Lou walked forward. He glanced over the casting circle, the slaughtered dog, and Mr. Howe's magician's costume. "Oh, I can't wait to hear this one."

Drummond could hold out no longer. His eyes closed.

WHEN HE FINALLY AWOKE, Drummond was in a bed at the county hospital. Apparently, he had been out for a day-and-a-half, but other than a broken arm and a splitting headache, he would be all right. Shortly after waking, Lou was informed and entered the room.

He looked around at the bland, functional space and snickered. "They're treating Cooper a lot better than you. But then, you're not a real cop."

"Charming as ever," Drummond said, the words creaking out of his throat.

"Dear Mr. Howe suffered some serious animal bites. Lost a lot of blood. He's in this hospital, too, recovering from it all. When he does, he's got a long list of charges to face."

Drummond nodded and said nothing. From the way Lou meandered back and forth at the foot of the bed, the way he spoke with an official capacity to try and mask his discomfort, Drummond knew — the man had questions. Questions that he did not know if he wanted the answers to.

"Those dogs," Lou said, drawing out the words as if he could discover meaning in them. "They were really strange looking. Best I can figure out, he was working on something new for his act. I don't know how the trick worked, but he created a heckuva damn illusion. Of course, that doesn't justify anything he did, but the best I can figure as to why he did it in the first place — probably thought the act would make him famous."

"Probably."

Lou's eyes fixated on Drummond. The relief, the desire to believe Drummond's agreement, turned his gruff face into a little boy. It lasted a few seconds longer than it should have. At length, he returned to his usual self. "Well, I came in here to let you know that your case is over. You won't be needed anymore."

"Fine," Drummond said. What else could he say? The police had taken control, and since Howe was connected to Crocker which connected to a cop shooting, there was no chance of Howe ever getting free. "I've got a question for you."

"Yeah?" The dread in that single word could not be mistaken.

"Just wondering — why'd you come into that house? You saved me, but why?"

Lou grinned. "You thought you were being sly, but I saw you saunter down the street. I had my hands full, and I figured you were following a lead. But when you didn't come back after a while, I began to wonder. I didn't know which house you went into, but after knocking on a bunch of doors, I found that little girl — Maggie. She told me to go to the blue door, and when I did, I heard the screaming."

"Yeah, but why? You hate me."

"Well, that's true. But it's like I said — for this case, you were my partner."

Drummond waited for more of an explanation, but none came.

"One more thing," Lou said, and checked that nobody could overhear him. "You ever get another one of these crazy cases — you leave me out. I don't ever want to see anything like that again. You got it?"

"Yeah, don't worry. You're not the first to say that to me."

Drummond laughed. Cooper would have a conniption when he learned that he finally had something in common with Ol' Lou.

CASE 13

MR. HOWE'S FINAL VICTIM

FEW CASES HAD COME Marshall Drummond's way since the death of Mr. Howe. The man had been an average stage magician — Mezmo the Magical — who toyed with the dangerous powers of witchcraft and lost. Ended up in jail. Less than two week later, Drummond read that Howe hanged himself rather than face trial. Considering the man had been involved in nearly killing a cop, Drummond marveled it took so long for a suicide or an "accident" to occur.

He didn't feel bad one bit. After all, Howe had tried to kill him, too. Oddly, the police — in particular, Detective Lou Piper — had saved Drummond's life. Then again, all of Drummond's cases tended to be odd, so perhaps he shouldn't think of anything abnormal as abnormal anymore. Without work, however, his current problem was quite normal — he needed money.

Rent on his office came due in a week, and since he illegally lived in the place, too, he couldn't afford to lose it. Couldn't afford to pay for it, either. Not unless he found some cash. Which was why he spent much of the day traveling from one coin collector to another.

During the Howe case, Drummond had spent a winter night with his old pal, Leroy Parker. The evening turned out to be the usual case of the unusual, and when it finished, he ended up with a gold coin in his pocket. The size of a doubloon, the coin had one side completely smooth and the other bore a small engraving — three symbols Drummond did not recognize.

According to Leroy, the coin was the autograph of the person who had created a mojo bag that gave them a lot of trouble that night. But both he and Leroy knew the thing held power of its own. Under normal circumstances, Drummond would have expected Leroy to keep the coin for further study. Old relics and supernatural curio were what the man loved. He gave it to Drummond because he thought it might help the detective hunt down Mr. Howe. That turned out to be unnecessary. With Mr. Howe dead, the spells he had attempted were dead, too. The coin was no more than a coin, now. And a coin had value.

Except not a single dealer could tell Drummond what the thing was worth. None of them had ever seen such a coin before. One even accused Drummond of trying to pass off a fake. When Drummond pressed to know what he would be faking, the man shut up and threw

Drummond out of the store. Others were intrigued, but most offered him sums based on the value of the gold plating (no solid gold, unfortunately). Not a lot, though. Not nearly enough. These dealers could smell a man's desperation and wanted to snatch this mysterious coin for next to nothing.

Two days into his search, Drummond visited Smythe Collectibles. The place looked a century out of date and smelled every bit as musty. Behind a wooden counter, Mr. Smythe hunched over a watch. He was a bony man with thick glasses and thin hair.

When bells hanging over the entrance rang, Smythe glanced up. "Welcome," he said, his voice a meek thing. "Feel free to look around. We've got stamps in the back corner, baseball cards there, and —"

"I've got a coin I'd like you take a look at," Drummond said, heading straight over.

"Oh, of course. I'll be right with you." He had a slight North Carolina accent but had clearly spent time elsewhere, too. As he put the watch away, he said, "You say you have a coin?"

"Yeah. A strange, little piece. Smooth on one side; a little writing on the other. Gold-plated, I'm told."

"And what do you want to do with it?" Smythe asked as he returned to the counter.

"Sell it, I think. Depends on what I can get for it."

"Then I suppose I should take a look."

Drummond fished the coin from his pocket and set it on the counter. Though the man tried to hide his reaction, Smythe let out a clear gasp. Just a short sound before he caught control, but Drummond had heard it.

Using a magnifying glass first and then a jeweler's eyepiece, Smythe inspected every inch of the coin. When he set it back on the counter, his fingers twitched, but he kept his hand on top of it. At length, he met Drummond's eyes. "You have a very unique piece here. If you wouldn't mind, I'd like to take it to some colleagues for their opinion on the pricing. I could have them look it over and offer a quote tomorrow."

"That won't be necessary. I've visited almost everybody in this city." Drummond reached out to pick up the coin, but Smythe did not move his hand. After an awkward pause in which Drummond glowered with cold threat, Smythe made an embarrassed sound and stepped back from the counter. Drummond swiped the coin.

As he left the store, Smythe followed, prattling on about making sure to come back in the morning, he could still offer the best price in town.

When Drummond walked out, he heard the distinct click of the door being locked behind him. He glanced over his shoulder. The store's CLOSED sign had been placed in the window.

Without hesitation, Drummond walked down the street, weaved around two derbies and a parasol, and ducked into the first alleyway. He leaned against the brick wall, lit a cigarette, and watched for Smythe. That man knew something about the coin — obvious enough from his behavior — and could be expected to act quite soon. Given the nature of how that coin came to Drummond, he had a dark suspicion as to where this might end up.

But as he waited, as he finished his cigarette and tapped out another, he wondered if maybe he was making a case where none existed. Maybe he itched to be active when he needed to acknowledge that the supernatural had simply been quiet of late. In fact, he really needed to accept that being a detective of the unexplainable required a second line of income.

He scowled. He had no desire to spend his nights hiding in bushes to catch unfaithful spouses in the act, but the bills were mounting up. As his mind swirled around these problems, his patience paid off. Smythe stepped out of the store, donning a dark bowler, and headed up the street.

Drummond had never had much difficulty following people. Even when his target tried to evade being tailed, he had a knack for keeping on his subject. He wasn't perfect, but most major league ballplayers would be envious of his batting average.

Though Smythe showed no sign or awareness that he was being followed, he sure made it difficult on Drummond. The man dashed down streets at the last moment, cut through alleyways, and tried to blend in with the other men wearing bowlers. All of this behavior only secured in Drummond's mind that he had been right about Smythe — that man knew about this coin. Perhaps knew a whole lot more.

After all, no way could Smythe have known that Drummond chose to follow him. That meant Smythe's behavior was based on an assumption that somebody might follow him at some point in time. The man had something to hide.

Twenty minutes of walking and more blocks than Drummond wanted to count, they entered a less populated area with several rundown buildings — tombstone remnants of the worst of the Depression. Old newspapers and trash that would never be picked up littered the sidewalks. The narrow confines blocked out enough sunlight that it felt like dusk had arrived early.

Drummond hugged a corner while observing Smythe approach a chipped door. He knocked. After a few seconds, the door cracked open and Smythe slid inside.

Hastening across the street, Drummond headed toward the building. Dim light broke through the seams between closed window blinds. Drummond tried the door. Locked. No surprise there. He walked around the perimeter and located a side door with a small overhead lamp. The bulb had blown out. In a nicer place, this would be for the help and for throwing out the trash. Also no surprise — the door was unlocked. People often forgot to check the servant door when locking up.

Drummond entered a severely disused kitchen. Thick layers of dust coated the pots and pans still sitting on an ancient woodstove. The icebox felt warm, and a small table against the back wall had been loaded with so many books and old magazines that nobody could ever eat there.

Crossing to the swing door that led into the main hallway, Drummond heard muffled voices echoing toward him. Considering the poor condition of the kitchen, he thought the door hinges might be underused, if not outright rusty. Indeed, he felt resistance when he pushed the door slightly open, but no screaming whine or rusty howl erupted.

"I'm telling you, I saw it with my own eyes," Smythe said from behind a closed door down on the left.

Another voice answered — a woman's voice. "Do not mistake my caution for doubt. You've never struck me as a stupid man, and it would be most stupid to bring hope yet not back it up."

"I would never lie to you. I only want to serve."

"You are sure, then?"

"There's no mistaking your coin."

"If that's true, why did you not simply purchase the coin from the man? Overpay, if necessary. It would be in our hands now."

Drummond had wondered the exact same thing.

Smythe's answer did not go down well. "Because the man who brought the coin to me was the detective. The same one who has caused all of your problems."

Damn. A witch. Drummond could think of no other type of woman who would suffer a downfall because of him. Not that he had any other thought in his mind, but hearing Smythe's words only confirmed that the woman he spoke with was a witch. He glanced back at the table — all that clutter. It should have been his first big clue. Witches loved to collect things.

So, a witch had made that coin. She then sold it to Mr. Howe who used it in a mojo bag to try to curse Leroy Parker. Drummond happened to be in the way at the time. Or maybe he wasn't in the way — Mr. Howe had wanted to hurt Drummond since their first meeting. Interesting enough as a piece of history — after all, Mr. Howe was dead — but why would this witch —

Something crawled over Drummond's foot. He glanced down and saw a rat. Large one. On instinct, he kicked his foot out, sending the rat across the room. It smacked the kitchen table leg, let out a loud screech, and skittered off to a hole in the wall. But not before disrupting several stacks of magazines. They slid down, hitting the floor with a clump that Drummond hoped only sounded loud in his head.

"What was that?"

Apparently, not only loud in his head.

"You idiot," the woman said. "He followed you."

Drummond looked to the servant door. If he ran out that way, either Smythe or the woman would easily see him dashing down the street. They would know without a doubt that he had been there. If instead, he hid nearby, remaining in the house, they would have doubts. And he might learn more.

He hurried over to what looked like an exit from the kitchen, but it only led to a walk-in pantry. However, at the back of the pantry, he spied another door — probably led down to the basement. Moving as fast as possible while keeping his noise to a minimum, Drummond eased the door open, stepped onto the slat stairs, closed the door, and waited. He put his ear against the wood to listen.

"It must've been a rat," Smythe said from inside the kitchen. "You have enough of them here."

"If you wish to pay for an exterminator, be my guest. But that was not a rat."

"I'm all for being cautious, and even a little paranoia is warranted, but I sincerely doubt this detective had any reason to believe I am connected to you."

"People have been underestimating Marshall Drummond for too long."

"You're a witch. Why don't you create a spell that will kill him? Be done with it all."

With enough menace that Drummond could hear it through the walls and doors, the witch said, "Of all people, you should understand that witchcraft is never free. Yes, there are spells that can kill a man wherever he stands, but the price tag for such witchcraft is not something I am willing to pay. Not something anybody I know is willing to pay. Unless you're offering."

"N-No. I suppose not."

"I'm glad you value your soul."

An unsettling hiss reached Drummond's ears from below. He glanced down the dark staircase. Basements. Always in the basements.

He did not want to know what he would find down there, but he recognized he would have to check it out. Not only because the curiosity would drive him crazy with insomnia for weeks, but also if a witch wanted to hide something down in her basement, it probably required Drummond to set it right. Nobody else in the world seemed to be doing so.

To reduce any wood squeals, he kept his feet to the outside edges of the stairs. He worked his way down. When he reached the bottom, he felt around for a light switch. The hissing grew louder and was accompanied by an even more insidious sound — the rattle of chains.

He glanced back up the stairs. Maybe he could ignore it. Maybe he wouldn't spend nights wondering what he had left down here. No. Because someday he would read in the newspaper that a sweet, old lady or an innocent child or a promising young student had been chewed to pieces by a strange animal attack. In between the reporter's lines, he would spot evidence of a witch, and he would know that he had let it happen. His hand found the switch, and he flicked on the lights.

A woman stood one foot away from a thick post buried into the dirt floor. A thick chain around her ankle tied her to the post. Her pale cracked skin and manic eyes peeked out from beneath a mane of wild black hair. Filthy rags covered her body. From the corners of her mouth, drool mixed with blood dribbled down to her chin. She stood crooked as if an enormous weight pulled her to the left, but from the way she held her arm close in, Drummond suspected she had been injured a while back and that the bones had poorly healed.

The basement smelled like an outhouse. A quick glance around and Drummond spotted a filled bucket in the back. A second bucket had been placed off to his right — the muck inside that one might have been food. All around this prisoner, the basement had been kept clear. The massive clutter had been pushed aside, kept out of her reach, so that she had access to nothing but the two buckets.

She stared at him. With her brow tightening downward, she opened her mouth. No teeth. A pitiful moan escaped from deep within as she stuck out her tongue. Covered with a gray film, veined with strands of bloodied mucus, she seemed to be mocking him while also begging for his sympathy.

But Drummond didn't have the time to feel anything. As he noticed the odd bumps and ridges near the center of her tongue, he heard the cocking of a handgun from behind.

"Will you please reconsider?" Smythe said.

The witch's voice from earlier answered. "No."

Drummond raised his hands. "I'm not a threat. No need to do anything stupid."

"You hear that?" Smythe said. "He thinks we're stupid. Let me kill him and we can be finished with this problem."

The witch said, "Are you willing to pay the consequences of such an action?"

"It's not a spell. It's a bullet."

"Consequences of killing a man who has friends with some in the police department. Marshall Drummond can't simply disappear without being noticed. Wherever you dispose his body, it will be found, and the police will search hard for his killer. Even those who don't like him would do so, because he's helped them out before. He's helped keep the police department from having to admit that we witches exist. Don't you understand this yet? It's his protection. Besides, you will get caught, and you will go to jail. And I guarantee that you will find an unfortunate accident while you're in jail. If not from the police department, then from my fellow witches. They would be too afraid that you might reveal something about us."

"Why must you turn everything into a threat? He's more a problem than anything else."

"Maybe. But he could be the answer I need."

Drummond did not know what to think about having a witch defend him, but he wasn't about to argue with the situation. Until the witch added, "If I'm wrong, and you still want to risk your life for the pleasure of killing a man, who am I to stop you?"

At least he heard Smythe let out a resigned sigh. "Mr. Drummond, kindly come back upstairs. Don't try anything or you will pay for it."

The witch grunted. "I said —"

"A bullet through his leg won't kill him."

As Drummond turned, keeping his hands up, he gazed at the stairs. For such a meek looking man, Mr. Smythe had a vicious streak in him.

And the witch behind him — Drummond had yet to see her. Climbing the stairs, he only glimpsed a silhouette as she re-entered the pantry toward the kitchen.

Mr. Smythe directed him down the main hall and into the room on the left. In its prime, it had been a receiving room — two upholstered couches, a large fireplace, portraits on the walls, books on the shelves, and an ornate table for serving drinks. But now, the room only hinted at its former grandeur. The couches were dusty and stained. The portraits were covered with sheets and blocked by boxes stacked tall. On the ornate table — a crack in the glass top had been matched by gouges along the sides.

"Please, sit," the witch said from a darkened corner.

Smythe indicated the maroon couch with odd white streaks down the center cushion. Drummond opted to sit at the far end. The entire time, Smythe kept his weapon aimed and cocked.

"You be careful with that," Drummond said. "I'd rather not have a bullet in my head by accident. Or on purpose, for that matter."

Smythe settled on the opposite couch, crossed his legs, and rested the butt of his revolver upon his knee. Not the safest way to hold a handgun. Drummond might have kept his eye focused on that impending threat if not for the witch stepping out of the shadows behind Smythe.

She wore a classy, conservative outfit. The kind of thing a secretary might wear when she knew she held more power than the boss. Her dark hair billowed down to her shoulders and curled inward at the bottoms. If he had seen her on the street, Drummond would not have been surprised to find out she wanted to be an actress. These two competing ideas — woman of business, woman of theater — played out in the way she moved and the stern yet provocative way she spoke.

Standing directly behind Smythe, she said, "You've heard enough to know that we're not going to kill you. Not yet."

"Then have your servant here put away that gun."

"I'm no servant," Smythe said.

The witch answered Drummond as if Smythe never spoke. "I would if I trusted you. Also, I don't want to go through the hassle of tying you up. As fun as that might be. But I promise you that if you behave, you will not have any bullet holes in your body."

Drummond removed his hat and placed it on his knee. "I guess I can't ask for a better guarantee than that."

The corner of her mouth twitched. "Look around you. What remains of this home is proof that there are no guarantees in our lives. Not too long ago, this was a proud and vibrant place. A glorious coven that had existed for close to a century resided within these walls. Now, only two witches remain — myself and my one sister."

"Would that be the charming woman chained down in the basement?"

"Her name is Sadie, and be sure to use respect when you talk of her."

"I meant no offense. I'm only trying to understand why you think I caused all this. I know I've fought against many witches in the past, but as far as I know, I've never come across you or your sister, Sadie. I'm certain I've never been to this house or know of your coven."

"I never said you did cause all this. But you have come across the gentleman responsible. He goes by many names, but I believe you know him as Mr. Howe."

Even if Smythe had not been holding a gun, Drummond would still have felt uneasy. The witch had avoided giving her name, suggesting that she feared he had access to powerful spells, yet she brazenly linked him with Mr. Howe. More than all of it, he noticed that this witch was not threatening him. Her tone had shifted to one he knew well. He had sat in his office enough times and listened to enough clients explaining how they got into trouble, that he recognized it right away. This witch wanted him to do something for her. And taking a job for a witch — that never turned out well.

"I don't work for witches."

"Then I have no use for you and Mr. Smythe may do as he pleases."

"I guess I work for witches."

Barely got a grin from her. "Smart man. Let's see if you'll be smarter still. Mr. Howe came to my coven because no other witch would deal with him."

"But you would?"

The witch's neck tightened under her clenched jaw. "While I am completely justified in blaming Mr. Howe for the demise of this coven, it would be untrue to suggest that we were thriving before his arrival. You see, we were one of the few covens who had attempted to break the bonds of tradition. That is, we did something that opened us to public visibility. We invested in the stock market. But that was the winter of '28."

"Bad timing might be a worse kind of witchcraft than your used to."

Smythe straightened and lifted the revolver. "Enough with the wisecracks."

"It's okay," the witch said. "He's right. The sorcery of the financial system did us in. A year later and we had lost most of our wealth. But we worked our way back to a sustainable life. Nearly there, anyway. Unfortunately, we were still in a position that we could not be picky with who we worked for."

Tapping his chin, Drummond said, "I take it that's when Mr. Howe showed up."

"He asked us to create a spell that would convert a human being into an animal. We agreed."

"You made the coin?"

"We did. But Mr. Howe thought he knew better than thirteen women living under one roof. He thought he could control the forces of nature better with his little bit of knowledge than the expert witches who had studied their entire lives. We learned from knowledge handed down generations upon generations. The arrogant fool learned from one book and screwed the whole thing up. But then, you were there."

Drummond started to see more of what had really happened. "He made a deal with others — people who knew even less than he did. Used them. They came for Leroy. Didn't expect me, though. Not that either of us were in a great position to defend ourselves." Drummond didn't want to think about that night he spent inside the body of a squirrel.

"Regardless, you handled the matter and stopped Mr. Howe from success. He, in turn, blamed us. He entered our home, raving about his right to rule us, and he performed a spell. A curse, I suspect."

"You don't know?"

"Like most things Mr. Howe attempted, this spell failed. Unlike most things, it failed with vigor. The concussive blast knocked out every one of us. When I awoke, I saw Mr. Howe leaving. I wanted to go after him, but I heard Sadie shrieking her throat raw. You see, Mr. Howe awoke before all of us. And he slit the throats of all our witches."

"Except for you and Sadie."

"My dear sister rose while he dealt with Phyllis. Sadie's shriek sent him running, and we've not seen of him since."

Drummond shook his head. "In all my dealings with Mr. Howe, he had others doing his dirty work. It's hard to picture him killing a woman. And eleven women? That's a lot of death."

"If you could have seen the rage I witnessed in his eyes, you would have no doubts."

"And Sadie?" He thought of that twisted woman in the basement.

"Seeing all those murders broke something in her." With a bitter chuckle, the witch tapped her fingers on the back of the couch. "Mr.

Howe failed at his curse but hurt her nonetheless. So, you understand now why I want him. He must pay for what he did. Naturally, we can't go to the police. Even if it had only been a single murder, witches and the police don't mix. But eleven? Far too sensational. Our existence, our coven, would be in all the newspapers, on the radio, and in the end, we would never see justice."

Drummond shifted in his seat, unable to get comfortable. "You're still looking for him." It wasn't a question. Merely a statement to stall. Because it did not take a brilliant detective to see where this headed, and the key piece of information this witch lacked meant everything to this case — Mr. Howe was dead. Drummond knew it. The witch, clearly, did not.

"I'll make this easy for you," she said. "Find Mr. Howe and bring him to me. If you do that, then I will pay you with one of the greatest pieces of currency a witch can offer. I will owe you a favor."

Trying to hide his shock, Drummond donned his hat and stood. "Doesn't look like I have much choice. You haven't outright threatened me, but I suspect if I turned you down, those threats would be coming. Besides, your friend Smythe makes enough threats for you."

"Thank you. Mr. Smythe will be joining you. In case you decide to change your mind."

Drummond touched the rim of his hat and gave the witch a nod. "I haven't seen Mr. Howe in quite some time, but I'll do what I can to find him." Cocking his head toward Mr. Smythe, he added, "Come on, lapdog. I'm not slowing down for you."

With that, Drummond strode out of the room and headed straight for the front door.

He put his hands in his coat pockets as he trudged along block after block. He didn't have any concerns over Smythe — the man had proven to be a great amateur. He never frisked Drummond, leaving the detective with the .38 in his shoulder holster. Not only that, but Smythe showed a severe lack of working knowledge of the weapon he held. That gave Drummond a little concern over the man. A fool with a gun might hurt those around him more than himself.

Picking up his pace, Drummond lowered his head and thought. He had to figure this out fast. Smythe would grow impatient — if not for his own purposes, out of fear of the witch. The biggest problem facing Drummond — lack of information.

Oh, he had the full story as told by the witch, but that could not be considered a trusted source. In Drummond's experience, witches lived in lies except when issuing threats. But they tended to weave those lies with the truth. Much of what she said probably had happened — just not exactly as she had portrayed it.

The part that sounded most off — Mr. Howe going on a murder spree in that house. Nothing about that resembled the man Drummond had known. Perhaps Howe's failed curse had scrambled his mind and led him to such vicious slaughter. However, when Drummond had faced Mr. Howe in the end, the man had acted quite clear and sane. Well, sane for an idiot who wanted to abuse witchcraft for his own purposes.

"Where are you taking us?" Smythe asked.

Drummond checked the road signs. He had not been paying attention and needed to come up with a quick answer. "The theater. It's where I first met Mr. Howe, and a good place to start searching for him." Sounded reasonable. As long as Smythe didn't think on it too much.

"No," Smythe said. Maybe he didn't need to think on it at all. "We need to go to your office first."

"Oh? Why?"

"I want that coin."

Well, well. Not only had the idiot failed to frisk Drummond for a weapon, but he also never checked for the coin. He simply assumed Drummond had taken it back to the office. But that brought a question to Drummond's mind.

"What do you need the coin for? I guessed, at first, that she was going to use it as a way to find Mr. Howe, but you've got me now."

"Call it insurance. In case you fail."

With a grunt, Drummond headed toward his downtown office as his mind fiercely went over everything that had been said. Something in Smythe's words rang within Drummond. His gut told him that the answer was there.

Insurance. That was the word that kept repeating in Drummond's head. If the coin could be used as he suspected — with a spell that would connect to Mr. Howe — then why bother with Drummond at all? Was this simply a witch's fanciful game? Entertainment? No — witches desperate as this one did not have time to toy with a person. Perhaps this was vengeance. The witch had spoken the truth regarding the desire of many in the witch community to hurt Drummond. Yet that didn't make a lot of sense, either. After all, she had him sitting on her couch at gunpoint. It would've been easy to torture him, kill him, or do any number of things to exact some measure of revenge. All of which suggested that she truly needed to find Mr. Howe and that the coin would not suffice. She needed Drummond.

But then why did Smythe want the coin? Insurance he had said — for what?

Rounding the corner, Drummond stared down the long avenue. They had seven blocks to go before hitting Fourth Street. From there, it would not be long to reach his office.

"I'm curious," Drummond said, hoping to get Smythe talking without the man realizing it. "How did you get involved with this coven?"

Turned out, Smythe opened up with ease. "I should've thought that much was obvious — I'm their fence."

"Really? I didn't think witches sold off anything they owned. Stolen or not."

A smarmy grin rose on Smythe's lips. "I suspect I could teach you a thing or two."

"I wish you would because none of the stories I've heard today are adding up." Drummond turned down a narrow alleyway, barely wide enough to fit two people. He waited until they had gone beyond the halfway point. Then he did what always worked for him when he couldn't figure out a problem — he stirred things.

With a short movement, he pivoted back and belted Smythe in the gut. Before the man could double over, Drummond brought his palm under Smythe's chin and pressed him against the brick wall. With his free hand, he dug into Smythe's pocket and pulled out the revolver. A sharp shove and Drummond backed up several steps, training his .38 on the gasping man.

Smythe's entire head shook. Not with fear. Not with regret. He showed no indication of dropping to his knees and begging for forgiveness. No — he glowered at Drummond.

"You are no better than the witches," Smythe said. "Y'all play your little games without ever caring about who gets hurt."

"I work hard to stop these witches from hurting people. You're the one enabling her."

"Are you that stupid? I thought you were the expert. Tell me, Mr. Detective, when has a coven ever allowed a man like me into their fold?"

That gave Drummond pause. "I assumed, given the state of her coven, that she was desperate."

Smythe lowered his head. For a second, Drummond thought he had started to cry. But then he heard the soft chuckling. "Desperate," Smythe said. "People think they know the meaning of that word, but they're all wrong. You want to understand desperate? Look into my eyes."

Smythe lifted his head and stared straight at Drummond. Something about that man's gaze lured Drummond to lean closer. That was all the man needed.

With surprising speed, Smythe popped Drummond on the nose and attempted the same maneuver used upon him moments earlier — digging into Drummond's pocket to get his revolver back. But Drummond had been in enough scrapes to know a counter or two. He blocked Smythe's searching hands and thrust his knee up. Connected with Smythe's thigh.

"What does this witch have over you?" Drummond said. "Or did she promise you something?"

Smythe launched forward thrusting both hands against Drummond shoulders and slamming him into the wall. "She stole my family — my Sadie."

"Sadie?"

"My sister. She seduced my sister with dreams of riches and power. Made Sadie believe she would be able to help me and the rest of our family dig out of the suffering we're under. Take the banks off our backs. But it was all a lie."

"Of course it was. Your sister was dealing with a witch."

Smythe flopped back on the opposite wall, breathing hard. "I tried to stop her. I begged Sadie to come back home. I promised anything that I thought might work, but she refused. I told her she was dealing with the Devil, but she insisted that she knew what she was doing. I even threatened her. But it was pointless. Look at what she's become."

"That was an accident."

"No. That was a curse."

Drummond picked his hat off the ground and brushed it clean. He had been stupid. Of course the witch had lied about Mr. Howe having failed. She didn't want to admit that a man had been successful pulling off a spell or two. Especially a curse. Which meant that she wanted Mr. Howe back for more than simple vengeance. She needed him in order to break the curse.

And Smythe wanted the coin as insurance — insurance to break the curse, too? It fit nicely. No — not quite.

"If Mr. Howe succeeded with his spell — and I can see that Sadie was his target — then why did he kill all the others? That sort of bloodlust still doesn't sound like him." Drummond set his hat on at an angle and looked over at Smythe.

"Well, let's go find him and you can ask directly," Smythe said.

Drummond leaned over and picked up his handgun. "Considering you're not on the witch's side in all this but merely trying to help your sister, then I think you need to know the truth."

"The truth?"

He checked around for any rocks, bricks, or other objects that could be used as weapons. Then: "Mr. Howe is dead."

"What?"

"Afraid so. The spells he continued to attempt eventually backfired."

When an attack did not come, Drummond half-expected Smythe to buckle and weep for his sister. But the small man clenched his fists and opened his mouth. He uttered a horrid cry like a wounded tiger drawing on its last reserves. Before Drummond could raise his arms in defense, Smythe launched forward.

He knocked away Drummond's .38. He punched Drummond in the gut, the ribs, the chest. Worked his way right up to the chin. He attacked with such viciousness that counter-attacks failed.

Smythe grabbed hold of Drummond's lapels and swung him to the opposite wall. But a metallic clink on the ground stopped them both. They looked down. The coin had slipped out of Drummond's pocket and settled next to a puddle of spit tobacco.

Smythe whispered a single thought, "I can still break the curse." Punching Drummond with a dazing blow to the side of the head, he then snatched the coin and bolted off.

It took Drummond a half-minute before he stumbled out of the alleyway and headed back toward the coven's house. The depths of anger that had been unleashed upon his body revealed the final piece. Mr. Howe did not kill the coven. Smythe did. All that rage which he used to pummel Drummond spoke well of murderous intent. It was possible that Howe had very little to do with the matter at all. Oh, he certainly cursed Sadie, but beyond that — Drummond could not be sure.

Gaining speed as he ran up the sidewalk, he thought about the witch's behavior. She had acted in control, like a former coven leader, but Drummond now thought he had it wrong. Smythe had been the one in control.

The man had said it himself — he loved his sister. He had attempted everything to bring his sister back. Tried to talk sense into her. Tried logic, love, bribery, any avenue that might have worked and probably several that had no hope. Yet when all failed, when his sister became a casualty of witchcraft, Smythe lost his sanity. He must have.

Driven out of his head by the loss of his beloved sibling, he snuck into the coven house in an attempt to rescue Sadie. That's when he saw her chained in the basement. That's when he really went mad.

Drummond winced at the sharp pain lancing up his side. That did not compare to the pain Smythe must have felt. In his ravaged state of mind, he combed through that house, exacting revenge on each witch he saw. He murdered the entire coven. All but one. He needed the head witch alive. Because he was not out for vengeance entirely. He needed her to break the curse. And she needed the man that made the curse — Mr. Howe.

Drummond turned down the last street and approached the house, the one far enough away from the general public, the one that would probably forever be haunted by the deaths of so many. The front door stood ajar. Pulling out his weapon, he entered.

Closing the front door, Drummond paused to listen. He heard movement coming from the receiving room. With his .38 at the ready, he slid down the hall until he reached the door. Crouching low, he scooted up to the knob. He didn't want to suffer a headshot when he opened that door, so maybe coming in low would save him that trouble.

When he opened the door, he found that both couches had been shoved aside, and Smythe trained his weapon on the witch. She drew a casting circle in chalk on the floor. Tears ran down her cheeks as she had set her mouth firm.

Smythe glanced up at the detective. "No need for such caution. The only one in danger here is the witch."

"I have bruises on my side to suggest otherwise," Drummond said. However, he stood straight.

"I apologize. But when it comes to my sister, there is no line I wouldn't cross."

"Is that what you told yourself when you murdered this coven?"

"I think you'll find that should you ever take this to the police, all the evidence points to Mr. Howe. But I took no pleasure in doing what needed to be done. They were witches, and witches only cause trouble."

"You're the one causing me a heck of a lot of trouble."

"You shouldn't be involved at all. I've been after Mr. Howe, not you. I nearly burst out laughing when you walked into my shop — with the coin, no less."

"You're saying it was my dumb luck?"

"And my good fortune."

Keeping his back touching the wall, Drummond eased along the side, hoping to get into a position that he could both stop the witch's spell and keep Smythe from committing yet another murder.

"It was him all along," the witch said. "He murdered my coven."

"I know," Drummond said.

Smythe kicked the witch in the side. "Be quiet."

The witch snapped at him like a rabid animal. "It's not often a man can pull one over on a witch. You should be proud."

"Shut up," Smythe said. "Finish the spell."

The witch looked toward Drummond, and from her trembling hand and her glistening eye, he knew the spell would not work. If it had been so simple, they would never have bothered looking for Mr. Howe in the first place.

"It's over," he said.

"Not until Sadie is free."

"She can't."

Rushing across the room, Smythe knocked down several books from the dusty shelves. "This is witchcraft. All of it. Don't you understand? They find things and curse things. They make people act unnatural. Anything is possible. As long as you're willing to pay the price. Isn't that right, witch?"

She kept her head bowed over the casting circle. "If it's possible to break this curse without the man who caused it, I don't know the spell."

Smythe grabbed her hair and yanked her back. "Then you can figure it out. That's what all those books are for."

Part of Drummond wanted to shoot Smythe in the leg and take control of the situation. Part of him shuddered at the idea of defending a witch. Especially one that would dance upon his grave should he be the man to fall. But as saliva leaked down Smythe's chin while the witch stared at the ceiling with terror, Drummond could not deny the overwhelming truth — the witch still controlled her faculties; the same could not be said for Smythe.

"Put down the gun," Drummond said. "I know it's terrible and it's wrong, but Mr. Howe is dead. That means you can't break this curse. You need to accept it so we can find mercy for Sadie."

Smythe swung his revolver toward Drummond. "And you need —"

Drummond fired. He would take no chances with a crazed man pointing a gun in his direction. But while his brain had only sought to disable Smythe, his instincts had another plan. Or perhaps Smythe moved in an awkward way causing the damage. Or maybe he shifted deliberately to take the bullet hard. The question of intent versus accident would bother Drummond for many nights to come. Whatever the truth, Smythe's neck opened and blood spurted out to the rhythm of his weakening heartbeat. He lived long enough to throw a confused gaze at Drummond. Then his eyes emptied as his body collapsed.

"Oh, thank the Mother," the witch said, dropping to her hands and brushing away the chalk casting circle.

Despite the witch's obvious relief, Drummond remained tense. He kept his weapon at the ready, pointed at the witch.

Wiping her tears, she lifted her gaze. "No need for that. I'm not going to harm you. At least, not today."

"What you said about the coin — was that true? Can you really not break the curse without Mr. Howe?"

"Unfortunately. But the coin does have value. It can be used to end the curse."

"Don't start your word games with me. It's been too long of a day."

"No games. Honestly. The curse cannot be broken — I cannot free Sadie from the rotting madness that has been placed upon her. But with this coin, I can end her suffering."

"A bullet to the head will end her suffering."

"No." The witch jumped to her feet but raised her hands as Drummond's finger dropped to the trigger. "You mustn't kill her yet. If you do so, her soul will be trapped in that madness forever. She'll wander the city afraid and alone as a ghost with no control over her thoughts or actions."

Drummond gestured to the coin on the floor. "But that fixes it?"

"It ends the curse before it kills her. She'll be able to move on in peace."

Drummond needed no time to decide. "What do we have to do?"

THE NEXT MORNING, Drummond sat in the back booth of The Sunrise Diner, sipping coffee, and gazing absently over the newspaper. He had slept little through the night and suspected he would sleep little more the following night. Or the one after that. Nothing but time would put to rest the horrible sounds he had heard. And maybe not even time could save him.

"You want anything to eat?" the waitress, Bobby Sue, asked.

Drummond forced a wink. "Your smile is plenty breakfast for me. That and this coffee."

She shrugged and sauntered off to the next table. Drummond's stomach grumbled, but he couldn't afford diner food. Couldn't really afford the coffee or newspaper, either, but he needed to step out of his office, needed some normalcy around him, and spending the morning at a diner was about as normal as Drummond's life would ever get.

With a shiver, he rattled the newspaper and scanned over the articles. He should have gone to the society pages. They would have been filled with inane and useless garbage with which to waste time and keep his mind occupied. Instead, his eyes fell upon a story detailing the tragic fire last night that claimed the lives of two women and a man. Firefighters reported that the occupants had most likely died of smoke inhalation during their sleep.

If only it had been so simple.

The truth — the reality that only Drummond would ever know — was that he and the witch walked down into the basement. She insisted that he come along. "In case I can't do it," she had said. He suspected she simply wanted an audience.

Standing at the foot of the stairs, he watched her approach Sadie. When the witch pulled out the coin, Sadie dropped to her haunches and stuck out her tongue. She knew. Enough of that poor girl's brain still functioned, and she knew what that coin meant.

And she welcomed it.

The witch turned the coin over. Drummond noticed the small marking on the coin matched those on Sadie's tongue. Indeed, the witch positioned the marking so that both tongue and coin lined up.

But when Sadie closed her mouth, she moaned. Smoke billowed from her lips and she spit out the coin. Drummond could hear the sizzle and smelled the burnt flesh.

Sadie whimpered.

"It's okay, sister." The witch picked up the coin. "I'll help you."

Stroking Sadie's ragged hair, the witch hummed until the girl calmed down. Then she placed the coin back into Sadie's mouth. Only this time, the witch clamped her hands around Sadie's head, locking her jaw shut.

The young girl flailed and spasmed. A horrid cry rattled in her throat. Smoke rose around them both, and Drummond could do nothing but watch.

With a flick of her chin, the witch dismissed him. As he turned up the stairs, he heard the witch's soft humming mixing with the death cries of the girl.

He could still hear them.

When he left the house, all was quiet outside. No fire had started yet. Drummond guessed that the witch brought Sadie's limp body up to one of the bedrooms. Tucked her in tight. Then she set Smythe's corpse on a couch, dug out the bullet, and doused him in alcohol. Especially around the bullet hole. She then led a trail of booze to the fireplace and hoped any investigation would see the story she wanted them to see.

But the last part that shook Drummond bad — the witch then dressed for bed, set the fire, and hurried upstairs. She settled in for the night and let the fumes and flames have their way.

The whole affair left Drummond uneasy. Disturbed. But then he turned to the next section of the newspaper and his attention fell upon a notice — since reaching out to the performer's management, the Afternoon Playhouse regretted to announce that the wonderful actor behind Mezmo the Magical had died in recent weeks. There would be no further magic from this talented fellow.

Drummond closed the newspaper and sipped his coffee.

CASE 14

A CASE OF INNOCENCE

AT THE END OF A CASE, especially a difficult case, Marshall Drummond liked to sit back with a bottle of whiskey and drink away whatever terrible images plagued his mind. He might turn on the radio, but on his way to finding a good Big Band tune, he would undoubtedly hear about Hitler, Roosevelt, and the rest of the madmen pushing for war. On occasion — and this was such an occasion — he found the warm embrace of a woman to be a far better elixir. Unfortunately, he had spent too many nights with too many ladies in his hometown of Winston-Salem — work had been rough of late. But in Greensboro, at the Silver Plate Diner, a particular woman who served as a waitress stood out. She had caught Drummond's eye months ago when he passed through the city, and this night, he found her more than willing to share a drink after her shift had ended.

The case he tried to forget had not been particularly harrowing. He had gone through far worse than a couple of missing boys. By the time he had located them, though, by the time he discovered that they had stumbled upon an old grimoire, by the time he drove all the way out to Greensboro and reached them late at night in Green Hill Cemetery, they had already decided it would be fun to try casting a spell or two. When Drummond rushed over to them, the one bled to death on a park bench while a corrosive hole ate him away from the inside. The other had lost his sanity. So, yeah, a stiff drink would not be enough to wipe away that night.

Bonnie, the waitress, had the kind of smile a man could get lost in. He could pretend the night marked the start of something rather than a meeting of the lonely and the troubled. While Drummond preferred a more romantic and honest relationship, he had an instinctual, animalistic side like anybody else. Once the drinks had set in, the knowing smiles had been exchanged, and a motel that asked no questions located, his blood heated up and all sense of gentleman propriety left him. They locked upon each other, breathing hard, kissing harder, pressing against one another with an individual desperation they shared.

They fell onto the bed — it protested with creaks and groans — and Drummond tried to ignore the dark stains on the brown walls, the cigarette burns in the bare carpet, and the fist-sized holes in the closet door. The place was small. Smelled as stale and overused as the ashtray on the desk in dire need of emptying. But then, neither he nor Bonnie cared about the décor or being cramped together. They did their best to take up the space of one person, anyway.

He started to shimmy off his coat, but she rolled him to his back, straddled him, and unbuttoned her blouse. She paused on the last button. "Now, you ain't going to be thinking I'm an Ol' Snaggletooth, are you?"

"Wouldn't dream of it."

"I ain't so young anymore. I don't want you lookin' at me and getting disappointed."

"Not on your life."

With a playful wink, she donned his fedora, letting her blouse open loose. She tipped the hat down and said, "Then sir, I think you're in serious trouble."

Drummond laced his fingers behind his head. "Oh? What did I do?"

"Would you buy that you stole my innocence?"

He laughed. "Got any other ideas?"

She reached behind to unclasp her bra. "Maybe we'll have to try a few things until we figure it out."

The room door burst open. The wood around the lock shredded with a loud series of cracks followed by two men stepping forwards. Bonnie's arms went to cover her chest as Drummond's hand reached for the .38 in his coat pocket. With Bonnie straddling him, he couldn't get the weapon out.

The man in front — tall, long coat, bowler hat, brown suit, dark eyes, and the grin of a bastard who took pleasure in hurting others — he fired twice. The first shot went into the wall above Drummond's head. The guy probably hadn't bothered with aiming. Just wanted to keep things confusing for his target. The second bullet pierced Bonnie's arm — the flesh right below the shoulder.

She cried out, clutching the wound as she fell to the side. Drummond used her momentum to roll them both right off the bed toward the back wall. As they hit the floor, he whipped out the .38, popped up from behind the bed, and put a round into the first man's head. As the body sank, the second man ran off.

Drummond bolted to his feet. He paused at the shattered doorway in case the second man decided to turn back and open fire. Poking his head into the hall, he saw the second man round the corner at the end. No point in giving chase. Not when he had Bonnie to worry about.

He bent over the dead man and took his gun — a Hungarian FEG 37M semi-automatic. Drummond preferred a good revolver, but he had to admit, the weapon had its charms. He patted down the body, but the pockets were empty. No wallet, no keys, no ID of any kind. A pro. Unless Bonnie turned out to be an underworld criminal secretly posing as a waitress, he had to assume the attack was meant for him. After all, the list of people willing to hire a gun against him was long.

Walking over to Bonnie, he swiped her blouse off the bed. He helped her sit up. Dark tears rivered makeup down her cheeks while her bottom lip sucked in and out rapidly. Blood trails flowed along her arm as her glazed eyes stared out at nothing.

"Sorry about this," Drummond said with a wink. "I try not to let my evenings get spoiled by gunfire."

Her brow crinkled. Apparently, humor would not be helpful.

With a gentle motion, he pulled her hand away from the wound. Then he said something far less helpful. "Oh, crap."

Thick green lines spread out under the skin like tree roots. That bullet must have been coated in something — a poison perhaps. He lifted his head to the hole above the bed. In one quick motion, he climbed onto the mattress while pulling a knife from his pocket. Only a few seconds later and he dug free the slug from the first errant shot. Though deformed, he could see enough. A pentagram had been painted on the back. Most likely, the rest of the casing had witch symbols drawn on as well. He glanced down at Bonnie. Poor girl had been shot and cursed in one action.

"Hospital," she said, the word coming out mushy. She wouldn't be conscious for much longer.

"Sorry, doll. Those docs can't help you. But I know a guy who might." He glanced around the room — the bullet hole in the wall, the damaged doorway, the dead body. "We should get out of here anyway. If I end up answering questions at the police station all night, you probably won't make it."

Harsh words, but she had passed out already. Clapping his hands together once, he said, "Okay, Bonnie, let's get moving." Awkward silence settled around him.

Pocketing the slug, he crouched down and positioned to lift Bonnie. He tried to be gentle. When he stood with her cradled in his arms, when he hefted her higher against his chest, he expected her to startle awake, cry out in pain, look about in confusion. She hardly stirred.

With midnight closing in, the city had shutdown. Still, Drummond scanned the empty streets as he carried Bonnie to his car. He propped her in the passenger seat with her head resting against the window. To anybody watching, she would appear asleep. One more quick glance up and down the street — clear — and he got behind the wheel, lit a cigarette, and drove off.

He knew exactly where to go. No real choice in the matter. Only one man he trusted enough to help in this situation — Leroy Parker.

THE OLD MAN LIVED DEEP IN THE WOODS to the south where he could delve into witchcraft and the occult without being bothered. As a black man, Leroy faced enough trouble with people. He didn't want to add to his burden by letting the whites know he understood magic. The fact that he studied such things in order to protect against them, to aid people, to help fight back, meant little. He knew the world well enough. Nuance was never a friend.

Neither was time.

As the city gave way to the towering pines, getting closer and closer to Leroy's far off home, Drummond dropped his foot heavier on the gas. He peeked over at Bonnie — perspiration dappled her skin, stained her blouse, and she let out soft moans with each bump that jostled the car.

"Hold on, doll. We're getting help."

After an hour, he spotted the dirt turnoff in his weak headlights. He parked on the side of the road — Leroy had downed trees and rolled rocks onto the path to prevent easy access. Not that it had ever been an easy drive, but now it was impossible.

A short bit of maneuvering and he lifted Bonnie out of the car. Her head lolled back. While not entirely dead weight, she certainly didn't help, either. With a grunt, he headed into the woods.

Twice during the difficult walk, Drummond had to stop and set her down. They were short rests, but rests nonetheless. Maybe he needed more exercise. Then again, maybe watching misused magic eat a hole in a kid had sapped his strength a bit. Either way, by the time he approached Leroy's rundown home — an over-sized, glorified shack — Drummond's sweat-soaked hair stuck to his forehead, his skin chilled in the night air, and his muscles complained with each step.

Though midnight had gone, Leroy sat on his porch with a bottle of wine at his side and a shotgun across his lap. When he saw Drummond, when he saw what Drummond carried, he shook his head. "Why is it you never come just for a visit? Always bringing me trouble."

"Sorry, old friend," Drummond huffed out. "Didn't know who else

I could trust."

Leroy already had the front door open and was clearing off the single table in the middle of the main room. Only one other room besides — a tiny bedroom off to the side. The kitchen simply took up one wall, another wall had a stone fireplace and chimney, and the rest of the room was comprised of books, papers, a comfy reading chair, and little else. As Drummond eased Bonnie across the wood table, Leroy returned with a stethoscope.

"Since when are you a doctor?" Drummond said.

"Shut up and stand back."

As Leroy listened to Bonnie's heart, Drummond waited. He felt a dash of pride that Leroy felt comfortable enough in their friendship to speak harshly to him. Most black men wouldn't dare say such a thing to a white man. But Drummond also felt a dash of guilt at even having these thoughts. Nobody should feel pride for simply having a normal friendship. It led him to a thought which troubled him on many nights — the witches had control of such great power, so why didn't they use it to fix some of the ugliest problems in this country?

"How long ago this happen?" Leroy set aside the stethoscope and pulled out a magnifying glass. He squatted to inspect Bonnie's wounded arm.

Snapping back to the moment, Drummond said, "Hour or two. I would've taken her to the hospital, but I worried they would cause more harm than good."

"Smart decision. See here."

Drummond crouched next to Leroy, and in the magnifying glass he spotted the slug buried in her arm. Four hard reddish-black pieces poked out of the slug like spikes made of crab legs. They pierced her muscle, and the horrid, poisonous lines spidering across her skin appeared to originate from these four points.

"You ever see this before?" Drummond asked.

"No. But then I ain't seen a lot of things before. I don't think we should remove that until we know about it, though. We could cause her worse damage than she got."

Drummond dug into his pocket and handed over the slug he had removed from the wall. "This one missed."

Leroy looked over the small hunk of metal, raised his graying eyebrows, and headed off to one of his many bookshelves. "This woman a witch?"

"Don't think so. I'm guessing the bullets were meant for me."

"You've certainly pissed off enough people to warrant it. Especially witches." He pulled out a small, leatherbound volume. "Then again, why not just curse you? Why go to the trouble of casting a spell on a bullet?"

"A lot of witches have tried to curse me and failed. Maybe one of them is trying to think of something new."

Squinting over the pages, Leroy said, "Come here. Look at this." He pointed to a page with several symbols and various pentagrams drawn out for reference. "You think any of these match the ones drawn on the bullet?"

Even with good eyes, it would be difficult to tell. The slug was a deformed version of the bullet. Thus, the symbols were also deformed. The closest to being readable was the pentagram, and even that could not be matched with absolute certainty.

Drummond shrugged.

Closing the book and holding it to his chest, Leroy pondered in silence. "Without knowing what we're dealing with, I'm afraid I can't do anything here."

"We can't do nothing. Can't let it attack her."

"I didn't say that. I said I can't do anything here. There's an old clearing deep in the woods. Covens from a century ago would have their solstice ceremonies out there. Powerful place. And that's where we take her. That's where we have a chance to save her."

While Leroy packed a few books and some other paraphernalia he thought he might need — candles, matches, and several unmarked vials — Drummond hastened outside to grab a wheelbarrow from behind the house. He brought it around front and dumped out the hose, some dirt, and a few rocks. Nabbing three towels, he lined the inside, and together, the men gently rested Bonnie into the wheelbarrow. Leroy set his bag of supplies next to her, gave it a moment of thought, and then added an old lantern.

"It's a bit of a hike," he said. "I'll push her for the first leg. You keep your eyes open."

Drummond's hand unconsciously patted the gun in his pocket as they trudged into the dark woods.

THE SINGLE WHEEL SQUEAKED with every revolution, and the sound sifted between the trees. Drummond could feel all the living creatures staring down upon them. With the whining wheelbarrow and the loud huffing, the men were noisy and brash — two unwelcome aspects for anything that hoped to survive the forest. But they were also humans — a single aspect which gave all other creatures pause.

Yet Drummond could not escape a deeper sensation of being watched. Not by the animals, though that feeling never went away, but by something else. Someone. His gaze roved the forest. Nothing. Nobody. Leroy must have sensed it, too. His pace increased.

At length, they switched jobs, and as Drummond pushed the wheelbarrow over roots and rocks, he saw Leroy's attention snap into the woods much the same. He wanted to ask if Leroy saw anybody, but the man would not have hidden such a thing. They walked onward. Perspiration returned, but eventually, they reached the clearing. Trying to hold back signs of exhaustion, Drummond set down the wheelbarrow yet still let out a relieved sigh.

Before he heard a sound, before he even lifted his head, he knew Leroy had been right about this location. In his time investigating the bizarre and unusual, he had seen several makeshift places of significant magical confluence. But this was not makeshift. This held a different energy. An ancient energy.

Looking about, he noticed that the ground had been tiled with carved stones that led to a central altar. Vines and leaves littered the area but kept a respectful distance from the center. Old statues of nude women raising hands upward as if caught in the ecstasy of casting a group spell surrounded the edge of the stones. Drummond counted thirteen statues — a permanent coven.

Leroy led the way to the altar, and without a word, enlisted Drummond's help in moving Bonnie onto the stone slab. The moment her body touched the cold rock, the air seemed to hum alive. Drummond swore he could hear it, feel it.

"This place was built centuries ago," Leroy said as he grabbed his bag of supplies from the wheelbarrow. "Legend is that the witches that created it wanted to make sure nobody ever found it by accident. So, on the first full moon after the summer solstice, they cast a powerful spell upon this land. It was so powerful, it turned them all into stone. Permanent guardians."

Drummond scanned over the statues once again. They certainly looked real enough. Either they had been carved by somebody approaching Michelangelo's level of talent or the legend bore some bit of truth.

With a shiver, he turned back. "What do we do next?"

Leroy struck a match and lit the old lantern. He set it on the corner of the altar. Then he opened one of his books. "Can't say how this is all going to go. I ain't ever done this before. But while I work it out, you stand guard and protect me from anything that tries to stop me."

As the depth of those words sank into Drummond like a stone chained around his ankle, Leroy pricked his thumb and pressed a crimson smudge onto Bonnie's forehead. Drummond rushed over to them.

"Hey, hey, you didn't say anything about doing blood magic."

Keeping his focus on Bonnie, Leroy said, "You know I don't want to be doing this at all. But are we going to let her stay cursed? Let it kill her? Or something even more horrible?" When Drummond didn't respond, Leroy nodded. "Then get back to protecting me and let me do what I have to do."

The night air dropped a few degrees. At least, Drummond thought it felt colder. He kept one hand in his pocket, resting on his .38, and he walked around the altar. Circle after circle, not wanting to see Leroy's dangerous work, not wanting to see the horrid statues. No matter what direction his eyes turned, he had to witness something twisted and wrong which he could do nothing about.

Until he spotted movement.

A shadow darting between two statues.

Drummond eased his weapon out. His eyes shifted from the statue of a witch bent over as if about to stomp the ground to another depicting a witch with her naked body open wide to the night sky. Where had that shadow gone? Maybe just an animal, but he didn't think so. Behind him, he heard Leroy mutter strange words as the man turned pages of a book. Then came the strike of a match and the crackle of burning wood.

As the fire grew, its orange light brightened the surrounding area. Dancing shapes played off the statues, but Drummond could see further beyond them now. He searched for the glow of eyes or the shine off glasses, the glint of a belt buckle or even the flash off a polished handgun.

"Five o'clock," Leroy said, his voice snapping sharp.

Drummond looked to the right and back. Emerging from the woods at the five o'clock position, a gunman appeared — long coat, bowler, brown suit, holding his weapon at his side. Same guy who ran off at the motel. He guarded a short woman with gray strands of hair poking out from a black veil. Deep lines carved up her baggy skin, and she hunched forward, moving with visible pain.

Raising his .38, Drummond said, "That's it. No further or I'll shoot."

They halted.

The old woman lifted her head, wincing at the action, and gazed beyond Drummond. She stretched for a better view of Leroy and Bonnie. Then: "You're going to hurt that poor girl."

When Leroy did not answer, Drummond said, "If you cared so much, you shouldn't have had her shot in the first place."

"Oh, don't be coy. You know very well that bullet was meant for you. But I suppose this will do just fine. After all, the point is to see the spell in action. Destroying you was simply an extra benefit."

"Don't mean to ruin your mood, but I haven't a clue who you are."

The gunman cocked a shocked glance at the old woman. Her mouth tightened into a perturbed dot. Drummond tried to look calm — a regular tactic when he needed to stall — and gave the woman a wink.

Clenching her teeth, she said, "I am Madame Strint. I would tell you to ask around and learn who you are dealing with, but I doubt you'll see the sunrise, let alone go chatting up people in the know."

"Awfully confident of you considering I'm the one with the gun ready. By the time your bodyguard twitches a finger, I could kill you both." Out of the side of his mouth, he said, "How's it coming, Leroy?"

"I ain't ever done this before," Leroy said with more than a hint of frustration. "Just deal with that witch and let me worry about this."

Madame Strint raised one hand and closed her eyes as if about to testify her religious faith. Her lips moved without a sound. Drummond had never seen a witch cast a spell this way — wasn't sure if they could — but best not to take a chance.

He squeezed the trigger and put a bullet in the gunman's leg.

The weapon's loud report startled the witch. She backed away, her eyes the widest yet. The gunman dropped to the ground, clutching his leg with one hand while trying to aim a shot at Drummond with the other.

As Drummond dashed off toward the edge of the clearing, he heard Leroy saying, "What the hell?"

But when Drummond jumped behind a large statue and peeked back, he saw that the gunman had not followed his run, had not tried to shoot him at all. Rather, the gunman trained his weapon on Leroy. And Leroy's exclamation had not been directed at Drummond's gunshot nor the gunman's threat. Drummond wished it had been.

In the center of the circle, Leroy stumbled away from the altar as Bonnie sat up. Her mouth hung open, saliva flowed free down her chin, and her entire arm had mutated into a marble of green and black. She turned her head, surveying the area with a calculating intensity yet also with an animalistic verve. She was a ravenous wolf that might be rabid.

When her eyes locked upon the gunman, she rose to her feet, standing on the altar, and glared downward. Dark fibers snaked out of the open wound on her arm. They twined around her limb until the infected area became a writhing nest. Less an arm, more a living mass.

Forgetting about his injured leg, the gunman scrambled back, kicking into the rocks and earth with both feet. "No, no, no," he said, leaving his handgun in the dirt. He found his bowler, smashed it on his head, and continued to work away from Bonnie — never taking his eyes off her, never getting up from the ground. He scooted and scooted until he reached the woods in little motions.

"Coward," Madame Strint said.

Bonnie lifted her head toward the sky, and Drummond thought she might howl. Instead, she let loose a painful groan as long, sharp teeth descended. They pushed out her human teeth, dribbling blood across her jaw and down her neck.

The sight froze everyone — including the gunman. If he had only continued his feeble backing away, maybe he would have succeeded. But shock took control. And so did Bonnie.

With a powerful thrust, she leaped off the altar and landed a few steps away from the gunman. He reached to his side, trying to find his weapon, but it was too far away. He gazed up like a mouse frozen at the sight of a hawk soaring down. As Bonnie loomed in, the gunman found the gumption to throw his bowler at her.

"Help." His voice weak and shaking.

He looked toward Madame Strint and opened his mouth. Drummond could not make out what transpired between them, but clearly the look she offered kept the gunman from uttering another word. Betrayed by a witch. What a surprise.

Drummond aimed his weapon at Bonnie's head. He thought he could pull off the shot, and even if he missed, he would draw her attention away. Not that he wanted to save the gunman or the witch, but he would be haunted by them — both figuratively and possibly literally — if he did not try.

But before he fired that .38, he had to talk with Leroy. If this curse could be broken, then it would be unjust to kill Bonnie. She had done nothing wrong — maybe choosing to sleep with Drummond had been a bad decision, but nothing beyond that. She certainly didn't deserve a bullet in the head.

Though only seconds in his mind, Drummond's debate cost him

crucial time. As he glanced toward Leroy for an answer, Bonnie pounced upon the gunman, lifted him off the ground, and in one hop, the two disappeared into the dark, thick woods.

Crap.

Leroy stepped up to the altar as Drummond and Madame Strint re-entered the clearing. The gunman's screams blended with the horribly satisfied grunts of a beast devouring its prey.

"We don't have long," Madame Strint said. "When she finishes with him, she'll come back here."

Drummond cocked an eyebrow. "Lady, we are not a we. You're on your own."

He made sure his friend had not gone into shock and gave the man a pat on the shoulder. Leroy stooped over his books, his bottom lip quivering as he searched page after page. "It should've worked. I know it. I did it exactly as it says."

"It's okay."

Madame Strint said, "You need my help."

Drummond glared at the witch, warning her off. She stood in the clearing, unwilling to go into the woods, unwelcome any closer to the altar.

"Don't be a stubborn fool." She put one foot out, hesitated, and stepped forward. "Your girlfriend won't be long now. You really want to have to kill her?"

"Pretending to care won't get you any safer."

"Oh, I don't care about her. She can die. That's fine with me. But I do have a healthy desire to stay alive myself. Seeing the viciousness in your eyes, I have the distinct suspicion that you'll let her rip me apart. But what do you think will happen after she's done with me?"

Turning his gun on her, Drummond said, "Maybe I should shoot you now and be done with you."

"You have more honor than that."

Leroy slammed the book back onto the altar. "Both of you — shut up. Drummond, put away your pistol. Witch, stop taunting him. Fact is that I'm going to need help here and if you both don't do your parts, we'll all end up dead and poor Bonnie will go on roaming the woods murdering people."

Narrowing his eyes, Drummond gripped his pistol tighter. But Bonnie let loose another series of grunting growls as she dug into more of her meal. Leroy was right. If they didn't fix this, all of them were doomed. Drummond lowered his head, sighed, and holstered the weapon.

Madame Strint wasted no time getting over to the altar. Not that a stone slab and a couple men would save her from Bonnie, but she probably felt safer anyway. People were funny like that. Drummond hated to admit it, but he also felt a bit better having the witch nearby. After all, having her work with Leroy meant there was a chance — hope for Bonnie.

With a brisk look at Leroy's books, Madame Strint said, "This is all wrong. You're being too tame with it. Blood magic is a brutal thing. Not meant for a gentle touch."

"Witch, I'm allowing you to help. You don't get to be rude."

"Oh, don't get huffy with me."

As she leafed through the pages, Leroy scowled. "This is your curse, ain't it? How come you don't know what to do to stop it?"

"Good question," Drummond said.

"Just because you create something, doesn't mean you can uncreate it. You boys know plenty on how to kill a thing, but I doubt either of you could bring it back to life. That's the way of things. Most times you do something, you don't get to undo it." She stopped on a page covered in heavy writing. "There."

Leroy shook his head. "Are you crazy?"

"What?" Drummond craned over the witch's shoulder, but he couldn't make sense out of the symbols on the page. A few he recognized, but far too few.

"This witch wants us to cast some seriously bad blood magic."

"Isn't all blood magic bad?"

Pointing to one part of the page, Leroy said, "That's a call for a sacrifice."

Madame Strint snorted. "Can't expect to cast real blood magic without sacrifice. For crying out loud, it's in the name."

"Well, I vote we use your blood, witch."

"I said I wanted to help you boys, but I'm not giving up my life for this. If that's your best, then you should go back to your first plan — shooting her."

Drummond put out a hand to quiet their bickering. He listened. He heard nothing. Quiet. No more snarls. No more gluttonous chomping. "She's done eating."

"Only done eating Jim. She'll be coming for us now."

With the shush of metal, Madame Strint whipped a hunting knife from an unseen sheath. Not bothering to argue further, she ran the blade across her open palm. Deep scars formed Xs over her hand, and Drummond wondered how many times she had performed this awful magic before. The new wound rivered blood along the ridges of her scars before splashing onto the altar. In a practiced motion, the witch flipped the knife, offering the grip to Leroy.

Bonnie appeared on the base of a statue portraying a dancing witch lost in ecstasy. Clinging like a lizard — limbs spread out to find purchase within each small ledge or tiny crevasse on the sculpture — Bonnie's muscles rippled. That horrid green-black coloring had spread across all of her skin. Even her hair had shifted — though that was harder to tell for certain because the gunman's blood soaked much of her chin, mouth, nose, forehead, and skull. She had practically bathed in his corpse.

She watched the altar — a look mixed of interest, wariness, and hunger. Drummond stared back. His own eyes promised pain and violence should she act upon the worst of her feelings.

He heard a sharp hiss from behind. Leroy had cut his hand and let his blood blend with the witch's upon the altar. Then Drummond felt a tap on the side of his arm. The blade had been offered to him.

Answering his expression, Madame Strint said, "We must all sacrifice."

Drummond paused. When he caught a nod from Leroy, he swiped the knife with a perturbed glare at the witch. One swift slice across the hand and he squeezed his blood out to mix with the rest on the altar.

Bonnie's creaking growl deepened. She jumped to the ground, scampered two statues over, and climbed up to get a clearer view of what transpired. Drummond guessed that either the curse interfered with her ability to think or she still could not believe in magic. Despite all that had happened to her, he would not be surprised at the latter being true. Most people loathed the idea of accepting a major change to their worldview. And magic? That was far more of a change than many could handle.

"Now what?" Drummond asked.

The witch sauntered around to the opposite side of the altar. "Now?" She raised her lips in the approximation of a smile. Or perhaps a sneer. Drummond couldn't tell. With a surprising display of strength, she slammed her hand flat into the puddle of blood. "Now?" she said, the words oozing out like an open sore. "Now, I do what should have been done long ago."

Bright blue light burst from beneath her hand as if she electrified the blood. The light filled the cracks of the altar, reaching down to the ground and spreading out toward the statues. The rich aroma of a campfire rode up on the air, and Drummond swore he smelled the sweetness of candy, too.

When the witch lifted her hand, the electricity stuck to her palm. Flashes of light flooded the night, strobing across her face, brightening moments of madness in her eyes. She cackled.

Leroy jumped back as Drummond pointed his weapon at her. But neither man had a chance to speak. A bolt arced out of Madame Strint's hand and blasted across the .38. Drummond felt the shock straight through his arm. He fumbled back several steps, dropping the handgun as his muscles spasmed. A second bolt struck Leroy, forcing a guttural yelp from his lips as he doubled over.

Holding her hand out as a clear threat to keep Drummond and Leroy back, Madame Strint moved toward Bonnie. "It's okay, dearie," she said, her old voice suddenly soft, firm, and young. "I know you're scared, but you've got nothing to worry about. Not with me. I'm going to take good care of you."

"I knew it," Leroy said. "You can't ever trust a witch."

Bonnie scurried around to the far side of the statue as she watched the witch with a curious eye. Madame Strint continued to approach and gently put out her hand. "You don't understand it, but you are a very special woman. Most special. With my help, you're going to be so powerful."

"Don't listen to her," Drummond said, hoping the sound of his voice might get through to wherever Bonnie's human mind resided in that creature. "She only wants to use you."

Madame Strint thrust her dangerous hand forward. Another arc electrified the air as it crossed the circle and burned into Drummond's shoulder. "Those men wanted to kill you. They even accepted my help, thinking I would betray the very spell I created, the wonderous magic that is transforming you into a mighty warrior. The only real betrayer is Drummond. He offered you a night of passion, and instead, he plots to murder you."

Bonnie cautiously placed her hand into Madame Strint's. They held still a moment, each looking into the other, and the longer they stood there, the more a bond grew between them. Drummond could see it. Trust forming before his eyes.

"Any ideas?" he asked Leroy.

"We can't go near them without getting shocked, and I don't know this kind of magic well-enough to stop her. Heck, I didn't really know enough to help Bonnie, but I had to try. Really, it's all up to your girlfriend, now."

An idea hit Drummond with a jolt far harder than the witch's magic. "Bonnie," he yelled, and the creature that had been Bonnie turned her head.

"Ignore him," Madame Strint said.

"Bonnie, I know you're still in there. You take a good look at that witch, that old woman — she's just like an Ol' Snaggletooth."

Turning her head as if that odd name required a lot of brainpower to process, her gaze came to rest on Madame Strint. Drummond could see the recollection hit Bonnie — a flashing memory of the woman she had been only hours earlier. If more of her had still controlled the creature, then perhaps the witch would have been safe. But the beastly side had taken over bit by bit, leaving Bonnie's rage unchecked.

In a swift motion, she flung out her cursed arm. The snaking nest whipped at Madame Strint. The witch tried to protect herself, but the flashes of electricity did little to stop the fuming creature. Light peeked through the thickening mass of vines, yet they continued to emerge from Bonnie's arm and wrapped around the witch without pause.

It happened so fast that Drummond had no time to realize he held his breath. One moment he urged Bonnie to recall Ol' Snaggletooth. The next, the witch writhed on the ground, cocooned in the creature's cursed and growing flesh.

He might have stood there and watched in horror through all that would follow, but the creature turned her head toward the altar. For an instant, the stark light of the witch's arcing blasts brought out the real face of Bonnie. Just a touch of humanity wrapped in a sorrowful gaze.

"Go," she said, her voice grating against the night.

Drummond tried to keep hold of Bonnie's image, but the flash of light vanished. The night reclaimed the creature. She turned her salivating maw toward Madame Strint.

A hand fell upon Drummond's shoulder. Leroy.

"Come on," Leroy said. "We have to go."

"We can't leave her."

"We can't help her. We tried, but if there's a way to stop that curse, she's destroying the only one who knows the answer."

"But —"

"Marshall, trust me. You did right. You did all you could. She's going to live out here on squirrels and raccoons for a while. Until that curse does away with her. Nothing for it now."

As he pulled Drummond from the statues, the altar, and the circle, the sounds of cracking bones and torn flesh rattled the air. The flashes of light ceased as the screams began. But Leroy continued guiding Drummond further back until the trees blocked out all existence of the horrors they had witnessed.

HOURS LATER, after Drummond left Leroy's home and drove back to his office in Winston-Salem, he sat at his desk and stared out one of the three large windows. The moon had come out, it's pale blue painting the darkened room. He didn't want the lights on. He could do without any electricity for the rest of the night. Maybe for even longer.

Leroy hadn't said a word the entire walk back and merely offered a knowing nod as a goodbye. They both had been through enough together. Words weren't needed. But now, alone at his desk, Drummond wanted to hear a voice — any voice — that might vanquish the slurping and gnawing and satisfied swallowing that echoed in his head.

From the bottom drawer of his desk, he pulled out a bottle of whiskey and a glass. He twisted the top off and inhaled the deep smell promising oblivion. The whiskey made its music splashing into the glass, and while it wasn't the sound he needed, it would have to suffice.

He tipped back the glass, letting the drink sting his throat, and didn't stop until he drained the entire thing. Then he poured another. Holding the glass for a moment, he winced. "Sorry, Bonnie. You deserved better."

CASE 15

WHISTLES

AS THE TRAIN CROSSED A RURAL ROAD, it warned cars with a howling scream, but only a flash of green light startled Marshall Drummond awake. He bolted upright. His Fedora rolled off his face, tumbling onto the passenger car floor. Holding still amongst the crowd of men smoking pipes and cigars while they read the afternoon papers to the rhythm of the train, he scanned their faces — nobody out of place. Rumbling back toward Winston-Salem from Raleigh with an orange-pink sky ending the day, everything appeared normal.

Except that green light.

Intense like staring at the sun yet pale as a ghost. And nowhere to be found.

Perhaps he had dreamed it. Wouldn't be the first time his work infiltrated his sleep. Being a private investigator for the bizarre came with a lot of baggage nobody warned him about.

With a sigh, he reached down and swiped his hat from the floor. Not remembering a dream, especially one that had abruptly woken him, left his nerves jangling. Drummond did not like anything that even smelled of an omen. Then again, looking at the newspapers with their headlines screaming about Germany's invasion of Poland, it seemed silly to worry about possible omens when real dangers unfolded right before him.

Drummond wiped the sweat from his brow before setting his Fedora back on. The September furnace of North Carolina roasted all the men in the passenger car. Even with the windows open, the temperature continued to rise. Probably didn't help that the engine blasted heat back their way.

He considered resting his head again in hopes of letting the rhythmic wobbling of the train lull him back to sleep. Even closed his eyes. But another flash of green light brightened against his lids, and he knew there would be no more sleeping that day.

Cracking a peek, he spied a greenish ball floating above the heads of several smoking gentleman. More importantly, despite its brightness, not a single person took notice. Only Drummond.

He had been in Raleigh investigating a potential haunted house at the request of a friend but found no evidence to support those concerns. However now, seeing that hovering, ball of bright-pale energy, he wondered if he had made a mistake. Some ghosts had been known to attach to people — supposedly attracted to the warmth of the living. Perhaps he had picked up a stray.

Except this bit of ghostly energy shot out the back door. Seconds later it returned. Then out again. Then back.

The few ghosts Drummond had come in direct contact with did not behave like this. Then again, he had never seen a ghost like this before. Maybe this wasn't a ghost at all. Whatever it was, though, something about its movements suggested to Drummond that it wanted to be followed.

Then again, maybe I'm just bored.

Either way, he did not think it would be prudent to leave a ghost — or whatever it was — zipping around a bunch of living people. If anything happened, anything that revealed itself to these folks, there might be a panic. And a panic while stuck in an enclosed space like a train car would not end well.

Getting to his feet, Drummond sidestepped into the aisle and headed toward the back. He passed through another passenger car. Less crowded, less businessmen. A few families, a handful of women, and some hats peeking over the top edges of newspapers. Still plenty of smoke, though. This was tobacco country, after all.

Several steps through, Drummond paused as the green light flickered out. Before he could focus on any one passenger, it burst bright near the far end. He strode across the car and followed the light into the next — a near empty dining car. The trip across North Carolina wasn't long enough to warrant full meal service, but Southern Railways still provided a waiter to serve coffee and tea. He was a young man, dressed in a full green and yellow uniform, and stood behind a silver cart in the back.

The light Drummond had followed now hovered over a woman sitting alone with a cup of coffee. The green flared before winking out completely. Drummond waited by the entrance, but the light did not return. Removing his hat, he combed his fingers through his hair and approached the woman.

She was in her late-20s, petite, wearing a faded floral dress that must have been special in the past but now had become serviceable. The kind of thing that once screamed poverty, until the crash of '29 turned so many people poor. A brown hat cuddled her head rather than shaping it, though it did have a small, red feather.

She had not touched her coffee — no lipstick mark on the rim. She simply sat there, watching the land pass by. Dried trails on her cheeks told him she had been crying.

"Excuse me, ma'am. I'm sorry to bother you, but may I ask you a few questions?"

She turned her head, slow and patient. Her eyes narrowed. "I thought the police were done with me."

Drummond lowered to the bench opposite her. "I'm not with the police. They were questioning you?"

"There's no story here. Trust me. You're wasting your time and your newspaper's money."

"Not with the press, either. My name is Marshall Drummond. I'm a private investigator. By any chance, back in Raleigh, were you at 370 Plum Street in the last few days?"

Speaking with a slow cadence — not out of Southern tradition but rather a cautious planning of each word — she said, "I do not know that address. Did my husband's name come up there as well?"

Drummond gazed over the tops of the few diners. He hoped to see that green light again. Hoped it might pull him away from this woman. No such luck. "I think I've made a mistake. I thought you might have been involved in a case of mine, but it's clear you have your own matters to deal with. My apologies, Mrs. —"

"Tagger. Mrs. Penny Tagger." She put out her hand.

With a gentle clasp, Drummond motioned to get up. "Again, my apologies."

Before he could stand, however, she said, "Did you know my husband? Is that why you're here? Your case has something to do with his death?"

"His death?" Drummond settled back. "I'm not sure. If you don't mind, would you please tell me what happened? It's probably nothing related to my case, but I'd rather know for certain. Besides, we still have to reach Greensboro before we go on to Winston-Salem. Or are you stopping in Greensboro?"

"No, we're from Winston-Salem. Though, there isn't a we anymore." Squirming in her seat, Penny said, "Is this really necessary? I've already told everything to the police. I don't know if I can go through it again."

"I wouldn't ask you to if it wasn't important. You see, your husband—"

"I know all about him." She reached into her purse and pulled out a handkerchief balled tight. She pressed it on her eyes, then held it beneath her nose. "Still smells like him." A frustrated huff, then: "I'm a good woman, and I've been a good wife. I don't deserve what happened. Having a bunch of strangers hounding me about it isn't going to make it any easier."

Drummond thought about all the people on the train. "Lives might be at stake."

Her eyes widened. "Lives? Over Ralph? Mr. Drummond, you can't possibly have the right person?"

"If we're lucky, I'm wrong. Let me hear what you have to say, and we'll figure it out."

She shifted her gaze out the window as if the rolling scenery turned the clock back. "Well, the short of it all is that Ralph was a trumpet player. Pretty good one, too. That's why I didn't report him missing or think anything strange when he didn't come home at first. He goes on the road plenty, and if things turn out well, if a bandleader picks up a couple extra gigs, well, Ralph goes along. Playing trumpet isn't a great way to make a living, but it kept him happy, and that's far more important than money. And he always comes home and he always pays the bills. Did, anyway.

"I suppose I always knew he was unfaithful. Didn't want to believe it. Didn't believe it. But I knew. Anyway, he was discovered in an apartment in Raleigh, and it took the police a while to find out who he was and then find me and then have me come out to Raleigh to identify him. Apparently, while he did admit to the woman that he slept with that he was married, he gave another woman's name as his wife. I mean it's one thing that he was unfaithful, but he could at least credit who I was. I should've been the most important thing to him, right? You're a man. Tell me. Even if you've got a mistress, surely your wife is the most important."

Drummond couldn't get a clear read on her. Betrayed, saddened, regretful, or full of vengeance — he had no idea which way to play things that would keep her talking. He opted with the truth. "Not married. But I believe in loyalty. I've never cheated on a woman, never will. Afraid I can't tell you what goes through the minds of men that do. I've never understood it myself."

"Then I guess I should have married you."

Neither one laughed. Drummond said, "So, you were in Raleigh today to identify your husband and give yourself an alibi to the police."

"Alibi? No need for that. They never asked. He died of a heart attack. While he was … with her."

Drummond took sudden interest in the fold of the napkin on the table. "I'm sorry."

With a bitter chuckle, she said, "I wish he had been murdered. Then the police would have to keep his body as evidence or something. Instead, I'm stuck lugging that lumpy fool all the way back home to be buried."

"He's here? On this train?"

"The coffin is in the back with all the other useless luggage." She dabbed at her eyes again. "You know what really hurts? The thing that really gets under my skin? It's that I'm truly sad. I loved him. Loved him and miss him and I don't think I'm going to be able to live without them. The bastard. Deserves all the misery death can bring."

Drummond knew she meant every word — the tears were real but so was the way her hand clenched that handkerchief. White knuckled and shaking. She didn't know whether she wanted to mourn him or murder him. Probably a good thing she never had to make the choice.

Easing to his feet, he offered a slight nod. "Thank you for your time. Again, I'm sorry to have disturbed you, but you've been very helpful. And — my condolences."

At the transit door between cars, Drummond asked the young waiter, "How far back is the luggage car?"

"Three, sir. Two passenger cars and then the luggage. Can I help you with something?"

"Is there somebody in there?"

"Oh yes, sir. We always have someone stationed there to make sure that nothing gets stolen. You ain't got to worry about that."

Drummond put his fedora back on and crossed into the next car. Nearly empty. Same with the next one. Only a handful in each car.

One fellow caught Drummond's eye, though. He wore a dark pinstripe suit two sizes too big like a kid playing grown-up. His hair had been slicked down and a sheen of sweat coated his brow. The entire time Drummond walked through the car, this man jumped between eyeing Drummond and trying not to make eye contact.

At the back, Drummond opened the door to the luggage car. Strange. He expected it to be locked.

Stepping in, he found the car filled with bags and trunks, a small chair next to a small table, a lantern, and a copy of Chandler's The Big Sleep. No sign of the guard. One thing Drummond did see — a coffin.

Simple, pinewood, with the nails pried up. He stared at those slivers of metal and noticed the dents in the coffin's lip where a crowbar had been used. Not good.

He searched over the top and sides of the coffin but found no witch symbols or any writing that would suggest spells. That did nothing to ease the tightening between his shoulder blades.

He put his hand on the lid and paused. Ghosts could not be seen by most people, certainly not by Drummond, so this one had to put in a huge effort to form that little green ball and make it last as long as it did. Some caution seemed like a good idea.

"Ralph, if you're in here, I'm not trying to disturb your body. I think it's you who brought me this way, so I'm trying to do my job for you. Trying to find out what's going on. Please, do me a favor — don't hurt me."

It was as close to a prayer as Drummond had made in years. It would have to do.

He lifted the lid and pushed it aside. Ralph barely fit in the narrow confines but managed to snuggle his trumpet in the crook of his right arm. He wore a simple black suit — probably used it every night for gigs. The cuffs were frayed and the underarms stained.

Drummond checked the inside wood. Clear. He tugged on the Ralph's shirt collar to inspect the neck and shoulders. Nothing. He shifted the shirt up to check the man's belly. Not a single witch symbol, word, or spell to be found.

He then pulled down the man's bottom lip. Still nothing. But when he opened Ralph's mouth, Drummond uncovered the first hint of something off — the two incisors were missing as well as one of the front lower teeth. Probably gold or gold fillings.

Either the luggage guard pried out those teeth or he had a deal with somebody else who did the dirty work. Didn't matter which way, though. The luggage guard had to be in on it.

"Okay, Ralph. Looks like somebody on this train has your teeth. I'm guessing that's what you want me to return to you."

"Hey, what're you doing in here?"

Drummond lifted his head to find a jelly-faced man with a donut belly. Short, curly red hair stood out against a Southern Railways green shirt with yellow trim. Dark suspenders kept up his saggy pants.

Stepping back from the coffin, Drummond thrust his hands in his coat pockets and cocked his head to the side. He knew this pose often intimidated people — especially guilty people. Made them think he had sized them up already and had special knowledge they couldn't dream of possessing. "I'm a private investigator, and we can make this real easy. You return the things you stole from this corpse, and you won't have any other trouble. No jail time, won't get fired from your job, nothing. I only want to make sure things are handled right for Ralph here."

"You son of a —"

The curly-haired luggage guard did not leave time to finish that statement. With speed that made Drummond reevaluate his judgment of the man, Curly knocked Drummond hard in the side. Nearly cracked a rib. Stepping back to reset for a fight, Drummond raised his fists.

"Nice move." The words wheezed out a bit. "You a boxer?"

The answer took the form of two sharp jabs followed by a deep gut punch. Grabbing Drummond by the back of his coat, Curly wrenched him straight up.

"How about we try this again, tough guy?" Curly said. "Only this time, you can tell me what you were stealing from that coffin. And don't give me that crap about being a PI. Who do you really work for?"

Though his knees still wobbled and he had yet to get a full breath of air, Drummond knew how to take advantage of an opening. The pugilist wanted to talk which meant he had let his guard down for a moment. Drummond summoned what strength he could find and drove a sharp uppercut into Curly's jaw.

Stunned, the man stumbled back several steps. Drummond followed through with two more punches — hitting the arm and chest. When that failed to produce results, he rammed forward, digging his shoulder into the sternum and driving Curly straight to the back of the luggage car.

They crashed to the floor. Hardshell cases and leather bags tumbled over them. Drummond pushed through the pile to his feet. Breathing heavily, he pulled back his fist for one final strike. If this didn't work, Drummond worried Curly might get standing again and pummel him right to the front of the train. But as he swung forward, another arm locked around his and pulled him back.

Drummond's gut soured. Of course, the partner had come in to help. Without even looking, Drummond knew what he would find — the man with slicked down hair and a pinstripe suit far too large for his narrow frame.

But where Curly had the moves of a seasoned fighter, Pinstripe had no concept of how to control his body. He pulled on Drummond's arm with too much force, and the two men fumbled backwards. Only the luggage car door kept them from a hard fall. A small miracle that saved Drummond. Because Curly clambered to his feet, snapped his suspenders in place, and charged forward like an enraged bull.

Drummond had enough. He racked his elbow back, catching Pinstripe in the cheek, and smoothly sidestepped to get out of Curly's way. To avoid crushing his partner, the big man performed an awkward pivot like a cartoon elephant dancing away from a mouse. The comical display gave Drummond all the time he needed.

He pulled out his .38 and waved it between the two until he had their undivided attention. "I am not in the mood to do a lot of paperwork tonight," he said, spitting a glob of blood onto the floor. "So, I'm going to give you one chance. Do what's right, and you two can walk. Play games, and you'll both be arrested."

"For what? You're the criminal here," Pinstripe said, his voice high and whiny.

Curly said, "That's right. I saw you break into that coffin and Chet here will back me up."

"I will. You got no right to be mess around with Whistles."

"Who's talking about whistles?" Drummond shook his head. "Boys, knock off the act. When I came in here, somebody had already pried up that coffin lid. I checked the body. Ralph's missing some teeth. Gold, I'm thinking. Now, you two put those back, and I'll do as I said. Last chance."

With his hands up by his shoulders, palms out, Chet said, "You got it all wrong, mister. We'd never steal from Whistles. He's a friend."

"Ralph is called Whistles?"

Curly pointed to his mouth. "On account of his teeth."

Drummond suddenly felt very stupid. "He doesn't have gold teeth, does he?" Both men shook their heads. "And that's why he's called Whistles?" Both men nodded.

Chet said, "We did open that lid. Sorry if that's illegal. But he needed to be buried with his trumpet. That's important. He would've wanted it that way, and the band wants to make sure he gets it. The band was his life."

Drummond lowered the .38 and heard both men sigh — Curly with relief, Chet with shaking fear. "Let me run this together — Chet, you're a musician. In the same band with Ralph. And you decide that he needed to be buried with his trumpet. You bribed the luggage guard here to help you out, look the other way while you opened that coffin. That about right?"

Curly said, "Except he didn't have to bribe me. Whistles was one of the greatest trumpet players I ever seen. Tons of feeling when he played. Always in the pocket. Wherever Southern Railway went that he was playing, I tried to get at least an hour off to go listen. I'm real sorry that he died."

Though he had one more question, Drummond's instincts told him these men spoke the truth. "Let's say all of this is correct and that you really did break into this coffin to let Ralph go to the grave with his trumpet. Why? I mean, why did you wait until getting on this train? Why not deal with it at the mortuary? They'd handle that for you."

"His wife," Chet said. "We asked, but she refused. Said that trumpet caused her more pain than most things in life, and she'd be damned if she let Whistles sleep forever with it."

"That's just wrong," Curly said. "A musician has to be buried with his music."

Drummond tapped his chin. "Boys, I want your help. I need to examine this body, so I want you two blocking the connection in the passenger car. Make sure nobody comes in here. I won't be long."

The train lurched into a curve, and Curly said, "You better hurry. I know that turn. We'll be in Greensboro soon. Short stop and then on to Winston-Salem."

The two men left the luggage car, though both peeked over their shoulders — Chet with nerves, Curly with concern. Once alone, Drummond used the sleeve of his coat to wipe the sweat from his face. Stifling enough to begin with, but fighting two men in an enclosed train car only made the heat worse.

Drummond scanned over the body again. He started with the mouth — checked those missing teeth. Looking closer now, he saw that the gums did not have gaping holes or torn tissue. If Ralph had gold teeth that were yanked out, there would have been damage, but the gums had healed over long ago.

"Looks like those two idiots are honest idiots."

The name Whistles made sense, too. With those gaps in his teeth, he probably had quite a musical way of talking. Plus, as his wife had pointed out, he liked to chase the ladies. Probably could manage a heckuva whistle with the aid of those missing teeth.

Next, Drummond picked up the trumpet snug in Ralph's right arm. Looked normal — not that Drummond had inspected many trumpets in his life. Judging by the dents and scuffs, the instrument had been well used. He checked inside of the bell for signs of spellwork. Nothing. Placing the trumpet back, he noticed Ralph's right hand had bruising on the knuckles.

"Looks like you put up a fight. What happened? You finally slept with the wrong woman? Angry husband shows up and things got a little too violent?"

Pushing back, Drummond's brow scrunched tight. If Ralph had died at the hands of a jealous husband, then Drummond would have to go back to Raleigh to complete the investigation. And since Ralph's ghost energy was involved, since no sign of witchcraft could be found on the body, it suggested somebody in Raleigh had a hand in all this. Worst of all — nobody had hired Drummond for this case. He couldn't get paid. But he couldn't walk away, either. It wouldn't be right to lead this ghost haunt the world and cause problems for others.

"Well, Ralph, I'm guessing you want me to go fix this, and while I ain't happy about it, I'm willing to do it. But we're pulling into Greensboro, and I've got to let Curly hammer this lid back on. After that, I won't be seeing your corpse ever again. Unless I'm digging it up, and I don't do that for free. So, if you got any strength left and you want me to see something, now's your chance."

Drummond stood with his hands out, listening to the train rattling on the track. He turned a bit to the side expecting to pass through a cold spot that would give away a ghost's presence. When nothing changed, he brought his hands together in one quick clap. "Okay. I guess this is it for now. Unless you plan to follow me —"

Blinding green light flared over the coffin. If light could be angry, this one certainly was. It crackled in the air. Drummond shielded his eyes and shuffled closer.

"Okay, okay. I got it."

The light slowly dimmed into nothing, leaving behind the smell of burnt wood. Drummond saw scorch marks on the inside of the coffin. Left side. By the hand. He bent closer.

Ralph's fingers had been curled under making a fist. Odd choice for laying a man to rest. Like the right, the knuckles on this hand were bruised — dark purple and yellowish-brown. Drummond reached in and slid open the hand, half-expecting to find a pentagram or some other symbol carved into the palm. Instead, he found something equally disturbing. The hand was clean, but the ring finger was missing.

A piece of metal poked from further down the side. Drummond had to press Ralph's leg inward so that he could pinch the edge of the metal and pull it out. A dinner knife. Southern Railways insignia carved at the base of the handle.

Drummond crossed over to the passenger car. To Curly, he said, "You can go clean up in there. I'm done."

As Curly resumed his duties, Chet glanced up from a seat by the window. "You turning us over to the cops? We busted?"

"Nothing wrong with trying to bury your friend in a decent way."

"Then why do you look like you're going to punch me?"

"Do I? I better change the way I look." Drummond readjusted his hat. "After all, I want to have a nice chat with a lady."

He walked back towards the dining car.

Penny was gone. Her coffee had been cleared and the tablecloth brushed down. The train slowed further. Almost there.

He called over the waiter. "You remember me?"

"Of course, sir." The young man spoke politely but did nothing to hide his tiredness now that the train neared Greensboro.

"The lady I was talking with — when did she leave?"

"Not long after you did."

Drummond strode into the next passenger car. His eyes darted from face-to-face, searching, searching. People stood, gathered their belongings, and lined up at the exits. Out the window, Drummond saw a larger crowd pooling together to climb aboard. He looked forward as the train jerked to a complete stop. No time to check each car. Instead, while the passengers disembarked like ants scattering a disturbed mound, he crossed his arms and stared out the platform.

Don't be there. Don't be there.

Maybe he was wrong. Maybe she was innocent. Maybe she would stay on the train and go home to Winston-Salem, and he would have to go to Raleigh tomorrow to investigate new angles. But then he saw that brown hat with the red feather weaving through the crowd. It bounced about like a warning light as she made her way toward the stairs.

Damn.

He stepped off the train and hastened after her. While climbing to the bridgeway that led into the station, he thought of all Penny had said. The philandering husband, the long trips away, the loneliness of a musician's wife. Based on her clothes and the pine box, Drummond guessed she did not expect to be left with much money — she didn't even want him buried with his most prized possession. Perhaps a trumpet could be sold for rent money.

Heading through the station lobby, he watched Penny exit the main doors. He followed her. At least, her lack of money would benefit him — she couldn't hire a cab. On foot, then.

Walking through the streets of Greensboro, keeping close enough to see her but far enough away to avoid her suspicions, Drummond recalled the way she got choked up at the table. Perhaps she had put on a show for him, but those tears seemed real enough. Only now, he thought she had not cried over the loss of her husband — she may actually have loved him a little — but rather, those tears fell from being shaken up at sneaking into the luggage car and cutting off Ralph's finger. Not an easy task for most.

Drummond recalled that when she had pulled out her handkerchief to dab at her eyes, the cloth had been balled up and looked hard. She probably held the finger in that handkerchief. Pulled it from her purse out of habit and then tried to cover up what she held with some well-timed tears.

Anger fed this woman. Anger and the blind hope that magic would solve her problems. But it never did. No matter how many clients he warned, they never listened — magic was a false shortcut

After a half hour, it was clear she headed toward a wealthier section of the city. Sadly, that confirmed all of Drummond's suspicions. Time to end this.

"Mrs. Tagger."

She froze. Bowed her head. Then rolled her shoulders back, took a deep breath, and turned around. "Mr. Drummond."

Walking up to her, he said, "You don't want to do this."

She looked around and saw what Drummond already knew — they stood on an empty street. Nice homes with nice yards but no people. The wealthy husbands were out at work, the bratty kids at school, and the numb wives drank away the afternoon out in the back by the pool, away from the eyes of their neighbors.

"I'm not doing anything illegal, and you are not the police."

"True, but the consequences of what you're planning to do will be far worse than anything the Law could inflict. You may wish for jail when it's over."

She made a good show of confusion. "What on earth do you think I'm going to do? My husband's already dead."

"Unless you've suddenly moved to Greensboro and have a job as a maid, there aren't many reasons for you to be walking up this street. But I happen to know the woman who lives four houses up on the right loves to get visits from people like you."

"Like me? Poor?"

"Desperate. Angry. Spiteful, maybe."

She chuckled — forced and pitiful. "I really have no idea what you're talking about."

"Cut the act lady. Madame Kriss lives in that house. Don't know how you found out about her, but since you're holding Ralph's finger wrapped in your purse, I'm thinking you know exactly who and what she is."

"And that is?"

"A witch. Over a hundred years old. Not much magic left in her, but you're hoping it'll be enough."

This time, while she forced another chuckle, her cheeks reddened. "Really? A witch?"

"Before you go into that house and make that deal, let me tell you what's going to happen. Because I deal with this kind of thing for a living. See, I'm a private investigator who handles people like you, those who get in over their heads with people like Madame Kriss."

Whirling back, Penny stomped up the street. "I don't need to listen to this."

Drummond came to her side. As expected, her sudden tantrum masked the outright dread on her face. "Witches don't work for free. I'm guessing you know that much because you wouldn't be here if you thought they wanted money. But I can see in your eyes, in your walk, in everything about you that you don't know what she will want. Well, lady, a witch always wants to make a deal. And those deals always go bad."

"You're talking nonsense. Madame Kriss is a respected member of the community. She comes highly recommended."

"Con artists often do. And witches can be some of the worst cons there are. They give you hope, maybe even a taste of what you wanted, but they never are clear on the price."

"Maybe I'm willing to pay."

"You think what you're going to do will cause Ralph pain, get you some vengeance, and it might. What that witch will neglect to mention is that cursing a ghost will keep it around forever. He'll haunt you. Until you're dead. Maybe even after that."

"This is the most ridiculous —"

"If you don't want to listen to me, at least take my card. Because in a few weeks, you're going to want to break this curse. And I don't work for free, but you'll pay. Because you'll never get a decent night's sleep again. The walls in your house will thump all night. You'll be seeing shadows that aren't there. You'll be living a nightmare of pain equal to whatever you inflict upon him."

On the right side of the street, the ground sloped upward, placing the witch's house on a low hill. Enough to overlook the other homes with a condescending gaze. The front door opened, and a tall, bald man stepped out. He had thin, pale skin — a skeletal look in a pinstripe suit that fit far better than Chet's. He placed his bony fingers on the porch railing and stared at Penny.

Drummond took a large step forward to block her way. “Your husband cheated on you. It hurts. I understand that. But don’t throw your life away on him. Hasn’t he taken enough from you already?”

Her face drained. “You think I’m doing this over the women? I didn’t care that he slept around. I preferred it. Better that than having to sleep with him myself.”

“I think he died from messing around with a married woman. Ticked off the wrong guy. I saw all the bruises on his …”

The look on Penny’s face, the shaking of her chin, brought those bruises straight into Drummond’s mind with such clarity that he did not need her to say anymore. They were yellowing bruises — old, healing. She looked down at her clasped hands. He wanted to hug her, offer some form of consoling, but he only stood there.

“How long?” he asked.

She sniffled. “The first time happened on our honeymoon, if you can believe that. He hid it well. Always did. Always in places that no proper woman would leave uncovered.”

They stood in silence like the trees. Then, Drummond said, “I’m sorry to ask, but I have to — did you have anything to do with his death?”

She shook her head. “It was just happy news. That’s all.”

“But you knew about Madame Kriss. Have you already made a deal with her? Is that why Ralph is dead?”

“I’m telling you the truth. I don’t know how he died or why. But yes, I knew about Madame Kriss. I had been asking around.” She glanced up at the odd man standing on the balcony. “I intended to have her cause him pain. Maybe make him impotent. Get some payback for during his life. And now that he’s dead, I figured a witch could accomplish a lot more.”

“Not this witch. This one will double-cross you. I wasn’t lying when I told you Ralph’s cursed ghost will haunt you.”

Penny looked directly at Drummond. Her eyes puffy and red but her mouth a firm line. “He shouldn’t be allowed to get away with this. Death is too good for him.”

“If you’re determined to curse him, you don’t want to get yourself cursed, too. That’s all I’m saying.”

“You don’t understand. You’re a man. You don’t know what it’s like to live with the brutality. You don’t know what it’s like to deal with the fears.”

“I know that Madame Kriss is not the answer.”

"I got pregnant once. Ralph punched that right out of me."

Drummond swallowed bile back down his throat. It swirled with a boiling rage in his gut. There was no talking her out of this. There never was. But he still had one option to make this right and protect her. Closing his eyes, unable to believe the words that were about to come out of his mouth, he put out his hand. "Give me Ralph's finger."

"What? Why?"

"Because I'm going to take care of this for you."

"I'm perfectly capable of dealing with Madame Kriss myself."

"You're not listening. She's a bad witch. All witches are bad, but some are worse than others. In my line of work, I know a lot of the ones throughout North Carolina. There are a few that owe me a favor. That's a big deal, by the way. Witches don't like to ever owe favors to anybody. So, you give me that finger, and I'll see justice done in a way that doesn't get you haunted."

She gazed up at the man on the balcony once more. "Why would you do this for me?"

"Like I said, if I don't, you'll be knocking on my door asking me to help you anyway. It's a lot easier to do it now than have to break the curse a month from now."

"And how do I know you won't be the one to double-cross me? Not follow through."

"I'll give you my card. Ask around. Whoever told you about Madame Kriss knows other witches as well. And they all know me. If I'm lying to you, you can cut off another finger before you bury your husband. Besides, after what you've done, the only way to get him to rest is to return his finger, and I certainly can't do that now — we both missed the train back to Winston-Salem."

Drummond dug through his coat pocket and pulled out a bent card with his name and address. He presented it to her in one hand, keeping the other out and open. Though she deliberated for a moment, he could see the relief in her eyes. The desire to have a better option.

"I'm going to trust you." She took the card and gave him a balled-up handkerchief. "But if I have to, I'll come back here. I'll make whatever deal I must with Madame Kriss. You understand? And I'll put you into that deal as well."

"No need for threats." He pocketed the handkerchief. "Come see me in two days. I'll tell you exactly what happened, and I'll make sure the curse leaves some kind of proof for you. Fair enough?"

Turning back toward the train station, Penny walked away. Without looking back, she said, "Two days."

Drummond waited. He wanted to make sure she did not double back to visit Madame Kriss. Once she was well on her way, he glanced up at the house. The bald man had gone back inside. Drummond stuck his hands in his pockets and turned up the street. He had a solid forty-minute walk ahead of him to reach the witch he knew would do this the right way. Especially after she heard about Penny's abusive circumstances and the lost baby. Of course, he might end the day owing this witch a favor. Not a good result for him, but at least he knew Penny Tagger would not suffer for it.

Strolling along the well-groomed streets, he tipped back his hat. He knew the area well. There were no graveyards on the way. So, he took a good breath, and started to whistle.

CASE 16

THE UNWANTED DEATH OF CLARENCE TUCK

CHAPTER 1

GUIDING THE RAZOR DOWN HIS STUBBLED CHEEK, Marshall Drummond listened to the sandpaper scratching with an odd sense of pleasure. Such a simple sound. He didn't shave as often as he should, so when he bothered, he found the act meditative. At least, he tried to make it that way. As a private investigator of the strange and bizarre, most of his time filled up with complicated matters that defied explanations for those who refused to believe. So, to find a moment, any moment, that could be quiet and simple — like shaving — he figured he should savor it.

A knock at his office door shattered that peace. He finished up with some fast, unpleasant swipes along his jaw, rinsed his face, and pulled the drain plug. The knock continued.

"Just hold it a minute," he called from the half-bath.

Standing in his undershirt, he pulled his suspenders up and headed across to his desk. Three large windows overlooked the afternoon traffic. A sea of dark suits and hats bobbed along the sidewalk. A new Chevrolet Special Deluxe drove by — good looking car that promised 1940 would be a good year. At least, that was the advertising. Drummond didn't know if he could agree as he opened the drawer holding his old .38, loaded and ready. The knocking got louder.

"Open up. It's me," a gruff voice said.

Drummond paused. He knew the voice — not one he expected to ever hear. Opting for a cigarette instead of the handgun, he strolled to the door.

With one elbow against the jamb and one hand clutching a file folder, Detective Lou Piper scowled in a rumpled suit and beaten hat. "Your office ain't that big. Why the slow answer? You got something illegal going on in here? Or maybe some*one*?"

"Take a look around, if it'll brighten your day. But be careful what you touch. You might end up getting a witch's curse."

Ol' Lou still refused to believe in anything beyond what he could see, but given that he witnessed a spell which controlled dogs, turning them into quasi-human tough guys, Drummond had wondered if he might come around to reality. Instead, the old, tough mule ignored every bit of evidence that contradicted what he *knew* to be the truth. Yet as he entered the office, his eyes warily roaming the desk, the chairs, and the couch — careful with what he touched. Which begged the question: "What the heck are you doing here?"

Noting the blanket crumpled at one end of the couch and the remnants of hasty shaving, Lou scrunched his brow. "You living here?"

"Well, Mr. Rockefeller, some of us can't afford more than one residence. Some can't even afford one. I consider myself quite lucky."

"Yeah? Be lucky for me, and shut up with the wisecracks. I got a serious case, and Captain has me bothering with cranks like you."

Sitting at his desk, Drummond said, "Gee, I thought you had given me a little respect after our case together."

"A little. I'm only calling you a *crank* this time." Lou set his bulk in Drummond's only other chair. "Since you're living here, you got anything to drink?"

That sent a warning through Drummond's chest. Whatever had brought Lou here, the man was shaken by it. Drummond went to his bookshelf and pulled out *Moby Dick*. Inside the hollowed book, he had a flask of whiskey.

From his desk drawer, he produced two pony glasses, filled them up, and passed one over. "What's all this about?"

Lou glanced down at the file folder locked in his hand. "Let me make one thing clear — I don't believe in any of this crap. Only reason I'm here is because your old pal, Cooper, can't take it anymore. Says he needs a break from you and all this weirdness. I don't know why it all now fell on me to deal with you, but nobody wants this case and Captain put it on my desk and that's the way of it. If I want to keep my job, I play ball. But it doesn't mean I like it or you or any of this. And it don't mean I believe a word of it."

"You feel better now you got that out? How about you let me see the file and we can get this over with?"

Lou lifted the file before setting it back. "It's not just that I don't buy into this stuff you claim happens. It's that this case is disturbing but it ain't none of your thing. It's just a murder. We don't need you."

Stubbing out his cigarette, Drummond shook his head. "Of course not. That's the way this always works. You boys end up with something you can't figure out, and you bring it to me as a last desperate attempt to solve the matter. But it's always *none of my thing*. Then, after I take care of it all, you change whatever happens so you don't have to admit that I actually know what I'm talking about, and you can file it away without losing your jobs. That sound about right?"

Reddening, Lou stabbed a thick finger at Drummond. "This is why nobody likes you. I shouldn't have to come down here and be insulted by a prick who couldn't even hack it as a beat cop. Especially when the department pays you as a consultant for this nonsense." With some effort, he stood. "Forget I was here. I'm not doing this ever again."

"You came all this way. At least, let me see the file." Drummond kept his voice neutral, but inside he cringed. Lou was right about one thing — the department did pay. Drummond hated the idea of letting that money walk out the door. Living in his office had become drab and unpleasant about five minutes after he moved in. That was months ago.

Lou halted at the door. His desire to leave and his duty to the department clashed across his scrunched face. With a wheezing huff, he stormed back and slapped the file on the desk. "You watch your mouth. One more thing I don't like, and I'm leaving. If you're lucky, I'll leave without cracking you across the head."

Using more willpower than he ever had against a witch, Drummond refrained from a snappy comeback. He turned his focus to the case file. As he opened it, a part of him flushed with impressed surprise that he hadn't said something and ended up brawling in the office.

Maybe I'm maturing, he thought. But then the corner of his mouth lifted. *Nah. I only want the payday.*

Unfortunately, a cursory scan of the photos and paperwork promised there would be no money coming his way. He still searched through it all anyway. Maybe he would find one nugget of the unexplained that could be turned into some cash.

The photographs told the story more than the poor grammar of the police report. The victim was a forty-one-year-old, white man who worked as a janitor at the Triumph Picture House. Between films, he cleaned the theater, restrooms, and halls. During the showings, he cleaned the projector room or rested in the basement — apparently, lived there, too.

That's where the body was found. Sprawled on the floor next to a hot plate. Drummond noticed the edge of a plain frame bed — blanket and sheets on the mattress but no pillow. Cement floor, brick walls — clean other than the blood.

Then there was the reason Lou stood at the desk breathing heavy and ready to break Drummond's nose. The body — Clarence Tunk.

"All of that was done after Clarence was killed," Lou said.

That referred to one of the most horrific murders ever presented to Drummond. The victim lay flat on the cement, stripped naked with his arms stretched overhead. The skin on his face had been removed, leaving behind all the muscle, bone, eyeballs, and teeth. Scalp remained. Hair, too. The rest of his body appeared untouched — except for the abdomen. Like the face, the skin below the ribs had been cut away with precision and patience. No hurried tears. No jagged edges.

The man's innards had been removed and segregated into three piles to the side. Drummond didn't see a clear reason to put one organ in a pile over another. In fact, the lungs had been placed in two different piles, but the kidneys shared the same one. Drummond couldn't tell exactly from the photos, but the report spelled that much out.

"Well?" Lou said, louder than necessary.

Drummond closed the file and handed it back. "You're in luck. Not one of mine."

"You sure?"

"Yeah. It's a terrible mess, and whoever did it has more than a few screws loose, but that's no form of witchcraft I've ever seen. Just some sick mind at work."

"Look again. You got to be absolutely positive. I mean, did you see what that bastard did to the guy's guts? You're telling me that's not some bit of … well, y'know."

Keeping the file closed, Drummond swigged back some of his whiskey. "Maybe he wants you to think it's the work of a witch or maybe he really believes he's casting spells or something, but what you see in those photos won't accomplish anything. This is not a case for me."

Lou's shoulders dropped and he let out a rush of air like a marathon runner finally crossing the finish line. He snatched the file. "Good. Great. Whew." He walked toward the door with a fresh hop. "At least now I can get the boys back to focusing on real policework."

"I'll be sending a bill for this time."

"I don't care. Ain't my money." Before he left, Lou glanced back and shook his head. "Look, I appreciate you looking at the file, okay? But take some advice — whatever's wrong between you and Cooper, you better fix it. I won't be doing this again, and there ain't nobody else who wants to deal with you, either. If you want to be getting the consultant money, Cooper's the only one you got on your side." He appraised the office with a trained eye. "I'm pretty sure you don't want to lose out whatever you can make off us. Unless you like living here." He knocked twice on the doorjamb and whistled down the hall.

One of the difficulties with Drummond's job — lack of customers. Even a normal PI found it challenging to get cases on a regular basis, but add to that the specificity of the supernatural and the opportunities for work diminished fast. As a result, Drummond meandered through his morning routine — coffee at the corner diner, reading the newspaper, taking a walk around the block — but his mind kept going over the murder of Clarence Tunk.

He had told Ol' Lou the truth — nothing in that file spoke of witchcraft or any other magic. Yet he doubted the Winston-Salem police would get far in solving the matter. Not out of incompetence. They were a good group of cops, and even hardnosed Lou knew how to do his job. But the disturbing nature of the crime — the unnatural sense of it that pushed the department to send the file over to Drummond in the first place — that would linger amongst them all. They would try their best, but part of them, a bone-deep part, would fight against them, afraid to learn the truth. Whatever it turned out to be.

Drummond looked up from his thoughts to find that he had walked all the way to Patterson Avenue. Midway along, on the other side of the road, stood the Triumph Picture House. The marquis announced a new film — *Road to Singapore* starring Bing Crosby and Bob Hope. Drummond considered going in, asking a few questions as he bought some popcorn, maybe poking around the back until either he got caught or the picture started. But all of that required purchasing a ticket and the food — money he did not have to spend. Especially since nobody would be paying him for the work.

He turned back. This wasn't his case. If he wanted to pound pavement, he ought to do it in search of work. Weaving around the few people startled by his shift in direction, he turned for home when he heard the music.

Soft, somber piano. A delicate hand playing a meandering tune like someone whistling alone in the woods. A private expression of thoughts meant only for the person making it.

Drummond headed up the street, drawn to the gentle notes, and found they emerged from the depths of a rare and used bookstore. Moe's Books — a narrow place made narrower by the overstocked shelves towering to the ceiling. The heavy aroma of old paper pressed in, and the main light source came from the sun fighting its way through the storefront window and down the three tiny aisles. At the entrance, an unmanned desk and a cash register made for a tight step against the wall. The place was a claustrophobic's nightmare.

All except for that music. The lightness of the wandering melody over a slow, methodical tempo danced above the cluttered store. It called Drummond down one aisle, his shoulders brushing books on either side, until he reached the back. There he found a staircase leading to the second floor and an upright piano flush against it. He also found a woman playing the enticing song.

Standing between *Biographies — A thru J* and *History — Civil War,* Drummond watched this lady as she dazzled the keys with effortless joy. She had dark hair to her shoulders that stood out against her pale blue dress. Her bone-thin frame suggested she had suffered like most through the economic hardships of the last decade, but the sound she produced from that piano promised she would overcome her woes.

She stopped mid-phrase, stiffening as if the cold of a ghost had passed across her back. "It's not polite to stare," she said, and her voice prickled Drummond's skin.

"Sorry about that," he said, pleased that his voice didn't crack like a teenager. "Your playing drew me in. It's beautiful."

She closed the lid over the keys. "Thank you," she said with an accent from somewhere in Europe.

"I'm Marshall Drummond. You are?"

"Miriam Rosen." She finally turned towards him, and Drummond felt as if he had been punched in the chest. Her deep eyes and soft mouth held a dark sadness that he found oddly seductive. He wanted to wrap his coat around her, hold her close, and promise to handle whatever problems she faced.

Maybe I am a teenager. "Miss Rosen, it is a pleasure to meet you."

"It'd be more of a pleasure if you bought a book. My father would certainly appreciate it."

"I'll consider that." He threw a winning smile at her — the one that had worked on many diner waitresses throughout North Carolina — but she merely stared back. Then: "You've got a lovely accent. Where are you from?"

Her eyes turned away. "Sulza. It's a town in Germany. A wonderful place. I loved it there."

She stood, coming up to his nose, and when she passed by, he noted a faint, flowery scent. He said, "I don't mean to continue being rude—"

"Then don't."

He chuckled. Walked right into that punch. "Well, if you don't mind me asking, what is that perfume you're wearing?"

As she sauntered up the aisle, she grinned back at him — a hesitant smile that she tamped down the moment it flashed out. "We don't sell enough books to afford perfume."

"Then I guess it's just you. They should name a flower after you. A Miriam flower."

She offered a polite tilt of the head, and Drummond wanted to smack himself in the face. He spouted foolish nonsense like a love-sick schoolkid. But he followed her, part of him working on the next moronic thing to say.

When they reached the front desk, a short, chubby man crossed his arms and scowled. "Why aren't you up here?" he said, his heavy accent rounding the words. The thick glasses resting atop his bald head flopped down onto his nose, and he fumbled to reset them.

"Sorry, Papa. I was helping this gentleman find a book."

Mr. Rosen appraised Drummond with a suspicious eye. "Where's the book?"

Seeing an opportunity, Drummond said, "It's a bit dark, but my interests tend toward more of witches and the occult."

"Scary stories? We have Poe."

"Non-fiction. I usually have to go out-of-the-way to find anything. I happened by your place and thought I'd see if I was lucky."

Miriam walked around her father, placing a calm hand on his shoulder. "But I couldn't help him. I don't know these aisles as well as you."

Mr. Rosen softened a bit. "Oh. Well, then, I can certainly help you. We don't have much on the subject anymore, but there is a book back here called *17th Century Witchcraft in North Carolina.* Perhaps that will suit?"

As the man headed down the far aisle, Drummond waited. He looked at Miriam. She looked back. And they both shoved down the laughter threatening to erupt.

"Sorry," she said. "I hope you can afford a book. He won't stop until you buy something."

From the back of the store, Mr. Rosen said, "Ah, I found it."

Not much time left. Drummond said, "Have dinner with me."

"Tonight?"

"Any night."

She glanced toward the sound of her father's approaching steps. But she shook her head. "Papa would not approve."

"He doesn't even know me."

"Are you suddenly Jewish?"

"No."

"Then Papa would not approve."

When Mr. Rosen returned, he carried a hefty tome. "This is all I have at the moment. Published a few years ago and in decent condition. You people seem to love this witch stuff. I can't keep much of it around, but I'll keep an eye out for you, if you wish. For when more arrives."

"It'll be fine," Drummond said.

Even though he shouldn't have bought the book, Drummond paid the full fifty cents anyway. Carrying the book out of the story, he shook Mr. Rosen's hand and tipped his hat to Miriam. Once on the sidewalk, he peered across at the Triumph Picture House. People strolled by the building, cars rumbled along the street, life pressed on.

Pushing back his hat, Drummond snickered. He had no case and no date. He had an empty pocket, too. The only thing this excursion provided was a book he didn't want.

"Great job," he said and headed back to his office.

THE DAY CONTINUED IN A QUIET WAY. Drummond spent much of the time leafing through his new book. It had little new to present; however, there were several photos he had never seen before. But in the end, the book offered nothing factual that he didn't already know. Still, he placed it on his bookshelf — a memento of meeting Miriam Rosen.

He started drinking early that afternoon. Daydreams of Miriam played around his head even as he tried to banish them. She had a haunted beauty, and he hated that it attracted him. Something about her dug into his chest, made him want to hold her, protect her, ease her burdens. He drank more and reminded himself that she came from another world — one that had no place for him. She had no place in his world, either. He knew that. Best to put her out of his mind. He drank some more.

By dinner, he considered going to one of his usual diners and seeing if one of his usual waitresses could help him forget the day. But when he stood, the office swayed deep and he flopped back into his chair. He laughed. For several minutes, he sat at his desk contemplating if the effort to swim the room to his couch would be worthwhile. Lost in this complex calculation, he fell asleep.

When the cold chill woke him, moonlight cast stark shadows across the floor. He sat up in his chair, the sudden motion tumbling rocks through his head while twisting his stomach with iron clamps. He placed a hand on his desk for stability and waited to see if he would throw up. Thankfully, the nausea drifted down. But the cold air remained.

He knew right away the temperature outside his office held steady at a comfortable seventy. Autumn would bring on the cold nights soon enough, but not yet. No. This cold came from a source he knew well — the dead.

When he lifted his gaze, Drummond saw the man floating several inches above the office floor. Pale skin, mournful eyes, body completely intact. Considering Drummond had seen photos of this man's eviscerated corpse only hours earlier, he counted it a blessing that Clarence Tunk manifested with a less disturbing appearance.

Despite having seen a few ghosts throughout his career, Drummond could not be casual about the experience — not on the inside, at least. His pulse ramped up while the cold labored his breath. Yet on the outside, he kept his fingers from shaking as he pulled out a cigarette and leaned back in his chair.

"I know you're newly dead, but you've gone through the effort of showing up. Might as well tell me why."

Clarence lowered his brow, concentrating like a student learning algebra. When he opened his mouth to speak, bits of his cheek peeled off. Damn. Drummond knew this could happen — some ghosts, traumatized by their deaths, became locked in that moment. They re-experienced it in a terror-filled loop for eternity. Horrible way to live the afterlife. Also made communicating with them a pain in the neck.

"Is this why you're here? You want me to help free you?"

As Clarence's face shredded away, he managed a few words. *"Lies… have … been …"*

"So soon after your death, your type usually wants vengeance or simply to have your murder solved. I don't do revenge — usually — and the police have your case."

"Virginia …"

"Fine. I'll give them the clue, okay? Is this Virginia a lady friend? Or the killer? Hmm? Don't strain. Being a ghost can be hard at first. Sometimes forever. Look, considering the extreme nature of the crime, I'm sure the police will put in every effort to get you justice." Or they'll put in every effort to bury the case, but Clarence didn't need to hear that.

With his belly opening, the ghost howled. His haunted pallor dimmed, became translucent, and Drummond thought the visit might have ended. But mustering his strength with a determined hunching of his shoulders, Clarence found solidity again. He pointed a skeletal finger at Drummond.

The ghost shot forward. Shrieking like a passenger train screaming its emergency brakes, he blasted across the room. His bloody, pale flesh fluttered like soaked ribbons as he swept through the office desk and then through Drummond.

When the chill hit, Drummond shouted. Muscle memory had brought his fists up even as he shoved back in his chair. Sweat dampened his brow. With his heart thundering in his ears, he scanned the office.

Empty.

Seeing a ghost, feeling the death chill, hearing a strained message — that always got his pulse going. But this had been different. Perhaps because Clarence's ghost came from the freshest dead man Drummond had ever seen. Perhaps because the nature of his death had been so brutal that it radiated the man's pain and sorrow. Or perhaps something had gone wrong for Clarence — beyond being murdered.

Scooting the chair back to his desk, Drummond jotted down the few words the ghost had managed. He finished his cigarette, visited *Moby Dick* for a few swigs, and let his body shudder several times. After ten minutes, the horrid sensations subsided, leaving behind a more familiar, more welcome feeling — the itch to figure this out.

CHAPTER 2

WINSTON-SALEM ON A WEDNESDAY never broke any records for Most Wild Nightlife. Too many hard-working folks needed to rest up in order to toil through another day come morning. Making cigarettes and other tobacco products for most of the nation required hard factory labor, and since that labor formed the backbone of the city, Drummond had little trouble making his way to the Triumph Picture House unseen. He passed only two people and neither wanted to be bothered — they had more interest in whether to rent a room for twenty minutes or simply duck into an alley.

If he had a choice, Drummond would have waited until morning to deal with the crime scene. Unfortunately, he had already turned down the case. He guessed Lou and the rest of the department would not be helpful granting him access now. They certainly would not go out of their way to provide any information they already had gathered. So, he had to do it himself, and that meant inspecting the crime scene that night — before anybody could intervene.

He strolled by Moe's Books and couldn't stop from peeking in the dark window. All peaceful and cozy. Another world, indeed. He tried to recall the last time he spent a night feeling peaceful and cozy that didn't involve a pint of whiskey. But then, spending his life dealing with the ghosts of rotting corpses tended to disrupt things.

He crossed the sleeping street and ambled down the theater alleyway. Around the back, he found a short run of stairs leading to the basement doorway. He cracked the glass with his elbow, then pushed through with his fist in his hat, clearing away the remaining shards before reaching through to unlock the door.

The basement had cement floor, pipes running along the ceiling, and a boiler taking up half the space. When it kicked on, it sounded like a locomotive. Shelves overstuffed with ticket rolls, replacement seat cushions, and popcorn boxes lined one wall. In the nearest corner, stacks of old cardboard standups promoting films that never succeeded now decomposed, as forgotten as the films themselves. If any of them had been for good shows, they would have been swiped away by fans, collectors, or employees.

Working through the room, Drummond spotted a door at the end, next to the stairs leading upwards. Clarence Tunk's room. The door stood open. From the darkness inside, he heard clothes rustling and thick breathing. Drummond's pulse quickened. He reached for his .38 but the click of a revolver stopped him. Out of the darkened room, a large man emerged holding a .38 of his own.

The man stood too far away for Drummond to attempt a desperate attack, and in the dark, there didn't appear to be a good place to run for cover. Only option left — talk. "Hey, pal, I didn't realize anybody was here. I'm not trying to muscle in on your shelter."

A flashlight popped on, blinded Drummond for a moment, then followed with an exasperated sigh. "You stupid idiot. I could've killed you." Lou flicked on the basement lights.

Trying to hide his own relief, Drummond said, "I know cop pay is lousy, but you don't need to sleep in a crime scene. I'm sure you've got at least one friend, and if you're lucky that guy's got a couch."

"I'm the only one of us who legally should be in here, so you ought to cut it with the jokes. Unless you'd like to spend the night behind bars. Then again, I've seen that you've got your bedroom in your office, so maybe jail would be a pleasant change." Lou holstered his weapon. "What are you doing here, anyway? You said this wasn't your case. You lie about that?"

"I didn't think so when I said it. I still don't think so. Not like you mean."

"Crap. Here we go."

"Well, why are you here this late at night? And why isn't the scene marked out? Doesn't look like anybody's gone over this basement at all."

Rubbing the back of his head, Lou said, "Yeah, that's part of why I'm here. It's like I told you this morning — nobody wants to touch this case."

"They're going to let it go cold that fast?"

"Captain said I've got until end of the week to either make an arrest or move on to the next case."

"At least that explains Clarence's visit this evening. Most victims worry they'll be stuck forever, can't move on, with their murder unresolved."

Lou tightened up like a fist. "Damnit, I don't want to hear that kind of stuff."

"Okay, okay. I'll try to keep it out of the conversation. But I'm here now, so maybe you won't mind if I poke around, too?"

"Long as you share anything you find."

"Anything?"

"Except for the weirdo crap. You find solid evidence from the world of reality, let me know."

With an unceremonious wave of the hand, Lou ushered Drummond into the small room Clarence called home. Drummond saw the unplugged hotplate, the rumpled mattress on a rusty frame, and the bloodstained floor. It all matched the photographs minus the body. Against one brick wall, outside the photo's frame, Clarence had an old student desk. Small, wooden thing. Empty, though. No papers, no books, a complete blank. He checked the single drawer. Not even a pencil.

Drummond turned his attention to the walls. No witch symbols. He looked through the bedding and sifted through the trash. Not a single hint of witchcraft. Not that he expected anything — he had told Lou that morning nothing in the photos looked like a Drummond case — but it sure would have made matters easier. Instead, he had a wandering ghost who thought the case could be solved with a strange haunting as motivation.

"I'm not finding anything helpful."

"Me, neither," Lou said. "And this isn't my first time looking. At least, when I tell Captain the case went cold, I'll know it actually did."

Drummond paused. Wedged between the front end of the mattress and the wall, he spotted a slip of paper. First pass through the room, he dismissed it as the mattress tag, but at this angle, it looked distinctly like torn paper.

"I might have one clue for you."

"Oh, yeah?" Lou didn't sound too hopeful. "I'm all ears."

Drummond shifted closer to the wall. "Didn't want to mention it since you won't like where it came from, and I figured I might find something here to help out and be done with it all."

"Out with it, already. What do you got?"

"A name. Virginia. Not much to go on, but the name meant enough to Clarence Tunk that he went through an awful painful bit of trouble to get it to me."

Lou's thick lips folded in as he suppressed a sour face. Then: "You're right. I don't like it."

"I know you can't use it as direct evidence, but —"

"I'm back to nowhere again. Simple is that." He cracked his knuckles and stomped out of the room. With a swift motion, Drummond bent down, swiped the paper scrap, and followed Lou into the rest of the basement.

Lou closed the door to Clarence's room. "This case is pretty much dead. I suppose I needed to convince myself of it, but you saw for yourself. There ain't nothing in there for clues. Maybe the autopsy will show something. I doubt it, though. Victim suffered through being gutted once already."

Drummond put his hands in his coat pockets, tucking the paper scrap secure in the process. "You're trying to convince yourself and doing a lousy job. This won't go away."

"Maybe not for you and your freakish nightmares, but in a week, it won't be my problem."

"It's just a name. Look into her or you'll be stuck wondering for the rest of your life what you missed."

Lou frowned as he nudged Drummond toward the exit. "Yeah, well, I'll keep doing my job until Captain says the case is over, but I ain't laying bets on finding much."

"It's your optimism that I admire."

Drummond ignored the string of curse words echoing from behind as he headed out. When he left the theater and strolled along the empty sidewalk, he knew he had to work even harder on the case. Because Clarence Tunk floated over the middle of the road, staring at the theater like a lighthouse widow watching the sea.

"I delivered your message. The police know about your friend, now. Are we done?"

But Drummond could feel the cold of the dead still following him. The chilled sensation went down his hand and into his pocket. That ghost would not let him out of this so easy.

"Okay, pal, I'll look." At the next streetlight, he brought out the paper slip. An address. Part of one, at least. Most of the important bits had been torn off, but he could make out the last two digits of a number — 72 — and the street name read clear enough — Tobias Road. However, Drummond's arms prickled far more than any ghost chill could cause when he saw the symbol next to the address — a circle with a diamond inside and four wavy lines poking out in the compass directions.

"That can't be good."

CHAPTER 3

THE SUN ROSE A FEW HOURS LATER, and Drummond grabbed only thirty minutes of that time for sleep. With a normal case, he would have placed his hat over his face and allowed the world to drift by while he caught up. But even if he tried, he had no doubt Clarence would chill the room until frost appeared on the walls. That ghost's determination far exceeded anything Drummond had ever encountered before.

So, under the morning's pink hues, he made a plan. Nothing complex. Just a simple list of how to proceed. He hoped it would keep Clarence out of his way.

Step one — make coffee. Step two — drink coffee. Step three — look up that symbol.

The first two steps went smoothly. He had done them enough, and muscle memory handled most of the intricacies. As his mind grumbled awake, he brought down two books of witch iconography he had on the shelves and got to work.

After a half-hour, he had come up empty. He checked through the books yet again, but even the three symbols that approximated the one on the paper didn't pass any logic test. The closest match marked the transition from one spell to the other. Sort of like a period at the end of a sentence. The other two symbols concerned animal husbandry. None of those made sense to be marking a street address nor to be of interest to a janitor of the Triumph.

Closing the books, Drummond leaned back in his chair and let another sip of coffee clear the fuzziness in his head. He looked at the paper slip again — *72 Tobias Road.* The rounded markings of at least one earlier number poked along the torn edge. Maybe a three. Maybe an eight. If the person writing this had terrible penmanship, Drummond could see a five, six, or nine as well. And if he could argue for those, then he had to throw in two and zero. Heck, only one, four, and seven were the definite exclusions. The prospect of knocking on every door on every

Tobias Street in every city and town in North Carolina excited him as much as watching a pile of dirt. But before he explored the wonders of a monotonous task, he had one other avenue to go down.

Grabbing his hat and coat, he headed out, making sure to tell Clarence, "Don't worry, pal, I haven't given up."

The fact that his idea meant another visit to Moe's Books and another chance to see Miriam had nothing to do with his enthusiasm. Well, almost nothing. Well, perhaps everything.

But when he entered the musty, narrow aisles, he found only her father.

"She's giving home lessons today," Mr. Rosen said. "Teaches piano. Most lessons she does here in the back, but some people have their own pianos and will pay extra to have her shlep out to their homes."

"Sorry to have missed her," Drummond said, removing his hat as he followed the man to the front desk, "but I came here to see you."

Mr. Rosen wagged a stubby finger. "Do not lie to me. I'm not a fool. At least, as a father I'm not. Oh, I saw quite clear the way you looked at her. You had a look we all know. Why be surprised? I'm not so old I don't remember being young."

"I'm not so young myself."

"Young enough. But she's not for you."

"Because I'm not Jewish?"

"That's certainly at the top of the list."

"There's a list now."

Sighing as if resigned to have this conversation, Mr. Rosen said, "I'm the father of a beautiful daughter. There's always a list."

"Maybe if you talk with me, you'll realize that I'm not —"

"No." Mr. Rosen snapped a book firmly closed. "My Miriam lost much escaping a war. You will only cause her to lose more. Show me some respect, show Miriam some respect, and leave her alone. Don't break her heart falling for a man she can never be with."

Rubbing the brim of his hat, Drummond said, "I'm sorry. I've offended you."

"No apology needed. I'm not offended. You strike me as a decent man. I think you'll do right by her."

He hadn't meant to get this open with Miriam's father, and it certainly had not gone the way he wanted, but Drummond couldn't stop his curious mind from asking one last question. "What if I had been Jewish?"

Mr. Rosen's stern mouth twitched upward. "Oh, why then, I think you'd be worth getting to know. I'm not sure what kind of prospects you have, but you have a job, and that puts you far above a lot of schlumps out there. But God did not make you a Jew. So, I'm afraid you are out of luck."

Drummond clicked his tongue. "Can't say I'm much of a religious man, anyway."

"Ah, well, another strike against you. You'll have to be satisfied with the millions of non-Jewish women out there in the world." Mr. Rosen put out his hand. "I do wish you the best of luck."

Shaking hands, Drummond said, "I wasn't lying when I said I came here to see you. I had hoped to see Miriam, too, but I'm here today for work."

"Oh?"

"If you don't mind, I've got a question for you. When you brought me that book on witchcraft, you said you've had a hard time keeping the stuff on the shelves."

"That's right. Quite a few people share your interest."

"Would one of those people happen to be a fellow from across the street — Clarence Tunk?"

"Certainly. He comes in here every week. Why are you interested in him?"

"I'm sorry to tell you he's dead. Murdered."

Drummond had said it plain and fast on purpose — trying to gauge the reaction. But Mr. Rosen showed nothing beyond mere acceptance.

"Shame. He was a good customer."

Odd reaction, but Drummond decided not to push on it. Mr. Rosen came from a violent situation. That could account for his lack of reaction. If evidence pointed otherwise, Drummond would have plenty of chances to follow up. He also didn't want the bookseller on the defensive.

"I'm helping the police investigate the death, and some aspects of the case made me think he might know some people who also liked to learn about witches and such."

"I see." Mr. Rosen stiffened. "I'm not one to give out names."

"I'm just looking for anybody that could shed light on who Clarence was. His room didn't say much about him, and he didn't appear to have many close friends."

"But you're doing so to help the police."

Drummond knew enough about Mr. Rosen now. He played it both into the man's expectations as well as straight. "I'm doing so mostly because the police are paying me. But if somebody with a serious interest in witchcraft killed him, then that person may not be stable. I'd rather not see another death, if I can prevent it. Only problem is that I don't have much to go on. Then I remembered what you said about people getting these books, and well, I came right over."

Mr. Rosen gave the matter some thought — serious thought. Drummond wasn't sure if he had overplayed, but he couldn't change it now. Besides, he had told the truth.

Licking his finger, Mr. Rosen began leafing through his accounting register on the desk. "There was a woman he met here awhile back. Not particularly attractive, I thought. I know that's not a nice thing to say, but look at me — I'm no catch, either. Anyway, I thought he could do better. They would come in together sometimes to look through the books. Always the occult section. But she never paid for anything. Always him. So, I don't have her name or anything here." He stopped at a page and brought his face close to a long column of names and figures.

"Is that Tunk's purchases?"

"No. This is the other gentleman, Mr. Tunk's rival, Mr. Arthur Fitzroy."

"Rival?"

"Mr. Fitzroy started coming to the store several months ago, said he was new to the area, and he often buys books from that section. Not exclusively, mind you. He also likes history and a little fiction. Mostly Wells — writes the time travel story, the Mars one, and such. I have to admit, he surprised me."

"How?"

"Mr. Fitzroy does not look like the usual readerly type."

"There's a type?"

"There's a type for everything, and Mr. Fitzroy struck me more as the type to be a heartless landlord who drinks too much and hates his wife. But there we see God plays with us. He makes Mr. Fitzroy a reader, after all."

"And Fitzroy doesn't like Clarence?"

"I wouldn't know."

"You called them *rivals*."

"I can only say that whenever I got a shipment of books, the two of them would be in competition to grab what they considered the best stuff. In fact, I don't know if they ever met. They each simply knew that there was another customer trying to get hold of the same books. I never told them the other's name."

"You wouldn't happen to have an address for Fitzroy, would you?"

Mr. Rosen nodded. "Of course. How else can I mail him specific orders when he can't pick them up?"

Drummond waited. When no further information came his way, he held back a frustrated sigh. "Would you please give me the address?"

A stern scowl tightened Mr. Rosen's face as he wrote the address on an index card. Before he handed it over, however, he stared at the card. "I do not like giving names, let alone addresses, so you should know that I take this very seriously. I'm only telling you anything because of the circumstances. If Mr. Fitzroy did indeed murder Mr. Tunk, then justice must be seen to. But right or wrong, particularly if you are wrong, Mr. Fitzroy must never learn that you got this information from me. Do you understand?"

"You got nothing to worry about. I know how to keep my sources private."

Still, he hesitated. At length, though, he thrust the card over, unable to look at Drummond, biting his lip, and shuddering. Drummond pocketed the card, and for a moment, he wanted to assure Mr. Rosen that this would be helpful, that Clarence Tunk would have appreciated this, but he held back. Whatever bothered the man about giving up a name went far deeper than street-code ethics. Drummond guessed it had more to do with the war, and that made him think it was none of his business.

Instead, he muttered his thanks and hastened out of the store. Once he walked a short distance away, he checked the address. A bit of a drive across town. Which meant Fitzroy had been going out of his way to swipe occult books before Clarence could get ahold of them.

TWENTY MINUTES LATER, Drummond parked on the street in front of a line of rundown rowhouses. Not a nice-looking area. Not the kind of place to raise a family.

He knocked on the door, and a tall, gaunt man answered. The man wore a stringy beard, wire-frame glasses, and the face of a mean drunk. A chewed cigar stuck out the side of his mouth.

"Arthur Fitzroy?"

"Yeah. Who're you?"

"Marshall Drummond, private investigator. I've got a few questions to ask you. May I come in?"

"No." He tried to close the door, but Drummond stuck a foot out to block it.

"Clarence Tunk is dead."

Fitzroy paused, his cigar threatening to fall. A long snort. Then: "Clarence is dead, huh? That's awful. Real sad. I'll be sure to write his mother."

"You don't sound too upset."

He shrugged but offered nothing more.

"Don't want to know how he died?"

"Don't care."

"Murdered. And unless you want the police to show up thinking you killed him, you better let me in."

Muttering a few foul words, Fitzroy walked deeper into the home, leaving Drummond on his own. Drummond figured this was as close to an invitation as he would get. He entered the house.

More deep than wide, the narrow home had been decorated with the care of a man who thought bathing was an optional activity. Dirty dishes in the sink, trash piling over the can, a foul odor drifting from the bathroom. Not much more. Not even a bed.

Drummond had seen it before. The Depression had technically ended or was about to end — radio news went back and forth on the subject as fickle as the weather — but there were plenty of people still hurting. Might take another half-decade before everyone could afford a home again. Fitzroy had a place which meant he had more money than a lot of better people.

"I'd offer you a drink, but I'm afraid I'm rather empty at the moment." Fitzroy paused, perhaps hoping Drummond would pony up for a beer or two. When he met only quiet, he spit in the corner and kicked a wooden stool toward his unwanted guest. "It's all I got to sit on."

Sitting low would be a horrible disadvantage should anything bad happen. The longer Drummond looked over Fitzroy and the shambles of the apartment, the more prepared for bad he wanted to be. He pushed the stool back. "I wouldn't dare deprive a man of his only seat. I can stand."

"Well, I ain't sitting when you're standing." Fitzroy raised his lip in a sneer. "That'd be rude."

Drummond's mind added up the sparse apartment, the criminal look, and the reaction to Clarence's murder. He didn't like the sum, but he decided to cut straight to it. "So, Arthur —"

"Arty. Nobody calls me Arthur."

"Okay. Arty. How long you been working for a witch?"

That snatched Fitzroy's attention. He clenched the cigar in his bared teeth as his eyes darted about. Drummond knew the look — an internal frenzy caused by one of two possibilities. One, Fitzroy's brain was catching up to the situation and wondering how much trouble he was in, how much he should admit to, and how to get out of whatever mess he had stepped into. Or two, he was a fine actor putting on a show to deflect suspicion from the murder he had committed.

Stuttering his words a tiny bit, Fitzroy said, "A witch? What the heck are you talking about?"

"Let me put it simple for you — you've barely got any money and I've been around people like you a whole lot. You're a desperate criminal willing to do anything for a buck. Now, I happen to know that you and Clarence fought over getting hold of books on the occult. Only there aren't any books in here, and you don't strike me as the reading type. So, now I've got to wonder, who needs those kinds of books that's afraid to buy them outright? Who would need to pay a guy like you? Only one answer I can think of — a witch."

Spitting once more, Fitzroy stabbed his cigar in the air to make his points. "First, Mr. Detective, I hardly knew Clarence at all. Don't really know nothing about him. He just happened to buy a lot of the books I wanted. And second, the idea that there are witches —"

"You can stop right there. Your reaction to the mentioning of witches is too late." Drummond placed his hands at his sides, hoping to look at ease. "Right now, I only need you to give me her name. Tell me the witch you're working for and you'll probably never see me again."

"That's all you want? No problem. I wrote it down over here." Fitzroy took two steps and bolted for the door.

Drummond slipped in behind, and with a sharp shove, thrust Fitzroy forward. The man's hand bent hard at the wrist as he tried to grab the doorknob. He barked another slew of foul words but ended up face into the wood. Drummond continued forward, using his shoulder to lock Fitzroy against the closed door. He took hold of the man's injured wrist and pulled the arm back. A little twist and Fitzroy cried out.

"You don't know what you've gotten into," Drummond said.

"Hey, you can't do this. I ain't done nothing wrong. Just bought some books."

"See what I mean? You haven't a clue."

"Buying books ain't illegal." Fitzroy thrust his head back, trying to bash Drummond's nose.

Twisting the man's wrist harder, Drummond rammed him flat into the door again. "You're right, Arty ol' pal. Nothing illegal in North Carolina law about buying books. But you're working for a witch, and those women have another whole set of laws they've got to follow. Whoever hired you, she's trying to get these books without any other witches knowing. You understand now? You're being used. Unless … oh, Arty, you didn't fall for her, did you? Tell me you're not doing this out of love."

"No," Fitzroy said, no longer struggling.

The defeat in his voice allowed Drummond to ease up. "Then tell me."

"Her name's Elsie, and I ain't in love with her. She pays me for the books."

"Madame Elsie?"

"Elsie Gerald, far as I know."

"You make a witch deal with her? She blackmailing you? What aren't you telling me?"

Fitzroy motioned to be let free, and when Drummond backed off, the man rubbed his wrist as he took a seat on the stool. "Nothing like that. I get paid and keep quiet. That's it. Heck if I even believe half this witch nonsense. But she sure believes it."

"Why you? If you don't have a witch deal with her, what's to keep you around?"

"Look, I didn't have a roof over my head before I met Elsie. She saw me sleeping in a gutter and offered me the job. Since then, she's always paid me fair, and look now — I got a place to live."

"Yeah? You'll make even more money now that Clarence isn't around to snatch up those books. Is that what happened? You decided to get rid of the competition?"

"I ain't no killer."

"Maybe. But you're going to give me Elsie's address and a description of her or I'll have the Winston-Salem Police Department turn your life over while they try to pin that murder on you."

Fitzroy glowered at Drummond, but he knew enough not to argue.

CHAPTER 4

MOST TIMES WHEN PRESENTED WITH A CASE, Drummond could tell right away whether or not the case ventured into his territory. But as he drove toward the southern end of the city, he had to admit that he had misjudged this one badly. Poor Lou would not be pleased the next time they spoke. Then again, Drummond had learned how to talk around the supernatural to make circumstances more palatable to the police.

The neighborhoods became a little nicer as he drove. Nothing fancy, but the houses didn't share walls and weren't sitting atop one another. A lot of them had rooms for rent, and according to Fitzroy, one such home would be where to find Elsie Gerald.

But this wasn't a mere suspect. This was a witch. One who knew she had broken some witch rules. Nothing drastic, but she had gone to the effort of hiring outside help to purchase some books — ones she assumed other witches didn't want her to have. That meant she didn't want — or couldn't afford — to get on the wrong side of those running the North Carolina witch community. Like the Hull family. All of which gave Drummond pause. Elsie could be more dangerous than an average witch. No sense in busting down her door just yet. Instead, he parked up the block and watched the house.

The lunch hour came and went. If Drummond had known he would be in a stakeout that day, he would have packed a sandwich. At five after one, right when he decided he would grab some food nearby and set up a proper stakeout tomorrow, a young woman stepped out the front door.

Fitzroy had said she was young, maybe mid-twenties, and that she had dark hair, bobbed. Also, she was thin to the bone, walked a little hunched, yet had great legs, and a cute little nose. Fitzroy's words — *a cute little nose.* Drummond thought that detail indicated Fitzroy had fallen for the witch despite the man's protests. But just as likely, the witch had cast some kind of charm on him.

Regardless, the woman heading toward the sidewalk fit the bill. She wore a simple skirt and blouse — the kind of thing that drew little notice. Turning away from him, she walked two cars up and climbed into a '39 Packard. As she pulled away, Drummond started up his car and followed.

She drove downtown, never performing any odd turns or maneuvers to suggest she knew she had a tail. She headed right by his office, even slowed down. Drummond wondered if Fitzroy had called the witch, warned her that a detective had been poking around and was coming to see her. He didn't recall a phone in Fitzroy's place — couldn't imagine the man had enough money for a phone — but a friendly neighbor or a pay phone on the street could have solved that problem.

Elsie pushed onward, working her way through traffic, and turned east. She parked in a small lot next to a lawyer's office — Springfield & Shand. Both named lawyers had reserved spots, but there were still a few others. Drummond could not get away with parking there. Much too visible. He lucked into a space not that far beyond, though, and watched Elsie in his rearview mirror.

She entered the offices, and he checked the time — 1:25 pm. Either she was early for an appointment or late for work. Older witches rarely needed another job. Given enough time, any witch worthy of the name had the reputation and regular clients to afford a basic living. But Elsie's youth implied she had yet to earn those things, and the longer she spent in that office, the more likely that she was working as a receptionist.

Of course, she could be a lawyer, too. Many witches held high profile jobs, but they were usually older women who worked such jobs for most of their lives and didn't get into witchcraft until later. Plus, Drummond knew women had been fighting to be lawyers for close to a century. Technically legal but frowned upon in many parts of the country. Heck, women's suffrage had passed over two decades ago, and North Carolina had still not officially ratified the 19th Amendment.

But a lawyer would have started working early in the morning, would have had a briefcase or an armful of papers, and would have had one of the private parking spots in the little lot to the side. On top of all that, being a female lawyer in Winston-Salem, especially one so young, would have made the newspapers when she had started. Drummond could not recall any such articles. A few minutes later, a woman dressed similar to Elsie exited the office looking tired from a long morning's work and miffed at having to wait for her afternoon replacement. That settled it for him — part-time receptionist.

Hours went by. Drummond's stomach complained. He never had

that lunch, and he couldn't risk dashing off for a bite. Part-time could mean just about anything, and her lousy work ethic meant she might get fired at any moment. He waited and watched.

She worked until 5:30. She didn't drive back home, though. So, he followed her car further east.

Reaching her destination, she got out, and walked up to a blue house with white trim. Funny thing about that house. A quiet group of witches lived there. Thirteen of them. The Tolson coven.

The youngest of the Tolson ladies had recently celebrated her fifty-seventh birthday. The oldest turned ninety-two in a couple of months. Drummond knew about all the women in that house. Though a coven, and a group of knowledgeable witches, they had decided to live a life of retirement. If they practiced any magic, it never reached a level that brought eyes upon them. As long as they didn't hurt anybody, Drummond let them be. He kept tabs on them, though — just a precaution.

Elsie strode up to their porch and knocked hard on the door. No answer. Strange because Drummond knew several of those witches never left the house. Apparently, Elsie knew it, too. She knocked harder. Still no answer.

"Avoiding me won't stop anything," she yelled.

The front door opened — enough so that a brown-skinned woman could poke her head out. Rebecca, sixty-five, joined the coven after arriving from Mexico City. The two women spoke, but Drummond couldn't hear any of it. Body language told enough, though. Despite Elsie's insistence, anger, and threats of some kind, Rebecca refused to let her in.

At length, the coven door closed. Elsie stood ramrod, clenching her fists, and staring at the door. When she stormed back to her car, Drummond considered approaching the house and trying to find out what had happened. But no matter how gentle the witches lived their lives, they were still witches. They wouldn't reveal anything — not without gaining something in return. And finding out information about Elsie was nowhere close to worthy of making a deal with a coven.

Besides, following Elsie had already provided a lot of information. Might as well keep the tail going for a bit longer. In fact, Drummond spent the final hours of the day watching Elsie visit a few pawn shops, pick up some groceries, and stop at an unmarked store well-known to witches for getting basic spell supplies like candles, salt, chalk, and various animal bloods.

While following this young witch around, an idea had formed. On one side of the situation, there was Elsie. Many witches lived and worked their craft in a solitary manner. Without a coven, the options were limited. As a young witch, she clearly had no mentor, no coven, nobody to help her along. If she did have such a person, she wouldn't be bothering the old Tolson coven and she wouldn't be paying Fitzroy to find her books. After all, a coven or a mentor had plenty of books to share with a student.

So, in desperation, Elsie hired Fitzroy and scoured bookstores for every possible written word on the subject of witchcraft. Probably only found one good book in fifty, but that would be better than zero. Whether Fitzroy was truly taken with her, under the sway of a spell, or nothing more than a man who saw an opportunity to make some dough, Drummond couldn't be sure, but he didn't think it mattered much. Fitzroy's job was simply to find the books.

On the other side of this situation, there was Clarence Tunk. He had a recent interest in the occult. Perhaps growing to something like an obsession. He probably thought Fitzroy was a kindred spirit, probably had no idea the man he snookered out of a book now and then actually worked for a witch.

Until one day, Clarence got ahold of a book — something special that Fitzroy recognized right away, something Fitzroy knew Elsie wanted. In fact, when he told Elsie about the book, she had to have it. Or perhaps Clarence tried to sell it to Fitzroy at an exorbitant price. Or perhaps Clarence actually knew about Elsie and tried to circumvent Fitzroy altogether. Went straight to the young witch and offered her the book. Whatever the particulars, the result remained the same. That night, either Elsie or Fitzroy or both crept into the Triumph Picture House and murdered Clarence. They then cleaned down the room and took all the books — including the one Elsie sought from the start.

Drummond's main problem with this theory — why cut apart the body? No matter how novice a witch she was, she would already know destroying a corpse that way would not help in any spell. No matter how novice a criminal Fitzroy was, he would already know that making a spectacle of a corpse only brought more attention to the case.

When Elsie parked near her home, Drummond continued pondering this sticking point as he drove back to the office. He grabbed a pre-dinner of whiskey and water before sitting back in his chair and setting his hat over his face. No matter what logical or reasonable scenario he could come up with, he didn't see any sense in the final act of desecrating

Clarence's body. He needed more information, and better, a new line of approach. Otherwise, he would be stuck following Elsie around another day. Not a pleasant thought.

DRIFTING OFF TO SLEEP while thinking through a case happened often. Especially when aided with whiskey on an empty stomach. Drummond might have made it to morning, might have awoken with a thick tongue, an aching head, and an overall sense of tiredness — the usual morning routine — but the cold startled him to consciousness, and his woozy brain wondered if he had left a window open. As he cleared up enough to think, he recognized that specific cold — not the chill of Mother Earth, but the frosty sensation of a ghost. Clarence was back.

Moonlight painted the floorboards with the window pattern. Drummond thought about turning on the lights but held back. Instead, he flicked a match against the bottom of his shoe, and as he lit a cigarette, he surveyed the room.

Nothing.

"You wake me up for a progress report?" Drummond took a drag and puffed the smoke out to the side. "I found Elsie Gerald." Did the room get colder? "She seems eager to learn witchcraft without the help of witches. Maybe you can find some way to tell me how you're connected to her? What do you say?"

No answer.

Either Clarence lacked the strength to manifest visibly or he had decided to play games. The answer to that, however, came fast. A raging wallop of energy smashed into Drummond's chest, toppling him back over his chair. The cigarette spewed into the air and landed on the floor. Drummond slapped his hand against it, trying to stop a fire from catching, while Clarence unleashed.

The ghost remained unseen, but his anger blazed a trail throughout the office. Papers flew into the air, books shot off their shelves, the client chairs lifted to the ceiling and splintered onto the floor. Drummond's phone crashed off the desk with a ring while his coffee mug cracked plaster off the wall.

Clambering to his feet, Drummond said, "Stop it. I can't afford to fix all of this."

Like a torpedo cutting through the waves, Clarence shot through the room, knocking aside anything in his path — a path that led straight to Drummond. The ghost plowed through the detective. A frigid shot infiltrated Drummond's gut, bruised his ribs, and raked out his back. The hit sent him against the bookshelf, banging his head on the wood, causing a flash of light in his eyes before the office spun.

Then, quiet. This squall of ghostly power finished in a rush like it had begun, leaving newspaper pages and file folders fluttering down like autumn leaves.

CHAPTER 5

WHEN THE DIM GRAY of morning arrived, Drummond decided to take a walk around the block. Clear his head, go over the case, figure out a next step. Halfway along, he remembered the slip of paper from Clarence's room. The symbol on it looked like something a novice witch might draw — an attempt at the real thing, but incorrect and a bit sloppy.

Drummond hurried back to his office. From the bookshelf, he brought out a street atlas for North Carolina cities — one of the first acquisitions he had ever made when he hung out his shingle. Slumping over the large book, he dug into the work. Usually, research of any kind filed down on every nerve in his body. He would squirm in his seat, itching to knock on doors, interview suspects, stakeout a location — anything that made him feel as if he made progress. But this time, he actually enjoyed to work. He couldn't point to why, but something about hunting down all the possible Tobias Streets that had addresses ending in 72 felt like tailing a good lead. Each step closed in on answers — even if he didn't know all the questions yet.

When he finished, an hour later, he had four complete matches written down out of fifteen Tobias Streets in the state. Two in Winston-Salem, one in Greensboro, and one in Burlington. With the day still stretching ahead of him and the frosty threat of a ghost pushing hard at his back, Drummond grabbed his hat, coat, and gun.

Okay, Elsie. Let's see what you're planning to do on Tobias Street.

A short drive, and he rolled up to the first place in Winston-Salem. He parked one house over and approached on foot. The homes on this Tobias Street had been packed in tight with little to suggest much effort had been put into their construction. Cheap to make, cheap to buy.

He knocked on the first door. A hefty woman with a cigarette in one hand and a baby in the other answered. The impatience on her face matched the disdain in her eyes as she looked him up and down. He decided to play it straight, asked her if she knew Clarence Tunk or Elsie

Gerald, and accepted her caustic denial as honest.

The second door didn't go much better. An unemployed husband well into a six-pack slushed his way through a few answers while his wife lurked several steps behind. Nothing helpful came from the exchange.

Drummond drove off to Greensboro next. That Tobias Street property had been an old warehouse. But now, only rubble remained as workers went through the process of clearing away the demolished building. He poked around a bit, searching for hints of witchcraft, but nothing jumped out to claim his attention.

That left Burlington.

The city boasted a Tobias Street on the outer-edges, deep into the wealthiest section. The further along the winding road, the larger the houses and the wider the land. When Drummond finally reached mansion number 1372, he wondered if he would have enough gas to make it back to civilization.

He pulled into a horseshoe driveway with a flowerbed centerpiece. The house rivaled a Greek temple — white stone, thick columns with fancy tops, and statues of mythic figures nestled into narrow alcoves. It reminded Drummond of something out of that book by Fitzgerald. At least, he thought it did. He never finished *Gatsby*.

Numerous delivery trucks lined the street while workers hoofed one dolly of boxes after another into the home. Drummond parked near one truck laden with produce. When two black men walked by wheeling half a pig, Drummond strolled behind and followed them straight in.

He wandered through the bustling kitchen, weaved around several maids carrying floral arrangements, and entered a side door leading to the main ballroom. The massive room had been decked out for whatever this party would celebrate, though Drummond wasn't sure rich people needed a reason. Might just be worth throwing a party now and then to say *ain't it great being rich*.

Other than an ostentatious display, however, Drummond didn't see anything that suggested this house was his target. He turned to leave, but two things stopped him cold. First, he saw that the dance floor had a special design tiled into it — a circle with a diamond in the center and four wavy lines at the compass points. Second, a man with a blue ascot, a blinding white shirt, and a bright grin that cost more than Drummond's lifetime earnings.

"Usually the party-crashers don't show up until the party actually starts," the man said. Even from several feet away, the smell of alcohol rolled ahead of him.

"Sorry to bother you. I'm a private detective, and I thought this house might be involved in something I'm working on. But I made a mistake. My apologies for barging in."

The man put out his hand. No slurring of his words, but he had certainly taken an early start on the festivities. "A private detective? How thrilling. I'm Taggart Stahl. And you are?"

"Marshall Drummond." He shook Taggart's hand and offered his business card.

But Taggart's eyes bugged wide. "Marshall Drummond? *The* Marshall Drummond? Why, it is a great honor to meet you. I've enjoyed following your work."

"My work?"

"Oh, come now. How many people, detectives or not, spend their days handling cases that involve those things we cannot see? I consider myself a watcher, personally." Stahl tittered. "Like most people that are fascinated by the occult, I'm also too cowardly to actually jump into the fray of it all, you see. But you, well, those of us in the know have all heard about the man willing to face down a witch, fight back a ghost, and break a curse or two."

"I didn't realize anybody had noticed." Drummond held still. Any movement and his disgust would spew out either in words or expression. His cases dealt with people in bad situations, people traumatized by the supernatural, people fearing their lives would be cursed for eternity. It was not entertainment for the rich. His eyes ticked around the room. Nobody appeared to be listening — too much work to be done.

"It's not easy, I admit, to follow a career of somebody in the shadows. Perhaps that's part of the excitement of it all. Hunting down every morsel of information in hopes that I'll glean some greater picture of what has occurred." Stahl's head turned toward the sound of clicking heels and a stern woman's voice. "Well, so much for having an enthralling conversation about witchcraft. That would be my sister, Kennedy. If you're in luck, she'll turn to another room before we see her."

"I take it she's in charge of the party."

"And everything else in my life. Apparently, I lack the aptitude for organization. But she'll be ordering me to go do something in a moment. Ironic that the least fun person I know puts on the best parties. Still, what a pall on this momentous meeting. And I so wanted to offer you a drink and hear your incredible stories. I'm sure you have many."

Drummond would have preferred torture by rusty saw over listening to Taggart Stahl blather any further, but he had a job to do. At least, he could make one final jab for the case. "I'm afraid I have to go, and it seems you have work, too. By the way, you wouldn't happen to know the name Elsie Gerald?"

"No. Is she involved in your case?"

"I don't know. What about a man named Clarence Tunk?"

Taggart made a show of thinking — actually put a finger to his cheek and rolled his eyes toward the ceiling. "Tunk. Hmmm. Sorry. I don't recall that name. Is he part of your case?"

"You have nice day, Mr. Stahl. Enjoy your party."

Snapping his fingers, Taggart's face opened as if he had discovered a new continent. "Wait, I do know that name. He worked some of our events, I think. Helped clean up the place after."

"When was the last time he worked here?"

"I haven't the foggiest notion. You'd have to ask Kennedy, and she's rather busy at the moment. But I have a wonderful idea." From his pocket, he produced a thick, black envelope and handed it to Drummond. "You are now officially invited to tonight's gathering. I insist you come. My sister may be a pain in the backside putting this together, but she does an amazing job. It'll be a peachy blast, no doubt. And if not, there will be plenty to drink. You must come and share at least one of your many adventures with us."

"I'm not sure I should."

"Nonsense. And since my sister will be there, you can ask her all the questions you want then. It'll be perfect for you and a great honor for me."

Pocketing the invitation, Drummond tipped his hat. "In that case, the honor will be mine."

"Oh, and please, bring a date along. The more, the merrier, of course," Stahl said with the merriest of smiles.

"I'll see what I can do."

"Black tie, of course."

"How else would you have a party?"

Taggart's amused grin dropped when his sister called out his name. With a guilty wink, he hurried away, snatching several glances at Drummond as if afraid the detective was an apparition that would disappear and never return.

Back in his car, headed toward Winston-Salem, Drummond tried to make sense of Taggart Stahl. Between the symbol on the floor and Taggart's admission of an interest in the occult, Drummond knew the mansion on Tobias Street matched the address Clarence Tunk had left behind on a torn paper. But if Taggart connected to this, why did the man pretend not to know Clarence? And why would he invite Drummond to the party? Could he really be so interested in a detective of the occult that he would ignore all the obvious signs to get away? Or maybe the man had been too drunk to make a good decision?

Drummond's thoughts returned to Clarence, trying to piece together a connection. The best he could come up with — Taggart told the truth that Clarence had been hired along with the rest of the help for the party. He was a janitor, after all, and somebody would be needed to clean the bathrooms, if nothing else. That suggested Taggart may have been honest when he said he didn't really know Clarence. But if that were true, why would Clarence tear apart the address of a good job? Lots of possibilities came to mind, but none backed with any evidence — or even a gut feeling.

Once he arrived in Winston-Salem, he drove across town to Holdsworth Tailors. Several years back, Drummond had helped Mr. Holdsworth out of jam involving a haunted basement and a dead witch. The old man paid well but also promised to help Drummond if he ever could. Well, tonight he could. And less than an hour later, Drummond left the store with a tuxedo on loan and a favor called in.

One thing remained — a date.

On his way to Moe's Books, Drummond picked up a half-dozen carnations from a lady selling flowers on a streetcorner. As he gave the lady two bits, he wondered how fast he would go belly up continuing to take on cases that didn't pay anything. Ghosts made for terrible clients.

"Well, well," Miriam Rosen said when Drummond entered the store. "Didn't think I'd ever see you again."

She sat at the little desk to the side, her dark eyes burning through the air. Drummond hated to admit it, but he felt a jump in his chest. Like he was happy to hear her voice. No, it was more than that. Something stirred deep in his core. Something that hadn't been awake since a lovely woman named Catalina had been in his life.

"You going to just stand their gaping at me?" Miriam asked.

Snapping back his focus, Drummond offered the flowers. "These are for you."

"I figured that out a few minutes ago." She smelled them and curled her lips. "Nice."

"There's a party tonight. Big one at a mansion in Burlington. I was hoping you might join me there."

A sharp laugh escaped her. Then she caught the look in his eye. "Oh. You're serious. Maybe I wasn't clear last time. You and your rich friends are not going to want me around." She put a hand to her mouth, and in a loud whisper, she added, "I'm Jewish."

"You're also classy, smart, and I'll bet you fill out a cocktail dress like a movie star."

"I doubt your friends will care about anything beyond the Jewish part."

Drummond clicked his tongue. "Probably not. But then, they aren't my friends. I don't know any rich people."

"You're crashing the party?"

"No, no, I've got an invitation. It's more of a professional visit. But I still need a date, and I still would like that date to be you." Drummond felt a trickle of sweat run down his side. It had been a long time since he had to work this hard or feel this nervous over a lady.

She came around the desk and leaned on the front edge. With a piercing stare, she observed him, and he wondered if this was how suspects felt when he interrogated them. But he had nothing to feel guilty over — at least, nothing regarding her.

At length, she sagged with a huff. "These are lovely flowers, and I thank you for the offer for what I am sure would be a fascinating evening. But nothing has changed from the last time we talked. My father would never consent to have me dating a *goy*."

"What's that?"

"You. A *goy* is a gentile. A non-Jew."

"Is your father here?"

She nodded. "In the back."

Drummond peeked down an aisle that stretched into ominous darkness. "If I can convince him to allow this sacrilegious event, would you be willing to go?"

"Anybody capable of changing Papa's mind on something like that — I would have to go just to find out how you did it."

"Then I guess I have no choice." Removing his fedora, Drummond headed to the back.

Mr. Rosen sat in a lumpy armchair paging through a dusty volume. His head bent low as he struggled to read the type on the page despite his heavy prescription glasses. When he heard Drummond's steps, he looked up, his jowls wobbling, and he offered a welcoming smile.

"Back for more on witchcraft. I forget names, sometimes faces, but I always remember the books people purchase. Of course, you had an eye on more than my books."

Drummond flustered, not expecting the old man to call out his interest in Miriam. "Um, that's what I wanted to ask you about?"

"More about Mr. Fitzroy? I told you all I can."

"No." Drummond held back his relief — not spotted yet. Of course, he had to admit his interest, but at least, he could approach it on his terms. "Everything's fine with that. I don't need to bother you about him."

"And how are you enjoying it? The book you bought."

"Haven't started yet. Been busy with work."

"Mr. Fitzroy again? You must be careful. One shouldn't let work get in the way of the pleasures of life, and reading a book is near the top of the list of great pleasures."

"Except I can't afford books without work."

"A dilemma we all face." Mr. Rosen chuckled as he set his book aside. "I'm afraid I don't have much more on witches unless you want fiction, and we're done with the Mr. Fitzroy business. So, what can I help you with today?"

Clearing his throat, Drummond said, "I came to ask about your daughter."

Mr. Rosen's mirth vanished. He gave his head a firm shake. "I'm sure you're a good lad, but I cannot permit you to see her in that way."

"I only need her as my date this one time. I have to go to this party for a work matter. There's nothing romantic about it."

He gazed up to study Drummond. "I can't tell if you believe that, but I'm no fool. When you looked at her before, you look at her a lot. I know that look. A father sees too many of that look upon his daughter — even if she's ugly, and my daughter is not ugly. I'm sorry, but for you, she's not available."

"If it's because I'm not Jewish, I understand, but —"

"No," Mr. Rosen said with the sharpness of a blade. "You've not been there. You haven't seen what's going on. We left Germany only a few years ago. 1938. Already they make things bad for us. Some of my family went to Canada. Some to England. But others refused to believe it could get any worse. But it has. I read the papers now, and over here you're told about poor Poland or Austria. But about us, nothing. We're supposedly refugees being relocated because of the ongoing conflicts. Lies. The Jewish papers have all the truth you need. You want to know what's really going on over there? Murder. The Germans are killing Jews for nothing more than being Jewish. And nobody says a word. Not the papers. Not the government."

"I've heard rumors, but most people can't believe it could be true."

"It's very true. It's also true that most people simply don't want to hear about it because they don't want to do anything about it. Easier on the conscience to pretend not to know. So, the answer is *no,* Mr. Drummond. You will not be seeing my daughter for the precise reason that I cannot trust anybody not Jewish — not with most precious Miriam."

Mr. Rosen dropped back in his chair, grabbed his book, and acted as if he could read it with ease. His face had puffed red, and he breathed heavily while turning a page — apparently, he could speedread, too. Drummond wanted to say something more, but the message couldn't be clearer.

He walked back up the aisle to find Miriam sitting at the desk. Setting his hat on, he said, "I don't think he likes me much."

She shrugged. "I warned you."

"Give him a little time and he'll warm up to me. Maybe one or two hundred years."

"Lucky for you I'm thawing a bit quicker." She put out her hand. "Good day, Mr. Drummond. I hope you'll visit us again sometime."

When he gently shook her hand, she pressed a piece of paper against his palm. He left the store and walked a full block before stopping to see what he held — more out of habit than any fear of being followed. In his hand, he found the torn half of a stationary note. It read — *Public Library. 7:30.*

He glanced down the street, half-expecting to find Miriam standing outside her bookstore. He saw only the crowd, but he smiled anyway.

CHAPTER 6

DRUMMOND HAD BEEN TO A FEW SWANK PARTIES over the years, but nothing prepared him for the audacious display of wealth the Stahls had pitched upon the quiet town of Burlington. From the uniformed valets to the uniformed caterers, from the dazzling chandeliers to the impressive ice sculptures beneath them, from the string quartet greeting arrivals in the lobby to the twelve-piece big band serving the dancers in the ballroom — walking through the Stahl mansion provided one moment of awe after another. Through it all, Drummond's pulse beat hard. But it had been doing so since he picked up Miriam at the library. The party only made it worse.

"Quite a shindig," she said, one hand holding his arm.

"Don't start thinking this is a regular occurrence. This ain't my life. I'm mixing business and pleasure tonight, that's all."

"Well, I hope I'm not the business."

He winked at her. "Never."

From the moment he watched her walk to the car, Drummond knew he had lost any fight against treating her as part of work. She wore a simple, straight dress that stopped just shy of her heels. Ivory with thin straps over bare shoulders, a choker of pearls, and elbow-length gloves — she shined. She also made him look like he belonged no matter how uncomfortable he felt.

"Marshall!" Taggart Stahl's distinct voice called out.

Drummond marveled that anybody could pick out an individual man in this sea of penguins, but he guessed the rich man's eye became accustomed to black tie events. Heck, some supposedly wore a tux every night for dinner.

"I'm so glad you came," Taggart said, taking several unsteady steps before he reached them. He had his hair slicked. From the champagne in his hand and the glaze on his face, he looked slicked all around.

"Don't call me Marshall. Only my mother does that." Drummond shook the man's hand and introduced Miriam.

"Lovely to meet you," Taggart said, making a ridiculous bow before kissing her gloved hand. "You look positively fetching, as my mother would say."

"Thank you for the invitation. This is a wonderful party."

"That's all my sister's doing. She's the brains behind these little get-togethers." He glanced around before leaning in. "Truth is — I don't even know what we're celebrating."

Sharing his conspiratorial whisper, Miriam said, "I won't tell a soul."

Laughing, Taggart sloshed his champagne. "Oh, Marshall, this one is quite impressive. I hope you both have a delightful evening. I must go play my role of gracious host, but perhaps we can meet later tonight. I'd love to show you my private collection of occult curiosities."

Drummond bristled at the man's cavalier mention of the occult — as well as using the name *Marshall* again. "Sounds grand," he said, and the words felt foolish in his mouth. "I never got to meet your sister. Kennedy, right? Where is she? I'd like to talk with her."

Either too drunk or too foolish, Taggart merely bowed again. "I must bid you adieu for now."

In seconds, their host disappeared amongst the other black-suited partygoers. Drummond wanted to scout around the ballroom, and if he could, meander through the house a bit. He didn't expect to find anything glaringly obvious like a photo of Taggart and Clarence after a rousing tennis match or even a school photo proving they were in the same graduating class together. No, their lives were so far removed from each other that the only thing making sense to Drummond would be Clarence hired to clean up this place. But home cleaning — especially mansion cleaning — that was usually the realm of maids, not janitors. Still, a stroll through part of the house might turn up something useful.

Before he could guide Miriam toward one of the back exits, however, the band launched into an instrumental version of Dorsey and Sinatra's slow and popular *I'll Never Smile Again*. She clasped his hand and said, "Dance with me."

They walked onto the dancefloor. With one hand on her waist and the other holding her hand, they started to move in time with the music. She gazed up at him, and a tremor tapped across his skin.

Closing her eyes, swaying with the music, she licked her gentle lips. "I want to thank you for a wonderful evening."

"It's a bit early for that. We just got here."

"The way you spoke with our host tells me the business portion of your night has already started. I thought you should know that I had fun anyway. I've never seen a place like this before. I promise I'll remember tonight."

"Now you're making things sound like there won't be a second date."

"There won't."

"Because of your father."

"Sorry, but that's the way it is. No real point in dating a guy — even one as handsome as you — when it can't go anywhere."

"Yet you went out with me tonight."

"I was bored. That's the problem with the fellas my father wants me to date. They're all boring. But they're also my only options, and time's ticking away."

"Well, forgive me for saying so, but I think you're making some lousy choices. Your father isn't the one that's got to marry one of these guys, have their kids, all of that."

"I just want this one night." She rested her head on his chest. "If he even found out about it, it would break his heart. He's done too much for me to betray him like that."

"Then why risk it at all?"

"I guess I'm selfish."

"I don't know about that."

She held him tighter. "The war is only getting worse. Papa got us out before things became too ugly, but I saw enough. I learned."

"Learned?"

"We only have today. Now. It can all be taken away in an instant. Papa clings to tradition. Thinks the old ways will protect us. Me — I don't mind dating a *goy* tonight if I might lose everything tomorrow."

"As the *goy* in question, I'm honored. But if this is the only night you get to be free of all your family obligations and religious requirements, we better make it worthwhile." He lifted her chin, bent down, and before he kissed her, he felt a flutter in his chest. He hadn't felt that since his first time. Pausing at the sudden sensation, he saw the desperate passion in her eyes, the need to make the most of the night, and he offered a silent hope for the war to end soon. People shouldn't look like that.

She held still at first, but when he didn't pull away, she opened her mouth a little. Their lips met with a stirring blend of urgency and care as if they had cast a delicate spell. She tasted of champagne. The music swirled around them, the party disappeared, and only the touch of her lips registered in his brain. When they parted, she pressed against him. Another slow song began, Glen Miller's *Blue Orchid,* and they moved like a gentle tide. They stayed on the dancefloor for two more numbers before sidling up to the bar for a refresher. Taggart slipped in beside them.

"The two of you are a delight to watch," he said.

Drummond cocked his head. "You're watching us?"

"Oh, I watch everybody. People are fascinating to observe." Taggart downed a gin and tonic, the ice clicking in the glass as he set it on the mahogany counter. "I have to confess, though, that I dislike all of this elbow-rubbing. Not for me. It's much more of my sister's doing. But now that I've made my appearance and shaken hands with the important people that I was ordered to shake hands with, I hoped to show you my collection. That is, if you're interested."

Miriam said, "I am."

"Then I won't even bother waiting for Marshall's answer because he is a gentleman, and any gentleman worth his salt knows that what a lady wants, a lady should get. Please, follow me, and I will take the two of you to see some amazing curiosities."

Snaking through the crowd, Drummond followed Miriam as she followed Taggart out of the main ballroom. They crossed through the halls of the house — the party echoes trailing after them — until they reached a rather plain door that led to Taggart's study. The oversized room boasted two large bookcases filled with books that appeared to never have been taken off the shelves and an enormous desk filled with papers piled high but probably never looked at.

"You'll find this interesting," Taggart said. From one desk drawer, he pulled out a Colt .32 Detective Special — a revolver used by the police and rarely seen in civilian hands. "What sort of gun do you carry?"

Drummond tried to play it calm, but the careless way Taggart gestured with the weapon in hand threatened a bad outcome. He hastened over and took the Colt away under the pretense of checking it out. "Nice piece," he said, and it was. Well-crafted, nice balanced weight. He glanced at the chamber as he rolled it — four rounds. "You shoot something recently?"

"Not at all. Why?"

"You're missing a bullet."

Taggart frowned as he snatched the weapon back. "I suppose I forgot one when I loaded it." He returned the Colt to the desk before gesturing to a narrow doorway that could easily be mistaken for a storage closet. In fact, it led to a confining staircase that went downward.

They entered a miniature museum. A small room converted to

highlight Taggart's precious collection. Deep red walls with gold trim, dim lighting, several round tables dotting the layout with his unique finds under glass, and a metal door on the far end. Several macabre oil paintings hung on the walls. But what first caught Drummond's eye — odd symbols had been centered near the ceiling on each wall and above the doors. Like the symbol on the dancefloor, these bore no relation to any witch symbols he had ever come across.

Taggart stopped in front of a tattered piece of cloth. "While I'm clearly not trained enough yet in firearms, my interest in the worlds beyond our senses started several years ago. I know a lot about it, but I'm afraid I don't know enough to truly evaluate all my wonderous finds. I hope you won't see anything mundane in here, but please, be honest. If there is something that shouldn't be in here, do tell. I only want the best."

Looking at the cloth, Drummond tapped his chin. "What's this about?"

Miriam stared at him. "I thought you were a detective."

"Oh, he most certainly is," Taggart said, with a ravenous gleam, hungry for more information from his guest. "In fact, dear, your date this evening is the best detective of the unnatural world in all of North Carolina. Probably all the country. I'd venture to add the entire world, but that seems a bit grandiose, and I'm hardly one for exaggeration." His eyes widened, waiting for a pat on the head. When it didn't come, his lips rolled in and he gestured to the cloth. "This is a shroud that was worn by a witch while she burned at the stake in 1729."

"Where'd you get it?" Drummond asked.

"I bought it several years ago. My sister and I were touring Europe before things soured over there, and while in Greece, I found a little shop of odds and ends run by an old lady. All sorts of strange things for sale. Most, even to my uneducated eye, were hardly worth looking at. But when I saw this, I could practically feel the energy coming off it." He brought his face close to the shroud and inhaled deeply. "You can smell the smoke."

"Little place in Greece, huh? Did the seller tell you anything about how she got hold of this?"

"Not that one. She was rather curt. Wanted me to make my purchase and leave her store. It never occurred to me at the time, but you don't think she stole this, do you?"

"You better hope not. Specific items like this can belong to specific covens. Like heirlooms. It's part of their history. If this coven still exists, and if they ever find out you have their sister's shroud, you'll be in a lot of hot water."

"Good thing I can hire you, then."

A glass cake dome stood atop a serving platter against one wall. Like all the finds in this museum, a small lamp hung over it from the ceiling. But the display was empty.

"You going to tell me there's a ghost in there or something?" Drummond said.

A cold wash covered Taggart's features in a blink. He shook it off fast. Then: "I'm afraid I no longer have what was once a great success of my collection — cursed diamonds."

"Really?" Miriam peeked over from across the room.

"A few nicely cut diamonds — nothing rather large — but the story is that a wealthy widow, distraught and lonely, fell in love with a younger man. She wooed him, and in short time, he asked her to marry. But he had no real interest in her. Just her money. The night before the wedding, he went into her safe, took stock certificates, bonds, cash, and of course, the diamonds. In her betrayed rage, she sought out a witch and offered her own blood to curse those diamonds. You see, blood magic is one of the deadliest types of magic there is. The young man disappeared after that — for a short time, anyway. There was a search for him. Apparently, you can look up a few articles about it, if you know where it actually all happened. But they couldn't find him. Until a few weeks later, a fisherman came upon a body face down in the river."

"Do you believe the story?"

"I suppose there might be some truth to it. I can tell you one thing for certain — I've made sure never to touch them directly. Still, they were stolen from me, too. So, perhaps I was cursed."

Taggart chuckled at his misfortune, and Drummond wondered what it would be like to have so much money that losing a handful of diamonds only meant an amusing anecdote to share.

"What's this?" Miriam pointed to a shriveled ball of material on another table.

Thrilled at her interest, Taggart rushed over. "That, my dear, is an actual shrunken head. Or I should say that the man who sold it to me promised he had performed the shrinking rite himself."

As Taggart continued bestowing tale upon tale regarding various objects, Drummond's attention turned toward three jars — Egyptian Coptic jars. He glanced up at the symbols on the walls once more. They didn't look like hieroglyphs. Still, he decided not to close out the possibility that Taggart or someone in this household attempted an Egyptian rite upon poor Clarence. Although, while Drummond knew the Egyptians removed the organs, he did not recall anything about cutting off the face.

"What do you say to that, chum?" Taggart smiled at him while Miriam stood behind with a guilty expression.

"I'm sorry. I was lost in these incredible relics you have. What did you ask?"

"They are incredible, aren't they? So, yes, I was informing your better half that tomorrow evening my sister and I will be hosting a private séance. I thought you might like to attend — both of you, of course."

Straightening tall, Drummond swiped a peek at the closed, metal door. "As much as I'd like to accept, I'm afraid the lady has made it clear this is a one-time outing for us."

"Really? I'm sorry to hear that. The two of you seemed rather fond of each other."

Miriam walked over to take Drummond's hand. "You men only ever hear what you think a woman is saying instead of what she really is saying."

Drummond winked. "Perhaps you should speak slower."

"If you want to see me again, this séance would be a perfect opportunity."

He looked to Taggart. "The lady is interested."

"I should think you would be, too," Taggart said.

"Oh, I am. But I'm not sure I can make it tomorrow night. I'll send word by the afternoon, if that's okay."

"If that's what it must be, then I suppose it will have to suffice. But I do hope to see both of you there. It would make the evening special for me." Heading to the stairs, he added, "We should get back. I must make second appearances now and all of that. I'm sure you'd be happy to dance some more or drink or whatever pleases you."

With that, they returned to the main ballroom. Drummond and Miriam did enjoy a few more songs, but they each wandered off into their own thoughts. An hour later and they both concluded that the night had waned for their date. It only took a shared look and they quietly made their way to the door.

Driving back, Drummond thought about those Coptic jars. He knew he should be focusing on Miriam, and he wanted to, but his mind kept returning to those jars. And that metal door. Taggart never once explained where it led or warned them away from it or mentioned it in any manner at all.

At the library, Miriam got out and walked around to the driver's side. She leaned in the window and kissed Drummond — more than a goodnight peck, less than a goodnight offer.

"You love your work, don't you?" she said.

"Maybe. When I get a problem stuck in my head, it won't go until I deal with it."

"I guess that means we'll be going to the séance tomorrow night."

Drummond clicked his tongue. "Only if you agree to go on a real date with me. This séance will still be partly business. I want one that doesn't double as any kind of work."

"You're asking me out on a third date before we've even had the second. Sheesh, I hope you don't jump ahead in all romantic matters."

"I can take my time when I should."

"You only get a handful of dates before I have to shut you out."

"Right. Because of Papa."

"You know, you might be good at the detective thing, after all."

Drummond laughed a short burst. Then: "Pick you up at the library again? 7:30?"

"See you then."

As she walked away, Drummond waited. He watched her legs and hips, savoring each step. Taking his time.

CHAPTER 7

DURING THE HOURS before he managed to fall asleep, Drummond's mind bounced between Clarence and Miriam. Both bothered his detective's sense. To have died in such a brutal fashion meant that Clarence died for a reason. But nothing about the little information Drummond had acquired suggested any motive. Or any firm suspect. Or anything. He had a handful of disparate pieces and one symbol that made the slightest connection.

As for Miriam — she was a woman. That was enough mystery right there. But she also walked a tightrope between her father's expectations and her own youthful desires. Except it was more than that. Something bad had happened in Germany. War, of course, but something more, too. It left her with a fatalistic need to capture every moment she could before they were all snatched away.

"Then again," Drummond said to his empty office, "maybe I'm half-drunk and full of it."

He liked to think he knew a thing or two about romance. The only thing about her that he knew for sure — he couldn't kick her out of his head.

HE SHOULDN'T HAVE BEEN SURPRISED that Clarence visited him again that night. However, being wrestled out of a pleasant dream about a certain bookseller's daughter left him befuddled for a moment. He rubbed his face and tried to put the world in its proper place. But when he felt icy fingers around his neck, he woke up full and clear in seconds.

At first, his body held still, straining to breathe as the grip tightened. In the dark, he tried to see his assailant, to judge size and strength, but then his brain finally had enough information. Nobody straddled him. Nobody held him down. Nobody choked him. Those things were happening, but not a living soul was in that room except for him.

Drummond's muscles quaked down to his feet as if he stood naked on an iceberg. He felt just as alone, too. No help would be coming, and he couldn't punch his way out. Not when he couldn't strike at his enemy.

All he had was his voice.

"Clarence," he managed. "Stop."

The fingers eased. Not by much. Not enough to save his life, but enough to speak more.

"Clarence, I can't help you if I'm dead."

A deep moan erupted from all sides. The weight on Drummond's body and the vice on his throat both lifted simultaneously. Books flew off his shelves, his framed investigator's license crashed to the floor, his phone lassoed through the air until released against the wall. It rang out as it widened the hole in the plaster.

Then silence. Stillness.

"Not really helpful," he said, his voice already scratching. He knew Clarence had gone, but it felt good to say anyway.

Rubbing his neck, hoping the whiskey he had left in *Moby Dick* wouldn't burn too hot going down his injured throat, Drummond started cleaning up. One thought kept spinning in his head — he couldn't take much more of this. He had to solve the case fast or his unwanted client would kill him.

FOR THE NEXT SEVERAL HOURS, Drummond smoked and stared out at the city. He watched the sun paint the buildings with morning gold. And he thought about the case. So little to go on, yet he reviewed each tiny morsel in his head. Because that night's attack was not the act of a ghost frustrated at a lack of results. That was a ghost losing control. Drummond had heard that it could happen. A ghost could go mad in a sense and lose all connection to the world that it understood. It would become a haunting spirit, violent and destructive. The name danced on the edge of his thoughts until he saw people walking to work and it hit him — *poltergeist.*

Two facts pointed to the idea that Clarence still clung to his ghostly sanity. One, he stopped breaking up the office and didn't start again. Two, Drummond was still alive. Clarence had backed off from strangling him.

Not soon enough, Drummond thought as his bruised ribs and throat reminded him.

He glanced back at the ruins of his office. Clean up would have to wait. He had a day, maybe two, before Clarence could no longer be handled easily. Not that solving a murder and getting a ghost to move on was ever easy, but it sure beat an exorcism.

He wanted to start right away. Unfortunately, nobody would see him so early in the morning. Plus, he was hungry. And tired. He could feel the bags puffing under his eyes.

A short walk and he ended up at Telly's, a new diner only two blocks over. Most times Drummond had walked by the place, teenagers filled the booths. But no teenager would be awake with the sun still creeping to start the day. So, worth a try.

The place was packed. A line of suits and hats filled the counter, and all the booths were taken, too. Drummond tossed a nickel at the boy selling papers by the entrance and ended up at a tiny table for two jammed against the back wall near the restrooms. The waitress bounced over, took his order — coffee, eggs, toast, bacon, nothing fancy — and rushed off to deal with the next customer.

Despite the crowd, Drummond found comfort in the simple ritual of coffee and the newspaper. The aromas massaged his head, and the murmur of the starting day awakened his body. He read over the headlines — the war in Europe continued to worsen as Hitler claimed his people had a given right to take back what had always belonged to them. That argument may have made sense for parts of Austria taken during the Big One, but anybody with half-a-brain could see the man intended to use this as an excuse to takeover countries that didn't belong to him. Especially since he already had done it in Poland.

Drummond thought of Miriam. From the way she told it, he could picture the daily promises from Hitler that the Jews were being moved for their own good. They would be fed one claim after another, and somehow, they would cross their fingers and hope that this time the claims would be true. But things would only get worse. Perhaps Mr. Rosen had been right to grab his daughter and get out of the country. The States had its share of problems — especially for Jews and colored folk — but Drummond figured most of those people would be happy to stay here rather than deal with a worse situation across the ocean.

Happy? That seemed the wrong word. Miriam's smiling lips flashed in his head. Her enticing eyes called to him. Yet she always carried a somber undertone. She wanted to grasp a fleeting sense of happiness from him. That was all. Her father wanted to keep her alive, build a future, but she couldn't see how a future mattered when tomorrow might not even exist.

Maybe that was her true interest in the séance. If she could see a ghost, hear a voice from the spirit world, maybe she would get a sense of the continuity of existence. In a strange way, maybe contacting the dead would help her connect to the living — to life.

Or maybe I haven't slept enough and my brain has static. He drank more coffee.

When he got back to the office, he figured two things had to be done. For the first, he hoped it wasn't too early to call Lou. He would have preferred a visit to the police department, but neither the captain nor Lou would have appreciated seeing him stroll into the building. After a short game of phone bureaucracy with the front desk and a few choice words from Lou, he managed to get a meeting at a floral shop on 7th Street — not far from the station.

Drummond arrived ten minutes early, scoped out the place to make sure they could talk in private, and bought a half-dozen roses to give to Miriam later that night. He figured the shop should make a little something for hosting this meet.

When Lou arrived, he snapped a finger at an old Russian woman behind the counter. "The usual." The woman nodded and went into a back room. "What?" he said to Drummond's surprised look. "I have a lady friend."

"Congratulations. And please offer the lady my condolences."

"I know I brought this case to your attention," Lou said, standing amongst the petunias and lilies, "but don't start thinking I like you."

"Never crossed my mind."

"You look crappy, by the way."

"Had a rough night. Kind of related to the case. You get anywhere with it?"

Lou readjusted his suspenders before settling his bulk forward. Probably worked wonders at intimidating suspects. "If I have my way, we'll never work together again, but since ugly things happen sometimes, you better wise up. I don't owe you anything. Especially information. Only reason I'm giving you my time is so that I can end this case enough to satisfy Captain."

Drummond had a lot of thoughts on all of that, but he merely nodded. "I'll do my best to keep the scary bits away from you."

"I'm not scared. I just don't believe any of it."

"I could say that you don't *want* to believe any of it, that the entire police department pretends these things aren't happening but you all know they do, or that your true fear is Captain deciding you really are the new Detective Cooper and you'll start getting the bizarre cases all the time. I could say all of that, and I think I'd be right. Instead, however, I figure you and I need to stop insulting each other and focus on dealing with Clarence Tunk. So, how about you be a pal and tell me what you know about the guy?"

Lou raised a meaty fist as his face tightened. "I swear, you better pray Cooper gets back to taking on this crap. Otherwise, I'll send you into the hospital more than once." He held still, waging an internal war, until he finally lowered the threat and spit out a sigh. "Fine. Didn't take much digging to find out about Clarence. He wasn't trying to hide himself cause he ain't got much to his name worth hiding. You already saw his place. Things don't get much better for him. No bank account. A grocery tab near the theater that he pays monthly. Not much of a drinker. The only interesting thing is that he has a sister."

"Let me guess her name. Virginia?"

Folding his arms, Lou flashed a cocky grin. "Nope. Not a name. It's the state."

"How's that?"

"According to the theater owner where Clarence worked, he wrote on his job application that he came from Lynchburg, Virginia. So, I called the local department to see what I could see. Thought a guy making the effort to live as quiet as he did and then got killed the way he did might have a sheet. Turned out mostly clean — just a shoplifting charge from when he was a teen — but when I explained what happened to Clarence, the police I spoke with got nervous. Said Clarence has a sister in Lynchburg. Her name's Vera."

"Vera from Virginia. What's her story?"

"Two things worth telling. Seems that while Clarence lived here in squalor, sister Vera had quite a comfortable life. Not rich, but according to the police, ol' Clarence had been sending her money every week. Lynchburg's a small enough town that people noticed. They all thought it was a local boy done good situation. But also, according to the police, there had been a few complaints against her about not paying bills. So, maybe she overextended or maybe she never had that much to start and only put on an act."

"And the second thing?"

"That's the part that got them nervous. See, Vera walks into the station a week ago saying her brother's life was in danger. Said that she heard he was getting involved in some dark stuff, she thought witchcraft, and that she had a dream he would be dead. She wanted the police to call down to Winston and have us check up on the guy."

"I take it the Lynchburg police never called."

"Why would they? This was all over a dream, at the time, and there was no crime committed."

Drummond didn't like anything he heard. "Any chance you came across a handful of diamonds?"

"Diamonds? No. What are you on about now?"

"Nothing. Taggart Stahl said he was out some diamonds, and I thought maybe Clarence stole them."

"Well, if he did, he didn't talk about it."

"I don't think he did it, though. From what you've said, Vera would've been noticeable if an increase in the money came her way, and he didn't seem particularly fond of spending money on himself. I don't see why he would risk stealing diamonds, anyway. Doesn't fit with anything we know about him."

Puckering his mouth as if he had eaten a bad lemon, Lou said, "I hate to hear the answer, but I've got to ask — you think he was doing all this for the … weird part of it?"

"Relax. Whatever Clarence had gotten involved with, it wasn't witchcraft."

"He seemed to think it was. At least, his sister thought that he thought so."

"Yeah. Sounds like he was getting suckered on a grift of some kind."

"Maybe he figured that out. Got angry and went to confront the grifter. Things went bad, and he ends up dead."

"Maybe. But why desecrate the body like that?"

"Sending a message to others is usually the case."

"With mobsters, sure. But with Clarence Tunk, a picture house janitor?"

"Then a cover up. Make it so gruesome nobody would ever want to start looking in the right place. Heck, if we didn't bother with you as a final stone to turn, this case would already be filed away cold." Lou got his flowers — a full dozen. "Your turn. What have you found out?"

Drummond glanced from beneath his hat. "You really want to know?"

"Of course not. But that don't make a difference. Spill it."

He spilled. Glossing over the details he knew would make Lou uncomfortable to the point of not listening, he explained that Clarence had an unknown connection to the Stahl family in Burlington, that they pretended not to know him, and that Taggart Stahl and his sister had a deep interest in the occult. He excluded all mention of Fitzroy, Elsie Gerald, and books on magic. Nothing from that angle would sit well with Lou. But Drummond also admitted that he had been invited to a séance that night and planned to attend.

"Those ain't real, though," Lou said. "Right?"

"I don't think so, but I haven't dealt with any before. One certain thing we do know — a lot of séances are faked. They're a form of grift."

CHAPTER 8

THOUGH HE HAD MOST OF THE DAY STILL AHEAD, Drummond felt the pinch of time. He briefly considered that perhaps Elsie Gerald worked with the Stahls in some way, but he could find no evidence pointing to a connection — other than Clarence. No, that was simply his brain trying to make matters easier. Put the competing suspects into one lump. Best thing to do would be to clear one of the suspects. Narrow things down.

He had an idea how to do just that.

Checking his watch — 9:07 am — he called Moe's Books. Thankfully, Miriam answered in a soft, charming, touched-by-morning voice. When she heard him, she said, "I know I'm irresistible but you can wait until tonight."

"Sorry, but this is a business call. I'm hoping you can help me out. The books Clarence Tunk recently purchased — I'm looking for the titles of the rarest or most expensive. The ones that stand out as having real value."

"I can look, but Papa would know the answer better than I would."

"Somehow, I doubt he'll be too accommodating for me."

She snickered. "Probably right. What would you have done if he had answered the phone instead of me?"

"Hung up like a frightened schoolboy and never called again."

That got more of a laugh. He also heard pages turning as she looked through the financial register. While he waited, Drummond grabbed a few books off the floor and set them back on the shelves. Not much of an effort at cleaning up Clarence's mess, but at least Drummond had tried.

"Two purchases stand out," she said. "Both were the last ones he made."

Drummond grabbed a pencil and paper. "I'm listening."

"First was *The Complete Witchcraft Compendium* by Xavier Milton. That's a recent publication according to the entry here — 1937. And it's expensive. Ten dollars. But the other book is both expensive and rare. It's just called *Our Spells* by Madame Collette Bardet, and it's from 1782."

"Anything else? Maybe what the books looked like on the cover?"

"I never saw them. I'm just reading the register entry."

He wrote both titles down. "Thank you, doll. I'll see you tonight."

"I'm counting on it."

Pocketing the slip of paper, Drummond headed for his car. The idea that he had two witches to visit and a séance to attend all in one day would have turned his stomach if he allowed himself to think about it. Instead, he kept his mind on the one step in front of him. Unfortunately, that step was visiting the first witch.

DRUMMOND DROVE TO HIGH POINT for this unsettling task of the day. The drive would take forty minutes, and that time gave him the opportunity to consider what these books meant, go over the photos in his head, and consider using one of the best sources he had — Leroy Parker.

Leroy lived alone, deep in the woods to the south, and he had a strong interest in the occult. He had helped Drummond numerous times and would be thrilled to jump aboard this case, too. But Drummond had to be careful. Using a man like Leroy over and over meant more than relying on the man for answers. It also meant failing to learn other ways to obtain information. Get too comfortable with any one behavior — even as simple as using the same source — and bad things tended to happen. Drummond never wanted to see what that would mean for Leroy.

When he parked on a side road off North Main Street, Drummond questioned if he had made the right choice. He only knew of Madame Magnolia by reputation — an unusual witch with less of a mean streak and more of an open heart. But that didn't mean he should lower his guard. All witches were witches. They played by specific rules. Then again, looking at Madame Magnolia's home, Drummond wondered if some witches ever bothered with the rulebook.

She lived in a three-story, brick townhouse with manicured hedges pacing a wrought-iron fence that outlined her property. The front door had been made of oak, stood a foot higher than standard, and boasted a massive lion's head knocker. As Drummond climbed the porch to buzz the doorbell, he noticed the steps were white marble. Just like the Stahl mansion.

Ever since that nasty business of being hunted down and burned at the stake for centuries, witches tended to hide their activities. More importantly, they hid the fruits of those activities. With experience, witchcraft could be quite profitable. Clearly, Madame Magnolia had a lot of experience. But her willingness to flaunt her wealth probably put her at odds with other witches.

Elsie also broke with the rules, secretly taking books and, presumably, teaching herself witchcraft without the rest of the community knowing. Unfortunately for her, she lacked the reputation and skill to break the rules with impunity. No matter what she might think of herself or what she hoped to attain, for now, Elsie Gerald was no Madame Magnolia.

Drummond buzzed the doorbell again, and when he contemplated giving that giant lionhead knocker a try, a tall, elderly gentleman answered the door. He wore a fine suit and moved with the stiffness of propriety. He had dead eyes. Glaring down over his large nose without lowering his head, this butler said, "Madame Magnolia meets only by appointment."

"What luck. I have an appointment."

"You most assuredly do not. If you insist on continuing this belligerence, I'll be forced to contact the police."

"Go right ahead." Drummond dug a business card from his pocket and held it out. "While we wait, please let the witch know that Marshall Drummond is here to see her. Since I'm pretty much the only detective in North Carolina dealing with the supernatural, I suspect she'll know who I am."

The butler turned his mouth further down, nearly off his face, before he snatched the card away. "Wait here." He closed the front door.

After seven minutes, the door reopened and the perturbed butler stepped aside. Drummond entered, and the butler gestured to a stiff-backed chair next to a coat rack. He did not offer to take Drummond's coat or hat.

"No, no," Drummond said, taking care of it himself, "I wouldn't want to bother you from not doing your job."

"Sit. You'll be summoned momentarily."

Before Drummond could throw off a comment about not being a dog, the butler walked away. Fine. If it meant getting to chat with Madame Magnolia, he could play along. He sat in the chair and waited.

He pulled out a pack of cigarettes but didn't see an ashtray anywhere. Not even a ritzy standing one that the wealthy often scattered in every room. In fact, this lobby boasted only the coat rack, the chair, an oil painting of tobacco fields, and a plain side table. Strange and sparse decorations for both a witch and the rich. The latter liked to flaunt all that they could afford with big displays of artwork and style. The former tended to collect everything they could get their hands on as if piles of newspapers and jars full of rabbit feet equaled a fabled dragon hoard.

Somebody started playing the piano in a nearby room. First running scales and then performing *Chopsticks*. Drummond followed the sound through a sitting room with high-backed teakwood chairs and into the adjoining room with a baby grand. A girl, probably around eight, sat on the bench and drilled more scales. She wore a blue dress with a blue bow in her hair.

"That's my niece," a sweet voice said from behind.

As Drummond turned, so did the niece. Standing in the archway between rooms, an old woman smiled without showing her teeth. She was a frail, tiny thing — under five feet and pushing a hundred pounds after a seven-course meal. But the sharpness in her eyes told the true story. This was not a woman to be toyed with. That sharpness — it promised not only intelligence, but ruthlessness.

"Madame Magnolia," Drummond said, thrusting out his hand.

She bent low and put her arms wide. "Come on, Sylvia. Give Auntie a hug."

The young piano player rushed over to embrace the witch. "Did you hear me playing? I'm getting better."

"Of course. Whenever we practice at something, we get better. Isn't that right, Mr. Drummond?"

"That's usually the way of it," he said.

With a kiss on the cheek, she turned her niece back to the piano. "You go on and finish. I've got to speak with this man, and when I'm done, maybe we'll have some ice cream. Does that sound good?"

"Ice cream always sounds good to me," Sylvia said, rushing off to finish her practice.

Without looking back, Madame Magnolia said, "Mr. Carlson, we'll be in the study. Please bring some refreshment."

"Yes, ma'am," the butler said, only a few feet away behind Drummond.

Happy that he didn't flinch, Drummond pushed on ahead to follow the witch. He had never heard the butler approach. Either Mr. Carlson walked with incredible stealth or he had some unnatural help. Drummond found both answers unsettlingly plausible.

Madame Magnolia entered a dark wood study with a proper desk in the center, a clawfoot couch that ran the entire length of the back wall, two tall windows that gazed upon the downtown street, and a wall of books without an ounce of dust. The large room had plenty of floorspace — wide open floor. Not a single pile of clutter.

She lowered on the edge of the couch near the middle and gestured to the spot next to her. Drummond sat. Holding statue still, she waited as Mr. Carlson appeared with a rolling cart. A tray of fruit and cheeses sat on the middle shelf, and the tray on top had two tumblers of brandy.

As he moved to set these out, the witch put up her hand. "No need. We can handle it ourselves. Besides, from the look in Mr. Drummond's eyes, I don't think he wants to stay too long."

Mr. Carlson curled a disgusted lip at Drummond before making a slight bow and exiting the room. After a moment of stillness, Madame Magnolia tilted her head toward the brandy and waited for Drummond. He stared back at her. But he saw no upside in provoking the woman — not when he had come with his hand out — so he walked over, grabbed the tumblers, and passed one to her. A few polite sips and he set it back on the tray. Good stuff, but he hadn't come for the booze.

"You have a lovely home," he said, not sure how to play things just yet.

The witch stiffened as if insulted, the danger behind her eyes piercing out, but in the next breath, the polite hostess returned. "It serves its purpose. I think I'd be happier with some land, but if I bought a mansion with a couple dozen acres, there would be other problems."

"From the witch community?"

"Some. But I'd draw the attention of the Hull family, and they were a painful group to handle even before they controlled the use of magic in the area. Worse, I might get noticed by the Reynolds family which would bring my life into a whole different type of scrutiny."

"Not interested in hobnobbing with the richest people in all of North Carolina? Probably one of the richest in the country."

She tapped a ring against her glass — she wore seven — and glanced out the window. "I like quiet. I don't want notoriety. I don't seek out trouble. Dealing with the rich tends to ruin all of that." She sipped her brandy. Then: "So does dealing with you."

"Yet we're still chatting."

"I didn't become successful by throwing every desperate soul out of the house."

Drummond grimaced. "I suppose the desperate are your best customers."

"Certainly the most lucrative. When I think about how much you know of my kind, I can only assume you're quite desperate. Or insane. Why else would you dare come talk with me, seek out a deal with me? Not that I'm complaining. Just incredulous."

"You worried I'm playing some kind of angle?"

"Dear, I'm old, not stupid. Everybody's always playing an angle. Now, stop digging for free information like a pig digging for a tasty morsel and start spitting out what you want."

The large townhouse grew around him. The long couch spread further along the impossible walls, the tall windows stretched to the infinite ceiling, and this little woman loomed overhead. Just a feeling, he promised himself, but part of him would not have been shocked if the world had grown around him. Or if he had shrunk.

Shaking off the weird sensation, he said, "I need a ghost ward."

"I see. How much do you think such a thing is worth?"

Straight into negotiations. That reminded him that these deals existed because witches wanted things, too. Sometimes they were desperate themselves. Her sudden impatience cracked off the last of the strange feeling she had induced, leaving Drummond sharp and ready. "Might be worth some information."

Madame Magnolia rocked forward with eager eyes. "Not offering money. You really do know about witches."

"Part of the job. Probably wouldn't be alive if I hadn't learned a thing or two. Now, I need the ward to be the most powerful you can make. The kind that can protect me from a ghost that's lost his way."

"You think you have information that valuable?"

"Once I have the ghost ward, I'll tell you what I know."

"That hardly seems fair."

"When has negotiating with a witch ever been fair?"

She tittered. "That's the deal you want? I make you a ghost ward, and in exchange you tell me something, but you won't say what about. Doesn't sound like I'm getting much of anything."

Drummond sipped more of the brandy. "I'm confident you'll feel otherwise once you hear. It's the kind of information that might help you in dealing with the witch community. Maybe even ease a few minds that don't approve of the way you live."

"I'm hearing a lot of *might* and *maybe*, but nothing to make me want to accept this deal. Here's what I'll do. I will make the ghost ward, and I will hold it. Then you will tell me what you know. To be clear, that means you tell me everything this is all about. If I'm satisfied, I'll give you the ward."

"Now it seems like I'm the one not getting anything. Just a big *if*."

"You came to me. Leave and my day can go on as peaceful and happy as it was before you got here. I've got a date for ice cream, after all."

He walked into this knowing he didn't have much wiggle room. He just didn't expect it to tighten so fast. Part of him had hoped to trick her into giving the ward over before he said a word. Then he would have offered up the bare minimum. Should have known better than to try fooling a witch.

"Fine," he said.

Sliding off the couch, she put out her hand. "Your finger, please. Doesn't matter which one."

He hesitated.

"I'm not going to cut it off," she said, both amused and insulted.

He poked out his pinkie. Fast as a jaguar, she rushed forward and snatched hold of the finger. Her other hand whipped around as a fist with one of her many rings led the charge. Drummond had a split second to notice the tiny tack at the end of the ring before it pricked his finger. A blood droplet formed. Madame Magnolia used another ring to smear the blood against its set amethyst.

Trying to keep the fear from reaching his voice, Drummond said, "Blood magic? You never said it would require that."

"You didn't ask."

"Isn't my blood more than enough payment?"

"That's not the deal we made. The ward for worthy information. You said you wanted the most powerful ghost ward I could make. Well, that requires blood magic."

Without another word, she left him alone in the room. He watched the door, his chest tight and breath held. Waiting for the return of Mr. Carlson. But when no perturbed butler entered the room, Drummond reached into his coat pocket for a cigarette.

He broke the first one he pulled out. Dropped the second. Once he got it in his mouth, he needed three attempts before he could strike a match.

Exhaling a long stream of smoke, he tried to regain some composure. He had confronted witches before. He had even made deals with them. This witch, however, nicked at a primal nerve within. The kinder she behaved, the calmer she spoke, the more he wanted to bolt from that house.

His eyes scanned over the numerous books in the room. Reading the titles, he wondered if he might stumble upon the two stolen from Clarence Tunk's room under the Triumph. That would have made the case easier and saved him a trip. He found plenty of unsettling titles — *The Chaotic Soul, Curses for Beyond the Grave, True Death* — but no such luck with Tunk's books.

Another shaking drag, knocking the cigarette halfway down, and he peeked at the door again. Every synapse in his brain screamed to leave. Forget the ward. Get out.

He stood. Yeah. Leave now, regroup, figure out a better angle.

But the tiny old witch filled the doorway as she returned.

"That was fast," he said, his voice not quite normal.

"I've made a lot of wards in my time."

She ambled toward the long couch and sat with a little hop. In her hand, she held a green, stone pendant, rectangular with a leather strap to tie around the neck. A pentagram had been carved at the top and clear witch symbols read vertically down. At the bottom, a dark bump marked the end like a period. Drummond knew that bump contained his blood.

Finishing his cigarette, he looked for some place to stub it out. When she offered no help, he pressed it against his shoe and held the butt in his hand. The grandmotherly look on her face did not mask the witchy look in her eyes — she wanted payment and would not be distracted.

Drummond swallowed down the concerns battling within and stayed focused on appeasing the witch before him. He had two directions to choose from, and it was a coin toss in his head. "You ever hear of the Stahls?" he finally said. "Brother and sister — Taggart and Kennedy Stahl. They've been running a séance scam for a bit."

She closed her hand over the ward. "That's your information? A séance scam?"

"I realize all séances are scams but —"

"Not all."

"Really?"

"In the right hands, a true séance can make a connection with a ghost. But I would have heard about the Stahls, if they had the right hands."

"Yeah, well, the part that would interest you is that they might be branching out. They've got a whole collection of occult pieces — shrunken heads, witch's shroud, and even some Coptic jars."

"Whose shroud?"

"Don't know. I only saw it briefly. Apparently, she was burned at the stake."

"Sadly, that doesn't narrow it down much. Is that it? Is that all you have to offer me?"

His temple twinged. "A witch's shroud, one worn at the time of her death, must hold energy."

"Some. Perhaps. But hardly going to make it worth more than the cloth itself. I'm sorry, but that's simply not enough." She put the ward in her pocket. Drummond felt it like losing a big bet on the ponies — all that opportunity gone in an instant. He opened his mouth, about to blurt out the name Elsie Gerald, but his detective instincts held him back. That piece of information was too valuable. But perhaps he could bring matters closer to Elsie without giving her up.

"Don't ignore this," he said. "It's more than you'd expect."

"I expect that you'll say anything to get this ward."

"A man connected to the Stahls, connected to their occult interests, was murdered recently. His body desecrated. His organs pulled out and set in three piles. Not exactly the Egyptian way, but clearly inspired by it. Now, you don't commit murder like that unless you have a good reason. I think we both know the reason. If you ignore the possibility that these people are hunting down the secrets to magic, and if it ever gets out that you could have done something to stop them but chose not to, I think the other witches around here might be a little angry. The Hull family would definitely be angry."

She took all of two seconds to think it over. "Okay, Detective, here is how you will earn this ward. You will do your job — detecting, that is — and find out if the Stahls are a serious threat to witchcraft or simply enthusiastic amateurs trying to improve their scam. I'll give you three days. The full moon arrives then, so if you betray this deal, I can cast a nasty reminder. I'll also shatter the ward."

"That sounds fair." What else could he say? Then: "You should know the murdered man is also the ghost that's bothering me. If I'm going to do this job right, I'll need that ward up front. I'll work better with it, and as you've pointed out, with a full moon, you can destroy it."

Madame Magnolia brought the ward out again and placed it in his hand. He hated the relief rushing over his body.

"Three days. Not a moment longer."

Drummond didn't wait for the butler. He gladly showed himself out.

CHAPTER 9

RETURNING TO WINSTON-SALEM, Drummond decided his visit with the witch had gone about as well as he could have hoped. For starters, she didn't put a curse on him. The deal he made only required him to do what he would have done anyway — try to solve Clarence's murder. The Stahls may not have anything to do with it, but he had offered them up to Madame Magnolia partially on a hunch, partially to keep her interested. Add the ghost ward he now had around his neck and he had to admit the whole thing went better than expected. All of which left him with a few final matters for the day.

Back at the office, Drummond grabbed the phone, spent a short time with the operator, and soon listened to the ringing of Vera Tunk's line in Virginia. He still had an hour until Elsie left for work. Gaining a better understanding of Clarence meant gaining a better understanding of why he made the choices he made, and the only name Drummond had of anybody who really knew the man was his sister.

Vera answered in a vibrant voice. No concern that the caller might be after her for unpaid bills. No worry that her brother was in danger. Nothing but the cheerfulness of a lady eager to chat away the afternoon.

But after he introduced himself as a private investigator, her tone shifted. She grew quiet. Then, in a resigned tone, she said, "He's dead, isn't he?"

"I'm afraid so."

Another pause. "You said you're a PI. Why aren't the police handling it?"

"They are. But I've been brought in to help."

Silence on the line that stretched into an uncomfortable itch. Drummond waited, let her dangle with whatever thoughts raced through her. When she finally spoke, he knew he had caught something. She sighed. "Go ahead. Ask your questions. I've got nothing to hide anymore."

Anymore. Drummond sat straighter at his desk. This call sounded more important with every word she spoke.

He considered slow-playing matters, treat it like a police detective. But Vera had shifted priorities in his head. Now, Lou would have to handle gathering information on Clarence's background. If anything popped as important, he would share it. As for a slow play, the stone against Drummond's chest reminded him that this case had a time limit on it. Two really — a week for Lou, but only three days for Drummond. Might as well cut right into it.

"How long ago did Clarence take an interest in the occult?"

Drummond heard her voice catch, but she pulled together quickly. She said, "Long as I can remember, he liked spooky stuff. Horror movies and such. But he never got into the real thing until recently."

"When he started working for the Stahl family?"

"Before that, but it definitely became something more once he met them."

"How long ago was that?"

"I don't know. He worked for them at least a year. Cleaning their pool, tending the house, that kind of thing. So, sometime in the last year."

"Did they pay well?"

"He got his fair share. But he insisted on also working as a janitor at the Triumph. I mean that was the job that brought him to North Carolina, but the sister, Kennedy, she sounded keen on him. I think she would have gladly given him a room in their mansion for free. She ain't much to look at, but for that kind of money, he could've swallowed his pride. Whenever we talked, I would ask him, and you know what he would say? He'd say that he loved the movies too much, that he figured he'd never get to be on the silver screen himself, but he wanted to be around it — even if it meant sweeping up after the show ended at the Triumph."

"Sounds like you talked a lot."

"Once a week, every week."

"Those are expensive calls."

"He called from the Stahl home. They didn't seem to mind."

"With two jobs, he must have made good money himself. He sent you plenty. A good brother."

"He is — was. Our parents died when were little, and he always made sure to take care of me since. I suppose that's part of why he ended up with the Stahls. Their parents also died when they were young."

Drummond tapped his chin, taking his turn to pause a moment, until he saw it. Some of it, at least. "When did he start helping with the séance scam?"

"That ain't no scam. Miss Kennedy, she ain't got a lot going for her, but she got the gift. She can commune with the spirit world. I seen it myself. Went and visited Clarence and he took me to a séance she run, and let me tell you, that woman spoke in a voice not her own. She knew things about me she could not know. Scared me awful. Wasn't long after that visit, she asked Clarence to run things with her. I mean that brother of hers is not so reliable, so I guess she needed somebody she could count on, but Clarence ain't the kind of person you'd ask to go into business with. That's when I knew certain she had eyes for him."

"Why not go into business with him?"

"He's got no ambition, for one — *had* no ambition, I should say. I ain't used to that."

"Takes time. Did Clarence ever sound worried about the work he did for the Stahls? Did he ever say anything that worried you?"

"Nothing like that. I only got worried when I had that dream. Well, I called it a dream to the police, but that was on account that they'd never have listened if I said a vision from the spirit world came to me, warned me that my brother was in danger, that he would die soon. And that's what happened, isn't it? He died. Real shame, too. He had been saving up to move away."

"Where to?"

"He never said. I'm guessing he would've gone wherever he could find work, but it would've been west. I mean the whole Winston-Salem job was always meant to be a short time. Move down there, get some money, and start working toward the west — toward Hollywood. Not that he'd do anything there, but that was where he tried to get to."

"Your vision didn't happen to mention who killed him or why?"

"It's obvious. The spirits killed him. As to *why* — how are we to ever understand the minds of creatures like that? But I can hear it in your voice. The doubt. The suspicions. The day those diamonds went missing, I told Clarence somebody was going to blame us. But the Stahls never did nothing about it. Didn't even call the police. They trusted Clarence. Never once pointed a finger at him. And why should they? He worked hard and never took no short cuts. The fact that you even think he would steal from them is ridiculous."

"I'm not accusing —"

"That's enough, Mr. Drummond. I'm tired of hearing doubt from folks and seeing how y'all want to twist it so that Clarence was a bad person. I know he wasn't no angel, but he did right by me. Always."

"But —"

"Goodbye." She hung up.

CHAPTER 10

RUSHING TO THE HOUSE where Elsie rented a room, Drummond lacked the time to think over all he had heard from Vera. That would have to come later. As he parked the car and well before he settled to watch the house, Elsie hastened out the front door, straightening her hair and clothes, clutching her keys in one hand. He could see the worry on her face that she might be late for work. Well, she should be worried. The chances for getting downtown to the law offices in time were slim.

That played in Drummond's favor, though. The more pressured she felt, the less she paid attention to her surroundings. She could have walked right by Drummond and never noticed a man sitting a car staring at her.

After she drove away, he strolled to the front of the house and knocked. An elderly man answered — wire thin, silver hair, bent over a cane. Twisting his back in an attempt to face his visitor, the man squinted. "Yeah?" he said, louder than necessary. Probably deaf, too.

"I heard you had some rooms to rent."

"Yeah."

"I'd like to rent one."

"Yeah?"

"But I was hoping to see the room first. Get a feel for it."

"Yeah."

He stepped aside to let Drummond in. The house looked cozy and well-cared for. Either the man had a doting wife or he had hired a regular maid service.

"Collin? Who is it?" a woman called out.

Drummond could see her down the hall as she peeked from the kitchen. She looked about as old as Collin, wore a frilly apron over a brown skirt, and had jowls down to her hefty chest.

"Is that your wife?" Drummond asked.

"Yeah." Collin shuffled down the hall as his wife walked by him, wiping her hands on her apron.

"Hello," she said, her voice in a near-falsetto. "I'm Mrs. Leader. You are?"

"Carson. Fred Carson. I'm interested in your room for rent."

"Well, welcome Mr. Carson. I think you'll find everything in the Leader house is tiptop and well worth your time. Come now. I'll show the rooms. We have two available right now, so you can take your pick." She brushed by Drummond and led him up the stairs. "Rent is four dollars a week or you can pay for a whole month and I knock off a few dollars. Bathroom is shared at the end of the hall."

She stopped at the first door on the left and opened it. An empty room, wood floor, tan wallpaper with brown floral print, dome light in the center with brass trim, two windows, one closet. Clean. Not bad for a rental room in a decent neighborhood. Better than Clarence's place.

"No alcohol or other shenanigans allowed," she said. "We run a quiet and respectable home here. You have a job, Mr. Carson?"

"Yes, ma'am. I'm a janitor over at the Triumph Picture House."

"That's on the other side of town. Why are you getting a room here?"

Mrs. Leader continued her interview, trying to disguise the whole thing as casual conversation, and when satisfied, she clutched her hands in front of her belly. Drummond spotted the tight grip and noted the anxiousness behind her eyes. He had met her criteria, and now she wanted the income from another boarder — desperate for it, by the looks.

She stood at the door as he walked the small distance from one wall to the other. "I think you'd be a good fit here, don't you? When do you plan to move in?"

Drummond's turn to secure some information disguised as casual conversation. "That depends. I'm not entirely sure this is the right place for me."

"Oh? Is there a problem?"

"Seems like a nice, quiet place to live."

"It is."

"But how many others live here?"

"Two at the moment. Mr. Shoemaker is upstairs, he's been with us for three years now, and right here across the hall is Ms. Gerald. She's new. Moved in about three months ago. That's it. Both are quiet, decent people. Haven't had any trouble, and they keep visitors to a minimum."

Acting bashful, he said, "If you don't mind, I like to have some privacy in a room like this. I want to spend a little time alone to see what impression I get if I'm actually living here. See how quiet it really is and get a sense for how it feels. That sort of thing. Do you mind?"

"Not at all," she said, her eagerness fluttering her voice. "I'll be downstairs with Mr. Leader. You take as much time as you need."

Drummond tipped his hat and turned away, facing the windows as if in serious consideration. He listened as she clumped along the hall and down the stairs. When things grew still — and surprisingly quiet — he counted to thirty before moving.

Careful not to creak the wood flooring, he slipped out and crept up to Elsie's door. The lock was nothing difficult. Rental rooms in an old house did not boast topline security. Even a novice thief could pick these doors open.

With one ear on the stairs and one on the keyhole, he worked the lock. It took him longer than he wanted to admit, but eventually, the simple device clicked free. Drummond gently turned the knob and pushed open the door. But then he heard Mrs. Leader.

"What are you doing here?" she said.

From a distance. From downstairs. Still, he looked over his shoulder, expecting to see her disapproving jowls shake in anger. Instead, he saw an empty hallway.

The voice of a young woman answered, "I'm so silly. Got all the way to work when I realized I forgot my purse. Just grabbed my keys and left."

"I swear, Ms. Gerald, some days I worry you'll forget your head if it ain't attached to your body."

Elsie made a polite laugh as her feet touched the first stair. Drummond closed her door and stepped back toward the empty room. He wanted to hustle, but moving too fast would make a lot of noise. Rather than risk notice, he took gentle steps, keeping to the rhythm of Elsie climbing up. Hopefully any floorboard sounds would be masked by the stairs.

When he reached the empty room, he eased the door mostly closed — kept a sliver open to watch Elsie as she walked down the hall. She toggled her key in the door and did not appear to realize it had been left unlocked. After she entered her room, Drummond leaned against the wall and released a breath he had been holding.

A short moment later, she emerged from the room, locked the door, and walked away. Drummond listened to her footsteps recede, gave another thirty count, and walked to the top of the stairs. "Mrs. Leader?"

The old woman came round and glance up at him with a hopeful grin.

"Have you decided?"

"I do like the house."

"It is a charming place to live."

"The other room for rent is down this hall?

"Yes, that's right."

"Do you mind if I try that one out?"

Plastering her smile wider, she said, "You go right ahead. The door's open. Take your time."

"Thank you."

"Oh, think nothing of it. You just come on down when you're ready."

Drummond made sure to thump his steps as he walked to the empty room at the far end. He bought more time, and hopefully, it would be enough. Standing at the door to the other rental, he waited a moment before repeating his silent steps back to Elsie's room. Then he started the process of picking the lock all over again.

This time he had no interruptions. He slipped into her room.

The place looked as if Elsie had moved in a decade ago, not a few months. Like most witches, she had built strange collections, and her hoard of baubles filled every inch of the room, blocking out most of the sunlight. A tweed couch in the center looked to be the only piece of furniture. The deep impression of Elsie's body backed up the idea — she slept on it as well as sat.

I'm in the same boat, Ms. Gerald.

A stack of shoeboxes fashioned a side table on one end. Elsewhere, Drummond noted a box filled with used candles, a collection of birdhouses, lumpy pillows piled in the corner, and numerous feather boas hanging off the curtain rod over one window. Mason jars — some empty, some filled with various colored liquids — dotted the room with no visible pattern or reason. Just like a witch.

Thankfully, also like a witch, Elsie valued her books above all. Wooden crates set upon each other formed a series of bookshelves, each book spine out, and no clutter blocked access.

He didn't think to bring a flashlight, so he slid the boas aside to let in some sun — he would have to make sure they were returned to their proper place or else she might figure out somebody had been snooping around. From his pocket, he pulled out the slip of paper with the titles of Clarence's most recent valuable and rare acquisitions. One by one, he went through Elsie's collection.

When he reached the end, he went back to the top and double-checked. But the result did not change. Elsie Gerald did not have

Clarence's books. That didn't clear her of the murder entirely — she could have the books elsewhere, Fitzroy may have sold them to some other witch, or maybe she sold them herself — but those other possibilities were thin. They did not match with witch behavior. Any books like the ones Clarence had would have a notable position on a shelf like this.

As he reset the boas and left the room, he had to admit he was hopeful at the result. She was too young to start murdering people. The longer she stayed away from the ugly side of witchcraft, the better her chances of surviving. Plus, from the little he had seen of her, she would not have done well in prison.

Mrs. Leader met him at the bottom of the stairs with an expectant look. Something on his face clued her in. "Not to your liking?"

"Both rooms are wonderful, but I'm very particular. I'm sorry." He wanted to leave it at that, but the disappointment in her got him talking more. "They're close, though. Perhaps if I don't find what I want, I'll come back and rethink my choices."

"They'll go fast. I don't often have vacancies," she said, but only half-heartedly.

Drummond thanked her for the time and left.

CHAPTER 11

THE REST OF THE DAY had been spent in his office — thinking. He sat at his desk, paced the floor, and stretched on the couch while his brain examined every fact and supposition he had in the case. Because he had more than he realized. And less.

On the *more* side, he knew that Clarence Tunk was complicated beyond the first impression. The man had moved to Winston-Salem for a janitor's job at an old theater. Clearly, he and his sister did not have much money back then. If they had, why not head across the country for Hollywood? Or perhaps he wasn't bright enough or confident enough to take a chance on himself like that. Yet he had some of those qualities because he caught the eye of Kennedy Stahl. Working for the Stahl family brought money — which he dutifully sent back to his sister and kept little for himself. Eventually, the Stahls roped him into helping with their séance scam. At this point, the story grew murky. Maybe Clarence acted like his sister — believing in the scam. She said he became obsessed with the occult. And then what? How did Clarence leap from partner-in-crime to victim?

On the *less* side, Drummond could be wrong about all of it. It was just as possible that some disgruntled séance customer took out his anger upon Clarence. Or perhaps the murder had nothing to do with the scam. Perhaps Clarence simply bumped into the wrong person — Fitzroy or Elsie acting out in a way that made no sense. Drummond didn't think so, though. Vera sounded credible to him, and the behavior of Taggart lent credence to much of the suppositions. Still, there were far too many holes in what Drummond could piece together.

He mulled over the case some more as he shaved, dressed, grabbed the flowers from the morning meet with Lou, and headed to the library. When he spotted Miriam waiting, all thoughts of Clarence Tunk, the Stahl family, the séance, and witchcraft vanished. She looked amazing.

Wearing a sleek dress that hugged her with a gentle embrace, she walked over like she had been born to royalty. Everything about her — the jewelry around her neck, the lines of her jaw and cheeks, the soul in her eyes — promised that she had been formed from an exquisite source and reminded him that he would only be permitted a brief time with her. She wasn't destined for him in the long run. Drummond decided right then that he could live with it. As long as he could enjoy the limited time he had. He smiled big for her as she eased into the car.

Miriam rolled her eyes and blushed. "I'm hardly all that. Do you like the dress, though? My friend, Betsy, let me borrow it. The necklace, too."

He leaned over and kissed her cheek. "I'll be sure to thank Betsy for her good taste." He presented the flowers. "For you."

"They're beautiful, but you've given me so many flowers, I'm running out of explanations to Papa about where they're coming from."

"Then he'll never see them." Drummond tossed the flowers out the window, and Miriam giggled as they drove off.

Heading to Burlington, Drummond had to force his eyes to stay on the road and his thoughts on the séance. But both drifted to Miriam at every opportunity. He knew she was just another person, not some goddess brought down from on high, yet he couldn't stop placing her in such majestic terms.

He shook his head. *Marshall Drummond, you are smitten like a schoolkid.*

"Do you believe in any of this for real?" she asked.

"The séance?"

"All of it. At the party last night, Taggart said you investigated this kind of thing. You even bought a book on witchcraft from our store. I've been thinking about it today and —"

"Thinking about me, huh?"

"Well, despite your flaws, you are quite an interesting man. But honestly, do you believe in it, or is your job to debunk these unusual things?"

"What's the answer you're looking for?"

The playfulness in her voice dropped away. "The truth, of course. Why would you even ask such a thing?"

"No offense, but it's been my experience that most people don't like the truth. Especially about this sort of thing. I tell them what I do and they twist it around into whatever their brains can handle."

With a dark undercurrent, she said, "I can handle a lot." Softer: "Please."

Drummond hesitated. He didn't want to scare her away — she'd be gone on her own accord soon enough — but he didn't want to soft-sell the matter. In his life, he had few people he could confide in. Maybe that was why he had fallen so hard for her so fast. Maybe he needed more than a warm body in bed.

"Okay. Here's the truth." And he told her.

He started with the basics — witches, ghosts, witchcraft. He dispelled the myths — flying on broomsticks, eating children. Finished with the unknown — things beyond ghosts, the séance. He made sure to emphasize that he had been at this for quite a few years but hardly knew enough to be considered an expert. There was far more to the world than he understood, and he had seen enough to know magic ran deeper than anybody could understand. Above all, though, he knew that every bit of it was dangerous. Not to be approached with a casual fascination.

"You have to respect it," he said. "Like fire. It can be useful, even beautiful, but if you don't take care around it, lower your guard for just a second, and you'll probably end up burnt."

"And tonight?" she said. "Are we in danger?"

"Absolutely. That's why I agreed to come. I figured you planned to go no matter what."

"You figured correctly."

"So, I came to protect you. That is unless you changed your mind. I'd be happy to turn us around, go find a nice diner, have a bite to eat."

"Sorry. No such luck."

"Guess I'll have to accept that. But, in all seriousness, don't go too far from my side."

She held back a comment, opting for a knowing grin. Then: "Since the séance is something that you don't know a lot about, it might work. It might be fine."

"In the right hands, I'm told it can work. But Taggart Stahl is just playing at it. Why? We're you hoping to talk to somebody from beyond the grave?"

"Isn't that the entire point?"

He wanted to ask her the obvious question — who did she want to speak with? — but the haunted hints riding her voice warned him off. It didn't take a seasoned detective to notice that there had been no evidence of her mother or any siblings around — just Miriam and her father. They had left Germany right as things were heating up, and even in the beginnings of war, bad things happened to good people. Chances were strong that one or more of the Rosen family died trying to escape the country.

Drummond crossed his fingers that he was wrong, though. Not only for the lives of Miriam's family, but because the odds favored the Stahls to be con artists and nothing more. He would hate to see Miriam's hopes dashed.

CHAPTER 12

WHEN DRUMMOND PULLED into the long horseshoe drive, his third visit to the mansion, it couldn't have been more different. The first time, the place bustled with the organized chaos of a construction crew — an endless stream of people going in all directions, each with a clear purpose as they prepared for the evening's party. The second time, the party itself, had been a fantastical, garish display filled with amusement, music, and an odd, desperate desire for acceptance permeating the air. This time, however, the enormous house felt dead and lonely — like the first burial in a family graveyard deep in the woods.

Most of the lights were off, giving the windows a cold, unwelcoming presence. No workers. No music. No partygoers. No laughter. Nothing but an open front door with dim candles flickering inside. Standing at the top of the stairs, a large man barely contained by a suit and tie waited to greet the evening's attendees.

Drummond escorted Miriam into the house — the large man merely bowing and gesturing down the hall. Candles had been set up periodically to light the exact route they were expected to follow. No surprise — the candles led them through the house, into Taggart's study, and down to the miniature museum.

"Wonderful, you're here." Taggart held his arms out to embrace Miriam, his speech already sloppy with alcohol. He winked at Drummond. Gesturing to a bald man with a white beard and a frail, wrinkled woman, Taggart said, "Allow me to introduce Mr. and Mrs. Rockwell. Our final guest should arrive shortly, and my sister will begin soon after that. Does anybody require a drink?"

Mr. Rockwell peeked at his chain pocket watch. "A libation is the least of what you should offer us. We were under the impression that for two thousand dollars, we would be having a private experience."

Mixing drinks off a rolling bar that had been brought in earlier, Taggart said, "I apologize for the confusion, but there is no possible way to have a private séance. This type of ritual requires a spiritual energy that comes from a group. It simply would not work with the two of you alone. Plus, tonight we have Mr. Marshall Drummond here — a notable investigator of the spirit world. He will verify the authenticity of the night's events. After all, I want you to be satisfied that you've spent your money well."

"I'm not satisfied by any of this. The reason I'm here, the only reason, is on account of my darlin' Emily wants to speak with our deceased son, Billy. I, for one, do not believe in any of this."

"I'll have to ask you to try. Doubt within the group tends to cloud the energies involved and can make it difficult for us to have a successful contact."

That comment and a stiff drink appeared to assuage Mr. Rockwell's unhelpful attitude. His wife's gaze fell upon everyone with an apologetic grin honed over decades of dealing with her husband. Then she lowered her head.

Miriam strolled around the room, taking in the various trinkets she had missed the previous evening. With drink in hand, Taggart approached Drummond.

"Sorry about that," he said, handing over a gin and tonic. Drummond wondered if it was the only drink the man knew how to make. Taggart went on, "He's quite obnoxious. The old man's been sour from the moment he arrived."

"For two thousand dollars, I'd be sour, too. Half of which is going to me, by the way, if you expect my help to *verify the authenticity*."

"Oh, don't worry about that. I'm sure we can sort something out when the time comes."

Spoken like a true grifter. Not that Drummond had any intention of supporting this scam or making a deal with Taggart. Making deals with witches was bad enough.

Lowering his head to Taggart's ear, he said, "You got a bathroom down here?"

"Good thinking," Taggart said. "After the séance, we'll have plenty of drinking to do. Might as well empty up before you fill up." He slapped Drummond on the back. "Upstairs. Out the study and to the right. You'll see it."

Drummond clambered up the stairs and into the study. He had no need for the bathroom, but he did have an investigative curiosity to satisfy. The final guest would have to come this way, so he had no worry of missing out on the séance. Still, he figured he should scan the shelves as fast as possible. Tapping his chin, he started reading the book spines from the top left.

When he reached the bottom right, he felt both relieved not to have found either of the titles as well as frustrated. If the Stahls didn't have the books and Elsie didn't have the books, then where were they? Whoever killed Clarence took those books, and Drummond found it hard to swallow the idea that the killer didn't know their value. Pondering the possibilities, he returned to the gathering as Taggart's drunken laughter filled the stairwell.

At length, the final guest arrived — a lithe man dressed as if he had just come in from riding horses. Even carried a crop. He flipped his thick, black hair to one side with a practiced maneuver and pumped Taggart's hand. "Good to see you again, chum. Has the drinking begun without me?"

Settling into his friend's manner with great comfort, Taggart said, "Wendell, my dear, the drinking always starts without you, but it never tastes as good until you arrive."

Both laughed as Wendell headed straight to the rolling bar. Drummond caught a look pass between the Rockwells — apparently, they did not think much of Wendell. Couldn't tell if it was Wendell's attitude or simply an old money versus new money thing, but Drummond could feel the shifting tensions curtail the serene, mystical atmosphere Taggart had aimed for. Then again, he was just trying to take their money, so the show would go on regardless of the audience turning up their noses. As long as they paid — which it appeared had taken place prior to the séance — the rest didn't matter.

Miriam returned to Drummond's side. Leaning close, she whispered, "Notice anything missing?"

"The shawl?"

With a playful pout, she said, "How did you know?"

"I didn't notice until you said something. But it's the only item in this room that has any real potential worth."

"What about the shrunken heads? Certainly, people would pay a lot for that kind of thing."

"Maybe so, but it's of no interest to the kind of people I deal with."

Three slow knocks sounded at the closed, metal door. Taggart clapped his hands. "My sister is ready."

Like a magician starting a show, he stepped in front of the door and flourished a deep bow. "Welcome, welcome, my dear guests, to a night unlike any other. Some of you know me well. Some know me only by reputation."

Mr. Rockwell snorted. "Not something to brag about."

Other than a perturbed glare, Taggart betrayed no notice of the insult. "In a moment, you will step through this door and into the world that is around us all the time yet unseen by nearly all. The spirit world. It is not to be taken lightly. I must warn you even at this late stage." Here, Taggart turned his head to Mr. Rockwell and stared hard. "Do not enter this room if you are not prepared with an open mind. Do not enter this room if consumed by doubt. What you are about to experience cannot be played with lightly, and I have no desire to see any of you injured … or worse."

Drummond half-expected a roll of thunder cued up as part of the show. To his credit, Taggart avoided that cliché. Instead, he simply stepped aside and lowered his head with a humbleness that fooled no one.

Miriam's fingers laced tight with Drummond's. His pulse quickened with her excitement. As if they prepared to enter a traveling circus big top. But when they stepped into the next room, all of Drummond's pleasure vanished.

Crimson velvet curtains covered the walls, sucking the candlelight the Stahls insisted on continuing to use. A long table dominated with chairs lined on either side. Using candlewax, a crude casting circle had been drawn in the center of the table. More of the odd symbols surrounded the circle as well as two candles at each compass point. As far as scams went, he thought the Stahls put in a strong showing. But they would have to do a lot better than merely set the mood if they wanted to bilk more out of their marks.

At the head of the table, Kennedy Stahl sat with the witch's burnt shawl draped over her head and shoulders. Nice touch. She bowed over a book, hiding her face from all. But what froze Drummond's heart, what caught his breath and set his nerves alight, was this book sitting closed under her gaze.

A grimoire.

He had seen enough of them to recognize it instantly — the oversized shape, the lack of writing anywhere on the cover, and of course, the cover itself. Many of the most serious coven grimoires were bound in human skin — something Drummond never forgot after encountering it once. The shape looked thick and rippled. Waterlogged. As if it had been lost at sea long ago. Indeed, when Kennedy opened the book, the pages crinkled and several stuck together. Most of the handwritten instructions on the coven's spells had become blurred, illegible. That happened when using blood for ink and then subjecting it to long periods submerged.

Drummond grabbed Miriam's wrist and turned away. But Taggart had closed the metal door and gestured to the table. Standing still, Drummond weighed the possibility of punching Taggart in the jaw, busting down the door, facing off with the hired muscle acting as a bouncer, and dragging an angry and embarrassed Miriam to his car. Not only did that set of ideas look bad, but he would still have the same problems to deal with — Clarence Tunk's ghost and the deal with Madame Magnolia.

"Everything okay?" Miriam asked.

"Sure," he said, as they sat at the table. He made sure to put himself between Miriam and Kennedy, keeping his eyes on the book.

Kennedy lifted her head, eyes closed, and sat back in her chair — a small, portly woman with a square, stern face. Releasing a long breath, she pulled everyone's focus. But where her brother had drawn interest like a carnival barker, Kennedy commanded attention with an obvious, earnest belief in the task at hand. Her posture, her expression — even in silence she had made clear that she controlled the night ahead.

This exuded confidence only served to worry Drummond more. First thing real witches learned was a cautious, healthy respect for magic. In fact, it had been Drummond's experience that the more bravado a witch displayed, the less he had to fear from her witchcraft. A woman like Madame Magnolia could be a doting grandmother in one moment, negotiate a witch's deal in the next, and cap it off by calmly preparing a blood magic ward, all without raising her voice or boasting of her prowess.

Kennedy's performance had been meant to create a similar sense of gentle power. And it did for the others. But for Drummond, she had failed. If she had managed to acquire any useful magic from that water-damaged book, she would be as surprised as Drummond. But bad magic, failed magic — that could be unpredictable.

Taggart locked the door with a heavy thud before sitting at the end opposite his sister. "Mistress Kennedy, I have brought before you five worthy souls who wish to commune with the spirit world."

Drummond caught Mr. Rockwell's eye, and the old man snickered. Mrs. Rockwell and Wendell appeared transfixed by Taggart's sister. Miriam looked caught between wanting to believe and suspecting fraud. But it was Taggart's hokey line — *Mistress Kennedy* — that allowed

Drummond to relax. This was a grift. Nothing more. A stage show for the gullible, and the Stahls had merely invested in authentic props.

With a thin nod, Kennedy leaned over the book once more and turned the pages. Taggart motioned for everybody to hold hands. Drummond happily obliged with Miriam but hesitated to make any contact with Kennedy. She held both her hands out to complete the circle and kept her head bowed low. Drummond slipped his hand in hers, inwardly shuttered at the clammy feel, then waited for the next step in this sham production.

The performance continued with some call and response between Taggart and Kennedy. Not a bad show, but nothing Drummond gave a serious thought about. Worth two grand? Doubtful. Though, he supposed if it gave Mrs. Rockwell solace in the loss of her loved one and, in doing so, gave Mr. Rockwell peace in his household, then perhaps the value of the evening was a matter of perspective.

That all changed when Kennedy let go of Drummond's hand. She turned a few pages in the grimoire, stood, and reached her palms over the casting circle. At first, Drummond dismissed it as more of the scam. Perhaps a distraction while Taggart flicked a switch under the table to start a light show or a shaking chair or thumps in the walls. But then, Drummond glimpsed the open page — the circle of wax matched that in the grimoire. The symbols, runny and ruined, looked closely the same.

Kicking back his chair as he bolted to his feet, Drummond clamped down on Kennedy's wrist and yanked it away from the casting circle. "Stop. Turn the lights on. This is over."

Wendell laughed. "Well, well, it looks like the brave detective is a bit scared."

Mr. Rockwell banged his fist on the table. "Now see here, young man, we paid good money for this séance and we expect to get what we paid for."

"That's the problem," Drummond said, locking daggered-eyes with Kennedy. "This isn't a séance anymore. It's a summoning."

"What does it matter what you call it? It's still nonsense that we paid for."

"No. You paid for a séance — a chance to communicate with the dead. This summoning is an attempt to bring the dead back. It's very real and very dangerous."

Kennedy's mouth continued to mumble words as she turned her focus back to the casting circle. Drummond glanced at her brother. He looked both amused and worried. This was only a money grab to him, but with Drummond taking things seriously, Taggart had to be shaking a little.

"I don't care," Mrs. Rockwell said, her voice stronger even as it cracked. "If I can hear him or see him or touch him — I'll take whatever you can offer."

Pausing her spell, Kennedy wrenched her hand free. "You are no longer welcome here, Mr. Drummond."

"Don't do this. It won't work the way you want." Drummond motioned for Miriam to back away from the table. "That spellbook is not correct. Not anymore. The symbols you've drawn are wrong."

"I know exactly what I'm doing."

Drummond turned to Taggart. "If you believed half the praise you've given me, then believe me now. Your sister is about to do something awful. She's no witch. She has no training. And I've seen horrible things happen when amateurs attempt heavy magic."

Though he made no motion to stop her, Taggart inched his chair back. "Sis? Perhaps Mr. Drummond is right. Perhaps we're not ready for this next step."

The Rockwells kept their places, but Wendell rose to his feet and tipped his head toward his friend. "I'm afraid I've just recalled an important appointment I must attend. Good to see you, old friend." He went to the door, but it would not open. "Taggart, there seems to be a problem with the lock."

Taggart paled.

A quick peek over his shoulder, Drummond saw that Miriam had retreated into the far corner. She watched the room with cold, analytical seriousness. A twitch of her shoulder gave away her nerves, but a stern jaw proved she could keep control.

Looking back, Drummond saw that the lines of the casting circle glowed a soft blue. He had held off from swiping his hand across the circle — doing so during a casting could cause an explosion of energy. In such a confined space, he didn't want anybody getting hurt. But now, there appeared little choice. Unless he tackled Kennedy out of the way. Yet that might cause an equal amount of damage. It would be a more dangerous move if he dealt with a real witch. With an amateur — hard to say what would happen.

"Last chance," he said, his hand wavering between the casting circle and the witch wannabe. "Either stop this now, or I'll stop it."

Wendell pounded on the door. Mr. Rockwell pounded on the table. And a louder pounding reverberated through the walls.

All motion stopped as the reality of ghosts and magic crashed into both the doubters and believers of the room. Wide-eyed fear trembled in every gaze. Even Taggart had lost his amused smirk.

"Arise, spirit of the dead." Kennedy's voice echoed despite the dampening curtains.

Drummond's fingers curled tight. He didn't want to punch her, but a slap seemed too minor to break her concentration and all other choices might get others hurt. "Don't make me do this," he said.

She lifted her gaze towards him. Her eyes blurred, the color smearing like the writing in the grimoire. Blood teared down her cheeks.

Startled at the sight, Drummond stepped back. Having kicked at the door to no avail, Wendell spun towards the others, caught a view of Kennedy, and screamed. He rushed the table. "No, no, no. We can't have this!" He swept his arm across the wax circle, and though he mostly brushed over it, his finger chipped a small piece free. Breaking the circle.

Wendell lifted off the ground and flew back parallel to the floor. When he hit the curtained wall, he disintegrated in a splash of blood and particles. As the gore painted the Rockwells' backs, Taggart toppled out of his chair, slamming into the floor with a resounding crack. Mrs. Rockwell covered her mouth, moaning as her face turned a nauseated green. Miriam gasped, and when Drummond looked down, he saw Taggart's stunned head turned completely around.

"Good Lord," Mr. Rockwell said, stumbling to his feet while pushing back from the table. One hand clutched his chest, and he dropped to his knees. His wife, however, did not come to his aid. Like Miriam and Kennedy, she transfixed upon the manifestation forming in the casting circle.

"Billy? Is that you?" Mrs. Rockwell said, horrified hope creaking through her voice.

But it wasn't Billy. Drummond recognized that right away, and he suspected Kennedy did, too. Lost in a false belief that she could still maintain control, that she ever had control in the first place, Kennedy continued reciting the spell, adding intensity to her words and tension to her outstretched hands. But Mrs. Rockwell's false belief was equally determined.

"Billy? It's Mama. I've missed you so baby. I love you."

Standing, pressing her hips against the table, she leaned forward, putting her hands out toward the pale, shimmering soul. But Drummond knew this trapped ghost was Clarence Tunk. Worse — this was Clarence Tunk suffering from his inability to move on and now shackled into a casting circle. The poorly designed spell and its interruption left Clarence's right side deformed. The arm had shriveled and much of his face slurred together like dried mud.

He watched Mrs. Rockwell, his brow knit tight, his chin trembling. Confusing enough to be a ghost trying to get justice for his murder, but to hurt this way left him troubled and angry.

"Clarence," Kennedy said. He whipped towards her, grunting like a beast. Clasping her hands to her heart, she went on, "Clarence, darling, it's me. You remember me, don't you, darling? Kennedy. Don't you remember all those hours we spent uncovering the secrets in this book? The way you looked fondly at me and pretended not to notice when our hands brushed together, or the heavenly gazes between us as we grew tired from our late-night studies. You meant everything to me."

"No, Billy, listen to Mama. I know you. I would always know you. No matter what has happened. Look at me. Look at Mama."

Clarence turned toward the imploring woman. Through the ghost's pale, translucent form, Drummond saw the way he watched Mrs. Rockwell, perhaps believing her words.

"Clarence, you helped me learn the art of the séance. You helped me learn how to tap into true magic. You love me. I know it."

"Billy, Mama loves you and you love Mama."

Even without years of knowledge confronting the paranormal, Drummond could see what would happen. Back and forth the two women pulled Clarence's attention, causing greater confusion as their tone and word betrayed greater desperation. Clarence lashed out.

Thrashing his good arm in a wild arc, he sent out a blast of energy, a vicious force of pain and frustration. It sliced Mrs. Rockwell's head clean off. Kennedy shrieked as she fell back. But Drummond did not see her demise. He had lunged at Miriam, instead. Tackling her to the ground and covering her body with his.

He knew from the start that the broken circle could not contain a ghost. Especially a furious ghost. Drummond felt the weight of Clarence's attacks against his back. But the ghost ward held. No icy blast cut through Drummond's spine. No tormented suffering reached through and into Miriam. For several moments, Clarence bashed into the ward's protection. When he finally understood he could not get at the last living beings in the room, he let loose a growling wail before dissipating in the air.

Drummond kept still over Miriam. Listening for any sign of further rage, hearing only his heartbeat and her shallow breaths. Pushing back to his knees, he looked at her. "Are you hurt?"

Coming up to meet him, she gazed into his eyes, stunned and stunning.

He opened his mouth to repeat the question, but she covered him with her own kisses. Locking tight against his mouth, she wrapped her arms around him as if to guarantee they both had lived through this experience. He kissed her back, reaffirming that they were indeed okay, full of warmth and passion and living need. When they finally broke, breathing hard and licking their lips as if to remember the taste, Drummond stood.

He slid the grimoire over and flipped to the front of the book. It read: *Our Spells* by Madame Collette Bardet. He had expected it, but somehow seeing the confirmation in print jarred him. Too much death over this thing. He closed the book and tucked it under one arm.

Taking Miriam's hand, he said, "Stay close. Don't let go of me. I'm wearing a ghost ward, and it's the only thing that will get us safely out of this place. Understand?"

Shivering and nodding, she pressed against his side.

Peering over the edge of the table, Drummond finally saw what had become of Kennedy. He guided Miriam around the other end. Nobody needed to see that. The shredded corpse was gruesome enough to fill a lifetime of nightmares, but her burned-out eyes and charred mouth threatened to sour his stomach forever.

The others didn't look much better. Even Mr. Rockwell, dead from a heart attack, still clutched his chest. His eyes had bugged open into a horrid moment of frozen terror.

The door out of the séance room, the same one Wendell had been unable to budge, opened without resistance. Though moving with wary steps, Drummond guided Miriam back upstairs and through the winding maze of the mansion. If Clarence watched them, he never attacked. Apparently, the ghost understood the concept of the ward quickly enough. Whatever staff the Stahls had employed, they could not be found. The hired bouncer lay at the bottom of the wide, white marble stairs — face down in his own blood. Nobody lived in that mansion anymore.

CHAPTER 13

THEY SPOKE LITTLE ON THE WAY BACK to Winston-Salem. She rested her head against his arm, shuddering on occasion, as he put together more of the case. He had the pieces now. A common enough story of meeting the wrong people and unrequited love. A uniquely tragic story of amateur witchcraft.

Clarence Tunk had moved down to Winston-Salem in search of a better life. Not only for himself, but for his sister, Vera. After their parents had passed, Clarence and Vera relied upon each other. Simple as that.

He needed a thriving city with plenty of opportunity, closer to his dream of Hollywood but not too far from his sister and her questionable financial problems. Winston-Salem fit the bill. And, indeed, Clarence found work, made money, and dutifully sent it back to keep his sister comfortable and out of trouble. He lived a frugal life, but not one without any comfort. The bare room under the theater had clearly been wiped down in an effort to hide information after his murder. But had he truly lived in such a meager way, Drummond found it hard to believe the place would have been so immaculately clean.

Eventually, Clarence met the Stahls. While the specifics remained unclear, Drummond guessed one of two strong possibilities: either Clarence had been hired to work as staff for one of Taggart's many parties and while doing his job struck Taggart's fancy, or Clarence bumped into Kennedy at Moe's Books, both looking over the occult section. Mr. Rosen mentioned Clarence being in the store with a woman — it could have been Kennedy, but it could easily have been Vera, too.

However the first meeting came about, Clarence soon spent a lot of time with the Stahls. Most importantly, Kennedy fell in love with him. A harsh looking woman, and a demanding one, she never got to be the star of these parties that she took the responsibility of throwing. Drummond suspected she had little dating experience. At some point, probably at

Taggart's suggestion because he thought it would be amusing, they brought Clarence in on their séance con. He would provide the noises coming from the walls or the moving table or whatever version of the scam they initially had attempted. It probably would've gone on like that for a while, and Kennedy would never have found the courage to express her true feelings for Clarence. As she had said to his ghost, she would continue to watch him, praise him, but in the end, he would move away — possibly across the country for Hollywood — always in search of a better life for Vera and himself.

That's how things soured. All during this time with the Stahls, Clarence had been acquiring books for his personal interest. But also to beat out Fitzroy. After all, if Clarence had a book of some worth, he could sell it to Fitzroy and make a tidy profit. Fitzroy wouldn't mind because he would just turn around and sell it to Elsie for even more. In this way, Clarence began to save up for that Hollywood move.

Except one day, Clarence found the grimoire, *Our Spells* by Madame Collette Bardet, in Moe's Books. He probably would have missed it, but Kennedy was with him, and she knew what power it held. Not only the power of witchcraft, but the power of luring Clarence.

The book fascinated them both, and Drummond suspected part of her conversation with the ghost that evening described the truth — that they spent hours into the late nights pouring over difficult research, trying to decipher the mysterious grimoire. But while Kennedy did work hard side-by-side with Clarence, while she stared at him and dreamed of him, while she brushed her hand against his and longed for more than a brief touch, he never noticed. He never acknowledged any of it. He never had any interest.

That much was true. Given the nature of Clarence haunting Drummond and finding a lack of evidence pointing to any other serious relationships in the man's life, Drummond concluded that either Taggart, Kennedy, or both were responsible for Clarence's murder. Best guess — Clarence stashed the grimoire at his place and then announced he would be moving away. Kennedy expressed her strong feelings for him in a desperate attempt to make him stay. When he rejected her, she reacted violently. In a rash moment, she grabbed Taggart's gun — the one missing a bullet — and she put a hole in Clarence's head.

Then came the shoddy cover up. That was Taggart's doing. He brought Clarence's body back to the room under the theater, mutilated the face to hide the bullet wound — it wouldn't work, but he didn't know that — and opened up the organs to further throw off any police investigation. His own interests recalled the Egyptian Coptic jars, so he went with that for his ritual theme. Next, he cleared the room, taking everything that might point somebody to the Stahl family. At Kennedy's insistence, he swiped all the books on witchcraft and the occult for her research — especially the grimoire — but he missed that small slip of paper with the partial address that fell behind the bed. The more Drummond thought on it, the more it sounded true in his head. When he finally reached the library corner, he had discounted all other varying theories.

"Looks like we're here," he said.

Miriam raised her head and peeked out the window. "I don't want to be alone."

They held each other in the still night. He kissed the top of her head. "I don't know if that's a good idea."

Her grip on him tightened. "Please."

He headed to his office. Part of him wanted to ask her what she would tell her father, what staying at his place would mean for them, what these events had done to the way she looked at him. Part of him didn't want to know.

Once inside the office, Drummond prepared two stiff drinks. She undressed in the bathroom, donning his robe, and settled on the couch, drink in hand. She looked more than lovely. Downright alluring. But he had one more job to do that night.

Removing the ghost ward from his neck, he handed it to Miriam. "Wear this. It'll keep you safe while I'm gone."

"You're going to leave?"

"I'll be back in a few hours. I have to deliver this book."

"Then take me with you."

"Trust me. You do not want to visit the house of a witch. Especially not tonight."

"A witch? A real one?"

"Very real."

"But you will be back."

"Have you seen yourself in a mirror? Of course, I'll be back."

One long-lasting kiss threatened to pull him in for the night before he found the will to step away. He picked up the grimoire, went out to his car, and headed to High Point.

* * * *

FIVE MINUTES TO FOUR IN THE MORNING and Drummond followed Mr. Carlson to a large, well-stocked kitchen. Everything sparkled clean. The green tiled floors had been washed to perfection. Not surprising in the least — Madame Magnolia would insist on the best work from her people. Considering the threat of displeasing a capable witch, Drummond imagined her people worked beyond their best for her.

She wore a pink robe over an old-fashioned sleeping gown. The combination created a sense of bulk counter to her actual small frame. Though her face looked puffy from having her sleep disturbed, her intense focus on Drummond promised an entirely clear mind.

"Well?" she said, standing next to a counter lined with jars labeled *flour, sugar,* and *salt.*

Drummond launched into a full account of the evening and the backstory that had led to it. He told her all he knew about Clarence Tunk and the little more he suspected. He told her of the lead up to the séance performance, the various guests, the wax casting circle, the grimoire, the botched spell, and the horrendous results. Then he set the grimoire on the counter, keeping one hand on it.

"Thank you for the ward. It saved my life. I trust that giving you this book will make us even."

She could not hide her hunger for that book. "Oh, yes. You can consider our deal completed."

He slid the book to her. Finding the self-control to stop from grabbing the grimoire and rushing off to her study to pour over every page of the book, she merely placed her own hand atop the cover. Drummond waited a moment. When it appeared that they had reached the end of the meeting, he turned to go.

But she said, "This isn't done, yet."

"Witches can do a lot of things I don't like, but I've never known your kind to go back on a deal. I've more than delivered, and you said yourself the deal was completed."

"Oh, it is. For us. But for you, there is still a ghost. From what you've told me, I'm fairly certain it's worse than that."

"Worse?" Drummond faced her again.

"Even in death, a mother would not mistake her child. When the Wendell gentleman destroyed the circle and Kennedy Stahl failed her spell — something we both know was doomed to happen since she had none of the correct writing — well, the result was not simply an angry ghost of Clarence Tunk. She also summoned Billy Rockwell. The two forced into the same broken circle."

"That melted side of Clarence?"

"Two ghosts occupying the same space. Locked together now. And unless you wish to be wearing ghost wards for the rest of your life, you'll need to fix this. I can show you the spell to cast. It will be more than a mere incantation, but you'll do fine."

"You do it, then. You've got the ability."

"I'm not the one they're after. Besides, do you really want to make another deal with me? Or any witch? After all, ghost wards don't last forever. If you let this abomination continue to exist, you'll have to regularly make witch deals for fresh wards. And not only for yourself, right? Your Jewish lady will need them, too."

Gritting his teeth, he said, "I'm no witch. How am I going to pull off a spell?"

"I'll do the heavy lifting before you leave, have it all set up so even a child could do it. You're at least as smart as a child, I should think."

"I suppose you won't show me this spell for free."

Her hand rubbed a circle on the grimoire. "This book is worth far more to me than we had agreed for. I think you've earned a little more help from me."

Drummond did not like that. Getting the spell without a deal meant owing her unofficially. The way a man would owe a friend or a colleague. A debt based on word not contract. It reeked of starting a relationship with this witch, and he wanted to keep it business. But that was the point. Madame Magnolia had put him in the position of either accepting her generosity and thus beginning a long-term association that would create greater problems down the road or insulting her by rejecting her offer and thus setting himself up for greater problems down the road.

"Oh, don't look so troubled," she said. "I'm not that terrible a witch. Unless you cross me."

With a resigned gaze around the kitchen, unable to believe that such a momentous decision occurred in such a mundane room, he thrust his hands into his pockets. "I might as well hear about this spell. At least I'll get rid of Clarence and Billy."

"Smart decision." She hefted the book off the counter. "Sit. I'll be right back. Would you like some coffee? I can have Mr. Carlson go brew a pot. The night isn't over for you."

She shuffled out of the kitchen, humming to herself, and Drummond knew right then that he couldn't let this happen. He would be indebted to her long after he paid back this favor. In fact, without a clear deal in place, he might never get out from under her control. Allowing that he might be overreacting, he decided it wasn't worth the risk.

At the same time, he still had the problem of this ghost. He knew other witches, a few that would undoubtedly know a similar spell to whatever Madame Magnolia sought, but most wouldn't even let him through the front door. Those that did would want too high a price for their help.

When she returned to the kitchen carrying a smaller, modern book, Drummond perked up. Another book made him think of Clarence and the bookstore and Fitzroy and —

"I appreciate you offering to give me this spell for free," he said.

"Think nothing of it. Someday in the future, you'll find a way to repay my kindness."

If he hadn't been sure, he was sure now. "I don't like owing people. So, I think we should make a deal right away."

She set the book on the counter, a flash of disappointment crossing her brow. "I'm always happy to make a deal, but I'm afraid you don't have anything I want. You barely pulled off paying for the ghost ward."

"That's not quite true. I have one thing you'll want very much."

"And that is?"

"A name. A young woman who is secretly trying to learn witchcraft. She's not your average amateur. She's the kind of person who has been getting ahold of real spellbooks and attempting real spells. I give you her name, and you've got plenty of options. You could report her to the other witches, force her to join the community, or have those in charge get rid of her. That would help your relationship with the other witches even more. Or you could take her under your wing. Plus, I'm sure you have plenty of other choices I don't want to know about."

Running her fingers over her rings, Madame Magnolia said, "I never thought of you as the kind to give up another person."

"Witches are bad enough, but at least the spells you cast are controlled. You target a specific person and that's the end of it. Amateurs cause too much harm to others."

"Like the remnants of your séance."

"Exactly. Do we have a deal?"

"I give you this spell and you give me the name." She deliberated for mere seconds. "Fair enough. I agree."

She then explained the spell, and Drummond provided her the name Elsie Gerald.

CHAPTER 14

AN HOUR LATER, Drummond parked a block down from the Triumph Picture House. He walked the empty street going over all the instructions Madame Magnolia had given him. It really was simple.

She had spent twenty minutes infusing a brackish liquid with most of the spell. That liquid sloshed in an old perfume bottle sitting in his coat pocket. He merely had to use the liquid like ink to draw a casting circle and two specific symbols. Nothing complex. Basic shapes to house the ghost's two names. Then set fire to the circle, say a few words, concentrate on the flames, and wait.

Simple.

Yet as he turned down the alleyway leading to the back entrance of the Triumph, Drummond doubted any of this. When dealing with the paranormal, he had learned from the start that nothing ever went smooth and simple. Madame Magnolia's steady confidence in the plan only made him doubt even more.

Nobody had fixed the backdoor window yet, so he had no trouble entering the building. He flipped the lights on. No reason to grope around in the dark when the police had no real interest in solving the case and most citizens would still be asleep.

Clarence's room looked as bare as before — nothing had been visibly touched since Drummond's previous visit — yet it all appeared different now. Drummond could pick out the faint lines where books of witchcraft had once cluttered the plain desk. He could picture where the stacks of paper crammed with notes on symbology had been piled on the floor. He spotted where Clarence's address book had sat on the edge of his mattress when Taggart hurriedly tore it apart, not realizing a sliver had fallen under the bed. Drummond pictured it all with ease. This wasn't an empty, sterile hovel for an empty soul. This room had been packed with the furious passion of a man obsessed in unlocking secrets he only glimpsed.

"If you're in here," Drummond said, his voicing falling dead on the cold walls, "I've come to help you move on."

He lowered to the spot where Clarence's blood had stained the floor. As he set about drawing the casting circle with the witch's concoction, he listened for any sign of the ghost. He heard nothing. No matter, though. When the spell kicked in, the ghost would come.

Writing their names turned out to be the hardest part of the preparations. Witches wrote words and symbols with all sorts of odd ingredients — mud, salt, water, blood. Drummond, however, lacked the practice at forming legible letters with magic-infused ink. When he finished and evaluated his work, he decided it didn't look half-bad.

"Better be enough," he muttered as he pulled out a match and struck it against the hard floor.

It sparked up, and he held the amber flame close enough that he could feel the heat against his chin. Still, he shivered. He had a good idea of what would happen in the next moments, and part of him resisted taking the step forward.

"This can be a painful, angry experience for a ghost," Madame Magnolia had said when she explained the spell. "It will get violent, and as long as the circle burns, so does the ghost. Once the flames cease, the ghost will have moved on. Until then, it will come after anything near the circle. But you needn't fear. No matter what the ghost does to your surroundings, you can trust that my ward will protect you. Just keep your concentration and you'll be fine."

But Drummond no longer had the ward. It hung around Miriam's neck.

His stomach gurgled, and he chuckled. His body didn't care what might happen. Dawn neared and he hadn't eaten in many hours. He was hungry.

That simple reality brought with it the clear idea that this ghost would continue to react in a dangerous, deadly way unless he stopped it. Same way his hunger would demand food regardless of the situation. The ghost and his hunger knew what it wanted, needed, and no other aspects of reality mattered.

Drummond let the match fall to the circle.

The flames ran along the liquid with a blue-green tinge. A scent of burnt bacon filled the room. Drummond's stomach muttered again.

On his knees, bent forward so his face felt the heat of the fire, Drummond said the words Madame Magnolia had instructed. A series of sounds, really, and as promised, a child could have done it. If he spoke another language, he had never heard it before, but he thought that in this case, the sounds were less a true incantation and more of a way to help the caster overcome his nerves. Nonsense words meant to ease his mind by giving him something to do. Because the witch had made clear the spell would take time. He would need patience. So, he spoke the sounds ten times as prescribed, then sat back on his heels, and watched the flames.

And waited.

The fire did not crackle like it would have in the woods. Rather, a soft and steady hiss came from the burning circle like air slipping out a small tire puncture. The dim light of the flames flickered into the shadows under the bed and desk. And against the walls.

Drummond stared at the wall near the corner under the bed. He had missed it when searching the room with Lou, but lit up by the strange colored fire, it looked so clear, so obvious now. One of the bricks appeared lighter than all the others.

When he moved towards the bed, the flames of the circle heated up, rising tall for an instant. The witch said that would happen, and when it did, he would know that the ghost had arrived. Drummond returned to the circle and, following instructions, repeated the incantation three times.

According to Madame Magnolia, Drummond had to sit as still as possible before the casting circle and focus. The spell would do the rest. "Oh," she said, "you might feel the ghost try to break through your ward. Ignore that and stay at the circle. Your energy feeds the circle. If the ghost is particularly nasty, he might be able to push the field produced by the ward. If that happens and you are moved away. Simply return to the circle. That's why you must concentrate. The longer you remain there, the more energy the spell will take in, and the faster it will work against the ghost."

Drummond surveyed the sparse room, wondering if he might see any sign of the ghost. "Clarence … and Billy, listen here. I'm trying to help you. All I want to do —"

A punch to the jaw. Hard enough to dazzle lights in Drummond's eyes. The ghost shrieked, the sound bouncing from wall to wall. At least, any contact with him would cause the ghost some pain, too. As he held still, his eyes attempting to see through the blurry watering, he hoped that fact would stop Clarence from throwing too many more sledgehammers like that first one.

With a cleansing breath, Drummond straightened in front of the circle and thought about sending whatever energy he could in its direction. This time, the pain-soaked shriek came before the attack — the spell starting to work perhaps. But the attack still came.

Frozen hands grabbed Drummond, lifted him off the floor, and threw him into the desk. The wood legs snapped, and the plain piece of furniture collapsed under his weight. Ignoring the bruises throbbing at his back, he clambered to his feet and returned to the circle.

The spell was definitely working now. If it hadn't been, Drummond would be dead. After all, the ghost had splattered Wendell against a wall with one strike.

When the third attack came, Drummond knew he was right. The longer the spell lasted, the weaker the ghost became. Ice gripped around Drummond's waist and hurled him into the doorway. He scrambled back to the circle only to be rolled in the other direction, tumbling into the hot plate.

The walls banged as if giants stomped on all sides. Drummond curled into a ball, covering his ears as he waited out the rage. When the sound ceased, he used the nearest wall to get onto his feet. Swiping his hat off the floor, he stumbled back to the casting circle. He felt the scrapes on his arms and bumps on his forehead. Minor stuff so far, but the witch never indicated how long the entire spell would take. He started to have a dark suspicion that she had omitted that detail on purpose.

Staring into the blazing lines of the circle, Drummond tried to capture some of the warmth from the small flames. The repeated assaults from a ghost left his skin prickled, and shivers rippled throughout his body. A deep groan reverberated through the room, and Drummond wanted to tell the ghost he felt the same way.

Though the spell had clearly weakened Clarence and Billy, the ghost still had plenty of strength. The next round of punishment arrived like being trampled under a stampede. One moment, Drummond watched the flames of the circle. The next, an unseen mass plowed into him, sliding him to the doorway, and thumping across his body over and over. Endless frozen punches.

Desperate to finish this ordeal, he crawled toward the circle. But a frosty grip locked around his ankles and dragged him back. His thighs and flanks burned. The wrath of this ghost shocked Drummond's system. When the chilled fingers took hold of his hair, wrenching back his head, when he realized his face would be smashed into the hard floor, he strained his eyes toward the casting circle. It was all he could do. Send his energy in thought and deed toward that small, burning circle.

The ghost wailed, dropping its hold on Drummond. The bed spasmed on its metal legs. Shreds of the wooden desk flew into the wall.

Like a soldier belly crawling under enemy fire, Drummond pushed back towards the circle. His muscles screamed at him. Pain dug into every motion. But when he reached his destination and focused on the fiery circle, the storm of wood clattered to the floor.

A new, guttural howl pounded through the air. Drummond braced for another attack. But the ghost did not punch him, did not throw him, did not try to tear him away. Instead, Clarence clamped onto Drummond's arm and twisted it at an odd angle.

The ghost hissed and shouted and cried at the pain of the spell and the pain of touching a human being. It sounded weaker. But with no warning and a sharp jerk, the ghost bashed into Drummond's elbow.

Drummond screamed his throat raw.

A clear snapping sound and the arm hung limp at his side. Pain seared up into his shoulder. Sweat drenched his face. He flopped over, his cheek pressing against the cool floor. The room grew fuzzy at the edges, and his mind lurched between the agony on his side and the singular command that he had to keep watching that damn casting circle. Focus. Concentrate.

But as he endured arctic blasts to his back and legs, his mind wavered. He kept his eyes on the dimming green-blue flames, yet he saw Miriam. She grew out of the fire. He pictured her at the piano that first day they had met. He saw her charming smile and her brilliant eyes. The flowery smell of her skin, the champagne taste of her lips. Yet he also recalled the darkness beneath the surface. She and her father had escaped a war, and that sort of pain healed slowly — if ever. But even that only made her more to him. More beautiful, more intelligent, more the kind of a woman that meant something.

Too bad he would die soon. At least, he would die with her lovely smile in his head.

His body rocked with every hit, but he hardly felt anything. His senses had numbed to the pain. Part of him wondered why the ghost toyed with him. Why not kill him already? For that matter, why had the attacks become so weak? They nudged against him instead of tossing him throughout the room. The flames of the circle had weakened, too. But as these questions entered his mind, the room darkened, his vision blurred over, and soon he could think no more.

CHAPTER 15

THE INITIAL MINUTES after he awoke mushed together much as the minutes before he had fallen unconscious. Sadly, instead of waking to images of Miriam, he stared at the bulbous nose of Ol' Lou Piper. A call had come in about a possible break-in at the Triumph, and Lou grabbed it, worried somebody might mess with the crime scene. When he found Drummond, he admitted that he felt anger. But seeing the weird private investigator's condition, Lou opted to help out, instead.

Sitting on the edge of the bed, he had made a sling by ripping a strip off the bedsheet. He said the rest of the injuries looked like they would heal on their own. Didn't feel that way to Drummond.

Every limb, every joint, every inch of skin throbbed or burned or stung as if tiny needles pierced open wounds. If this all healed on its own, it would take a long time. At least he had the satisfaction of seeing the charred remains of the casting circle. The flames had died out. The ghost had moved on.

"I'm guessing I don't want to know," Lou said, "but I'm going to have to report something. What can you tell me?"

Drummond went through the story once again. He didn't water it down, but he didn't go out of his way to talk about ghosts and magic, either. In the end, he offered Lou one bone. "Look, I know you don't believe any of this, but these people do. That's the thing you've got to understand. They believe it deep in their hearts."

Lou had been taking notes on a small pad. He stuffed it in his coat pocket. "Kennedy Stahl killed him because he didn't love her, and her brother, Taggart, he covered it up. Then she kills Taggart and bunch of other rich folk in a scam gone wrong. Kills herself, too, for some reason. Guilt, I suppose. That's pretty thin."

"Yeah."

"And it don't explain what you're doing here and how you got all beat up."

Drummond thought for a moment. Lou didn't want the truth. He was asking Drummond for a plausible explanation, something he could put in a report that didn't make him sound looney. When Drummond came up with the answer, he straightened fast, sending a ripple of sizzling fire up his back.

Wincing, he said, "Under the bed, in the back corner, there's a brick different from the others. Newer looking. Knock it open, and I think you'll find something worthwhile."

Lou pulled the bed away from the wall and lowered to the floor with a heavy grunt. It didn't take him long to release the brick. After all, Clarence had never sealed it up permanently. He always wanted easy access to his little hiding spot. When Lou returned to his feet with more grunting, he held a well-worn, rawhide pouch. He loosened the string tie and dumped several small diamonds onto the bed.

With a thick snicker, he said, "Well, well. The bastard stole the diamonds, after all."

"I didn't think he had it in him. The Stahls didn't either, but you can leave that out. Add in Vera's need for money, and it looks like you've got all the motive you could want."

Sifting his fingers through the diamonds, Lou gave a more appreciative grunt. "That's why they killed him. The séance was a cover for this group — maybe they stole the diamonds from someone else. Whatever the case, the whole thing went pear-shaped last night, and resulted in a lot of deaths." He thought through how this new fiction matched up with the evidence. "You said the one guy, um, Wendell, that he's dead, too, but nobody will ever find anything more than his blood, right?"

"Yeah. Trust me, you don't want to know more than that."

"In that case, we can pin the séance murders on him, too. Then you came here to recover the diamonds, which I'm sure you intended to hand over to me later, but this Wendell character came round and jumped you. Took you by surprise, otherwise, I'm sure you would have won the fight."

"Thanks for making me look better than losing to that beanpole."

"Don't start thinking I like you. Just trying to sell it. Anyway, Wendell can't search the room with you around and maybe he's injured, too, so he runs. I get the disturbance call, find you, we recover the diamonds, and you get some of the credit for solving the case." He scooped the diamonds back into the pouch. "This could work. Hey, you sure you don't want to go to the hospital or nothing?"

"I'll take care of it later. I want to go home and rest."

"I got all I need. You come down to the station tomorrow and give an official statement, but I think I can make this all sound good enough to satisfy everybody."

Drummond wobbled out of the room, out of the theater, and let the morning sun warm his face. He would see his doctor later in the day, and he would have to talk with Madame Magnolia about those diamonds. No matter what, he couldn't let Lou suffer under a curse — which meant he would have to make another deal to get the curse lifted off the diamonds.

Drummond tried to sigh despite his arguing ribs. He didn't want to think about any of it. For now, he only wanted to know if Miriam had stuck around. He wouldn't blame her for leaving. He was more than a couple hours late getting back, and she had her Papa to answer to, but he hoped to see her anyway. After all, she had promised him a third date.

WHEN HE OPENED the door to his office, he smelled her floral scent. And he smiled.

CASE 17

LATE NIGHT CALL

MARSHALL DRUMMOND SCREECHED HIS CAR to a stop, the right tires bumping onto the sidewalk of a rundown tenement on the edge of Winston-Salem. Flying up the stairwell, sweat drenched his half-buttoned shirt. Two floors up. Three more to go. He kept hearing the woman's voice — desperate, haunting, afraid.

The call had come at 2:32 am. He had been in a deep, uncomfortable sleep on his office couch. Being Winston-Salem's sole detective of the bizarre and being a profitable business rarely thread together. Hitler's war didn't help. That couch had played the part of his bed for too long. After four shrill rings, his brain finally recognized the sound as reality and not the start of a weird dream.

"Please, come," a woman said. "238 Candle Street. Apartment 5-C. Hurry."

Drummond planned to say something about the late hour, about her call ruining his sleep, and about his fee doubling after midnight, but before he could utter a word, she added, "I don't want to die."

Four floors. Heart racing faster than he had driven through the slumbering streets. Those final words blazed in his head. She meant them. No hyperbole. He had heard enough authentic fear to know when he faced the real thing.

He burst onto the fifth-floor landing, one hand keeping his Fedora from leaping off his head, and sprinted to the door marked 5-C. It stood ajar. Lights were on. Slowing his approach, he pulled out his .38 and perked up his ears. Though a dark chill covered his skin, his long coat remained open. The commotion of his arrival had not awoken anyone — at least, nobody poked a head into the hall to inquire. Nobody rushed out of 5-C, either. Not a fleeing criminal. Not a frightened woman who had made a desperate call. With one hand gripping his weapon, the other pushed the door fully open.

The woman lay sprawled on the floor. Her eyes were locked open, staring at the ceiling — a needle lodged in her arm.

Drummond shook his head as he rested his weight against the doorjamb. Through heaving breaths, he said, "Well, crap."

From down the hallway, he heard the clink of a bottle. Maybe just a cat or, considering the quality of the building, a rat. Without bothering to look, he hustled into the apartment and closed the door. If the noise had been a tenant finally awake enough to see what happened at this hour, Drummond didn't relish getting caught with a dead body. Not by a civilian. Too many bad results would come from that scenario.

The woman's apartment looked rather nice for the area. A real effort had been made to spruce up the single room. Though sparse, each piece of furniture had been well-cared for, and several landscapes had been hung on the old wood walls. A radiator clanked under a slim window. A narrow writing desk bore a typewriter and harbored the only chair. Next to it, a low dresser — chipped paint but otherwise in good condition. Lines on one wall marked the rectangle of a Murphy bed stowed away, and a shallow closet faced it on the opposite wall. If not for the dead drug addict on the floor, Drummond would have guessed a respectable gal lived here.

He had to think. First obvious step — call this in. It would make for a long night of explaining himself over and over to the officers who caught the case, even if they knew him, but in the end, they would check the phone call to his office and match it against the coroner's estimated time of death. With his story clearing that obstacle, they would let him go, warning him to stick around town.

One big problem — no phone. A swift scan of the room again. Nothing. In a tenement like this, he should never have expected a private phone. Probably had one at the end of the hall on each floor, or if the landlord preferred sadism, only one phone in the main lobby downstairs. The call to Drummond's office could be traced to such a phone but not to a specific person. Unless somebody witnessed this woman making the desperate call, Drummond had no way to prove she had contacted him. Heck, he could have phoned his own office from here to establish an alibi before murdering her.

Except they wouldn't see her as a murder victim. She overdosed. Simple as that. Drummond's presence complicated matters, but most officers had a way of ignoring spooky late-night calls that would muck up a simple case. They'd probably dismiss him as an ambulance chasing PI trying to scratch a couple coins out of this unfortunate incident. One look into his bank account, and they would be thoroughly convinced.

Yet Drummond had heard that voice. This woman had feared for her life.

Okay, then. No police. At least, not while he was in the apartment. He could perform his own quick investigation and slip out before sunrise. Let somebody else find the body and report it. If he was careful, nobody would ever know he had visited, and even if the police learned of the phone call, he could deny following up on it.

Patting sweat from his brow, he gazed down at the woman and shook his head. Why would she call for help if only to shoot her arm full of poison?

Perhaps she had attempted suicide and regretted it after injecting the drug. She then raced to the phone and called him. Except the needle remained in her arm. Even if she had ignored taking it out in her panic to make the call, it would have fallen out as she rushed or stumbled down the hall. Plus, unless she had an athlete's stamina, the exertion required to reach the phone would have gotten her blood pumping faster, pushing the drug through quicker, and killed her long before she returned to her room. So, no suicide.

An accidental overdose? That didn't add up, either. For one, she called him. She was terrified. Her simple phrase — *I don't want to die* — could have been a regretful overdose, but it sounded more like a person afraid of a threat. She knew that something or someone endangered her life and wanted help. Drummond supposed she could have made the call, panicked afterward, and then shot up in an effort to calm her nerves. But the apartment's appearance discounted that idea — it was too neat, too loved.

Every inch of the tiny room told the story of a woman who cared for her life. Only the location suggested anything related to drugs, but even as the Depression slipped into the past, people still ended up in unlikely, dirt-cheap places in order to survive. The typewriter, the scant but respectable wardrobe hanging on a wood rod, the organization of every object — it suggested she worked as a secretary or in some clerical capacity. Nothing hinted at drugs beyond the needle.

Squatting next to the body, Drummond looked closer at her arm. Smooth, creamy skin. Not a single mark of previous usage.

She was thin, but not sickly so, and had her curly, blond hair cut in a stylish bob. Brown eyes, full lips, round cheeks, gentle neck, healthy frame, firm legs, and painted toenails. Not a single mark of the ill-health or self-abuse associated with an addict.

So far, he had a working woman struggling to survive economic hardship with not a single, visible sign of drug use — in her apartment or on her body. She had felt under attack or looming attack and called for help. Which brought up the most unsettling question — why did she call him?

She obviously had time to make a call, so her assailant had yet to reach her. But why not call the police? Or if she called after being forced to take an overdose, why not call a doctor or hospital? Why call a detective like him? Heck, how did she know he existed in the first place?

He scanned over the row of books lining the back ledge of her writing table. Nothing about the supernatural or witchcraft. Just some romance novels.

Perhaps this was a setup. Except if that were the case, why hadn't the police arrived to find him hunched over the body? Or the flash of a camera to blackmail him with the photo?

There was also the possibility that he had been set up by one of his many enemies in the witch community. But if that were true, where was the casting circle or the witch symbols or anything to suggest he had been the object of a curse?

"What is going on here?" he muttered to the empty room.

A glance down at the body once more. He had hoped to avoid disturbing her, but without any other visible explanations, he needed to inspect her closer. Any witch markings — tattoos, burns, or even carvings in her skin — would be hidden from daily view.

But when he rolled her to the side in order to view her back, the coldness of her skin shocked him. He stumbled away a few steps. She fell back, rigid as a log.

Drummond had never worked as a coroner nor as a medical examiner, but he had seen more dead bodies than most people. While he couldn't pinpoint the exact time of death, he knew for certain that rigor mortis usually didn't start until at least two hours after death. Two hours before she had called him.

His skin prickled.

Standing back from the body, seeing the entire apartment in a new light, he removed his hat and let out a slow breath. Logic said that a different woman could have made the call. Somebody who had stumbled upon the victim and wanted to help. Or somebody involved in the scheme — whatever it may ultimately be. Experience, however, knew better.

He set his hat back on. Time was short. When daylight hit, he had to be out of the building, or he'd get caught up in a police investigation. Normally, not a problem. But when magic got involved, the police grew fidgety. They didn't want to know about such things, and that often led to a quick arrest of the nearest suspect — close the case fast. Drummond had no intention of being the nearest suspect.

Scanning the apartment, he said, "Miss, are you in here?"

Nothing.

"If you're a ghost, I can help you. Isn't that why you called me? That call must've used everything you had, so maybe you're tired. But I need you to give me a little something right now. A thump on the wall or move your chair, or heck, just pass through me and I'll feel the cold. Something to let me know you're here."

Still nothing.

He might be wrong, but his gut told him otherwise. He held motionless, listening, watching, his intense focus locked on a search for any slight change in the room.

When he saw it, he could not believe his eyes. Her fingers twitched. Not much. Barely any motion at all. But coming from a corpse, that slight motion created tsunami waves of proof.

"Hello, there," Drummond said, frowning as he crossed his arms.

Before he asked the question — why had she chosen to move those fingers when she could have shown herself in far easier ways? — he knew the answer. She was trapped inside that body. Her ghost unable to move on, unable to roam — still alive. Alive-ish, anyway. Yet locked down in that corpse.

"Maybe." The word spoken aloud carried more weight, and he had to admit that he was guessing. But he was a good guesser. In fact, his ability to make such thought-leaps had served him well over the years. Right now, he would put his trust in that fact.

Until he learned more.

"Okay, Miss. Time for you to give me some answers."

His first stop — the writing desk. Sifting through her letters and bills, he found the easiest piece of information — her name. Natalie Pearson.

After a few minutes reading, he learned that Ms. Pearson was twenty-four, single, and employed at the front desk of a dentist's office. She kept regular contact with her mother who lived on a farm in Alamance County. Father deceased. One brother in the army.

Browsing the book titles again, nothing popped out, but Drummond combed the apartment with more serious consideration. She liked to draw but lacked much skill. Played the piano since she was young — kept all her instruction books though she lacked a piano to play upon. Ate a lot of canned beans cooked on a hotplate. Despite the money from steady employment, she lived a jobless lifestyle. A few of the letters from Mom suggested Ms. Pearson sent most of her income home. A dutiful, family gal.

When he finished his circuit of the apartment, nothing pointed to the use of or even an interest in witchcraft. He rested his eyes on her prone body once more, knowing what needed to be done but loathing the idea. Maybe he should ask her. Set up a simple system — twitch the right hand for *yes* and the left hand for *no*. It might work. But if moving that body were easy on her, she would have done so sooner, and while Drummond knew little of this curse, he knew enough about ghosts. Interacting with the corporeal world was strenuous, difficult, and often painful. Best to keep it to a minimum — even if that mean some embarrassment.

Which returned him to the body. Crouching at Ms. Pearson's side once more, he said, "My apologies for the indignity, but I have to examine you."

Moving fast and with his most professional demeanor, he unbuttoned her blouse. She wore a bra with a high-waist girdle reaching right up to her ribs. No marks on her torso that he could see. When he moved to unclasp her bra, he noticed that she still wore her work clothes. Either she had been out late that night or her death had occurred long before she would have normally dressed for bed. No symbols or marks on the breasts or under them.

He then unzipped the girdle. Nothing on the stomach. He rolled her to the side to inspect her back. Then the legs, hips, crotch, and buttocks. Nothing. He put everything back to a respectable appearance. Ms. Pearson had kept healthy and clean.

Except for the needle sticking in her arm.

The hypodermic consisted of the needle, a metal casing, and the glass vial nestled inside. Markings on the casing indicated volume units, and a cutaway allowed Drummond to see that half the vial's contents remained unused. Right away, he could tell this was not a normal drug. He had seen heroin and morphine before. They were not red, milky concoctions like this. They did not look like pale, spoiled blood.

As he gently handled the needle, careful not to remove it — not until he had better information — he noticed something etched on the underside. Two symbols. Not anything he recognized, but there were a lot of witch symbols. More than any single witch could learn in a lifetime. Or two.

Though Drummond could not identify the symbols, he had dealt with spells and curses long enough. With only two symbols and no casting circle, these would not accomplish much. They could hold power, possibly, but only enough to keep a spell alive for a time.

Added all together and it suggested that the liquid was a potion of a sort. He had learned long ago that such things existed but rarely came across it. Most witches — at least, most witches in the Carolinas —

preferred to cast spells directly. Those that liked to make potions proved a different breed, and one he had little knowledge about.

His old pal, Leroy, would probably have the answers, but he lived in the middle of the woods, a solid hour away, and had limited access to a telephone. By the time Drummond drove out there, found the old man, maybe got an answer or at least a clue, and drove back, Ms. Pearson's body would be discovered. The police would get involved and mire the whole situation in procedure. No. Drummond was on his own.

He figured he needed to know three things — what potion he dealt with, who bore responsibility for it, and how to stop it from whatever it had done. Other facts like motive and opportunity mattered for criminal prosecution, and though they might help Drummond, they weren't necessary to dealing with magic. At first glance, none of what he needed would be easily acquired. However, Drummond knew his work well, and the first glance often lied. Information abounded.

To start with, the room showed no signs of violence. Also, when he had arrived, the door was freely open. No splintered jamb. No kick marks. So, this wasn't a forced attack. Ms. Pearson knew her attacker and let the person enter without fear.

Drummond could discount a witch's direct involvement, too. The lack of witchcraft paraphernalia suggested as much, but the blunt yet bland way he found the body coupled with the use of the hypodermic solidified the proof. If a witch had been the one in this room, she would have either hidden her actions by removing the needle and staging the death — perhaps as a suicide with a forged note on the typewriter — or she would have made a brazen statement — casting circle on the floor, blood symbols on the walls, perhaps carvings into the skin.

Ms. Pearson might have owed money to a person or group that associated with magic. But she had a job and lived on the cheap. She also had plenty of possessions in the room that could have been pawned off, and nothing appeared to be missing. Plus, the kind of people who killed over owed money would have broken the door down or banged up the place. They would certainly have ransacked every drawer for jewelry, loose coin, and anything of value. Still, none of these inconsistencies meant Ms. Pearson wasn't dealing with a loan shark or other unsavory character, but Drummond didn't give the idea much credence.

In fact, Drummond saw little to suggest that Ms. Pearson associated with many people at all. He looked through the small trashcan next to the writing table — no ticket stubs to a picture house or a theater. He checked the table — no matchbooks to a bar or restaurant. He searched the rest of the room — not a single remnant pointing to any kind of social life. She had her letters to her mother, but mostly she lived through her work and her books. A solitary life. Not the kind of person to end up this way.

Like turning a faucet fully open, a rush of movement overcame Ms. Pearson's body. Her legs, arms, hips, and head all spasmed. Drummond swore he saw worry in her eyes.

The moment this sudden seizure ceased, Drummond heard the rumble of an approaching car. His watch read 3:14. He stepped aside the window and peeked onto the street below.

A well-kept 1939 Pontiac parked four cars up from his old beater. The driver, a doughy man with dark hair, hurried around to open the door. But the passenger had sat up front and after opening the door, the driver did not wait. He rushed toward the building before hastening back to the car.

"I left her right up there," the man said before realizing he spoke too loudly on an open street at three in the morning. Lowering his voice but still speaking loud enough for Drummond to hear most of the words, he went on, "I know, I know. I'm sorry. But you made the damn stuff. You could've told me she'd end up like that. I wouldn't have come for you."

Not the way an employee would speak to his boss. Clearly a lackey, but Drummond thought the driver worked with the passenger as much as for the passenger.

"Thanks for the warning," Drummond said to Ms. Pearson.

He looked at the door. It would be easy to slip out before these two men arrived, but that meant leaving Ms. Pearson behind.

"We need to hide you," he said. "Any ideas?"

He didn't expect an answer. Spoke out loud merely to help himself think. But with a jolting motion, Ms. Pearson's dead arm rose straight up, then flopped overhead. One stiff finger pointed toward the closet.

Drummond held back a wisecrack. Her action must have hurt something awful. "Okay, doll. Let's get you in there."

Lodging his grip under her arms, he dragged the dead woman across the floor. Her body moved with all the grace of a wood plank. His lungs burned from smoking too many cigarettes lately, and his sweating hands slipped. The sudden absence of dead weight caused him to lose his footing, and Drummond crashed to his backside.

The two men climbed the stairs, their clumping steps growing louder. Scrabbling back, Drummond took hold of Ms. Pearson once more. When he reached the closet, he pushed aside a few hanging dresses and attempted to ease the corpse in. But the body wouldn't stand, and the limbs wouldn't cooperate.

If this had been a stage play, it would have been a comedy. Probably a farce. All he needed was a nosey neighbor with bad eyesight to mistake him for Ms. Pearson. A drunken audience would help, too.

By the time he had Ms. Pearson situated and out of sight, he heard the two men coming down the hall. Drummond had intended to share the closet with the corpse, but he didn't see how he could fit without dislodging her. Even if he managed to avoid that horror, if he accidentally knocked over a hat box or a dress, the noise alone would give them away.

Too late to bolt from the room. No other place to hide and spy from. "Looks like it's going to be bluster and bull."

He spun the one chair in the room to face the door. As he sat, he placed his .38 on the writing desk, also pointing at the door. A few calming breaths, and he narrowed his view on the knob while he focused his thoughts on how he wanted this to play out.

But a luxury like Time did not come his way. The footsteps stopped. The knob turned.

The doughy driver entered first. He looked even smaller now, sweating through his workman's shirt, lines forming alongside his suspenders. Behind him came the passenger — a flat-nosed bruiser wearing a suit with the jacket on the shoulders like a cape. Very European. The kind of guy that had spent most of his days shaking down people and somehow got promoted to bossing around a few underlings.

The driver focused on the floor, expecting Ms. Pearson's corpse. "What the —"

"Evening, gentlemen," Drummond said.

Both men startled, their eyes snapping up before their heads followed. The man-in-charge reached for his coat, but Drummond patted the .38, and with the shake of his head, he kept the man from doing anything stupid.

"You want I should take care of this shlump?" the driver said.

With a raised eyebrow and a smack on the ear, the man said, "You want to take a bullet?" Then to Drummond: "My apologies for barging in. We thought the place was empty."

Trying to hold back his surprise, Drummond reassessed the man. This cool politeness suggested more than a dumb bruiser. Easing his hand off the .38 — not too far off, though — Drummond said, "Oh, you thought the place had somebody in it. Just not a living somebody."

"C'mon," the driver said, rolling from one foot to the other. "We don't have to take lip from this guy."

Folding his hands in front of him, the man said, "Forgive us. It is late and Eddie here has had a rough day."

Eddie snarled but settled back a step.

Once satisfied that the immediate danger had subsided, the man nodded. "You got a name?"

"Drummond. Marshall Drummond. I'm a private investigator."

Not even a flinch. "I'm Duke."

"Just Duke?"

"It's enough for you." With a display of patience he probably did not have, Duke forced a gentle grin. "Now that we're better acquainted, Mr. Drummond, how 'bout you tell me what you did with the young lady's body."

"I'm not quite sure what you're —"

"Thing is, you don't know what you're dealing with."

"Looks like I'm dealing with a couple low-level criminals who are messing with witchcraft."

Duke tried to hide his surprise. The driver, however, looked gobsmacked. Nobody spoke for a moment, and Drummond noticed how Duke reappraised the room. Maybe searching for witch symbols or some other sign that Drummond had set a trap.

At length, Duke said, "I guess you've got the upper-hand. The girl. Your gun. So, hurry up. I'm listening."

"Nothing much to hear. Name the witch you're working for. I know you don't want to — probably more afraid of her than anything and that's smart — but you can be smarter. Help me out with a little information, and I can help you get free of whatever she's holding over you."

Even as the words left his mouth, Drummond knew he had made too many assumptions. That Duke wanted out from the witch's grasp, that he would give her up easily, that he would give up anybody easily — all wrong. The confusion flashing in Duke's eyes confirmed the mistake.

With a disgusted sneer, Duke said, "If you think I would ever let a witch —"

He never finished describing the limits he placed on a witch because Ms. Pearson slid halfway out of the closet. Part of Drummond marveled that she had stayed hidden for so long.

The air stilled. Only for a breath. All three men exchanged surprised glances. All three men calculated their next moves.

Eddie got the jump. A split-second too late, Drummond snatched up the .38, but Eddie had already launched towards Ms. Pearson. For his part, Duke eased back toward the doorway.

Drummond swung his aim toward Eddie as the pudgy man dropped to the dangling corpse. "Back off," Drummond said.

But Eddie ignored the warning. He grabbed the arm with the needle and checked it over. As he positioned his hand to resume plunging that sick serum into her veins, Drummond fired one round into the wall.

The blaring blast that filled the room would be heard throughout the building, but Drummond figured nobody would bother phoning the police. Many would sleep through it, and those rattled awake would most likely assume a car had backfired or thunder cracked from above. Within the room, however, Eddie had the sense to raise his hands.

"You're screwing everything up," he said, red-faced and clenching his fists.

"That's the idea." Side-stepping across, Drummond motioned for Eddie to join Duke. "I'd rather not let you harm a young gal trying to better her life."

The men could easily back out the door and run off. Fine by Drummond. For the moment, he focused on saving Ms. Pearson from whatever calamity these men had planned. Once he got her fully living again — or worst case, fully dead — then he could deal with locating the witch behind Duke and Eddie.

With a slight shake of the head, Eddie said, "Look, pal, you're in the deep end now, and the last thing you want is catching our eye on you."

"Ah, good. Mixed up threats."

"What the hell do you —"

"Eddie." Duke's single utterance silenced his driver.

"Seems to me, you two fellas are the ones in trouble. Your witch is going to be mighty disappointed that you failed tonight."

"I've tried to explain, we don't work for a witch. Never would."

"That's odd," Drummond said, using his free hand to take hold of the needle in Ms. Pearson's arm. "If you don't work for a witch, then how is it you know about witchcraft and symbols like the ones on this?"

"No! Wait!"

Drummond didn't often strive for the dramatic moment, but as he yanked the needle free, a satisfied gloat tinted his face as he heard Duke's panicked cry.

Panicked?

Both Duke and Eddie stared beyond Drummond with horror. And

their eyes lifted — up towards the ceiling. Drummond's shadow lengthened across the floor. Not his shadow, though. Hers.

"Damn," he muttered, peeking back and up.

Ms. Pearson floated in the room. Her eyes as dark as her growing shadow. The veins on her face pulsed with that same darkness. Both arms tensed at her sides, her hands spread wide.

Drummond backed away until he stood in line with Duke and Eddie. "You didn't think to warn me about this?"

"You were protecting her and threatening us."

"You could have mentioned she was a witch."

"I assumed you knew who you worked for."

"I barely know what part of the city I'm in."

Duke kept his focus on the floating witch as he snapped a finger at Eddie. "We've still got a job."

With a shaking nod, Eddie lowered to one knee and pulled a leather pouch from his trousers. He unrolled it on the floor — more hypodermics, more vials of milky red liquid. While preparing another shot, he snatched glimpses of the witch. She hissed and growled as her body contorted in the air.

"The half-dose we already got her with is slowing her down," Duke said. "We need to take advantage while we still have a chance."

"A bullet will put her out of her misery."

"She's not a horse. And there's a chance you'll hurt somebody innocent."

Drummond holstered his pistol. "Okay. This is your game. How do we play it?"

Gesturing to the apartment, Duke said, "This place is small. Somewhere is her cache of supplies."

"I've checked the place out. First thing I did when I came in. Nothing. I didn't even think she was a witch at all."

"She's more than that. Or less, I guess." Duke shot a scornful eye at Eddie. "You're too slow."

"I-I'm trying." Eddie slopped some of the liquid onto the floor as he attempted to refill a vial.

Drummond thought pressuring the guy only made him slower, but before he could debate speaking his mind, he learned that Duke had been right. Eddie was too slow — the witch finally found the strength to attack.

She cut through the air — claws out, mouth open and salivating, a horrid creaking in her throat — heading straight for Eddie. Drummond expected Duke to intervene, to help his partner, but Duke stepped back. Not cowering but observing. As Drummond motioned to help, it was too late. Ms. Pearson slashed at the man's arm.

Eddie yelled and dropped the vial to clutch his wound. The glass tube shattered on the floor, the red potion soaking into the wood. The reek of onions gone bad filled the air.

"Idiot," Duke said.

"I can make another."

"Hurry. I'll find that cache while you waste more time. And don't drop our last vial."

No time to get between these two. The witch had swung around, her eyes blazing darkness as she turned her attention on Drummond.

"Lady, you've really disappointed me." Drummond stepped away from Duke and Eddie. He didn't like the idea of bullfighting a witch, but if he kept her attention, then maybe these other two could finish their plan — if they really had much of one. "I know you witches don't like me, but calling me in the middle of the night as a set up — couldn't you at least let me get a full rest before toying with me?"

She hissed and launched at him. Drummond dodged aside. She slammed into the closet wall — clothes and hangers tumbling to the floor.

A quick view of the room — Eddie swirling together another vial of their potion, Duke rifling through the writing desk. "I've already looked there," Drummond said.

Slamming the desk drawer closed, Duke moved to the radiator.

"Nothing there, either."

Duke spun on Drummond. "I know how to do this."

While a smart comeback would have been satisfying, Drummond lacked the time. The witch blasted from the closet, swiping her claws as she repositioned. No need to wave a red flag. Her attention had locked on him, her nostrils flared, and she rolled her neck with a crackle.

Waiting to be slashed into streamers sounded like a bad idea, so Drummond charged ahead. She launched down upon him, and they clashed together in the middle of the apartment like two gladiators.

Though he rotated his body, she managed to catch his hip, igniting a jittered shock along his flank. He snapped a strong jab to her jaw. Her head rocked back, and her feet touched the floor for stability.

Drummond grinned. For a second. But the witch rocketed into the air, her hand curled into a fist that caught him in the gut as she flew by. He dropped to one knee, coughing and sputtering phlegm.

"The Murphy bed," Duke said.

The witch's head snapped toward the bed hidden in the wall. Of course. Drummond hadn't searched there because Ms. Pearson's body had blocked the way of swinging it down.

Duke dashed across the small room. The witch dashed after Duke.

"The serum's ready." Eddie held the prepared hypodermic overhead, and that outburst saved Duke's life.

The witch paused for an instant, unsure of what threat would prove worse. Duke, however, never stopped. With a flourish, he wrenched down the Murphy bed.

As Drummond regained his footing, he saw the black blanket with red stitching that formed a series of witch symbols. Two oversized books were nestled tight in sown pockets. Though he couldn't make out the titles, the oiled-skin look of the covers told enough — old texts of spells or curses. Mounted on the wall-framing, four red candles awaited use, and on the inside wall, a large casting circle. Not as useful as one drawn on the floor that a witch could sit within, but useful nonetheless. Hidden from daily sight.

A loud screech erupted from the witch as she dove for Duke. Her decision made, she could not change course. She snagged Duke in the back, digging her claws deep. With a yelp, he tried to twist free. No luck. The witch slammed him against the wall, hissing and spitting in ecstasy.

Though Drummond's gut still ached, he wobbled across the room with some speed. Snatching the needle from Eddie's shaking hand, Drummond stayed focused on Duke's writhing pain. The man bellowed for help. The witch yanked a gouge of flesh before digging in for more.

Careful not to give himself away, Drummond refrained from yelling anything, rushed forward, and collided into the witch's back. In the confusion of being sandwiched between her victim and her assailant, she may have missed the sharp prick in her skin as Drummond administered the serum. She knew it well, though, when her body spasmed, when her muscles failed her, when she flopped to the floor once more reduced to a corpse.

Eddie hurried to aid his boss, but Duke swatted him away. Covered in sweat, the man said, "Hurry. Finish this."

Nodding vigorously, Eddie hastened to the witch. He pulled a charcoal stick from his pocket and wrote three strange symbols on her forehead — symbols that reminded Drummond of the ones from the first needle.

"Good," Duke said. "Make sure to fill her with all of the potion."

Drummond glanced at the needle. "I did."

Sliding against the wall until he sat on the floor, Duke nodded. "Then we're done."

"No, not yet."

"Why? What did I miss?"

"Telling me what the heck is going on here, for one. Why did it matter that you found her supplies? That needle did the trick just fine. And who are you fellas? And what is this woman? I've dealt with plenty of witches, and they don't act like this."

As Eddie drew a circle around the witch's body, Duke produced a silk handkerchief and patted his forehead. Drummond considered leaving. He wanted answers, but maybe it would be better to go back to his couch in the office and get some sleep. Forget tonight even happened.

"I am Duke Blanchard, and I think you know exactly what we are. Like you, we're witch hunters."

"Sorry, pal. I'm a private investigator."

"But you know of witches."

"I investigate matters of the strange. I don't seek it out, don't hunt it down. You two — you go around killing witches?"

Waggling an index finger, Duke said, "We always offer them a chance to reform. Ms. Pearson refused even to admit she practiced the craft. That was the need to find her paraphernalia. Don't want to kill an innocent, after all."

"The floating dead woman with blackened eyes wasn't enough proof?"

"We have rules. Otherwise, we'd be nothing but hoodlums." Duke stood, brushing his suit down. "I appreciate your attempt to help tonight. It shouldn't have gone this way, but Eddie panicked when the witch's body fell semi-dead."

Eddie clenched his jaw. "You never told me that'd happen."

With an embarrassed grin, Duke leaned toward Drummond. "His first time in action. Well, we'll finish here and be on our way. I don't think you'll have to worry about witches for a while. They tend to grow quiet in an area once we've dispatched one of their kind."

Drummond wanted to dispatch that cockiness from Duke's face, but instead, he set his hat on and headed to the door. No use arguing with bigots. Especially bigots with something to truly fear. After all, witches did have real power. The fact that they were still women, still human, meant nothing to these two. Drummond had been around enough idiots like this to know he couldn't change their minds. After all, if they ever saw witches as actual people, they'd have to come to grips with all the murders they had committed.

Duke and Eddie exchanged a look in silence. Then Eddie began cleaning up. Over the next twenty minutes, he would clear away all evidence of witchcraft — going so far as to paint over the markings on the wall. The furniture would return to its rightful places, too. When they left, nobody would be able to tell anything terrible had occurred in that apartment. Not even the police.

"Wait," Duke said as Drummond stepped into the hall. "My card. In case you ever need to be rid of another witch. Eddie and I travel all over the country, but my service takes messages and I call in every day. If you need me, I'll find out."

Drummond pocketed the card. Biting back the urge to say something nasty, he nodded toward Ms. Pearson. "What're you going to do with her?"

"We'll take her to a nearby city and have her cremated before dawn."

"I suggest Greensboro. It's closest."

"I appreciate the information. Thank you."

He flicked the brim of his hat and left. Once behind the wheel, he drove down the block and turned away. When he thought he could no longer be seen or heard, he floored the accelerator. A few trucks and late-night drivers were on the roads, but most folks either slept or had started a pre-dawn routine. He cut half the drive time by speeding, and when he blustered into his office, he dove straight for the phone on his desk.

"Morning," he said when the desk sergeant answered. "Is Detective Lou Piper in yet?"

"Detective Piper won't be in for a few hours."

"You'll want to call him in for this. I've got a couple murderers he'll want to catch. They're headed to Greensboro right now."

CASE 18

GIFT FOR A TRUE FRIEND

MARSHALL DRUMMOND NEVER FOUND IT EASY to keep friends. This fact only became worse when he hung out his shingle as Winston-Salem's only private investigator of the bizarre and supernatural. Apparently, some people found dealing with witches, ghosts, and magic scary. However, Drummond had one friendship that never failed — Leroy Parker. Not only had Leroy proven to be a loyal friend, but he had become an invaluable resource for many of Drummond's cases.

Leroy's deep interest in the occult provided Drummond with a sounding board and a research specialist — highly important considering Drummond hated bookwork. More than that, Leroy was honest and trustworthy. These qualities, and many more, explained why Drummond drove an hour outside of Winston-Salem, braving the treacherous icy roads, and trudged through the December snow to reach a barely warm cabin in the middle of the woods all to deliver a holiday gift.

As a lover of knowledge, Leroy preferred the solitude of his book-filled cabin over the companionship of his fellow man. With his favorite subject being the occult, he had to remain cautious and vigilant — witches did not like when others learned their secrets. Leroy found isolation an excellent way to evaded witch curses. As Drummond shivered in the wet cold, he had to agree. A witch would have to be mighty pissed-off to bother seeking Leroy in this weather. But above all else, Leroy preferred his lonely cabin because it kept him away from most white men. He enjoyed a measure of freedom in the woods that he could never achieve being black in the city.

Drummond cinched his coat tighter and lowered his Fedora. His boots cut through the fresh snow, the bitter wet soaking his socks and chilling his feet. He adjusted his grip on the neck of a whiskey bottle with a yellow bow around it. Not only a gift for Leroy but an apology for not having visited in a long time.

"Not a step further," Leroy's gruff voice called out. "You're trespassing. Come any closer and I have every right to put you down."

Raising his hands, making sure Leroy saw the whiskey bottle with the ribbon around the neck, Drummond said, "Is that any way to treat a friend bringing gifts?"

A pause. Then: "Drummond?"

"Yeah, it's me. Will you lower the shotgun or rifle or whatever you got aimed on me?"

Leroy's laugh carried across the forest, and Drummond heard a double-barrel shotgun being set against the porch of the cabin.

"Well, come on in. It's cold out there tonight. We don't need to be freezing anything important."

Brushing off snow as he entered the small cabin, Drummond inhaled the air with a smile. A mixture of cigarettes and wood fire — the delightful aroma that blended friendship with a warmth equal to how they would soon feel once they had whiskey in their bellies. The cabin consisted of a large room with a small bedroom attached. In the large room, a table took up the center for eating, researching, and anything else a table could be used for. The fireplace crackled on the left side while the kitchen dominated the right. In between, every imaginable book on the occult lined the walls.

Leroy grabbed two glasses and plunked them onto the table. Always an observant fellow, he gestured toward Drummond's left-hand which had not been removed from his coat pocket. "You here for something besides holiday drinks?"

Bowing his head and wincing guilt, Drummond pulled out a small brooch — two birds kissing on a branch. Silver with little flecks of gold trim. No jewels. It was all Drummond could afford.

"I'd like it to be a gift for my gal."

Leroy nodded. "But you want to make sure she doesn't get anything extra along with it."

"Exactly. It's not like I could buy this brand new. The shop I got it from had plenty of trinkets that looked questionable. Miriam puts up with a lot dating me. She shouldn't get a witch's curse or worse from a gift of jewelry."

Picking up the brooch, Leroy said, "Anything for a friend."

An hour went by as Leroy studied the handiwork of whoever made the brooch and then compared his findings against several of his books. Drummond sat at the table. He wanted to open the bottle of whiskey, but Leroy could not be bothered until he found an answer to the brooch question. Until then, Drummond would have to wait.

Another twenty minutes went by before Leroy closed the fourth book he had stacked into a tower. With a gentle smile, he slid the brooch toward Drummond. "I think it's completely safe. No curses, no strange histories, nothing to worry about. She's going to love it."

"Thanks, pal. I'd say that's a finding worth celebrating."

Leroy chuckled. "I like the way you're thinking."

But as he reached for the whiskey bottle, the heavy thud of boots on the porch was followed by a sharp triple-knock at the door.

"You expecting somebody?" Drummond asked.

"I wasn't even expecting you."

The knocks became a hard pound. A weasel voice said, "Come on. I know you're in there."

Drummond pulled out his .38 and checked the weapon. After a knowing look with Leroy, he stepped into the side bedroom and closed the door, leaving a crack open to peer through.

More pounding on the door. Leroy gave Drummond one final look — concern beading like sweat — and he answered.

Two men burst into the cabin. One stood tall and lanky, wore filthy overalls, and carried a Springfield bolt-action rifle. Probably his daddy's from the poor way he held it.

Darting his eyes about the cabin, the man said, "You got to help my brother."

Though not as tall, the brother was equally thin. Drenched in sweat with sunken eyes and pasty skin, he looked like he might keel over at any moment.

"Cody, sit down," the gunman said.

The sick-looking brother found his way to one of the chairs at the table. He flopped down with a sigh as if expending his last reservoir of energy.

Inching forward with the Springfield, the man said, "You're Leroy Parker, right?"

Leroy nodded. He had too much life experience and was too smart to speak.

"All right, then. You're going to help us."

Cody gazed up at his brother. "Hank, it don't need to be this way."

"Shush. I'm handling this."

He nudged Leroy's shoulder with the rifle's muzzle. "You're going to do exactly what I say. You don't, and I'll put a hole right through your head."

"Yes, Mr. Hank," Leroy said. "I'll take a look at your brother right away."

Drummond eased the bedroom door closed. All he had wanted was a quiet evening in the woods and a nice holiday drink with his friend. Was that too much to ask?

He double-checked that his weapon was fully-loaded before crossing the room to its one window. He unlatched it and pushed it open all the way. The bite of winter cut into him as he flopped over the edge and into the snow. Ice melt soaked his pants and somehow trickle down his back. He decided right then that killing these two men might be the best option.

Hank's muffled voice blared out in anger. Leroy must have been stalling. That got Drummond to his feet and scurrying around the front.

Staying low, Drummond approached the porch. He couldn't recall a squeaky step or any loose boards, but he moved slow and careful just in case. He figured he had a little breathing room because Hank would not have come all this way just to kill the guy he needed to help his brother. But having extra time did not mean Drummond would come up with anything good to do.

Pressing one foot onto the porch step, Drummond cringed. He put his weight down and expected to hear Hank yell, come racing out, and blindly shoot. But the step did not squeak, and there was nothing for Hank to notice. Once on the porch, Drummond sidled next to a window and peeked in.

Cody had his arm on the table, and it looked wrapped in a metallic cast from wrist to elbow. Hank stood near the front door, holding the rifle up and using it as a sight toward whatever he looked at. Not a very effective approach in this situation, and Drummond thought he'd take advantage of it.

With a gentle touch, Drummond placed one hand on the door. If he shoved it open, Hank would whirl around, using the gun to align his eyesight. Drummond could duck beneath the swinging arm of the gun and charge ahead. Or he could use both his arms to block the swinging weapon, and then utilize that spinning momentum to send his own body around. He could shove his back into his enemy and deliver an elbow to the chest. The third option would be to duck the weapon and immediately shoot forward while thrusting his hands up. If Hank reflexively squeezed the trigger, the bullet would lodge into Leroy's ceiling as Drummond's hands lodged in Hank's gut.

He was capable of all three moves, but it turned out to be unnecessary.

"Look here, look here." Good old Leroy. Of course, he noticed the front door opening and made sure to pull the assailants' attention. Drummond had no trouble entering the cabin and pressing his weapon against the back of Hank's head.

"How about we start this whole night over?" Drummond said.

Hank did not share the sentiments. Nor did he cooperate by acting in any manner that Drummond had expected. With an oddly practiced move — as if he had experienced a gun against the back of his head before — Hank cocked his head out of the way and whirled around on Drummond. With his free hand, he struck, gaining time to bring around the rifle. Drummond stumbled back. He couldn't let Hank take aim, but that didn't give Drummond time to aim either. As he banged into the doorway, Drummond shot blind.

His weapon blared out, sending a flash of light into the cabin. With a shriek, Hank dropped to the floor. He clasped his kneecap and curled into a ball.

When Drummond regained his footing, he took a quick scan of the room. Cody had not moved. He wouldn't dare — Leroy held a hunting knife against the man's wrist. Walking over to the kitchen area, Drummond grabbed a towel and tossed it at Hank. "Don't want you bleeding to death, and I don't want Leroy mopping his floor all night. And quit whining. It's annoying."

As he watched Hank wriggle up against the wall and tie off his bleeding knee, Drummond noticed the most heartbreaking results of this scuffle. His bottle of whiskey had smashed on the floor. What a waste.

He swiped the rifle and ejected the remaining bullets. Once empty and double-checked, he handed the neutered weapon back to Hank.

"Now, anybody want to explain what's going on?"

Leroy said, "It's over here."

Holstering his .38, Drummond stepped behind Leroy and glanced at the table. The metal cast on Cody's forearm — more like an ancient bracer — had intricate, meaningless designs. But mixed in with these brass flourishes, somebody had burned a pentagram near the wrist. Witch symbols dotted the outside of the circle.

"That ain't good."

Leroy glanced up. "They want me to get it off him."

"Can't say I blame them, but why did you boneheads go with such a violent approach? You could've just asked."

Cody scoffed. "This black guy ain't going to help us. Never would unless we forced him."

Glancing down at Leroy, Drummond said, "You have bad blood with them?"

"I got bad blood with most white folks. You're the exception, though the last few times you've come here, I got nothing but trouble."

"Now hold on. I didn't bring these fellas. They were coming whether I was here or not. And that time we got cursed together, I think I'm the one who should be complaining."

Cody kicked at the table. "Stop bickering and get to helping me." Looking pastier than before, Cody said, "I'm real sorry about the way we came in here. We didn't think you'd want to help us. We figured you'd figure that we deserve this — once you hear how this all happened."

From the floor, Hank said, "You shut up. They don't need to know nothing."

Drummond crossed over to Hank and nudged the wounded knee with his foot. "I got more bullets. You want to go for the other knee?" Hank didn't respond which Drummond took to be a sign of acceptance.

He pulled a chair at the table and sat. After sharing a look with Leroy, he decided it best to give the young man a bone. "Look, kid, I know you're scared of whatever's going on, but you've got my word. Leroy here is the best. If you want to find out what this thing is, what it might do to you, and what you've got to do to get it off, he's your best bet. You must've known that to some degree otherwise you wouldn't have come here."

"Mr. Leroy's got a reputation."

Leroy said, "And you were out of options."

Cody nodded.

With a single clap of his hands, Drummond said, "See that, Cody? You didn't have to come guns a-blazing after all. Now tell us what happened, and we'll see if we can fix that."

Swallowing hard Cody said, "It all started back in '31."

"Sheesh," Drummond said, knocking his knuckles on the table. "You had this thing on you since 1931?"

"Oh, no, sir. That's just the first time I saw the lady in the blue dress." Cody paused as Leroy turned the metal bracer to the side. He motioned for Cody to continue. Then: "I was only eight, and I was fishing out on the pond in the woods out back of the family farm. She just appeared there like out of nowhere. Hank thinks I don't pay enough attention, and that might be true, I have a hard time sometimes, but all's I know is that at one moment I was fishing by myself, and next moment there's this lady in a blue dress on the opposite side of the water. She said I was a handsome young man, and I told her I'd never seen such a pretty lady before, and that was the truth. She must have liked that because she said that maybe someday when I was older, she'd come back and see if I became a handsome man."

Drummond glanced at Leroy. "This sound like anything you know?"

Leroy said, "Could be lots of things. Some cultures believe in the incubus that seduces you into losing your soul. But none of the seduction stories end up with a metal arm."

"Okay, kid. Give us the rest."

Cody straightened. "I didn't see her again until last week. Hank and I had finished the day's work on the farm, and I headed out to the pond. I've always loved relaxing by the water. I think I may have forgotten all about that lady, but when she appeared, it rushed right back into me."

"You actually saw her appear this time?"

"No, sir. She stepped out from behind a tree. Looked exactly like she did back in '31."

"Oh, no," Leroy said.

Ignoring Cody's panicked expression and Drummond's curious one, Leroy left the table for his bookshelves. As he searched through the pages, Cody tried to speak, but Drummond hushed the boy. In a low voice, he said, "Let the man work."

At length, Leroy returned with one book and opened it flat on the table. He pointed to a drawing of a young woman with a devilish grin.

"That's her," Cody said.

"This book calls her a *nicheto*, but she goes by lots of names. Different cultures, different religions, many of them have a version of the *nicheto*. Basically, they live off health and youth and vigor of young male adults. You sleep with this woman?"

"What?" Cody reddened as his voice raised a pitch.

"No shame in it. She's a fine-looking woman. But I got to know if you slept with her, and if you did, was she your first?"

"Well, gee, I don't see how that's really —"

From the floor, Hank said, "Just answer the question. We need to fix this and get me to a hospital."

Cody rolled his lips in but nodded. Leroy turned the page and pointed to an illustration similar to the contraption on Cody's arm. "When you woke up afterwords, you had this on your arm, right?"

Again, Cody nodded.

Drummond said, "Let me get this straight. You meet this woman, sleep with her, while you're in blissful dreams after, she puts this thing on your arm, you wake up, and she's gone. That about right?"

"That's the strange part," Leroy said. "She should've stayed."

"Oh?"

"The whole point of seducing the boy was to get that contraption on him. With that she can nurse his soul right from his fingers. It's the whole point of this. Why would she leave?"

Squirming in his seat, Cody said, "Well, you see, she did leave a note."

Drummond waited but nothing more was said. Finally, he smacked the table. "And?"

"And what?"

"What did the note say?"

Acting bashful once more, Cody said, "Oh nothing you need to hear about. Just pillow talk kind of stuff."

"He's lying," Hank said. "He can't read, and neither can I."

Wiping the frustration from his face, Drummond said, "I swear, you better have brought that note with you or I'm going to put a bullet in your knee to match your brother's."

Fumbling as he raced into his pockets, Cody produced a folded piece of paper. He threw it onto the table as if it might bite him. Drummond snatched it in a quick motion and made sure to glower at Cody for a moment before turning his attention to the note.

For Leroy's benefit, Drummond read aloud. "My dear sweet Cody, from the first time I met you, I decided you were going to be one of my greatest conquests. But now that I have won, I feel empty. More than any other man I have known, you are so innocent and earnest. You love your brother, your family, and want nothing more than to provide for them through your farm. Normally I don't know my victims. But somehow, through each sweet kiss and each soft caress between us, you kept talking about them, and I kept listening. I hope you can forgive my lies that put you in this situation. I decided to spare you, but I cannot remove the soul catcher. Nothing can. I wish I had realized how special you are before attaching it. I might even be so bold to say that I might love you. Enjoy your life. Live it with all the honesty you showed me tonight. For you have been spared, and that is no small gift."

Drummond let the note fall to the table. He scratched his chin before shooting an inquisitive look at Leroy.

"Don't look at me. This is a first as far as I know."

Cody said, "What's that mean?"

Using the wall for support, Hank pushed up to standing. "It means that either you are the greatest lover in the history of mankind or the luckiest fool I've ever known. Merry Christmas, brother. She's letting you live."

"What about this thing on me, this soul catcher?

"Sounds like it don't ever come off. That right, Mr. Leroy?"

Leroy skimmed over the rest of the entry in the book. "If there's a way to remove it, it ain't here."

"Guess we just got to cut off my brother's arm."

"Hey." Cody looked terrified until he saw the smirk on Hank's face.

"Come on. We got to get my leg fixed and figure out how you're going to live with that thing." Hank glanced at Drummond and Leroy. "Thanks, I guess. Sorry about your whiskey."

Drummond said, "Sorry about your knee."

With some awkward maneuvering, Cody acted as a crutch for his brother. The two men shuffled outside into the snow to find their way home. Drummond closed the door and turned back to his old friend.

"That might be the strangest case I've ever dealt with."

"If you can call it that."

"Why not? They came in with supernatural troubles, and we solved that for them. Just happened to simply be reading a note that did it." Drummond sat at the table. "Too bad we don't have that whiskey to celebrate our victory."

Leroy opened the cabinet in the kitchen. "Says who?" He pulled out a bottle of whiskey with the same yellow bow. "I figured it be a good gift for you, too."

Drummond laughed. "You are a true friend." The remaining hours of snow and holiday spirit went by uneventfully. Other than the whiskey, Drummond could think of no better gift.

CASE 19

THE MAGIC FIX

DRUMMOND
PARANORMAL
INVESTIGATOR

STANDING IN THE DOORWAY of Ms. Racheal Cohen's apartment, Marshall Drummond tried to shake off the disturbing morning. He needed to concentrate. Searching the apartment to uncover how Ms. Cohen ended up in her predicament outweighed the rest.

With a careful turn, he surveyed the one-bedroom space. Small with a sink, counter, and icebox tucked in one corner, a shallow closet against one wall, and a narrow door leading to a tiny bedroom. Clean and organized. Drummond had no doubt that the cabinets above the counter would reveal the contents neat, straight, and possibly alphabetized.

No bathroom. Poor lady had to handle matters in a shared room elsewhere on the floor. The apartment had a rug of striped concentric circles, and the walls had several paintings. None of it fancy or expensive.

Might as well start with the obvious.

He strode to the circular rug and pulled it back. Nothing but wood slats underneath. It would've been nice and easy if he had found a witch's casting circle, but everything about this case promised to be the opposite.

Things had started while walking back to his office from a good diner breakfast. Drummond had his Fedora pulled low against an unexpected rainstorm. Well, unexpected to him. The three people under a large umbrella outside his building had come prepared. Even more unexpected — when he reached them, he discovered the owner of Moe's Books, Mr. Rosen, standing with an old gentleman wearing a Jewish skullcap and a white fringed garment under a black vest. Between the men, Miriam Rosen smiled.

Despite Mr. Rosen's disapproval, his daughter had spent months using any excuse to escape his watchful eye so that she could visit Drummond. Dates of dancing, eating, a movie, a play, and of course, many hours exploring the surfaces of Drummond's physique. Mr. Rosen had been clear that Miriam could never be with Drummond long term. Drummond was a *goy* — a non-Jew — and that ended any future for them.

"I don't care," she had told Drummond once after a rigorous bit of physicality. "If you had seen Germany, you'd know. Better to enjoy what life you have now."

Ms. Cohen's apartment showed a woman who appreciated life through order. She filled it with books and figurines. Each in its place.

Nothing pointed to her being a witch, though. If he had not seen her, he would have assumed she was a normal person with a penchant for literature.

But he had seen her.

The elderly gentleman standing in the rain with Miriam and Mr. Rosen had been introduced as Rabbi ben Scholl. He had come to Winston-Salem five years ago to oversee the building of the city's first and only synagogue. In the process, he fell in love with North Carolina and its tiny Jewish community. He decided to stay.

"What's this about?" Drummond asked.

The Rabbi glanced along the street before bending closer. "A witch," he whispered.

He lived in a two-story house one block up from the synagogue — a short drive in the Rabbi's Model T. Nice, quiet neighborhood yet still connected to a wide road that led back into the heart of Winston-Salem. Plenty of men with skullcaps and fringe walked in the diminishing rain.

Once inside, Miriam excused herself to make coffee, and at that moment, Drummond wondered why she had come along. Not that he minded — any excuse to see her was welcome — but he considered her role might be as insurance. They may have feared he would refuse to help. He tried to be understanding. After all, just because Germany was the enemy didn't mean every American would welcome the Jews.

The Rabbi invited Drummond into his study. A heavy wood desk dominated the room. Two stiff-backed chairs sat aside endless books stacked in piles against overflowing bookshelves.

"My people have a strange relationship with magic," the Rabbi said, wasting no time as they sat.

Drummond had seen it before. Many clients couldn't discuss these difficult matters unless protected by walls they knew. For most, the act of hiring a paranormal detective meant their world had been shattered. Suddenly ghosts, witches, magic, and such were real. These clients sought familiar ground before they could talk. For the Rabbi, it appeared to be his study.

The Rabbi continued, "We are a practical people. We study and debate the Torah. We live quiet lives in this wonderful land. We try to avoid trouble. On the other hand, in the Torah, we find men like Moses. With help from above, Moses predicted the future, parted a vast sea, and led his tribe through a punishing desert. Magic flowed through him. So, you see, we believe in magic of a sort. But there is a small group within us that believes we all should wield magic."

Miriam entered with three steaming cups on a silver tray. "You're just getting to believing in magic?"

"Miriam!" Mr. Rosen scowled.

"It's okay," the Rabbi said. "I do tend to ramble, but I wanted Mr. Drummond to understand how we see what we see."

To divert attention from Miriam while also keeping these men on track, Drummond said, "I take it you have a witch problem."

Licking his lips, pulling in small hairs from his thick beard, the Rabbi thrust a single finger in the air. "Ms. Rachael Cohen. A good, Jewish girl. Helps those around her. Follows the Torah. Stays within the community."

Drummond ignored the pointed glare from Mr. Rosen. His daughter, however, clanked a coffee mug on the table.

Before she could voice her opinions, the Rabbi continued, "Last night, Ms. Cohen's neighbor called for me. Mr. Davison heard strange noises coming through the walls. When I showed up, I found … well, you'll see. If you will follow, you should meet Ms. Cohen."

The men headed toward the basement door. When Miriam stayed behind, Drummond glanced back. "You're not coming?"

She shook her head. "I'm not welcome."

He wanted to say something kind but knew Mr. Rosen heard everything. Any small gesture of caring would be picked up, and Drummond might cause Miriam more trouble. He opted for a simple nod.

As he searched Ms. Cohen's apartment, he wondered if perhaps Mr. Rosen had been right. Not in excluding his daughter — that custom, which carried over into many religions, lacked creditability and imagination. Rather, Drummond considered that dating Miriam, no matter how strong their feelings, might only bring the young lady suffering. At best, their relationship would end bittersweet.

But what if their time together sullied her reputation? He knew little of the Jewish people, yet he had seen many cultures mistreat their most-prized sex. Then again, Miriam knew what she wanted, what she risked, and what her community demanded. She chose to spend time with Drummond, anyway. Who was he to deny her?

In Ms. Cohen's kitchen, things proved to be as orderly as expected. In fact, the only disruption was the cracked soup bowl in the sink — the remnants of chili stained the sides — and the spoon that didn't match the other cutlery. Drummond looked for signs of struggle. Nothing. That was information itself. The lack of witchcraft evidence, the abundance of nothing — Drummond concluded rather than a witch, Ms. Cohen was the victim of a witch. Especially considering the woman he had met in the Rabbi's cellar.

Dark and damp place, that cellar had a concrete floor outlined by a brick foundation. Low ceiling, musty smell. Dim light from the rainy day peeked through a small rectangular window near the top.

Hunched over in the cramped space, the Rabbi led Drummond toward the back corner. Long before he saw Ms. Cohen, he heard metal clinking. A heavy chain connected to a bolt in the wall leashed the young woman by a leather strap around her neck. Drummond held back any shock.

"Please," the Rabbi said with a bashful squint. "We don't know what to do. That's why you're here. To help us. To help her."

Walking closer, Drummond caught a sour odor like ammonia. When he finally saw Ms. Cohen, he understood. She was barely human.

Bent over and hooting grunts like an ape, her eyes blazed at him with a mix of hope and hatred. Between the shadows and shafts of gray light, he noticed a greenish tinge to her skin. It had a flaky texture like a peeling sunburn. Saliva dribbled from her half-open mouth, and razor-sharp teeth daggered beneath her lips. Blood dotted her bottom lip where her teeth continually dug in.

"She's getting worse," Mr. Rosen said. "When the Rabbi called me over, she looked more normal. She smelled better, too."

The Rabbi said, "You are the best in the city with this sort of matter, yes?"

"Who told you that?" Drummond asked.

"Miriam." Mr. Rosen gave Drummond an accusing glare. "She overheard the Rabbi and I talking and said you might handle these things. We asked around, and you've built a reputation with those who know."

Drummond winced. A *reputation* would be good for gaining business, bad for dealing with business. Last thing he needed was a bunch of witches targeting him because he got too good at his job.

Then again, as he finished his search of Ms. Cohen's apartment, he wondered if he was any good at all. He hadn't found a single thing that could be called helpful, let alone a clue. Labelling Ms. Cohen a victim simply shifted the burden outside the apartment.

However, *outside* did include the neighbors. The Rabbi had said that a neighbor called worried over strange noises through the walls. Remembering his old beat cop days, Drummond decided to take the methodical route. Interview all the neighbors on the floor until he found the right one.

On one side, he met a woman with a baby, a toddler, and a hangover. She said nothing useful and plenty rude. On the other side, nobody answered. But the apartment across the hall won the prize.

Mr. Joshua Davison, a portly fellow who worked at the corner bakery, said he had heard odd noises from Ms. Cohen's apartment. "So loud, in fact, I couldn't believe it didn't bother the whole floor, in fact."

"And you called the Rabbi?"

He shrugged. "Who else should I have called?"

"The police."

"I heard no crime committed, and quite frankly, the police aren't friendly to our people."

Drummond opened his mouth to protest, but Mr. Davison wasn't exactly wrong. Though modern-thinking men existed throughout North Carolina, even on the police force, Drummond couldn't deny that a greater number still clung to a dream of returning to the South of old. Some mystical time when black people loved being slaves and all white men lived lives of wealth and ease. As for the Jewish people — well, they didn't exist in that fiction.

"Anything else?" Mr. Davison asked, he cheeks a bit red, his fingers jittering at his side.

"You okay?"

"A little off, in fact. But that's all."

"That why you're not working? A bakery is usually an early morning kind of job, isn't it?"

"I have a cold. You'd better not stand any closer. Wouldn't want you to catch anything."

He motioned to close the door. As Drummond turned to leave, his gut itched about this guy. Something was wrong. Then the man added: "How does she look, anyway?"

Strange way to ask. *Is she okay? Is she sick? What's wrong with her?* Anything like that would have passed over Drummond without a thought. But asking how she looked suggested *something* had happened to change her. That led to another thought — the small problem with the initial call to the Rabbi that was out of the ordinary.

Drummond grabbed the jamb before Mr. Davison could close the door. "I have a couple more questions."

"I really need to get some rest." Davison's face paled.

"The Rabbi sent me, and since you called him, I'm guessing you care what he thinks. Should I tell him that you didn't want to help?"

"I did help. Made sure Ms. Cohen got cared for, in fact."

Drummond perked up. He loved when a suspect made things easy. "That's right. The Rabbi said you called because you heard strange sounds through the walls." He glanced behind at Ms. Cohen's door. "You don't share a wall. Any sounds from her apartment had to go through her door, across the hall, through your door, and you had to recognize those sounds as coming from her place instead of anywhere else in the building."

Mr. Davison's face blanched as he drifted back several steps. His lip quivered. "It's not my fault."

"Never said it was." Drummond entered the dingy place. Hit by the sharp stench of garlic mixed with an unwashed body, he resisted the urge to cover his nose.

"Go away."

"You were in that apartment."

"Please."

Drummond took another step, and Mr. Davison's face dropped. The realization, the acceptance, that he had been caught, that he had no escape, that he would have to confess to his crimes, washed over him with a cold shudder. Drummond has seen it before. Next came either tears or belligerence.

Mr. Davison found a third option.

He rushed toward the back wall that looked over the street. Screaming the entire time, Mr. Davison hurled himself through the window. The shattering glass blended with his terrified cries. Before Drummond managed another step, he heard the wet thud on the street below. New screams erupted from horrified pedestrians.

Drummond held still.

He fought the urge to look. If he gazed upon the scene from the shattered window, someone might spot him. He would have to spend hours at the police station clearing his name, something he had done more than once in his career.

Avoiding the police meant he had to hurry. Soon, they would be called to investigate. He needed to be gone. But not before investigating on his own.

The layout of the apartment mirrored Ms. Cohen's, but it lacked her cleanliness and organization. Dirty dishes, pots, and a cutting board filled the sink. Layers of dust piled in the corners. A stained mug formed a new ring among many on a wood table next to a torn couch. A sharp, spicy smell filled the place — not sweet confections one might expect from a baker but rather a savory, garlic aroma. Onions, peppers, and spices, too. It reminded Drummond of the cooking in the Mexican part of the city where all the tobacco fieldworkers lived.

From below: "That's Mr. Davison!"

Crap. Now, he had to worry about a neighbor coming up to Mr. Davison's apartment.

Taking a final survey of the main room, Drummond moved toward the hallway. He froze. Sitting on the kitchen counter, barely visible under a filthy towel, he spied a book. The tattered cover had a six-pointed star set in a circle. Not exactly a witch symbol but close enough.

He swept open the book. The strange, blocky characters did not resemble witch writing. In fact, it looked more like the writing in Rabbi ben Scholl's study. Hebrew. Pocketing the book, Drummond left the apartment.

On the street, a crowd gawked at the horror splashed against the sidewalk. He had seen enough dead bodies, and he expected to see more before his life concluded. Still, as he walked away, a guilty twinge plucked his chest. Mr. Davison would not have killed himself had Drummond not knocked on the door — at least, it wouldn't have happened then.

But that guilt left fast. Messing with magic set Davison up for his grim death. Not Drummond trying to save a young lady.

Soon, Drummond stood in the Rabbi's stuffy study. At his desk, Rabbi ben Scholl hunched over the book Drummond had retrieved while Mr. Rosen sat nearby watching with an eager eye. Miriam prepared tea in the kitchen. Drummond had never seen her act so domestic. He found it both charming and disturbing as if he witnessed Greta Garbo baking a cake.

At length, the Rabbi settled back, his chair groaning. "Mr. Davison was a disturbed man, an unholy man."

"Then it is witchcraft," Drummond said.

"It is Kabbalah — the more mystical version of Judaism. Numbers hold great significance, and numerical relationships are highly important."

"Okay. What evil thing did Mr. Davison do to Ms. Cohen with magic numbers?"

The Rabbi shook his head. "Not that simple." He tapped the book. "The number in question is thirteen."

"Ah," Mr. Rosen said as if this explained the entire situation.

Drummond folded his arms. "You're going to have to be more

specific."

When the Rabbi opened his mouth to speak, Miriam entered with the tea. He waited until the tea was served. He said nothing the entire time.

Miriam remained comfortable under their gazes, pouring the tea as if her presence hadn't changed the room. After snatching a quick glance at Drummond, she left. The Rabbi and Mr. Rosen sipped their tea twice before setting the cups down with soft clinks.

"The number thirteen," Rabbi ben Scholl said, "holds great significance. Both good and evil."

Mr. Rosen cocked his head toward Drummond. "Surely, you're familiar with the *bar mitzvah*."

"Something about becoming a man, right?" Drummond leaned back against a bookshelf.

The Rabbi nodded. "At age thirteen, a boy is initiated into manhood by leading the *bar mitzvah* service at the synagogue. It is an important and wonderful moment in a young boy's life."

"Don't women get them, too?"

Mr. Rosen ruffled, but Rabbi ben Scholl said, "That started recently. 1922. Rabbi Mordecai Kaplan performed the first *bat mitzvah* with his daughter in New York City. Not everybody thinks this is a good idea."

"Is that why Mr. Davison hurt Ms. Cohen? She have a *bat mitzvah?*"

"Remember, thirteen is a number both good and evil. On the one hand, it represents unity and our ability to rise above evil influences. But on the other hand, many see the number appear in Kabbalah's darker magical practices. Because of his horrible reaction when you questioned Mr. Davison, we can assume that he intended no harm for Ms. Cohen. He felt guilty and punished himself."

"Whether or not he regretted anything doesn't matter. It's done. How does the number thirteen help Ms. Cohen now?"

The Rabbi tilted his head back as he perused his bookshelves. With a grin, he rose and removed one dusty volume before settling back in his chair. Flipping through the pages, he went on, "The use of thirteen and Mr. Davison's actions lead me to believe that he cast a spell to either help Ms. Cohen in some way or win her affections."

"A love spell?"

"A potion, more likely. Easier for the beginner. But magic is an unstable use of the universe's energies, and it can be difficult to handle."

"You got that right." Drummond had witnessed many novices achieve horrendous results.

"There are several spells centering on thirteen ingredients, and one of them — ah, yes, here it is — a spell for attaining the heart of another." The Rabbi grew quiet as he read. He then checked Mr. Davison's book. "Yes, yes. Mr. Davison had attempted a version of this spell, but several of the ingredients are rare. Difficult to find in America. He writes in the margins his substitutions that, to his mind, seemed equivalent."

Drummond clicked his tongue. "Spells never like substitutions."

"Very true."

"Okay. We know where Davison went wrong. Can we fix it?"

Tapping on the tattered book, the Rabbi said, "You think I'd tell you this if there was nothing to do?" Turning to a new page, he added, "Knowing what he has created, we can use the opposite to undo it. This is a list of thirteen ingredients needed to heal Ms. Cohen." He handed the book to Mr. Rosen. "I believe Miriam can assist you with this."

Mr. Rosen paused, clearly displeased with being removed from the room. His hesitancy, however, only met the Rabbi's expectant eyes. Finally, Mr. Rosen took the book with a tiny bow and left.

Drummond wished he could switch places with Mr. Rosen because that man was wrong in thinking he had been cut out of some higher-level planning. No. Drummond saw through this — the Rabbi wanted to speak in private, and it wouldn't be a pleasant conversation.

"I understand you've been spending time with Mr. Rosen's daughter."

Bingo. Well, Drummond had to hand it to the Rabbi for being direct. He figured he could respond in kind. "That's none of your business."

"Miriam and her father are part of the community. I'm a rabbi. Part of that responsibility is ensuring the young make wise and healthy choices. The two of you — no good can come from such a relationship."

"She's been through a lot and —"

"We all have. She is not special in this. But ruining her future is a poor way to live." The Rabbi gestured to the seat Mr. Rosen had been occupying. "You strike me as a good man. An honest one. Surely you see that the world is not willing to accept a Jewish girl and a *goy* together. And you don't seek marriage anyway."

"She knows that." Drummond flicked out a cigarette. "I suppose that's partly why she likes me. I'm not complicated. She can't marry me — you've all made that clear — so, she's blowing off steam from the horrors she lived through. Once that's done, she'll be done with me. I don't expect more."

"You young folks think you understand the world, but you don't."

"Maybe you should worry more about the rest of your community. A *goy* didn't throw himself out a window rather than face how he ruined a sweet gal with magic. Seems to me, you all should be thrilled that I'm a decent guy who treats Miriam well."

Mr. Rosen entered with a glass of brackish liquid. "It's ready."

Snatching the glass, Drummond thumped to the door leading into the cellar. Why did everybody lock their horrors in the cellar? Did that really help hide what crawled beneath them?

He ignored the creak of the wooden steps, the drop in temperature, and the growing ammonia stench. This might be terrifying to Rabbi ben Scholl and Mr. Rosen, but Drummond had faced worse than a love potion gone wrong. He didn't underestimate the danger Ms. Cohen possessed, but she was a rabid animal, not a cursed witch. He could handle this.

As he strode toward the darkened corner, he plastered on a calming smile. "Easy there, now," he said as if soothing a crazed dog. "I'm sure you're thirsty. I've brought you something to drink."

The swirls of brown liquid in the glass gave off an unpleasant aroma. With this being the cure, Drummond wondered how nasty the original potion must have been. Especially since Davison botched the whole thing.

Inching closer, he listened to the woman's snarling and snorting. He stayed alert. Any sudden change and he would dash for the stairs. Ms. Cohen's body and mind had been altered to the point that she did not think rationally, probably did not think animalistically, either. Whatever thoughts traversed her disturbed brain, they belonged to creatures of witchcraft.

But, if he hadn't taken too long finding this cure, if Mr. Davison lacked any true skill, then a glimmer of Ms. Cohen might remain inside. She might find the strength to claw her way into consciousness. Drummond set the glass on the floor and backed away.

"Drink up. You'll feel a lot better."

He had no idea if she understood him, but hunger and thirst did not require thought. She merely had to answer the calls of her grumbling stomach and her parched throat.

The growling increased as she emerged from the dark. Her decaying skin looked worse, greener, more scaley. The ammonia reek strengthened, and Drummond worked hard to mask his disgust.

She approached the glass, sniffing with cautious curiosity, but always watching Drummond, too. He grinned.

"Can't blame you, kid. I wouldn't trust anybody, either."

His gentle tone received a good reaction. Her tense muscles eased as she squatted at the glass. With fingers that had thickened — threatening to became paws — she lifted the glass to her nose. Snapping back, she winced, and threw the glass aside. It cracked against the wall, and the potion splashed upon the floor.

She barked, eyes blazing yellow. Lunging into the air, her chain snapped hard. A painful yelp, and she fell to the ground. Momentum slid her legs forward, and she ended on her backside.

"Sorry, kid, but I ain't getting close enough to bite. Seen that too many times." He watched her crawl back into the darkness. A whiff of the drink's horrid remnants hit him. "How did Davison get you to drink that stuff?"

The answer came fast. He hurried upstairs.

As Rabbi ben Scholl and Mr. Rosen crowded towards him, eager-eyed for news, Drummond stormed into the kitchen. Miriam startled. She had been smoking a cigarette and staring out the window. A pinprick touched his heart. He had seen her do this during other cases. She had been worried about him.

Keeping her arms down — fighting the urge to hug him — she trembled out a smile. "You okay?"

"Fine. We need more of that awful potion."

The Rabbi entered behind him. "I was sure one dose would be enough."

"She didn't drink it. Too foul smelling. But I remembered something from her apartment. An empty bowl of chili. Gobbled down. Davison's apartment smelled of it, too. He must have disguised his potion with food."

"What is chili?" Mr. Rosen said from the doorway.

"Mexican staple. Cowboys used to eat it on the range. Still do, I imagine."

The Rabbi scratched his bearded chin. "A bowl in the sink is hardly proof that Mr. Davison —"

With a plead in his eyes to get Miriam working on the potion, Drummond then turned to the men. "Ms. Cohen's apartment was impeccably kept. The bowl had a crack in it and the spoon didn't match the knife and fork in the drying rack. They weren't hers. Plus, there is no way she would have left a dirty bowl to dry up and become a crusty mess. I'd guess Davison brought her the bowl and spoon, she ate the food, put the bowl in the sink to wash, and before she could start, the potion destroyed her."

"Hmmm. Could be."

"So, we're going to make Ms. Cohen another magical meal. I've known some wonderful Mexican people, and I can make a decent chili. Oh, and Rabbi, you'll love this — it takes thirteen ingredients."

An hour-and-a-half later, Drummond held a bowl of hot chili. The actual meal only required thirty minutes, but the Rabbi's pantry lacked nearly all the ingredients. Miriam had to run to the southeastern end of Winston-Salem where the signs shifted into Spanish. Thankfully, this was a meatless chili. Scrounging together the money for meat would have been a challenge, and if they had needed pork, the Rabbi would have had serious problems.

Miriam formulated two glasses of the potion. "In case we need another backup."

"Smart." Drummond winked as he poured one glass into the bowl and stirred.

Navigating the stairs with caution, he made sure not to spill any of the precious food. As delicious as it smelled, it could not overpower the raw stink of Ms. Cohen. She growled with his approach.

"Don't be like that. You're going to love this. It's chili. You remember? Tasty, tasty."

He doubted his words meant much, but the food's mouth-watering aroma did all the talking necessary. Once she got the scent, her threatening grunts ceased. She hastened into view, her chain jingling, and when she reached its end, she sat like an obedient pet waiting for a treat.

Drummond inched ahead, offering the bowl, crouching low, trying to keep his free arm ready to punch or grab should action be required. "Be nice, now. I'm trying to help you."'

With a rapid motion, she snatched the bowl away. Not even bothering to move toward the dark, Ms. Cohen shoved her face in the meal and slobbered it up.

And nothing happened.

Drummond kept expecting a sudden jolt. A seizure, perhaps. Maybe a strange magic glow.

Instead, she licked the bowl. When she finished, she wiped her face with her hands and then licked whatever she found on her fingers. After that, she rose to her feet. Her muscles tightened as her eyes flared with a sense of life previously absent.

"More," she said.

Drummond cocked his head toward the stairs. "Sorry, lady. I think that was it."

"More." Arching back, she sniffed the air. "Upstairs."

"Yeah, I know, but we've got to be careful. Don't want things getting worse for you. Especially because you seem a little better."

With a single shift, Ms. Cohen looked smaller, weaker. She held out the bowl. "I need more."

"Let's see how that first meal sits."

"Please."

Taking cautious steps, he approached. He reached for the bowl. "I'll go see what else —"

Ms. Cohen's hand snapped out, clasped upon Drummond's wrist, and yanked him off balance. The bowl shattered on the floor. He stumbled forward, doubling over. In a flash, she wrapped her chain around his throat as she leapt upon his back.

He grabbed the chain — pulling down hard, trying to find air. He rushed backwards, hoping to slam her into the wall, but he tripped on a stack of old pots. They clattered and rang out. With Ms. Cohen hissing in his ear, he tumbled atop her, and while it wasn't the way he had intended, the hit loosened her grip.

Shoving the chain off, he rolled away. Gasping. Coughing. Sputtering in the cellar dust. As he pushed to his feet, weaving like a man struck in the head, he sought the stairs — or, at least, the limit of her chain.

But when she stood, the chain did not follow. He had learned the lesson long ago — all things are only as strong as their weakest point. She had not broken the metal links or ripped the chain free from the wall. Rather, Ms. Cohen simply broke the leather collar.

Shrieking, she launched forward. Drummond raised his fists. He didn't expect to do much, he still wobbled, but he would try. Except she jumped passed him, clawed her fingers into the plaster of the stairwell, and jumped from wall to wall like a horrifying giant insect. She scrabbled up the stairwell, leaving behind gouges in the wall.

Drummond followed. Each step required concentration. His lungs had stopped burning, but he still couldn't think straight. When he heard Miriam's shocked cry, however, he bolted up the remaining stairs.

From the hallway, the Rabbi and Mr. Rosen watched the kitchen in fright. Peeking in, Drummond found Miriam in a nearby corner, pressing a dishcloth to her forehead. Blood trickled down her face. And Ms. Cohen — crouched atop the kitchen counter, head deep in the pot of chili, her unsatiated moans echoing as she inhaled the spicy food.

The Rabbi said, "The potion hasn't worked."

"When she eats the rest, it'll kick in and …" Drummond's gaze dropped to Mr. Rosen's hand holding the second glass of the potion. "You didn't put that in the chili?"

Mr. Rosen shrugged. "Was I supposed to?"

"How else is she going to get it?"

"I didn't know. You never made the details clear. Besides, why would I ruin a perfectly fine meal?"

Drummond snatched the glass away, sloshing some of the awful liquid over the lip, and turned toward Ms. Cohen. Maybe he could slip it into the pot while she ate. He took one step forward.

With a vile hiss, she raised her head. Her flaking skin blew off with the motion and the rest of her decaying body swayed. She placed one hand on the counter for balance as her bloodshot eyes locked on Drummond. When he backed away, she returned to her meal.

"Give it to me." Miriam set the bloody dish towel aside. The gash on her forehead had little beads of red dancing like dark sweat.

"No," her father said. "That thing is too dangerous."

Keeping her eyes on Drummond, she said, "You already gave one full glass to her?"

"Yeah."

"Then I'll give her the second."

"I hate to agree with your father, but Ms. Cohen isn't in her right mind."

"I can see that."

"What exactly do you think you'll do?"

She gently removed the glass from his hand. She caressed his cheek with a bitter smile. "You'll grab her long enough that I can pour this down her throat."

Mr. Rosen gasped. "Absolutely not."

Even Rabbi ben Scholl chimed in. "I cannot allow —"

"Both of you, stop," Miriam said. "I survived the same Germany as you. This is nothing." To Drummond: "Let's not make Ms. Cohen suffer longer."

She was right. No time to worry about the rest.

"This is going to be ugly." He set his hat on the tiny kitchen table.

Moving with caution and taking short, sharp breaths, Drummond closed in on Ms. Cohen like an athlete preparing for his big moment. But this wouldn't be a hundred-yard dash or an attempt to break a world record. At best, this might be a boxing match.

Or wrestling.

Drummond intended to throw a few punches and knock out the

woman-creature. Looking at her now as she slurped chili, he thought he might be able to —

She snapped her head up. Chili splashed off her chin, and she growled. Drummond put his arms out wide — hoping he looked friendly even as he readied to snatch her in a bear hug. She had other ideas.

With a screech, she hurled forward, slamming into Drummond. They stumbled back. She scratched at him while scrambling her feet, her eyes locked on the hallway escape.

"No, no, lady." Drummond latched onto her wrist.

She swung back, clobbering his rib, but he held firm. As if performing a twisted dance move, he used her momentum to spin her so that her back faced him and the arm he held crossed in front. He locked her tight against his chest.

"A little help." He stared at Mr. Rosen and the Rabbi.

Both men took hesitant steps, but Ms. Cohen kicked at them. Drummond tried to use his free hand to lock her head in place, give Miriam a chance, but the poor creature thrashed about. If he didn't stay focused, he'd lose his grip entirely.

"Rabbi!" he barked. That got the old man moving.

Tottering into the kitchen, Rabbi ben Scholl uttered Hebrew prayers while his fingers jittered with uncertainty. "What can I do?"

Ms. Cohen raised a foot to kick at the Rabbi again. Drummond saw his opening. He arched back. With her balance off, she couldn't fight well. The two dropped to the floor.

"Grab her," Miriam said.

Before Drummond could throw out a sarcastic comment, Mr. Rosen appeared on the right and the Rabbi closed in on the left. They both took hold of the wild animal that had once been Ms. Cohen. This freed Drummond to lock his arms around her head — not enough to render her unconscious, but enough to keep her head back and her mouth open.

Though messy, Miriam managed to get most of the nasty potion down the creature's throat. They held her for another minute before her muscles relaxed. Another short pause, and Ms. Cohen had gone to sleep.

AN HOUR LATER, they sat in the Rabbi's study. Even Miriam had been allowed. They had brought a cot to the kitchen for Ms. Cohen. Her color had returned to a more human hue, and they hoped the rest of her would follow.

"Thank you." Rabbi ben Scholl pulled out a business ledger. "We appreciate this great service. How much do you charge?"

Drummond needed the money. He always needed it. But he waved the offer away. "Not interested in your cash." He looked toward Miriam.

Mr. Rosen said, "Absolutely not. My daughter will never be your bride."

With a slap of her knee, Miriam said, "I'll marry whoever I want. And Mr. Drummond is not proposing." She glanced at Drummond. "Right?"

"I'm not the marrying type, doll. But you all need to pay attention. Davison was one of your own. I'm not."

The Rabbi said, "All communities have bad men in them."

"But I'm not one of them. Mr. Rosen, I apologize for dating your daughter behind your back. From now on, we'll be in the open. I'm sorry if that upsets you, but until she tires of me, she should enjoy her life a bit."

The two men stared without further words. Perhaps they agreed. Perhaps they simply were too shaken by the night's events. Didn't matter to Drummond.

As he left the house, he thought of Mr. Davison being so enamored with Ms. Cohen that he lost his life trying to use magic for love. Suddenly, throwing away money for Miriam didn't seem so foolish.

Oh, no. Am I falling in love?

But that would be a problem for tomorrow. One he knew better than to rely on magic to fix.

CASE 20

DREAMS OF THE DEAD

MARSHALL DRUMMOND, Winston-Salem's best and only detective of the strange and bizarre, stared at the black phone on his desk and waited. More than ever before, he understood the temptation magic posed. He wanted that phone to ring with a job. Needed it. Another week without income might sink him. Plus, he was bored.

After twenty minutes, he let out a long sigh, leaned back in his chair, and crossed his feet on the edge of the desk. He set his Fedora over his face. Apparently, no work would be calling on him this morning.

A knock came at the door. Before he could do anything more than swing his body up, the locked door opened. An old lady, five feet tall and hunched over to four-and-a-half, entered the office. She wore a gray frock to her knees and veined legs poked out beyond. Her feet were bare. Using a dark wood cane, she thumped her way towards him.

The air dropped several degrees, and Drummond knew to hold still. Whatever this woman wanted, she brought the cold of Death with her. Which heavily suggested she was a witch. Even more reason to keep from moving.

With each step, she let out a small huff. When she finally stood opposite Drummond, the beaten desk the only barrier between them, she turned to face him. Her wrinkled skin puckered her features on one side. The other side had no skin at all.

Blood, tissue, and bone mocked him over a skull smile. Drummond sank back as if he could press through his chair to escape. But she did not threaten him. Merely stared as if waiting for him to speak. He opened his mouth, but no words came.

Unable to move, unable to utter a sound, he crinkled his brow, hoping that would be enough communication for this woman. She shrugged. Great. Neither of them knew what the heck was going on.

But before his frustration could find his voice, she reached toward the coffee table and placed down a creased cigarette card — trading cards used to stiffen a soft pack of cigarettes. The card on Drummond's desk depicted a biplane parked in front of a hangar. The old woman lifted her one eye and her gaping skull eyehole and pulled back her half-lips in a foul grin.

Drummond's eyes snapped wide open. His hat rolled into his lap. He was alone. The front door remained closed and locked. Morning traffic rolled by his open window.

With a shake of his head, he sat up, trying to rub the weirdness of the dream from his face. But he froze. A creased cigarette card depicting a biplane parked in front of a hangar rested on his desk next to his phone.

Of course.

Ignoring the fuzzy heat warming his forehead, Drummond inspected the card. He remembered collecting these things as a kid, and he knew adults made a hobby of it like stamps and coins, but he didn't know the dead liked to drop them around. The cards from his childhood tended to focus on famous figures of the West like Wyatt Earp or Billy the Kid or the various tribes throughout the country like the Cherokee or the Sioux. Cards of airplanes had been rather new — at least, new in the last couple decades.

Other than the method of delivery, nothing about the card appeared strange. No witch symbols hidden in the image. No odd energy radiating off the card. Not even an odor of death. Nothing.

The card didn't strike him as a threat. Unless a biplane crashed through the window to kill him. The old lady in his dream looked more regretful than hostile.

All of which led Drummond to the conclusion that while this was clearly a case of the bizarre, it probably did not involve a witch. He hoped not, anyway. But he needed to be sure, and that meant following the one clue he had — the cigarette card.

SIMON GROVE — a collector of anything people found value in collecting. From the normal like baseball cards and famous autographs to the oddities like shrunken heads and withered fingers. More than a good source for information on unusual items, Drummond had confided in Simon the truth about witches and magic. He had hoped Simon would help in procuring old witch tomes and unique ingredients, but the collector couldn't handle learning his reality was not what he had believed. He found excuses and denials, and ultimately, he kept his distance from Drummond as much as possible. But the detective needed a man who knew all about card collections, and there was none better than Simon Grove.

He had inherited his father's stamp collection, shifted into coins, then baseball cards, and when those weren't enough, he opened a shop so that he could gain access to all sorts of strange and wonderful items. Simon once showed Drummond his prized 1908 cigarette card celebrating the 5th anniversary of the Wright Brothers at Kitty Hawk. That popped into Drummond's head as he walked along the morning streets of Winston-Salem toward the shop.

Simon's pride over the card felt paternal. He protected and cherished his acquisitions. Mixing that with fear explained his negative attitude toward witchcraft. After all, if a man started collecting the books of witches, he invited their hatred and wrath.

Rather than enter the shop and be berated, Drummond opted to take a seat at the diner one block up. It was a new place — *Mama's Diner* — and if the day offered nothing else good, at least he got to enjoy the view of his waitress. With gams as long and shapely as hers, she should have left this town for Hollywood a year ago. She brought him steaming coffee and pointed to the payphone when he asked.

When Simon arrived, the man's scowl spoke harsher than the man had spoken on the phone. He took the chair opposite and set his hat on the table. "Only reason I'm here, only reason I even took your call, is cause of history."

"I know," Drummond said. "And it's out of respect for you and our history that I don't make that call lightly."

Simon looked far older than his years. One wouldn't expect running a shop to be dangerous, but during the worst of the Depression, Simon had to defend his business on more than one occasion. Often, quite violently. His once boyish face had age lines creating sharp angles. A deep scar ran along the left jaw — probably an altercation with a thief — and from the way he winced as he shifted in his seat, Drummond surmised his former friend had a bullet hole or two in his side.

Waving the waitress away, Simon said, "I want to be clear. I am not getting involved in any of your cases."

"Never crossed my mind to ask."

"Then what the heck are you here for?"

"Information." Drummond placed the cigarette card on the table. "This came my way. A new case — one that you won't be part of, I promise — but I need to know everything I can about this."

Seeing the card, Simon's scowl opened into curious surprise. He reached for it but snapped his fingers back. He scanned the diner as if he might spot a ghost or a magic glow in the corners. "Is it safe to touch?"

"Should be. It was sent as a message. If there's anything about it that could do harm, it would be harmful to me. Besides, I've been carrying it around all morning, and nothing's happened."

"Not a word of that was encouraging."

"Sorry, pal. Just trying to steer you straight."

After a hesitant thought, Simon snatched the card off the table and settled back. Drummond shook out a cigarette and lit it. He offered one to Simon, but the man didn't respond — too wrapped up in the card.

"This is wrong," Simon said. "Where'd you get this?"

"As the saying goes, *ask me no questions* —"

"Right. This card, though, it shouldn't exist. I mean it doesn't exist. It's showing a biplane in front of Hangar 7B — you can see the hangar markings on the building's corner right here. Those two letters above the hangar number, that's the airport code. This is Piedmont Airport in Greensboro."

"What part of that's wrong?"

"Some businesses team up with the cigarette companies to run special issue cards as an advertising thing. Movie studios, car companies — all kinds."

"Airports?"

"Not really. Showing off the planes in flight or famous aviators is still a big thing — probably going to become bigger if we get involved in that Germany war — but they never show the airport. And if they ever did, why would they do a run with Piedmont Airport?"

Drummond plucked the card out of Simon's hand and slid it into his coat pocket. "Thanks. Sorry to bother you."

"Hey, wait. What's this about? Where are you going?"

"You don't want to know what it's about. And where do you think I'm going? To the airport."

OVER AN HOUR LATER, Drummond parked in the Piedmont Airport lot. He strolled by the main entrance and headed toward the area reserved for private planes and related businesses — a flight school, a place to order gas delivery, even a small restaurant. Just beyond, a row of ten hangars lined up like giant houses designed by the same hand. Drummond never broke his stride as he zeroed in on Hangar 7B.

Large enough to house a DC-3 — a rather new plane that made commercial flying smoother, faster, and more enjoyable — the hangar had its big doors tracked back. Drummond halted. He lit a cigarette, took a drag, then thought better of smoking around airplane fuel. Grinding the stick under his heel, he stared at the dark hangar.

No plane inside. Not that he could see. But the morning sun splashed the backside of the hangar, rimming the edges in orange and making the interior even darker.

Drummond reached for another cigarette before he realized what he was doing. Damn. No matter how many times he dealt with the dead, his nerves still returned. Must be a good thing, though. If he ever found it mundane that he would soon enter a threatening area in the middle of the morning because he was summoned by a ghost in his sleep, well, he should hang it up. This was no job for a man without enough self-preservation sense to be on edge.

He walked into the hangar and stopped to allow his eyes to adjust. The smell of grease and gas floated through the cavernous space. A radio played somewhere deeper in, sounding hollow and lonely. Squinting, he made out the floor had never been paved — still dirt — and a lengthy table covered in tools ran along the left wall. On the right, about midway, a door stood ajar. The word *Office* had been painted on the frosted glass. Oil splotches marked where planes had been parked and had work done.

His eyes drew toward one back corner. Not sure why, but something about that area demanded his attention. As he moved toward it, as his vision continued to clear away the dark, the distinct buzz of a plane racing down a runway and lifting into the sky blanketed all other sounds. For a moment, only that plane existed. If not for that noise, he might have heard the man rushing him from behind.

As it happened, two things occurred simultaneously. First, he noticed the disturbed earth in the back corner. About the size and shape of an old lady as well as a second shape resting next to it. Second, something hard clunked the back of his head.

All went dark.

His skull pounded with each heartbeat. He would have preferred a hangover to this focused thumping. An army of soldiers marched in unison on that one spot of impact, and he thought there would be a goose egg large enough to make sleeping difficult for the next week. He'd also have to visit a doctor. Getting cracked on the head might have caused him far worse than a little time unconscious.

He wanted to touch the bruise, but coarse, frayed rope bound his arms to the wood chair he sat in. A quick glance at his surroundings. Looked like the hangar office. A narrow room with a worktable mounted against one wall, barely enough space for two chairs, and a small walkway behind — providing access to the bathroom on the other end. Papers littered the table along with a greasy chunk of metal which Drummond assumed came out of an airplane. It sat on an oil-stained cloth. A radio dominated the remaining space on the table. A mid-tempo song called *After You've Gone* by the Benny Goodman Trio rolled out.

The part Drummond wanted to ignore, the part nobody could skip over, sat in the other chair — a dead man.

He wore workman's denim overalls and had a red handkerchief sticking out of the left side pocket. Dirt and grease stained the knees and sides. He might have been sleeping, if not for the blood on the front bib. That, and the man's slit neck.

With his head angled back, the open wound gaped at Drummond like a puppet's mouth. Rimmed crimson, the blood had ceased pumping out long ago. All the man's gore had dried.

From behind the man, a small figure emerged. An old woman, bent over, using a cane. The room chilled as she thumped to the dead man's side.

Drummond didn't have to look to know that half of that wrinkled face would be nothing but bone and muscle and teeth. He looked anyway. Couldn't turn his head as a fresh rush of blood rivered out of the dead man's cut throat.

The dead man rose. He tried to speak, but that only caused the blood to flow stronger. The old lady merely stood by his side. When the man finally accepted that his throat wouldn't cooperate, he pointed at a photo next to the radio. It showed two men — one the dead man; the other a beefy man with a pencil-thin mustache and slicked back hair. The two wore work clothes, held wrenches, and smiled as they posed in front of an airplane.

Drummond snapped awake. He sat in the same chair, tied with the same frayed ropes, stuck in the same narrow office. But no corpse in the opposite chair.

Footsteps and humming came from the main part of the hangar. A little song and dance to accompany the radio. Some light-hearted play before making his appearance. Of course, his captor could be a woman — a witch — but this didn't feel like a witch's magic. This felt like the work of a twisted mind.

He scanned the room. In addition to the things he had seen in his dream, his gun sat on the table — far enough out of reach to be useless. Several cigarette cards had been fanned as if part of a poker game for one. Next to the cards, an open razor, dried blood covering the blade. Drummond didn't question it — the weapon used to cut the dream victim's neck.

The office door opened. Nothing dramatic. Nothing designed to instill fear. The door simply swung in as a man entered.

He looked ill. Emaciated. A thin mustache lined his upper lip, and his hair had been slicked back — possibly with the grease found in every cranny of the hangar. His bones pressed against his skin like he wore a thin gown, yet he moved with the strength of a healthy man. All about him suggested one who struggled to survive and somehow continued on.

Except his eyes.

He stared at Drummond, resting his boney hands on the back of the empty chair. Those eyes narrowed, mostly pupil, mostly dark holes. They screamed a maliciousness that reached into Drummond's gut and coiled around it like a snake wrapping around a squirming meal.

"You came here to kill me," the man said in a whispery voice, "but I caught you instead."

"I don't even know who you are."

The man tilted his head toward Drummond's handgun. "No need to lie. I can see lies in the air when you speak them."

Great. A nut job. Well, the guy wouldn't be the first Drummond ever had to deal with. Even in his beat cop days, he had to handle fools so drunk they might as well have been insane. But this fool in front of him didn't speak like he was missing a few cards in the deck. No, he acted more familiar, more like a man unhinged from playing with powers he could not control.

Drummond rocked back on the wood chair, causing it to creak. His ropes complained, too, but he achieved the casual look of a man comfortable with being held captive. "You been messing around with magic, haven't you?"

The guy's eyes widened. "I'm right, then. A witch sent you. Come to kill me so I can't learn their secrets?"

"No. I only —"

Whipping around to sit in the empty chair, leaning on his elbows so that his soulless eyes bore down, he said, "Tell me who sent you here."

Drummond held still. Despite his casual attitude, he had been paying close attention to what this man said and did. Drummond's life could end at any moment. This man's paranoia betrayed that simple truth. In fact, the more Drummond thought it through, the more he understood that only one small bit of information had stayed the man's bloody hand — who had sent Drummond to the hangar.

Working hard to maintain his relaxed appearance, Drummond knew exactly how to deal with this guy. "First thing, pal, is I need a name to call you."

The man said nothing.

"Have it your way. I'll call you Benny. You wouldn't, by any chance, play a mean clarinet?"

"Who sent you?"

"Benny, you got worse problems than that. I've seen this before. Some people, when they learn that witches are real, they start thinking they can control that power, too. Tap into it and make themselves rich or powerful or whatever they want. Is that what happened for you? Because here's the part you missed out on — magic is dangerous. It screws with your mind. Especially if you don't know what you're doing. And I'm sorry, Benny, but I can tell right away that you don't know what you're doing."

Benny's face reddened and his mouth turned down. With a bark, he launched forward, grabbed Drummond's shirt, and shoved hard until the chair tipped back. Drummond slammed into the floor, smacking the back of his head at the same point where his goose egg continued to grow.

Maybe I don't know exactly how to deal with this guy.

Trying to focus through the sparkling white light that filled his vision, he spotted a blood-stained bowl a few feet away. A charred piece of wood stuck against the coated rim. A photograph leaned against the bowl, too — another moment of the bulky man with a thin mustache and slicked hair standing next to his pal that now sported an open neck.

Benny righted Drummond back up. Sweat danced on that mustache as he strained for a few breaths before sitting. "You make me mad again, and I'll do far worse than knock you over."

"I'm starting to see the problem." Drummond quit the casual game and lowered to a serious tone. "You've been doing worse than exploring a little magic. You've been trying out blood magic."

Reaching for the razor on the table, Benny cocked an eyebrow. "You know nothing about nothing, except about a witch. You tell me who sent you, and I'll kill you quick."

"Can't really promise that one, can you? Not if you're going to keep casting blood magic. Dead man's blood won't do the trick. At least, for a novice like you. Is that what went wrong?"

Benny threw a sharp jab, catching Drummond on the cheek. For a bone-thin guy, he packed a wallop. Probably did some boxing back when he looked like the bruiser in the photos.

He bent to the floor and picked up the bowl. "Last time I'm asking. Tell me the name of the witch that sent you after me, or I'll drain your blood. Slowly."

"Wasn't a witch." Drummond had an idea, but it required the help of a couple dead people. Given the circumstances, that was better than nothing. "I had a ghost visit me in a dream. Old lady. You remember her. You shredded off half her face."

"You're lying." Benny didn't sound too confident. "I never heard of ghosts entering dreams."

"It's a new one for me, too, but it happened. That old lady took one of your cigarette cards and brought it to my office. I don't know how much you've learned about ghosts, but touching our world hurts them a lot. So, you've got to figure that she's really mad at you if she held that card all the way from the airport in Greensboro to my office in Winston."

"And she sent you here to kill me?"

"Don't really know. She left the clue that brought me here. Maybe she wants you dead, but I'm not in the vengeance business. I think she tried to tell me again. When you conked me on the head, I had another dream. She was there, and so was a fellow with a neck you cut open."

Benny glanced at the razor in his hand, then at the photo resting on the radio. "Casey. He shouldn't have been poking around my stuff."

"Look, pal, I'm not here to curse you or kill you or anything like that. No witch sent me. And like I said, I'm not in the vengeance business. Not for that old lady or her pal, Casey. I am here to help. You've got a chance right now to fix things. I know this blood magic can get in your head, make you take stupid chances. You've done some bad things, but it doesn't have to get any worse. Untie me, and let me bring you to a friend of mine. He's a detective with the Winston police. You confess what you did, and I'll see that they go easy on you."

His mouth dropped open in a wide laugh. "You say all that and have the nerve to call me stupid? I sure would be if I let you free and just walked to the police to admit I killed a couple people."

Drummond bowed his head, hoping to find some other angle that would work. But he doubted it. Which left him no choice but the one he wanted to avoid.

Raising his eyes, he said, "I'm sorry to hear that. You see, I'm pretty confident that both Casey and the old lady are in this room with us."

Benny stopped laughing.

"Now I'm not here to hurt you, but I suspect they are."

Benny looked around the office.

"They're both new to being ghosts, so they don't know all about it. For instance, if they get close enough to us or get emotional enough, we'll feel the air around drop in temperature."

A cold spot passed by Drummond, and Benny jolted as he clearly felt the touch of a ghost.

"Another thing they don't know yet, that they can harm us. That old lady already figured out how to pick up your cigarette card. If she shoved her hand into your head and did the same thing, endured the pain of touching our world, she could make you suffer, freeze you unconscious."

"What?" Benny jumped to his feet as the temperature plummeted. He lifted the razor, but he never got any further. His body stiffened, his skin prickled, his eyes rolled up, and he collapsed. His head clanged the blood bowl.

As he jittered on the floor, Drummond said, "Don't kill him."

But the ghosts didn't listen. Benny flopped from side to side and foamed at the mouth.

"Stop it." Drummond wriggled in his chair, trying to break free.

The air remained frigid around Benny. Every stuttering breath left his body in short puffs of smoke. His eyes bulged as he tried to scream, but only a soft whimper escaped his clamped jaw.

Then nothing.

No movement. No sounds. No breath.

THE TWO GHOSTS NEEDED TIME to recoup from killing Benny, leaving Drummond tied to the chair with nothing to do but think. He went over the events, starting from the beginning and tracing his conclusions, decisions, and actions throughout. Because something didn't sit right.

The dream had led him to the cigarette card which brought him to Simon which led him to the hangar and then to Benny. Simple enough. Admittedly, most cases did not play out so straightforward, but then Benny hadn't been too smart about hiding what he had done. Burying the bodies in the hangar where he had killed them — dumb. Repeatedly playing with blood magic despite the horrific results — dumb. Not learning how to protect himself from ghosts — dumb.

Drummond could have added far more to Benny's list of stupid, but he felt the cold presence of two ghosts close in on him. Before he could remind them that they were on the same side, or even worry that they might turn against him, he felt the rope around his right arm turn to ice.

The brown braiding frosted white and grew brittle. Drummond yanked his arm upward, and the rope snapped apart.

"Thanks," he said. "I can handle the rest myself."

He swiped Benny's razor off the floor and cut the remaining ropes. Once freed, Drummond promised to call the authorities. The ghosts' bodies would be exhumed and taken to their families where they could receive proper burials.

"After that, you should both be ready to move on. When the chance comes, take it. I've seen a lot of ghosts, and trust me, you don't want to go that way."

CLIMBING THE STAIRS TO HIS OFFICE, his mind had left the case and focused on his couch. He wanted sleep. Uninterrupted sleep without any ghost dreams. Maybe he could meet that waitress with the great legs, they could dance on a cloud to some good music — just not Benny Goodman. Yeah, that sounded like a wonderful dream. But when he found his office door unlocked, thoughts of sleep and waitresses vanished. He unholstered his handgun and gently pushed the door open.

A woman wearing a black veil knelt in the middle of a casting circle surrounded by blue, green, and black candles. Blood trickled down her arm. A hunting knife rested at the woman's knees along with a bowl of blood.

"Guess I should've listened to Benny," Drummond said, closing the door behind him. Trying to calm his racing pulse, he eased forward, locking his gun on the witch. "Who are you?"

She remained on her knees as she lifted her head. "That doesn't truly matter." Her voice floated with all the charm of a Southern lady raised on money. "Not today. After all, one witch is as bad as another to you."

"I take it you're the one who put those ghosts in my dreams."

"Of course. You didn't really think a ghost could do that on their own, did you? An old lady who had only been dead a short time, who barely knew the basics of being a ghost, suddenly discovers a new power that no other ghost has ever known. That doesn't make much sense, now."

As Drummond moved toward his desk, the witch merely sat still. She spoke without threat or anger, but her mere presence was threat enough. His desk had a few wards in the top drawer, not that they would help against a witch, but he couldn't think of anything else that would help. Unless he shot her, but that would be a last resort.

"I'm beginning to see," he said. "The guy at the airport — Benny's what I call him — he stole a book or two about blood magic. Stole them from you, I'm guessing. Or maybe you're part of coven and one of your sisters was the victim. You decide to have some fun at my expense. Planted that dream in my head, and at the same time, break into my office and set the cigarette card on the table. Since that card doesn't really exist, you must have conjured the image so I'd take the clues that led me to the hangar. Then you sit back and watch as the detective hated by much of the witch community stumbled upon a blood magic killer. From there, it wouldn't matter to you how it played out. Either I died, Benny died, or we both did. Whatever the case, you'd be happy."

"Not quite," the witch said.

"Oh, it's like that, is it? I wasn't supposed to live."

She winked.

"That's why you're here. Come to finish the job."

She snapped her fingers and pointed at him.

"I'm sorry, then, but I'm going to have to —"

The witch spread her fingers wide as she rammed her hands forward. Drummond's body jerked, and an unseen force shoved him in the chest while another force yanked him from the back. He smacked into the wall hard enough to cause his hands to clench. The one holding his gun squeezed the trigger.

A loud bang and a bullet lodged into the floor. Drummond's eyes widened. A couple inches closer and he'd have put a hole in his foot.

From the casting circle, the hunting knife rose in the air. It turned like a snake's head seeking out its victim. When the blade pointed at Drummond, it hurled across the office.

The fact that casting multiple spells simultaneously required a great amount of concentration and energy saved him. No matter how much time the witch had to prepare — and Drummond guessed this witch had been waiting several hours for him — she wasn't superhuman.

Controlling the knife meant loosening her grip on Drummond. He dropped to the floor as the blade lodged into the wall. With a glance up, he saw the hilt vibrating as the witch attempted to call it back.

This was his opportunity. Drummond launched forward, scrabbling along the floor, and tackled the witch. As they tumbled, he rolled her to the side so he could get behind her and lock her head in a sleeper hold. She struggled. Wrenching her backwards, he made sure to kick two of the candles aside. Hopefully, that would be enough to disrupt whatever other spells she had planned.

She didn't claw at him or kick him, though. Instead, she kept her fingers splayed as she reached for the knife. It wriggled in the wall. It inched outward.

Drummond tightened his grip, arching back. When he thought she would fall unconscious, she managed to twist her head and gasp a solid breath of air. Drummond readjusted, but he had already given her the moment she needed.

The knife shot out and hovered in the middle of the room. It spun towards them. If it had eyes, Drummond would have sworn it frowned at him.

Uttering a strained giggle, the witch managed to say, "You're going to die."

She clutched her fingers into a fist and thumped her chest.

But nothing happened.

She repeated the motion, but the knife remained still. Before she could speak, Drummond noticed moisture beading on the blade like an ice-filled glass on a hot day. The room turned cold.

Drummond let the witch go. She pushed off him, clambered to her feet, and went to grab the knife. But then she saw the frost on the blade, too.

"Doesn't look too good for you," Drummond said.

"You didn't send those ghosts to move on?"

"I told them to. But it'll be at least another day before they get a decent burial."

She stiffened as the cold touch of a ghost ran through her. Sneering at Drummond, she said, "They won't be here forever to protect you."

"I'd be careful, if I was you. Don't want to give them ideas. Tick off a ghost, and maybe they'll choose not to move on. Maybe they'll want to hang around to keep an eye on you."

The witch yelped at another icy pass across her skin. The floating knife dropped, clattering on the floor. With a begrudging glower, she backed away. When she reached the door, she stopped.

"I can learn plenty of spells to deal with you ghosts." To Drummond: "And plenty more to deal with you."

She stormed out. But making a final threat wasn't bright. Drummond wanted to warn her that these ghosts had killed Benny, but before he could say a word, the door slammed shut and the temperature heated up. The ghosts had followed her out.

He doubted she would live to see tomorrow. But he faced a bigger problem now: nobody was going to pay him for the day's work.

About the Author

Stuart Jaffe is the madman behind *The Max Porter Paranormal Mysteries,* the *Nathan K* thrillers, the *Ridnight Mysteries,* the *Parallel Society* novels, *The Malja Chronicles, The Pathway Ring* series, *Founders, Real Magic,* and much more. He trained in martial arts for over a decade until a knee injury ended that practice. Now, he plays lead guitar in a local blues band, *The Bootleggers,* and enjoys life on a small farm in rural North Carolina.

For more information about Stuart and his books, please visit *www.stuartjaffe.com*

www.ingramcontent.com/pod-product-compliance
Lightning Source LLC
Chambersburg PA
CBHW020349310726
48979CB00015B/2557/J

* 9 7 8 1 9 6 3 5 1 7 2 2 4 *